James Martineau

The Seat of Authority in Religion

The Seat of Authority in Religion

James Martineau

The Seat of Authority in Religion

ISBN/EAN: 9783742813770

Manufactured in Europe, USA, Canada, Australia, Japa

Cover: Foto ©Andreas Hilbeck / pixelio.de

Manufactured and distributed by brebook publishing software
(www.brebook.com)

James Martineau

The Seat of Authority in Religion

THE
SEAT OF AUTHORITY

IN

RELIGION

BY

JAMES MARTINEAU

Hon. LLD. Harv.: S.T.D. Lugd. Bat.
D.D. Edin.: D.C.L. Oxon.

THIRD EDITION
REVISED

LONDON
LONGMANS, GREEN, AND CO.
AND NEW YORK: 15, EAST 16th STREET
1891

PREFACE.

THE critical reader may possibly discover that this book has not taken shape at once *aus einem Gusse;* and he will at least excuse a few words in explanation of its origin and formation.

At the request of a literary friend in New England, editing a monthly periodical, I wrote, between 1872 and 1875, a series of theological papers which were designed, when complete, to present a compendious survey of the ground both of Natural and Historical religion as accepted in Christendom. Before the plan had been half worked out (i.e., after the appearance of fourteen papers), the periodical came to an end ; and in the absence of the motive of a fixed engagement, the further materials which I had collected were thrown aside, to free me for the studies in another field which have occupied me since. But the forlorn rudiment of an intended structure, with its scaffolding still standing and its roof rotting on the ground, never ceased to haunt and reproach me ; and when released from preoccupation with philosophy two years ago, I at once rushed to the fair field which I had uselessly deformed, and, with no little dismay, appraised the tumbled bricks and unhewn stone so long abandoned by the builder. Crumbling and weatherstained, they could no longer be trusted or wrought ; and nothing remained but to mould and quarry as well as build anew, accepting only the working plans from the past.

So great in the interval had been the gains of historical research, in regard especially to the growth of the Church in the first two centuries, that it was impossible to resume my task till I had overtaken the movement in advance by following the footsteps which led to the higher point of view. This recovery of a true position is now rendered comparatively easy by the striking improvement, in condensation, critical fairness, and literary form, of modern theological authorship: so that, under such guidance as that of Scholten, Hatch, Pfleiderer, Holtzmann, Harnack, and Weizsäcker, even a veteran student may find it possible, with no very wide reading, to readjust his judgments to the altered conditions of the time. To a fresh study of the early Christian writings in or out of the canon, under the lights of this newer literature, are due the third, fourth, and fifth books of the present volume, and a great part of the second chapter of Book II. All that precedes is, in the main, a reproduction of the American papers. That this part contains a summary of the same ethical doctrine as that which is more fully developed in the " Types of Ethical Theory " will not, I hope, be regarded as an inexcusable iteration. In its distinctive characteristic I find, in truth, the very " Seat of Authority " of which I was in search: so that there was no help for it, unless I were content with the mere exposure of illusory authorities unrelieved by the indication of any that is real.

I am prepared to hear that, after dispensing with miracles and infallible persons, I have no right to speak of " authority " at all, the intuitional assurance which I substitute for it being nothing but confidence in my own reason. If to rest on authority is to mean an acceptance of what, as foreign to my faculty, I cannot know, in mere reliance on the testimony of one who can and does, I certainly find no such basis for religion; inasmuch as second-hand belief, assented to at the dictation of an initiated expert, without personal response of thought and reverence in myself, has no more tincture of religion in it than any other lesson learned by rote. The mere resort to testimony for information beyond our province does not fill the meaning of ' authority '; which we never acknowledge till that which speaks to us from another and a higher strikes home and wakes the echoes in ourselves, and is thereby instantly transferred from external attestation to self-evidence. And this response it is which makes the moral intuitions, started by outward appeal, reflected back by inward veneration, more than egoistic phenomena, and turning them into correspondency between the universal and the individual mind, invests them with true ' authority.' We trust in them, not with any rationalist arrogance because they are our own, but precisely because they are *not* our own, with awe and aspiration. The *consciousness* of authority is doubtless human ; but conditional on the *source* being divine.

PREFACE TO THE THIRD EDITION.

Since the issue of the second edition of this book, numerous reviews of it have appeared which I cannot treat with silence, as if they gave me nothing to learn. Such of them indeed as simply pronounce, *ex cathedra*, the critic's judgment of approval or condemnation, after a fair report of its contents, may well be left to speak for themselves; they give legitimate guidance to readers who see reason to trust them. Others which, under the influence of theological antipathy, do but travesty the book, or pick out from its contents such phrases or thoughts *ad invidiam*, as may best repel the reader, spring from a state of mind inaccessible to words of mine. But there remain a few to which I owe an insight into the defects or weak points of my own exposition, and by negotiation with which a possibility seems open of essential concurrence on the theory of Authority. I hope it will not shock my critic in the *Spectator*, or Dr. Dale in the *Contemporary*, if I say that, on this fundamental point, I see my way to substantial agreement with all that they press upon my attention.

Through a common inadvertence, these reviewers address themselves to a different question from that with which this book attempts to deal. By the terms of the title I limit myself to the treatment of " Authority *in Religion*." They have pushed the discussion beyond these bounds, and answered me by fetching in from alien territory examples of authority which do not come within my definition. Were I to admit all that is said about them, no position taken up in the opening chapters of this volume would be affected in the least. The *Spectator* mistakes me in saying that I " repudiate and almost deride the notion of *any kind of authority* except that which the conscience enforces on the nature of man."[*] On the contrary, I expressly distinguish two kinds of authority, one of which has nothing to do with the conscience ; viz., authority for intellectual assent to what I learn from persons better informed ; and authority for reverence and devotion to the claims of higher character and diviner life : the one, authority over the understanding ; the other, over the will.

I do not disparage the former as an adequate ground of new knowledge ; I only contend that it has no tincture *of religion* in it ; it justifies a belief to the reason ; it originates and demands no worship in the heart. When a judge upon the bench accepts information elicited from a competent witness, he performs a rational act, and nothing more. And so do readers at home, when they assure themselves of the existence of foreign countries on the report of travellers who have visited them. And could messengers pass from world to world and bring with them means of accrediting their story of things invisible, no less *reasonable* would it be to welcome the extended knowledge, but also no more *religious.* Far from thinking that " we should no more lean upon the word " of such a visitor " than upon the word of a dreamer or the guess of an historian," I should say, When once satisfied that the reporter *is* such a messenger, we should be fools, did we not accept his tidings ; to do so would be an act of mere common sense ; not, I submit, of religion. The gain is simply tantamount to a filling-in of the cosmic map and the human history, with similar significance (of mere phenomenal knowledge) to the men of science and to the saints. Touching no springs of spiritual life, and susceptible of no inward verification, it lifts no soul into nearer union with God. The second-hand belief which I take up from a witness who

<hr>

[*] Aug. 23rd, 1890.

knows what is incognizable to myself you cannot draw into the essence of religion. But the primary homage which reveals to me my relation to the beauty of holiness and the mandate of the highest Will, you can never part by one hair's breadth from the essence of religion.

Is then religious authority a mere "subjective" rule, "which conscience enforces on the nature of man"? A power which can "enforce something on the nature of man" must be above that nature and not a piece of it: and if conscience be taken in this sense, as an authority *over* humanity, felt within but with appeal descending from beyond, it passes into a Divine reality, communing with us as person with person, seeking the assimilation of spirit with spirit. And this is precisely the relation which opens upon our view when the moral intuitions spread forth their contents in articulate consciousness. If therefore by "subjective" be meant an affection limited to the human subject, the epithet marks precisely what this experience rejects: the authority felt to be *over us* is *eo ipso* objective; alighting upon consciousness, but from an illuminating source known only as Divine. This is not exclusively "subjective," unless all inspiration is so; if this word is to be applied, by way of reproach, to all that is given us in consciousness, how can you exempt the greatest prophet from it? Does not his inspiration arrive at him in the shape of thought and feeling? and if in his case thought and feeling can carry in it an immediate report of its Divine source, what is to hinder the moral experiences of humanity from bringing with them the same light? I own that this style of criticism deeply humbles me, not by its efficiency, but by its inappositeness, showing as it does how absolutely I have failed to put even the best class of readers in possession of my meaning. The whole purpose of the first Book in this volume is to show that religious authority is necessarily objective and supernatural: and my critics charge me with contending that it is purely subjective and natural.

The relation of a child to his parents, far from embarrassing the doctrine for which I plead, very happily combines and illustrates the two types of "authority;" the rational, wielded by those who know more, and the religious, vested in the higher and larger personality. In both instances we may speak of the attitude of the dependent nature as one of "trust"; but the word will cover quite a different state of mind in the two cases: in the first, the mere contentment with a witness's report in the absence of first-hand vision; in the second, the waking echo of the heart to the mandates of the riper soul, with the uplooking love inseparable from such secret sympathy. It is the latter only which has a sacred character; and if once obedience begins to be demanded to what is felt to be unjust or base, the inner piety instantly turns round, and makes a rebel even of the child. For want of the inner verification, the sanctity of the act is gone; and if the will complies, it is under protest and with self-contempt. Without the element of personal trust based on moral veneration within the scale of a common righteousness, character and life remain outside the sphere of religion.

Dr. Dale is so far from disapproving the stress which I have laid on the "inner witness of the spirit," that he rather censures me for overlooking the great part assigned to it by Calvin, Owen, and other reformers of the Puritan type.* There is justice in this complaint; the more so as the fact to which he calls attention was familiar to me and had much to do with the attraction I have always felt, in spite of doctrinal divergence, towards the divines of that school. But writing with a view to contemporary wants I naturally represented Protestantism to myself as exhibited in its literature since the time of Locke: and that alone must be taken as embraced in the scope of my argument.

"The inward witness," without which the authority of no sacred text is brought home to us, Dr. Dale would fain render valid for more than it attests. By an inference from analogy

* *Contemporary Review*, Sept. 1880, p. 107.

he stretches it as an elastic shield over an indefinite expanse of scripture which has it not: "the real power of the New Testament," he says,—"its *authority* for myself,—must come from those parts of it in which I find God and God finds me; but it does not follow that I am free to say that only in those parts is there any divine light and power": "parts of our Lord's teaching, and parts of the teaching of the apostles, which have not 'found us yet may find us some day.'" * Then, when that day comes, they will acquire religious authority: meanwhile, they remain without it. And, while awaiting their chance, are they to be treasured as enigmatical oracles that must be left to declare themselves? If not, are they not exposed to equal possibilities of rising into the Divine, or sinking into the ignobly human? Am I to hang in suspense till the injunction, for instance, "Give not that which is holy unto the dogs, neither throw your pearls before swine, lest haply they trample them under their feet and turn and rend you," "finds" me as a word of light and love?

Something remains to be said in order to relieve the critical portion of this volume from certain imputations to which it has been mistakenly exposed. Without either re-opening the many controverted questions with which it deals, or resenting the many hard words which I feel to have done me wrong, I will simply clear away such misapprehensions as may be removed by a bare recital of facts. In my former Preface I described the origin of this book as an intended summary of the results of theological study up to the year 1875 ; the suspension of the design and the diversion of my chief attention to philosophy. till 1887–8 ; and my devotion of two years to reading myself into such new literature as brought fresh evidence into the questions on which I had previously pronounced. In speaking of this batch of supplementary study I unfortunately expressed my gratitude for the vastly improved structure of German theological writings, and for the saving

* P. 410.

of the student's time through such excellent literary workmanship, mentioning half a dozen authors by way of example. Taking advantage of this passage, more than one of my critics have treated it as a complete map of my travels on theological ground, and have rebuked the arrogant levity of such ill-secured judgment. As " a disciple of that grossly one-sided book ' Supernatural religion ' " I am said simply to " reproduce the exploded absurdities of the Tübingen school " : [*] and, according to Professor Sanday, I think it enough, in dealing with " the most perplexing of human problems,' " to go to a few of the latest German writers, not to weigh and test their hypotheses, and explore all round their data, but simply to take their conclusions ready made, translate them into English, and spread them broadcast as a new Gospel." [†]   And it is considered a sufficient proof of one-sidedness that I do not quote Bishops Lightfoot and Westcott, Ezra Abbot, Schürer, or Professor Ramsay.[‡]

Whether this attempt to discredit a writer whom you think " better left unread " [§] is less or more of a wrong than the omission to quote one from whom you regretfully dissent, I do not pretend to decide. My answer shall be a mere transcript from my memory. The critical contents of this volume result from the direct study, seldom intermitted through more than sixty years, of the Scriptures themselves and the cognate literature affecting the early Christian Church ; and are not got up at second hand from " the ready made conclusions " of any theological school, though deeply indebted to the insight gained by the labours of several. The book on " Supernatural religion " I have never seen, and know only from Bishop Lightfoot's answer to it. Westcott, Ezra Abbot, and Schürer I have read with much warm appreciation, but without altered conviction ; and the last of them with the irresistible inference that scholarly judgment is verging

---

[*] *Baptist Magazine*, June 1890.
[†] *Expository Times*, Sept. 1890, pp. 283, 284.
[‡] *Ib.* p. 284. *a*.   [§] *Ib.* p. 284. *b*.

more and more towards a negative verdict on the Johannine question. During the growth of the Tübingen school, I was guarded against any unquestioning surrender to the influence of Baur by habitual reading of Ewald's " Jahrbücher der biblischen Wissenschaft," so far as the enthusiasm of one man of genius can countervail the intellectual grasp of another. All this, I am well aware, amounts to just nothing at all when compared with the resources of some of my learned critics ; but however small it may be, I submit that it is not the reading of a partisan, but is fairly divided between the opposite sides of the chief questions on which I have touched. If I have not quoted this or that opponent of my case, it is not for want of attention to his plea, but simply because the line of reasoning I was following could apparently afford to let it alone ; and in the instance of the late Bishop Lightfoot, because his chief controversial work leaves on me the same impression which Pfleiderer has put on record as his own.*

In his strictures on my view of the Fourth Gospel and the Ephesian traditions respecting the apostle John, Dr. Dale, at the word of Irenæus, accepts Polycarp as a personal disciple of the apostle ; and, not content with assailing my doubts on the subject with legitimate arguments, suggests in the following sentences that, in support of my opinion, I manipulate the evidences unfairly by omission of important texts: "As Dr. Martineau satisfied himself that Irenæus made a mistake in supposing that Polycarp was a disciple of the apostle, he *naturally omits* all reference to the letter of Irenæus to Victor, bishop of Rome (A.D. 190–198 or 199), in reference to the Paschal Controversy, in which he says that Anicetus, a previous Roman bishop, was unable to persuade Polycarp to give up the Asiatic custom of keeping Easter, ' because he had always observed it with John, the disciple of our Lord, and the rest of the apostles with whom he was associated.' And it is also natural that he should omit to

* " The Development of theology in Germany since Kant, and its progress in Great Britain since 1825." p. 397.

notice the passages in Irenæus's great work 'against Heresies' (about A.D. 185), in which he refers to John's residence at Ephesus. But the letter of Polycrates, who was bishop of Ephesus at the end of the second century, to Victor, in defence of the Asiatic observance of Easter, ought, I think, to have been mentioned. Polycrates says, 'For in Asia great lights have fallen asleep which shall rise again in the day of the Lord's appearing ; Philip, one of the twelve apostles, who sleeps in Hierapolis ; moreover, John, who rested upon the bosom of the Lord and bore the sacerdotal plate, both a martyr and teacher ; he is buried in Ephesus.' This testimony is very important." *

The reader may estimate the justice of this rebuke if he will turn to p. 285 of this volume, where he will find the passages which it was 'natural for me to omit,' from the letter of Irenæus to Victor, and from that of Polycrates to Victor ; and to p. 192, where he will find quoted from Irenæus 'against Heresies' the other missing reference to John's residence at Ephesus.

* *Contemporary Review*, Sept. 1890, pp. 399, 400.

CONTENTS.

CHAPTER II.

BOOK III.

DIVINE AUTHORITY INTERMIXED WITH HUMAN THINGS.

CHAPTER I.

CHAPTER II.

BOOK IV.

SEVERANCE OF UNDIVINE ELEMENTS FROM CHRISTENDOM.

CHAPTER I.

CHAPTER II.

CHAPTER III.

CHAPTER IV.

BOOK V.

THE DIVINE IN THE HUMAN.

CHAPTER I.

CHAPTER II.

BOOK I.

CHAPTER I.

GOD IN NATURE.

IF we ask ourselves what was the earliest impression produced by the spectacle of the universe on the mind of man, we can no longer, like Milton, imagine him standing alone upon the grass of Eden, and answering with adoring thoughts the gaze of the vaulted sky. The solemn tones of the Puritan poet give forth quite another music from any that really lay at heart in the childhood of the world. Yet it is admitted on all hands,—not less by those who ridicule than by those who revere the tendency,—that, to the eye of primitive wonder, the visible scene around would at first seem to be alive; day and night to have in them the lights and shades of thought; summer and winter to be pulsations of a hidden joy and grief; the eager stream to be charged with some hasting errand; and the soft wind to whisper secrets to the forest leaves. This sympathy with the action of Nature,—this ideal interpretation of the world,—which looks through the physical picture of things, and is touched by more than their physical effect, is, moreover, a specially human characteristic, confessedly due, not to the endowments which we share with the other animal races, but to the higher gifts of a constitution in advance of theirs. It is, therefore, an enriching faculty, and not a deluding incapacity from which the happier brutes are free. Say what you will of the superstitions to which it may lay us open, who can contemplate its primitive manifestations without a profound, though it be now a compassionate sympathy?   And when, among the prehistoric vestiges of man upon this earth, we find already a grotto for his dead,* where, after the farewell funeral feast, he shuts them in, with their weapons by their side and their provisions for their journey into unknown fields, who does not feel in these simple memorials a pathetic dignity which other natures do not approach?

In the apprehension, then, of the human observer, using his most human faculty, this visible world is folded round and steeped in a sea of life, whence enters all that rises, and whither return the generations that pass away.   This is religion in its native simplicity, so far as it flows in from the aspect of the physical scene around, and ere it has quitted its indeterminate condition of poetic feeling, to set into any of the definite forms of thought which philosophers have named. Doubtless, it is an ascription to Nature, on the part of the observer, of a life like his own: in the boundless mirror of the earth and sky, he sees, as the figures of events flit by, the reflected image of himself.   But for his living spirit, he could not move; and but for a living spirit, they could not move.   Just as when, standing face to face with his fellows, he reads the glance of the eye, the sudden start, or the wringing of the hands, and refers them home to their source within the viewless soul of another; so with dimmer and more wondering suspicion, does he discern, behind the looks and movements of nature, a Mind, that is the seat of power and the spring of every change.   You may laugh at so simple a philosophy; but how else would you have him proceed?   Does he not, for this explanation, go straight to the only Cause which he knows?   He is familiar with *power* in himself alone; and in himself it is *Will;* and he has no other element than will to be charged with the power of the world. Is it said to be childish thus to see his own life repeated in the sphere that lies around him, and to conceive of a God in the image of humanity? to project, as it were, his own shadow upon the space without, and then render to it the

* At Aurignac in Haute Garonne. See Lyell's Antiquity of Man, ch. x. pp. 192-3.

homage of his faith?* The objection might naturally enough be urged by a disciple of Schelling or Cousin, who supposed himself able to transcend his personal limits, and take immediate cognizance of the Infinite and Absolute. But surely it comes ill from those who have carried to its extreme length the Protagorean maxim, that "man is the measure of all things;" who have laid it down as a rule that we know nothing but our own feelings and ideas; and who have construed back even the material world into an ideal reflex of the order and permanence of our sensations.†

The objection, however, is as little considerate as it is consistent. For if we are to conceive of mind at all, elsewhere than at home, where are we to find the base of our conception, the meaning of the words we use, if not in our own mental consciousness? Not in religion only, but in every sphere of understanding, self-knowledge is the condition and the limit of other knowledge; and if there were laws of intellect, or affections of goodness, other than our own, they must remain forever foreign to our apprehension, and could be no objects of intelligent speech. Be it an order of thought of which we see traces beyond us, or a purpose of righteousness, or an expression of power, we have no means of imagining it at all, except as homogeneous with our own. Either, therefore, the very structure of our highest faculties is unsound, and the constitution of our reason itself condemns us to unreason; or else the likeness we see between the world within and the world without, in its idea and its causality, reports a real correspondence, the answering face of the Divine and the human, communing through the glorious symbolism between.

It is, at all events, acknowledged as a fact, that this religious interpretation of the world is natural to man, and therefore holds him, till it is dispossessed by some superior claimant, with a certain right of pre-occupation. Next, it must also be admitted, that, simply as an hypothesis, it is adequate to its purpose; i.e., that, if tried through the whole range of the phenomena, it provides a sufficient cause

* Mill's Logic, book iii. ch. v. 8, 9.

† Mill's Examination of Hamilton, ch. ii. xi. Grote's Plato, ch. xxvi.

for all. It may be open to an objector to say that an infinite Divine Will, eternally acting through the universe, is *more* than we want, to give account of what we find; but he cannot say, that it is *less*. It supplies an inexhaustible fund of causality, equal to every exigency, and incapable of being thrown upon engagements which it cannot meet. It is only when you add on to it superfluous explanations of your own; when you affect to know, not only the power wherein, but also the reason why; when you presume to read the particular motives whence this or that has sprung; when you charge the lightning flash with vengeance, or treat a blighted harvest as a judgment upon sin; when you discuss the course of a comet, or a trembling equilibrium of the planets, as a preparation for the judgment day; when, in short, you fill the fields of space with the fictions of your spiritual geography, and pledge them, without leave, to act out the situations of your drama, that you are sure to be brought to shame, and turned into the outer darkness prepared for the astrologers. But keep to the modesty of simple religious faith, which, however sure of the ground and essence of things, knows nothing of the phenomena, and lets science sort them as it will; say humbly, " How this and that may be, I cannot tell, nor am I in the secret why it is not other; I only know it is from Him who shines in the whole and hides in the parts : " and, stand where you may in time or place, you hold the key of an eternal temple, on which none can put a lock you cannot open.

If, then, the recognition of divine causality is admitted to be primary and natural to man, to be dictated by just the faculties that lift him above other tribes, and to be adequate to the whole field it proposes to embrace, how is it that in many a mind it is weakened by the spirit of modern knowledge, and meets there with beliefs and tastes which seem to be ill at ease with it, and by supercilious looks to take repose and courage out of it? Has anything really been found out to disprove it? Has any chamber been opened and found empty, where it was thought God was sure to be? Has any analysis reached the hiding-place of his power, and entered its factors on the list of chemical equivalents? Has any

geologist succeeded, not only in laying out the order of phenomena into well-reasoned succession, but in passing behind
phenomena altogether, so as to attest a vacuity in the sphere
of real being; and, after his long retreat through the ages,
has he slipped out at the back door of time, right into the
eternal, and brought word that there is no Mind there? Let
us calmly review, one by one, the characteristic achievements
and auguries of recent science, so far as they are supposed to
affect religious conceptions, and estimate what they have
done to disturb the theistic interpretation of the world.

The first grand discovery of modern times is the immense
extension of the universe *in space.* Compared with the fields
from which our stars fling us their light, the Cosmos of the
ancient world was but as a cabinet of brilliants, or rather a
little jewelled cup found in the ocean or the wilderness. Wonderful as were the achievements, and sagacious as were the
guesses, of the Greek astronomers, they little suspected what
they were registering when they drew up their catalogues of
stars : skilfully as they often read the relative motions and
positions of the wandering lights of heaven, so as to compute
and predict the eclipse, their line of measurement fell short
even of this first solar chamber of nature; and, for want of the
telescope, their speculative imagination soon lost itself in
childish fancies beyond. The concentric crystal spheres, the
adamantine axis turning in the lap of Necessity, the bands that
held the heaven together like a girth that clasps a ship, the
shaft which led from earth to sky, and which was paced by the
soul in a thousand years, except when the time was come for
her to be snatched, in the twinkling of an eye, to the mortal
birth,—these things, presented in one of the most solemn and
high-wrought passages of ancient literature,* give us the
standard of the Greek cosmical conception in its sublimest
dreams. That Plato should deem that fair but miniature
structure not too great for some sort of personal management;
that he should provide a soul to fill it, ever-living and self-
sufficing, thinking out its order, and gleaming through all its
beauty, and making it an image of eternal good,—this, it is
said, is not wonderful; the theory was not wholly dispropor-

* Plato, de Republ., X., 614 C–621 B.

tioned to the scale of the phenomenon. But what has now become of that night-canopy of his, and all that it contained? It has shrunk into a toy; and with it, we are told, its doctrine must go too. That which he deemed a millennial journey for a human traveller has been measured for us by a messenger swifter than the flash of Plato's thought,—a messenger that could run round the earth eight times in a second.* What would the philosopher have said, had he known that the beams flung from the pole-star when, as a youth of thirty, he was detained in his sick room from the last hours of Socrates, could only just reach his own eye,† when, at fourscore, he was about to close it in death? As for the paler rays of the milky-way which he describes, many a one that started in the hour when Plato was born, we are too soon to see; for they are not yet half-way. Is this stupendous scene, we are asked, inhabited and wielded by One Sole Will? Can we stretch the conception of personality, till it is commensurate with the dimensions of such a world? Must not the problem be flung in despair into the shadows of fate, to be scrambled for by the rude and nameless forces which can do we know not what?

To this vague apprehension, which seems to oppress many minds, thus much must be conceded: that a compact little universe, every part of which our thought can visit with easy excursions, and which can lie within our conception as a whole, is better fitted to the scale of our capacities, and less strains the efforts of religious imagination, than the baffling infinitude which has burst open before us. But ease of fancy is no test of truth; and the mere inability of panting thought to over-take the opening way is no reason for retracing the steps already made. To let our own incapacity cast its negative shadow on the universe, and blot out the divineness because it is too great, is a mere wild and puerile waywardness. How does the *size* of things affect their relation to a Cause already infinite? The miniature Cosmos which we owned to be divine is still there, with all its beauty and its good, only embosomed in far-stretching fields of similar beauty and repeated good. It is not pretended that the vast quantities with which we deal in-

---

* The speed of light equals 192,000 miles per second.
† Plat., Phaedo, 59 B.

troduce us to a different *quality* of things; that they take us into lawless regions, and turn us out from a Cosmos into a chaos. On the contrary, the same simple but sublime physical geometry which interprets the path of the projectile, the phases of Venus, and the sweep of the comet which has no return, is still available in the most distant heavens to which the telescope can pierce; and the star-traced diagrams of remotest space are embodied reasonings of the same science which works its problems on the black board of every school. Nay, the very light that brings us report from that inconceivable abyss is as a filament that binds into one system the extremes of the Cosmos there and here; for, when it reaches the telescope, it is reflected by the same law as the beams of this morning's sun; the prism breaks it into the same colours, and bends them in the same degrees. So confident do we feel that there is not one truth here and another there, that no sooner does a luminous ray out of the sky reproduce in its spectrum the same adjustment of lines and colours which our incandescent chemicals have been made to paint upon the wall, than we pronounce at once upon the materials supplying the solar and stellar fires. Nor do the nebulæ, composed of gaseous matter of various density, with brilliant nucleus and fainter margin, leave it doubtful that the laws of heat and expansion, which have been ascertained by us here, carry their formulas into those vast depths. It is plain, therefore, that, in being thrust out beyond the ancient bounds, we are not driven as exiles into a trackless wilderness, where that which we had owned to be divine is exchanged for the undivine; the clew, familiar to our hand, lengthens as we go, and never breaks; and, with whatever shudder Imagination may look round, Reason can find its way hither and thither precisely as before. What, indeed, have we found, by moving out along all radii into the infinite? that the whole is woven together in one sublime tissue of intellectual relations, geometrical and physical, the realized original of which all our science does but partially copy. That science is the crowning product and supreme expression of human reason; what, then, is the organism which it interprets, and renders visible on the reduced scale of our understanding? Can the photograph exhibit the symmetry of beauty and the expressive lines of thought, if no mind speaks through the original? Can the dead looks of matter and force fling upon the plate the portrait, alive with genius, and serene with intellect? Unless, therefore, it takes more mental faculty to construe a universe than to cause it, to read the book of nature than to write it, we must more than ever look upon its solemn face as the living appeal of thought to thought, the medium through which the eye of the Infinite Reason gazes into ours, and wakes it to meet him on the way. The Cosmos-tracks all have the same termini; and whoever moves upon them passes from mind to mind; God, thinking out his eternal thoughts on lines that descend to us, from cause to law, from law to fact, from fact to sense; and we, counting our way back with labouring steps, from what we feel to what we see, and from what is to what must be, till we meet him in the eternal fields, where all minds live on the same aliment of the ever true and ever good.

Whether, in the movements of reason, he descends to us, or we ascend to him, it is by the path of law which stretches across the spaces of the world, and which is in one direction the wayfarer's track, and in the other the highway for our God. Is it not childish, then, to be terrified out of our religion by the mere scale of things, and, because the little Mosaic firmament is broken in pieces, to ask whether its divine Ruler is not also gone? Do you fear, because the earth has dwindled to a sand-grain? So much the more glorious is the field in which it lies; so much the more numerous the sentinels of eternal equilibrium, the brilliant witnesses of order, rank upon rank, that pass always the same word, " There is no chaos here." Do you pretend that the dimensions are beyond the compass of a personal and living Mind? How, then, has your own mind, as learner, managed to measure and to know it, at least enough to think it something beyond thought? Cannot the Creative Intellect occupy and dispose beforehand any scene of which your science can take possession afterwards? And if it is too much for the resources of mind,—which, at any rate, is supreme among the things we know,—how can it fail to be, in higher measure, beyond the grasp of anything else? Does the order of *one* solar system tell us that we are in the domain of intelligence, but the balance and harmony of *ten thousand* cancel the security, and hand us over to blind material force? Shall a single canto from the epic of the world breathe the tones of a genius divine; yet the sequel, which clears the meaning and multiplies the beauty, take from the poem its inspiration of thought, and reduce it to a mechanical crystallization of words? Does reason turn into unreason, as it fills auguster fields, and nears the Infinite? Such a fear is self-convicted, and cannot shape itself into consistent speech: it is the mere panic of incompetent imagination, which the steadfast heart will tranquillize, and the large mind transcend. We are not lost, then, in our modern immensity of space; but may still rest, with the wise of every age, in the faith that a realm of intellectual order and purest purpose environs us, and that the unity of nature is but the unity of the all-perfect Will.

The second great discovery of modern science is the immense extension of the universe *in time*. This also disturbs the hearts of men, by the dissolving of many a venerable dream, and forces on them unwonted and unwelcome conceptions, the significance of which we must try to estimate.

If for this purpose we deign to consult the witness of history, and listen to other men's thought ere we venture to work out our own, we encounter at once a singular rebuke to the precipitancy of theologic fear. As if to evince the perseverance of religious faith, and its ready adaptation to the intellectual varieties of mankind, a conspicuous proof presents itself on this very field, that one age may consecrate a belief which to another may appear simply impious. The imagination of Christendom has selected and drawn out from eternity two limiting epochs as supremely sacred,—the creation and the dissolution of the world. These two—the opening scene of the divine drama of all things, and its catastrophe—have enclosed for us the whole *terra firma* of humanity, nay, of physical nature itself, between opposite seas of awe and mystery. All the beauty and horror, the tenderness and wrath, the pity and hope, which piety can wring from the soul of genius, have been shed upon these moments, to make them real by their intensity. The imagery of ancient hymns—the " Lucis Creator Optime," and the " Dies irœ, dies illa ; " the masterpieces of art in the cathedrals of cities, and still more, perhaps, the plebeian pictures by the road-side oratory ; the majestic epics of Dante and Milton ; the glorious music with which Haydn ushers in the light of the first day, and Spohr draws down the shadows of the last,—have deeply fixed those supernatural boundaries in the fancy and feeling of Christendom. Yet those very conceptions, that the universe had come into existence, and that it would pass out of it, are pronounced by Aristotle totally inadmissible, as at variance with the divine perfection ;* and so strong was the reverent feeling of the ancient philosophy against them, that even Philo the Jew, in the face of his own Scriptures, was carried away by it, and wrote a special treatise to prove the indestructibility of the world. Far from beginning with a genesis and ending with a destruction of the heavens and the earth, both of them sudden alike, the Greek philosophical piety shrank distressed from paroxysms of change, and never felt itself in the Divine Presence except where the evolution was smooth and the order eternal.† The more it retired from phenomena to their ground, and, while among phenomena, the more it dwelt with regular recurrences which might go on forever, the nearer did it believe itself to the Supreme Mind. Its favourite symbols and abodes of the godlike were not the earthquake, and the smoking mountain, with its " blackness and darkness and tempest and voice of a trumpet and sound of words ; " but the sphere, most perfect of forms, because like itself all round ; and the rotatory movement of the fixed stars, because self-sufficing and complete, without the varying speed and even reversed direction of the less sacred planetary lights ; and the symmetry of proportionate numbers, and the rhythm of music, and the secure steps of geometrical deduction ; whatever is serene and balanced and changeless, and seems to ask least from causes

* Aristot., de Cœlo, I. 3. II. 1. Met. xi. 1074. a. b. Conf. Philo, de Incorruptibilitate Mundi, 9.

† Θεοῦ δὲ ἐνέργεια ἀθανασία. τοῦτο δ' ἐστὶ ζωὴ ἀίδιος   Aristot., de Cœlo, II. 3.

beyond itself,—is the chosen retreat of the Hellenic type of devout contemplation. The peculiarity has its origin in this, that while the Hebrew traced the footsteps of God in time and history, the Greek looked round for him in space and its cosmic order : so that the one met the sacred fire flashing and fading in the free movements of humanity, the other saw it fixed in the unwasting light of the eternal stars.

It would seem possible, then, for the universe still to remain the abode of God, even though it should never, as a whole, have come into existence, but should have been always there ; and that actually, under this very aspect, it has put on its divinest look to some of the greatest intellects of the human race. This may well re-assure us if, for the doctrine of absolute creation, we are called to substitute entirely new conceptions of the genesis of things. A century ago, all the lines of research which pushed their exploration into the past bound themselves to meet at a starting-point about six thousand years away. Intent upon this convergence, they virtually predetermined their own track in conformity with it. One after another, as they followed the trail of their own facts, they found that they were likely to overshoot their rendezvous, and must either twist the indications of direction from their natural sweep, or else demand a longer run. Even for the mere human phenomena, the allowance of history was evidently too small. Along the great rivers, which were the earliest seats of civilization, were found memorials of ancient dynasties which could not be compressed within so narrow a chronology. Remains of art, disinterred from surprising depths, beneath annual sand-drifts and fluviatile deposits, measured themselves back thousands of years too far. The genealogy and rate of change in languages asked for more room to work. And the races of mankind, especially if they were to claim a common ancestry, could not make out their family tree, unless it were a more venerable stock, with roots in the soil of an older world. Meanwhile, the naturalist, hitherto content to classify and describe the forms of life now upon the earth and in the waters, was introduced by his brother, who had been taking notes among the rocks, to an entirely new realm of plants and animals,—a realm which compelled him to arrange its kinds by a rule of succession, one after its forerunner, as well as by a rule of analogy, one like its neighbour; and hardly had organic nature, instead of remaining a mere picture of what is, become also a history of what has been, than, even before any attempt at measuring the intervals, the beads of the chain declared themselves in numbers far too great for the thread on which they were to hang. A less indefinite reckoning, however, was not far off. The geologist, by patient and irresistible induction, established a series of sedimentary rocks; and showed that the crust of the earth, to a depth far exceeding the measure of our highest mountain-chains, has been formed and re-formed; its continents depressed and elevated, its valleys scooped out, its sea-lines changed; nay, even its oceans filled, its climates turned from tropical to glacial, by the agencies which are at work around us now, but which are so slow that a single generation can scarcely see them stir. Within the millions of years which are thus gained, the physiologist finds scope to move, and thinks better of the small causes of change at his command, for deriving kind from kind, and bridging the chasms which seem to keep the families of creatures distinct. And he suggests a law, gathered from the art of man in modifying plants and animals, and legible enough in many natural samples, at the touch of which the barriers between species give way; the separating intervals become derivative; and a provisional character is assumed by even the broadest distinctions, not excepting (some will tell us) that which parts the organic from the inorganic world. To complete this conversion of the Cosmos born in a week, into a growth through immeasurable ages, enters the hypothesis, that the whole solar system was once an incandescent nebulous mass, whose rotation, as it cools, has flung off in succession its outer rings, and left them to condense in their orbits into the planetary spheres; each, in its turn, to solidify round its molten centre into a habitable world, till the sun alone retains its self-luminous glow. There is nothing to hinder speculative science from pushing the same analogies into the remotest stellar fields; and the resulting picture would be, of an eternal Cosmogony, by uninterrupted development, with no starts

from nonentity into existence, no leap from stage to stage
of being, but with perpetuity of the same methods and the
same rates of evolution which have their play around us
now.

For our present purpose it is superfluous to draw any line
between what is established certainty, and what is conjectural
vaticination in this picture. Suppose it to be all true; and
consider what difference it makes to our religious conceptions.
The essence of the difference between the older and the newer
doctrine lies in this: that the causality which the former concentrates, the latter distributes; the fiat of a moment bursts
open, and spreads itself along the path of perpetuity. Whichever way it acts, it is plain that the sum of its work is still
the same, and demands neither more nor less in the one case
than in the other. The element of time is totally indifferent
to the character of the products it turns up; and it takes as
much power to grow a tree in a century as to create it in a
night. Neither the magnitude nor the quality of the universe
is altered by the discovery how old it is: whatever beauty,
whatever intellectual relations, whatever good, gleaméd from
it and reported its divine inhabitant to those who deemed it a
thing of yesterday, are still there, only with glory more prolonged, for us who know it to be a less recent and a less
perishable thing. It is not degraded by having lasted so long,
that we should set it down to a meaner source; it is not
dwindled or reduced, that we should give it to a minor power.
We want, in order to render account of it, precisely what was
wanted before; and the only change is not in the cause, but
in the date and manner of the effects; in the substitution, for
fits and paroxysms of volition, of the perennial flow of thought
along the path of law,—a method which surely more accords
with the serenity of perfect Mind. So long as we arrive at
last at the symmetry, the balance, the happy adaptations, of
the higher organisms,—at the constitution of the eye for
vision, and the hand for a designer's work, and the instincts
that move blindly into partnership of harmony,—there is not
less to admire and esteem divine, for its having been forever
growing richer and grander, and so having been long upon
the way. If you suppose that the less can produce the greater,

you leave the excess of the latter above the former without a
cause ; if you admit that it cannot, then, whatever you would
require as adequate to the last term must already be present
in the first.   This brings me to notice a singular logical
illusion which seems to haunt the expounders of the modern
doctrine of natural development.   They apparently assume
that *growth* dispenses with causation ; so that if they can only
set something growing, they may begin upon the edge of zero,
and, by simply giving it time, find it on their return a universe
complete.   Grant them only some tiniest cellule to hold a
force not worth mentioning ; grant them, further, a tendency
in this *one* to become *two*, and to improve its habits a little as
it goes,—and, in an infinite series, there is no limit to the
magnitude and splendour of the terms they will turn out.
By brooding long enough on an egg that is next to nothing,
they can, in this way, hatch any universe, actual or possible.
Is it not evident that this is a mere trick of imagination, con-
cealing its thefts of causation by committing them little by
little, and taking the heap from the divine storehouse grain
by grain?   You draw upon the fund of infinite resource to
just the same amount, whether you call for it all at a stroke,
or sow it sparse, as an invisible gold-dust, along the mountain-
range of ages.   Handle the terms as you may, you cannot
make an equation with an infinitesimal on one side, and an
infinite upon the other, though you spread an eternity between.   You are asking, in fact, for something other than time ;
since this, of itself, can never do more than hand on what
there is from point to point, and can by no means help the
lower to create the higher.   Time is of no use to your doctrine,
except to thin and hide the little increments of adapting and
improving power which you purloin.   Mental causation is not,
then, reduced to physical by diluting it with duration ; and if
you show me ever so trivial a seed, from which have come,
you say, the teeming world, and the embracing heavens, and
the soul of man which interprets them in thought, my inference will be, not that they have no more divineness than that
rudimentary tissue, but that it had no less divineness than
they have spread abroad.

It is a common feature of every doctrine of development in

time, that the course has been from ruder elements to more refined combinations, from comparative chaos to the Cosmos we behold. That a solar system should succeed to a cloud on fire; that a red-hot earth should put on a decent crust, and get the waters into its hollows, and the residuary atmosphere cool and pure; that the history of its life should begin with the lichens, the mosses and the ferns, and should reach to man,— constitutes a clear progression, and compels us to report, of our portion of the universe, that it is forever looking up. If this discovery had been opened to Plato and Aristotle, would it have added to their religion, or subtracted from it? Which terminus of the progression would their thought have seized, as the seat of the new light? Assuredly on the latest point of the ascent. As it was not in the raw material, but in the realized order of the world, that they read the expression of divine reason, as the *end in view* can only come out at the last, thither it is that the eye of their philosophy would have turned; and they would have accepted the law of progression as enhancing the sacredness of the great whole, as intimating ideal ends beyond what they had found, as the sign of even more and better thought at the heart of things than they had dared to dream. "Did we not say," they would have asked, "that this Cosmos was full of Mind, shaping it to such beauty as was possible, and directing it to the best attainable ends? And see here the very pressure and movement of this inner mind; for the beauty rises in glory, and the ends are stepping on to more perfection." No one, probably, who is familiar with their modes of reasoning, will doubt that this is the kind of impression which would have been made upon those philosophers by the modern law of progression. But how do its popular expounders deal with it? By a singular inversion of attention and interest, they fix their eye on the other end of the succession, the crude fermentation of the earth's seething mass, and virtually say, "You think yourself the child of God; come and see the slime of which you are the spawn." Need I insist that the antithesis is as false as the insinuated inference is mean, inasmuch as no secondary causation excludes the primary, but only traces its method and order? It is quite right to complete, if you can, your natural history from first to last. But if you would estimate the type or project of a growing nature, with a view to see whether it carries anything which you can suppose to be divine, is it the more reasonable to look at the stuff it is made of, or at the perfection it attains to? If it *were* the work of God, which of these two would bear the stamp of his intent? There is no wonder that you miss the end in view, if you will look only at the beginning ; and that the intellectual character of the finished product is not apparent in the lower workshops of Nature, where its constituents are mixed. As well might you expect to find the genius of a poem in the vessel where the pulp of its paper is prepared. Causation must be measured by its supreme and perfect effects ; and it is a philosophical ingratitude to construe the glorious outburst to which its *crescendo* mounts by the faint beginnings of its scale.

Would you think the aspect of things to be more divine if the law were reversed, and creation slipped downwards on a course of perpetual declension? Would you turn your present conclusion round, and say, " See how the higher creates the lower, and all must begin from God"? on the contrary, you would justly take alarm, and cry, " There is no heavenly government here ; the tendency is through perpetual loss to chaos in the end; and, if there were ever an idea within the aggregate of things, it is a baffled thought, impotent to stop confusion." Nowhere, surely, would atheism be more excused than in a world that runs to ruin. Would you, then, prefer, so far as piety is concerned, that the universe should be a system of stationary good, either without a tide at all in its affairs, or with periodic ebb and flow, rising forever with a flood of promise, and forever sinking with disappointing retreat? Does the movement of living Mind speak to you with power in this oscillating pendulum, or this perpetuity of rest? Or would they not rather throw upon you the silent shadow of an eternal Fate? May we not say, then, that, of the three possibilities conceivable in the course of Nature, that law of progression which is now registered among the strong probabilities of science is the most accordant with the divine interpretation of the world?

I conclude, then, that neither of these two modern discoveries, namely, the immense extension of the universe in space, and its unlimited development in time, has any effect on the theistic faith, except to glorify it. A tissue of intellectual order infinitely wide, a history of ascending growth immeasurably prolonged, surely open to the human mind which can read them both, everything that can be asked for a spectacle entirely divine. No one, indeed, could ever have supposed that religion was hurt by these discoveries, had not Christendom unhappily bound up its religion with the physics of Moses and of Paul. Setting aside any question of authority, and looking with fresh eyes at the reality itself, who would not own that we live in a more glorious universe than they? Who would go to a Herschel and say, "Roof over your stellar infinitudes, and give me back the solid firmament, with its waters above and its clouds beneath; find me again the third story of the heavens, where the apostle heard the ineffable words?" Who would demand of a Darwin, "Blot out your geologic time, and take me home again to the easy limits of six thousand years?" Who, I say, not in the interests of science, but in the very hour of his midnight prayer, would wish to look into skies less deep, or to be near a God whose presence was the living chain of fewer ages? It cannot be denied that the architects of science have raised over us a nobler temple, and the hierophants of Nature introduced us to a sublimer worship. I do not say that they alone could ever find for us, if else we knew it not, *Who* it is that fills that temple, and what is the inner meaning of its sacred things; for it is not, I believe, through any physical aspect of things, if that were all, but through the human experiences of the conscience and affections, that the living God comes to apprehension and communion with us. But, when once he has been found of us,—or rather, we of him,—it is of no small moment that in our mental picture of the universe, an abode should be prepared worthy of a Presence so dear and so august. And never, prior to our day, did " the heavens " more " declare his glory," or the world present a fitter temple for " Him who inhabiteth eternity."

If God cannot be distinguished from the universe except by being placed outside, the loss, from modern scientific conceptions, of empty time and empty space, is the loss of him. To the childish imagination, to distinguish is literally to set apart; and objects of thought, from which you abolish all quantitative interval, become confounded. Hence the prevailing terror lest what we had taken to be two should prove to be only one, and the doubt whether that one must be called All-Nature or All-God. So long as the world was supposed to be only ten-score generations old, it was easy enough to separate the provinces of God and Nature. There was a definite date imagined at which its powers were set to work and put in charge of the order of things, and, prior to that date, nothing in existence but his lonely infinitude. Different domains of time were thus marked off as receptacles of supernatural and of natural existence; and, though the Divine Life continued all through, its activities were regarded as delegated since the creative hour; and human piety, in order to stand face to face with its supreme object, had to fling itself back into the abyss of duration " before the mountains were brought forth, or ever he had formed the earth and the world." His proper realm was above the firmament and before the origin of things; and as soon as the heavens had been spread, and the land and sea stocked with the creatures of his hand, he *rested* from his work, and entered on a sabbath, which would only cease when a new heaven and a new earth should be called into being. No doubt, during this long sabbath, he was not supposed to be entirely without part in this scene of things; but it was chiefly in human, or, if in physical, in exceptional affairs, that any agency of his was traced: and the very phrases used to describe it, implying always some *interrention* of righteousness or mercy, assume a certain natural order, which would else take its own course to other ends; for whoever *overrules* steps upon a field beyond his ordinary *rule.* Setting aside such interpositions, we may say that the courses of the universe, so far as they proceed by regular law, were conceived to be the result of secondary powers or forces of nature, distinct from the Divine Will during their term of agency, and in contact with it only at their first adjustment. He was the first term of causation ; they were the *second*. The natural was theirs ; the supernatural was his. Whatever was assigned to them was taken one remove from him ; whatever was reserved for him was kept at one remove from them. So that the larger their domain became, the more did his retire into the residuary space beyond the boundaries of knowledge, a space which, though it is forever infinite, is also forever blank.

By this treaty of partition between science and religion, natural forces were installed in full possession of the cosmos in time, and the Divine Will was prefixed to it to be its origin. When, therefore, it appeared that no commencement could be found ; that cosmical time goes back through all that had been called eternity ; that for the prefix of an almighty fiat no vacancy could be shown, the natural forces seemed to have secured the system of things all to themselves, and to leave no room for their first appearance in succession to an earlier power. Faith, terrified at the prospect, vowed for a while still to search somewhere for the crisis of their birth ; and, while inexorable Discovery penetrated the past, taking the centuries by thousands at a stride, she kept beside upon the wing, watching with anxious eye for the terminal edge which looked into the deep of God ; till at last, weary and drooping, she could sustain the flight no more, and, to escape falling into the fathomless darkness, took refuge in the bosom of her guide, not to be repelled or crushed, as she had feared, but, as we shall see, to be cherished and revived.

For though the natural forces have lost their birthday, and seem to be old enough for anything, they gain no higher character by their extension of time ; and do not, by losing their sequence of date, lose their dependence of nature. They are no more entitled, by mere longevity, to serve an ejectment on the divine element, than is the divine element to claim everything from them. The reasons for recognizing the Infinite Mind as supreme cause are in no way superseded by the *age* of this or any other globe. It was not because the world was *new* that we had resorted to the thought of God ;

not because having, in the course of our researches, alighted
upon a chaos at one date, and a cosmos at another, we wanted
a means of bridging the chasm between them ; but because
the world was orderly and beautiful,—an organism of intellectual relations, the original of all our science and art, which
tells its story only to the interpretation of thought and the
divinations of genius.   And *this* it still is, and by its very
antiquity is shown, so far as we can tell, to have forever been.
The added duration extends the claims of both agencies alike,
the natural and the divine ; it enables neither to extrude the
other ; but it obliges us to revise the relation in which we had
placed them to one another.   They can no longer be treated
as successive in time.   Are, then, the natural and the divine
to be regarded as both of them present on the scene ? and, if
so, how do they make partition of the phenomena between
them ?   We are thus led at once to the third great characteristic of modern science,—its doctrine of the correlation and
conservation of forces.   Let us look at it in itself and in its
religious bearing.

So long as each science pursued its way, without regard to
its neighbours, the force with which it had to deal was simply
taken up at its entrance on that particular field, and escorted
to its exit ; and hence was apparently treated (perhaps only
apparently) as though there it were born and there it perished,
coming nowhence and going nowhither.   If a flash of lightning struck a tree, the electricity was traced to the cloud, and
spoken of as if it were original there.   If two bodies of equal
mass and velocity met from opposite directions and brought
each other to rest, the impinging forces were taken as
(mechanically) destroyed.   If this idea of force coming out of
nothing and going into nothing were really ever entertained, it had to give way as soon as the sciences lost their
isolation and were contemplated together.   When applications
of heat were found to evolve electricity, the flash of lightning,
ceasing to be spontaneous, fell back into questions about the
temperature of the clouds ; and from the shock of solid bodies
both heat and electricity were developed : so that the masses
whose motion was cancelled to mechanical measurement only
handed over their history to inquirers in another field.

Attention once being drawn to this migration of phenomena in their natural series from one science to another, instances crowded in so fast that the rule soon acquired a wide generality. There is not, in fact, a process in art or nature which does not illustrate it. The combustion of ordinary fuel is an example of chemical action, resulting on the one hand in light, on the other in heat: the heat, when applied to water, first simply raises its temperature; then, ceasing to do this, spends itself in producing vapour, and metamorphoses itself into elasticity, and becomes available to the inquirer as a store of mechanical power. Every railway telegraph that rings a bell has its electric current generated by magnetic or by chemical arrangements, and resulting in mechanical motion and in sound; while, in every photograph, we have light at the first point, and chemical change at the last. Need I say how this transmutation of power claims to cross the boundary from the inorganic to the living world? how the solar rays, acting on the ingredients of the soil, deliver them into the vital structure of the plant, and build it up into maturity? how the plant again becomes the nutriment of the animal, and the senses of the animal respond to the light and sound of the outer world, and pass on into the elaborations of thought, and enter into the determinations of will? And, in all this transmigration, the movement is in no single irreversible direction, but is strictly reciprocal: as heat will earn for you mechanical power, so will mechanical action, as is shown in the friction of every machine, develop heat; as you may make magnets of electricity, so will moving magnets give you your electricity again.

These effects have not only been ascertained over a field of vast extent, but, in numerous instances, been *measured*, so as to justify the statement that the quantity of force which vanishes in one form is identical with that which consecutively re-appears in another. The general inference is, that the distinction of forces into various kinds is only apparent, not real; depending on the medium of their manifestation, not upon anything in their intrinsic nature: that all the force behind the changes of the world is *One*, whether it assumes the mask of this or that order of phenomena; that nothing is ever added to it, nothing taken from it; that it circulates reciprocally from form to form of manifestation, being always capable of returning by any steps which its laws may enable it to take. This conception of force is the more readily embraced, because *motion*, which is its perceptible effect, has at the same time been similarly simplifying its varieties of kind: heat, colour, sound, chemical, electric, and magnetic action, being all resolvable into motory vibrations of different and even assignable velocities.

Here, then, we have Science abolishing her own plurality of natural powers, and, as her latest act, delivering the universe to the disposal of One alone; various in its phases, but in its essence homogeneous. It is impossible not to press the inquiry, How are we to conceive of that essence? *Which* of its phases represents it most truly? Does it more resemble a universal elasticity, like steam? or a universal quivering, like light? or a universal conscious mind, like thought in man? or must we say that probably it is like none of these, and that all its phases *misrepresent* it? To answer these questions we must resort to the fountain-head, wherever it be, whence Science drew what she has to say about this hidden power. Where did she learn to think about it, and to believe in it?

Not, it is confessed, in her own proper field of observation and induction. Nothing comes before us there except what speaks to our perceiving and comparing faculties. Phenomena, one after another in time; side by side with one another in space; like or unlike one another in aspect; those are all that, with such resources, we can ever hope to find. The things that happen being visible or audible or tangible, you can see or hear or touch; and you can write down the order in which they occur, so as to know in future what you are to expect. But the *power* behind, that turns them out on to the open theatre for us to look at,—call it chemical, electric, vital, as you may, *that* does not come into the court of eye or ear, and could never cross your thought, had you no faculty but such as these. So little disputable is this, that philosophers of the newest school forbid us, on the strength of it, to ask about causes at all, as lying beyond the range of the human faculties; and would limit us rigorously to the study of phenomena in their groupings and their series. The restriction, however, is too severe for even their own observance; and, in spite of themselves, words denoting not simply sequencies but energies continually occur in their writings.

Indeed, as I have elsewhere observed,[*] " the whole literature of science is pervaded by language and conceptions strictly *dynamical;* and if an index expurgatorius were drawn up, prohibiting all pretensions that went beyond 'laws of uniformity,' it would make a clean sweep of every treatise, physical or metaphysical, from the time of Thales to our own. Comte himself speaks of 'the mutual action of different solar systems,' and of 'the action of the sun upon the planets :' he says that 'the mathematical study of astronomical movements indispensably requires the conception of a single force :' he speaks of the 'thermological actions of a system mutually destroying each other ;' and of a 'character special to the electrical forces which presents more difficulty than the molecular gravitations.'[†] And Mr. Mill tells us that the 'contiguous influence of chemical action is not a powerful force ;' that 'electricity is now recognized as one of the most universal of natural agencies :' he speaks of 'a force growing greater' and 'growing less ;' of the 'action of the central forces ;' of the 'propagation of influences of all kinds ;' and distinguishes 'motions, forces, and other influences :' and 'the motion with which the earth *tends* to advance in a direct line through space' he calls 'a cause.'[‡] Whence this perpetual resort to an idea which lies out beyond that simple 'order of phenomena' of which alone, it is said, we are competent to speak ?"   Bain is apparently conscious of the inconsistency in which such use of dynamical language involves the disciples of his school ; for he rebukes it thus : "To express causation we need only name one thing, the antecedent or cause, and another thing, the effect ; a flying cannon-shot is a cause, the

---

[*] Study of Religion, B. II. ch. I. pp. 162–164 (1st Edn.).

[†] Philos. Pos. II. pp. 254, 250, 560, 708.

[‡] System of Logic (3rd Ed.).   Vol. I. pp. 489, 501.   Vol. II. pp. 33, 34. Vol. I. pp. 335, 352.

tumbling down of a wall is the effect. But people sometimes allow themselves the use of the additional word *power* to complete, as they suppose, the statement; the cannon-ball in motion has the power to batter walls; a pure expletive or pleonasm, whose tendency is to create a mystical or fictitious agency, in addition to the real agent, the moving ball."[*] If the author of this criticism would try the effect of it upon an officer of engineers, he would find that the "expletive" which he derides was not without a meaning to persons acquainted with cannon-balls, and that the "mystical" element was actually reducible to figures, and the object of innumerable problems far from being insoluble and still further from being fictitious.   Nay, the very language which he criticises he, too, is unable to avoid: he tells us of "moving power expended;" of "primal sources of energy;" "gravity," he says, "is an attractive force; and another great attractive force is *cohesion*, or the force that binds together the atoms of solid matter."[†] No struggles of ingenuity avail to prevent these self-variations: the theory of these writers is refuted by their vocabulary. With more consistency, and surely with deeper insight, the authors of the doctrine of conservation which we are reviewing have said in effect, "We grant you, force is not a phenomenon which can be observed; but it is indispensable for the conception of all phenomena; and, quarrel with it as we may, it will always be supplied in thought: it is as much their intuitive background of origination, as space of their position, and time of their succession, and has no less good a right than these to a place among the assumptions of science. Its justification is in its own necessity; its guarantee is in the very structure of our faculties; before which you can never present a change without awakening belief in a power which issues it."

Thus it is admitted that our own mind carries us behind the phenomenon as seen, and, supplementing it by an act of necessary thought, precludes us from conceiving it at all except as dealt out by a power. We believe this dynamical axiom on its own account, precisely as we believe, though we

[*] Mental and Moral Science, p. 400.
[†] Inductive Logic, pp. 35, 38, 121.   .

never experience, many things besides our own trains of sensation and inward change; precisely as we believe in the
presence of an external world, in the infinity of space, in
the immensity of duration,—all of them lying around, and
not within the sphere of our personality, and all therefore
out of reach, if we know only what turns up within ourselves.
But if we accept the idea of power *because* it is given us in
necessary thought, we must accept it also *as* it is given us in
thought: there is no other rule by which to fix and clear it.
What, then, *is* that idea of causality which mingles for us
with all our impressions of this moving world? What *kind*
of haunting presence is it which, under this name, our intuition spreads behind the scene? And what part of our nature,
what function of our reason, is it, which sets it there? The
answer is neither doubtful nor indistinct. There is but one
source which can tell us anything of causality at all, viz., our
own exercise of voluntary activity; and there it is that we
learn what it is to put forth power, to meet resistance, to
produce effects. Were we merely passive; were eye and ear
only beaten upon by the pulsating elements, so as to have
vision and sound, but not to look and listen; did we only lie
still to feel, and never start up to act, all that fell upon us
would stream through us like the images of a dream; and,
though we should be forever suffering effects, we should never
ask about a cause. And this is approximately the case of
creatures that are meant to feel and live, but not to *know*.
But add on the other half of our nature; let the lines of
energy go forth from it, as well as flow in upon it; above all,
set its organs and movements at the disposal of a free and
reasonable will; and with the active the cognitive faculties
will rise to their completeness: the causality within will
apprehend the causality without; and a power will be invisibly
interfused behind the visible incidents of the world, the
counterpart of that which we wield ourselves. This personal
tension by which we pass from the centre to the circumference
of our field, and institute a movement, a look, an attention,
is power: if with attainment of ends, successful power;
if otherwise, still power, though frustrated. Nothing is so
intimately and directly familiar to us as this: it is coincident

with the spontaneous side of our life, as distinguished from the recipient: it is at no distance from our essence, and defines and constitutes our proper self. It is the point where the interval is lost between our being and our knowing : only in putting out force am I, in fact and thought, myself. True it is, I do not become aware of it, even in exercising it ; i.e., I do not make it an object of reflection, except in presence of the opposite phenomenon of passive sensation, especially of impediment or arrested movement. But, in thus waking up to what I have been about, the apprehension of energy issued is no *inference* from data, no hypothesis of thought which might be erroneous and deals with the unknown, but an immediate intuition of a reality supremely certain. Here at home, we have first-hand acquaintance with power ; and nowhere else can this experience repeat itself. Even in the reaction of objects upon us, we do not know how they deal with us, on quite the same terms on which we know how to deal with them ; but we are aware that their action is opposite : and on the principle περὶ τῶν ἀντικειμένων τὴν αὐτὴν εἶναι ἐπιστήμην, we extend to them the same attribute by which we have moved upon them. So that, in owning their causality, we proceed on a different guarantee from that which assures us of our own, and apply to them a category of thought which is, indeed, the only one possible, and which covers them by a necessary act of the intellect, but which is not identical with the central consciousness of egoistic power. Still less is there any first-hand access to the idea of force in the action of one external body upon another. As witnesses of such phenomena alone, we could never pass beyond the law of succession ; and whatever we think further is an element intuitively imported from our own dynamical experience. Were we only observers, therefore, we should not, I repeat, have the idea of power ; for it is beyond the reach of sight and of every other perception. Were we only *patients*, it would be inaccessible ; for then, in the absence of anything distinct from them, we should not *have* sensations, but only *be* sensations ; and could not escape from them to ask about their " whence." It is as *agents* that we get behind phenomena, instead of looking at them, and learn the secret of their origin ; and the causal idea which by an intellectual law we then apply to all observed phenomena is wholly supplied from this known fund of personal efficiency. In other words, by power we mean *will;* neither more nor yet less: the word has no other possible signification; there is no source which can add any new element to this primitive type of the conception; and if anything be taken away, it can only be the accessories which distinguish this from that variety of will, leaving untouched the central idea of living agency. The same law of thought, therefore, which guarantees to us our action of power, interprets that power into will, and fixes on the highest phase of force as that into which all others are to be resolved. And so this last and most refined generalization of science justifies the sublime faith, that the sole power in the phenomenal universe is the Divine Intellect and Will, eternally transmuting itself into the cosmical order, and assuming the phases of natural force as modes of manifestation and paths of progression to ends of beauty and of good.

The same conclusion arises from another aspect of the same law. I have said that the convertible forces may often be submitted to the test of actual measurement; and that the amounts prove to be identical before and after the metamorphosis. This would seem to imply that it was a matter of indifference to which side of the equation we looked for the principal and representative term; that the movement could be read equally well either way, and that the two sides were absolutely interchangeable for all purposes. Yet it is not so. In comparing the several forms of power, there are two dimensions of value which you have to estimate; not their *quantity only,* but *their quality too;* and of the latter no system of equivalents, no gauge of " foot-pounds," or other standard, takes any notice or gives any account. Having measured, e.g., the dose of light and heat expended in growing a definite portion of your food, suppose that you could further find the equivalent chemical action which reduced that food into the material of blood; and then the measure of vital force for assimilating the blood, and turning some of it into brain; and finally the store of nervous power laid out thence in the service of thought; these quantities, by the rule, must be all equal in amount ; but they leave the several stages, in their other dimension of quality, wholly incommensurable and inconvertible. What degree of the thermometer can be the equivalent of a stanza of " In Memoriam," or of a happy stroke of philosophical genius ? What photometric scale can give the value of a moral act of self-denial, or a glad sacrifice of love ? How many grains of the protoids or the fats are tantamount to a penitential psalm, or to the agony of Gethsemane ? Among your forces, then, equate and proportionate them as you may, there remains, besides the measure of their material media, an indestructible difference of dignity, which ranges them on an ascending scale, and forbids you to read them indifferently backwards or forwards, though their scientific numbers may be equivalent. Now, when we bring the One force into which all are resolved before the face of this ascending scale, on *which* step shall we find the term which coincides with it in character ? Where is the type of power which, not in amount only, but in kind too, is all-comprehending, and omits no requisite for exchange with all the rest ? Is it not obvious, that, as in quantity the less can never match the greater, so in quality the inferior can never, out of its own resources, convert itself into the superior ? while the higher, containing more than all that is wanted for the lower, can take the descending place by merely suspending what is superfluously good ? You cannot deny the prerogative of will to reduce itself to lower phases ; to forego its own freedom, for determinate law ; to pass, therefore, by descending transmigration, into the form of force, vital, chemical, mechanical : for it would indeed be perverse to insist that dead and blind power can transmute itself into living intellectual energy, yet deny that mind can divest itself of its voluntary alternatives, and pledge itself to the lines of lower rules. The conclusion, then, is again, on this ground, irresistible, that the One Power which appears under guise so various must, in order to be adequate to its highest demands, include all that its supreme phases display, and must be thought of, not as the gravitation that answers to our weight, not as the undulation which reaches us in the form of heat, not even as the vital current of our life, but as the soul of our soul, the fountain and prototype of our thought and conscience, with whom our relation rises at once from convertibility of force into communion of spirit.

What, then, has become of the secondary causes supposed to be set up at the creation as delegated administrators of this universe? They are merged in the primary will, which, instead of planting them as vicegerents outside itself, holds them as modes and rules of its own permanent action. Am I asked whether this is not pantheism,—this identification of the dynamical life of the universe with God? I reply, it certainly would be so, if we also turned the proposition round, and identified God with no more than the life of the universe, and treated the two terms as for all purposes interchangeable. If, in affirming the divine immanency in nature, we mean to deny the divine transcendency beyond nature, and to pay our worship to the aggregate of all its powers, the law of its laws, the unity of its organism; if we merely sum up in one expression its interior modes of movement, in anticipation of some unknown formula whence they may be all deduced, then, undoubtedly, we do but pass from part to whole, and rest in a dream of future science, instead of emerging into immediate religion. But, if this were our thought, we should choose some other phrase than *will* to denote the inner principle of the world : for it implies intellect and purpose ; and of these, assuredly, the winds and waves, the light and heat, the curving projectile, the oxidizing metal, the crystallizing fluid, the growing plant, are not conscious ; so that, in resolving their forces into will, we mean to affirm *more* than belongs to them *per se*, and to put their blind phenomena in relation to a consciousness beyond them which knows and wields them. It is precisely to mark this transcendent element, this presence of a living idea in objects that are not alive, that we avail ourselves of the word " will ; " and, but for this, we should else, with Spinoza, be careful to ward off the ascription of understanding and will from the immanent Cause. Schopenhauer, it is true, has tried to divest the word " will " of the intellectual part of its meaning ; to discharge from it all idea of thought or purpose, and thin it down to the significance of blind power from within. He has substituted it for the word *force ;* not that it may carry a larger sense, and suggest the notion of intentional aim ; but simply to mark the point of personal experience, the exercise of living activity, which gives us the dynamic idea. But he cannot go thither for his word, yet fetch it away in that starved and blind condition : expel from will all consciousness, all light, all direction upon an end, and it is will no more; nor will men ever consent to embrace within the language of volition the physical and the moral phenomena of the world,—the dash of the torrent and the struggle of human resolve,—unless it be to infuse an ethical character into nature, instead of driving it off from the chief faculty of man. In identifying, then, the natural forces with will, we mean, not that *it* is essentially no more than *they*, but that *they* are essentially no less than *it;* that their action is attended, therefore, by a living consciousness, and intellectual conformity with a given drift and law ; and since these concomitants are not intrinsic to the several objects (which are the seat of action, without feeling their own phenomena), they are present with a mind abiding in the midst, and supplying the ideal to what else were but material. Instead, therefore, of cutting down the conception of God to the measure of natural objects, and leaving it only as the sum total of their attributes, we elevate them to his standard, and supplement their sensible qualities by relations with invisible thought and conscious knowledge. Thus, he is not the equivalent of the All, but its directing mind ; conscious where it is unconscious ; seeing where it is blind ; intending the future, where it only issues from the past.

Here, then, is one way in which, if the expression may be allowed, God and the world part company : at the lower end of the scale of being there are natures included in his δύναμις, whose phenomena, unfelt by themselves, are under cognizance by him ; at the upper end of the scale, the distinction is again effected, from an opposite cause. There are natures individually sentient, rational, moral, whose phenomena, felt by themselves, are unfelt by him. The hunger or the rage of the wild quadruped, the pain of the wounded bird, the perplexity of human thought, the rapture of relieved anxiety, the remorse of insulted conscience,—these are experiences not predicable of him ; they are objects of his cognition ; but the only subjects of them are some members or other of the hierarchy of creatures. Here, therefore, we alight in the universe on something which is not included in his personal being ; something which must be treated as objective to him ; something which, as universal power, he causes ; which, as omniscient intellect, he knows ; but which, as infinite perfection, he cannot feel. As, before, he was more than the "All," here he would seem to be less than the All ; and the identity between God and nature, in which pantheism consists, is again disturbed, and the two schemes of thought are further distinguished. I need hardly add that he is " less than the All," not as inadequate to its comprehension and control, but as having immunity from some of its phenomena ; only as the life of the saintly and the wise is " less than " that of guilty folly by exemption from its compunctions and unrest. It is of the very essence of the perfect nature to miss such experiences as these. And it is the fatal necessity of pantheism, that by making the consciousness of God identical with that of all sentient creatures, by treating them as but the leaves, and him as the sap, of the great life-tree, it has to predicate of him every error and weakness belonging to them ; and make him, not cause alone, but subject, of all the sorrows and falsehoods of the world.

We may present the distinction between the two theories in another light. It is the peculiarity of pantheism to admit of *nothing objective to God*. In his causal relation, he is the inner side of nature, its principle of spontaneous development, the *natura naturans* which is forever emerging in the *natura naturata;* and for that Infinite Being there is no " beyond " on to which any transitive action can pass ; no self-escape in order to deal with what is *other;* but only an eternal weaving of the tissue of phenomena from some focus within towards some circumference that is not without. But when we adopt the idea of will to mark the essence of God, we do exactly the reverse of this : we thereby claim something objective to him, on to which his thought, his purpose, his power, may pass ; for it is the characteristic of will to stand face to face with an end in view : to distinguish itself from what is other than self, and look forth on things and persons around as the scene given for its activity. In merging, therefore, the forces of nature in the will of God, we expressly guard ourselves against drowning the objective field under the overwhelming flood of the divine; and stipulate that, in some way or other, be it by space and matter given, or by lending out and fixing at certain centres stores of delegated power, there shall be reserved a theatre and objects of possible action for an intending and effectuating mind. Whether or not the theory can be worked out, its idea and purpose evidently are to negative the first principles of pantheism.

But how are we to carry out this purpose, and provide a domain that shall be objective to God? Must we assume such a thing to have been already always there,—a primitive *datum*, eternal as himself? or must he be regarded as furnishing himself with objects, and causing the very field of his own causality? The problem lies on the ultimate confines of human thought; but, if I read it aright, neither of these assumptions is adequate to its solution, without the other; and we must use them both, in order to conceive without mutilating the divine relations to the universe.

To raise the question whether a pure subjectivity can give rise to its own objects is to propose an empty riddle. Its sense is zero; and the answer can only be its echo. An "absolute subject" is no less a contradiction in thought than a single-termed equation, or an uncaused effect. To be a "subject" is to have an "object," and hold an existence, not "absolute," but relative; and the moment we conceive of mind at all, or any operation of mind, we must concurrently conceive of something other than it as engaging its activity. *This* thing which occupies it, or *that*,—empirical particulars without number, may be later than the mind, and arise in the course of its history. But, when these are all withdrawn, there must still remain, coeval with itself and inseparable from itself, some field of possible experience to carry the requisites indispensable for thought in any form. God, therefore, cannot stand for us as the sole and exhaustive term in the realm of uncreated being: as early and as long as he is, must also be somewhat objective to him. To the primordial condition we are helped by our intuitive apprehension of the infinitude of *Space*, supplying a field already

there for the most ancient movement of thought out of itself.
Space, however, is not itself an object, but only the opportunity for objects; so that there is, perhaps, still need of
another *datum;* viz., *matter* occupying finite place. It is
quite possible, indeed, to refine upon this word and reduce it
to " solidified extension ; " to resolve solidity into resistance ;
and to conceive of points of space *hardened* by becoming the
depositories of a repelling force, forbidding all else to enter ;
and in this way to construe the material element back into
the play of omnipotence in space. But for those who find
it difficult to work out this last simplification, we may
concede matter also, or extended solidity, in addition to space,
as a *datum* of the problem, and as the rudimentary object for
the intellectual and dynamic action of the supreme subject.
Here at once is presented a field comprising an immense
tissue of relations ; all that can be evolved by the sciences of
measure and of number, or deduced among the primary
qualities of body ; and in thinking out the universe under
these conditions, the Divine Intellect moves in steps of pure
deduction on an eternal ground, and justifies the saying of
Plato, that God is the great Geometer.

But on this field of necessary truth there is no scope for
the alternatives of will, or the inventive exercise of creative
reason. These enter, however, at the next stage ; for when
the remaining attributes of body are filled in, it must be by
pure origination ; for no links of demonstrative thought
connect them with the prior group, nor can the keenest
insight discover that they might not have been otherwise.
When the circle is given, all the properties of its intersecting
chords, the relations of their tangents, the comparative size
of an arc's central and peripheral angles, are unalterably
determined. But why undulations in one medium should
produce sound, and in another light; why one speed of
vibration should give red colour and another blue, can be
explained by no reason of necessity. These things we must
attribute to that which alone can determine the indeterminate ; viz., a selecting will, making for itself rules of
uniformity, and betaking itself here to this order, there to
that. In thus formulating his power, and distributing it

through the material *datum*, God makes it *objective* in two senses. He puts it into that which is *other than himself*, and he parts with *other use of it*, by pre-engagement to an end. This is all that is required for the setting up of other natures, which are thenceforth a guaranteed presence on the field, secure of their own distinctive history. But the power lodged in them for the conduct of that history remains, in one sense, subjective to God. He is its eternal supply, the continuous source of its regulated ebb and flow in every inlet and channel of being; apart from whom the universal organism would cease its pulsations and collapse. To say thus much of his agency in nature is only to re-assert the ancient claim of a perpetual upholding or perpetual creation of the universal order by divine power. " In him we live and move and have our being."

It must be admitted, however, that this conception will not work satisfactorily except in the lower departments of creation, ere we have entered upon the stage which we occupy ourselves. The vast system of cosmical mechanics and chemistry, the structure of the solar and the stellar worlds, we readily contemplate as *a whole*, pervaded by universal modes of power, and subsisting as the organ of God's legislated will. But when we look at the other end of the hierarchy of originated being, especially at ourselves, of whom our knowledge is most intimate, it is no longer possible to retain this close interfusion of the divine and the created natures. Whatever not only lives, but feels and consciously acts, must have something of its own ; must appropriate the impressions it receives, and have the credit of the energies it puts forth, and cannot be regarded as the mere organ through which flows a foreign power. If my thoughts were passed through me by another ; if my desires, affections, resolves, were phenomena of a force upon its travels that chose to come my way ; if, further, the whole genius and knowledge of the human race, the moral struggles of its heroes, the literature, philosophy, and art of its cultivated nations, were but the ripplings of the Divine Reason upon a world itself the aggregate of divine powers,—there would, in fact, be only One Person in the universe, and the whole drama of our life and history would dissolve into an illusion. To provide for this higher class of cases which culminates in *personality*, we must recognize a further stage of *detachment* of power from its source than we have hitherto mentioned, and admit the conception of *delegated* force, lent out for a term, in order to work the conditions of a distinct existence, and relapsing when the term is over.   Of the so-called " natural forces," each one in the ascending scale is more special and specializing than the preceding, more characteristic of particular natures, and gathered around centres of individuality, till, at the furthest distance from universal gravitation, we emerge into the conscious *Ego* of intellectual existence which finally sets up *another person*.   This *planting-out* of power, and storing it at single foci, to be disposed of from within under given rules of life, breaks no allegiance to its sole Fountain-head, and establishes no second source for it, but merely determines that, on touching the conditions of living beings, it shall have a consciousness which is not God's, though known to him, and to which its further course of administration shall be for a while consigned.

Even then within the realm of undisputed physical law, and without emerging beyond the region of natural history, we meet with provinces of reality objective to God in various degrees, without prejudice to the identification of all power with his will.   But the full security against the dissolving mists of pantheism is first obtained when we quit the simply natural field in which nothing is possible but in linear links of succession, and stand in presence of the supernatural in man, to whom an *alternative* is given, and in whom is a real mind, or miniature of God, consciously acting from a selected end in view.   Here it is that we first learn the solemn difference in ourselves between what is and what might be ; and, carrying the lesson abroad, discover how faint a symbol is visible nature of its ideal essence and Divine Cause.   Here it is, that, after long detention in our prison of facts, the walls become transparent, and let us see the fields more than elysian beyond. The Eternal is more than all that he has done.   And if the universe, with all its vastness, is only the single actuality which shapes itself out of a sea of possibilities ; if its laws are but one function of thought in a Mind that transcends them every way; then, in being the indwelling beauty and power of the world, he does not cease to be the living God above the world and though the world were gone. Still more, if, within the local realm of his administration, there is an enclosure which he has chosen to rail off as sacred for a minor divineness like his own, for a free and spiritual life, having play enough from the thraldom of natural laws for responsible movements of its own; then, however resistless the sweep of his power elsewhere, here, at the threshold of this shrine of conflict and of prayer, he gently pauses in his almightiness, and lets only his love and righteousness enter in. Here is a holy place reserved for genuine moral relations and personal affections, for infinite pity and finite sacrifice, for tears of compunction and the embrace of forgiveness, and all the hidden life by which the soul ascends to God.

Here, however, we are carried on to ground which no natural philosopher can survey for us. Looking back on the path which has led us thus far, we meet, in the three great modern discoveries, respecting the space, the duration, the forces, of the cosmos, with nothing to disturb, and with much to elevate and glorify, the religious interpretation of Nature; and, through the falling away of puerile conceptions, at once to justify and to harmonize the impressions of devout minds in every age. The outward world, nevertheless, is not the school of the purest and deepest. It is not God's characteristic sphere of *self-expression*. Rather is it his eternal act of *self-limitation*; of abstinence from the movements of free affection moment by moment, for the sake of a constancy that shall never falter or deceive. The finite universe is thus the stooping of the Infinite Will to an everlasting self-sacrifice; the assumption of a patient silence by the Fountain-head of boundless thought. The silence is first broken, the self-expression comes forth, in the moral phenomena of our life, where at last Spirit speaks with spirit, and the passage is made from the measured steps of material usage to the free flight of spiritual affection. The world reports the power, reflects the beauty, spreads abroad the majesty, of the Supreme Cause; but we cannot speak of higher attributes, and apprehend the positive grounds of trust and love, without entering the precincts of humanity.

CHAPTER II.

GOD IN HUMANITY.

WHEN we wish to speak of the world as a system of established order, we borrow a word from the methods of human society, and say that it is a realm of *law*. The term very accurately describes *movement or action in conformity with rule, and restrained within definite and assignable conditions*; and this, its essential meaning, never leaves it through the whole range of its application. It is curious, however, to observe how this fundamental idea, as it passes from province to province of the universe, takes on new elements, and embodies itself in richer forms. Under its lowest aspect, we find it in the inorganic and insentient world, which is simply the unconscious theatre of its presence. The water, in its cycle from sea to cloud, from cloud to snow, from snow to stream, that finds the sea again; the foliage, that drops in winter, and is re-born in spring; the flower, that throws its stamens open to the sun, and folds them from the chills of night; the curving light, that shows us the sun before he has risen, and after he has set, and softens the night at either end; the gulf-stream, that warms the higher latitudes, and cools the tropic seas,—all these constitute an order which they do not feel, and weave a web of relations among things that do not see each other, and are disposed of by a power that uses them all without reporting itself to any. They follow a law which is made for them, and which, without consent or recognition of theirs, holds them in unswerving obedience. The mind in which their order is original does not enter them except as force, and wields them only as the diagrams and apparatus of its own thought.

When law takes possession of Animal Life, it plants a power of higher type within, and establishes a fuller system of relations. Instinct, everywhere adaptive, seems to take the adjusting activity into its own hands, and to manage its business for itself; yet, with curious partition of the work, selects the means without preconception of the end. The moth, which deposits its eggs on the only plant which will feed the future caterpillar, or, itself vegetarian, stores around them the kind of chrysalis which its *larvæ* will require; the salmon, which punctually ascends the stream, and intrusts its progeny to the fresh waters in which itself was born; the bird, that builds and hides its nest on the ground, or under the eaves, or pendent from the bough, and seems to get ready for its dangers and its time; the mother-ostriches, that club together to put all their eggs of yesterday into one nest, under charge of a male bird, and all those of to-morrow into another; the new-fledged fly-catcher, which at once snaps, without missing, at its prey, with true measure of the distance, and selection of the kind; the constructive beaver, the civic ant, the co-operative bee,—all are engaged in building up a balanced organism of relations, a beneficent interdependence, every part of which, even that which they directly serve, is wholly beyond their cognizance. They are not left, however, like the planet in its orbit, or the tidal wave, wholly outside, as merely vehicles of the order they display: their conscious life is drawn into it; they serve it with their feeling, they advance it with their strength, though it is absent from their thought. With a kind of incipient partnership in the economy of the world, they are admitted to its administration, but not to its counsels; and are the eager executants of purposes to which they are blind. Are these ends absent, are they non-existent, because unknown to the creatures of which they dispose? No: they are assembled elsewhere; and, from the perfection of the divine thought, work themselves out into realization, through the pressure of countless feelings, con-verging upon a final equilibrium of beauty and of good.

This form of law does not cease with the tribes below us; it rises into our nature, and occupies in it all the functions which our life has in common with theirs. The attempt of philosophy to invest us with a constitution violently different from theirs; to make everything derivative in us which is original in them; to substitute in us, for their spontaneous passions, the trained results of experience, and build us up out of associated pains and pleasures with next to nothing ready-made, is a wasted artifice of ingenuity, which forces, stronger than argument, will forever confute. The propensions which are the common stock of all animal existence; the passions which fence it from its foes; the affections which knit it to its kind, plainly enter our life on the same terms which are assigned to them elsewhere, and equally bear upon them the stamp of instinctive impulse driving blindly to its end. Who that has seen and laughed at the passionate boy, venting disappointment on his hoop or top, as well as on his playmates, can fail to recognize the same signs which appear in every provoked creature, of that resentment which springs against sudden harm, and, in the moment of danger, invests weakness with preternatural strength? And shall we admire, as provisions of instinct, the maternal cares of the swallow or the hen, and break the analogy when the same conditions light up a human life with joy and love and patient sacrifice? Nay, even when we take account of tendencies more special to man, the impulsive and spontaneous character which distinguishes instinct from reflection does not disappear. What more sudden flash can burst unbidden into the soul than the kindling of pity at the spectacle of woe? It is but an appealing look; and in the twinkling of an eye the seals are melted from the source of tears, and the hand is seized as with a spasm of succouring strength. It is the instant remedy for instant anguish; and as the sorrows of this world often cannot afford to wait, so is there ready in the soul a balm swifter than reason, and more healing than any skill. The difference between man and his companion-creatures on this earth is not that his instinctive life is less than theirs, for, in truth, it goes far beyond them; but that in him it acts in the presence, and under the eye, of other powers, which transform it, and, by giving to it vision as well as light, take its blindness away. He is let into his own secrets; though he too is snatched forward toward objects given to his nature, not found by either accident or art, yet he has this distinction: that he marks and remembers what they do to him; and when they offer themselves again, he now knows, in his

movement towards them, whither he is going; and what
before was a drifting in the dark, becomes a passage to an
end foreseen. It is this change of theatre for the natural
instincts, this removal of their life on to an illuminated stage,
where they have to act their parts in the presence of higher
direction,—this it is which adds a new character to law, when
it takes possession of the human activities, and which lifts it
at once from natural to moral. Other beings it sways, but
does not consult. Man it takes into complete partnership
with it and treats as its confidant. Its force was on the
planet; its feeling in the animal; its thought is in man.
Passing thus from physical to ideal, and asking, not the
obedience of matter, but the assent of mind, it drops its
coercive aspect, reports itself as duty, without the enforcement
of necessity, and simply leaves with the soul a trust of power
adequate to execute its own idea. And so man becomes "a
law unto himself;" not that he *makes* the law or can repeal
it, but that he has within himself the resources for recognizing it and for obeying it, and may consciously and freely co-
operate with that appointed order by which other natures are
swept along without their leave.

Now, how is this change in the character of law brought
about on its transplantation into our nature? What is the
provision for replacing the rectilinear sequences of natural
law by the alternative possibilities of moral law? In what form
is our consent asked to the right, and the warning given
against the wrong? And by what constitution of mind are
we qualified to give the true response? Has each one of us,
like Socrates, his good genius attending him, with voice ever
ready to check the incipient aberration? Or have we a certain
special sense for detecting in all actions, when they come
before us, some quality, otherwise occult, that distinguishes
the right from the wrong? Or is the quality not occult at
all, but just the superior pleasure to ourselves or others of the
action rightfully preferred, and do we approve by admeasurement of happy results? These are the chief doctrines prevalent about the ultimate ground of our moral sentiments. The
comparative criticism of them is the business of the systematic moral philosopher, and is full of interest, both historical

and psychological. But it would take us to our end by a needless circuit. It will be better for us to enter for ourselves the field of ethical phenomena, regardless of all its preoccupation, to consult afresh the nature on which we have to report, and simply register what there appears. The facts which we may find will incidentally controvert the fictions which we must exclude, and furnish a criticism while dispensing with the critic. Where, then, is the exact incidence, and what are the characteristics, of all moral judgment?

1. Whenever we pass a moral judgment, it is always upon a *person*, and not upon a *thing*. Both of these may affect us agreeably or disagreeably, may be received with welcome, or rejected with dislike ; but the admiration or aversion awakened by mere things, by the form of a tree, the plumage of a bird, by disproportion in a house, or discord in a song, are totally distinct from moral approval and disapproval. Be the annoyance ever so great which we suffer from these impersonal objects, be the tree such as drew down the humorous imprecations of Horace, or the house such as it has cost us dear to mend, we are simply hurt by them, not angry at them. And the very same disasters affect us differently according as they are or are not believed to have a personal origin ; the tile that falls and wounds us as we walk brings us only harm from the wind of accident ; but injury, to be felt as such, must come from the hand of mischief. Nay, so true is this, that, even in the case of acts distinctly human, it is not the *thing done*, but the *person doing*, not the product, but the cause, that we are impelled to judge. The same deed of crime may issue from a dark, neglected nature, and from one luminous and rich with the discipline of Christian opportunity ; but our feeling will verge towards pity in the one case, and burn with indignation in the other. And so when some sacrifice of love,— the tending of the sick, the support of the orphan,—is made by the poor, whose own need is scarcely less severe, and whose struggle might be held to excuse from such devotedness, we yield to it a homage which it would win in very different degree if it came from the strong, stooping easily to help the weak. For us, it is invariably, not the act, but the agent, that is mean or noble : him it is that we despise or honour ;

apart from him, and looked at as an object in itself, the act offers to no sense or faculty of ours any moral quality to cast the vote of our approbation. It may give pain or pleasure; it may be beautiful or ugly; it may be prolific or sterile; but cut off from its author, and treated as an external phenomenon, it takes its place, like health or disease, among natural facts, to which no ethical emotion is due.

Instances, indeed, are adduced, in which we seem to estimate outward objects in terms of moral appreciation. For example, we may "approve" the tone of a picture, the proportion of a sculpture, the decorations of a room; we may "despise" a mincing speech or a tawdry costume; and the surveyor may "condemn" a fortress or a frigate. But it is obvious that here we have only a figurative transfer of ethical language to judgments of taste and utility; and that the feelings expressed are purely æsthetic or technical, without the characteristics of moral sentiment. And the cause of this transference is not difficult to find. It is limited to cases where an end is aimed at, and a choice is made; and is never applied to the given objects of nature, which lie beyond conceivable variation. Works of fine art, and structures of mechanical skill, are products of will, involving alternative possibilities, and resembling moral action in carrying a better and a worse; and hence they draw upon them the same preferential language, though the thing preferred is not a greater righteousness, but a greater beauty or a greater use. The personal habits and creations, to which above all we apply this phraseology, are, moreover, the symbols of inward character; and, though betraying primarily no more than its cast of imagination, suggest by implication the probable presence of a corresponding type of ethical preference. It is still, therefore, not upon the phenomenon itself, but upon the personal source, that the sentence of our feeling is passed.

2. We must then enter the precincts of the agent's personality in order to scrutinize more nearly the precise point on which our moral appreciation settles. His action we may resolve into the three main elements of its history; viz., the impulse whence it starts, the movements which execute it, and the effects that follow it. No one can let his attention

rest for a moment on each of these, without confessing that it is *the first alone* which we approve or condemn, and which we accept as an expression of character. So long as this remains, and the spring of action has not changed its decree, our praise or blame will stand; though, by some arrest of execution, the intention is frustrated at its birth, or, by a change of outward conditions, the consequences are reversed. The holy purpose, broken off by paralysis of limb, or interrupted by sudden death, kindles our reverence as much as the highest triumphs of successful will; and those whose designs of love are blotted out in the darkness of some Calvary are none the less venerated as saviours by the world. And who does not own the defence of Demosthenes to be just, that the patriot and statesman is not to be judged by the event, but may yet have his claim on gratitude from a ruined country, and amid the wreck of baffled plans? Take away, on the other hand, the initial term, and suppose the same succession of events to complete itself by other means than the originating purpose; and the phenomenon, thus mechanically accomplished, slips at once from ethical into natural history; and, bring what it may of good or ill, it commands no love, and justifies no indignation. Without its prefix of impelling affection, the executive activities are but a muscular spasm; and, though they were to conjure up all imaginable felicities, would be as little praiseworthy as the sunshine and the rain. We conclude, then, that the moral quality lies exclusively in the inner spring, of which the act is born.

3. Yet, if there were *only one* such spring of action implanted in our nature, or allowed scope in our opportunities, it would be no object of ethical judgment. Who, for instance, could condemn any fury of resentment, if that passion had the soul entirely to itself, and there were no opposing pleadings pressing to be heard? or any voracity of appetite, if all consciousness were swallowed up in hunger? The creatures below us are apparently not far from this condition: they seem to be actually taken up by instinct after instinct, each in its turn, as if there were no other. They have, therefore, no problem; and nothing is possible to them but to become the organs of each present affection, and

let it hand them over to the next. It is precisely because
this is *not* the condition of our world, because no man is ever
noble without the opportunity of being base, or the slave of
a false service without the offer of a true, that we look on
human character as on an eventful drama, full of crises of
suspense, and, as we watch the stage, have our hearts ever
charged with a sacred anger or a thankful joy. When,
therefore, on seeing a human impulse break into life and
claim the field, we clap our hands, and cry, " Well done ! "
we always see a rival near ; and, knowing what conflict there
may have been behind the scenes, welcome the victor as from
a battle won.

4. If this be so, if it be on these conditions that our moral
judgments are passed, one weighty controversy may be at
once discharged. Where, it has been asked, is the birthplace, where the earliest school, of our moral sentiments ?
Do we gather them from the influence of our fellow-men ?
Are they the infection of education, the copy of social
opinion ? Are they imposed upon us by the will of predecessors and companions, mere rules, made in their interest,
and enforced by the sanction of their power ? Or are they
native to our own mind, and a true home-growth upon the
personal field ? In other words, are the primary verdicts
passed upon our fellows, or upon ourselves ? One simple
test would seem to decide this question. If the moral criticism express the view we take of others' conduct, if it is from
this as a beginning that our sentiments of right build themselves up, they must fasten their approval or contempt upon
what an observer can see and feel of the action which they
judge,—upon its visible characteristics of good and ill. Not
till it has quitted the agent's personality, and has gone
abroad into the light, charged with benefit or injury, will it
be qualified to earn our praise or reprobation. We have
seen, however, that it is by no means to these outwardly
perceptible features of its history, but exclusively to its
hidden springs within, that our sentence addresses itself:
there alone it is that we discern the clean and unclean, the
worthy and the base. Where, then, do we learn these appre-
ciations ? What should we know of these viewless seats of

character if we could only look out of our eyes at the movements of other men?   How could we ever interpret the
moral meaning of these signs, any more than a bird could
understand the tears of compunction, or the uplifted look of
prayer, if the key were not within us, in the motive affections
of our own hearts?   It is on the home enclosure, within the
private plot of our own consciousness, that we make acquaintance with the springs of action, and are forced to see them as
they are; and if here it is that we discern the sacredness and
the sin, our primary school of morals lies within ourselves,
and we may dismiss, as a play of ingenious fiction, all
attempts to explain our own conscience as a reflection of
other men's looks, and to elaborate the delicate sanctities of
private duty out of the coarse fibre of public self-interest.
That our fellows make demands upon us, that they expect us
to be just and true and merciful, is a secondary phenomenon,
which could have no place did they not presume us first to
make the demand upon ourselves; and their suffrages, however coercive, would speak to us with no inward weight did
they not issue from a moral apprehension like our own, and
reproduce from kindred witnesses the verdict, or the surmises,.
of our hearts.   The theory is not only an opprobrium to·
philosophy, but a poison to the world, which assumes that, to
begin with, men know nothing but the sentient difference
between pleasure and pain; and set themselves, in default of
distinctions more august, to work it up by artifice into semblance of a thing divine, virtually saying to each other,
" See! there is no conscience here.   Come, let us make an
image in its likeness, and build it of the clay of our own
wishes, and gild it over as a god; and we will set it on the
plain, where all men shall see it, and at the sound of our
trumpet they shall bow down and worship it."   When such
illusions have come to the end awaiting all idolatries, we
shall return to the simpler speech of less ingenious times:
" Brothers, we have all one conscience here.   Come, let us
confess together what it would have from us; and, to help its
weakness in each, let us declare its claims on all, and gather
the divine voices, scattered as they are, into a chorus of right
for our community."   Society, once tempted by flattery to

believe itself the *source* of moral law, is ever sliding towards dissolution ; but, while reverently living as its product and its organ, becomes ever firmer and more glorious.

5. If it be the inner spring of action to which all ethical quality attaches,—and even then, only on condition that it is not there alone,—our moral constitution reduces itself to the simplest form : it stands clear at once of every mystery, and of every arbitrary pretension supposed to be chargeable on the doctrine of a moral faculty. It is all contained in this : that, as the instinctive impulses turn up within us, one after another, and two or more come into . presence of each other, they report to us their relative worth ; and we intuitively know the better from the worse. The hungry child, who is ready to satisfy his appetite without a restraining thought, no sooner falls in with some Lazarus, fainting with starvation, than he feels in a moment the higher claim of pity, and either parts with the untasted meal, or, if not, finds it made bitter by compunction. An irascible mother, fretted with her cares, and venting herself upon the nearest vexation, strikes her idiot boy, and he falls beneath the unintelligible wound. With what instant anguish does she know how much meaner is the anger she has indulged than the compassion she has forgot ! Such examples are types of all our native self-judgments. And the consciousness we have of the relative excellence of the several instincts and affections which compete for our will—a consciousness inseparable from the experience of each as it comes into comparison with another, but incomplete till we have rung the changes on them all—is neither more nor less than *conscience.* The moral faculty, therefore, is not any apprehension of invisible qualities in external actions, not any partition of them into the absolutely good and absolutely evil, not any intellectual testing of them by rules of congruity, or balances of utility, but a recognition, at their very source, of a scale of *relative* values lying within ourselves, and introducing a *preferential* character throughout the countless combinations of our possible activity. I will presently consider what is the nature, and what the religious significance, of that moral authority which thus opens upon us. But, before proceeding to this

topic, I would pause for a moment on a single aspect of our exposition.

From the constitution of the human mind which we have traced, we see how it is that all great moral natures instinctively turn inwards; and by their native thirst for *divine knowledge* are carried to the fountains of *self-knowledge*. There it is, in the secret glades of thought and motive, that the springs of life arise, and the distinctive lights and shadows of good and ill are seen to play; and thither is the soul invariably led by the genius of duty. Even amid the brilliant distractions of Athens, it was to this centre that Socrates retreated from the speculations of science, and the dazzling ambitions of men, and disciplined himself to be the martyr of the first ethical philosophy, and the father of all others. Under the weight of empire, it was the chief care of Marcus Aurelius to commune with his own heart; and from that silent converse he brought a strength and harmony of virtue which shames the whole calendar of saints. As soon as the religion of Christ had had time to make itself felt, and to fix its spirit legibly in the hymn, the prayer, the literature, of the faith, the unsuspected contents of the human soul seemed to pour themselves forth in a flood of pathetic confession, and to open resources for a new and deeper drama of life. And, compare where we will the expression of ancient and of modern civilization, in their epics, their tragedies, their art, or their philosophy, the relative interest of the outward world pales in the later ages before the inner mysteries of our own nature. The broad canvas of history fascinates us less than the cabinet portrait of biography with its silent lips and meaning eyes; and, through the pomp of statesmanship and the din of revolution, we pierce with eager search to the play of individual passion and the conflict of personal character. This reflective tendency, this retirement within, is due to the hidden sense rather than the open discovery that here is the true seat of law,—the place of judgment, whence there is no appeal. And hence it is never in light mood, with noisy and jaunty step, but with hushed breath, and on the tiptoe of silence, that we draw near to look into these inner circles of the soul. Elsewhere, we can go familiarly in and out, and take our notes of what we find, without disturbance to the humour of the hour : but *there* we know there is a *sanctuary ;* and ere we reach it, an invisible incense breathes upon our hearts, and subdues us into involuntary worship. While the more external study of men, the scrutiny of them by intellectual eye-sight, is the constant source of cynical illusion, meditative self-knowledge is the true school of reverence, of sympathy, of hope, of immovable humility ; for there we see, side by side, what we are and what we ought to be ;—and of unquenchable aspiration ; for there too we meet, spirit to spirit, the almighty Holiness that lifts us to himself.

It is true, however, that the self-knowledge which is the special prerogative of man is his latest, as it is his highest, gain. And hence the simple program of his moral nature, though living in him in lines of light, remains unread ; and its very existence is as much disputed as if it were invisible. There is nothing surprising in this. The truth is too near for the average eye to see it ; and the vision, accommodated to outward things, overlooks what presses more closely on itself. If men could be quietly consulted one by one, taken into the closet of some Socratic questioner, schooled in reaching the confessional of thought, they would readily be made aware of their inward discernment of ethical differences among their incentives, and would own a law of God written on the heart. Were there only this private witness of personal consciousness, the evidence would seem to be all one way. But they go out into the public streets, and watch the variegated stream of population intent on different ends ; they frequent the courts, and listen to the contending pleas for a right suspended between two suitors ; they observe a nation, whose noblest citizens confront each other under the opposite banners of law and revolution ; they scrutinize history, and find the sanctioned usages of one age become the crimes of another : and, amid the din of this distracted field, the authority which looked so clear within seems lost in lawlessness without : all uniformity of rule is broken up, and of any consentaneous moral faculty scarce a trace remains. The throng of conflicting phenomena gives noisy answer to the silent inward pleadings ; and the secret conviction of a divine order, known to all, is beaten down by the confusion of the world.   Where, it is asked, is the pretended intuition of the right in a race which, by turns, has consecrated every wrong?   What is the use of a moral faculty which, if it can sleep while a Caligula or a Borgia triumphs, and saints are hunted down by inquisitors, and superstition plays off its pitiless cruelties, is no better than a moral incapacity?   Who would trust himself to the conscience of an African savage or a Mexican chief? Is it not plain that a standard which is constant for no two places or times must be the arbitrary creation of social necessity, the crystallization of traditional prejudice and usage, passing from the public fashion into the private feeling, and calling itself indigenous there, because not knowing whence it is ?

These considerations would have great weight against any doctrine of conscience which set it up as an infallible oracle, able to pronounce at sight on the ethical character of external actions.   Men, under such guidance, would have their moral perceptions perfect at once, and uniform everywhere, and could add nothing by way of growth or history, except so far as, with changing conditions, new lines of possible action came before them.   But if conscience is withdrawn altogether from the criticism of outward action, if it be taken simply for the sense we have of a better and worse among our inward springs of conduct, not only is its existence compatible with the conflicting judgments of mankind and the cross-lights on the field of history, but it affords the simplest key to these, showing precisely how they arise, and exhibiting them as the direct and inevitable consequence of the very plan of our mental constitution.   For instance :—

1. The *limited range* of conscience among barbarous tribes and people everywhere of immature humanity is precisely what we should expect, when we remember how few are the influences which have play in their life; and how scanty, therefore, is the set of moral differences to which their feeling has yet been introduced.   Our nature opens and turns out its forces only by degrees.   There is an infancy for the race as well as for the individual ; and, as nearly one-third of life must pass ere the child succeeds to the passions and problems

of the man, so, in the first attempt at society, and in its more retired parts, a large proportion of the human dynamics sleep. A small number of private instincts and affections appear upon the stage, and conduct the action of the piece; and since, even of these, one is usually off before another is on, the inner life is rather a succession than a conflict of powers; and there is little of that comparison and strife of incentives from which the moral self-consciousness is born. The Indian who, in a fit of suspicion, takes the life of his faithful wife or son, discovers with remorse how much nobler is the affection he has insulted than the fear he has obeyed. Or, perhaps, in the hot blood of victory, he tortures his captive till some look of piteous agony pierces to the seat of pity in his heart, and he finds something to which revenge itself must yield. But among these rudiments of a moral life, his years of simple experience pass away, and all the higher terms on the scale of human incentive remain undiscovered overhead, so that the very materials are invisible of the problems which they present; and to seek a verdict on them from his moral sense would be like carrying into the nursery questions of political libel or international law. Within the narrow circle of his existence, so far as it has emerged from the dominion of *successive* instincts, and fallen under the rules of a comparing consciousness, I do not think it can be shown that he mistakes or inverts the claims of his few natural affections.

2. The *apparent discrepancies* of ethical judgment by which, in different societies, the hero and the criminal change places, are also the necessary result of the unequal development of a uniform moral consciousness. To convince ourselves of this, we have only to remember that every verdict of approval is passed, not upon the action, but on its spring; and is, moreover, not absolute, but simply relative and preferential. Whenever, therefore, you try to settle the worth of any case of conduct, your eye fastens at once upon the feeling whence it has obviously sprung; and this, for the purposes of estimate, you set side by side with that other feeling which you take to be its alternative, sure to have the field if its competitor withdraws. Our sentence of approval, then, though it bears an absolute look, and only says, "The thing is *right*," really

means no more than the comparative decision, " *This* is better
than *that*."   Suppose that, meanwhile, I have been pondering
the same case; that I have referred it, like yourself, to its
true incentive; but that I have imagined a different alternative, and therefore instituted a different comparison, not, as
in your deliberations, with the term immediately below, but
with the term immediately above : is it any wonder that I
contradict you, and say, " The thing is *wrong* "?   And is it
not plain that, flat as the contradiction seems, it is not real ?
since my assertion that B. is worse than C. is no reply to
yours, that B. is better than A.   To both of us, by the very
constitution of our nature, a suppressed term of comparison
is indispensable ; and if that term should be not the same for
you and for me, our minds will never meet, and we shall
deliver judgments on different problems, though in form the
one decree affirms precisely what the other denies.   I know of
no seeming discordances of ethical opinion which do not
readily resolve themselves under the application of this
formula.   Nothing is more revolting to us in the Greek
civilization than the sacrifice of the weakly and infirm by the
exposure of infants and the cutting off of the old.   We treat
it as sheer inhumanity and irreverence, selfishly inflicted on
helpless victims in riddance of a burden of troublesome but
sacred cares.   We carry to it our Christian estimate of the
individual soul and its trust of life,—a trust which no maimed
conditions, no sorrowful lot, no waiting for release, can ever
cancel or disappoint : we think how large a part of social duty
is constituted by the humanities which shelter the weak and
nurse the sick and care for them that have none to help ; and
that all this should be cast away in order that the strong may
be stronger, and lives too brilliant should lose their shadows,
fills us with indignant horror.   But in this we proceed upon
comparisons which were impossible to the Greek ; whilst he
acted on a view of the world impossible to us.   Life, death, the
world, the individual, stood before him in relations which have
passed from our sympathy,—almost from our apprehension.
He inverted our order of reverence.   The *State* was to embody
for him the divine perfection of the cosmos, and its single
components were to be used like the seed-corn, or burned like

the weeds, according as they could adorn it with the beauty of their growth, or cleanse it by their swift decay. He recognized no rights in the personal life which could stand up against the wholesomeness of the community ; and no duties, except to yield itself unreservedly as the organ, or remove itself as the obstruction, of the public good. For one who was disabled from serving the commonwealth, there was no trust, no sacredness, no business, here: he could remain only to discover himself a cumberer of the ground ; and it was not only permitted, but required, whether from himself or from others, as guardians of the perfection of the world, that he should quit the scene which he deformed. In this view the sacrifice was made, not to self and private ease, but to an ideal of public good and divine order ; and the thing sacrificed was not that solemn opportunity, that inalienable trust, which to us the probationary plot must ever be of even the poorest cottiers in this husbandry of God, but a mere shipwrecked position on barren sands, where not a green thing would grow, and the circling sea cut off the continents of hope and love. The terms of the comparison, and the conditions of the problem in the ancient and the modern mind being thus different, it is no wonder that answers seemingly conflicting are given to questions really different.

In truth, it is only by thus retiring inward to the preconceptions and sentiments from which action is assumed to spring ; only, therefore, by consulting the moral consciousness itself, that these startling contrarieties of judgment can at all be understood. If we went by the external effects of action alone, approving of what did good, condemning what did harm, it would be much more difficult to explain the violent revolutions of ethical opinion. For the outward consequences do not, like the inner springs, change their adjustment and relation from age to age: they are palpable and measurable alike to the ancient and the modern, to Aristotle and to Mill ; and if the materials and the method of solution were thus impartially present to all observers, the opposite answers would hopelessly perplex us, and would but hand over the imputation against the consistency of conscience to stand as a charge against the uniformity of reason.

3. The *gradual growth* of moral discernment, and the mode in which it takes place, are also what we should expect from the preferential character ascribed to it. Till a spring of action appears upon the field and disputes possession of us with another, it has no place in our estimate at all; and when it has begun to visit us, it has to pass through its circle of comparisons with prior occupants before it can fall into order with the rest. We are far on in our career before the whole of even the primitive series of impulses, e. g., the parental affection, can have found us out. And, by various partnerships among these, as well as by conversion, through our self-consciousness, of the instinctive into the prudential, new and mixed incentives (e. g., the love of power, the sense of veracity, devotion to our country) are perpetually added, so as to enrich the contents of our nature and enlarge the scope of our moral existence. And what is it that quickens these elements into life? Is it in solitude that, like bubbles set free from the bottom of some sleeping pool, they one by one rise to the surface? No: it is in the eddy and the flow of life, as it chafes in its channel, and is turned by the rock, and ventures its leap, that all the force and the effervescence come out. We find our proper personality only in society; and it is by exposure to the light of other consciences that the colours of our own steal forth. Especially is it the play of inequality in the characters around us, the repulsion of those below, the attraction of those above, our level, that wakes up the forces of our proper nature, and, by compelling us to define our aspirations, turns the blind tracks of habit into the luminous path of a spiritual career. Am I thrown among associates who breathe a lower atmosphere, and who appeal to incentives which in my heart I cannot honour as the best? My secret ideal stands before me as it never did before; and, in my compunction if I am weak, in my resolution if I am strong, its authority looks down upon me with living eyes of pity or of help. Am I admitted into the company of greater and purer men, who move among the upper springs of life; who aim at what had scarcely visited my dreams; who hold themselves, with freest sacrifice, at the disposal of affections known to me only by momentary flash; who rise above the fears that

darken me, and do the duties that shame me, and bear the sorrows that break me down ? The whole secret and sanctity of life seem to burst upon me at once ; and I find how near the ground is the highest I have touched, and how the steps of possibility ascend, and pass away, and lose themselves in heaven. This is the discipline, this the divine school, for the unfolding of our moral nature,—the appeal of character without to character within. The sacred poem of our own hearts, with its passionate hymns, its quiet prayers, is writ in invisible ink ; and only when the lamp of other lives brings its warm light near do the lines steal out, and give their music to the voice, their solemn meaning to the soul. In this sense of interdependence we do, undoubtedly, owe our moral sentiment largely to others ; but only because they, too, bear *that* about them which we revere or abhor, and their character serves as the mirror of our own. In a *world morally constituted,* where the authority of conscience has at least its implicit presence in every mind, the ethical action and re-action of men upon each other will be infinite, and will so far prevail over the solitary force of the individual nature, that no one, however exceptionally great, will escape all relation to the general level of his time. The dependence, then, of the moral consciousness for its growth upon society is incident to its very nature. But to suppose, on this account, that, *if it were not there at all,* society could generate it, and, by skilful financing with the exchanges of pleasure and pain, could turn a sentient world into a moral one, will never cease to be an insolvent theory, which makes provision for no obligation : never, so long as it is true that out of nothing nothing comes.

4. As the growth of conscience, so its *decline* takes place in the manner we should expect, if it be a natural valuation of our springs of action as they arise. When some affection higher than your wont has dawned upon you, and claimed you with its divine appeal, if you simply recognize the call, and, cost what it may, go whither it may lead, though the feet may bleed and the strength may droop, your mind is clear with a new serenity and repose. The tension of anxiety is gone, the care for opinion dies away, and, by this step of elevation, you pass into harmony with the very heart of things. If, on the

other hand, you stifle or defy the appeal, and cling to the ease of your low level, you are torn with keen misery, while the angel and the fiend are contending for you, and then sickened with self-contempt, when the strife is over, and you have sent the sacred messenger back to heaven. The divine importunity will not return, or, at least, can never speak again in that warning voice, without reproach which you could scarce refuse to hear ; and, in its absence your shame and compunction will tire themselves out : the organs of your moral life, impaired by the shock, protect themselves from future pain by becoming benumbed, and refusing to give such delicate response again ; and, while your cheerfulness comes back at one entrance, your nobler hope goes out at the other. With disuse and rejection, the higher springs retire and vanish out of sight, not only abandoning us to our poor performance, but lowering the range of our very *problems*, and leaving us with a sinking standard for our thought as well as an enfeebled vigour in our will. While your face is turned upwards, and, on the angel-ladder, you are climbing nearer heaven, there are, even at midnight, lights on the steps above to show the way ; but once look downwards, and mingle with the descending troop, and one by one the lights go out aloft, and there is darkness overhead ; and, by mere invitation of relative brightness, you reverse the direction of your eye, and your foot is drawn to the step below. A moving nature, with its attractions set upon an ascending scale, must either rise or sink : nor, in such a constitution of things, is there any fact more natural and more awful than the " blindness in part " which is incurred by all unfaithfulness : so that as our actual becomes meaner, our possibility itself contracts ; and our debt of responsibility is ever growing, not only by the sin which we consciously commit, but by the lost sanctities which we have driven into the wastes of the unconscious and invisible.

On the whole, then, the moral phenomena of life, including those which are thought least reconcilable with an intuitive discernment of ethical differences, receive from it a fair interpretation. Its objective meaning, the religious significance of its felt authority, must still be reserved for separate treatment. Meanwhile, I take leave of the present part of my subject with one comment more: that each spring of action should bring with it, on its first encounter with another in our mind, a report, there and then, of its relative authority, is suitable, nay, indispensable, to our position as responsible beings. Unless and until I know the right, you cannot call me to account for the wrong. If I am to pilot my ship through waters I have never traversed, you must spread the chart before me, and forewarn me of the shallows and the reefs. It will not do to let me learn my lesson from experience, and fling me upon observation of the stars, and soundings of the ship, beneath, perhaps, the blackened heavens, and on the wildest sea: unless you would have me shipwrecked into skill, I must be taught the coast, and have my insight, ere I step on board. The foresight of prudence may wait for experience, and gather its breadth and refinement by degrees; for, during the process, we can but smart for our blunders, and are involved in no sin; and often enough we learn best when we are pupils of our own mistakes. But, while intelligence comes out at the end of action, moral discernment must be ready at its beginning, and be beforehand with the earliest problem that can arise; nor can it be that the wisdom needed for the first occasions of ethical experience is itself left to be the product of experience. On a journey so momentous, which can never be retraced, and on which the soul has its one chance of ascending to the high fountains of humanity and surmounting the Alpine glories of the world, it were a poor consolation for missing the passes, and being lost amid the swamps, that, at the end of her wanderings, she had learnt the way. No: skill and prudence are *found:* but conscience is *given.* And, accordingly, it is (within its range) the clearest and the tenderest in the dawn of life, while, as yet, the haze of unfaithfulness is thin, and no gathering clouds of guilt taint and intercept the purity of its light. And it is a sad substitute when, in later years, the native insight is replaced by the sharp foresight, and we compute, with wisdom, the way which we should take in love. Are we never to blend the fresh heart of childhood and the large mind of age, and so recover the lost harmonies of life?

If a true account has been given of the fundamental facts of our moral psychology, they cannot be left standing as independent and perfect in themselves. They do not fulfil the conditions of a self-sufficing system, but, like a truncated geometrical solid, compel us to look for a completion beyond their own boundary,—to ask, what would their form be if their idea were visibly carried out, and to what constitution of the world they are intrinsically fitted. Hitherto we have examined them simply or chiefly as parts of our inner experience. But one element is comprised in them which seems to be more than a mere feeling in ourselves, and to constitute a link attaching us to a scheme of things beyond: I mean the *authority* belonging to every better impulse of our nature as against the worse. For, wherever authority is exercised or felt, a relation subsists which it takes two members to constitute. Submission demanded from one implies rule imposed by another: parent and child, master and servant, teacher and taught, lawgiver and subject, exemplify the pairs formed under such relation, in which a higher directs a lower, and a lower looks up to a higher. Now, we have seen that the moral structure of the human mind carries in it, as its deepest essence, the consciousness of a binding authority, claiming our preference for the better incentive over the worse. It is based, therefore, on just such a dual relation, and compels us to ask, Where are the two required terms? *One* of them, it is plain, is *our own will*, on which the demand for right choice is made, and which, conscious of the appeal, is ennobled by yielding to it, or degraded by defying it; and which, in proportion to its fidelity, is admitted to a more elevated discipline. But where is *the other*, which prefers the demand, and administers the discipline? How are we to find and name this power, felt within, invisible without, which plays the part of a superior, and, in speaking to our will as bound to serve, wins assent from our heart of hearts? To this question, What *is* the ultimate authority which commands us? there are several possible answers. These we may pass under a brief review.

1. This authority is often resolved into the persuasive power of superior *pleasure*, or *exemption from pain*. No one incen-

tive, it is said, can claim any advantage over another, except on the score of happier effects. "Nature," says Bentham, "has placed mankind under the governance of two sovereign masters, *pain* and *pleasure.* It is for them alone to point out what we ought to do, as well as to determine what we shall do. On the one hand the standard of right and wrong, on the other the chain of causes and effects, are fastened to their throne."* "There is in reality," says Mr. J. S. Mill, "nothing desired except happiness. Whatever is desired otherwise than as a means to some end beyond itself, and ultimately to happiness, is desired as itself a part of happiness, and is not desired for itself until it has become so. Those who desire virtue for its own sake, desire it either because the consciousness of it is a pleasure, or because the consciousness of being without it is a pain, or for both reasons united ; as in truth the pleasure and pain seldom exist separately, but almost always together, the same person feeling pleasure in the degree of virtue attained, and pain in not having attained more." "Happiness is the sole end of human action, and the promotion of it the test by which to judge of all human conduct."† The ethical adequacy of this doctrine will be considered hereafter. Psychologically, it seems to me incorrect in assuming that we never act but for pleasure as an end ; for this description misses the whole of the *instinctive* life, during which we are propelled by blind impulse, and have to choose between our incentives, without as yet knowing what they will do to us. Pleasure is, in fact, the *fruit*, and not the *germ*, of the several types of natural activity : it is simply the satisfaction of reaching their various ends, and, but for their existence first, could never itself arise afterwards. No one, for instance, exercises resentment because he enjoys the pain of others : he enjoys that pain only because he is resentful. And, if you pity suffering, it is not in order to win the pleasures of relief : to your compassion you are indebted for its bringing a pleasure to you at all.

"It is by no means true," says Aristotle, "that the virtues

* Bentham's Introduction to the Principles of Morals and Legislation, chap. i. § i. p. 1.

† Utilitarianism, chap. iv. pp. 56, 57.

have universally any other pleasure in their action than that which is incident to the attainment of their proper ends."* If your nature is the seat of twenty primitive affections, each in love with its own distinct object, there is not one of them which will not be happy in its success : but shall we say, on that account, that they are not twenty, but only one ? and that happiness is your only aim, and absolute ruler ? You will justly protest that it is not the happiness that supplies the aim, but the aim that supplies the happiness. When some propension in us, and some external thing which suits it, find each other out, a satisfaction arises. But this pleasure which results from the completed relation, and is previously undiscovered, cannot be the source of the initial activity. To call it so is to make condition and consequent change places.

As we emerge, however, from the conflicts of impulse, and having learned their lesson, begin to look forward and compute our way, a balance of pleasure, or of exemption from pain, certainly becomes a just object of preference, and often decides our course. But, where it does so, it produces simply an act of *prudence*, such as might appear in a merely rational world able to economize its resources wisely, without any sense of moral distinctions at all. This is the impassable limit, beyond which the motive said to be omnipotent can never be carried ; and unless all human excellence is resolved into prudence, worldly or *other-worldly*, unless character is really without any higher region where self-regards can breathe no more, the sceptre of pleasure meets here the frontier of its sway, and carries no prerogative into the proper territory of *duty*. In order to explain away the felt *authority* of right, it has always been found necessary practically to abolish the distinction between prudential and moral action ; leaving them no other difference than that of the narrower and nearer, from the more comprehensive and far-sighted, economy of happiness. Both Bentham and Paley identify "authority" with the power of *fear*. With the former it is the *fear of other men :* with the latter it is the *fear of hell*. And, apart from these, there is, we are assured, no awful ground of choice between

* Eth. Nicom. III. ix. 5.

the possibilities before us. When you want to thrust your likings upon me, says Bentham, and to tyrannize over me with your tastes and fancies, you dress them up as a moral faculty, which advances upon me with a grand air, and pretends to have rights over me too royal for your private impudence to assume ; and, if I am as impressible by hobgoblins as the majority of men, your device may easily secure my obedience.* Were this account correct, and were the proclamation of right no more than an arrogant " ipse-dixitism," it is conceivable that I might manage to browbeat *another man*, and frighten him into submission to my sentiment. But how could I do so to *myself ?* How could I make one desire threaten another with the police ? for the police being also my own, and overhearing the whole game, will be apt to wink at both parties to the sham, and " make things pleasant " all round. At all events, it is obvious, that, if this history were true, the personal sentiments of conscience would be an ulterior superstition, by which, having imposed on others, we at last imposed upon ourselves : they would be an illusion of the second degree, impossible till the first had an integral and definite existence. Yet we have seen that the inverse order is a fundamental fact in our moral nature, and that self-judgment is the prior condition of all judgment of others. To this prior stage Bentham's analysis is ludicrously inapplicable.

Nor is Paley's account, though in the spirit of a sermon rather than a satire, one whit more satisfactory. It is given in answer to a different question : not, " Why should I care for *your* moral sense ? " but, " Why should I care for *my own ?* "—" Only," he replies, " because heaven and hell lie behind it." Take away the assurance of reward and punishment hereafter, and with these sanctions its authority vanishes : I may do as I like, and put up with the sentimental discomfort of my own remorse.† A more thorough-going misinterpretation of the elements of " authority " it is impossible to imagine,—dispensing with its essence, and insist-

* Principles of Morals and Legislation, ch. II. § 14, note.

† Moral and Political Philosophy ; chapter on the Moral Sense, last paragraphs.

ing on its appendages. Are we, then, to say, that if there
were no pains of hell, and joys of heaven, there would be no
duty binding upon men? and that, while the call and the
compunctions of conscience remain, duty can cease to be?
On the contrary, it is the external sufferings, wherever placed
in time, which it rests with us, in simple prudence or imprudence, to meet or to decline; and it is the internal appeal for
preference, and remorse for rejection, which it may be in our
power, but is never in our right, to tamper with by likings of
our own. Whatever impressiveness there is in the prospective
retribution belongs to it, not as a sentient expectation, but as
a moral award. Strip it of its ethical significance, and reduce
it to a naked affection of the sensitive nature; turn it from
an emblem of justice to an arbitrary, though calculable,
physical experience,—and all its solemnity is gone: if it
commands our will, it is of power, and not of right; and if
its strength is tested side by side with any deep conviction of
right, its emptiness of all authority will instantly appear.
Bring Paley face to face with a congregation of the Cornish
miners of his time to try his ultimate appeal; let him urge,
with his tersest good sense, his plea of long-visioned prudence,
" You had better take care, or you will go to hell ; " and, if
this were his last word (and he confesses that he has " no
more to say "), is there a passion which his message would
quell, or a heart which it would subdue? Or would the list-
less hearers stroll into tomorrow, unaltered from to-day? But
let a Wesley stand up before them, and press home upon them
the " conviction of sin," dwelling not so much on the future
anguish as on the present ruin of the soul, interpreting the
secret shame and self-contempt of its daily recklessness, re-
calling its memory of better life, appealing to its inward longing for higher things, and ineffaceable kindred with a holy
God, and we know by experience into what deeps such a voice
may penetrate ; how it reaches the dryest fountain of tears ;
how it casts the strong man to the ground ; how it bends the
stiff neck of pride, and makes the frozen heart flow down ;
how it may shake and convulse the habits of a life, and,
driving their evil spirit out, bring them to a composed and
wakeful order under the heavenly eye.

No such conquests are possible to the mere estimate of happiness,—to any prudence, temporal or eternal. Having no executive but the police of self-interest, it cannot pass into a province where interest has to be summoned, not to parley, but to surrender without terms. It may induce, but cannot command: it is invested with no authority; it is the source of no obligation. It may warn us against a blunder: it cannot awe us out of any sin. It has no voices to tell its bidding that can speak to us from above: they come to us on our own level, and bargain with us in our own coin. They cannot, therefore, lift us out of our own disposal to serve a higher law; for, say what you will, we shall never cease to feel, that, with our own pleasures and pains, if these be your ultimate resource, we may do as we like, and you can establish no right in them against us; and shall still applaud the noble inconsistency of our great utilitarian in declaring that " to hell he will go," rather than pay a lying worship to a tyrant God.* If he is right, as assuredly he is, then there is a claim upon us in veracity, an appeal to us in righteousness, which no extremity of consequences can cancel, but which will stand fast in the face of an infinitude of agony taken in place of a forfeited infinitude of joy. In the presence of that solemn claim we lose our personal rights, and have no liberty to twist the lips to falsehood, and bend the knee in hypocrisy: the remorse for such baseness is more than suffering, and has in it that which we are not free to incur. Though you show us the happy slopes of paradise on one side, and on the other take

* Mill's Examination of Hamilton, ch. vii. pp. 102-3.

" If, instead of the ' glad tidings ' that there exists a Being in whom all the excellences which the highest human mind can conceive exist in a degree inconceivable to us, I am informed that the world is ruled by a Being whose attributes are infinite, but what they are we cannot learn, nor what are the principles of his government, except that ' the highest human morality which we are capable of conceiving ' does not sanction them,—convince me of it, and I will bear my fate as I may. But when I am told that I must believe this, and at the same time call this Being by the names which express and affirm the highest human morality, I say in plain terms that I will not. Whatever power such a Being may have over me, there is one thing which he shall not do,—he shall not compel me to worship him. I will call no Being good who is not what I mean when I apply that epithet to my fellow-creatures; and, if such a Being can sentence me to hell for not so calling him, to hell I will go."

us through boundless torture-halls, the walls hung round with excruciating instruments, and the pavement thronged with fiends, none can challenge our title to defy the difference, and take the lot of proffered misery. · It is not, then, in this *sentient* element that we meet with the authority beyond us.

2. Can we find it, then, by dividing our own nature into two, and saying that there is a certain *better part of self* which has right of command over the rest? In one sense, such a statement is no doubt true. It is within the arena of our conscious mind that both sides of the moral fact—the announcement of the claim upon us, and the acceptance of the claim by us—present themselves : both are known to us by our own feeling, and form part of our own inner history. But, though the authority of the higher incentive is *self-known*, it cannot be *self-created ;* for, while it is in me, it is above me. Its tones thrill through my chamber where I sit alone : but it was not my voice that uttered them : they came to me, but not from me. They find me out in my sin when I would fain be let alone ; they reproach me till I go out to hide my tears, though I do not want to leave the mirth and song ; they make a coward of me, and shake me in my shoes, though I am for setting my face as flint, and hardening my joints as iron. I resist the claims of the right ; I wrestle with them ; I am beaten by them : or, I surrender to them ; I follow them ; I triumph with them : and how, then, can you say that they are but the shadow of myself? The authority which I set up I am able also to take down ; yet, do what I may, I cannot discharge my compunctions, and shut the door on them as on troublesome creditors who have nothing to show against me, and depend upon my will for any claim they have. No act of repeal on my part avails to release me from the obligations which turn up within my consciousness ; nor, by any edict of clemency to my own moral bankruptcy, can I say to myself, " I forgive thee all that debt." Nay, the very effort at oblivion only darkens the shade of guilt ; and he who stifles his self-upbraidings, and drowns his remorse, and tries to treat his transgressions as all his own affair, sinks doubly deep in immediate offence, and prepares the seed-plot for every future sin. Besides, if there is to be partition of

the human self between the functions of command and of obedience, what will our analysis give us for subject, and what for Lord? The former we know; but where is the latter? It is *we ourselves*, our *will*, our *personality, the whole of our voluntary nature*, that must be owned as under higher orders; that is, precisely our supreme characteristics,—those which distinguish us from mere creatures, and set us " a little lower than the angels." And, if these constitute the *subject-*term within us, nothing is left for the seat of lordship—if it is, indeed, but an element of ourselves—except the *impersonal*, the *involuntary*, the *unreasoning* affections which surround the will, and beset it with importunities they neither hear nor overhear. To a responsible will, nothing that is less than will can issue orders, and commit a trust; and, if we are really taught the lessons of conscience, assuredly we are not *self-taught*.

Moreover, if the authority which claims us were of this merely subjective nature, if it were the aspect which one part of self bore towards another, it would lie within the interior relations of the individual : and so it would belong to him, though he were in solitude; and, though he were in society, it would be valid for him alone. But neither of these things is true. Though the essence of our nature, as responsible and religious beings, is in the shrine of its self-conscious and reflective powers, it does not wake up there spontaneously to pay its secret worship; but, if left alone in silence, will fall back into the sleep of animal existence. It needs the school of sympathy and society, the appeal of objective character, the play of the like and the different, to fling into the soul the sweeping winds at which its chords speak out. We learn ourselves and others together; it is the reciprocities of life that deepen and enrich its solitudes; and in every age the ferment of the city has rolled around the closet of sublimest prayer. The acted drama of life, unless witnessed with mere callous criticism, reaches the springs of secret poetry in the heart, and the real startles the ideal from its repose. The moment we see a nobleness which is above us, we recognize it and own its claim, and are fired with possibilities we never guessed before. What does this bespeak,—this flashing of conscience from mind to mind, this consent of each to the moral life of all, this answering look of the outward and the inward,—but that the authority which claims us, whatever it be, is something far beyond the personal nature, wide as the compass of humanity, embracing us all in one moral organism, —a universal righteousness which reaches through time, and suffers no individual to escape? Surely it is a fantastic scepticism or a superfluous modesty which would treat all moral authority as a personal idiosyncrasy, and decline to apply it to others: saying, for instance, "It may be better for you to die for your country than to betray it and escape; but how can you tell that it is so for your comrades? it may be a peculiarity of your mental constitution not extending to theirs." If such a limitation is good in morals, it is equally justified in regard to intellectual truth which my nature constrains me to accept; and it would be only a proper self-restraint to say, "For my part, I think of space as having three dimensions; and I cannot think of two times as being together: but I speak only for myself, and have no right to expect assent from any one else." A late distinguished mathematician and logician (Prof. De Morgan) actually carried his intellectual modesty to this extreme; asserting that, of the infinite extension between the directions of two divergent straight lines, he certainly had a positive idea: but that other people might very possibly be without it; for that there was no telling whether all minds were made alike. But, of the two, which is the more legitimate postulate,—to assume a universal diversity of reason in different persons until concurrence is proved, and so far forth as it remains unproved? or to assume a universal sameness of mental constitution in mankind until we are obliged to allow for a certain range of difference? On the latter, it cannot be denied, all language is founded, all interchange of thought and feeling, all permanent literature, all progressive science; and were each mind that appeared upon the scene treated as a nature new and strange till it had made good its similarities, one by one, there could be no social organism, no spiritual culture, no historical life.

Moreover, the differential authority of one inward spring of action as against another we cannot believe at all, without believing it to attach to these principles themselves in their mutual relation, and to cling to them, wherever and whatever the mind be in which they appear. It is owned as a function inherent in them on every field which gives them scope to act, and not appended to them by the variable peculiarities of the individual agent. Accordingly, we make it the foundation of an undoubting claim upon others: nor, on behalf of any sane wrong-doer, should we for a moment listen to the plea that he has a moral constitution special to himself, for which ours is no rule; though we are quite familiar with just such exceptional conditions in the case of colour-blindness and similar infirmities of perception. Far from being valid for you, and not for me, this moral authority invariably gives the ideas of duty and of rights together; duties for me which are rights to you, duties for you which are rights to me. And the reciprocal claim is readily responded to: it takes no man by surprise: each one owns the title of our expectations from him, and, under the name of *Justice*, falls under the obligations we impose upon him. Unsupported by this inward acknowledgment ever ready in the mind, we should be unable, by the mere grinding of coercion, to command the sacrifices and abstinences which are now spontaneously submitted to.

The common sentiment of conscience is the very ground of public law, the assumption of private honour; and weaves us all into one texture of moral relations, which has neither continuous strength, nor pattern of beauty, till the single threads disappear in the whole, and take the order of the disposing will.

3. Though, however, authority cannot be administered by one part of self over the rest, though it must be acknowledged as a relation of person to person complete, still, since we are so dependent for our consciousness of it upon *society*, is it, perhaps, a thing imposed upon us by our fellow-men? May it not be the dominating influence of the *whole* over the part, like the discipline of the camp over the conduct of the private soldier? It is difficult to free these questions from ambiguity: but in no sense do they seem to me to suggest more than very partial truth; and, in any sense which substitutes social

power for the personal consciousness of moral differences,
they suggest nothing that is true at all. What do you mean
by the " whole " which environs the individual? How do
you think of the throng of his " fellow-men," of the " society "
around him? With what sort of nature do you charge it?
with what faculties and affections endow it? Is it conceived
of by you as an aggregate of separate persons, taken one by
one, without any consciousness of moral distinctions, and
combined simply for the greater strength of associated will,
and intent only on voting into existence convenient rules
which the reluctant shall be constrained to obey? If so,
then, in your dominance of the " whole over the part," you
give me only the relation of force to weakness, which has
nothing whatever to do with the relation of right to wrong.
Mere magnitude of scale carries no moral quality; nor could
a whole population of devils, by unanimous ballot, confer
righteousness upon their will, and make it binding on a single
Abdiel. Such as the natures are, separately taken, such will
be the collective sum: no crowd of pigmies can add themselves up into a God; and self-love multiplied by self-love
will only become self-love of higher power. Nor will accumulation in time serve you any better than aggregation in mass.
The highest capital of human wishes, paid up through all the
ages, although it may ruin the small dealer in such wares,
and drive his venture from the field, can make nothing just that
was not just before. At best, it can only enforce obligations
already there,—obligations which it cannot cancel, and did
not create. If, however, you will take " society " to mean the
affiliated multitude of *consciences*, the common council of
responsible men, then it is most true that the moral authority
which we acknowledge is brought to an intense focus in our
minds by the reflected lights of theirs; and we should but
dimly own it, did they not own it too. But how is it that
they thus work upon us, and mould us to a new docility?
Is it that they are principals in command, and we subordinates
in service, that, accepting their will as sovereign, we are
content to do their bidding? No: their function in this
matter is, not to fill the post of authority, but to join us on the
steps of submission below it ; to confess their fellow-feeling with

us, and accept their partnership under the same law.   Instead
of being our masters, they are but bondsmen, with us, of a
higher righteousness, which opens its oracles and seeks its
organs in us all.   And so, following out the moral authority
from my solitary nature to human-kind, I only widen, and do
not elevate, my position; I gain a larger view of its range,
but no higher insight into its source : I still am at the lower
term of this mysterious relation ; and must yet look up, if
perchance from the form of the other the cloud may pass
away.

4. And may we not say that the cloud already grows transparent, and gives promise of clearing away ?   The authority
to which conscience introduces me has its station, we have
seen, beyond the limits of my own personality ; with equal
certainty, beyond that of my neighbour, in whom my experience is simply repeated ; and, similarly, beyond that of any
and every man.   Though emerging in consciousness, often
with the sharpest surprise of feeling, it is *objective* to us all :
and is necessarily referred by us to the nature of things,
irrespective of the accidents of our mental constitution.   It
is with us as a holy presence, and guaranteed to us by all the
marks which distinguish existence from illusion.   It is not
dependent on us, as an invention or dream, but independent,
as a thing given us to apprehend.   Like any other reality
open to our cognizance, it dominates as known over our
faculty as knowing ; and, by its persistency, baffles the
subtleties and survives the mutabilities of our subjective
conditions.   If we pretend not to see it, it still makes itself felt,
like the sunshine, through the closed lids ; and we know that
the blaze is there without a cloud.   If we set ourselves to contend
against it, and pass on without giving it heed, it soon brings to
us its legitimate mastery, and spoils our usurped freedom by
timely prohibition and late reproach.   If we try to silence it,
it must be, not by refuting, but by insulting it ; and the sense
of shame it leaves as it turns away carries a constant echo of
the very sound we would fain escape.   Should we be resolutely intent on breaking the spell and ridding ourselves of
the haunting voice, the only possible way is to act, not upon
it, but upon ourselves ; to render our own organ of perception

too callous to hear it. But not even then is the witness securely dead. Some shock of self-knowledge, some pathetic breath of sorrow, some returning wave of retreating affection, may visit us with recovery, be it only for an hour or a day, from our moral deafness; and instantly the forgotten tones flow in again, bringing a contrition all the more passionate for its arrears, and so giving evidence that it is not *they* which have ever perished from the atmosphere, but *we* who have been asleep to music such as theirs. These are the characteristic notes of permanent objective existence,—the same that assure us of a world perceived beyond the range of our percipient nature; and from the conclusion to which they point there is no legitimate escape. All minds born into the universe are ushered into the presence of a *real righteousness* as surely as into a scene of *actual space.* And whatever certainty we feel that that space is unoriginated and infinite, and that, wherever a circle is, its intersecting chords supply equal rectangles, the same certainty must we feel, that, wherever *character* is, there must pity be rightful superior to selfishness, and honour to perfidy; and that, whatever may be our own stage of ethical attainment, we look into . unmeasured heights beyond.

5. But in what kind of world must we be, if this apparent certainty is not to be completely illusory? Suppose a human being to be standing, amid the tribes of natural history, and with a companion or two of his own race, in an *atheistic* universe,—dead space around him, blind matter before him, and a few equals near him, forming, with himself, the supreme term of the whole. Suppose further,—that we may begrudge nothing to the unconscious genius of " Nature,"—that, through some happy correspondences in the organic chemistry which set him up and made him what he is, his faculties and apprehensions have got correctly adjusted to the theatre on which he is planted, and bring to him only faithful reports of what is there. How, on such a stage, can he possibly have cognizance of an objective authority of righteousness higher than himself? For, actually, no higher would *be* there. His fellows are on his level, known to him only as himself over again. Other forms of life are below him, as his servants or

his foes. The earth is his bed, and the sky his roof. Often enough, no doubt, may these surroundings press severely upon him, and extort the cry of conscious weakness. But, whatever his physical dependence, he is without spiritual superior to give law to him : there is no one who has any title to dictate to his will : he is himself the supreme being in the known universe. If, therefore, he feels, as we do, a real and rightful authority over him ; if, face to face with him, there seems to stand a justice and sanctity that claims him,—his feeling is adjusted to the wrong world, and is out of place among things as they are. How should he recognize a better, and aspire? It is only the uneasy dreamer, who, stationed on the highest peak, still strains to climb, and finds no foothold on the yielding air. Why should he look up, when all is blank above,—darkness, and no stars? why kneel before nothing, fling out imploring arms into a vacancy, and sob forth his contrition into a silence deaf and dumb? A being placed amid such conditions must either be without moral intuition, and therefore something less than human, or, in having it, lie at the mercy of a brilliant but hopeless deception ; as if, by a strange mistake, there had strayed into him an apprehension visionary here, but proper to some divine realm, where a real government prevailed, of Spirit over spirits, and One perfectly holy communicated himself to minor natures, and empowered their answering consciousness to report back of him.

. No suspicion of illusion, however, against our primary faculties, can be entertained ; for we have access to no world but that which they present to us, and the account we cannot check it is our wisdom to take on trust. The moral intuition exists ; and the atheistic universe vanishes before its face. We know ourselves to be living under command, and with freedom to give or withhold obedience ; and this lifts us at once into divine relations, and connects us with One supreme in the distinguishing glories of personal existence, wisdom, justice, holiness. We have only to open and read the credentials of conscience, and this discovery bursts upon us at once. That sense of authority which pervades our moral nature, and tempers it with a silent reverence, places us under that which is *higher than we*, which has claims on our personality, and hovers over it, and keeps near its problems with transcendent presence. But the world of nature and outward phenomena has in it nothing that is thus superhuman; nor can matter and force, with their linear necessities and predetermined tracks of successive effects, give the free spirit its alternative law. And the world of humanity, however rich in saints and heroes who are above you and me, and may well discipline our hearts to homage, is here all in the same case with us, and bends low before the same vision. Seeing, then, that the impersonal cannot morally rule the personal, and that over living spirit nothing short of living spirit greater in elevation can wield authority, what remains but that we recognize the communion of a divine Visitant, and accept the light of conscience as no longer an unmeaning phosphorescence of our own nature, but as the revealing and appealing look of God? The wise and good of every age have variously struggled to express in adequate terms the solemnity of human obligation; but all the strivings of their thought have culminated in this: " The word of conscience is the voice of God." To this, indeed, all the indications lead. The law that is over us, we cannot fail to observe, is a *selective* law: it looks, as we have shown, at the springs of action *together*, announces a comparison between them, and tells the result: " *This* is worthier than *that*." Such a selective law can issue from nothing but a preferential will. In the realm of nature and necessity the forces move right on to their determinate end; compare nothing, and prefer nothing; and turn up, without pause or scruple, the sole possibility given them to execute. And this selective law speaks direct to a selective power in us: exalting *this* above *that*, it requires that we should do so too. It is the appeal of will to will: " This is my choice: be it yours also." And so it is nothing less than the bending of the divine holiness to train the human; the overflowing sanctity of the Supreme Mind, shed forth to elicit by free sympathy the secret possibilities of ours. But for this objective contact between his Spirit and ours,— between the divine life reporting itself to an apprehensive faculty in us,—it would be hard to understand how it is that the human mind can rapidly pass to moral levels unreached before; and that, at some epochs of its history, it seems to seize at a bound heights never sought, because never imagined. The philosophers who undertake to expound the dynamics of society are fond of telling us that the character of each period is the inevitable result and vital development of its predecessor, and might be predicted from an adequate survey of the prior phenomena. And doubtless vast lines of historical causation may be successfully traced through some of the levels of human life, linking differing centuries into a continuous system.

But, in the spiritual experience of nations and of races there are mighty paroxysms which break through the restraints of this law, when, as at the Christian era, a new type of mind and character, a fresh creation of moral beauty, bursts into blossom in an ungenial time, like a delicate flower from a rotting soil; or when, as in the seventh century, a people scarcely reckoned in the statistics of civilization starts into organized existence, and with fiery magnanimity sweeps over half the world as the missionary of a perishing truth; or when, as at the minor crises which have given birth to Protestant sects, whole populations have been carried off their feet by affections never felt before, and as truly remodelled, in habit, thought, and aspect, as if they had risen from the dead. No study of the antecedent aggregate of conditions enables you to give account of these leaps of transformation; else why are they not foreseen by some philosopher's appreciative eye? The utmost that your scrutiny can effect is to point to some predisposing influences which might affect the temper of the time, and warm many a mind into the ready fuel of reaction. This, however, goes but a very little way to meet the facts before us. Reaction is a swing back into the old; and here we have a seizure of the new,— a spring to loftier levels of original character, where speech has tones, and action, attitudes, and art, varieties of form, quite strange before. And whence the kindling power, the lightning flash of genius or inspiration, to pierce the passive fuel, and compel it into a blaze? Is this, too,—this living force without which a world ever so " predisposed " lies dead, and refuses to "react,"—the necessary product of the preceding age? and will you father the new ideals upon old, worn-out deformities? Is it from the Jewish rigour and self-assertion that you deduce the meekness and self-sacrifice of Christ, or from the Pagan dissoluteness that you explain the Christian purity? If so, why does not every odious form of character bring its own redemption, and corruption arrest itself, instead of spread? Thus to treat the contagion of vice as the seed-plot of holiness is indeed to seek "grapes from thorns, and figs from thistles." It must needs be that the redeemers of mankind arise in times which require redemption; but to assign this concurrence as an adequate account of their existence and characteristics is to overlook the living cause in the circumstantial condition. It is not merely with a stand against declension, with a tenacity of right habit in resistance to decay, with a protest of unspoiled feeling against sinking life, that we have here to deal ; *this*, perhaps, the inertia of lingering goodness already there might sufficiently explain : but it is the positive creation of fresh images of perfection, a recoil from the lower which already carries in it dreams of the higher, an expostulation with the present, which, not content with seeing the better past, presses into a previously unimagined future. This dawning of unsuspected lights within rare and exceptional natures is no mere human phenomenon, explicable by our reciprocal mental action : it betrays the overarching presence of brighter skies. Among the societies of men, it is ever the greater spirits that morally sustain the less ; and, as the scale of realized excellence ascends, the conscience of us all is ashamed to linger, and eventually rises too. We are lifted by the souls of mightier wing, and are set where otherwise our feet would not have climbed : and, were we without this hierarchy of moral ranks, there would be nothing ennobling in our interdependence ; and no healing would flow down, no reverence pass up, from link to link. Once upon the flat, upon the flat we stay. But what, then, is it that sustains the *summit-minds?* that kindles them with light they cannot borrow, and fires them with strength that no man can lend ? Have they escaped the law of dependence, and become

original springs, first inventors, of a non-existent righteousness? Go to them, and judge from the manner of their life
and the temper of their affections whether it be so. Do they
stand upon the earth as creative gods, with lordly mien, and
will that is all their own? Do they know their height to be
supreme, and stoop with the pity of a superior to the subject
crowd beneath? Or do you see them with still uplifted face,
and bending low before a Holiest of all? nay, with the very
light that most transfigures them glistening through the
streaming tears of a tender penitence? Is not their calm,
their strength, their fearlessness, more than any man's, free
from self-assertion, and an expression of pure dependence and
perfect trust? And the tender mercy which flows from voice
and hand as they mingle with mankind—is it theirs alone,
without a partner in it, and with only autocratic look towards
the sorrows it relieves? Or is it rather a divine compassion,
that moves through them as its organ, and glorifies with
sympathy a created spirit as it goes? No: they feel, not
less, but far more, than others, the law of objective contact
with higher mind as the condition of moral insight and
spiritual power; and unless we charge our highest witnesses
with illusions in that which is especially their own, and so
reject whatever we have that is supremely trustworthy, we
must carry that law beyond our mutual relations, and recognize the fires of God in the glow which kindles the summits
of this world.

This new and spiritual function ascribed to God is but the
just sequel, as we ascend the gradations of being, to his
prior indwelling in the world. As the forces of Nature are
his causality, and the instincts of the creature his seeing
guidance of the blind; so the alternative apprehensions of
conscience are the preferential lights of his moral nature, the
first reporting his power, the second his wisdom, the third his
righteousness. That it is the same one life which is the
ground of all is plain from the intertexture of the whole: for
it is amongst the instinctive impulses of the animated world
that the problems of ethical experience first arise; and it is
through the physical constitution of nature, and of our own
organism in particular, that many of the penalties of the

moral law make themselves felt. The causality of the world, therefore, is at the disposal of the all-holy Will ; and whether within us or without us, in the distant stellar spaces or in the self-conscious life of the tempted or aspiring mind, we are in one divine embrace,—" God over all, blessed for ever."

Here, too, we reach the precise point of transition from morals to religion, and step across the boundary from Pagan nobleness to Christian sanctity. Divine guidance has never and nowhere failed to men ; nor has it ever, in the most essential things, largely differed amongst them : but it has not always been recognized as divine, much less as the living contact of Spirit with spirit,—the communion of affection between God and man. While conscience remained an *impersonal law*, stern and silent, with only a jealous Nemesis behind, man had to stand up alone, and work out for himself his independent magnanimity; and he could only be the pagan hero. When conscience was found to be inseparably blended with the Holy Spirit, and to speak in tones immediately divine, it became the very shrine of worship : its strife, its repentance, its aspirations, passed into the incidents of a living drama, with its crises of alienation and reconcilement ; and the cold obedience to a mysterious necessity was exchanged for the *allegiance of personal affection*. And this is the true emergence from the darkness of ethical law to the tender light of the life divine. The veil falls from the shadowed face of moral authority, and the directing love of the all-holy God shines forth.

CHAPTER III.

THE sketch which in preceding chapters has been given of our human nature, has been drawn wholly from the interior; and how far it is true, how far a fancy picture, must be determined by each one's reflective self-knowledge. The facts to which it refers, and on which it rests its appeal, are not palpable and visible upon the stage of overt action, but lie behind the scenes, and can be affirmed or denied only by those who will carry their scrutiny thither. They are simply these. We are sent into the world, charged with a number of instincts, each, when alone, darkly urging us towards its own object; but all, when thrown into various competitions together, lighted up with intuitive knowledge of their own relative worth and rights; so that we are never left in doubt which of two simultaneous impulses has the nobler claim upon us. This natural estimate is what we mean by *conscience*. It has nothing to do with the values of external actions, but only with the comparative authority of their inward springs; it gives no foresight of effects, but only insight into obligation at its source. But this it does with revelation so clear, so solemn, so consentaneous for all men, that those who will not own it to be divine can never find a voice of which it is the echo in our humanity.

The problems of human conduct, however, may be approached from the other end. They may be looked at from the outside, and traced through their sphere of visible operation, in the hope of separating, by some serviceable rule, the actions which work well from those which work ill. Whoever moves along this path in order to take his measurements of human character, exercises a different order of sagacious habit, and naturally objects to every form of intuitive doctrine as " sentimental " or " mystical." The inward facts on which it rests are seen by a kind of light to which his eye does not readily adapt itself; and even if he recognizes them as there at all, he cannot believe them to be really indigenous to that indistinct and barren interior, and traces them to some winged seeds of accident blown over the fence by the winds of circumstance from the sunny fields of his favourite outer world. For him, the values of action are found, not up among its springs, but down in its issues; nor is one affection better than another, except as it bids fair to be more fruitful of beneficent deeds; so that all moral judgment is turned upside down, if we estimate the act by its incentive, instead of the incentive by its act. Once allow this inversion, and you provide, as he protests, an excuse for every well-meant enormity; for the mischievous asceticism and monstrous license between which superstition oscillates; for the bad faith deliberately shown to heretics; for the cruel persecutions against which the tender mercies of conscience have afforded no guarantee. This judgment by sentiment it is that hinders all rational agreement about the relative worth of actions, and leaves men to fling about their approbation at random, elevating into a virtue in one age what is punished as a crime in another. Not, he insists, till we turn them from the mutabilities of feeling to the appreciation of steady facts, and teach them to consult the external operation of conduct as the sole definite rule of admeasurement, will their chaos of contradictions fall into order, and the exactitude of science silence the wranglings of conflicting morals. Nor is it doubtful what the standard of valuation must be; for there is but one end given to our nature, viz. happiness; that is, the attainment of pleasure in its various kinds, and the avoidance of pain; and only as a means to this, or as a part of it, can anything else have place as a secondary end. This proposition, though never stated except for a controversial purpose, and in the face of those who deny it, has always been commended to its own self-evidence, as if it could dispense with the support of proof. Epicurus thought it enough to predicate of pleasure that it was the beginning and the end of desirable life, our primary and natural good, the source of every preference and rejection, the rule by which we estimate all

else at which we aim.* That it held this supreme position
was a first-hand certainty, as little needing or admitting
corroboration as the statement that fire is hot and snow is
white.† "Pleasure and pain," says Bentham, "govern us in
all we do, in all we say, in all we think : every effort we can
make to throw off our subjection, will but serve to demonstrate
and confirm it. In words a man may pretend to abjure their
empire ; but in reality he will remain subject to it all the
while. The *principle of utility* recognizes this subjection, and
assumes it for the foundation of that system the object of
which is to rear the fabric of felicity by the hands of reason
and of law."‡ "A man acts," says James Mill, " for the
sake of something agreeable to him, either proximately or
remotely. But agreeable to, and pleasant to ; agreeableness
and pleasantness are only different names for the same thing ;
the pleasantness of a thing is the pleasure it gives. So that
pleasure in a general way, or speaking generically, that is, in
a way to include all the specimens of pleasure and also the
abatements of pain, is the end of action."§ "The creed,"
says Mr. J. S. Mill, " which accepts as the foundation of
morals, Utility, or the Greatest Happiness principle, holds that
actions are right in proportion as they tend to promote happiness, wrong as they tend to produce the reverse of happiness.
By happiness is intended pleasure, and the absence of pain ;
by unhappiness, pain and the privation of pleasure." And
he states as " the theory of life on which this theory of
morality is grounded,—that pleasure and freedom from pain
are the only things desirable as ends, and that all desirable
things (which are as numerous in the utilitarian as in any
other scheme) are desirable either for the pleasure inherent in

---

* Epicurus ap. Diog. Laert. 128, 129. Τὴν ἡδονὴν, ἀρχὴν καὶ τέλος λέγομεν
εἶναι τοῦ μακαρίως ζῆν. ταύτην γὰρ ἀγαθὸν πρῶτον καὶ συγγενικὸν ἔγνωμεν,
καὶ ἀπὸ ταύτης ἐπαρχόμεθα πάσης αἱρέσεως καὶ φυγῆς, καὶ ἐπὶ ταύτην
καταντῶμεν, ὡς κανόνι τῷ πάθει πᾶν ἀγαθὸν κρίνοντες.

† Cicero de Finibus, I. 9. Negat opus esse ratione neque disputatione,
quamobrem voluptas expetenda, fugiendus dolor sit. Sentiri hoc putat, ut
calere ignem, nivem esse albam, dulce mel, quorum nihil oportere exquisitis
rationibus confirmare ; tantum satis admonere.

‡ Principles of Morals and Legislation, chap. 1. § 1.

§ Fragment on Mackintosh, Appendix A, p. 389.

themselves, or as means to the promotion of pleasure and the prevention of pain."* As this is the sole possible object of desire, so is it at once the solitary means of influence, the exclusive source of obligation, and the invariable standard of all good : and human actions must be approved in proportion as they apparently tend to increase human pleasures or abate human pains. " According to the Greatest Happiness principle," says Mr. J. S. Mill, " the ultimate end, with reference to and for the sake of which all other things are desirable (whether we are considering our own good or that of other people), is an existence exempt as far as possible from pain, and as rich as possible in enjoyments, both in point of quantity and quality." " This being, according to the Utilitarian opinion, the end of human action, is necessarily also the standard of morality; which may accordingly be defined, the rules and precepts for human conduct, by the observance of which an existence such as has been described might be, to the greatest extent possible, secured to all mankind ; and not to them only, but, so far as the nature of things admits, to the whole sentient creation."† To guard us against any partial or selfish application of this rule, it is added, that, in making our estimate, we must give no superior weight to our own share, but impartially remember that others' happiness is worth as much as our own ; and take care that " everybody shall count for one, and nobody for more than one."‡

Such are the two chief types of ethical doctrine : of which the one betakes itself to the inward impulses, and finds an order of natural ranks among them ; while the other resorts to the outward products in conduct, and applies a calculus of happiness for their admeasurement. Notwithstanding their seeming opposition, each doctrine speaks with a telling voice to some part or other of our nature : the one in tones of deeper harmony to the whispers of the meditative mind ; the other, in the sharper language of the courts and of the street. And each, too, it must be confessed, seems to leave us with a want unsatisfied. The one, fond of lingering aloft to breathe

---

* Utilitarianism, pp. 9, 10. † Ibid. p. 17.
‡ Ibid. p. 91.

a religious atmosphere, is too apt to miss its way and stumble, when held down in the tangle of human relations and engaged with the concrete problems of the hour. The other, while skilfully balancing the merits of social usage and personal habit, seems to strain itself out of character when it assumes the higher language of Duty, and can hardly fall into tune with the plaint of human confession, or the pathos of a saintly joy. Can we then distribute to each its proper part? Or must they treat one another as irreconcilable enemies, and fight it out till the sole empire has been awarded by the reason of mankind?

I. Let it be admitted at once, that the doctrine of Conscience cannot do the work which the doctrine of Utility accomplishes.

1. This becomes clear, the moment we ask what it is that these two lights profess to show us. The one is set up among the springs of action; the other is set down among its effects. The one tells us what present incentive is noblest; the other, what future results will be happiest; and though we must start by the incentive light of the former, we must arrive by the calculated signals of the latter. When we have flung our tempters aside, and given ourselves up to the right incentive, it may well be that only the first stage of our problem has been solved; for, with that one incentive many lines of action may be compatible; and among these it will yet remain for us to make our choice. Am I conscious, for instance, of a wrong against my brother? And have I conquered my pride, and resolved to make reparation? The question immediately rises, in what form shall I render satisfaction to his claims? Shall I make public confession? Or shall I go to his house and humble myself before him? Or, lest bitter memories should there prolong themselves with words, shall I repent in self-sacrificing and expressive action? Or, again: have I become ashamed of too self-indulgent a life amid the miseries of men, and determined to deny myself largely on their behalf? It is well; for Conscience requires no less. But what direction shall my purpose take? Shall I go into a monastery and give up my goods? Shall I found a hospital? Shall I organize and manage a reformatory? Shall I take pity on

the west-country labourers, and create there a model estate? These ulterior questions it would be absurd, and, except to a fanatic, impossible, to settle by any pretended intuitive light; they can be resolved only by careful study of each scheme in its natural working on the well-being of all whom it affects. If Conscience selects the right affection, Utility determines the fitting action; nor, without consulting it, is there any guarantee against the perpetration of well-intended mischiefs, which may bring the purest impulses into contempt. Viewed in this relation, the second doctrine supplements the first, and steps in to remedy its imperfect competency. Only, it must not enter before its time: not till Conscience has spoken, is Utility to be taken into counsel; it has a diploma for the executive Art of Ethics; but is an impostor in the primary Science.

2. In truth, the rule which it supplies, however indispensable for giving effect to our highest aims, is not really *Moral* at all, distinguishing right from wrong; but simply *Rational*, distinguishing wise from foolish. You condemn, on grounds of Utility, the institution of foundling hospitals, or the Catholic latitude of alms-giving, and prefer to spend your resources in lifting, by education and sympathy, some depressed class into permanent self-help? What is the difference between you and your mediæval-minded neighbour? Are you more *charitable*, or only more *sensible*, than he? Is it a distinction of *character*, or one of *judgment*, that separates you? Do you regret that he is not a *better* man, or only that he is not a *wiser?* If the benevolence of both arises under the same inward conditions, and from conquest of the same temptations, you assuredly stand upon the same moral level, and the interval between you is simply intellectual. You merit the same approval; of neither can we say, that he stands nearer to the love of God. And did we propose to convert your neighbour to your state of mind, it must be, not by the machinery of moral correction, but by methods of intellectual persuasion. Supposing our appeal to him successful, we shall save him in future from a *blunder* only, and not from a *sin*. Am I charged with confounding the morality of the agent and the morality of the act, and told that, though

tho alms-giver may bo a good man, his alms-giving is a bad act? I do not blindly confound them, but openly identify them, and unhesitatingly say that I know of no morality in an act except the morality of its Agent; nor can I approve of him as its doer, yet disapprove of it as his deed. *Bad* indeed, in another and *unmoral* sense, the act may be; it may be injudicious, may miss its end, and work harm instead; but bad it cannot bo, in the sense in which ho is good. Since, indeed, the moral quality attaches exclusively to the inner springs of affection, apart from which the most beneficent activities would bo but the munificence of nature, and not products of character, an act, once issued from its source, has already got its ethical complexion, which cannot bo altered by its later history.

The unqualified terms which I havo here used in ethically excusing nobly-prompted acts of mistake are deliberately chosen, in order to bring into tho strongest light the essential contrast between tho two theories which we are comparing.

"Tho Utilitarian moralists," as Mr. J. S. Mill very truly says, "have gone beyond almost all others in affirming that the motivo has nothing to do with the morality of the action."* Bentham habitually insists that tho words of praise or dis-praise which express our moral judgments have no application to motives; that tho epithets *good* and *bad*, *virtuous* and *vicious*, which properly belong to actions, and their conse-quences actual or contemplated, cannot bo attached to the springs of action, without giving rise to " practical errors of tho very first importance." Tho "Motivo," ho says, " is always some pleasure, or some pain; some pleasure, which tho act is expected to bo tho means of continuing or producing; some pain, which it is expected to bo tho means of discontinu-ing or preventing. A motivo is substantially nothing moro than this pleasuro or pain, operating in a certain manner. Now pleasuro is in *itself* a good; nay oven, setting aside immunity from pain, tho only good: pain is in itself an evil; and indeed, without exception, tho only evil; or else tho words good and evil havo no meaning. And this is alike true of every sort of pain, and of every sort of pleasure. It follows,

* Utilitarianism, p. 26.

therefore, necessarily and incontestably, that " *there is no such thing as any sort of motive that is in itself a bad one.*"* And a more explicit argument to the same effect he introduces with the following proposition : " As there is not any sort of *pleasure*, the enjoyment of which, if taken by itself, is not a *good* (taken by itself, that is, on the supposition that it is not *preventive* of a more than equivalent *pleasure*, or *productive* of more than equivalent *pain*) ; nor any sort of pain, from which, taken in like manner by itself, the *exemption* is not a good : . . . in a word, as there is not any sort of *pleasure* that is not in itself a good, nor any sort of *pain* the exemption from which is not a good ; and as nothing but the expectation of the eventual enjoyment of pleasure in some shape, or of exemption from pain in some shape, can operate in the character of a motive :—a necessary consequence is that, if by *motive* be meant *sort* of motive, there is not any such thing as a *bad* motive ; no, nor any such thing as a motive which, to the exclusion of any other, can with propriety be termed a *good* motive."†

Later Utilitarians have not been quite faithful to this paradoxical rule, that only Acts and not Motives are objects of moral appreciation. " VIRTUE," we learn from James Mill, " is the name of Prudence, Fortitude, Justice, and Beneficence, all taken together ; it is also, like the name of each of the species included under it, at once the name of the Affection, the *Motive*, and the Disposition."‡ And the statement is repeated with an addition : " Virtue, as we have seen, is a name which is given to each of the three, the Affection, the *Motive*, and the Disposition ; Morality is a name which is applied with similar latitude."§ With this account, so curiously at variance with Bentham's, the author's own practice is in harmony. When he speaks of " the man who takes the virtuous course, *that is, obeys the virtuous motive*,"‖ he not only allows a moral quality to the motive, but identifies the

* Principles of Morals and Legislation, ch. x. §§ ix. x. p. 169.
† Table of the Springs of Action, II. § 4. Works, Part I. pp. 214, 215.
‡ Analysis of the Phenomena of the Human Mind, ch. xxiii. vol. II. p. 288. J. S. Mill's edition.
§ Ibid. p. 302.   ‖ Ibid. p. 270.

morality of the act with it; and when he more than once
deplores the "feeble operation" of particular "motives,"
social, domestic, patriotic, philanthropic, and refers to the
higher associations which form them as among the "most
ennobling of all states of human consciousness,"[*] we see how
the artificial lines of system melt away at the first fervent
touch of moral enthusiasm. Not less distinct is Mr. J. S.
Mill's admission that "*with the worth of the agent*," though
not "with the morality of the act," the motive has "much
to do,"[†] and that, as a right action (by the Utilitarian
standard) "does not necessarily indicate a virtuous character,"
so "actions which are blamable often proceed from qualities
entitled to praise. When this is apparent," he says, "it
modifies our estimation, not certainly of the act, but of the
agent."[‡] Here, though the outward act is reserved for ethical
valuation on its own account, its inward spring is also allowed
to be a proper object of moral estimate; and the treatment of
motives as lying wholly beyond the sphere of approbation or
censure is plainly abandoned. To complete the history of
this surrender, the need of it has been still more explicitly
avowed by Mr. John Morley; who, not content with the
qualified concession just cited, urges that, in measuring the
morality of an act, it is impossible to omit its motive from
the account. "Might it not be said," he asks, "with all
deference to the thinker who has done so much to reconstruct
and perfect the Utilitarian system, that as the morality of
action depends on the happiness of all persons affected by it,
there can be no reason for excluding the agent from the
number of those persons; that his motive reacts with full
power upon his character, strengthening or weakening this or
that disposition or habit; and therefore that the effect of the
motive ought to be taken into account in computing the total
of the consequences of the act?" "At any rate, there is
nothing to hinder us, on Utilitarian principles, from praising
and blaming motives. We may judge motive and act apart,

* Analysis of the Phenomena of the Human Mind, vol. II. pp. 272, 273,
276, 278. J. S. Mill's edition.

† Utilitarianism, p. 26.

‡ Ibid. pp. 27, 28."

but the motive is judged equally."[*] These three writers then take off the interdict imposed by their predecessor, and allow the motive spring of action to come into court for judgment. In passing sentence on it, however, and in assigning their relative worth to the several kinds of motive, they merely extend to the inward fact the same rule by which they appreciate the outward deed; they estimate it by its consequences of pleasure and pain, and regard as groundless every verdict of approval or censure which does not, in the last resort, rest upon this basis. No intrinsic value is attributed to any incentive; no inherent relative authority, which imparts a moral character to resulting action; but only a greater or less power of producing or preventing happiness. Nay, more: this power chiefly consists in the tendency to create repeated acts of the same kind, whether of benefit or mischief; and such fruitfulness in homogeneous consequences affords the main reason for praising or blaming a given motive. So that it is only in a derivative way that the spring of conduct is admitted at all to ethical valuation; it simply borrows a moral character from the overt acts to which it leads; and they remain, after all, the sole primary object-matter with which the moralist has to deal; keeping an ethical complexion constant and defined through all possible changes of the inward impulse which may issue them.

In direct contradiction to this order of dependence, I submit that actions, apart from their motive source, possess no moral character whatsoever; that the hedonistic estimate and classification of them under this condition is a purely rational affair, which might take place in a world and among races wholly unmoral; that the differences which constitute duty, and introduce us to the shades of right and wrong, lie up among the mental incentives to volition; and that thence alone is any ethical complexion or obligatory aspect contributed to the external actions which we put forth. Among the springs of action are found, no doubt, both self-regarding and social affections, which, in their proper place, make binding upon us a consideration of others' happiness and of our own: but the pleasures thus drawn within the horizon of duty do not on

* Fortnightly Review, May, 1869, p. 532.

that account constitute and define it; nor is a disturbed vision or a false reckoning of them to be condemned as an immorality, but only deplored as an illusion. The calculus of consequences is an indispensable instrument for giving the best effect to the rightly-adjusted forces of character; only, to wield and apply it well is the function, not of goodness, but of sagacity. While therefore it is perfectly true that our proper business in life cannot be done by Conscience alone, but needs to be supplemented by the rule of Utility, the functions of the two are nevertheless successive and distinct; the one supplies the inner guidance of Obligation, the other the outer guidance of Reason; the latter is needed to give Duty a rational direction; the former, to give Reason a moral inspiration: but neither is entitled to usurp the language of the other, or to work what ought to be an amicable partnership as a means for plotting mutual ejectment.

II. The Utilitarian, however, is by no means satisfied with the place thus conceded to his doctrine. He claims for it a competency to the whole business of a moral theory; and declines any services from Conscience, unless he may himself have the credit of first calling it into existence by the power of his favourite principle, the universal desire of happiness. Let us, then, assume that man has no other end, no other possible spring of action, no other ground of obligation, than the attainment of pleasure (including the avoidance of pain); and consider whether such a constitution of his nature as an agent, planted in the midst of his rational faculties, is competent to supply him with a moral rule, and to explain his moral affections.

1. At first sight it would seem that, if pleasure is the sole possible end of action, I have only to do as I like, and the law of my life receives its fulfilment; and the very idea of any guide but inclination appears to vanish. But, to save us from so hasty a conclusion, we are first reminded that the inclination of the moment may clash with interests of wider scope; and unless I deny myself to-day's indulgence, I may only be preparing to-morrow's loss.* True enough, but this

* Οὐ πᾶσαν ἡδονὴν αἱρούμεθα, ἀλλ' ἔστιν ὅτε πολλὰς ἡδονὰς ὑπερβαίνομεν ὅταν πλεῖον ἡμῖν τὸ δυσχερὲς ἐκ τούτων ἕπηται, καὶ πολλὰς ἀλγηδόνας ἡδονῶν

merely warns us to do as we like in a discreeter way, and avoid the bankruptcy of the spendthrift by careful balancing of our accounts. The differences of human conduct rise to no higher level than varieties of prudence; and we are still no nearer to any conception of duty or of authority over us.

The next device for carrying us a step in that direction deserves and requires a fuller notice. We are told that pleasures differ, not only in quantity, so as to be reckoned by a calculus of amounts, but in quality too; so that, apart from their magnitude, some are more desirable than others, as being of a higher kind; and unless we subordinate the life of Sense to that of the Intellect and the Affections, we have not worked out the Philosophy of Utility to its last refinements. "It is quite compatible with the principle of Utility," says Mr. J. S. Mill, "to recognize the fact that some kinds of pleasure are more desirable and more valuable than others. It would be absurd that while, in estimating all other things, quality is considered as well as quantity, the estimation of pleasures should be supposed to depend on quantity alone. If I am asked what I mean by difference of quality in pleasures, or what makes one pleasure more valuable than another, merely as a pleasure, except its being greater in amount, there is but one possible answer. Of two pleasures, if there be one to which all or almost all who have experience of both give a decided preference irrespective of any feeling of moral obligation to prefer it, that is the more desirable pleasure. If one of the two is, by those who are competently acquainted with both, placed so far above the other that they prefer it, even though knowing it to be attended with a greater amount of discontent, and would not resign it for any quantity of the other pleasure which their nature is capable of, we are justified in ascribing to the preferred enjoyment a superiority in quality

κρείττους νομίζομεν, ἐπειδὰν μείζων ἡμῖν ἡδονὴ παρακολουθῇ πολὺν χρόνον ὑπομείνασι τὰς ἀλγηδόνας. Epicurus in Epist. ad Menœc. ap. Diog., Laert. x. 129. Totum hoc de voluptate sic ille (Epicurus) præcipit, ut voluptatem ipsam per se, quia voluptas sit, semper optandam expetendamque putet, eademque ratione dolorem ob id ipsum, quia dolor sit, semper esse fugiendum, itaque hac usurum compensatione sapientem, ut et voluptatem fugiat, si ea majorem dolorem effectura sit, et dolorem suscipiat majorem efficientem voluptatem. Cicero, Tusc. Disp. v. 95.

so far outweighing quantity as to render it, in comparison, of small account."*

Till this passage was written, the distinction on which it insists had never, I believe, been regarded as "compatible with the principle of Utility." No more direct contradiction can be exhibited than between Mr. J. S. Mill's statement, that "*neither pain nor pleasure are homogeneous*,"† and Bentham's that "the words *pain* and *pleasure* are names of *homogeneous real entities*."‡ That the variance is not accidental, in the mere phrase, but lies deep in the very conception of the doctrine professed by both, is evident from the fact that Bentham, in giving his complete enumeration of " the *elements* or *dimensions* of *value* in a pleasure or pain,"—an enumeration on which, he says, "the whole fabric of Morals and Legislation may be seen to rest," admits no gradation of kind, but limits himself to attributes which *any* pleasure may be liable to have,—*e.g.*, intensity, duration, certainty, absence of delay, freedom from alloy, fertility in ulterior pleasure.§

We equally miss the distinction between quantity and quality in the writings of the elder Mill. Where he distinguishes the different " classes of ends " which may move the will,—sensuality, for example, ambition, avarice, glory, sociality, &c.,—it is not by any gradation among them, but only in the ingredients of their composition ; and the pleasure they carry is named only as the common feature of them all ; occurring indeed " in company, or connection with things in infinite variety," now " with the form and other qualities of a particular " person ; now " with a certain arrangement of colours in a picture ; now with the circumstances of some fellow-creature ; " " but these are the accessories ; the essence is the pleasure."| In thus discountenancing the language of qualitative gradation, the Utilitarians of the last generation did but follow the example of the ancient Epicureans ; who, while affirming the superiority of mental to bodily pleasures

---

* Utilitarianism, pp. 11, 12.
† Ibid. p. 16.
‡ Principles of Morals and Legislation, ch. vi. § vi. note p. 76.
§ Ibid. ch. iv. p. 49.
‖ Fragment on Mackintosh, pp, 389, 390.

(of χαίρειν to ἥδεσθαι), resolved it into a difference of duration and intensity.* Mr. J. S. Mill indeed is too well versed in the philosophical literature of ancient and modern times not to be conscious of the novelty of his position: "It must be admitted," he says, "that Utilitarian writers in general have placed the superiority of mental over bodily pleasures chiefly in the greater permanency, safety, uncostliness, &c., of the former,—that is, in their circumstantial advantages, rather than in their intrinsic nature. And on all these points Utilitarians have fully proved their case; but they might have taken the other, and, as it may be called, higher ground, with entire consistency."†

If so, it is certainly strange that they withheld their foot from ground so obvious; for, once stationed there, they would have been saved half the trouble of "proving their case" at all. "The superiority of mental over bodily pleasures" speaks for itself, if there is a natural scale on which we already know them to occupy a higher place; unless it can be shown, that, by an opposite adjustment of "quantities," the relation is inverted. The older Utilitarians had good reason for avoiding this treacherous advantage. They would look with a just suspicion on this language of *ranks*, "higher and lower," "worth more and worth less,"—"superior and inferior," as not the native mode of hedonistic speech, but imported into its vocabulary from some mystic hieratic tongue. "Higher," "worth more," "superior," not as productive of more pleasure, but for no reason at all, except that some presumed expert is pleased to say so, surely in this we hear the voice of the "Moral-Sense-man," or of the "partisan of the principle of asceticism," who, as Bentham remarks,

---

* Beginning with the converse case of pain, the statement is as follows: Τὴν γοῦν σάρκα διὰ τὸ παρὸν μόνον χειμάζειν, τὴν δὲ ψυχὴν καὶ τὸ παρελθὸν καὶ τὸ παρὸν τὸ μέλλον. Οὕτως οὖν καὶ μείζονας ἡδονὰς εἶναι τῆς ψυχῆς. Epicurus apud Diog. Laert. x. 137. Omnia jucunda, quamquam sensu corporis judicentur ad animum referri tamen; quocirca corpus gaudere tam diu, dum praesentem sentiret voluptatem, animum et praesentem percipere pariter cum corpore et prospicere venientem nec praeteritam praeterfluere sinere; ita perpetuas et contextas voluptates in sapiente foro semper cum expectatio speratarum voluptatum cum perceptarum memoria jungeretur. Cicero, Tusc. Disp. V. 95, 96.

† Utilitarianism, p. 11.

has no better reason for objecting to an act than that "the commission of it is attended with a gross and sensual, or at least with a trifling and transient satisfaction."* What is this *second scale*, other than the familiar one of greater and less pleasure, by which each action is to be tested, with possible reversal of its former place? What attribute is it, whose comparative and superlative degrees are there spread out, as predicable, more or less, of all our objects of choice? It is vain to call it "quality" in the abstract, without telling us *what quality;* for comparison there cannot be, along a line of gradation, without *something to compare;* and if the attribute remains anonymous, represented in its absence only by an abstract x, the comparison is fictitious or illusory. Till Mr. Mill can name the property whose varying dimensions modify our estimate of happiness by mere amount, his new criterion remains in the dark. And when he names it, it must turn out, after all, to be a quantity; for, to be susceptible of a "more or less," yet *not* to be a "quantity," is plainly impossible. Yet, by the hypothesis, it is not quantity of *pleasure* with which we have here to do; *that* is provided for on the other and prior scale; and whatever else it may be,—call it dignity or nobleness or what you will,—it constitutes and attests an element of worth other than pleasurableness; and its admission is an involuntary surrender of the theory which it is intended to rescue. In spite of our absolute subjection to our "two sovereign masters, pleasure and pain," there is, it seems, some graduated attribute, not mensurable upon their scale, which may appeal with effective persuasion to our will.

Can any one doubt what this nameless attribute—or attribute of many names (for it is called "superiority," "eligibility," "desirableness," "preferableness") really is? I venture to affirm that it is simply the *moral quality* under a disguise, holding before its face the mask of pleasure, but with the serious eyes of duty looking through. The second scale, of *kinds* or *quality* of satisfaction, is not, in its source, a classification of pleasures at all, but just the natural hierarchy of our springs of action, our own conscious order

* Principles of Morals and Legislation, ch. ii. § xviii. note, p. 39.

of a relative rank in the impulses and ends of life. *Given* that felt hierarchy of claims, and undoubtedly it must tell upon our sensitive experience; to defy it, and live the life of a beast with the powers of a man, or of a selfish wretch amid the pleadings of suffering affection, involves a self-contempt and humiliation worse than death. But this is the anguish of a morally constituted nature; the pursuing shadow of conscience in its unfaithful flight. Take away that prior sense of relative authority; let there be no shame in self-surrender to the appetites, no consciousness of any call to intellectual aims as a worthier possibility, no constraining demand of duty from the social relations; let all these springs of activity be there, but not inherently distinguished as better and worse; let them bring their several ends before us, as candidates, with no other recommendation than the pleasurable experiences they may convey into an unmoral nature; and I know not on what ground we could longer say, "It is better to be a human being dissatisfied, than a pig satisfied; better to be Socrates dissatisfied, than a fool satisfied."* The one of these is "*better*" than the other,— the dissatisfied than the satisfied,—only when you refuse to try the case by the test of satisfaction,—that is of pleasure. The element of "superiority" which Mr. Mill's correct feeling recognizes can never be designated in the descriptive dialect of happiness. Who could rationally speak of the superior *happiness* of those who, for noble ends, or from honour that cannot stoop, have sacrificed their portion of life's immunities and enjoyments? of one, for instance, who has gone into slavery in order to redeem another, or of the martyr who cannot lie?

Suppose, however, these objections waived, and the distinction between quantity and quality admitted as an adequate account of the motives operative on the human will. Let happiness, if you please, be computed in two dimensions, not degree only, but rank as well; yet so long as I am engaged in selecting and arranging my own pleasures, and only taking care, that, among the plainer viands, my table is duly served with provisions of a more delicate cuisine, no moral phenome-

* Utilitarianism, p. 14.

non is reached, and the mark of the mere epicure is on me
still. Nay, its stamp is deeper and more ineffaceable than it
was before ; for when the proper object of the reason, truth in
all its breadth, the object of the imagination, beauty in its
depth, the object of the affections, the living groups around,
are set before me only as so many different varieties of pleasure, and I am drawn to them, not for themselves, but to
gratify my own intellectual taste and sympathetic sensibilities,
I push the claims of Self into shameless and desolating usurpation ; subordinating to them, not simply the lower elements
of life of which I am rightful master, but those higher ends
which I am bound to serve with reverence. Could I even
seize these angels of the way and detain them as my menials,
they would only become incarnate, and lose whatever is divine.
Self-culture, however balanced and comprehensive, not only
has no tincture of duty in it, but must be quitted ere a duty
can be done.

Nor is there a more subtle impostor in the world than the
sham self-sacrifice which you make in the interest of your
own perfection, or for which you stand ready in that "unconscious ability to do without happiness," which Mr. Mill says
"gives the best prospect of realizing such happiness as is
attainable."*   It may be true that "nothing except that consciousness can raise a person above the chances of life, by
making him feel, that, let fate or fortune do their work, they
have not power to subdue him ; which, once felt, frees him
from excess of anxiety concerning the evils of life, and enables
him, like many a stoic in the worst times of the Roman
empire, to cultivate in tranquillity the sources of satisfaction
accessible to him, without concerning himself about the uncertainty of their duration, any more than about their
inevitable end."†   But this invulnerable Stoic, who, under
the ban of fortune, tranquilly resorts to the virtues and
humanities as "accessible sources of satisfaction," lingers
still at the propylæum of the temple of Duty without real
worship of what is divine within. And his modern admirers,
who, in expressing their ideal of excellence, speak so often of
"cultivating their sympathies," "cultivating their moral

* Utilitarianism, p. 24.   † Ibid. p. 24.

feelings," "cultivating nobleness of character," do but foster self-homage, even when sounding the praises of self-abnegation. Elevate it as you may, we are called to something else than this. We are placed here, not to remain at home, dressing up our own personality to the last spiritual refinement, but to be carried out and borne away by the glories and sorrows of the world; to be the organs of a truth that may bring us only scorn, of a love of right that may meet no response, of a pity that sees nothing but the griefs it heals. And from this service of ends above us we are fatally removed by a theory which brings everything to the ultimate test of personal sensibility, and labels it as a kind or degree of pleasure. The animating genius of such a doctrine cannot be doubtful, and cannot be changed; there is but one possible habitant that can be owned as its resident Spirit; however dressed up with the borrowed characteristics of genuine Duty, still, under the cloak of heroism, or behind the mask of saintliness, and with the praises of martyrdom upon his lips, it is after all the figure of *Prudence* that looks out of the window, and tries to personate the supreme graces of humanity.

2. This, however, I shall be reminded, would hold only if the Utilitarian took for his rule the happiness of the individual agent; whereas he includes in the account the happiness of every one concerned. In the reckoning between my own happiness and that of others, he insists on my maintaining "the strict impartiality of a disinterested and benevolent spectator," and forbids me in the least to favour myself; and so appropriates the Christian injunction, "As ye would that men should do to you, do ye also to them likewise."* Now, it is perfectly true that the teachers of this doctrine, after grounding it on each man's necessary pursuit of his own pleasures, and affirming that this invariable "*end of human action*" is also "*the standard of morality*,"† do slip away from the rule of *personal happiness* which alone comes legitimately out of their reasoning, and announce instead the criterion of *public happiness.* The fact is honourable to themselves, but fatal to the logical structure of their system. For, what right have they to demand from me an "impartial" standing between

* Utilitarianism, p. 21.　　　　　† Ibid. p. 17.

the pleasures of another and my own? Have they not told me that I am by nature incapable of desiring anything but happiness? And to move my own desire, is it not my own happiness that they mean? How, then, can they turn round and say, "But, mind, it is to make no difference to you whether the happiness is yours or somebody else's. It is the pleasure of *quilibet*, and of equal value, as *suum* or *tuum*, abroad or at home." Surely I may reply, "Another's happiness is no doubt worth as much to him as mine to me; and you, who are outside us both, may be neutral between us: but to ask me to be indifferent about the ownership, provided somebody, it may be in China or the planet Jupiter, gets the pleasure which I miss, is to contradict your own assertion, that my only end is the gain of happiness."

The inconsistency here indicated appears in the strongest form in the writings of Bentham; but I am not aware that it has ever been relieved. What can be more startling than to find the same writer who demands from me perfect impartiality between my own happiness and that of others,—who insists that "everybody is to count for one, nobody for more than one," also giving the following sketch of the nature to which he appeals, and of his business with it as a Moralist? "Dream not that men will move their little finger to serve you, unless their advantage in so doing be obvious to them. Men never did so, and never will, while human nature is made of its present materials." "But they will desire to serve you when, by so doing, they can serve themselves; and the occasions on which they can serve themselves by serving you are multitudinous."* "To prove that an immoral action is a miscalculation of self-interest, to show how erroneous an estimate the vicious man makes of pains and pleasures, is the purpose of the intelligent moralist. Unless he can do this he does nothing; for, as has been stated above, for a man not to pursue what he deems likely to produce to him the greatest sum of enjoyment, is in the very nature of things impossible."†

If his only possible rule is "the greatest sum of enjoyment *to him*," what is the use of giving him another, that he must

* Deontology, vol. ii. p. 192.   † Ibid. vol. i. p. 13.

give equal weight to enjoyment *not* for him?   And if, as an
"intelligent moralist," you can ask him to sacrifice the less
to the greater happiness only when both are his own, why
renew the demand when against his lighter treasure the preponderance lies in the scale of another life?   In short, for a
mind sent into this world with one supreme impulse of self-
love, from which all others are secondary out-growths, it is
impossible to establish any obligation to self-sacrifice, any call
to the path of pain and the acceptance of Death to save a
blessing for happier survivors.   What cannot be *prudentially*
established, cannot be established at all.   *Why* should he
incur the privation, when it conflicts with the only good at
whose disposal you place him?   By what persuasion are you
to move him to throw away his all?   Either you must tell
him that the high consciousness condensed into an hour of
self-immolation will transcend all the possibilities he foregoes;
in which case you bid him consult for himself under pretence
of martyrdom for others.   Or else you must speak to him in
quite another tone; must remind him that he is not his own, and
can ask nothing for himself; that he is to be at the disposal
of an authority higher than he, against which he has no
rights to plead ; that, when he knows the true, when he sees
the just, when he is haunted by the appeal for mercy, a constraint which he cannot question is put upon him to be their
witness, however long their dolorous way, however agonizing
their Calvary.   And speaking thus, you altogether change your
voice, and from casting up the account-book of greater happiness are caught and carried away into the hymn of all the
Prophets.

Whence this evasive oscillation in the maxims of the
Utilitarian philosophy,—this unsteady shifting of the weight
of obligation from one leg to the other,—planting it now on
the footing of the agent's interests, then on that of the public
good?   It probably has its origin, not in any deep-seated
philosophical fallacy, but in a superficial accident in the
literary history of the modern school.   Its first apostle,
Bentham, was a jurist, rather than a philosopher, eager for
the banishment of fiction, barbarism, and disorder from the
intellectual system and practical procedure of English law.

At the substructure of all well-ordered human life he laboured
no further than was indispensable for his ulterior end; and
was content to assume, or to treat with scant analysis, the
few undisputed conceptions in his work. Instead of working
out, like Hobbes, an explicit theory of the origin of Society,
he throws the light and force of his thought upon a later
stage; and instead of looking about to find out how the Lawgiver came there, recognizes him as having been there so long
as already to have grown blind to his proper functions and
stiff with stereotyped habits. The great Utilitarian never
loses sight of him, and keeps him always at his side for purposes of discipline; boxes his ears pretty freely; strips off his
phylacteries, cuts through fold after fold of the texture of
maxims which impede his movements; and trains him to a
freer skill and a more natural step. Now it is to *him*,—the
Lawgiver over others,—and not to the subjects themselves,
that Bentham prescribes the rule, "Everybody to count for one,
and nobody for more than one." It is the Legislator's true
guide. From his height above the field *he* is to look impartially on and insist on fair play among the various candidates for their own maximum of attainable pleasure; by
restraining and moderating each, he is to maintain the
equilibrium most favourable to the collective sum. Plainly,
however, this office of his implies that no one else is expected
to be impartial, or to care except for himself; it is simply to
provide against the effects of an assumed universal self-love
that the Lawgiver is there. In other words, Law and Right
are the indispensable antagonists, instead of the products and
exponents, of Self-love; and have a rule to follow quite
opposite to any which individual interest can ever supply.
To reach that rule, there must be a Superior lifted above the
scene, apart from its impulses, and wielding Authority over
it; and but for this august presiding nature, capable of inspiring awe, the competing haste of beings surrendered to
their own pleasures and pains would lead only to a lawless
carnival. Where, then, and what, is this abstract Lawgiver,
with whom even Bentham cannot dispense, and whom he
supplies with a rule not valid for a race at the disposal of
their own visible advantage alone? It is simply Conscience

under a disguise, the inward Sense, inseparable from our nature, of an orderly authority amongst our springs of action : or, to chase it into the last retreat of truth, it is the Lord of Conscience, the Legislator of life, whose revelations of Right make themselves felt, with or without recognition, in every effort to clear the thought and purify the practice of human justice. But for such a power, it seems to be admitted in the very assumption of it, pleasure, as our sole end, would send us all astray. The Utilitarian inconsistency has arisen from transferring to the governed subjects a rule of impartiality originally meant for the guidance of their governor alone.

The Utilitarian doctrine has usually been connected with the opinion that pleasure, or exemption from pain, constitutes the only possible end of action. But it is capable of being held in conjunction with a different view of the sources of volition. There is nothing in it to prevent its disciples from accepting, as original in us, other affections than the desire of happiness for ourselves ; and it is natural to ask, whether the doctrine gains in validity by this psychological change. Suppose, then, that you amend your program of human nature, and allow to it, in addition to its fundamental self-love, an original and equal love of others ; and compute the effect upon our problem of this new condition. It certainly gives a good account of the facts that personal interest frequently gives way to social ; that the happiness of neighbours becomes an essential element in our own ; that therefore there is an approximate coincidence, in their practical working, between the rules of Prudence and those of Benevolence, and that where they conflict, the disinterested impulse has as fair a chance of ascendency as the selfish. Of the two affections at the disposal of which human life is placed, now one, and now the other, will be driven from the field, and the movement will sway and oscillate between the extremes of egoism and generosity. And so, if instead of two primitive forces of affection we admit ten, we should furnish the conditions of a corresponding variety of result. Turn ever so many impulses into the mind to have their play there, and it is certain that each will, some time or other, lead the game. But in such acts there is absolutely no moral phenomenon at all. They are actually, though partially, presented in the irresponsible creatures below us; in whose nature several instinctive affections are co-present on terms of equality, taking them by turns in each direction embraced within the compass of their being. The question to which we require an answer is not, Why self-love often *does* give way, but how, under certain conditions, all men know that it *ought* to give way. And this sense of Duty,—this consciousness of an obligatory order, this moral right of one incentive over another, is something totally distinct from the existence of the affections themselves and their assemblage on the arena of the same consciousness. If we are fitted up only with personal interests and various loves, without the revelation of any natural ranks of authority among them, there is no rational ground for the characteristic experiences of the Conscience; for that flush and glory of approval with which we look upon a victory of Right; for the shame of forgotten vows, and the remorse of irrevocable guilt; and for that pathetic play between the shadows of sin and the conquering lights of a divine trust, which fills the whole atmosphere of Christendom with the gleams and glooms of a stormy day.

The assumption, then, of an original social as well as self-regarding tendency does not convert the Utilitarian doctrine into an adequate theory of duty. Yet another alteration must be made in its draft of human nature, before its ethical and its psychological aspects are brought into harmony. If we were naturally endowed, not only with sympathy for others, but also with a knowledge that we were *bound* to consult for their happiness as for our own, then indeed we should be made upon the right pattern for the Utilitarian philosophy, and its method would work without a check from any part of human life. Such an account of the factors of our moral being, reducing them to self-regard, sympathy, and obligation, though too complex for the school which would gain by it, would indeed, as I believe, be an utterly illusory simplification; omitting or distorting the greater part of the incentives which urge the will and constitute the character. But it would at least lay the real foundation for duty; and the remaining controversy would lie wholly in the field of mental history and analysis.

That *something* must be conceded to the intuitive doctrine, and that the fabrication of the mature perceptions, intellectual and moral, from the elements of early sensation, has not proved a very manageable problem, seems now to be consciously or unconsciously confessed. For no otherwise can we explain the eagerness with which the experience-philosophers have seized upon Mr. Herbert Spencer's suggestion that our seeming axioms are not personal acquisitions, but an inheritance transmitted from the habits of our forefathers, and formed in them by an incalculably slow accumulation of personal experiments. If the so-called intuitions had already been satisfactorily resolved, if their analysis was as exhaustive as it professed to be, if there was no residuary function in them which, however often dissipated, insisted on coming back, there would have been no room for a new explanation ; and a theory which overleaped the boundaries of the individual life, and flung itself upon the illimitable resources of antecedent generations, would have been resented as a reflection upon the adequacy of prior expositions designed to be complete. Instead of this, Mr. Spencer's ingenious and fruitful hint has been welcomed with a zest which shows how much his help was needed. To estimate the amount of its evidence, and the range of its value, as it is beyond my competency, is happily not within the scope of my design. For one remark only do the exigencies of my subject seem to call. The doctrine of cumulation by inheritance can never help us to any genesis of moral faculty out of data that are unmoral. The transmission of improving aptitudes may render rapid and easy, processes which were slow and difficult ; rich and intense, feelings that were poor and faint ; immediate, perceptions that were mediate ; abstract, cognitions that were concrete. But it cannot give what it does not contain ; no induction, however wide and long, can yield us predicates never found in its particulars ; and from an experience, be it of one generation or of a million, into which at one end only the sentient element enters, at the other nothing that is moral will come out. To deduce the authority of Duty, and the disclosures of

Conscience, from " consolidated experiences of utility," is to violate the ancient rule, Οὐκ ἔστιν ἐξ ἄλλου γίνους μεταβάντα δεῖξαι ;* and to assign a cause which, when relinquished as inadequate in the individual life, cannot be shown to gain by extension any better relation to the effect.

The facts, then, of our Moral nature retain, as it appears to me, the character and significance ascribed to them in the previous expositions. In order to give them another aspect, the philosophy of Utility has to explain them away into something else from which their essence has departed ; treats their central thought as an illusion, whilst still appealing to it as a power ; and raises their external function into an authoritative importance to the claims of which the Conscience never will respond. It fails to take possession of Morals at their source, not less than the Intuitive doctrine to conduct them to their application ; and will never occupy its true place, till it is content to take up the Will already right in Duty, and guide it to an issue equally right in Reason.

* Aristot. Anal. Post. 75. a. 38.

CHAPTER IV.

GOD IN HISTORY.

ALL that has happened among mankind has arisen from the mutual play of the forces around them and the forces within them. The drama of ages has had this world for its stage, and our race for its actors, and could not have remained the same, had either been different. Suppose, for instance, the distribution of sea and land other than it has been within attested time, giving a new massing to the ice, and new currents to the ocean; or change the lines on which the mountain-ranges rise, so that the great rivers, whose reeds hide the cradle of all civilization, shall have a different flow; bury the old forests a little deeper; put the mineral veins out of reach; or take the cotton and the flax from the flora of the earth: and, by this modification of terrestrial conditions, you turn back all our actual past into the impossible. And in the same way, had man been constituted otherwise than as he is; had his appetites been less exigent, or his resentment less keen, or his affections less capable of ideal direction, or his faculty of speech no greater than a dog's,—then, also, an observer of the world must have witnessed quite another change of scenes. Nay, there are crises in human affairs at which the whole movement of the future seems to hinge on a single act of a single agent. Had Judas Iscariot spurned at first, instead of returning at last, the thirty pieces of silver, who can measure the change from that dropped link in the sequence of events? Had Mohammed broken the cobweb which was flung across his cave of concealment, and which seemed to tell his pursuers he was not there, the vehement life which Islam has breathed into so many nations would have been lost to the pulses of the world. Had the monastery at Erfurt deputed another than young Luther on its errand to paganized Rome, or had Leo X. sent a less scandalous agent than Tetzel on his business to Germany, the seeds of the Reformation might have fallen by the wayside, where they had no deepness of earth, and the Western revolt of the human mind have taken another date and another form. And so it would seem as if the many-coloured web of history were all woven by the threads of our volition, shot through the continuous warp of natural law without us.

Is there, then, it will be asked, no part left free for a Divine Agent? Is the story all told, when the scene has been physically described, and the actors have revealed their purposes, and played out their game? Or is there a deeper plot, which wields their conscious aims, and combines them for unconscious ends, and works out a catastrophe dissipating and transcending all personal dreams? How far there is scope for a divine education of mankind, without disturbing either factor of their history, and on what lines of change we are to seek its vestiges, will be evident by simply following out the principles which we have already gained.

If, indeed, the only way in which God could find entrance among the phenomena were as a *third factor*, over and above the theatre of nature, and the life of man ; if the question were, whether, when these two had done their utmost, there yet remained some unexplained effects for which he must be invoked,—we might well despair of finding room for any causality of his ; for it is obvious that the other two groups— the agency without, and the agency within—constitute a pair logically exhaustive, and absolutely close their ranks against any new partner on the field. Those who insist that nature and humanity suffice to account for everything, and need no *tertium quid* to complete the tale, tell us not simply a truth, but a truism, serviceable only as betraying their total misconception of the problem. Their tacit assumptions, that nature is a reservoir of atheistic powers, and that man is an insulated personality, —the product and reagent of those powers,—and that, till we discover some other realm, we may deny all other mind than his, are simply a prejudgment of the question by false definition and inaccurate division. There is no need of any outlying domain, beyond the scope of the phenomena we see and feel, to serve for us as the receptacle of God. Infinitely as his being may transcend the whole sphere of our cognition, it is not beyond nature, but within it, that we must find the action of his power: it is not beyond the human mind, but within it, that we must be conscious of his living spirit. We shall have, therefore, to break up the two factors of history in order to draw forth from them, and exhibit apart, such elements in them as may be divine.

This world, which is the outward theatre of history, is part of the great cosmos, all whose forces, as we have seen, find their unity in God, and whose laws are but the modes and order of his thought. In that field, he is not simply *First Cause*, but *Sole Cause;* all force being one, and no force other than his. Whenever, in accommodation to the vocabulary of science, we speak of a plurality of powers, we refer in reality only to several distinct orders of phenomena which are wrought out by the universal power, and which, by their different aspects, cover its identity with variable masks. Though this disguise is often used as a philosophic trap, and the laws of things are tricked out in the drapery of causality, it can impose on no one who follows the meanings of his words to their ultimate seats, and knows thought from thought under every dress. Thus the first factor, nature, falls back entirely to the account of the highest Will. And to this term, we must remember, belongs man himself, so far as he is simply a living thing,—a mammal in the museum of nature. He, too, is subject, like the clouds and trees and waves, to rules in which he has no voice : and within these limits he is merely a natural object, the seat of natural phenomena ; and the Divine Cause is operative in him in the same purely dynamic way in which he grows the forests, and moulds the hail. So far, therefore, as the birthday of our race upon this earth, the distribution and movement of population, the genius and habits of nations, the shifting centres of power, have been determined by the natural constitution of the globe itself, they fall directly under divine causation, and are included in the organism of the divine scheme. By referring these things to the soil and the sun, to the fruits and hunting-grounds, to the wood and metals, of the world, we do not take them out of the Supreme Hand, but, on the contrary, leave them unconditionally there; for, though the Creator goes beyond nature, nature lies and lives entirely in him. This *physical* agency of God, spreading alike through persons and things, through organic and inorganic being, can take no separate notice of human life and character, nor of the differences which distinguish us from each other in our lot and in our mind; but pledges itself to steadiness and consistency throughout a whole cosmical system, to the balanced good of which it is directed. So severe does this unbending uniformity sometimes appear, that it wrings from us passionate deprecations of pity and alarm; as when some rude force crushes, or some unearned malady tortures and prostrates, a noble and lovely life, the centre of a thousand hopes. But we must not be tempted to demand that the *whole* of Omnipotence should stand at the disposal of human ends. We must beware of saying that the physical conditions which influence the course of humanity are *meant* for these alone, and should be measured by the standard of our needs. They are only a local application to one planet (which, moreover, has other inhabitants besides ourselves) of laws embracing other worlds, and affecting, it may be, innumerable other things; and all that we can ask is, that, in their universal sweep, their operation here should have its estimated place. To us, side by side with the *moral* government of God, which goes by the *characters* of men, there must ever appear to be a yet vaster administration, which, still intellectual, is *unmoral*, and carries its inexorable order through, and never turns aside, though it crushes life and hope, and even gives occasion to guilt and abasement. Probably enough, this is only an illusion of ours; and, could we follow from world to world those laws which look so sad and stern below, we might find them working out elsewhere the spiritual ends which here they seem to disappoint; and might discover that the training of minds into the likeness of himself is not only supreme, but sole, among the designs of God. But, so long as we are confined to our provincial position in this universe, and can see no moral ends beyond the limits of mankind, there will remain outside these limits a simply natural divine order, which, so far as it educates us, does so only in passing on to other ends.

But, as we have seen, God is not only in nature, which spreads the scene of history, and in mankind, as natural objects belonging to the furniture of that scene; he is also in those higher endowments of our humanity which transcend the zoölogic limits, and enable us to become the actors in history, and to perform the parts. He has not only planted within us the train of passions and affections which carry us hither and thither as they take their turn at the helm, but has disposed them in a hierarchy of ranks, and by his own Living Spirit in the midst interpreted their relative authority, and made it felt. So that over us, as moral beings, are set other laws than those which are embodied in our animal organism, and in virtue of which we eat and drink, and sleep and wake, and laugh and weep, and fear and fight, and herd together in gregarious masses; viz., laws to which our *assent* is asked, and to which we render, if at all, an *elective* obedience. We are committed to the disposal of no imperious and overmastering spontaneity of force, but of a clear consciousness of relative worth among the claims that bid for us; and this revelation of authority, this knowledge of the better, this inward conscience, this moral ideality,—call it what you will, —is the presence of God in man. Twice over, therefore, does his life meet with ours,—his *physical* agency in the forces which he lends to our organic nature; his *spiritual*, in the apprehension which he gives us of the gradations of character and the supremacy of duty.

Do we thus admit into our being too much that is divine? Within so narrow an enclosure, must we fear that it will demand the whole space, and leave nothing for ourselves? It is a groundless fear. Far from encroaching on our proper personality, the second or spiritual divine element addresses itself to *minds* alone, and presupposes the co-presence with it of our will as a responsible subject and an effective power. Without this, it would have no function in us any more than in a sheep; to this only can it address its appeal, and offer free suggestion for free adoption. Its voice is not less strictly relative to the problems of character in us, than it is distinctly expressive of character in God. There cannot be one to command, unless, also, there is one to obey. Three orders of power, therefore, meet within the human being,—a physical, a spiritual, and a personal; the first conditioning his life as a creature or living thing, the other two as a moral nature; the former divinely presenting, the latter humanly answering, the responsible appeal.

This personal will, which is thus saved as the third constituent power in our nature, may concur, or may conflict, with either of the other two. It may resist, or strive to evade, the dynamic order of the world; as when we vainly defy the physical laws of health, or attempt enterprises with resources inadequate to their success. In all such cases of frustrated aim,—when, for instance, we are detained by storms from reaching the death-bed of a friend across the sea,—it is we in our personal life that are baffled by the divine order of the world. Our will, again, may resist, or it may adopt, the imperative intimations of conscience; either betraying the right to save a life of tainted ease, or meeting self-sacrifice, rather than incur the sin of unfaithfulness. And here the casting vote is ours; and, if the wrong is done, it is the divine agency, in its spiritual function, that is "grieved" and driven away. In this way are clearly distinguished the relative parts which the two agents, the divine and the human, play in the respective spheres of necessary law and of moral law. As in the former, in the outward field of nature, we often say that "Man proposes, but God disposes," so in the latter, in the inner sphere of conscience, we may reverse the rule, and say that "God proposes, but man disposes." God's part is done, when, having made us free, he shows to us our best: ours now remains to pass on from illumination of the conscience to surrender of the will. And thus we obtain at once the separating line between the divine and the human in that moral and spiritual life which involves the communion of both: the initiative of all higher good is with God; while it rests with man to be the organ of its *realization, or its loss.* If, as there dawn upon us purer lights, be it of truth or of duty, which promise to dissipate the lazy mists that fold us round, we refuse to lay ourselves open to them, and to take the path illumined by them alone; if, still worse, we try to appropriate their glory without accepting their obligations, and thus turn them into richer ornaments of self,—we do all that we can to be "without God in the world," and to reduce whatever is divine into the mere food of appetite or convenience. If, on the other hand, we freely give ourselves away to the true, the beautiful, the right, and reverence them as above us, and entitled to the sacrifice, then, whether we know it or not, we place ourselves at God's disposal, and become fellow-workers with him. Hence, all *dying out* of moral good is a human phenomenon, due to some canker of unfaithfulness; while all the new births of good are divine in their source, though human, also, in their accomplishment.

It is a true saying, however hard to a stoic's self-reliance, that it is beyond the power of man to lift himself: he can only prevent himself from sinking. It is not *we* that set the lights before us at which we aim : they gleam upon us from beyond us, if not by the immediate gift of God ; and our part is complete if we keep our eye intent to see them, and our foot resolute to climb whither they show us the way. The beacon aloft is given; the path to reach it alone is found. But there is another saying, not less true, needful to complete the story,—that whoever is faithful to a first grace that opens on him shall have a second in advance of it; and, if still he follows the messenger of God, angels ever brighter shall go before his way. Every duty done leaves the eye more clear, and enables gentler whispers to reach the ear ; every brave sacrifice incurred lightens the weight of the clinging self which holds us back; every storm of passion swept away leaves the air of the mind transparent for more distant visions : and thus, by a happy concord of spiritual attractions, the helping graces of Heaven descend, and meet the soul intent to rise. Though, therefore, it is not ours to elevate ourselves, we shall assuredly be sent for, if we will only go. But, then, this growing scale, this more and ever more of opportunity, must be referred to God ; and it gives us a mark by which we may track the lines of Providence in life.

It is from personal self-reflection that we learn this constitution of our nature, and find in it the boundary between the human and the divine. But its discovery would be impossible, and its effects reduced to zero, in an insulated life; as it is only in the presence of other minds similarly formed and affected, only in the visible play of passion and character around, under the appeal of the nobler and the shock of the baser, that the moral capacities can find development so as adequately *to be:* so, even if regarded as potentially there, they could not *be known* to us, but for the objective image of our own inner history in the living drama around us. The reciprocal action of a common nature in each and all not only multiplies, but absolutely conditions, its manifestation in any; and the divine relation to the conscience, being social not less than individual, may be followed out in the character of nations over the surface of the world, and will give traces everywhere of a common moral government. These traces will be found a homogeneous extension of individual experience.

Humanity, however, is not only a *many-lived* organ; it is also a *long-lived* organ of God: and its phenomena, besides enlarging themselves from the personal scale to that of collective society, acquire a certain cumulative power and volume from generation to generation, yielding results, which, being beyond the intentions of all the human agents in their production, must be referred to the divine administration of the earth. The aims of man, taken one by one, and then added up into a whole, are no adequate measure of the effects achieved by them as tenants of the globe; and its surface is rich in memorials which have been left as a heritage for the race, but would astonish no one more than the private agents in their creation. Who can think, without wonder, of the operation, in the long run, of a very simple and inconspicuous cause; viz., man's need of *fresh water* to relieve his periodic thirst? This it is which has led him to the banks of rivers for his first settlements; which has selected the site of mighty cities, and woven the network of the early civilizations; which has loaded the margins of the Nile, the Tigris, the Euphrates, and the Ganges with monuments of ancient art and more ancient piety; and, in short, traced the whole contour of historical geography. When men saw the marvellous product, and, under the shadow of palaces and temples, speculated on the origin of so proud a scene, it is not surprising if they fancied that it must have been fore-announced by the fates, and that the founders, well knowing what was given them to do, were all heroes and divine. But the naked Britons, who, before Cæsar's time, were encamped on the brink of the Thames, were placed there by the rudest exigencies of barbarian nature, without foresight of the modern London; and just as little was it any historic vision of the "Eternal City" that floated before the mind of Romulus and his band. Each increment on these small beginnings has been similarly made by the working of petty and temporary aims, yet with an aggregate result as much grander than its rudiments as the history of human society transcends the pettiness of retail trade. Nor is it only the material capital of civilization which thus outstrips the conception of its several contributors. The whole structure of human law—that august expression of the moral organization of our collective life—has its ground in the simplest of psychological facts; viz., the *inequality of the resentment*, in case of wrong, felt by the *injured* and by the *bystanders ;* inducing the latter, who cannot be worked up to the rage of the former, to interpose, and enforce their own more mitigated anger. But how little could they who first rushed in to stay the uplifted arm of vengeance dream of the Pandects, whose initial word they wrote, or imagine that mighty system of rights and obligations, of restraints and sanctions, of mutual service required and common protection guaranteed, which, expressing the formed and educating the unformed conscience of communities, secures their moral tissue by fibres ever firm and ever growing! The New-Zealander, who, when brought to London, wondered how, without flocks and herds in sight, or fields loaded with the fruits of tillage, the swarming city was fed day by day, yielded to a just surprise; the countless springs of private interest which easily effect so gigantic a result being inconspicuous, and unconsciously adjusting an equilibrium never before the agents' thought. But far more marvellous is the peaceful co-presence and orderly co-operation of millions of human beings, each charged with forces of passion and desire distinct from the rest and unheeding, for the most part, the unity of the whole. This new order of phenomena, beyond the range of our personal aim, sets us on the vestiges of God in history; and, by following out the individual moral constitution into its social manifestations, we shall trace an intelligible line between the divine and human agency in the vicissitudes of the world.

Let it be observed that the partnership which we have here to define subsists entirely between the *personal* and the *spiritual* constituents already discriminated ; and that with the *physical* agency, which God shares with none, our problem has no concern. As man has no part in it, except to be more or less subject to it, it cannot enter into any estimate of his claims. I do not forget, in striking out this element, that, according to the disciples of Mr. Buckle, I fling everything away, and leave only the effects and products of what I have cancelled. In his view, individual and personal forces, even when set up and consolidated, are as nothing in presence of the great system of natural law which builds about them the conditions of their action ; and are themselves, at one remove, the off-spring of that system. That "one remove," however, would carry us at a stride into the darkness which surrounds the origin of man, and hides his cradle in the reeds of unknown rivers, or the caves of nameless shores : and whether the germ of a new living form that lay there had every fibre still woven into the tissue of nature, and, if so, at what later epoch an untransmitted power was lent to its heirs to be their own, are questions of prehistoric speculation, on which it is irrelevant to pronounce. It is sufficient, that, within the limits of history, man has been agent as well as patient, and, however restrained by the conditions of the scene in which he stands, has himself variously modified its possibilities, and asserted his own causality against a thousand pressures of both material and moral resistance. That by variations in climate and soil, in distribution of land and water, in the relation of island and continent, and in the flora and fauna of both, the bodies and the dispositions of men must be affected, their numbers modified, their employments cast into different moulds, and their polities tend to divergent lines of development, is admitted on all hands, and has been frequently insisted on by writers who have treated of the sciences subsidiary to history. But to represent such external influences as all in all, and reduce history to a mere study of man as shaped by them, is surely no less an exaggeration than that opposite extreme of hero-worship which resolves it into a series of biographies. However difficult it may be, in accounting for events, to measure the respective shares of great personalities on the one hand, and circumstantial pressures on the other, both causes are alive upon the field ; and neither of them has any pretension to silence the other, and claim to tell the whole tale itself. Will you assure me that Christianity must have turned up in no very different form without Jesus of Nazareth, and the Reformation without the reformers, and the great inventions of printing, of the mariner's compass, of the steam-engine, without their particular inventors? I excuse myself from listening to so paradoxical a slight passed on the original inspirations and intense will of exceptional persons of past ages. Are you so captivated, on the other hand, by the brilliant genius, or the marvellous wisdom, of some favourite whom you admire, or some master whom you revere, as to lift him into free air above all earthly contact with his time, and forget that he was born in a local home, hemmed in by social habitudes, and able to drink only of the stream of thought from earlier times, and breathe only the air of his own? and do you resent the suggestion that his individuality was not the solitary cause of the new epoch dated from his life? I can only wonder at so strange a disregard of the restraining conditions against which even the intensest human energy matches itself in vain. Recognition must be given to both sets of causes ; and the reason for excluding the *physical* from our present reckoning is not that it is disowned, and treated as absent, but that it is neutral in the account which it aims to settle. That account lies between our *personal humanity* and God's *spiritual* agency in us, not his *physical* agency in nature ; and we carry our scrutiny into history only in so far as its character springs from the moral alternatives of our voluntary life and the divine relation with them. All else, even though happening to man, belongs to the theme of "God in nature;" this alone remains for the quest of "God in history."

What, then, is the kind of test by which, on this crowded stage, the two wills may be distinguished? Exactly the same as that which serves us within the inclosure of the individual mind. *There*, as we have found, it is God that *inspires* for man to *realize*. The *ideals* are his: the actuals that come out of them, or that fail to come out of them, are ours. We feel his authority, we know his look, in whatever stands before our thought as higher, and claims us as its own. We are conscious of unfaithfulness, we pass under eclipse of divine light, in refusing to rise to the appeal, and staying to do our own work upon the levels of ease. It is no otherwise on the large scale of history. Nations, as well as private persons, have their impulses and opportunities, their gleams of a better, their temptations to a worse : and here, also, to give the higher initiative is the divine part; to fling it away and forget it, or to follow it up the glorious ascent, is the human. Hence, on the principle that man cannot lift himself, but can freely give himself to be lifted, a simple rule emerges from tracking the steps of Providence through the ages. Where there is nothing to be seen but bare conservation of what good there is, or, at best, only a local extension of it to classes or regions not brought up to its level, the human will is the chief agent, working on its own prosaic and unaspiring flat, and content to stand alone. Where there is continuous growth, and advance to loftier stages of life and character, and the men of each generation leave the world better than they found it, there we are on the vestiges of the divine Agent, and trace his moral government in history. It is not, therefore, in the great *stationary* civilizations of Egypt or Eastern Asia, where reverence spends itself in locking up stores of truth and art, of faith and character, and guarding them as much from increase as from waste, and worshipping the golden key which shuts them from the air of heaven, that we can study the path of Providence through the ages. They are, indeed, wonderful witnesses of a certain stage in the education of mankind, which, but for their longevity, would have been lost to our knowledge, and impossible to our belief; but it is in the relations which link them to what is prior and posterior, and not in any history within themselves, that they claim a section in the divine scheme of the world. If we would recognize the living course of God's discipline for our nature, we must look to *progressive civilizations* which have not survived their function, and then been content to petrify into solemn mausoleums of dead ages, but which have had an influence far outliving themselves, mingling and throbbing in the very life-blood of the world, and tincturing in after-ages even the very minds that know them least. The few nations which have been capable of this creative and impelling action, have been made the depositories of successive divine trusts, each carrying our nature along some line of advance it had never tried before ; and all their movements have at times been brought by converging dispositions to meet and melt, and give a nobler volume to our humanity. There is, however, a theological prepossession, which we must beware of taking with us into the study of the world. It is common, and it is natural, to imagine that God is most intimately present to those who know him, and least to those who know him not : so that true or false belief respecting divine things may be taken as marks to show where in history his vestiges are to be found, and where they are not. In conformity with this view, the Jew has been habitually treated as within the sacred circle,—a subject of the kingdom of God ; the Gentile as beyond it,—an exile in the domain of the Prince of darkness : and nations have been regarded as favoured with divine light, according as they stood nearer the monotheism of the one, or were farther astray in the polytheism of the other. The history of men's thoughts about God would thus be identical with the history of God's own dealings with them; and to follow out the religions of the world would be to survey the track of his living communion with the human mind. How utterly such a rule would mislead us must be evident to any one who lays his heart open to the nobleness of Pagan virtue, and who is not afraid to see the meanness and cruelties compatible with Orthodox belief. It is plain, that, where (to judge by the *Regula Fidei*) God may seem to be best known, he often leaves no living sign, and the dry ground yields no tender grass and flowers to mark where his fertilizing dews descend ; and that, to minds from whose creed he appears quite hid, he no less often goes in the dark, and kindling before them the lamp of honour, or the star of truth, draws them, they know not whither, except that it is to a higher than themselves. No doubt, all religions in their primitive life do really express what commands the supreme veneration of the mind, and are then coincident with the divinest lesson that has yet been given ; and if their types of thought were as expansive as our nature, and content to take up and consecrate every rising growth of pure reverence and noble admiration so as really to embody whatever speaks to wonder and conscience, and to drop whatever has withered from the heart, then, certainly, would their history coincide with the history of God's spiritual education of our race. But since they soon set into mythologies, and crystallize into forms of speech and habits of worship little susceptible of change, they lose their power of taking up new thought and love, and turn to stone. The tide of living reverence flows by with a sweep of deviation, and, taking fresh channels, leaves the ancient temple stranded on the delta of the past, —monuments of an earlier humanity, but not sheltering the sanctities of to-day. As religion is the germ, and spiritual culture the ripest fruit, of society, their characteristic products are widely separated in time ; and it is inevitable that traditional faiths and maturer pieties should part company, and that the highest elements of mind and character should at last be found, not in the theology, but in the civilization.

If, however, theology is too narrow an enclosure to exhibit the divine vestiges in history, we should go too far a-field did we seek them indiscriminately over the whole area and through all the tracks of thought and art. In his zeal to set free the idea of *inspiration* from the limits imposed upon it by divines, Theodore Parker has left it inadequately distinguished from the ordinary exercise of the human intellect and will, and almost fused into one the *physical* action of God in nature and the *spiritual* in man. Thus he says, that " through reason, conscience, and the religious sentiments," and " by means of a law, certain, regular, and universal as gravitation, God inspires men, makes revelation of truth ; for is not truth as much a phenomenon of God as motion of matter ?" And, as if still more completely to erase the distinction, he suggests, that " God's action on matter and on man is perhaps the same thing to him, though it appear differently modified to us."[*]

To press this alleged analogy between the dynamics of nature and the inspiration of man is to fling the human personality away. God's "action on matter" exhausts *the whole action there is*, and is identical with the very *constitution of the material world itself:* so that, without it, matter, if existing at all, is no more than the passive *nidus*, or objective medium, present as the condition of the divine energy. If the case of man is the same, he, too, is reduced to virtual nonentity, and, without agency possible to himself, becomes the mere vessel of the divine. The laws of his several faculties, that is, the orderly connection and consecution of their phenomena, being the movement and march of God within the mind, nothing remains which can be predicated of the human self; for it is nothing short of the whole of his personal history which is thus conveyed over into the life of God. The more this doctrine is carried out into illustrative examples, the more serious does this difficulty become. The " Principia " of Newton, for instance, we are desired to regard as the product of inspiration ; and the *measure* of inspiration is said to be the amount of " natural ability evinced in the achievement of each work." But the " Principia " is a book of deductive reasoning, in which each step involves or necessitates the next, and lays the track of one continuous intellectual movement, the partition of which through its whole length between two minds is surely inconceivable. Who, then, is *the reasoner* answerable for the processes of demonstration ? Is it Newton ? Then are they activities of his personality, and are not to be looked for *ab extra*, in the operation of another life. Is it God ? Then the intellect of Newton is rendered otiose, with only the residuary function, at best, of a receptive and recording obedience. Moreover, if the movement and force of the natural faculties are to be deemed an inspiration from a superhuman source, we shall have to recognize as divine, not only the truth, beauty, and goodness to which they lead, but the false, the ugly, and the evil issues into which they go astray ; for these are results

---

[*] Discourse of Matters pertaining to Religion. Bk. ii. ch. viii.

of the same faculties, often in the same men, and interspersed among the tentatives of the same effort of genius. The individual mind is thus lost in God; and God is no longer clear of the imperfections of the human mind.

In order, then, to save the *personal* power in man, and to leave him any real partnership in history, we must concede to him a mental constitution of his own,—a trust of both intellectual faculty and moral will; and must limit the divine part to the intuitive *data*, from which every activity of our inner nature must start. Each power of the soul has its own appropriate object towards which it feels its way,—reason to truth, imagination to beauty, conscience to right. The presentation of these to us is not our own doing; the regular pursuit of them *is*. If we say that all these ideals unconsciously directing us are divine, we remove the limitations from the theological conception of inspiration, without flinging the human causality into the mists of the pantheistic abyss.

In trying to trace the divine initiative here and there in the education of the human race, we must throw out of the account the earlier and remoter portions of mankind, and take up only the threads which are visibly twined into the present.

There is but one influence in the world that has transcended in beneficent power the genius of ancient Greece; and the spiritual providence of God in the historical education of our race has drawn on it as largely to nourish the intellect of the later ages, as his natural providence has drawn on the atmosphere to feed the fires of animal life. It is not, however, from the gods, but from the men, of Athens that an exhaustless and refining light has penetrated the whole organism of human thought. If the temples speak to us still, it is not of Athena, but of Phidias; not by their rites and sacrifices, but by their proportions and their sculptures. Scarcely does Homer himself make their Olympus endurable; nay, it had already become revolting to Plato; and our patience with it has returned only because it is so far from us: and, after all, we are ever glad to descend with the old poet to the plain of Troy, and make him sing rather of the defiance of chiefs, and the talk and tears of women. It is the literature, the art, the political life, of Greece, that constitute its significance for the world, and form its contribution to the providential education of mankind. No more striking evidence could we have that the divine initiative may take other forms than that of theologic truth, and may lurk in the unconscious tendencies of a people's mind, rather than come to the front in their defined beliefs and external worship. If, in this instance, we lift the veil of their visible life, and, passing behind, interpret for them the inspiration of which they were the subjects unawares, we shall find it in a haunting feeling of an *indwelling divineness* embodied in the cosmos, and interfused through all its parts, including man as one of them; for, to the Greek, the universe and human life never appeared as in their essence *antithetic* to the divine, but rather as clothing and manifesting it, and moulded by its inner thought. To him the brilliancy of the heavens and the beauty of the earth were no dead picture, asleep on this or that stretched canvas of dimension, but were alive, and looked at him through waking eyes expecting their response. Through all the products of his genius, from the early mythology to the philosophy which destroyed it, this feeling of a background of gods behind all that appears is traceable as their creative inspiration. In one view, his very polytheism is due to the tenacity of this implicit religion; for it consisted, in its origin, rather of a *succession* than of a *copartnership* of gods: and, if an original unity passed into a later multiplicity, it was because the power first conceived was too dark and rude, too convulsive and gigantesque,—adequate, perhaps, to the period of primeval night, and half separated elements, but no more fit for the elaboration and the rule of the finished cosmos than a hyperborean barbarian to be Archon at Athens. Hence, as the theogony descends from Chaos, Ouranos, and Gaia, through Zeus and Metis, to Prometheus and Athena, a progress is evident from the more material, indeterminate, and violent to the more intellectual, orderly, and fair, culminating at last in the reason, the arts, and the civic union of mankind. As the universe fell into intelligible order and clearer beauty before his eye, the Greek resorted to more gods, because he wanted better gods, yet could not let the old ones go. Nor does anything more finely express his faith in the ascendency of mind and order everywhere, than the Oresteia of Æschylus, with its conflict between the elder Erinnues and the younger divinities of Light and Thought, ending in the recognized authority of civic justice, and the removal of wild vengeance to hide itself in a grove beyond the walls. Human society itself thus comes to be regarded as the divine, set up on earth ; and its laws, its rights, its culture, and its harmonies, are the tentative miniature copies of a real but unapproachable perfection. And what was only felt in the mythology advanced into distinct theory in the philosophy. The whole language, not of Plato only, but of Aristotle, is pervaded by the assumption of the inherence of thought in things, and of the correspondence between the steps of natural evolution from generic conception to individualization, and the inverse steps of our mind from phenomenon to law in ascending grades : so that all our knowledge is a communion of intellect within us, and intellect without us,—a thought on our part respecting what itself is also thought. The same word *truth* served to express what was *real* and imperishable in the world, and the *apprehension* of it by us; and the word is the same, because no difference was felt in the things. This dominant peculiarity of the Greek, while it is the key to his own intellectual development, has transmitted a thrill of power through the mental culture of the world. Engaged on the beauty of the cosmos, and its claim to be reflected in human life, the Athenian genius, shedding its subtlety and vividness and strength through a marvellous language moulded to its ends, has touched the most delicate springs of thought, and at once brightened the finite margin of things with images of loveliness, and deepened the background with infinite problems. Scarcely greater has been the enlargement of the physical universe by the brilliant discoveries of modern times, than the gain of intellectual space and light by the Hellenic race ; and while its own theology has perished, and its temples have crumbled away, it has imparted to the religion of succeeding times that sense of an immanent divineness in the world, of a mingling of thought with the very substance of things, which has forever made the visible beauty, truth, and good a symbol of the invisible.

Different in every way, and ethically far higher, has been the function intrusted to the Hebrew race; viz., to live upon the earth for thousands of years, whether in society or in long exile, as subjects of an immutable justice and mercy, and bear an unswerving witness to the *moral government of the world.* As the Greek interfused the divine essence through the *cosmic space*, so did the Jew follow the divine footsteps down the tracks of *historic time*, and make the course of history a highway for his God. True, *he* also owned the power of God in the heavens and the earth, as their Creator and the Lord of all; but they stood in a different relation to their Author. Their life was not his life; they were not the organism of his manifested being, and he the soul of their rhythm and beauty, so that both together were but the outer and the inner side of the same divineness,—its transient glance and its eternal rest. He was separate from them, and looked down upon them from a heaven above the heavens. He set them up as the decorations and furniture of his universe; he worked them as his instruments. He sent the elements upon his errands, turned them hither and thither as blind executants of his momentary will, and would in the end fling them and all nature aside as the worn-out implements of an imperishable perfection which needs them not. They are his works,—monuments of his acts of skill and power in the past,—but are not what can tell the story of his thought in the present. Once for all, the Almighty had spread the firmament, and hung up the stars, and upheaved the mountains, and set bounds to the deep. He spake, and they *stood fast.* But his *life* was with the sons of men, to give them truth, to guide them right, to weed out the worthless, to organize the faithful, and make all things work together towards an everlasting righteousness. The architecture of the universe doubtless spake his glory; but it was only the scenery of a drama, whose plan disposed of all the nations, and unfolded itself through all the ages.

The first conception of that drama, formed by the Jewish mind, was certainly small enough,—a simple tissue of family vicissitudes, gradually widening into a larger design, embracing the providences of a group of federated tribes. But the faith in justice, the vision of a righteous plan, once given, sufficed for all the exigencies of an expanding life, and drew into it province after province of the spreading world which captivity or colonization opened to Jewish experience. The area of the divine stage seemed to become broader with every age, the actors more numerous, the plot more vast. Damascus and Tyre, Nineveh and Babylon, Antioch and Alexandria, appeared upon the stage which once stretched only from Dan to Beersheba; and the domestic piety traditional in the family of the Oriental sheik opened its heart to take the world into the embrace of its providence. The perseverance and the progress of the fundamental conception may be traced through the post-Maccabean literature, till at last, in the Book of Enoch, the whole known history of mankind—distributed into ten periods, like a poem in ten cantos—is presented as a divine epic, realizing at the end, by extinction of all that hurts and defiles, that *civitas Dei* which had been in contemplation from the beginning. It must be owned that this widening thought was long in bringing wider sympathies. The hard line between the Jew ordained for glory, the Gentile for perdition, only wavers and softens a little, remaining, though obscurely, pitilessly there. But at length the broader piety subdues the heart to a broader humanity. In the Apocalypse of Ezra, the scanty limits of salvation haunt the very soul of the author: he bewails them in pathetic tones; and, though he tries to banish the complaint, he evidently feels, that, at the cost of so sweeping a retribution, the kingdom of God is too dearly purchased.

With this fruitless touch of pity, however, he leaves the problem where it was. But how tenaciously the great idea of continuous historical development was held as the key to the providential plan, is evident from the comparisons by which he illustrates the course of humanity on our earth. It is like the order of the seasons, which cannot be inverted, but must pass through its regulated round; or like the successive births of child after child to the same mother, till the family is complete, and the organism of relations constitutes a moral whole. Who can deny that this theory, fairly carried out, must foster a temper at once prospective and humane? With the living God to lead them on, the centuries must brighten as they roll, or, if a darkness broods over them, must burst into richer sunshine after the passing storm. The golden time, the perfection of society, the purity and beauty of humanity, lie in the future, not in the past; and life is to be spent, not in sighs of regret, but in the joy of hope and the power of faith. By this grand and profound conception, the unity of God descends upon the fragments of the world, and passes through the conflicts of time, flinging its embrace around alienated men, and fastening the separated links of history. Whatever mistaken interpretations of concrete events may have marked the course of this belief, it has brought home to us the moral oneness of our humanity, and has no less bound into a system the phenomena of historic time than the law of gravitation the bodies of external space.

The mind of both Greek and Jew had a prevailing tendency *outward*,—upon the spectacle of nature, and the spectacle of man. The instinct of the one was to set the universe before it in an order of beauty and of thought; that of the other to set the fates of nations before it in an order of divine justice. The one gave a cosmical, the other a social and political faith. The effect of this objective tendency is apparent through all the differences which separate their conceptions of the best life. Their ideal of human perfection is, in both instances, thrown into the form of *a state:* it is planted out and embodied in a social organism ruled and pervaded by reason in the one case, by righteousness in the other. When Plato says, " Unless philosophers obtain the government of states, or kings and rulers become philosophers, there can be no hope of any end to the evils of commonwealths, or, as I believe, to the sufferings of humanity,"* he truly paints the Hellenic dream of an intellectually harmonized society. When the Hebrew prophet says, " The dominion shall be given to the saints of the most High, whose kingdom is an everlasting kingdom,"† he is intent upon that vision of a divine common-

* Republic, 473. C.   † Dan. vii. 27.

wealth, which, for the Christian, has passed into the heaven above, with its shadow only in the Church below.   In neither case was *the individual* regarded as in himself a whole, competent to have ends of his own investing him with inalienable rights, and imposing on him duties with which none could intermeddle.   He was to serve only as *material* for building up a structure of composite grace and statelier proportions,—a plinth of the palace, a "living stone" of the temple, an element lost in the collective beauty, or a support invisibly present in the edifice of holiness.   He had no claims apart from the civic or sacred social unity to which he belonged, which alone redeemed him from his solitary insignificance, and conferred upon him whatever importance or dignity he had, and which had an absolute title to dispose of him, through all the factors of his being, in the interest of its own perfection.   The immense power of this preconception is evidenced by the strange centralization and the revolting communism of Plato's Republic, leaving nothing to private life except in the lowest stratum of the community, and ordering, without scruple, the affairs of birth and death, the number of permitted lives, the diet, the occupations, the training, the abode, the possessions, of every citizen.   It is but a modification of the same fundamental assumption, that, for his relation to God, the Jew was dependent on his nationality.   His religion was an ethnological distinction.   It was not he, it was his tribe, that held a place in the regards and purposes of the most High; and, if he forfeited his place in the sacred caste, he fell under divine as well as human excommunication. His piety, therefore, was mainly patriotic and domestic,—a martyr's faithfulness to the guardian of his people, an inherited worship of the God of his fathers; and all its more private applications were but inner circles of derivative affection embraced by this wider circumference.

Need I say that there yet remains a vein of character unopened by these workings of thought, penetrating and powerful as they are? To check the tyranny of the social idea, there is needed a third inspiration,—a sense of the claims and the possibility of *individual perfection* as a supreme end, entitled to hold its ground even against the pretensions of apparent social good. Under its first rude form of self-subsisting courage and manly independence, Plato already recognized at a distance this type of character as special to the northern barbarians; and, for ages after, it vindicated and secured its place in history by stormy heavings of a freedom seemingly wild, yet not without secret centres and invisible lines of loyalty and obedience, pouring them in desolating floods over the lands of the enervated Latin populations. When their rough work was done, it became clear that their characteristic feeling of inward freedom carried in it nothing lawless and ungenerous, no senseless defiance of things right and sacred. On the contrary, it was a fresh fountain of affection and devotion, hitherto but little known, where the reverence which tinges life issues direct from the personal consciousness as its spring, and spreads thence to the nearest homefields of life, and onward till it freshens and fertilizes the landscape fading in the horizon. The Teutonic independence, in its aspect towards divine things, becomes that sense of personal relation between the single soul and the Spirit of God, which is the mainspring of the private sanctities, and releases the heart from the constraint of law into the freedom of love. The Germanic piety, in all its native movements, has been marked by a peculiar inwardness and spiritual depth, strongly contrasting with the more objective faith and casuistical self-scrutiny of the Latin churches. The mystic devotion of Eckart, of Tauler, of the Theologia Germanica, finding its way at last into Luther's doctrine of "justification by faith," expresses that self-abandonment of the soul, that merging of it in the life of God, which, though breathing the most passionate humility, can spring only from the sense of essential and ultimate affinity with him.

In claiming this subjective and solitary religion as the special Teutonic inspiration, I do not forget its occasional and striking manifestations elsewhere. Here and there, in all ages, an inward and meditative piety has possessed the intenser natures. It dictated many a tender phrase of the Hebrew poets. It was so perfectly embodied in Jesus Christ, that it shapes his very lineaments in our imagination. Its pathetic tones and sweet quietude return upon us in the lives and words

of the older Christian mystics. But these are exceptional and
scattered phenomena; and not even the authoritative image
of the Son of God availed to give large extension to this kind
of devotion, till its appeal fell upon a nation just ready to find
its native genius, and to rebel against the externality of sacerdotal Christendom. From the time when Luther gave voice
to the passionate struggles of his heart and conscience, and
told how he found the perfect peace of a surrendered nature,
there has been 'a deep and wide response among his people,
and thence throughout the world, to his gospel of faith and
communion of the Spirit; and the lonely pieties which need
no priest, and which, in humbling the soul before God, set it
erect before man, have passed from the rare recluse to form
the habits of multitudes and the ideal of churches. Nay, this
inwardness and reflectiveness of mind has spread far beyond
the bounds of religion: it has found its way into philosophy,
into poetry, into art, and deepened the whole spirit of our
western civilization.

Our modern religion is a triple cord into which are twined,
as strands once separate, the Greek, the Jewish, the German
elements of thought and feeling, and which, where it is perfectly woven, combines the strength of all. To fabricate such
a texture is the work of countless hands through many ages.
The genius of each progressive nation unfolds itself at first in
isolation or in opposition. The culture of the Greek was indigenous, of the Jew was separatist, of the German born in
conflict. And the *distribution* of the several factors of the
higher civilization has been effected by other nations than
those in which they were original; the Romans becoming for
the world the purveyors of the Hellenic and Jewish ideals, and
the Anglo-Saxon race of the Teutonic. But, when the various
agencies have played their part, the dividing barriers which
rendered each source provincial finally disappear; and a field
is opened by the providence of God in which the distinct
streams pass into confluence and swell into mightier volume,
and flow on with more fertilizing power. Not, indeed, that
any of the tributary fountains of civilization can come down
to us untainted,—the limpid vehicles of perfect truth. All
bring with them elements both pure and impure; and it must

still be the problem of our wisdom to precipitate the latter, and lead the former to nourish the roots of whatever is fair and fruit-bearing. It yet remains, therefore, for us to consider how to fling down the evil, and reserve the good, and recognize whatever has divine claims upon us in our historical inheritance of religion.

still be the problem of our wisdom to precipitate the latter, and lead the former to nourish the roots of whatever is fair and fruit-bearing. It yet remains, therefore, for us to consider how to fling down the evil, and reserve the good, and recognize whatever has divine claims upon us in our historical inheritance of religion.

BOOK II.

CHAPTER I.

THE CATHOLICS AND THE CHURCH.

The present, it has often been said, virtually contains within it the whole past. The products of art, of literature, of law, may largely perish, and leave many a former age with scanty monuments to bear witness of its genius; but its character and ideas, mingling with the life of the succeeding generation, tincture that newer time, and, however traceless in the fresh colour of the immediate hour, could not be withdrawn thence without changing its hue throughout. We cannot say that this law of transmission has any selective power to swallow up the evil, and hand down only the good; and, if the stream of history grows clearer as it flows, it is not that the current will not carry down both alike, but that the purifying interposition of reason and conscience arrests the turbid elements, and tries to let only the sweet waters through. In proportion as this interposition fails, the fountains of life and the marshes of death send down their contents together. Prejudices pass with truths; the seeds of vices are entangled in the same eddy that bears the virtues; and, rich as the crop may be in the fields below, there will still be tares appearing between. Every later civilization is of necessity a mixed product, large with the accessions, but tainted with the impurities, of earlier experience; and, whatever treasures it has taken up into it from the faiths and philosophies of nations variously endowed, it cannot escape its heritage also of human imperfection, or be spared the duty of severing the good from the evil. Our historical inheritance of religion is richer in the elements of truth and the sources of moral power than any ever intrusted to any previous age. We live environed with a sublimer nature, we are conscious of a more sacred humanity, we own a wider providence in history, than was opened to our forefathers. The cosmic intellect was less august for Plato, the communion of the Spirit less deep for Tauler, the moral drama of the world less grand for Isaiah and for Paul, than for us. But along with this progressive truth are many lingering errors, grown worse from their misplacement in a larger scene. The ampler our horizon, the more does the clinging mist around us hide from view; and we are but lost in the expanded universe, if we apply to it only the rude and petty measures hung up in the monkish cell. In the courses of history, be it remembered, there are two agencies ever at work,—the perfection of God, and the imperfection of man; and the present in which we live is the result of both. How, then, shall we separate the divine from the undivine? How discharge the perishable fancy, and hold fast only to the eternal reality? What sacred authority shall stand for us in the field of thought, and divide between the living and the dead?

To answer this question properly, we must ask another. The two elements in our religious inheritance, the divine and the human—are they likely to be blended and interfused throughout, so that the criterion which shall sunder them is needed everywhere? or do they sit apart, though on the same field,—the one railed off within some sacred enclosure; the other poured around it, and hiding it from view, and here and there assuming its likeness, but never mingling with its living power. Surely we should naturally expect that whatever divine influences have been shed upon the world must freely spread through the recipient capacity of our humanity, act in its functions, and share its risks. In nature there is no force but God's; in conscience yet unspoiled, there is no light save his; but it is the specialty of history, that there he concedes to man a partnership with himself, and lets everything arise from the confluence or the conflict of both wills. It seems, therefore, hardly conceivable that an historical revelation should be pure and simple, even for an hour. Mingling with human faculties in the first soul it enters, taking the vehicle of human language in passing from mind to mind, committed to the custody of human tradition in surviving from age to age, drawn into the intensest ferment of human thought, and struggling through the seething deep of human passion, and guarded from change, if at all, only by the crystallized imperfection of human institutions, it becomes more closely interwoven with the liabilities of our life at every point, till you can no more withdraw the supernatural from the natural than you can distinguish in the tree the cells formed in a spring shower a hundred years ago. If it be so ; if, to borrow the Scripture image, the sacred leaven diffuses itself thus through the whole mass of our humanity, and in quickening our nature is dissolved into it,—then there remains no rule for separating what is divine and authoritative, except the tests by which, in moral and spiritual things, we know the true from the false, the holy from the unholy. External criteria,—that is, *un-moral* rules for finding moral things, *physical* rules for finding spiritual things,—there can be none. Reason for the rational, conscience for the right—these are the sole organs for appreciating the last claims upon us, the courts of ultimate appeal, whose verdict it is not only weakness, but treason to resist.

This close intertexture, however, of the human and the divine in our historical inheritance of religion is by no means admitted by its chief trustees. They are possessed with the idea that they have actually got divine truth enclosed within a ring-fence, still pure and integral after all these ages,—a paradise of God, where his voice is heard, and his presence is felt, planted amid the profane wilds around. Two claims are preferred to this exceptional position,—one by Catholics on behalf of " the Church ; " the other by Protestants, on behalf of " the Bible." They agree in assigning to something outward an authority before which the inward protest of even our highest faculties must sink in silence : they differ in attributing this authority to a *corporation* in the one case, to a literature in the other. In the latter case, the Holy Spirit, having once created the books of Scripture, remains, as it were, stereotyped there, and liable to all the disadvantages which Plato charges upon written language,—that, though you would think the page alive with the thoughts it has, it looks up at you always with the same face ; is dumb to the questions you ask ; and, if tossed about in contumely or mistake, cannot defend itself, but needs its father to help it.* In the former case, the Holy Spirit perpetuates its work by taking for its organ an ever-living hierarchy, which is there to speak in every age, to interpret and supplement the dubious text, to correct the aberrations of reason, and relieve the perplexities of conscience. To this Catholic theory let us first turn ; the more so, because, to punish our imperfect exorcism of evil spirits at the Reformation, it is fast returning from the dry places of controversy in which it could never rest, and, finding in many minds the mediæval chamber swept and garnished, enters in to resume possession.

The Church then is, in this view, not simply a divine establishment historically continued in the administration of certain original trusts, but a living body, permanently and for ever animated by the Third Person in the Trinity, who, since the day of Pentecost, has occupied this organism, just as the Second Person was united with the humanity of Jesus. And if, in this case too, we do not speak, as in his, of an incarnation, it is not because the divine embodiment is less assured, but because the human persons are many and successive, and the body is corporate. The Holy Spirit had in all times, and even in heathen nations, been the secret source of natural grace, and rational apprehension of divine things ; and has enabled men to know God as the Author of Nature, to feel him in the suspicions of conscience, and to knit society together by his laws. All this, however, was but an invisible and scattered influence, present everywhere, instituted nowhere. But now, having created on earth the mystical body of the Christ in heaven, the Holy Spirit has opened a special abode, and established an organized and visible agency for distributing a higher and supernatural order of grace. His presence, no longer contingent on individual fidelity, has become unconditional and constant, and—whether by diffusing

* *Phædrus, 275 ad fin.*

the light of the incarnation, or by the consecrating power of the seven sacraments, or by gifts of vision, prophecy, or miracle, or by the efficacy of preaching—continues the characteristics of the first age, undiminished to the last. If you ask how you are to know, when you see it, this field of sacred wonders, crowded with daily miracles, a perfectly definite answer is immediately given,—there are *four* divine marks, or "*notes*," which make any mistake of the true Church of God impossible; viz., its *Unity*, or identity in all times; its *Sanctity*, as the one home of holy men; its *Universality*, or identity in all places; and its *Apostolicity*, or exact reproduction of the first and model age. Visibly bearing these characteristics, the Catholic Church claims to be the exclusive trustee of revelation, the sole channel of supernatural grace, the infallible witness and interpreter of divine truth.

That so stupendous a claim should appeal to tests so inadequate would be impossible, were it not that it has had to confront nothing but pretension weaker than itself, and already pledged to its most vulnerable premisses. If we take for granted, that, somewhere upon earth, there must be a divine institute, and only one, for the distribution of grace and the organization of true dogma; and if the only question be, whether what we find at Lambeth, at Geneva, or at Rome, looks most like this long-lived and world-wide establishment, —these "notes" serve readily enough to pick out the Catholic Church; being, in fact, invented for this very purpose. As between different pretenders to the same ideal, they may be conclusive. But if we dismiss that ideal assumption, and look first at what is real; if we relieve the Church of her rivals, and ask her to begin at the beginning, and speak to us from the primitive ground of humanity alone,—then we shall need other marks than these to convince us that there is nothing diviner upon earth than a spiritual corporation which can have a Borgia for its head, the councils of Ephesus and Constance for boards of justice, and the index and encyclicals as its expressions of pastoral wisdom. . Nor is it difficult to say what the other tests should be to which the issue should be brought. In reasoning with the Catholic, we have always this advantage, that he admits a natural reason, a natural conscience, a natural religion; nay, that the light which we have through them is a grace of the same Holy Spirit which makes his Church the depository of higher, but homogeneous gifts. When, then, from my prior ground of Nature, I approach the reputed enclosure of supernatural grace, what vestiges of its divine character shall I inevitably seek? None other than I have learned already, and seen gleaming through the minds and characters of noble personalities, and from the answer of conscience known to be given me from above, truth, justice, pity, purity, and self-sacrifice; and, in the reputed supernatural order, I can acknowledge nothing which contradicts these revelations of the natural order. If one and the same spirit is the living breath of both fields, there can be no change of moral atmosphere on crossing the boundary: the light must be akin in both, refracted by the same media, and flinging the same tender tints, and differing only in clearness and intensity. By this criterion, then, of moral reason and conscience, let us try the validity of these "notes" of a divine institute, secured from human contamination.

1. The UNITY of the Church throughout all time owes its effect on the imagination to the contrast it seems to present with the endless variations of human opinion, especially in the regions of higher speculation. While the ambitious intellect has been visited by a thousand perishable dreams, and has constructed worlds out of the frostwork on its windows till the next sunshine melted them away; while philosophies and heresies without number have put forth their gaudy blossom in the morning, and withered before night,—the one thing that has been patient through it all, and unchanged alike by fancy or by force, has been, it is said, the teaching and worship of the Church. The very creeds that are on the lips today, the very prayers that take up the yearnings of the heart, have been charged with the faith and piety of Ambrose and Chrysostom, of Benedict and St. Francis, of Alcuin and Bernard. This persistency, it is urged, belongs to the immutability of God, and shows that we are here within the compass of the divine thought, which has no shadow of turning; not of the human, which is as the passing

cloud. "In the unity of the Church's doctrines," says Balmez, "pervading as it does all her instructions, and the number of great minds which this unity has always enclosed within her bosom, we find a phenomenon so extraordinary, that its equal cannot be found elsewhere, and that no effort of reason can explain it according to the natural order of human things. It is certainly not new in the history of the human mind for a doctrine, more or less reasonable, for a time to be professed by a certain number of learned and enlightened men: this has been shown in schools of philosophy both ancient and modern. But for a creed to maintain itself for many ages by preserving the adhesion of men of learning of all times and of all countries—of minds differing amongst each other on other points; of men opposed in interests and divided by rivalries—is a phenomenon new, unique, and not to be found anywhere but in the Catholic Church. It has always been and still is the practice of the Church, while one in faith and doctrine, to teach unceasingly; to excite discussion on all subjects; to promote the study and examination of the foundations on which faith itself reposes; to scrutinize for this purpose the ancient languages, the monuments of the remotest times, the documents of history, the discoveries of scientific observation, the lessons of the highest and most analytical sciences; and to present herself with a generous confidence in the great lyceums, where men replete with talents and knowledge concentrate, as in a focus, all that they have learned from their predecessors, and all that they themselves have collected: and nevertheless we see her always persevere with firmness in her faith and the unity of her doctrines; we see her always surrounded by illustrious men, who, with their brows crowned with the laurels of a hundred literary contests, humble themselves, tranquil and serene, before her, without fear of dimming the brightness of the glory which surrounds their heads."[*]

Before accepting the challenge to account for this magnificent prodigy, we must first assure ourselves of its reality,

[*] Protestantism and Catholicity compared. Written in Spanish by J. Balmez. Translated from the French by C. J. Hanford and R. Kershaw. London: 1849. P. 13.

and, if it exists, must measure its amount. That through
the life of the Church there has persisted a certain common
essence of sentiment, never lost amid secondary changes, and
that to this common essence is due the allegiance of great and
good minds to Christianity, is beyond doubt; but with this
central genius of. the religion to identify the characteristics of
the Romish Church, as if they were its equivalent in permanence and power, is to contradict the whole course of Christian
history.   If Clement of Rome could be called to the scene of
his labours, and placed before the high altar of St. Peter's
to-day, do you think he would find himself at home, and know
when to kneel, and when to bow, or even dimly guess the
meaning of it all?   Or if, before Clement of Alexandria you
could lay the Tridentine Decrees, would they so speak to his
habitual thought and faith, that you could count on his signing
them with joyful assent?   Notoriously there is neither dogma
nor rite in the system of the Church, which has not a long
history to tell of its growth into settled form.   It took two
centuries and a half to determine the relation of the Son of
God to the Father; nor will any one who is even slightly
acquainted with the ante-Nicene literature affirm that
Athanasius would have been content with the doctrinal
professions of Justin Martyr, Irenæus, and Tertullian; all of
whom, in their "economy" of the divine nature, distinctly
subordinated the Second Member of the Trinity to the First.
For three centuries more, it remained unsettled whether
Christ had more than one nature and one will; the forces of
opinion swaying to and fro for generations before a predominance was won, and opposition driven from the field.   How
little concord had been reached respecting the Third Person
of the Trinity, more than fifty years after the Council of
Nicæa, Gregory Nazianzen tells us in these words: "Of our
thoughtful men, some regard the Holy Spirit as an operation,
some as a creature, some as God; while others are at a loss
to decide, seeing that Scripture determines nothing on the
subject."*   A year later, the bare phrase of the original Nicene
Creed, "I believe in the Holy Ghost," was enriched at the
Council of Constantinople by the added attributes, "the Lord,

* Oratio 39: De Spiritu Sancto. Gr.: 1555 (written about A.D. 380).

the Giver of life, that proceedeth from the Father; that with the Father and the Son is worshipped and glorified; that spake by the prophets;" and not till the year 589,[*] and then only in Spain, was the recital introduced, that the Holy Spirit proceeded from the Son as well as from the Father.

Similarly, only for a far longer time, did the conception of Christ's redemption remain indeterminate and variable; so that, even as late as the time of Anselm (who died 1109), it entered upon a new stadium of its history, and lost the characteristic features of its patristic prototype. In both doctrines, indeed, it was taught that Christ had paid the ransom which rescued men from the powers of hell; but, when we ask *to whom* he had paid it, Irenæus and Origen, Augustine and Gregory of Nyssa, reply, that it was paid to *the Devil*, who, by his successful offer of temptations, had become absolute proprietor of men, but who forfeited his right by being himself tempted to put to death the sinless Son of God, and, having fallen into this trap, was obliged to surrender his spoil.[†]

[*] At the third synod of Toledo, held on the conversion of the Visigoth King Recared from the Arian to the Catholic Church. Conc. omn. Coll., tom. xiii. p. 106, *seq.*

[†] Irenæus adversus Hær., V. xxi. 3. Grabe, 1702, p. 433. "Quoniam in initio homini suasit (i.e., Apostata) transgredi præceptum Factoris, ideo eum habuit in sua potestate." Comp. V. i. 1, p. 393. "Potens in omnibus Dei Verbum et non deficiens in suâ justitiâ, juste etiam adversus ipsam conversus est apostasiam, ea quæ sunt sua redimens ab ea, non cum vi, quemadmodum illa initio dominabatur nostri, ea quæ non erant sua insatiabiliter rapiens, sed secundum suadelam, quemadmodum decebat Deum suadentem et non vim inferentem, accipere quæ vellet, ut neque quod est justum confringeretur, neque antiqua plasmatio Dei deperiret."

Orig. in Epist. ad Rom. ii. 13. Lommetzsch, tom. vi. p. 139. "'Redempti sumus non corruptibili pretio argenti et auro, sed pretioso sanguine' Unigeniti. Si ergo 'pretio empti' sumus, ut etiam Paulus adstipulatur, ab aliquo sine dubio empti sumus cujus eramus servi, qui et pretium poposcit quod voluit, ut de potestate dimitteret quos tenebat. Tenebat autem nos Diabolus, cui distracti fueramus peccatis nostris. Poposcit ergo pretium nostrum sanguinem Christi, . . . qui tam pretiosus fuit ut solus pro omnium redemptione sufficeret."

When the transaction is thus conceived as a recovery from Satan of a possession to which he had a legal right, it is easy to understand the stress which is laid on God's having managed it without " *violation of justice;*" i.e., instead of arbitrarily using the power of a superior, he proceeds juridically, and, keeping within the terms of the contract, *did the Devil no wrong,* taking no sinner out of his hands till he himself had gone beyond his bargain, and

Anselm, on the other hand, denying the Devil's claim altogether, transfers the debt to the righteousness of God, to which, he contends, the sacrifice of Calvary renders more than an equivalent for the sins of men.* While the later doctrine superseded the earlier, it could not secure its own position, but served as the starting-point of a new polemic, in which Abelard, Duns Scotus, and Thomas Aquinas appear on opposite sides.

No part of the Church system carries more definite pretensions to a supernatural character than its group of *sacraments*. They are its instituted vehicles of grace, or securities from sin, intrusted to the charge of its consecrated ministers, and withheld from the people only at the peril of their salvation. Yet their number, their mode of administration, nay, their very idea, remained undetermined for more than a millennium; and first attain to some exactitude in the hands of Peter Lombard. Even in the case of the earliest and least disputed of the Christian rites, a different construction was put upon its very essence after eight centuries of usage.

made the mistake of passing death upon the sinless. What these theologians admire is, that, even to the Devil, God was just, and observed fair play, —a position very different from the modern thesis, that, in the incidence of penalty on the innocent in place of the guilty, there is no infringement of ideal justice. August. de lib. arbitr. iii. 10, ad init. "Servata est in peccato justitia Dei punientis. Nam et illud appensum est æquitatis examine, ut nec ipsius diaboli potestati negaretur homo, quem sibi male suadendo subjecerat. Iniquum enim erat ut ei quem ceperat non dominaretur. Nec fieri ullo modo potest, ut Dei summi et veri perfecta justitia, quæ usquequaque pertenditur, deserat etiam ordinandas ruinas peccantium. . . . Verbum Dei, Unicus Dei filius, Diabolum,—quem semper sub legibus suis habuit,—homine indutus etiam homini subjugavit, nihil ei extorquens violento dominatu, sed superans cum lege justitiæ."

The device by which Satan was caught, viz., the disguise of a divine and sinless nature under human form, is praised as a successful stratagem or trick. "᾿Απατᾶται καὶ αὐτὸς τῷ τοῦ ἀνθρώπου προϐλήματι," says Gregory of Nyssa, "ὁ προαπατήσας τὸν ἄνθρωπον τῷ τῆς ἡδονῆς δελεάσματι." Orat. Catoch. c. 26. Tom. iv. p. 84. Paris: Morell. 1638. "Oportuit hanc fraudem Diabolo fieri, ut susciperet corpus Dominus Jesus," says Ambrose, Expos. in Evang. Luc. lib. iv. ad Luke iv. 1.

* Cur Deus homo, ii. 20. "Quid misericordius intelligi valet, quam cum peccatori tormentis æternis damnato et unde se redimat non habenti Deus pater dicit, Accipe Unigenitum meum et da pro te; et ipse filius, Tolle me et redime te? Quid justius, quam ut ille cui datur pretium majus omni debito, si debito datur affectu, dimittat omne debitum?"

Pope Zachary had declared (about 742) an invocation of the Trinity essential to its validity.* But, when the difficult task of converting and baptizing the Bulgarians had to be accomplished, Pope Nicolas I. (A.D. 858–867) waived this condition, and pronounced baptism in the name of Christ to be sufficient.† In John of Damascus (in the first half of the eighth century) we find but the two Protestant sacraments; in the Dionysian books, probably belonging to the same century, there are six; and in a similar enumeration a little later, Theodore Studita gives a sacramental place to monkish vows.

These facts are but samples of endless variations, constituting in their succession the very substance of ecclesiastical history. So undeniable are they, that, to cover them and take them up into its adoption, the Church has invented its theory of " development," according to which the ever-living oracle reserves its judgment upon a doctrine till the contradictions and controversies of men require that the truth should be rescued from peril, and planted among sacred things : so that there is, for each dogma, a period when it is emerging from its germ, and throwing out its life in tentative forms. And only when, at last, it has struggled into the explicit thought of Christendom, does the divine interpreter define the form in which it is to set. Thenceforth nothing but unity is found. If this be so, then the life of each doctrine is sharply divided into two periods by the verdict of the Church, lying freely open to doubt and variation prior to that verdict, but, from the moment when the judge has spoken, closed against the interrogating intellect, and registered among the conditions of salvation. Living in the former period, you may go wrong without offence; living in the latter, your heterodoxy is perdition : under the very same conditions of thought, your relations to God are inverted. The definitions

* "Quicumque sine invocatione Trinitatis lotus fuisset sacramentum regenerationis non haberet. Quod omnibus verum est," etc. Epist. x. Concil. omn. Collectio Regia. Paris: 1643. Tom. 17, p. 393.

† "Hi profecto si in nomine sanctæ Trinitatis, vel tantum in nomine Christi, sicut in Act. Apost. egimus, baptizati sunt (unum quippe idemque est, ut sanctus exponit Ambrosius) constat eos non esse denuo baptizandos." Responsa ad consulta Bulgar., c. 104. Sacros. Concil. Labbé., tom. viii. p. 548.

of tho Church have thus tho effect, not of simply declaring, but of constantly altering, the terms of acceptance with God : and if, being in error, you die tho day before a Vatican decree, you may pass to tho seats of tho blessed ; if tho day after, you join tho Dovil and his angels.

And what becomes of the imposing unity of tho faith, when thus interpreted ?   It is limited to tho second and post-decretal period of every doctrine.   It is not tho permanent fact pervading tho religious thought of tho faithful, but only tho ultimate ratio in which their divergences resolve themselves ; not tho continuous life of their waking mind, but tho *terminus ad quem* they work and tend, and where at last they rest and sleep.   It has been sometimes objected to tho political economists, that they are so engaged in tracing to tho last results tho laws which they investigate, as to forget how long is tho road thither, and how brief tho pause there. They point to certain movements of profits towards tho same level, to tho equalization of wages by free distribution of labour, to the benefits of machinery in cheapening production, and enlarging tho employment-fund, but, in contemplating these futurities, hardly remember that they are in "no man's land ; " that tho actual life of generation after generation is spent in approximating towards them ; and that meanwhile tho mixed conditions of a process of transition may fill the present with struggle and suffering.   A similar remark may bo applied to tho Catholic Unity : it is an ideal tendency forever approached, but in no full sense historically reached.   However many theological points have been professedly settled, every ago that was not dead asleep has teemed with controversy ; and all that is intellectually great and morally noble in tho past life of Christendom— its richest literature, its finest humanity, its truest saints— will bo found in connection with tho growth rather than tho definition of faith ; not in tho stationary, but in tho moving periods.

Still it will bo said, " The post-decretal unity seems indisputable : however energetic tho previous strife, it sinks to perfect peace when judgment has once been given."   This assertion it was difficult to test so long as tho precise seat of judicial authority in matters of doctrine was undefined; for it was easy to discover that there were flaws in every decree which failed to bring the required unanimity, and to disavow it as not duly ratified. Now that the once floating and distributed infallibility is concentrated on the popes, as their personal and official attribute, we have to look no further for the divine unity of the Church than to their decisions, formally pronounced in the exercise of their teaching and magisterial functions; and the phenomenon which is claimed is neither more nor less than an entire consistency, pervading the whole series of Papal edicts on matters of faith and morals. That this claim is totally inadmissible will appear from a recital of a few well-attested facts.

During the reign of Justinian (A.D. 527–565), both the Court and the Church were violently agitated by disputes respecting the union and the distinction of the divine and the human constituents in the person of Christ. The extremes were marked, on the one hand, by the name of Apollinaris (Bishop of Laodicæa, about A.D. 362), who so intimately blended the two as to suppose them eternally one, and to believe that the Son of God, instead of being incarnate first on earth, already brought his humanity with him from heaven; and, on the other hand, by the name of Nestorius (Patriarch of Constantinople, A.D. 428), who so discriminated the two as to hold them in co-existence without sharing the same predicates, and, in particular, to deny that Mary could properly be called the mother of God (θεοτόκος). The opposite opinions not only separated individual Christians, but gave a party-colouring to the very map of the empire; the Egyptians and their Palestinian neighbours, where chiefly the mystic and cremite life was fostered, inclining to the former, i.e., the *monophysite* doctrine; while the patriarchate of Antioch in the East, and the greater part of the West, though not shrinking from the phrase "mother of God," sharply distinguished the two natures united in Christ. Through the usual tendency of such subtle disputes to win for themselves some human interest by concentrating the quarrel on personal representatives, the monophysites in Justinian's time set their hearts on condemning by authoritative anathema three

Syrian theologians,—Theodore of Mopsuestia, who had been the teacher of Nestorius; Theodoret, Bishop of Cyrus, who had written against Cyril, the great champion of the other side; and Ibas, presbyter in Edessa, who also had censured the doctrine, and questioned the consistency, of Cyril. It so happened, however, that, in the minutes of the fourth ecumenical council at Chalcedon (A.D. 451), there were resolutions on three articles (*capitula*),* recognizing the orthodoxy of those writers, and reinstating the two survivors of them in their ecclesiastical offices; so that the proposal to condemn them was a proposal to rescind the acts of an authority regarded as supreme.

In this controversy of the "three chapters," as it was called, Pope Vigilius was exposed, on the human side, to conflicting influences. He owed his primacy to the Empress Theodora, and was pledged to her monophysite fanaticism. He was at the head of a clergy resolute to uphold the Council of Chalcedon, and was himself in sympathy with their zeal. He was in the power, and for six years was virtually the prisoner, at Constantinople, of the emperor, intent on repealing the three articles without further disturbance to the authority of the council. Whether he had guidance enough, on the divine side, to steady him amid these deflecting forces, and hold him to the simple line of truth, we may estimate by the following facts. In the autumn of A.D. 540, he professed his adherence to the fourth as to the previous councils, and his concurrence in the anathema of the Eastern patriarch against the monophysites.† In a letter to the empress, written in 544, he avows himself a monophysite.‡ But when an imperial edict, in the same year, condemned the three articles of Chalcedon, and Vigilius was summoned to Constantinople to give it his support, he abides by his first profession, and through 547 persists in his refusal.§ Next year, however, he formally pronounces against them in a document, —his "*Judicatum*,"—signed by himself and several bishops

* Concil. Gener. Eccl. Cath., tom. ii. Rom.: 1628. Act 8, 9, 10, p. 944, *seqq.*

† Epp. 4, 5. Concil. omn. Coll., tom. xi. p. 514, *seqq.*

‡ Breviarium Liberati, cxxii. Concil. omn. Coll., tom. xii. p. 490.

§ Sacrosancta Concil. Labbé., tom. v. p. 323. Nota Sev. Bin.

assembled at Constantinople.* The obedience of the West being still unsecured, Justinian issued in 551 a second edict, renewing the condemnation of the three articles.† Vigilius now declines once more to join in the condemnation, not only when it proceeds from the emperor alone, but also when, in 553, it is confirmed by the fifth ecumenical council at Constantinople. Nay, he defends the *capitula* in a special manifesto, his " *Constitutum ad Imperatorem*," bearing with his own the signatures of sixteen Western bishops.‡ Even this was not his last word. In the following year, he addressed to Eutychius, patriarch of Constantinople, a formal retractation, declaring that he has been the instrument of Satanic delusion, but that now, delivered by Christ from all confusion of mind, he subscribes to the anathema he had so often resisted.§ Whether it was the function of his infallibility to discover his delusion, or of his delusion to be sure of his infallibility at last, the sequel does not help us to determine. No time was allowed him for further tergiversation ; released from Constantinople by his submission, he died on his journey back to Rome.

Such variance from himself in a supreme spiritual guide is too startling to be often repeated in history. But variance of the popes from each other is a more frequent phenomenon, and is equally fatal to claims of unity ; for, where a uniform infallibility is asserted of a perpetual dynasty of rulers, they virtually become a single undying personality, and it matters not whether the official acts which we compare proceed from many members or from one. The further progress of the controversy about the person of Christ soon made it apparent that Roman prelates might contradict and anathematize their predecessors. The decision that there were in Christ two natures, left out—disaffected and in the cold—large bodies of Oriental Christians whom the emperor wished to conciliate, and restore into Catholic communion ; and, to meet their demand for a less divided Christ, it was suggested by the Emperor Heraclius, with approval on the part of the patriarchs

* Sacrosancta Concil. Labbé., tom. v. p. 328, *seqq.*
† Ibid. p. 683, *seqq.*   ‡ Ibid. p. 337.
§ Concil. omn. Coll., tom. xii. p. 21, *seqq.*

of Constantinople (Sergius) and of Alexandria (Cyrus), that, if the two natures were placed at the disposal of one active principle, or will (ἐνέργεια Θεανδρική), this dominant unity would satisfy the scruples of the alienated party, without compromising the decisions of the Catholics.* But the chasm opened by nearly two centuries of controversy was too deep and wide to be bridged by a phrase; and the proposal made in the interests of peace proved but the beginning of a fresh strife. It was in vain that an emperor and two patriarchs sustained it. A poor monk, Sophronius from Palestine, sufficed to upset it: he had only to raise the cry that the *one will* was but *one nature* come back again, and the flame was soon rekindled which had driven the monophysites beyond the confines of the Church. True, he was kept silent for a while; but, having become patriarch of Jerusalem in 634, he deemed it his duty to sound the note of alarm, and watch over the purity of doctrine given him to guard.† He addressed himself to Pope Honorius, in the hope of a judgment at once more authoritative and more favourable than Alexandria or Constantinople had yielded. But Honorius, while regretting the importation of a new ambiguity into an old dispute, gave the same verdict which the other metropolitans had given, and insisted that there could be only one will in Christ; else there would be room for conflict between the wills divine and human. Twice were imperial edicts issued in this "*monothelite*" sense, —first by Heraclius in 638;‡ then by Constans, ten years later, threatening terrible punishment against all the disobedient. Meanwhile, however, the temper of Rome was changed. The turn of the tide was just traceable in the immediate successor of Honorius; but John the Fourth, who followed, pronounced his anathema against the doctrine of one will§ in a synod of A.D. 641; and at the first Lateran Council, held by Martin the First in 649, the imperial edicts, and the patriarchs who had supported them, were solemnly condemned, and the doctrine of two wills decreed to be orthodox.‖ Such bold defiance of the civil power exposed

<hr>

* Concil. omn. Coll., tom. xiv. p. 588.   † Ibid. tom. xv. p. 86.
‡ Ibid. tom. xiv. p. 504; xv. p. 152;   § Ibid. tom. xiv. p. 560, segg., epist. 2.
‖ Ibid. tom. xv. p. 260, segg.

this heroic ecclesiastic and his supporters to cruel sufferings, but with so little effect, that, in 680, a sixth ecumenical council had to be held at Constantinople for further deliberation ; and, under the guidance of Pope Agatho, the doctrine of two wills was defined and adopted ; the. only resisting bishop was deposed ; and, among the past upholders of the opposite opinion, the Pope Honorius was anathematized by name.* This denunciation of the Vicar of Christ was formally communicated by Leo the Second, who had succeeded to the Papacy ere the council closed, to the bishops of Spain ; † and, in a letter to the Emperor Constantine, he speaks of Honorius as one, " qui hanc apostolicam ecclesiam non apostolicæ traditionis doctrinâ lustravit, sed profanâ proditione immaculatam subvertere conatus est." ‡ Yet Leo and Honorius were both infallible, and represented on earth the unbroken unity of divine truth.

The questions of sin and grace, in which the genius of Augustine and the moral strength of Pelagius came into conflict, had the effect, no less than the early Christology, of entangling the Church in contradictory decisions. Two African synods—held in A.D. 416 at Carthage and at Mileve, under the overshadowing influence of the Bishop of Hippo— decided that Pelagius, by allowing to man free power to do the will of God, infringed upon the province of divine grace, and rendered infant baptism superfluous ; and they memorialized Rome to put down such errors.§ Innocent the First at once acceded to their request, and, in virtue of his apostolic authority, excommunicated Pelagius, his friend Cælestius, and all adherents to their doctrine.∥ This was one of the last acts of a pope who eminently represented the spirit of the Western Church. His successor, Zosimus, was a Greek ; and when, in A.D. 417, the well-reasoned counter-statement of the accused came up for examination, it impressed him so favourably, and so distinctly disclaimed the consequences fastened upon their teaching, that he declared himself satisfied, reported to the African Church in favour of their

* Concil. omn. Coll., tom. xvi. p. 509.   † Ibid. tom. xvii. p. 6.
‡ Ibid. tom. xvi. p. 586.   § Ibid. tom. iv. pp. 357, 364, 375.
∥ Ibid. tom. iv. pp. 60, 65.

orthodoxy, and added a warning against giving ear to the calumnies of ill-disposed men.* It was not to be expected that a keenly-agitated question should be set at rest by two conflicting Papal verdicts delivered within a few months of each other. The African party convened a new synod at Carthage, in 418, and carried nine articles of condemnation against their opponents ; and, not disdaining a more effective weapon, drew from the joint emperors, Honorius and Theodosius, an edict, visiting with exile and confiscation of goods all adherents of the Pelagian heresy. Zosimus recoiled before this display of determination. He not only ceased to shield the accused; he cut them off from the communion of the Church, anathematized their doctrines, and addressed a circular letter to all bishops, visiting Pelagianism with an express condemnation, which they were required to sign.† Perhaps, however, though at the cost of temporary inconsistency, the Church struggled into unity on this matter at last ? On the contrary, eleven and twelve centuries later, the very same strife broke out anew in the University of Louvain, and so divided, first the Augustinians and the Molinists, next the Jansenists and the Jesuits, that repeated appeal had to be made to Rome, fresh heresies to be created, fresh subscription enforced, without, after all, setting the dispute at rest.

The history of ecclesiastical legislation with regard to the exercise of diabolical arts affords a striking practical refutation of the pretension to persistent unity. If it affords, indeed, an argument less formally complete than the contradictory edicts hitherto cited, this is only because no Papal decree, so far as I am aware, has yet frankly repudiated the old demonology ; and though it has silently disappeared from the language of faith, and the processes which assumed it have passed into desuetude, the canons which treat of it are unrepealed ; so that, judged by its statutes, the infallible Church may be taken as still upholding the reality of sorcery. But in effect it has outlived that monstrous superstition, and, through the lips of its scholars and intellectual guides,

---

* Concil. onin. Coll., tom. iv. p. 394.
† Ibid. p. 418, with passages there referred to.

speaks, like the rest of the world, with shame and compassion
of the miseries which so poor a delusion inflicted on mankind.
This is an entirely new state of mind; and, if it be right, it
condemns as wrong a series of church-edicts extending over
seven hundred years. The "Old Catholics," indeed, would
persuade us that this modern spirit is only a return to the
early doctrine of their communion. "For many centuries,"
they say, "the popular notions about diabolical agency,
nocturnal meetings with demons, enchantments, and witchcraft, were viewed and treated as a folly inconsistent with
Christian belief. Many councils directed that penance should
be imposed on women addicted to this delusion."* They
appeal, in proof, to an old canon found in the collection of
Regino, Abbot of Prüm, at the beginning of the tenth century,
and known by the mistaken name of the canon of Ancyra.†
This document (which probably speaks the sentiment of the
seventh century) certainly treats the popular belief in the arts
of the magician and the diviner as a heathen superstition,
which the servants of the Church are bound to root out from
their diocese; and requires them in their preaching to deliver
the people from their delusion. But, unfortunately, this is
not all. Far from teaching "the nonentity of witchcraft,"
the edict distinctly recognizes its reality and its supernatural
character, only treats it as a devilish instrument of delusion,
instead of a divine endowment of knowledge and power.

* The Pope and the Council. By Janus: authorized translation from the
German. P. 249.

† Libri duo de causis synodalibus et disciplinis ecclesiasticis. C. 371.
Wasserschleben: 1840. Bishop Burchard (who died in 1025) first gave the
credit of this decree to the ante-Nicene synod held at Ancyra, in Galatia,
A.D. 315, in his Magnum Decretorum Volumen, book x., where it is reproduced. The twenty-fourth canon of Ancyra, however, though on the same
subject, is very different, simply enacting that "those who, in conformity
with Gentile usages, resort to divination, or introduce persons into their
houses with a view to devise incantations or means of expiation," are to
incur certain penances; and entering in no way into the doctrinal grounds
of this prohibition. See Routh's Reliquiæ Sacræ, vol. iv. p. 126, for the
original text. In the Acts of Pope Damasus, a decree of a Roman council
(A.D. 382) is cited thus: "Omnes maleficos, sacrilegos, augures, aliisve super-
stitionibus vacantes, excommunicandos esse. Feminas illas, quæ a dæmone
illusæ putant se noctu super animalia ferri, atque cum Herodiade circum-
vagari, eadem sententia plectendas esse."—Concil. omn. Coll., tom. iii.
p. 421.

L

Some women, it says, having turned to Satan, have been misled by his deceptions, and pretend to have ridden on certain animals by night, in company with Holda and a number of women, over a great part of the earth, and to have been called away to their service. Unhappily they have not been the only victims of superstition; but countless numbers have been led by them to accept this delusion as reality, and to fall into the Pagan error of supposing that there is some other divine nature besides God. The clergy, therefore, must emphatically preach to their parishioners that all this is a false show, put into men's minds not by a divine being, but by an evil spirit; viz., the Devil, who assumes the form of an angel of light. As soon as he has made himself master of some woman by the force of superstition, he changes himself into forms of disguise, and occupies the soul he has captured with visions or dreams—now bright, now sad—of persons known or unknown, causing all sorts of aberration; the victim believing that all this is material fact, instead of mental phantasm. Hence it is to be publicly proclaimed that whoever believes things of this kind loses the faith; and that whoever has not the right faith of God is none of his, but belongs to the Devil, in whom he believes.*

We have here, not a denial of the sorcerer's phenomena, but simply a transference of them (1) from the objective to the subjective field; (2) from divine to diabolic power. The doctrine is in harmony with the idea traditional in the Church through all its previous centuries,—that the outside world of the unbaptized, the unconverted, the heathen, was under the dominion of Satan, from which the Christian theocracy alone afforded an ark of refuge. And, in the struggle between the two realms, the Pagan divinities and oracles and usages were regarded as the great hiding-places of disguise for the evil spirits, whence they put forth their superhuman power to beguile the souls of men. Against these snares there was no protection but the true faith, which enlisted omnipotence on the believer's side. "*Dæmones fides fugat*," it was said; and in every act of faith, like prayer to God, nay, in every symbol

* Gratian: Decret., p. II. Caus. xxvi. qu. v. c. 12.

of it, like the sign of the cross, or the uttered name of Christ, there was power to drive the fiends away. Of every baptism, *exorcism* of evil spirits formed a part, the response to which, on the part of the baptized, the *abrenunciatio Diaboli* ("I renounce the Devil and all his works"), remains to this day. Inasmuch as the polemic against Paganism consisted, not in denying the preternatural facts, incantations, oracles, possessions, atmospheric changes, and anomalies of animal life, nor in claiming them for the providence of God, but in snatching them from the pretended divinities, and making them over to the Devil and his tribe, the effect of this enlargement of his domain inevitably was to intensify the popular belief in his agency, and horror at his manifestations.

It is no wonder, therefore, that, in the thirteenth century, we find this belief so extended and confirmed, as not only to render an ignorant population excitable to frenzy, but to corrupt the very fountains of authority, and fill even Papal edicts with contemptible hallucinations. Yielding to a report from his inquisitors in Germany, Gregory IX. describes in a bull of the year 1233 the ceremony of initiation practised by certain heretics, on whose speedy punishment he insists. With evident good faith he relates how the novice pays the homage of a kiss on the hind-quarters to the Devil in the shape of a toad as large as a goose, a duck, or an oven, or of a black tom-cat lifting his tail for the salutation; how, at certain stages of the proceeding, there appears, in place of these incarnations, a pallid man of mere skin and bone, with jet black eyes, whose kiss, cold as ice, drives the Catholic faith clear out of mind; and, again, a figure, shaggy below, but, above the hips, brilliant as the sun; how to this personage the disciple is introduced by the president, as a devotee, a shred of his coat being offered in pledge, and, being accepted, is handed back to the charge of the master; and how, by horrid rites, these miscreants carry out their doctrine that the Devil will prove in the end to be the true God, and change places with his rival.* The proceedings of the

---

* Epist. Greg. IX. Th. Ripoll, Bullarium ord. Predicat. i. 52. The occasion of this letter is described by Labbé, Sacros. Concilia, tom. xi. pp. 478, 479.

inquisitor, Conrad of Marburg, founded on this bull, bear witness to the terrible earnest in which these statements were made. To each of the accused the alternative was offered,— to confess his kiss to the toad, the cat, and the pale man, and save his life; or to protest his innocence, and be burned alive.*

Neither scruples of humanity, nor the dawning light of a returning intellectual civilization, disturbed the resolute persistency of the Church in this superstition. Murmurs, indeed, were heard against the intrusion of Papal officers, selected from the regular orders, on the judicial functions of a foreign episcopacy, and on the national rights of French and German subjects; but the pope, who could bear down such constitutional resistance, had no theological contradiction to expect. This is evident from the celebrated bull of Innocent VIII., issued at the end of A.D. 1484, for the express purpose of ratifying the authority of his inquisitors over places not expressly named in their first credentials, and giving them paramount jurisdiction over every place in Germany where they chose to open their court. The whole tension of the edict is directed against a local and political obstacle; and, in its definition of the crime which the commission is appointed to try, there is still the quiet assumption of its reality, which could only be made in the face of its universal recognition. It complains of the extensive prevalence of diabolical arts, which are employed to blight the fields and orchards, to prevent the increase of flocks and herds, and even the human race, to afflict life with strange maladies, to draw men into apostasy, and induce unheard-of crimes; it attributes these to the direct agency of Satan; it empowers the bearers of the pope's apostolic letters to visit such offences with fine, imprisonment, and other punishment; and threatens all who obstruct them with the wrath of Almighty God and his blessed apostles Peter and Paul.†   To aid in carrying out

* See the Letter of the Archbishop of Mainz to the Pope, in Alberici Chron. ann. 1233.

† The bull, " Summis desiderantes affectibus," is given in Hauber's Bibliotheca, acta et scripta magica: 36 Stück 1739-1745. St. I., p. 1, seqq. See, also, Gustav Roskoff's Geschichte des Teufels: book II. p. 222.

this edict, the inquisitors, Jacob Sprenger and Heinrich Krämer, published in 1487 their "Malleus Maleficarum," or "Witches' Hammer," under the patent of the Emperor Maximilian and the sanction of the pope,—a complete hand-book of sorcery, which for upwards of two centuries guided the proceedings in such cases, and had almost the force of law. It affirms the reality of magic, and the origin of its power in a personal compact with the Devil, of monstrous progeny from licentious relations with demons, of an influence of the heavenly bodies on the moral actions of men, of the magician's ability to bewitch people with preternatural hate or love. Betraying a singular scruple against the infliction of capital punishment without confession of the crime, it gives instructions for extorting confession on the rack ; previous to which, however, it is desirable to get a holy angel to cancel the Devil's control over his victim, otherwise he will make her insensible to pain : and no terror you can apply will make her speak. The decree which called this manual into existence, and appears as its preface, applied to Upper Germany alone ; but succeeding popes, Julius II., Alexander VI., Leo X., Adrian V.,* by the issue of similar edicts, drew land after land within the "magic circle," with such effect, that in the diocese of Como alone, there were, during the earlier part of the sixteenth century, no fewer, on an average, than a thousand trials, and a hundred executions at the stake.†

So far, it must be confessed, the Church, in its teaching and discipline on this matter, had not forfeited its unity ; nor can we say that there is more than a difference of degree between the earliest doctrine of demoniacal possession, and the epidemic superstition which lighted up the fifteenth and the sixteenth centuries with fires of human sacrifice. But how is it that no voice is longer raised on behalf of the infallible edicts which scattered over Europe the torches to kindle those fires ? that the only plea for them now urged is, that the barbarism of the age, not the rule of the Church, is

---

* This last, a fair sample of the whole, may be seen in Concil. omn. Coll., tom. xxxiv. p. 588.

† Barthol. de Spina, de Strigibus, c. 12.

responsible for them, and created the same results in the communities born of the Reformation? Such a defence is simply an echo of the indictment, surrendering the Church to the pressure of barbarism, and the illusions of idolatry, within the very province which it claims for legislation, and so far waiving its pretensions to supernatural insight. Yet no higher ground of justification can be taken in consistency with recent history. Not only have the prosecutions for sorcery gradually disappeared,—a fact which might be explained by the resistance of princes, and the "usurpations" of the civil courts,—but from the Inquisition itself we have a memorable confession, bearing date 1657, that its commissioned judges had long been guilty of irregular procedure and unwarrantable use of the torture-chamber, to the sacrifice of many innocent lives. The murdered victims of the authority which cannot err were beyond the reach of this apology ; but it introduced restraints and alleviations, which, enforced as they were by the altered spirit of the times, rapidly rendered harmless the tribunals so long the terror of Europe. Catholic theologians now speak, like other men, with habitual contempt of the belief in sorcery. The perplexing question is how this state of mind · can be pieced on to the decrees of Gregory and Innocent, so as to leave unharmed the sublime "unity" of the faith in all ages ?

In the year 1616 Pope Paul V., with the Congregation of the Index, condemned as "false, and totally opposed to the Divine Scriptures," the work of Copernicus, "De Revolutionibus Orbium," which achieved for all time the miracle of Joshua, "Sun, stand thou still ! " In 1818 Pope Pius VII., in full consistory, repealed the condemnation. In the interval, the Holy Office prosecuted and sentenced Galileo, in 1633, for suspected adherence to the Copernican heresy ; and in 1741 the Catholic editors of Newton's " Principia " apologized for that work in these words: " Newton, in this book, assumes the hypothesis of the motion of the earth ; and the author's system could not be expounded except on the same hypothesis. Hence we have been obliged to assume a character other than our own ; but we declare our obedience to the decree of the supreme pontiffs against the motion of the earth." In the present day, Catholics are Copernicans, like other people; and what was heresy once is heresy no more. How to embrace both judgments within the limits of infallibility, and resolve the contradiction into a higher unity, might puzzle even a Hegelian, but has not proved, till very lately, beyond the resources of Ultramontane advocacy. The divine exemption from error affects only decisions *ex cathedra;* and though these are not necessarily bulls issued directly by the Pope, but may be resolutions of a Roman "congregation," they must, in that case, fulfil two conditions,—they must receive the approval of the Holy Father; and they must be published by his express desire. Now, the second of these conditions, we are assured, fails in the decrees of 1616 and 1633; and the latter cannot be shown to satisfy either condition.* Under permission of this ingenious but precarious argument, the condemnation of Galileo was set down in 1866 among the human mistakes of a pontifical congregation. But in 1867, fresh extracts from the minutes of Galileo's trial, preserved in the archives of the Inquisition, were published by M. Henri de l'Épinois, which distinctly show, both that the proceedings simply carried out the instructions of the Pope, and that, by his direct command, copies of the sentence were forwarded, " that these things may become universally known " to all apostolic nuncios, and all inquisitors into heretical pravity, to be publicly read in solemn assembly, in presence of the principal professors of the mathematical art.† Thus the human mistake is at once metamorphosed into a divine decree; and, treated as a pretender yesterday, is on the throne of supreme authority to-day. As the unity of the Church cannot be restored by sacrificing the inquisitors of Paul V., perhaps some flaw may be looked up in the repealing act of Pius VII.; and everything may be set right by putting the sun in motion again, and re-enacting the Ptolemaic system.

Neither, then, in the stability of her doctrines, nor in the

* See the Authority of Doctrinal Decisions, which are not Definitions of Faith. By William George Ward, D.Ph. Essay viii., the Case of Galileo, 1866.

† See, for an interesting account of this recent and important discovery, Mr. Sedley Taylor's paper in Macmillan's Magazine, December, 1873: Galileo and Papal Infallibility. The statements in the text are from this essay.

consistency of her tribunals, does the Church give evidence of any immunity from the laws of ordinary growth and change. Nor, even if we could shut our eyes to the fluctuations of opinion, and look only at the cluster of beliefs which her artificers have held together by screws and holdfasts, till little else but the rivets remain, should we see in this residuary orthodoxy anything persuasively divine either in its source or in its character. How has it arisen? Have we here a real unity among minds free to act, and yet restrained from aberration by the inner strength of divine conviction? Or is it an illusory unity, produced by the simple process of expelling all variety? It is notorious that the whole history of Christendom is darkened by controversies, at once fierce and tedious, ending always in cutting off the outvoted minority as a withered branch, and proclaiming the triumphant majority, which was left in possession, to be the only true Church. Even, therefore, if this invariability held good (and no perversion of history can carry it back into the first two centuries), it would bear witness, not to the immanent action of the Divine Spirit, but to the oppressive weight of human tyranny. What, indeed, is it but that very attribute of *stationariness*, which, in all other historical fields, we treat as the sure mark of a kingdom of darkness, not of a realm of supernatural light? Everywhere else, in China, for example, or in ancient Egypt (as it has been erroneously imagined), the fact that centuries teach nothing, and change nothing; that thought and belief at the end of fifty generations are just where they were at the beginning; that they have no more to say to God or man in an old world than in a new,—is justly regarded as an opprobrium and sign of inward poverty; the proof of a dead conservatism, that wraps in a napkin the mere shrivelled form of a divine life, and confounds the perpetuity of its mummy with immortal being.. Why should we attribute the highest divinity to a crystallized church, and the lowest humanity to a crystallized civilization?

2. No one can desire to deny the claim of SANCTITY for the Catholic Church, if he have studied its influence through dark and troubled ages, and on a long train of devout and devoted minds. That Church has proved its capacity to defy every

injustice except its own, to pity every suffering needless to
itself, to banish every darkness deeper than the cloister-shade.
It has worked out an ideal of character—and approached it in
many high examples—truly original as compared with the
standard of Pagan times, and marked, without sacrifice of
force, by a depth and sweetness and patience of self-surrender
never known before. But these are Catholic phenomena only
because they are Christian. They have reappeared in all the
great sections of divided Christendom : they are a growth
from the new piety and tender humanity which have been the
response of the heart, wherever the eye of Christ has fixed its
look. Who dares to claim these as marking an ecclesiastical
monopoly of supernatural grace ? To make good his case, he
must prove that they specially pervade the whole organism,
and present the proportions of the holy and the unholy far
otherwise than we find them in the world without. This
surely is the least that can be looked for in that " mystical
body " which is " permanently united with the Holy Ghost,
the Sanctifier." Yet who can say that the Church has less
to deplore within her pale that is offensive to her saints than
in society around ? License has seldom been carried farther
than by some of the " holy fathers " on the throne of Peter.
If by *sanctity* be meant some occult quality which magically
appeals to the favour of God, it is of no avail in evidence,
being itself out of sight. A "note " that is invisible is a contradiction and a nonentity. If the word denote self-dedication
to a perfect Moral Will, this interior state of mind will
manifest itself in an habitual elevation of aim, purity of
life, disinterestedness of work, quickness of compassion, and
balanced loyalty to truth and love, legible to every eye familiar
with the language of character. When I pass through Church
history in search of these, I doubtless find them, but in such
sparse and partial gleams from a wilderness of passion and of
wrong, that secular history itself, though less inspiring in its
supreme heights, is less dreary on its ordinary levels, and less
dreadful in its darker depths.

There has been no exemption within the sacred precincts
from the vices and crimes which deform all human society.
For ages, Pagan and Christian, it seemed the fate of Rome to

be the tragic theatre of the world; but the darkest sins of the declining empire are paralleled by the revolting crimes of an ascendant Papacy. Though the Holy Father, Rodrigo Borgia, and his son Cæsar, the cardinal, were fortunate enough to have no Tacitus to tell their story, the disgust and horror of mankind have done the work of history, and saved from oblivion a picture of flagitiousness, treachery, rapine, and murder, unsurpassed in the records of guilt. A pope who gained the apostolic succession by bribery, and who quitted it by the poison-cup which he had mingled for another; who dissolved his daughter's marriage that he might wed her to a prince; who made his son a cardinal in boyhood, and, to do so, fathered him on the husband he had wronged; who allied that son with the Orsini faction, and, when the end was gained, screened him in the betrayal and murder of its chief; who, while preaching a crusade against Bajazet the Turk, bargained with him to murder his rival brother Djem, then prisoner at Rome, and won the poisoner's price,—is certainly a singular abode of the Holy Ghost, likely to radiate something other than the beauty of " sanctity " upon an obedient world. The orgies of the palace, the assassinations in the street, the swarm of flourishing informers, the sale of justice, of divorce, of spiritual offices and honours, turned the holy seat into an asylum of concupiscence and passion, and startled men into the belief that Antichrist was come. " Roma, gentium refugium, et arx populorum omnibus sæculis, nobilis jam carnificina erat." " In urbe gladiatorum nunquam licentia major, nunquam populo Romano libertas minor."* Can we say that this corruption was new and rare,—a transient stain on the white robe of a saintly Church? Alas, the long-established " nepotism " of the popes; the legislation of the councils of the previous centuries in restraint of a dissolute priesthood; the denunciations of Wicliff; the confessions of Æneas Silvius, himself a vicar of Christ, who openly treats the most ordinary rules of chastity as counsels of perfection, meant only for exceptional men;† the popular satires of a dawning literature,

<hr>

* Raphaelis Maffei Volaterrani Commentaria Urbana: Anthropologia, lib. xxii. Rom.: 1506.

† See his letter to his father, announcing the birth of a natural son, quoted by Gieseler, Eccl. Hist. div. v. c. 2, § 138, note 9.

—all bear terrible witness to a protracted and deep-seated moral putrefaction. Can we say that it was local, a lingering curse on the ancient capital of Paganism, still doomed to be the *colluvies gentium?* More than a century before, the experiment of removal had been enforced by political conflict; and of the new court at Avignon we have, in Petrarch's Letters, the report of an eye-witness, who calls it the third Babylon, the shameless abode of cruelty, avarice, and lust,* where honour, innocence, and piety are of no avail against gold ; and heaven and Christ themselves are put up to sale. Is a distinction drawn between the private character and the official functions of the successors of Peter ? "Sanctity" is an attribute which admits of no such distinction : it belongs to the indivisible will or personality ; it is a tincture of reverence in the conscience, of sweetness in the affections, of quietude in the sacrifice of self; and to say that a man who is licentious in conduct, and perfidious in human engagements, can be holy in all public relations, is an insult to the primary apprehensions of right. Besides, draw the line where you will, it will not serve you here. If, as there is reason to believe, John XXIII. poisoned his predecessor, Alexander V., to secure his apostolic chair ; and, as is well known, Paul II. and Alexander VI. granted dispensations for robbery and fraud, on payment of money to a crusade ; and Clement V. gave to King John of France and his queen absolution, through their confessor, for the breach of any oaths and engagements, past and future, which it might not be convenient to them to keep ; and Innocent III. declared worthy of death all who had a scruple against taking an oath ; and Boniface IX., as though he represented Simon Magus, instead of Peter, established the sale of benefices into an organized rapacity, and took money from all candidates alike, the rejected as well as the admitted,—are these violations of the most sacred human obligations, committed on the steps, or from the very seat, of the Papal throne, private or public ? Do they still leave the epithet "holy" applicable, without profanation, to their perpetrators? If not, and if, for several centuries, examples like these infected the Church through Western Christendom with revolting moral

* See the Liber sine Titulo, Epist. 10.

disease, how can any instructed man prefer, without a blush, the claim of " sanctity " for an institution marked by such experience ?

If we are asked to try the case, not at the headquarters of the system, but by reference to the moral ideal which, in her most characteristic and highest examples, the Church has offered to mankind, we can admit the claim only under weighty reservations. The Catholic training has certainly fixed in the mind of Europe a conception of perfect character in many respects purer, larger, deeper, than was present to the ancient world ; has elevated duty and affection by making them part of the confidence between the soul and God ; and, for hardihood of resolve against the ills of life, has substituted a patience, sympathy, and trust, inwardly quieter, but infinitely stronger. But then, all ecclesiastical honour for this type of character is contingent on its co-existence with orthodox belief, in the suspected absence of which the attitude is reversed at once, and the half-canonized disciple becomes the excommunicated. The Church has made many saints, but has also murdered not a few. Do you say that she is sacred for making so pure an ideal, and deny that she is profane for marring it ? In his eighteen years of office, Cardinal Thomas de Torquemada had burned alive, it is computed, eighty-eight hundred victims, and punished ninety thousand in various ways,* not for offences against the moral law, or crimes against society, but for thoughts of their own about religion, which only God, and not the pope, had allowed ; or for being Jews that would not be apostates ; or for refusing on the rack to confess what they had never done. When this man had carried in Spain his terrible resolve to clear the land of infidels, and procured a royal edict requiring the whole Jewish population (not less than three hundred thousand) to vacate the country within four months, leaving all their gold and silver behind, Isaak Abarbanel, gaining audience of Ferdinand and Isabella, pleaded for his people with expostulation so pathetic, and offers so profuse, that the royal will, softened by compas-

---

* See, for the grounds of this statement, Histoire Critique de l'Inquisition d'Espagne. Par D. Jean Antoine Florente. Paris, 1818. Tom. iv. pp. 251, 252.

sion and cupidity, was on the point of giving way; but, with his usual instinct for critical moments, the great inquisitor appeared, and with lifted crucifix exclaimed, "Judas of old, for thirty pieces of silver, betrayed his Lord; and now, again, your majesties are ready to sell him for thirty thousand pieces of gold. Here he is! take him, and sell him quickly!" That voice, touching the springs of a true shame, brought the false fanaticism back. The bribe was flung away, and with it the relenting pity too; and, ere the summer was over, Spain had lost the best element of her population, and added new traditions of heroism and hatred to the life of a people whose history is little else than a memory of exiles.* In estimating the ecclesiastical ethics, are we to give credit for the saints, without deduction for the inquisitors? Shall we celebrate the graces of humility, tenderness, and self-devotion in the one, and not recoil from the pride, the injustice, the inhumanity, of the other? It is vain to tell me how conscientious these persecutors were. There lies the very charge I make against the Church,—that it has put into the conscience what has no business to be there; has treated error of thought as if it were unfaithfulness of will; and misguided the affections of men by rendering it possible for them to hate what is most lovable, and honour, if not love, what is most hateful. The whole conception of an "orthodoxy" indispensable to the security of men's divine relations—a conception which has had a regulative influence through all ecclesiastical history—is an ethical monstrosity, in the presence of which no philosophy of duty is possible, and every moral ideal must be dwarfed or deformed. Under its oppressive tyranny, the intellectual virtues, which have their exercise in the effort to see and say things as they are,—candour, sincerity, openness to light,— have withered away; and in their place has been formed that peculiar temper—dogmatic in assertion, unjust in criticism, evasive in reply—which has always clung to the clerical order, and left the simple love of truth as the adornment, almost exclusively, of lay life. Nay, this desolating notion has poisoned the social affections of men with rankling suspicions, and

* See I. M. Jost's Geschichte der Israeliten seit der Zeit der Maccabäer. Th. vii. c. x. Berlin, 1827.

spread through their communities a system of espionage. Even in ages when heresy was visited with torture and death, the edicts of councils and popes have invited children to detect and report the swerving faith of their parents, sisters to lay traps for brothers, and friend to betray friend. The "robe of righteousness" falls of itself from the form, however stately, of a Power which can thus consecrate the most odious crimes as favourite varieties of goodness.

The creation of artificial sins does not stop with the guardianship of doctrine, but extends to the field of practical concerns. The rising commerce of Southern Europe, especially of Genoa and Venice, with the consequent extension of monetary transactions, in the twelfth and following centuries, brought up for settlement new problems of contract and exchange, which the supernatural guides of morals were expected to solve. All their decisions proceeded on the assumption that it was contrary to the divine law to charge or to pay anything for the use of money; and that, unless a loan as returned was identical in amount with the loan as received, there was robbery or fraud in the transaction. Again and again,* by Alexander III., by Urban III., by Innocent III., was this doctrine laid down, and violations of it in practice threatened with excommunication; and in the sixteenth century it was made the plea for prohibiting all mercantile partnerships which guaranteed to the member of a firm any fixed return upon his capital, and all negotiation of bills of exchange, except the final presentation for payment to the house addressed. The principle was reaffirmed and explicitly defined by Benedict XIV., in five canons, promulgated in 1745; and in 1793 the Bishop of Quebec was advised by the Propaganda, that guardians of children must not put out to loan,

---

* As early even as the Council of Illiberis, in Spain, held before the Council of Nice, we find legislation against "usury." The twentieth resolution of that Council, while visiting the offence with excommunication, treats it more sharply in a clergyman than in a layman : "Si quis clericorum detectus fuerit usuras accipere, placuit eum degradari, et abstineri. Si quis etiam laicus accepisse probatur usuras ; et promiserit, correctus jam, se cessaturum, nec ulterius exacturum ; placuit ei veniam tribui. Si vero in ea iniquitate duraverit, ab ecclesia esse projiciendum."—Routh's Relig. Sac. vol. iv. p. 269.

with interest, the trust fund committed to their charge.[*] A rule which made all banking business a breach of "commutative justice" and "the divine law" could not be expected to keep its ground in the economy of modern Europe ; and, since the beginning of the present century, the Roman authorities, with more prudence than candour, have evaded the problems of this nature which have been submitted to them ; contenting themselves with a simple reference to the existing canons, or recommending that conscience should not be disturbed. Nay, through the whole period of this prohibitory legislation, no royal or mercantile house was more deeply implicated than the Papacy itself in money-dealings with the capitalists of Italy, who certainly did not come to the relief of the Roman indebtedness, or the support of the Roman profusion, without security for adequate returns. Brokers and lenders, who elsewhere fell under malediction as the "mammon of unrighteousness," brought their treasure and their transactions to Rome or Avignon, and found themselves in a paradise of privilege and peace.

Were we permitted to treat these errors and defects as parts of a simply human history, they would take their natural place in the gradual ascent of European society into clearer light and higher conscience, and would bear favourable witness to a religion that could work itself free of them, and join in the sentence which condemns them ; but when they appear as attributes of a divine institute, included in the unchangeable teachings of the Holy Ghost, as a deliverance of the inspired custodian of faith and morals, they so wrap up Christianity in obscurantism, and weight it with wrong, that its beauty is hid, its progressive life impeded, and its claim to supernatural sanctity rendered totally inadmissible. Even in " The Lives of the Saints " as personal portraits alone, judged without any reference to doctrinal mistake, we have little more than a great conception spoiled, a noble instrument of moral education applied to the nurture of childish tastes and feeble superstitions, instead of to the culture of a manly reverence and a

† See, for a good summary of the facts, Papal Infallibility and Persecution, Papal Infallibility and Usury. By an English Catholic. London. 1870.

guiding love. "Consider," says a distinguished Ultramontane, "the saints of the Church. How singularly like to each other! how singularly unlike to all besides! It is a part of Catholic doctrine, that the Church is actually infallible in proposing these holy beings to the love and reverence of the faithful. Moreover, the practice is earnestly inculcated on every Catholic, of studying carefully their acts and lives, as the one highest and truest exhibition of Christianity, as presenting the one type of character most acceptable to God, —the type of character by approximating to which, and in no other way, can men become better Christians."* No more winning hope can be held out to a devout mind than that of being thus drawn towards God through the example and communion of those who are nearest to him; but, among the many collapses that await a high-wrought religious imagination, there is hardly a greater descent than from the saint of pure thought to the saint of the calendar. The loss of clear biographical interest in a legendary tissue of trivial miracles and visions, the stiff and narrow conception of character, the exaggeration of ascetic severities and spiritual contemplations, the strained opposition between the secular and the divine life, produce an indescribable disappointment in the reader of the Catholic hagiology, giving him no living friend to his spirit, but leaving him in the presence of something between the doll and the idol. So, at least, it is with the mass of such literature. And when we turn to the greater figures of authentic history, now glorified with the beatific crown, we might feel many a doubt, were not the award infallible, whether it sits well on the head that wears it, and would not now and then be more becoming on modest but heretic brows, which the canonized persecutor bound with thorns of agony. If, in our dreams of a perfection truly holy, we might follow the Christlike image, we might, perhaps, desire for the historical niches of our sanctuary a series of saints less ill-humoured than Jerome, less ferocious than Cyril, less arrogant than Becket, less jealous than. Bernard. Many an unpretending human biography, telling its story in the dialect

---

* The Authority of Doctrinal Decisions which are not Definitions. By William George Ward, D.Ph., 1866. P. 100.

of nature, rather than of grace, has spoken to the heart of higher things, and stirred the conscience to nobler aims, than the wonderful tales of monks and martyrs, whose very dust and relics are said to dispel the powers of ill.

These many vestiges of moral imperfection compel us to feel that we here stand in a mixed and human scene; nor can we find, as we look round, any simply divine enclosure, that we should take the sandals from our feet, and say, " This is the house of God: this is the very gate of heaven."

3. By the CATHOLICITY, or UNIVERSALITY, of the Church is meant, " not mere extension, but also identity in all places."* It is therefore the same character, relatively to a wide area, which is expressed by the word *unity*, relatively to long duration, and must be estimated by similar methods. The grand rule of Consensus—" Quod semper, quod ubique, quod ab omnibus "—is divided by these two notes; the " semper " constituting *unity;* the " ubique," *Catholicity;* the " ab omnibus," resuming both. What is this, we are asked, which in every latitude, and all round the world, has a persistency attaching to nothing human,—not even to the features and colour of men's bodies, much less to the expression of their inner nature? No language, no polity, no code, no schemes of thought, no rules of art, can bear travelling and colonization without rapid change of type. Nor among the elements of civilization does religion in itself enjoy any immunity from this general rule. But here is a system, which, from Scandinavia to the Cape, from the St. Lawrence to the Colorado, preserves its character intact,—which is steady through varying nationalities,—which neither freezes in arctic snows, nor dissolves in tropic heats,—which, through the Babel of human tongues, speaks ever the same venerable words, and holds forth the same visible symbols, embodying an unalterable faith, and enforcing on the conscience an inflexible moral law; so that the miracle of Pentecost might any day virtually repeat itself; and visitors from every clime, meeting under any sacred roof, would find themselves in no strange sanctuary, but would hear proclaimed, in tones they can interpret as their

* The Temporal Mission of the Holy Ghost. By Henry Edward, Archbishop of Westminster (Cardinal Manning). 2nd ed., 1866. P. 69.

own, " the wonderful works of God."   Whence can this marvel of steadfastness proceed, but from the presence of objective truth, and the guardianship of the divine Spirit?

Whatever of argument there may be in this appeal to the imagination admits of a very simple reply. The truth of God, it is urged, is self-consistent and uniform. Yes. But not everything which is self-consistent and uniform can claim to be the truth of God ; other causes than the presence of the divine element may arrest the growth of variations. There is a monotony in blindness, as well as in perfect sight ; where the sun never rises, as where it never sets : and whether the sameness is that of abiding darkness, or of certain light, can be judged only by the conditions which attend it. If it is found among minds and wills freely played upon by the influences which modify thought and character, their concurrence affords a fair presumption of their having fallen into harmony with the reality of things ; but if it appear only within a fence of severe restraints, where an audacious spiritual power has secured a universal abjectness, the subjective uniformity stands in no relation to objective truth. When observers East and West, gazing through perfect instruments on both hemispheres, bring in the same report of successive constellations seen at differing hours, it is because one movement carries, and one heaven overarches all ; but when blindfolded men are led about by a skilled practitioner, and made to tell the visions they behold, their agreement only proves that they stand in the same relation to their prompter, and, because they see nothing, can see anything that he desires. Error, you say, is various, while truth is one. Yes ; but passive obedience is something short of either, and keeps men standing, where, if they do not wander, it is only because they cannot move. You must first let them be free to lose themselves on the open plain, and seek the infinite horizon wherever any heavenly glow may seem to call ; and if then you find them all moving along the same radius, with eye intent on the same meridian, and face ashine with the same beams, you may well be sure that the light of some divine reality is there, and intersects the trackless wilds with a true pilgrim's road. But, till then, cease to " talk so exceeding

proudly " of a feature, which, with equal reason, every Buddh-
ist and even every Freemason may make his boast.

It would affect us strangely did we find a vast and scattered
society, consisting wholly of one-eyed people ; but the wonder
would vanish, if we learned that it was a rule to put out the
other eye during the novitiate, and to remove out of the way
all who objected to the operation.   Such a monocular phenomenon is the orthodoxy of the Church.   It has got its one old
picture of divine things, as seen through a single highly chro-
matic lens, and represented by the hand of a rude art ; and
resolutely refusing to reproduce it with the slightest variation,
or to look through a second organ, it simply drives off all
persons who are endowed with stereoscopic vision, and have
gained a little insight into the deeper perspective of things.
In a result thus brought about, there is nothing wonderful,
except the infatuation which produces and admires it.   That
there are none but true sheep under the chief Shepherd means
only that every goat is turned out of the fold.

In the uniformity which is claimed, there would be something of diviner look, had it been effected by prevention,
instead of by penalty and expulsion.   Had the Apostolate at
Rome been able to say, " See the concord that reigns and
ever has reigned within the circuit of my charge ; no disturbing doubts, no conflicting thoughts, no insurgent wills, awaken
any trouble here : the certainty my children need, I am able
to afford ; the truth for which they begin to sigh, I administer
betimes ; the usages and discipline their wants demand, I
prescribe in season, ere a cry is raised,"—this indeed would
well become an organ of spiritual wisdom, intrusted with the
spiritual guidance of mankind.   Instead of this, the Church
has never succeeded in maintaining peace and concurrence
within her precincts.   Her discipline has been exercised, not
in warding off, but in punishing and cutting out, variations.
The initiative has always been taken, not by herself, but by
errors and heresies within her bounds that compelled her to
speak ; and it is not too much to say that every council has
been called, every Papal edict issued, because *Catholicity had
already been lost.*   And the remedy was always the same,—a
long struggle of parties for ascendency, ending in a short and

sharp amputation of the weaker. So frequently has this process been renewed, and so brief have been the intervening terms of rest, that, prior to the last century, scarcely can a half-century be named during which the Church has not had a divided life on some question ultimately settled by authoritative definition. To give instances is little else than to set down the heads of all ecclesiastical history, from the quarto-deciman controversy of Polycarp and Anicetus at Rome, A.D. 160, which left Asia Minor and Italy with different Easter usages, to the condemnation of Fénélon's "Maximes des Saints," in 1699. Heresy, it must be remembered, is a product of the Church, and, ere it could be excommunicated, has been in communion, often with such tenacity as to leave it doubtful for a whole generation what hand would carry off the banner of orthodoxy. The great ecclesiastical heroes won all their victories over fellow-disciples,—Tertullian over Praxias, Athanasius over Arius, Augustine over Pelagius, Cyril over Nestorius, Hincmar over Gottschalk : the battle-ground was within the sacred enclosure, and its discordant din mingled with the hymns of worshippers. A visitor to Phrygia in the latter half of the second century would hear nothing but of the Paraclete and the millennium ; returning to Rome, he finds that type of Christianity condemned. Crossing to the schools of Alexandria, he listens to a mystic doctrine of Christ's divine nature, in which his human history seems to melt into a bright cloud ; removing to Antioch, he recovers the humanity again, and hears the clearest lessons drawn from the sacred life in Palestine ; but is put off with only a poor account of the higher essence of the Son of God. A lapsed Christian of the third century, who in Spain would be driven from the church-door, had only to take ship for Italy to find entrance into communion again. The long strife between the Latin and the Gothic theology ; the yet longer between Rome and Constantinople ; the swaying to and fro of the eucharistic doctrine for two centuries, till, by the condemnation of Berengar in 1050, transubstantiation won its place ; the Albigensian crusade ; the rival schools of Scotus and Aquinas ; the polemic passages about the immaculate conception, about indulgences for the dead, about the seat of supreme ecclesiastic power; the divisions on grace and free will, first between Dominicans and Molinists, then between Jesuits and Jansenists,—all these things must be forgotten before the claim of Catholic concurrence can be pressed with any avail in evidence of an internal peace supernaturally secured. Nay, what more do we require for the just estimate of this claim than the spectacle of the ancient Church in Europe since the Vatican council of 1870? Whither must we go to hear the veritable voice of the traditional consensus? Must we mingle with the Genevan Catholics, and listen at the feet of Father Hyacinthe? Or kneel before the altar of some "Old Catholic" church, and give ourselves to the word of Döllinger or Rheinkens? Or mingle with the acquiescent multitude, that will swear to any words, contradict any history, betray any inherited trust, so long as they are covered by the dome of St. Peter's? The illusory nature of a "universality" that breaks in pieces, and then allows a fragment to label itself as the whole, in virtue, not of identical essence, but of greater size, is in our time laid bare before the eyes of all the living.

4. Finally, for the last "note" of divine authority we are referred to the "APOSTOLICITY" of the Church. If this word were meant only to mark the historical origin of the Church from the labours of its first missionaries, it would express no more than an indisputable fact; but it is intended to denote "conformity with its original power, the mission and institution of the apostles,"* and to claim the sanction of apostolic example for the creed and cultus, the constitution and administration, of the Church. For persons of historical culture to put forth such a claim for the first time in an historical age would exceed the measure even of ecclesiastical courage, so utterly fictitious is the picture of Christian antiquity, and so uncritical the reading of the early Christian memorials which it implies. It is a formula which lingers on, like an inherited casket emptied of treasures, from a time when so much only of Scripture and history were quoted as might seem to give some colour to orthodoxy, and some support to a theocracy. Hardly can a more pervading contrast be

* The Temporal Mission of the Holy Ghost. By Henry Edward, Archbishop of Westminster. P. 69.

found than between the primitive and the mediæval Christianity which are here identified. I do not refer to the
accidents of time and person alone, striking as these will ever
be to the popular imagination,—to the poverty of apostles
and the princely magnificence of pontiffs,—to the simple
prayer-meetings of the upper chamber at Jerusalem or the
proseucha at Philippi, compared with the splendid scenery
and pompous offices of the Roman basilicas,—to the fraternal
simplicity of the scriptural lessons, so unlike the Papal bulls,
in which an over-acted humility transparently covers an
assumption more than royal. These differences, and more
than these, may be conceded to the transition from an incipient to a reigning Church. But far deeper than these, in the
fundamental conceptions of the religion itself, and in the
whole spirit and tendency of its administration, there is an
essential opposition between its first and its last stages. The
early gospel was the escape—gradual in the Petrine circle,
taken at a bound in the Pauline—of the free prophetic spirit
from ritual and sacerdotal restraints : the Catholic Church is
the re-enthronement of a priesthood over the world. The
former accepted no mediator except One who came to abolish
mediation, and himself withdrew to heaven, that there might
be no distraction from the divinest Presence : the latter
appropriated the open treasury of grace, and kept the key,
and set itself up as sole agent in divine affairs. The one
proclaimed, that, as instruments of peace with God, oblations
and atonements had vanished from the earth, snatched away
by the ascending Christ ; and that, with him, humanity itself
had passed into the Holy of holies : the other rebuilt the
altar, invented a new offering, arranged the sacramental
train, and restored the daily sacrifice. The one rent away
the veil of untrustful fear that interposed between the private
soul and God, and sent the conscience charged with sin to
breathe its prayer, and shed its tears, within the Divine
embrace itself ; the other established the confessor's box in
every temple, and enjoined its occupant to find its way into
every home. Who will tell me that the apostle Paul was
a pontiff ? that he confessed Aquila and Priscilla ? that he
elevated the host at the Corinthian supper, and withheld the

cup from the profane? It is no wonder that to his Galatian
and Roman Epistles the mind of Luther, in its first revolt
from the existing system, flew for refuge, and that there he
found an indomitable strength; for, within the whole compass of thought and feeling on divine things, there is hardly
to be found a more precise and radical contrariety than
between the spiritual gospel of their author and the priestly
system that takes his name in vain.

Even without pressing this extreme contrast, we find no
evidence, in either the memorials of other apostles, or the
writings of the next age, of any likeness between the Papal
Church and its presumed prototype. Besides Paul's striking
sketch of the mode of celebrating the communion at Corinth,[*]
we have other notices of the Christian usages in their religious assemblies, carrying us forward into the next century.
Let any one read Pliny's letter to Trajan,[†] and fix in his mind
the image of the simple meeting there described, of the alternate hymn to Christ at daybreak, of the mutual engagement
to innocent and holy life, of the common meal in pledge of
brotherhood; let him turn to the later and fuller picture,
drawn by Justin Martyr,[‡] of the baptismal or the Sunday
assembly, the reading, the exhortation from the presiding
brother, the prayer, the distribution of bread and wine, the
alms, and the visit to the poor and solitary; and, with these
scenes in his mind, place him in view of the altar of St.
Peter's at the celebration of high mass. Will he see in the
drama before him—in its vestments, its incense, its genu-
flections, its signal-bell, its wafer for the church and its cup
for the altar—a reproduction of that early communion?
Will the gorgeous symbols tell their tale, and speak to his
heart the things that he knows, and seem only to glorify the
genius of his religion? Or will they look like the language of
quite another story, in which those Bithynian and Ephesian
disciples could play no part, and the apostles who established
their usages would be strangely out of place? Perhaps it
must always be the fate of a new spiritual life, infused from
purer heights of inspiration, to droop into lower levels when

[*] 1 Cor. xi. 20-33.   [†] C. Plinius Traj. Imp. Lib. x. Ep. 96.
[‡] Just. Phil. et Mart. Apologia, i. ch. 65-67.

the first divine impulse ceases to sustain it, and it passes into the custody of a less responsible humanity. But, in the genealogy of degenerating ideas, there is nothing more marvellous and more humiliating than that Christ and his first missionary band should be held responsible for the vastest hierarchy, the most theocratic absolutism, the completest sacramental system, that the world has ever seen. That which they chiefly lived to destroy has found its way back into existence, and flaunts their names upon its banner as the sanction of its boldest claims.

It is needless, at present, to ask whether, if the pretension to apostolicity were made out, the model on which the Church had framed itself could claim, on that account, to be altogether divine. That is a question still in reserve; and without reference to it the proof appears to me complete, that the Church is no exception to the rule of mixed agency—divine and human—which runs through all history; that within its enclosure, as without, truth and error, holiness and guilt, the spirit of God and the passions of men, are blended into one tissue, and spread out together the pattern of the ages. To separate these opposites, it is vain to make mechanical divisions, and draw boundary lines in time or space, and say to those who are seeking consecrated ground, "Lo, here! and Lo, there!" as if you could turn them into a fold secured by a patent of inviolable sanctity. Other tests are needed,—to apply which is no surveyor's task, but a work of inward apprehension, of moral analysis, and spiritual discrimination. There are always plenty of people ready to take this trouble off your hands; and you can escape it, if you are so minded, but only with this result: if the insight of conscience is dispensed from determining your religion, your religion ceases to be security for your conscience.

CHAPTER II.

IF, somewhere among the communities of Christendom, there is a sovereign prescription for securing " salvation," the Roman Catholic Church has obvious advantages over its competing claimants for possession of the secret. Regarded merely as an agent for the transmission of an historical treasure, she has at least a ready answer for all her Western rivals, and a *primâ facie* case of her own. They have, to all appearance, quite a recent genesis, their whole tradition and literature lying within the last three centuries and a half; and, in order to make good their title-deed as servitors of Christ, they must carry it over a period four times as long, during which it was lost, and identify it at the other end with the original instrument of bequest. ˙ Her plea, on the other hand, is, that she has been there all through ; that there has been no suspension of her life, no break in her history, no term of silence in her teaching; that, having been always in possession, she is the vehicle of every claim, and must be presumed, till conclusive evidence of forfeiture is produced, to be the rightful holder of what has rested in her custody. If you would trace a divine legacy from the age of the Cæsars, would you set out to meet it on the Protestant tracks, which soon lose themselves in the forests of Germany, or the Alps of Switzerland? or, on the great Roman road of history, which runs through all the centuries, and sets you down in Greece or Asia Minor, at the very doors of the churches to which apostles wrote ?

But it is not only to its superiority as the human carrier of a divine tradition, that Catholicism successfully appeals. It is not content to hide away its signs and wonders in the past, and merely tell them to the present, but will take you to see them now and here. It speaks to you, not as the repeater of an old message but as the bearer of a living inspiration ; not as the archæological rebuilder of a vanished sacred scene, but as an apostolic age prolonged with unabated powers. It tells you, indeed, *whence it comes;* but, for evidence even of this, it chiefly asks you to look at *what it is*, and undertakes to show you, as you pass through its interior, all the divine marks, be they miraculous gifts or heavenly graces, by which the primitive Church was distinguished from the unconsecrated world. This quiet confidence in its own divine commission and interior sanctity simplifies the problem which it presents to inquirers, and, dispensing with the precarious pleas of learning, carries it into the court of sentiment and conscience, addressing to each candidate for discipleship only such preliminaries as Peter or Philip might have addressed to their converts,—as if there had been no history between. No Protestant can assume this position ; yet he can hardly assail the Roman Catholic without resorting to weapons of argument which may wound himself. Does he slight and deny the supernatural pretensions of today,—the visions, the healings, the saintly gifts of insight and guidance more than human ? It is difficult to do so except on grounds more or less applicable to the primitive reports of like phenomena in the first age. Does he insist on the evident growth, age after age, of Catholic dogma, as evidence of human corruption tainting the divine inheritance of truth ? The rule tells with equal force against the scheme of belief retained by the churches of the Reformation : there is a history, not less explicit and prolonged, of the doctrine of the Trinity and the Atonement, than of the belief in Purgatory and Transubstantiation. Does he show that there are missing links in the chain of church tradition, especially at its upper end, where verification ceases to be possible ? He destroys his own credentials along with his opponents' ; for his criticism touches the very sources of Christian history.

The answer of the Catholic Church to the question, " Where is the holy ground of the world ? Where is the real presence of the living God ?"—" Here, within my precincts, here alone,"—has at least the merit of simplicity, and is easier to test than the Protestant reply, which points to a field of divine revelation, discoverable only by the telescope, half-way towards the horizon of history. It has no absolute need to make its title good by links of testimony running back to far-off sources of prerogative; no age of miracles to reach and historically prove, as a condition of its rights today. It carries its supernatural character within it; it has brought its authority down with it through time; it is the living organism of the Holy Spirit, the Pentecostal dispensation among us still; and, if you ask about its evidence, it offers the spectacle of itself. Though it is the oldest of churches, it asks recognition by credentials of the passing hour. Though it alone has lived through all Christian history, it least affects an antiquarian pomp, knowing no difference between what has been and what is, and in its retreat from the movement of the world being hardly conscious of the lapse of time. Itself the sacred enclosure of whatever is divine and supernatural on earth, it has no problems to solve, no legitimacy to make out, no doctrine to prove, but simply to live on, and witness of the grace it bears.

To the Protestant, on the other hand, there is no spot railed off from modern life as absolutely sacred, no continuous vehicle of inspiration, no personal or corporate authority for the supernatural guidance of mankind. To him, revelation is an inheritance. During one privileged generation it flowed from living lips; but afterwards, passing into a mere record that could never grow, it became more and more deeply buried amid the natural products of historical experience. Thus, for him, the divine and human are everywhere mixed, and need the application of thought and conscience to sever them. He finds himself, with his religion, in the eddying currents of the recent ages, and feels their conflicting forces meeting in his mind. He has been borne along by them to points so little suspected, that he looks round to discover where he is, and, according to his mood, is sometimes enamoured, sometimes frightened, by the aspect of a position so new. How does he stand with regard to the old land-marks? or, if they are gone out of sight, can he still find his way? Is he to seek guidance by going to the standards half effaced, or by looking round for himself upon the present, and choosing the path of clearest promise? No one who measures the changes of the world can be surprised at this perplexity. The faith of Christendom, essentially historical, has inherited its clearest memories from its primitive times, and turned towards them a gaze of regretful homage; but thrown into the contests of the passing hour, and co-existing since the Reformation with an unexampled progress of discovery, it could not remain purely retrospective, the passive trustee of departed sanctities. It was impelled to learn the language of a new time, and show its unexhausted fitness for the human soul, if it would vindicate its place in a universe so changed. This self-adaptation to the wants of a later culture created the whole religious literature, and much of the speculative philosophy, of modern Europe. Natural science, crowned with dazzling triumphs, affected every department of thought with admiration of her precise method and her favourite evidence of sense; and religion became fascinated, and undertook to shape itself into logical and objective form. The increase of social liberty gave a wider scope to every man's free will, and a deeper experience of responsibility; and no appeal on behalf of religion became so effective as that which spoke of its adaptation to the wants of tempted and aspiring men. In thus availing itself of modern auxiliaries, Christianity receded from the high ground of ancient authority, and descended into the field of intellectual conflict. Rationalistic tests were applied to its whole structure and contents. Believers being encouraged to pass judgment on their beliefs, doubters could be denied the privilege no longer: hence the two contrasted tendencies observable in the religious feeling of our day, in answer to the question, "Forwards, or backwards?" All churches that by the toil of venerable men have got together a body of established doctrine show symptoms of apprehension; all of them refusing to advance; some insisting on the one impossible attitude of standing still; and others, like men weakened by the fear of death, terrified into open repentance, and vowing, if they may only be spared, to retrace their steps, and yield to the temptation of thought no more. These last plainly disown the Reformation; would put back the clock to the night of 'Luther's birth, and reconvert the Bible into a sacerdotal trust, thinking it easier to root out the whole produce of that great era than to leave it growing, yet prevent its spreading. In its feebler forms, the same reaction, without the support of any consistent theory, simply appeals to taste, and avails itself of the resources of ecclesiastical symbolism. Men who cannot find sufficient assurance to play the priest, or forget themselves enough to cast out Satan, can sigh over " neology," warn off human reason from the sanctuary as if it was some destructive maniac, and invoke historical veneration to seize and manacle the fiend. It is the dream of these archæological Christians to restore some golden period of the Church, and by reproducing the forms, to tempt back the thought and characteristics of " the good old times ; " and doctrines and practices are judged, not by their truth and worth to the living, but by the standard perceptions of dead men centuries out of reach. The present is looked upon as degenerate and profane ; and, to correct its tendencies, old literature is republished, early art revived, and traditional models of life are re-animated, as if the stone figures upon the tombs opened their folded hands, rose up, and walked. Whatever is beautiful, magnificent, and tender in the worship, the architecture, the sacred biography, of the mediæval church, whatever was benign and picturesque in the sway of a mild priesthood controlling a barbarous nobility, whatever is captivating in the idea of a peasantry surrendered to the guidance of a beneficent and cultivated clergy, is brought so persuasively to view, that we feel as if, in passing from our forefathers' time into our own, we stepped from the cool silence of a cathedral to the hot chaffering of the street. In short, everything is done to incline us to trust in the past, and distrust the present. And thus has been provoked into activity the opposite disposition, to repudiate as obsolete our spiritual heritage from the past; to begin afresh, and live today as if it were alone in time ; to breathe the morning air as if it were new-born, instead of sweeping down the Alpine valleys, and across the purifying seas, of another zone. We are asked to set aside the divinest influences transmitted to us by history, as impertinent obtrusions between the soul and God, and retire wholly to the oracle within, for private audience with God.

Both these tendencies, as often happens with extremes, are, I should say, right in their love, wrong in their hate; their negative spirit, false; their affirmative, true. The historic God and the living God are alike realities, the same Eternal, there and here; and only when his recognition in one aspect is interpreted into denial of the other, does his oracle become apocryphal, and his worship an idolatry. This artificial contrariety, however, has been established by the narrowness of men; and imposes on us the inquiry, whether, in the drama of the past, we meet with any episode purely divine, and step upon absolutely consecrated ground; whether especially the apostolic age, with its productions, really merits the pedestal of exceptional infallibility, whence it is made to pour rebuke on the profane tendencies of modern life.

According to the Protestant's theory, divine revelation is permanent only in its effects. In itself it is a past transaction, supernaturally interpolated in the history of mankind, and completed in the first century of our era. From that era, the source for him of all divine authority, he is now separated by threescore generations; and whatever is true in heavenly things, whatever is holy, must cross that interval ere its tones can reach him. For his knowledge of it, he is dependent on its *records*, created by the first actors or observers on that sacred stage, and handed down by successive witnesses of their identity: and it is only as native to that age, and stereotyping its inspired voice, that the Christian Scriptures speak to him as " the word of God." Could he suppose them to have been born outside that circle of special revelation in place or time, to be the production only of impersonal rumour, or a secondary age, his reliance on them would be gone, and they would descend from their consecrated height to mingle with the mass of human literature. His first essential, therefore, is to trace them clearly home to that exceptional period, and to the body of first disciples within it. If this be once secured, all else appears to him readily to follow. Does the New Testament which we read today really come from the group of apostolic men who turned the death of Christ into the birth of Christendom? Then is it a faithful record; for its authors have every title to be believed, which ample opportunity and disinterested sacrifice can win.   But further: if it is faithful in its account of facts, it is authoritative in its statement of doctrines; for among the facts are various miracles, imparting a superhuman character to the chief figure of the story, and specially a direct descent of inspiration on his first missionaries, which made them vehicles of a testimony higher than their own, and which guarantees the truth, not of their narrative alone, but of their whole course of religious thought and teaching.   And so is forged a three-linked argument which joins divine and human things: if the facts are real, the doctrines are certain; if the books are authentic, the facts are real; that the books are authentic, adequate testimony proves.

There may, perhaps, be logical devotees whose enthusiasm loves to reach their God by long and painful pilgrimages of thought; but it would not be a happy thing for natures of more direct and impatient affection to be left thus dependent for knowledge of divine things on literary, antiquarian, philological evidence, judicially balanced, analogous to that which scholars cite in discussing the Homeric poems, or the Letters of Phalaris.   We are not permitted, it would seem, to take our sacred literature as it is, to let what is divine in it find us out, while the rest says nothing to us, and lies dead : all such selection by internal affinity is denied us as a self-willed unbelief, a subjection, not of ourselves to Scripture, but of Scripture to ourselves.   We are required to accept the whole on the external warrant of its divine authority, which equally applies to it all; to believe whatever is affirmed in the New Testament, and practise whatever is enjoined.   In escaping by this path from the Catholic Church, we are merely handed over from an ever-living dictator and judge to an ancient legislation and guidance, still with the same idea of somewhere disengaging ourselves from human admixtures, and finding some reserved seat of the purely and absolutely divine.

Neatly as the Protestant argument is compacted, it will not bear the strain which is put upon it.   Each of its links is in fact unsound.   And, even though no flaw were visible in them, still the conclusion is demonstrably false.

How far have we, in the Christian Scriptures, the testimony of eye-witnesses to the events and teachings which they relate ?

If direct and rigorous proof were required, it would be impossible ever to trace a book on our shelves today to the hand of a specified man in ancient Athens, or Rome, or Jerusalem. Even productions prepared for immediate public recital by their authors, like the Histories of Herodotus, the Odes of Pindar, the Orations of Cicero, speak to us out of darkness and silence ; and the multitudes that heard them at the games, or in the forum, have vanished without a vestige left ; and there is no voice among them all to vouch for the identity. Still less can we expect that writings published only by the copyist should be attended from the first by their own credentials ; with the Dialogues of Plato, the Treatises of Aristotle, the Annals of Tacitus, we look for the signature of no witnesses, the seal of no notary. Far less than this suffices, in all ordinary cases, to make us as sure of our author as if we bought the book from his own advertisement. If it is mentioned and cited as his, while he still lives to own or to disclaim it ; if its influence is visible in the immediately succeeding literature, like that of Lucretius, or Catullus, or Virgil, though without notice of his name ; if, from his own time onwards, it passes for his without question in the presence of a critical age,—we accept the confidence of others as a ground for our own. The presumption is in favour of a book being in its authorship what it professes to be ; and whoever would deprive it of the benefit of this rule must produce some counter-evidence, from its history or from its contents, at variance with its pretensions. In the vast majority of instances we proceed wholly on this presumption, and unhesitatingly repeat in our libraries the labels which have come down to us unchallenged ; and, however puzzled we might be to prove our accuracy in any particular case, e.g., to establish off-hand the literary rights of Erasmus or Montaigne, our general habit is undoubtedly justified by a prevailing experience, which it sums up and applies. Yet an indolent confidence in such a rule may leave openings for mischievous and long-enduring mistakes, not only in ages when printing was unknown and men of letters were few, but in the full daylight of modern intellectual intercourse.

A curious example of this is furnished in connection with

Lord Bacon's name. In 1648,—thirteen years after his death,—appeared a volume of " Remains of Francis, Lord Verulam, some time Lord Chancellor of England," including, among essays and letters previously unpublished, a tract entitled " The Character of a Christian, set forth in Paradoxes and seeming Contradictions." In 1730, Archbishop Sancroft revised this essay for Blackburn's edition of Bacon's collected works ; and it has ever since kept its place among his writings, though not without hesitation on the part of some of his editors,—Montagu, Bouillet, and Spedding. Except in the last instance, the doubt was not any divination of literary criticism, but arose from arbitrary preconceptions of Bacon's theological position. The piece opens thus : " A Christian is one who believes things which his reason cannot comprehend, who hopes for that which neither he nor any man alive ever saw, who labours for that which he knows he can never attain ; yet in the issue his belief appears not to have been false, his hopes make him not ashamed, his labour is not in vain. He believes three to be one, and one to be three; a Father not to be older than his Son, and the Son to be equal with his Father ; and One proceeding from both to be fully equal to both." To the eighteenth-century imagination it was inconceivable that startling contradictions like these could be the grave expression of sincere religious faith ; and it is no wonder that Bayle, Cabanis, and others of the French philosophers, as well as the Romanist, Joseph de Maistre,* should appeal to them as an evidence that Bacon was an Atheist, veiling his contempt for " believing Christians " under a colourable exposition of their creed. With less excuse have writers of our own time reproduced the same construction ; Heinrich Ritter treating the essay (which he pronounces authentic) as the " effusion of a scepticism afterwards suppressed," † and Mr. Atkinson seeing only irony in " the ridiculous light in which he has placed Christian dogma in his paradoxes," and adding, that " it seems equally vain to argue that

* In his Examen de la Philosophie de Bacon, 2 vols. Paris : 1836. (Posthumous.)
† Geschichte der Philosophie, book x. p. 318, 1851.

they were not his writings, or done only as an exercise of his wit.*

The allusion in this last clause is to Dr. Parr's judgment, that "these fragments were written by Bacon, and intended only as a trial of his skill in putting together propositions which appear irreconcilable." †   Here, then, we find a book passing current through two hundred and twenty years of the most recent history, under the name of a renowned philosopher, popularly read, criticized by literary men, argued on by metaphysicians and the chiefs of science throughout Europe, and regularly admitted as an important datum in the history of opinion: yet, all the while, this essay, which is not Bacon's at all, existed in numerous printed editions, with the name of the real author, Herbert Palmer, B.D., Master of Queen's College, Cambridge, and a parliamentary member of the Westminster Assembly of Divines.   He gave it to the world July 25, 1645, as a second part of his " Memorials of Godliness and Christianity," with a protest against a surreptitious and imperfect edition which had by some means been anonymously issued the day before; so that it had been in circulation for three years before the appearance of Bacon's " Remains ; " and afterwards new editions continued to follow, without availing to detect the mistake.   Had Palmer himself been on the stage when his literary offspring stepped forth in philosopher's garb, doubtless he would have stripped off the borrowed cloak, and shown the plain Puritan beneath.   But he had passed away in 1647 ; and few of his readers, it is probable, ever looked into the pages of the founder of the Inductive Method.   And so the re-discovery of the true authorship was reserved for the curious and admirable researches of Dr. Grosart within our own times.‡

The tenacity of a literary illusion is increased, whenever, in addition to the ordinary sources of error, any romantic or reverential feeling is enlisted on its side.   Of this we have a

---

* Letters on Man's Nature and Development, p. 174.

† Basil Montagu's Bacon, vol. vii. pp. xxvi.-xxviii.

‡ For a full account of this discovery, see his (privately printed) Lord Bacon not the Author of the Christian Paradoxes; being a Reprint of Memorials of Godliness and Christianity by Herbert Palmer, B.D.   1865.

memorable example pertinently cited by Toland at the end of
the seventeenth century, in the Εἰκὼν Βασιλική, or " Image of
a King," a book professedly written in his own defence, by
Charles I., during his imprisonment, and published in 1649,
shortly after his execution. Its seasonable appearance, its
stately manner, its rhetorical outpouring of pathetic sentiment, raised it somewhat above the level of a party manifesto,
and gave it a strong hold upon public feeling. And, though
its authenticity was immediately called in question by Milton,
its almost universal reception was not arrested, and carried
it rapidly through nearly fifty editions ; and to its influence is•
to be attributed, in no small measure, the High-Church conception of the " Royal Martyr." After the Restoration, the
spell of mystery was rudely broken ; and Dr. Gauden, Bishop
of Exeter, avowed himself the author. But to have the interest of its story thus reduced to fiction was more than loyal
admirers could be expected to bear : and, refusing to believe
the bishop, they insisted on still having the autobiography of
a king. And hence, when, in 1699, Toland, in his " Life of
Milton," reproduced and corroborated the poet's critical
judgment, he added, not without reason, this reflection : that
if forty years of modern daylight, when criticism is awake and
keen, and conflicting parties in the state are intently watching
one another, suffice for the establishment of such a fictitious
claim, it cannot surprise us, that, in the early Christian times,
many spurious productions found their way into circulation
under the names of Christ and his apostles.· When Blackall,
replying to this remark in a sermon before the House of Com-
mons, defended in the same breath, as alike authentic, the
Christian Scriptures and the Εἰκὼν Βασιλική, the appositeness
of Toland's historical parallel seemed to be admitted by both
parties ; and the earlier era could be protected from the suspicion of mistaken authenticity only by the process, no longer
possible, of excluding it from the later.

In order to fall, with whatever restrictions, under the rule
that, in the absence of counter-evidence, a book may be assigned to the author from whom it professes to come, it must
carry in itself such profession, and must not merely have
attached to it, by way of external heading or description, some

repute of authorship, coming we know not whence. To writings intrinsically anonymous no unaccredited rumour, however current in the course of years, can lend the weight of personal authority; and rarely can we hope, if they have preserved their incognito through one generation, ever to recover the story of their origin, and identify the pen that wrote them. In their case, we are thrown entirely upon the evidence of *age:* and, as the most accurate determination of date would still leave us unacquainted with the witness whose statements are before us, it cannot secure the correctness of his testimony, but ,only exclude the appendix of errors which tradition annexes with growing time. To know the birthday of a book is still a long way from a settlement of its parentage.

Of the New Testament writings, six letters of Paul, viz., 1 Thessalonians, Galatians, Romans, 1 & 2 Corinthians, Philippians, must have the full benefit of the presumption which accepts a book on its own word. Here and there, no doubt, as at the conclusion of the letter to the Romans, a passage may be found with possible traces of a later editorial hand; but, in general, the contents are in perfect accordance with the reputed author's position and character, so far as these are known. Considerable as the differences are between the earlier and the later Pauline letters, they all find a natural place in the history of a growing mind, and give even a stronger impression of personal unity than the most constant reiteration of doctrine and illustration. This impression from within is corroborated by such external testimony as we have. True it is, more than a generation elapses, before we find an allusion, in Clement of Rome, to the first Corinthian epistle as Paul's. But this testimony, late as it is, is the earliest which the scanty Christian literature of the time permits us to expect, and, being unopposed, suffices to assure us, that, in this first group of writings, we are really in contact with the primitive expression of the new faith.

The other epistolary writings, which set themselves forth under an apostolic name, remain unattested till the fourth generation from the death of Christ, and in nearly all of them there are such evident traces of a post-apostolic time, so many thoughts unsuited to the personality of the reputed author, that the ordinary favourable presumption is broken down; and, however excellent the lessons which they contain, we must confess, as we receive them, that we listen to an unknown voice.

The remaining constituents of the New Testament, the Apocalypse and the whole of the historical books, are, in spite of their traditional titles, practically anonymous. They offer us no personal warrant for the accuracy of their contents; and we are left to find out for ourselves the probable story of their origin, and the value of their materials. This in itself is surely a startling fact, utterly fatal to the claim of infallible authority constantly set up on behalf of Holy Writ. How is it possible to prove a divine right to be believed respecting a book that comes out of the dark, with no competent witnesses to vouch for it, and no self-confession of the hand that wrote it? On what ground can we attach a superhuman weight to the testimony of a masked and veiled witness, who does not even tell his name, or say how near he stands to the things which he relates? The evidence which he gives may have more or less of credibility, according to its degree of self-consistency, of verisimilitude, of apparent originality, and of agreement with parallel reports; but it can never acquire personal authority, or rise above the level of current tradition. The historical value of this tradition, variable from section to section of each book, has broader differences in the three synoptics, in the fourth Gospel, and in the Acts of the Apostles, as will be readily seen from a brief summary of the facts of each case.

§ 1. *The Synoptical Gospels.*

In gathering up the most ancient vestiges of our Gospels, we find the evidence respecting them fall naturally into two stages. In the last quarter of the second century, the notices of them are accompanied by *their names*, which are absent from all prior citations of words now extant in them. This significant fact comes out forcibly, on comparison of Irenæus (who flourished, says Jerome, chiefly in the reign of Commodus, i.e., A.D. 180 to 193) and Justin Martyr, whose extant writings were probably produced between A.D. 147 and 155.* The former quotes the Gospels under their present titles, and gives amusing reasons why they can be neither more nor fewer than four; and why those Christians who use only one must be in the wrong: "Since there are four quarters of the world in which we are, and four chief winds, the Gospels, which are to be co-extensive with the world, and to be the breath of life, blowing incorruptibility on men, and vivifying them, must be four." Besides, the gospel is given by Him who sits above the cherubim, which is a fourfold figure; and it answers to the Beasts in Rev. iv., which are four; and it must correspond with God's covenants through Adam, Noah, Moses, and Christ, which are four. "These things being so, they are all vain and ignorant and rash men, who spoil the beauty of the gospel, and decide on either more or fewer forms of it than have been mentioned; some, to take credit for finding more than the real number; others, to reject the ordinations of men." † Irenæus was not a wise man; but he would not have resorted to this fantastic reasoning, if he had been in possession of real historical grounds for the statements he wished to support. It is clear that he had nothing to tell, except that, by that time, the Gospels which we now have were prevailingly accepted, under the titles which they have borne ever since, but that there were Christians who held by some one of them alone, and others who did not restrict themselves to four.

Stepping back a generation, we find in Justin Martyr traces of a different state of things. In his pages there are copious citations both from the Old Testament and from certain Christian "*memoirs*" evidently embodying the gospel history; and, in the latter case, there is no difficulty in finding the corresponding passages in our synoptical Gospels. But whether it was precisely these that he had before him, is

* It is usual to refer the First Apology to the beginning of A.D. 139, the Trypho to the same year, the Second Apology to 162 or 163; but Prof. Volkmar appears to have made out his case for correcting this chronology, and treating the Second Apology as a mere appendix to the first. The whole of Justin's extant writings would thus be subsequent to the time when M. Aurelius was raised to the proconsular power, and associated with Antoninus Pius. Theologische Jahrbücher, von Baur und Zeller, 1855, S. 297 and 412. (Die Zeit Justin's des Martyrers kritisch untersucht.)

† Irenæus, Hær. III. 11.

rendered doubtful by two peculiarities. 1. He never names, never alludes to, their authors or their number, but quotes as if from a single anonymous production. 2. There is a want of verbal agreement with our texts, so nearly invariable, that, out of a vast number of passages, only five are exactly true to Matthew or Luke. The contingencies of memoriter citation will not explain this singular phenomenon; for the same differences are constant through repeated quotations of the same passage: they resemble remarkably the variations observed in the Scripture texts of the Clementine Homilies, a production of the same period; and they differ, both in frequency and in character, from concomitant inaccuracies in citing the Septuagint version of the Old Testament, where the memory alone is answerable. These facts imply that Justin drew his quotations from some source textually different from our Gospels,—an inference confirmed by the further fact that he adduces, from the same memoirs, *matter* which is not found in our Gospel narratives; e.g., " Wherefore the Lord Jesus has said, 'In whatever ways I shall find you, in the same also I will judge you;'"* and again: " When Jesus came to the river Jordan, where John was baptizing, as Jesus descended into the water, a fire also was kindled in Jordan; and, when he came up out of the water, the apostles of this our Christ have written that the Holy Spirit lighted upon him as a dove."† Comparing these phenomena with the citations of Irenæus, we seem to be in contact, at the earlier date, with the unfashioned materials of Christian tradition, ere yet they had set into their final form, with some elements still present which were ultimately to be discarded, and others not yet incorporated, which could not have been absent, had the author been acquainted with them.

Does, then, the external evidence conduct us to the person of a known eye-witness, and enable us to say who it is that vouches for *this* statement, and who for *that?* On the contrary, it carries us back out of the period of definite names into one of indefinite floating tradition,—tradition called indeed " apostolic," but by the vagueness of that very phrase betraying its impersonal and unaccredited character. His-

* Dial. cum Tryph. c. 47, 19.   † Ibid. c. 88, 7, 8.

torical memorials which are to depend for their authority on the personality of their writer cannot afford to wait for a century ere his name comes out of the silence. The remaining records of the ministry of Christ have an origin so obscure, that it is impossible to say who is answerable for any part of them.

If, in default of outward testimony, we closely scrutinize the internal structure of the synoptical Gospels, we are met by a series of phenomena which virtually reduce them to a single source, and show that we are not in contact with three independent reporters. The same recitals are repeated in either two, or all of them, with such resemblance in substance, in arrangement, and even in language, as totally to exclude the possibility of original and separate authorship. In the fourth Gospel, which is really the production of a single hand, we fortunately have a measure of the amount of common matter which may be expected to appear in two or more independent accounts of the ministry of Christ. Two-thirds of its matter is peculiar to it; and the rest, though dealing with incidents related elsewhere, presents them under aspects so new, that the identity is often difficult to trace, or is even open to doubt. But if the whole text of the synoptics is broken up, as it may naturally be, into one hundred and seventy-four sections, fifty-eight of these will be found common to all three: twenty-six, besides, to Matthew and Mark; seventeen to Mark and Luke; thirty-two to Matthew and Luke; leaving only forty-one unshared elements, of which thirty-one are found in Luke; seven in Matthew; three in Mark, comprised within the compass of twenty-four verses. The agreements in the parallel narratives are not so complete as to exclude diversities in the accessory circumstances: they are greatest in the parables and other discourses of Christ, and in the marking epochs of the story, the calling of the apostles, and the transfiguration; though, in the most momentous of all,—the last Passion,—the deviations are considerable.

Is it said, that the fourth Gospel, being supplemental, purposely avoids what has been already adequately told; while the other three, written on the same subject, viz., the Galilean and the final stages of the life of Christ, necessarily reproduce the same incidents?   Even if we could admit this untenable view of the fourth Gospel, no more similarity of design will explain the accordance of the others.   The synoptists deal with the events of fifteen months, of which more than fourteen are assigned to Galilee; and the whole are supposed to have been spent by them, or their informants, in attendance upon the steps of Jesus.   But we hardly realize to ourselves how little of this story is really told.   Of the four hundred and fifty days comprised within it, there are notices of no more than about thirty-five; while whole months together—now three, now two—are dropped in total silence.   The evangelists, when they speak, know how to recite with sufficient fulness.   The day in the cornfield (Matt. xii. 1–xiii. 52) occupies one-tenth of Matthew's history of Christ's ministry; the day of the Sermon on the Mount, one-eighth (v. 1.–viii. 17); a day in the Temple, nearly one-fifth (xxi. 18–xxvi. 2).   The day of the blighted fig-tree occupies more than one-seventh of Mark's Gospel (xi. 20–xiii. 37). And five days claim, in Luke (xx. 1, to the end), more than one-fourth of his narrative (excluding the legends of the birth and infancy).   It appears, therefore, that *twelve-thirteenths* of the ministry which they describe is left without a record; and that the three Gospels move within the limits of the remaining one-thirteenth.   How could this possibly be, if they came, whether at first or second hand, from personal attendants of Jesus, cognizant of the whole period alike, or, if absent at all, not all absent together?   Even if they were independent selections from a mass of contemporary memorials, preserving fragments only of the life of Christ, they could not all alight upon materials lying within such narrow range; for the flying leaves, scattered by the winds of tradition, would be impartially dropped from the whole organism of that sacred history, and, when clustered by three disposing hands, could never turn out to be all from the same branch.   The vast amount of blank spaces in which they all have to acquiesce betrays a time when the sources of knowledge were irrecoverably gone; and their large agreement in what remains, that they were only knitting up into tissues, slightly varied, the scanty materials which came almost alike to all.

Still more evident is the derivative character of our Gospels when we study their verbal coincidences and differences. No two witnesses, however perfect their substantive agreement, will tell any part of their story in identical words; and did their recitals contain even a single sentence, other than a quotation, cast in the same mould, we should infer that their statement had been dictated, or artificially got up. Even of the remembered words of another, unless brief and incisive, they will give divergent reports, meeting only here and there upon some striking phrase, but moving in the intervals without contact in terms, though parallel in drift. Most of all is this diversity inevitable, where the words remembered were spoken in one language, and the witnesses deliver their report in another. That they should hit upon concurrent translations, no one will regard as possible; yet in our synoptical Gospels, there are from three hundred and thirty to three hundred and seventy verses common to all; and, besides these, from one hundred and seventy to one hundred and eighty common to Matthew and Mark; from two hundred and thirty to two hundred and forty to Matthew and Luke; and fifty to Mark and Luke. Comparing with this range of partnership the amount of individuality in each, we find that the first Gospel has three hundred and thirty verses of its own; the second, sixty-eight; the third, five hundred and forty-one.[*] Some of the coincidences occur in common citations from the Old Testament, where all the narrators deviate from the Greek of the Septuagint, without betraying, by closeness of rendering, any controlling influence from the Hebrew.

While these facts certainly reduce our evangelists to mere editors of previous materials, room is still left for a considerable play of variety, either in their selection or in their treatment of these materials. Even in the midst of prevailing agreement, both substantive and verbal, striking discrepancies emerge in the telling of the same story. The first Gospel

---

* See Reuss: Geschichte der heiligen Schriften neuen Test. § 179. In the different Gospels the same words are often differently divided into verses. In Mark especially the verses are shorter. Hence the margin of variation in counting the agreements by verses.

supplies a series of such cases by its curious tendency, as by some defect of binocular vision, to see its objects twice over; as in the cure of *two* Gadarene demoniacs,* the restoration of sight to *two* blind men near Jericho,† the combination of the ass with the colt at the entry into Jerusalem,‡ the reviling of Jesus on the cross by *both* robbers, instead of by one.§ The Jericho miracle was wrought, according to one account,‖ on going into the town; according to the others, on going *out* of it. When the twelve are sent upon their Galilean mission, they are ordered, in two reports, to take *no staff;* in the third, to take *nothing but* a staff,—a difference trifling in itself, but noticeable in its relation to the early handling of Christian tradition. At times we can scarcely fail to see that the same story, in different versions, has been inserted twice, as if it related successive incidents ; as, in the case of the miraculous feeding of the multitude, counted now as five thousand, and now as four thousand,¶ of the Pharisees' demand of a sign,** and of their reproach of exorcism by Beelzebub.††

Through how many recensions the Christian tradition passed before it set into the form under which our Gospels present it, it is beyond the resources of criticism to decide. But the traces of successive additions as well as of composite structure are sufficiently distinct, not merely in the finer phenomena of language, but in the broad veins of thought and sentiment. Mingled with the genuine teachings of Jesus, and often obtruding a rude interruption upon their purity and depth, appear sentences manifestly thrown up by the controversies and pretensions of the apostolic and even the post-apostolic age. The whole theory of his person,—that he was Messiah, what was the meaning of his death, what the range of his kingdom, and when would be the time of his return to take it up,—was a posthumous and retrospective product, worked out by disciples who could not bid adieu to so divine an influence,

---

* Matt. viii. 28. Comp. Mark v. 2.

† Matt. xx. 30. Comp. Luke xviii. 35.

‡ Matt. xxi. 2, 7. Comp. Mark xi. 2, 4, Luke xix. 30, 33.

§ Matt. xxvii. 44. Comp. Luke xxiii. 39 ; here, however, Mark agrees with Matthew.

‖ Luke xviii. 35.   ¶ Matt. xiv. 15, xv. 32.

** Matt. xii. 38, xvi. 1.   †† Matt. xi. 34, xii. 24.

and who, in delivering it over to the world, made their own conceptions its vehicle, and fused into one his supposed future and his real past.   Eager to attribute to him beforehand all that they thought about him afterwards, they will have it that he claimed the Messiahship, yet would not let it be mentioned ; that he contemplated and fore-announced his death and resurrection, yet without succeeding in preparing them for the event ; that he authorized their look-out for his return from heaven, yet without ever naming *himself* as coming *back*, but only a third person, the mythologic " Son of man," as " coming," to wind up the drama of human things ; that he sided with the Jewish Christians, and wished only Israelites to belong to him ; that, on the contrary, he foresaw how the Jewish appeal would comparatively fail, and the gospel must be preached to all nations ; that he provided for the long conflict between the Petrine and the Pauline gospel, and gave the headship and the keys to Peter ; that he entered into the far distant question whether converts should be baptized as at first, into *his* name, or, as in the second century, into the name of " the Father, and the Son, and the Holy Spirit," and gave his voice for the Trinitarian formula.   In all these cases, and they are but samples, the anachronism must be felt by every one who has closely studied the infancy of the Christian Church ; and of the two or three strata of unhistorical material which overlie the primitive and unvitiated tradition, the newest can scarcely have been deposited before the third or fourth decade of the second century.

Out of writings thus constituted, how is it possible to make an authoritative " rule of faith and practice " ?   Composed of mixed materials, aggregating themselves through three or four generations, they report no authorship in any case : and no date, except of their unhistorical accretions.   Imbedded even in these, there is doubtless many a gem of original truth preserved ; and in the residuary portions which are the nucleus of these, we approach, no doubt, the central characteristics of the teaching and the life of Christ.   But the evidence of this is wholly internal, and has nothing to authenticate it except our sense of the inimitable beauty, the inexhaustible depth, the penetrating truth, of the living words they preserve and the living form they present. Of our witnesses we know nothing, except that, in such cases, what they tell as reality, it was plainly beyond them to construct as fiction.

If our points of contact are thus few, and are rather felt than seen, with the *ministry* of Christ, what can we say of the *birth and infancy*, which lie still thirty years behind? Even were it true that apostles were our reporters, it would be strange that precisely the evangelist who, as the "beloved disciple," was nearest to Jesus while on earth, and gave a home to Mary ever after, should be silent of what she alone could tell, and should thus drop the only link that could save our connection with that remoter time. But left as we are, in the absence of all apostolic guarantee, to the mere verisimilitude of unaccredited tradition, we have no outward support against the false chronology, the irreconcilable contradictions, the historical prodigies, and the fabulous mode of conception, presented by the two stories of the Nativity. They do not belong to the kind of record that can commend itself by self-evidence; and other evidence they have none. Yet every Christmas celebration attests how large and fundamental a place in the faith of Christendom is held by the incidents of that poetical mythology.

§ 2. *The Fourth Gospel.*

There remains, however, yet another Gospel, which, if the tradition of its origin be true, takes us out of all obscuring mists, and brings us into clear historical light. Whether or not it rightly bears the name of the apostle John, it is, at all events, free from the doubts and complications arising from the process of growth out of prior materials of different dates : it needs no analysis into component elements; it is plainly a whole, the production of a single mind,—a mind imbued with a conception of its subject consistent and complete, and not less distinct for being mystical and of rare spiritual depth. It is no wonder that the strife of opinion in regard to the origin of Christianity concentrates itself upon this point ; for while the problem is simple in its form,—was the hand which wrote this book that of John?—an affirmative answer to it wins everything at once, an original portraiture of the person of Jesus, an authentic account of the duration and plan of his public mission, and a measure of his divine claims. So long as the synoptical Gospels retained their position as original and independent witnesses, doubts respecting the fourth Gospel touched only that higher estimate of Christ's nature to which it gave the chief sanction ; and, even if they prevailed, there was still the triple history of his life in its more human aspect to fall back upon for solid though less sublime assurance. With better understanding of the work of the earlier evangelists, the Johannine question has become more vital, and is discussed with a passionate eagerness, which, however natural, and even pathetic as the mark of religious anxiety, is apt to discolour the evidence, and distort its proportions before the eye. While confessing the strongest drawing of sympathy towards the characteristics of this Gospel, I will endeavour to give an impartial summary of the facts.

A. *External Testimony.*

In one of the most masterly defences of the authenticity of the fourth Gospel, it is said, "No one who knows the state of the external testimony to the authorship of the Apocalypse and Gospel will hold that it *adds much*, in any way, to the decision of the question. Neither of them receives any explicit testimony till the time of Justin Martyr, about the middle of the second century; when the two Johns, having been both disciples of Christ, probably enough were already confused. Within ten years both are explicitly acknowledged."[*]

This disparaging comment on the external testimony seems to imply that, even if it were better than it is, it would only come in by way of *confirmation* to a decision resting on other grounds ; but that, as it is, the confirmation goes for little. Prior, however, to the external evidence, or in its absence, what case could there possibly be,—I do not say admitting of "decision," but presented for "decision" at all ? Let there be *no history* of a book, let it come into our hands without a record of its source, and by what scrutiny of its literary characteristics, by what marks of individuality, shall we refer it home to some one among the myriad shadowy hands that crowd the darkness of the past? No such divination is possible; and wherever a critic pretends, by the mere keenness of his unaided eye, to have detected the writer in some unheard-of quarter,—like the Zürich scholar who made out that this very Gospel was certainly the production of Apollos,*—we justly look on the pretension as audacious, and its proofs as a waste of ingenuity. We are absolutely dependent, for the first suggestion of an author's name, on the witnesses who speak of it; and any disabilities attaching to these witnesses must seriously affect our reliance on their report, and throw a greater burden on the internal confirmatory proofs. The primary and substantive evidence is testimonial; which, once given, may gain weight by various congruities, or lose it by incongruities in the writing itself; but which, if not given, can be replaced by neither.

The fourth Gospel does not materially differ from the others in the date of its earliest citation with the reputed author's name. Theophilus, a convert from heathenism, elected in 176, A.D., to the see of Antioch, addressed to his Pagan friend, Autolycus, a defence of Christianity, in three books, which is still extant, and which approximately reveals its date by a list of the Roman emperors carried to the death of Marcus Aurelius, A.D. 180. In the second book we meet with a passage beginning thus : " Wherefore the sacred Scriptures teach us, and all that have the Spirit ($\pi\nu\epsilon\upsilon\mu\alpha\tau\delta\phi\rho\rho\upsilon$); of whom John says, ' In the beginning was the word, and the word was with God ; ' showing that at first God was alone, and in him was the word."† Here, near the end of the third generation from his death, we are introduced for the first time to the writer of the fourth Gospel ; still without any distinctive epithet identifying him as one of the Twelve; for in classing him with prophets and partakers of the Spirit, he does but place him in the same line with the Sibylline versifier, from whom he gives copious extracts similarly

* Die Evangelienfrage. Denkschrift. Zürich. 1858.
† Ad Autolycum, ii. 22.

recommended.* For the complete designation of the author, we have to wait for Irenæus, who says, " Next, John, the disciple of the Lord, who also lay on his breast, himself put forth the Gospel, while staying at Ephesus in Asia;"† and his frequent quotations abundantly prove that the book which bore his name was no other than our fourth Gospel. The lateness of this testimony is thought to be compensated by the peculiar opportunities with which the witness was favoured ; for in childhood he had seen the aged Polycarp of Smyrna, the disciple of John ; and he still retained the memory of the old man's look and gait and speech. And though Irenæus' place was in the Western Church, he never lost his interest in the affairs of the Asiatic Christians, and freely appeals in controversy to the local traditions handed down through the successors of Polycarp to his own time. So great was the advantage which he thus enjoyed, that we should expect him, in any encounter with persons who did not acknowledge the fourth Gospel, to confute their doubts by direct information drawn from Polycarp and the Johannine churches. Yet what is the fact? He actually *does* engage in controversy with just such persons,—with " Some who of late do not admit the form of tradition which is according to the Gospel of John.";   But instead of establishing the authority of that Gospel by simply stating what he knew about its apostolic origin, on the testimony of personal disciples of John, he resorts to the absurd arguments already noticed, that there must be four Gospels because there are four winds. Not only does he thus disappoint us of his early memories, when we should be glad to have them : but, when at last we get them, they do not prove particularly trustworthy ; for he assures us, on the authority " *of the Gospel*," and of all the old men who in Asia had known John, the Lord's disciple, and of those who had known other apostles besides, that Jesus lived to be more than fifty years of age ! §

In estimating the value of Irenæus' evidence, it is necessary to distinguish between what he believed and what he knew. He doubtless believed that the Apostle John, after banishment

* Ad Autolycum, II. 9, 36, III. p. 129.   † Adv. Hær. III. 1.
‡ Ibid. III. 11.   § Ibid. II. 39.

to Patmos in the persecution under Domitian, lived at Ephesus till the time of Trajan (A.D. 98–117), and there wrote the fourth Gospel. He knew by memories treasured through some forty years what Polycarp had in his youth heard tell about the life of Jesus from surviving eye-witnesses of it, including John. Had Irenæus reported the contents of Polycarp's recitals, he might have saved for us some missing element of tradition respecting the ministry of Christ; and we should have known as fact, that it was current at the close of the apostolic age. But his silence leaves us none the wiser for his contact with the martyr : from whom we have no reason to suppose that he learned anything about the composition of the fourth Gospel or the other Johannine writings. For his beliefs on such matters he was, so far as we know, not less dependent than others on the common Christian tradition of his time, and was in no position of authority, enabling him to confirm or to correct it. The current assumptions cannot claim exemption from criticism, in virtue of his assent to them.

Yet, surely the bare fact of the young Polycarp's resort to "the Lord's disciple John," settles one important point,—viz., the actual residence of the apostle in Asia Minor ; and so far favours the ascription to him of a Gospel having its probable origin there. So we should say, if Polycarp had gone alone in his visits to the aged "disciple." But we hear of them also from one who went with him, and who, in doing so, introduces us, as Eusebius remarks, to a different John, viz. "*the Presbyter.*" This fellow-learner (and afterwards forerunner in martyrdom) is Papias, "the ancient man, companion of Polycarp," who also collected the reported sayings of Christ, and had recourse, in verifying his materials, to two of "the Lord's disciples," *John the Presbyter and Aristion.* Since, in their joint search for the same thing, Papias depended on the "Presbyter," and Polycarp on the "Apostle," it is natural to ask whether both do not rest on the same personal authority, under different designations ; and whether, in that case, as Papias speaks for himself, Polycarp only through the memory of another, the real historical person is not the *Presbyter John,* mistaken by Irenæus for the *Apostle.* The conjecture receives some negative confirmation from the extant epistle of Polycarp to the Philippians; in which no mention is made of the Apostle John, though the writer assails the same heretics with whom, according to tradition, the apostle had contended at Ephesus, and against whom the Johannine letters are directed. On the other side may be set the positive mention by Papias of *both* Johns at Ephesus, though his personal relation was with the Presbyter. He has no weight, however, as an historical authority for matters beyond his own experience; and would be as liable as any of his neighbours to take up with the current Christian belief, in the latter part of the second century, that the closing years of the Apostle John's life had been spent at Ephesus.

Unless, therefore, we know the basis of that belief, its recognition by Papias tells us nothing. There need be no mystery about its origin. It came from the assumption, popularly made then, as it is now, that the Book of Revelation is from the pen of the *Apostle* John. The Seer and writer makes no such profession: he calls himself only "*servant*" of Jesus Christ, and "brother and fellow" of his readers (i. 9); his angelic guide calls him one of the fraternity of "prophets" (xxii. 6), who, in the early Church are always secondary to the Apostles (1 Cor. xii. 28): and when, in the crystal light of the New Jerusalem coming down from heaven, he sees the names of the twelve Apostles inscribed on her twelve foundation stones (xxi. 14), no one can suppose that he reads there his own. These indications were easily overlooked in an uncritical age. And when once the John of the Apocalypse had been identified with the Apostle, the tradition found in the book itself all that was needed for its completion. The author was in "tribulation," doubtless as an exile, in Patmos "for the Word of God and the testimony of Jesus" (i. 9). This could only be in Domitian's persecution, A.D. 95, to which indeed allusions are to be found in xvii. 6, 11, 14. The messages with which the Seer is charged to the seven churches (ii. iii.) imply his relation to them collectively as habitual apostolic agent. And that the first letter is addressed to Ephesus indicates that city as his place of residence. If, as is probable, it was from that

centre that both the Apocalypse and the fourth Gospel, though
at different times and from different hands, passed into circulation, this local coincidence would extend the Apostle's
name from the one to the other, and complete the tradition
that, after his release from banishment, he lived and still
wrote at Ephesus into or beyond the first decade of the second
century.

The story then which, towards the end of that century,
emerges in the writings of Irenæus, of the Apostle John's
removal to lesser Asia and residence at Ephesus, has no
support from external testimony, but is itself built up by false
inferences from the very books which it is supposed to
authenticate. Not only does its late date indicate this, but
the silly fables mixed up with it when it does appear; e.g.
the caldron of boiling oil which only served to the apostle for
a harmless bath, and his orthodox flight from the water in
which he saw the heretic Cerinthus bathing, lest the roof
should fall. When, from such fictions of later tradition, we turn
to the Christian literature of the first quarter of the second
century, in which, as mainly the produce of Asia Minor, we
may fairly look for witnesses to the Apostle if he were there,—
to Luke's two histories, the epistles to the Ephesians and
Colossians, the 1 Timothy, the Ignatian letter to the Ephesians,
we find an absence of Johannine characteristics, and a silence
in regard to the Ephesian tradition, more significant than the
credulous statements of Irenæus.

When we enter upon the series of *anonymous* citations, the
limits within which we can appeal to them in evidence of the
existence of the book are by no means easy to determine.
Two principal causes of doubt hold the problem in suspense :
we cannot with any certainty date the quotations; and we
cannot be sure that they are quotations at all, and not
rather,—inversely,—an earlier expression of some thought
pervading the theology of the age or school, and ultimately
fixed in the language of the fourth Gospel. The first of these
causes comes into play when we alight upon the book in the
Gnostic circles of the second century; the other, when we pass
farther back to the Epistle of Barnabas.

Among the heresiarchs who threatened to absorb Christianity

by planting its founder and its God among their æons, there
was no greater figure than that of Valentinus: whose influence
is attested by the eagerness of ecclesiastical opposition,
especially as represented by Irenæus and Hippolytus. As he
is known to have gone to Rome about A.D. 140, and not to
have lived beyond about A.D. 160, his use of the fourth Gospel,
if it could be proved, would add nearly forty years to its
ascertained term of existence. That it was used by his
disciples in the next generation is indisputable; for one of
them, Ptolemæus, addressed a letter to the Lady Flora,—a
member of the school,—which has been preserved by Epiphanius; wherein he says, ''Besides, the Saviour claims
the creation of the cosmos as his own, inasmuch as all
things were made by him, and without him was nothing
made.'' And another—Herakleon—wrote comments on the
Gospel, some passages of which have been handed down by
Origen. Yet, while they used the book, it is surprising how
little its historical authority seems to have weighed with them;
for, in the face of its obvious chronology and plainest narrative,
they attributed to the ministry of Jesus a duration of only a year,
and taught that he lived on earth eighteen months after his
resurrection.* That Valentinus himself had in his hand the
Gospel which became such a favourite with his followers there
was no ground for supposing, till the discovery of the long lost
Philosophumena attributed to Hippolytus: for in the account
of his system by Irenæus,† and of the passages of scripture
adduced in its support, we find only texts from the Old Testament, from the synoptics, from Paul, tortured into applications
which they will not bear; while not a single Johannine text
presents itself, though to every reader the most apposite
quotations must occur, as lying right in the way, as at once
supplying a good argument and sparing a bad one. Thus, in
support of the position that before Christ no man had known
the supreme God, the irresistible appeal is not made to John
i. 18, "No man has seen God at any time; the only-begotten
Son, who is in the bosom of the Father, he has revealed
him." This silence becomes the more striking, when we turn
to an appendix in which Irenæus reports the later Valentinian

* Epiphanius: Hær. xxxiii. 3.   † Adv. Hær. I. 8, 1–4.

expositions given by Ptolemæus; for here, at last, we meet with the Johannine texts which we so strangely miss in a system which moves among æons named "Logos," "Only-begotten," "Life," "Grace," and "Truth." The natural inference would be that the master had not yet seen the book in which the disciple found a welcome ally.

But Hippolytus, we are assured, with the treatise of Valentinus lying open before him, actually produces from it passages out of the fourth Gospel, and so corrects this negative inference. His account of the Valentinian Gnosis is introduced by these words: " Valentinus and Heracleon and Ptolemæus, and all their school, disciples of Pythagoras and Plato, following the principle recited, established their own numerical scheme ; "—" The above-mentioned monad is called *by them*, Father ; "—" The Father, says *he*, was alone unbegotten."* Who is the "*he*" that says this? How are we to identify him within the previous plural "*them*," whence he emerges? We can only reply, he is *that one of them* whose book was before Hippolytus as he wrote ; but *which* of them fulfils this condition we cannot tell. When therefore, farther on, the writer similarly states, "Hence, says he, the Saviour's words, ' All they that came before me are thieves and robbers,' " (John x. 10,)† it is quite arbitrary to fasten this quotation from the fourth Gospel upon Valentinus in particular, as distinguished from Heracleon and Ptolemæus. Come the citation from whichsoever of them it may, the words of Hippolytus would stand exactly as they are. There is nothing, therefore, here to disturb the indications given by Irenæus, that the fourth Gospel first came into the hands of the Valentinians in the second generation of their sect. Exact dates cannot be confidently given ; but the most recent and probable conclusion assigns Ptolemæus to about A.D. 180, and Herakleon to a time ten years later.‡

---

* Hippol. Philosophumena, vi. 26.   † Ibid. vi. 35.

‡ The case of Basileides and his alleged citations labours under precisely the same defect of proof as that of Valentinus, and requires no separate notice. He also is mentioned in the same breath with his later followers ; from any one of whom the quotations adduced may have proceeded ; the plural subject being followed by the verb in the singular,—" Basileides and Isidorus, and the whole χορὸς of these men falsely allege (καταψεύδεται) "

Equally unsuccessful is the appeal to Marcion as a witness to the existence of the fourth Gospel. That he made no use of it, but in constructing his system resorted only to Luke and ten of Paul's Epistles, is admitted on all hands. This selection, however, was due, we are told, not to unacquaintance with the Johannine writings, but to deliberate rejection of them, as unsuitable to his purpose; and there is certainly some passionate language of Tertullian which gives a colourable aspect to this assertion. Marcion was induced, says this vehement controversialist, by the second chapter of the Epistle to the Galatians, " to destroy the standing of those Gospels which are published under the names of apostles and apostolic men, and, by taking away reliance on them, transfer it to his own."* And again he says, " Had you (Marcion) not purposely rejected some of the scriptures that oppose your opinions, and corrupted others, the Gospel of John would have confuted you."† Here, no doubt, the exclusive use by Marcion of a few writings arbitrarily detached from their usual companions is treated as a repudiation of the rest; and since, at the time when Tertullian wrote, the canon was made up, and all its parts would be alike to him, it is not wonderful that the fourth Gospel, being absent from the Heresiarch's list, is classed among his rejected books. To infer from this loose language that Tertullian knew Marcion to have been in possession of the Johannine Gospel would be unwarrantable. He probably knew nothing about it; but, presuming that what was scripture now had been scripture then, resented, with all the heat of his African rhetoric, the dishonour inflicted on the Church by so fastidious an anthology of the Bible. It is the less likely that Marcion's disregard of the fourth Gospel was intentional, because from Hippolytus we learn that his follower Apelles already used it,‡ and from Origen that passages of it were cited by later Marcionites. And who can believe, that, with his anti-Judaic design to construe Christianity into a universal religion, Marcion would

<hr>

&c., vii. 20. As the sect still existed in the third century, such passages supply no determinate chronology.

* Adv. Marc. iv. 4.   † De Carne Christi. c. 3.
‡ Hippol. Philos. vii. 38.

have taken Luke as his text-book, if the next Gospel had been ready to his hand? It would have saved him a large proportion of the trouble and odium he incurred in making a synoptic speak sufficiently like Paul, and supplied him with many a formula weightier than his own for the expression of some favourite ideas. In the case, therefore, of both these sects, the evidence points to the same conclusion,—that the Gospel was known to their second generation, but unknown to their first. If so, it passed into circulation between A.D. 140 and A.D. 170.[*]

This inference is supported by another witness, producible from the same age. A controversy began at Laodicea in the year 170, on the question whether Christians ought to keep, or not to keep, the paschal feast according to the Jewish rule ; one party maintaining that, as Jesus kept it with the twelve before he suffered, so should his followers, and appealing to Matthew's Gospel in support of their opinion ; the other insisting that Jesus in his death was himself the true passover, and closed forever the typical celebration ; resting their case on the fourth Gospel. This latter doctrine found a zealous advocate in Claudius Apollinaris, bishop of Hierapolis in Phrygia ; and in a fragment of his, preserved in the Paschal Chronicle, occurs the following distinct reference to the narrative in John xix. 34 : " He who was pierced in his holy side, who poured out of his side the two purifiers, water and blood, word and spirit, and who was buried on the paschal day, having been put into a sepulchre of stone." It is singular that, though this is cited as a set-off against the authority of Matthew, on which the opponents rely, it is not put forth under the name of John, so as to make apostle answer apostle. In the anonymous character of its citation, as well as in its date (between A.D. 170 and A.D. 180), it agrees with the Valentinian and Marcionite evidence.

Till within a few years, the citations which we have passed under review afforded the only clear vestiges of the fourth

---

[*] This chronological conclusion from the history of the Valentinian Gnosticism coincides exactly with that which Pfleiderer deduces from the internal development of Christian doctrine in his admirable work, Das Urchristenthum, seine Schriften und Lehren, S. 778.

Gospel before the later decades of the second century. There was especial reason for surprise that no notice of it appeared in the Clementine Homilies, a Jewish Christian production (probably produced at Rome about A.D. 160–170), pervaded by an intense hostility to the Pauline Christianity and the doctrine of the godhead of Christ, and not likely therefore to be sparing of criticism on a Gospel which carries that doctrine on its front, and goes far beyond Paul in its revolt from Judaism. But throughout the eighteen and a half homilies contained in the solitary Paris codex, only two phrases which might be, yet need not be, Johannine could be detected. In 1838, however, Dressel found in the Vatican Library a second MS., containing the missing close of the book; and in 1853 published the whole twenty Homilies. In XIX. 22 we meet with the following unquestionable reference to the narrative in John ix. 1–3: " Hence, too, our Teacher replies to those who asked him, about the man blind from birth and endowed by him with vision, whether he sinned or his parents, that he was born blind,—' neither did this man commit sin nor his parents; but that by means of him the power of God might be made manifest, healing the sins of ignorance'."* Yet here, two remarkable features are to be observed : (1) The citation is not word for word in agreement with the Gospel ; and the principal deviation of phrase is found also twice in Justin Martyr ;† (2) the doctrine which the passage elicits from the man's congenital blindness, is entirely at variance with that of the fourth Gospel ; the Ebionite writer deducing the blindness *retrospectively* from some " sin of ignorance," some unconscious disregard of the Mosaic law on the parents' part ; the author of the gospel explaining it *prospectively,* as the condition provided for the light-giving " works of God." Both these features may be due to the writer of the Homilies, who, in borrowing from the Gospel, may have made his own

---

* Ὅθεν καὶ διδάσκαλος ἡμῶν περὶ τοῦ ἐκ γενετῆς πηροῦ (John τυφλὸν) καὶ ἀναβλέψαντος παρ' αὐτοῦ ἐξετά[ζουσιν καὶ ἐρωτῶσιν] εἰ οὗτος ἥμαρτεν ἢ οἱ γονεῖς αὐτοῦ ἵνα τυφλὸς γεννηθῇ, ἀπεκρίνατο · οὔτε οὗτός τι ἥμαρτεν, οὔτε οἱ γονεῖς αὐτοῦ · ἀλλ' ἵνα δι' αὐτοῦ φανερωθῇ ἡ δύναμις τοῦ Θεοῦ, τῆς ἀγνοίας ἰωμένη τὰ ἁμαρτήματα. XIX. 22.

† Apol. I. 22. Πηροὶ ἐκ γενετῆς. Dial. c. Tryph. 69. ἐκ γενετῆς πηροὶ καὶ κωφοὶ καὶ χωλοί.

alterations in language and in thought. But the evangelical citations in the Clementine Homilies have a peculiar complexion, which suggests another explanation ; not one of them is found in Mark ; only four could come from Luke ; more than a hundred present themselves, only not verbatim, in Matthew ; and eight are in no canonical Gospel. These phenomena indicate the use, by this writer, of some source unknown to us,—a source which might also be resorted to by the author of the fourth Gospel. An evangelist, writing in the post-apostolic age, and wishing to give a fresh version of the ministry of Christ, would not break with the historic past, and draw on his own invention for his biographical construction ; but searching among the traditions, fixed or floating, of Christ's acts and words, would work up what best suited his new design. These same materials would be equally available for other writers, and might therefore reappear in several forms. Some of them actually do so appear in our synoptical Gospels; and others, in the second century, may no less have repeated themselves, with similar varieties, in the less historical pages of Christian compilers and advocates of that age. We cannot, therefore, safely infer, from the agreement of an anonymous citation with a passage in one of our evangelists, that it is *taken from* his Gospel, and proves its contemporary existence. Were we, however, to admit the inference in the present instance, it would still leave our previous chronological conclusion undisturbed.

The farther we go back, the more do we encounter this strange phenomenon,—of seeming citation fading into mere resemblance, which might be accidental, and which memory would hardly leave so incomplete. Often as a passing phrase of Justin Martyr seems to have in it something of the Johannine *ring*, the sound dies away, and changes too soon to come from that full-toned source ; and there is but one passage on which any stress can be laid as a probable quotation. It runs thus: "For Christ said, ' Unless ye be born again, ye will not enter into the kingdom of heaven.' But that it is impossible for those who have once been born to enter the wombs of those that bare them, is plain to all."[*]

* Apol. i. 61.

On reading this we turn at once to John iii. 3, 4, as its Scripture source : " Jesus answered and said to him, Verily, verily, I say to thee, unless a man be born from above " (for that is the true reading), "he cannot see the kingdom of God." Nicodemus saith to him, " How can a man be born, being old ?   Can he enter again his mother's womb and be born ? " [Jesus answered] " Verily, verily, I say unto thee, Unless a man be born of water and spirit, he cannot enter the kingdom of God."   Among the differences between the two passages we may especially notice, (1) That Christ addresses in the Gospel *one* person only ; in Justin, a *plurality*.   (2) The regeneration in Justin is only a being "born *again ;* " in the Gospel a birth "*from above.*"   (3) Justin says, " Ye *will* not enter ; " the Gospel, " He *cannot* enter."   (4) The Gospel speaks of the "*kingdom of God ;* " Justin uses Matthew's phrase, " the *kingdom of heaven.*"   All these differences might arise from the looseness of *memoriter* quotation, intent upon the sense rather than the words.   But in that case they are personal to Justin, and, as accidents of his literary mood, will not appear again.   It so happens, however, that in Rufinus's version of the Clementine Recognitions we find the same passage, with all these four differences reproduced : " Verily, I say to *you* [plural], Unless a man shall have been born *over again* of water, he *will not* enter into the *kingdom of heaven.*"*   This concurrence of two independent writers in a set of variations on the same text must be due to some common cause ; and what else can it be than the use by both of them of a source deviating from the fourth Gospel in these points.

Nor can we well doubt that that source embodied an earlier tradition, on which the Johannine version afterwards refined : for the re-birth, which in the former is boldly identified with baptism, and amounts only to the entrance on a *new* life, is elevated in the latter into a fresh creation by " the Spirit," the initiation from above into a *divine* life.   That this higher doctrine is a later emergence from the other, must be evident to any one who has studied the history of religious ideas.   It

* Amen dico vobis, " Nisi quis denuo renatus fuerit ex aqua, non introibit in regna cœlorum," vi. 9.

is probable, as Volkmar has shown,* that the Johannine
passage, with its doctrine of new birth, is only the divine
saying of Christ, in its last stage of metamorphosis,—"unless
ye turn," and become as little children, ye will not enter the
kingdom of heaven (Mat. xviii. 3).

The absence of distinct Johannine quotations in Justin
Martyr is the more remarkable, because he was obviously
influenced, as might be expected from a Platonist, by the
Gnostic conceptions which were afloat in his time, and which
embodied themselves in many of the phrases characteristic of
the fourth Gospel,—λόγος, μονογενής, σάρξ, πνεῦμα, ἄρτος Σεοῦ.
His mind was drawn into the same current which sweeps so
broad and strong through the work of the evangelist, but only
at its first and feeble drift; and his tentative and wavering
movements in its direction would have been not less impossible, had its full tide set in, than it would have been for Plato,
had he known the Newtonian physics, to explain as he does
the equilibration of the earth in space.† The Logos doctrine,
especially, he presents in a far less determinate and developed
form than it assumes in the Gospel,—in a form that might
naturally come after Philo, but could only precede the evangelist.

The recovery of the Greek text of the Epistle of Barnabas,
and the natural affection of Tischendorf for everything contained in his Sinaitic Codex, have revived the interest of theologians in that production, and, for a while, given it a weight
greater than justly belongs to it in the decision of the Johannine
controversy. If it could be assigned, as Weizsäcker‡ supposes,
to so early a date as A.D. 80, or even to the reign of Nerva
(about A.D. 97), as Hilgenfeld contends; § and if, further, Keim
were right in affirming the author's evident acquaintance with
the fourth Gospel,‖ this piece, intrinsically of no great significance, would solve the most important problem in sacred
criticism. An impartial judgment will hardly find in it
materials for winning so considerable a result. The dates

* Ueber Justin den Märtyrer, c. iii. Zürich, 1853.
† Phædon, 108, E, 109, A.
‡ Zur Kritik d. Barnabasbriefes: S. 21, *seqq.* 1863.
§ Nov. Test. extra Canonem Receptum: Barn. Epist. Prol. xi. *seqq.*
‖ Geschichte Jesu von Nazara: B. i. p. 141–143.

suggested for its composition are recommended by evidence so slender as to remain simply conjectural; and they are rendered improbable, by some indications, which can hardly mislead us, of a later time. A passage, for instance, in Matthew's Gospel is quoted with the formula, "*As it is written,*"—a phrase never employed but of the Old Testament books, which were read as sacred scriptures; and the Christian books were not placed upon that level till some way into the second century.* The whole cast of thought and sentiment is in harmony with this indication : Judaism is left behind, except as furnishing a fund of types of Christian incidents. The Pauline period and manner are in the past, with the controversies that formed their characteristics ; the Alexandrine theology is in the ascendant, turning the literature of religion into a frost-work of precarious imagery and correspondences, yet still with a lingering play about biblical texts and histories, and not yet elevated into a speculative gnosis, aspiring to be philosophical and spiritual at once. These are the features which mark the first quarter of the second century. By the aid of a passage in the sixteenth chapter, the date may perhaps be more precisely fixed. Contrasting the local and legal worship of Jews with the spiritual temple of the Christians, the writer appeals to the Jews' own Scriptures: "The Lord saith, ' Heaven is my throne, and the earth my footstool. What house will ye build for me, or where is the place of my rest ? ' Know that their hope is vain. And again he saith, ' They that have destroyed this temple themselves shall build it up.' It is coming to pass : for through their going to war it has been destroyed by the enemy ; and now they themselves, as servants of their enemies, will have to rebuild it." The reference here, there can be little doubt, is to a contemporary event of the second Jewish war under Hadrian, occasioned by the rebellion of Barchocbarr, A.D. 132–135, when the temple was utterly destroyed and its platform levelled. The Jews, even then hoping and entreating that it might rise again, were permitted to commence a reconstruction. But, when the work was finished, the temple was dedicated to Jupiter Capitolinus.

---

* See Barnabas und Johannes, von H. Holzmann: Zeitschrift für wissensch. Theologie. 1871. p. 350.

This was what was "coming to pass," and proving that " their hope was vain." *

If, in reading the Epistle of Barnabas, we assumed that all the elements of Christology which transcend the synoptical Gospels must be drawn from the fourth, we should certainly pronounce it dependent upon both. The pre-existence of " the Son of God," his superhuman nature, his " manifestation in the flesh," are dwelt upon in a way foreign to the earlier evangelists. But so are they even in the undoubted Pauline writings, and more emphatically in the epistles to the Hebrews, the Colossians, and the Ephesians; the growth of doctrine continually receding from the first Messianic form, and passing through many stadia to the ultimate definitions of the creeds. Two of these stadia are represented by the epistle of Barnabas and the Johannine Gospel respectively; and our immediate question is, Which occupies the earlier place? The chief indications of precedence in the Gospel are two. Barnabas represents the death and the resurrection of Christ as acts of *his own*, in conformity with a command of his Father,† just as the evangelist does (John x. 18); and he takes the brazen serpent as a type of Christ,‡ like John iii. 14. But neither of these representations is so peculiar as to have no possible source but the fourth Gospel. Paul (Phil. ii. 5–8) treats the humiliation and sacrifice of Christ as voluntary; and though he ascribes to God the raising him from death to heavenly life, the post-apostolic age was not content without carrying the Saviour's agency through the whole economy of redemption, and making it all the execution of a predicted and intended plan. We find, accordingly, this same idea in other writings of the period; e.g., the Sibylline oracles and the Ignatian letters.§ There is no reason to suppose that any one of these writers borrowed the conception from another : it lived in the Christian imagination of their time, and, drawn thence by all, was originally applied by each. As for the brazen serpent, it is only by singling it out from the forest of types by which it is

---

* Cf. Pfleiderer, Das Urchristenthum : S. 667.

† C. 5.   ‡ C. 12.

§ Orac. Sib. viii. 313. καὶ τότ' ἀπὸ ὀφθαλμῶν ἀναλύσας. Ign. ad Smyrn. 2. ἀνέστησεν ἑαυτόν ap. Holzmann, B. & J. p. 338.

environed, and setting it forth as if it stood alone, that the critic can suggest a suspicion of its being a stolen analogy. When the whole of the Old Testament is ransacked for prophecies and types, and objects and incidents innumerable from Abraham to Isaiah are turned into evangelic symbols, how should the serpent in the wilderness escape? or, if resorted to, be more symptomatic of imitation than any other equally artificial play of fancy? The author of the Wisdom of Solomon had already treated the brazen serpent as "a sign of salvation," inasmuch as "he that turned himself towards it was not saved by the thing that he saw, but by Thee that art the Saviour of all; * to say nothing of the manifold use of the same emblem by Philo.† Had the writer of the letter really been reproducing John iii. 14, he could not, have missed, as he has missed, the whole tone of that passage; least of all, have dropped the one essential word ($\dot{v}\psi\omega\vartheta\tilde{\eta}\nu\alpha\iota$), in which (as again John xii. 32) the whole life of the thought is contained.

While these slight coincidences imply no interdependence of the two writers, there are differences on a much larger scale which completely separate them. Barnabas (v.) affirms that Jesus, when appointing his apostles, selected men "lawless beyond all measure of sinfulness," in order to show that he came to call not the righteous, but sinners, to repentance. Could any one write thus who knew the words which met Nathanael at his call, "Behold an Israelite indeed, in whom there is no guile"? or who had before him the story of "the disciple whom Jesus loved"? There was a time in the post-apostolic age when, partly an antinomian impulse, partly the fact that one of the twelve had been a "publican" and the Gentile apostle a persecutor, gave rise to this extravagant conception of the character of the first missionaries of the 'gospel; and no slight approach to it is made in the exaggerated self-disparagement attributed to Paul by the writer of 1 Timothy i. 12–15. The epistle of Barnabas advances upon this; but it is not an advance in the Johannine direction, or compatible with the presence of such an influence.

* xvi. 6, 7.

† De Agricultura, § 22, Legg. Alleg. B. II. § 20, 21, referred to by Holzmann, B. & J. p. 340.

In the evangelist's account of the appearance of Jesus after he had risen from the dead, there is no notice of the ascension ; and the interviews with his disciples which are recorded (not reckoning the appendix, ch. xxi.) are at the beginning and the end of a period of eight days.* In the epistle of Barnabas the cessation of the Jewish sabbath, and the substitution by Christians of a Sunday celebration, are justified by the consideration that "on the eighth day " (i.e. the day succeeding the seventh, or the first day of the week), " Jesus both rose from the dead, and appeared, and ascended into heaven."† This is in accordance with the form of tradition which is preserved in Luke's Gospel, and probably with the more ancient materials which formed the basis of the whole synoptical history ; and it is quite conceivable that from this side the writer of the Epistle may have been in possession of such a version of the facts. But he could never have reproduced it, without a hint of hesitation, if the fourth Gospel, with its plain contradiction, had been present to his hand.

But the decisive, though not the most palpable test of the relative order of these two productions lies in their different conceptions of the person of Christ. On his divine side, he appears in the epistle as "the Son of God," to whom the Father addresses the words, " Let us make man in our image," who is Lord of the earth, who has appeared in the flesh, and died to abolish death, and risen again to show the way of life beyond.‡   The Christology is not indeed a reproduction of the Pauline type of doctrine ; for, instead of admitting that Christ "was born of the seed of David according to the flesh " (Rom i. 3,) the author denies his humanity, saying that " he is not the son of man, but the son of God."§   This ignoring of heredity and of a human soul in Christ, approaches Docetism ; but is saved from it by the assumption of an *Incarnation*. But in deviating from the Pauline point of view, the writer by no means reaches the Johannine. We nowhere come across the characteristic doctrine of the fourth Gospel with its subsidiary conceptions, the Logos, co-essential with God, and immanent in the world as its light, its life, its truth. No one

* XX. 1. 19, 26.   † C. 15, *ad fin.*
‡ C. v.   § C. xii.

who has stood in presence of the Johannine Christ, and entered into the marvellous thought whence the delineation comes, can pass to the epistle of Barnabas, without being consciously thrown back upon a balder and prior theology, which could never be reproduced by one trained in the higher school. Unless we invert the natural seasons of growing thought, the Epistle could only arise when the Gospel was still in the future.

Can we, then, sum up the testimony of our witnesses to any definite result ? From various quarters the line of their evidence seems to converge upon one time for the origin of this Gospel. Probably not known to Justin (about 155), but possibly to the author of the Clementines (about 170) ; not in the hands of Valentinus (about 160), but in those of his disciples, Ptolemæus and Herakleon (180 and 190) ; not used by Marcion (about 150), but by Marcionites of the next generation ; cited by Apollinaris (about 175) ; for the first time *named* by Theophilus of Antioch (about 180) ; the fourth Gospel would seem to have become known in the sixth or seventh decade of the second century, and to have ceased to be anonymous in the eighth. Time must be allowed, prior to these dates, for its gradual distribution from the place of its nativity to the literary centres of the church and of the Gnostic sects. But even the most liberal allowance, which, consistently with the habits of the age and the organization of Christendom, can be claimed for this purpose, will leave us a long way from the apostolic generation. We cannot confidently name any earlier date than the fifth decade of the century. This conclusion will not be affected, even if we allow Justin to have had the Gospel in his hands.

Whether, however, the internal evidence will confirm or correct this provisional conclusion still remains to be seen.

B. *Internal Character.*

The oldest account we have respecting the authorship of the fourth Gospel is contained, not indeed within its own proper text, but in the Editor's Appendix, which counts as its last chapter. There it is expressly referred to " the disciple whom Jesus loved ": " This is the disciple who testifieth of these things and *wrote these things :* and we know that his testimony is true " (xxi. 24).   As there is no reason to believe that the Gospel ever appeared without its supplementary chapter, we learn from these words that it was not given to the world in its alleged author's lifetime : for the very purpose of the recital which they close is, to remove the surprise at the death of one supposed to be reserved " till the Lord should come." This motive would be most operative *soon* after the disciple's decease, if he and it were well and definitely known, and his departure occasioned a shock conspicuous in date and place. But if he were simply an unnamed member of a group dispersed, there would be nothing to prevent whole decades passing that were silent of his life or death, and the prophecy would first be charged with failure through the mere absence of any claimant on supernatural longevity. The correcting answer therefore to the charge of failure, viz., that the supposed prophecy was never uttered, might come at any time, and does not require to be brought within the limits of the apostolic generation. And in issuing a gospel as a production of " the beloved disciple," the editor, at whatever date, was bound to give the correcting answer : for if the Evangelist " who wrote these things " were the very person pointed out for survival, why can he not speak for himself? What need of an editor to formulate and accredit his own deepest personal experiences ?

Turning from the appendix to the Gospel itself, we do not find the author claiming identity with " the beloved disciple." Once only does he speak of the *source* of his narrative, as coming from an eye-witness : in relating the incident of the spear-wound in the side of Jesus, he says (xix. 35) : " And he that hath seen it, hath borne witness, and his witness is trustworthy."   These are words that can inform the reader only of a third person's testimony. And though the following clause, " And he (κἀκεῖνος) knoweth that he saith true," has been supposed, as a declaration of consciousness, to be predicable only of the writer himself, the inference is barred by the demonstrative pronoun ἐκεῖνος, which no speaker can use of *himself.* It is as if the author said, " And *that* is a man who does not speak at random, but only when sure that his word is true."

The eye-witness thus characterized is left, without further mark. The conjecture that he was "the beloved disciple" rests only on the previous mention of that disciple as standing beneath the cross with the three Marys (xix. 25–27). But the narrative does not forbid us to think of others also as being near : nor is it easy to see why the author, who so emphatically insists on the value of his eye-witness, should silently forego the advantage of his identity with the favourite disciple. ·

To the Evangelist then, the eye-witness, whether he were " the beloved disciple " or not, was an outside person ; and his editor alone is responsible for the statement that the " witness " in question " wrote these things.'

But further, neither Evangelist nor Editor identifies "the beloved disciple " with John, the son of Zebedee. Three times he appears in the Gospel,* twice in the Appendix ;† in every instance, under the veil of the same general description —" the disciple whom Jesus loved." He is not introduced to the reader till the last supper needs him to draw from Jesus the secret of the betrayer's name ; when it is said " There was at the table reclining on Jesus' bosom one of his disciples, whom Jesus loved. Simon Peter therefore beckoneth to him, and saith unto him, ' Tell us who it is of whom he speaketh.' He, leaning back, as he was, on Jesus' breast, saith unto him, ' Lord, who is it ? ' Jesus therefore answereth, ' He it is, for whom I shall dip the sop, and give it him.' " The second passage relates the dying injunction to the disciple to be as a son to the mother of Jesus : and the third, the visit to the empty sepulchre, at which " the other disciple outran Peter." This completes the picture which is given us. In two of the instances the unknown figure is associated with Peter, in each case with a curious suggestion of a certain advantage over him, and yet concession to him, of a leading part as chief. But the *incognito* remains unbroken. Had we been left to the fourth Gospel alone, we should never have heard of either James or John. Of those who formed the inner circle of

* xiii. 23. xix. 26, 27. xx. 2–5.   † xxi. 7, 20.

"disciples" ("apostles" they are not called) the writer names but seven; and among them the sons of Zebedee are not found. As the Evangelist recognizes the limitation of this inner circle to *twelve*, he leaves us to seek " the beloved disciple " among the unnamed five. The mode in which the Church tradition worked out the problem has already been indicated. The synoptic gospels supplied the list of missing names. Ever since the Apocalypse appeared, the seer was known to bear one of them : and to whom was Jesus Christ more likely to convey the Revelation which God gave him of things to come, than to " the disciple whom he loved," to whom he had con-fided the traitor's name, and committed the guardianship of his mother ? And so it was inferred that the Prophet John was no other than " the beloved disciple," and therefore " the beloved disciple " the younger son of Zebedee.

The conclusion seems forced upon us, that the Apostolical authorship of the fourth Gospel receives no adequate support from either claim on its own part, or competent external testimony.

Does the *internal character* of this Gospel commend it to us as probably the authentic record of an intimate disciple? The moment we ask this question, we feel the need of some standard by which to measure the probability of its statements. The deep and tender sympathy which the evangelist awakens surrounds him with eager advocates, who find his story self-evidently true, and who think it enough to say, that dramatic episodes like the cure of the man born blind, and the raising of Lazarus, could be drawn only from the life; that the conversation at Jacob's well, and the discourse before the betrayal, transcend the inventive range of mere spiritual genius ; and that, unless Christ were really of the higher nature assigned him in this Gospel, his personality would not be on a scale adequate to such a result as Christendom. But such subjective rules of possibility are valid only so long as they encounter no objective contradiction ; and must be subject to correction from historical fact where known, and to a comparison of parallel testimonies where doubtful. In Josephus, in the synoptists, and in the writings which mark the successive phases of Christian doctrine, we have some means of checking and testing the narrative of the evangelist ; and in every instance we meet with grounds for distrusting his pretension to be an original witness. No companion of Jesus could have placed the scene of the Baptist's testimony to Jesus in " Bethany beyond Jordan,"*—a place unknown to geography ; or have invested Annas as well as Caiaphas with the prerogatives of high priest ;† or have represented that office as annual ;‡ or have so forgotten Elijah and Nahum as to make the Pharisees assert that " out of Galilee ariseth no prophet."§   No Israelite, sharing the memory of the λαὸς Ξεοῦ, could, like the evangelist, place himself superciliously outside his compatriots, speak of their most sacred anniversaries as "feasts *of the Jews*," and reckon the Jews among the common ἴξνη of the world ; still less, display towards them an ever pitiless and scornful spirit, and treat them as children of the Devil, deaf to every divine voice, and doomed to die in their sins.   They appear on the canvas of his narrative, painted with a monotony of shadow which has no character in itself, and serves only to throw forward the effulgent figure in the centre : there is nothing too silly for them to say, too wicked for them to do : they pervert all that they hear ; are destitute of any spiritual apprehension ; care only for " signs and wonders," and for these chiefly when, by means of them, they " eat and are filled."   Is this the tone of a son and a brother even to the kindred he has left ? does such bitterness of insult suit the temper of the beloved disciple, the bosom friend of Him who wept over his Jerusalem ? Is it possible that we are here in presence of one of the twelve, who looked askance at Paul's emergence from Judaism, and threw on himself alone the responsibility of his dangerous Gentile gospel ?   With Paul, neither heart nor faith was ever

---

* John i. 28 (the true reading is Bethany, not Bethabara).

† John xviii. 19, 22, 24.   " Annas therefore sent him (' not *had* sent him ') bound to Caiaphas the high priest."

‡ John xi. 49, 51, xviii. 13.   H. Holtzmann attributes this mistake to the author's familiarity with the practice in Asia Minor of annually changing the high-priest of the new temple dedicated to the worship of the Emperor ; the year being called by his name.   Lehrb. d. Einleitung in d. N. T. 460 (2te Aufl.).

§ John vii. 52.   See 1 Kings xvii. 1 ; Nahum i. 1.

so alienated from the traditions and inheritance of his people
as we find the spirit of the fourth Gospel to be. So far as he
was an exile from them, he grieved at the separation : he
looked back on them with regretful affection, and forward to
reunion with yearning hope. The universal religion which
he had gained was not opposed to theirs, but its proper consummation, if they would only take it all. They were cus-
todians of its oracles, the organs of its historical conveyance ;
and, when their dark hour was past, they would enter into
its imperishable light. That, while the Gentile missionary
speaks of his brethren in this tender voice, one of the elder
apostles should set his face as flint against them, and treat
their place in the world as the stronghold of all that is earthly
and undivine, is hard to conceive ; and the contrast suggests
rather the suspicion that we are transported into the age of
Marcion and the anti-Jewish Gnostics, whose Christianity
was not a development but a defiance of the Israelite religion.

If the synoptical materials embody traditions flowing from
the original apostolic circle, and represent the order of ideas
prevailing there, every feature which strongly contrasts the
fourth Gospel with them renders it improbable that it proceeds from the same group of disciples. So great and all-
pervading is that contrast, not only in historical matter and
literary form, in the scenery, the chronology, the order, of the
story, but in the whole theory of religion assumed, and the
personal delineation of Christ, that the improbability reaches
a high intensity. The single omission of all demoniacal
possessions by the evangelist conclusively removes him, in
time and place and culture, from the Palestinian school. If
narratives of this class presented merely cases of ordinary
miracle, in which some morbid deflection of nature was
corrected by the beneficent interposition of God, a selecting
hand might conceivably drop them out in favour of other and
more striking samples of the same type. But the "casting
out of evil spirits" does not belong to the same category as
the raising of the dead and giving sight to the blind : it is
cited with a different significance, and is the expression of a
different Christology. The bodily and mental disorders which
supply the material for these incidents are not human

infirmities, remedied by a divine healing art, not short-comings in creation, set right by the Creator; but are themselves as preternatural as their removal,—a violent *raid* committed on helpless men by demons of superhuman power, who can be driven off only by Messiah with his superdemonic power. The whole proceeding in this case lies out in the mythological sphere, where evil spirits have free range to play with their victims till the advent of One who is to sweep them from the upper world, like pirates from the sea. The interest of the transaction is in the encounter of these natural foes, in the instinctive recognition of their superior and destroyer by beings more knowing than men, and in the shriek of final defeat by which they confessed their vanquisher. It is as a special and decisive mark of Messianic identity that the synoptical exorcisms are offered; and the important part which they play in the earlier Gospels shows how strong was the hold of this evidential argument on the minds of the Palestinian Christians. No one who was tinctured with the Jewish demonology could fail to feel its force; and the absolute disappearance of it in the fourth Gospel indicates that we are there transported to a different spiritual climate, where this kind of mythology cannot live.

Nor is it possible to piece together, as expressions of the same personality, the synoptical *discourses of Jesus* and those of the fourth Gospel; and the same circle of disciples cannot be answerable for both. If it be true (Mark iv. 34) that "without a parable spake he not unto them," no address of his is given us by the last evangelist; for of this picturesque and winning type of public teaching, so locally true, so personally characteristic, not a single instance appears in his narrative. Instead of these coloured lights upon the Teacher's doctrine, we have it wrapped in dark disguise: the concrete language of life, born in the field, the boat, the olive-ground, is exchanged for the abstract forms of philosophical conception; the terse maxims of conduct and epigrams of moral wisdom, for doctrinal enigmas and hinted mysteries of sentiment. The simple directness with which, in the earlier reports, the speaker advances to his end, and leaves it, is here replaced by the windings of subtle reflection, and the repetitions of

unsatisfied controversy. We pass from the breath and sunshine of the hills to the studious air and nocturnal lamp of
the library; and exchange the music of living voices, never
twice the same, for a monotonous pitch of speech, which flows
unvaried through the lips of Jesus or the historian, of Nicodemus or the woman of Samaria, of this disciple or of that.
We find Jesus quoting before one audience what, months
before, he had said to another, and charging on later opponents the persecution he had suffered at the hands of earlier,
as if the scene and the actor had never changed,*—a sure
sign that the thread of narrative connection is not the living
sequence of history, but the author's own memory of what he
has recently written. Hardly, indeed, does the evangelist
attempt to conceal his own hand in the free composition of
his dialogues; for unlike the open-air addresses of the synoptists, or the confidences of Jesus with the inner circle of disciples, some of the most impressive of them, as the conversation with Nicodemus and at Jacob's well, have no witness but
the interlocutors themselves, who cannot be supposed to have
taken notes in the service of future history.

When an actor in some great crisis of human affairs reads
the record of it which has been left by his companions, and
finds it recall to him many things which they have not told,
and perhaps disturb him by false lights thrown on real transactions, he may naturally resolve to complete and correct their
work by contributions of his own. In executing this purpose,
he will necessarily work upon their main program, and find
room within its outline for filling in the forgotten details, and
retouching the faded or mistaken colours. The story will act
itself out on the same field and in the same period: only it
will be enriched by new episodes, and gain some varieties of
light. But the fourth evangelist, totally disregarding the
organic scheme of his predecessors, constructs the history
afresh; so that the sparse points of contact (only four prior
to the last act) † are but tantalizing concurrences, that supply

* Compare John x. 25, 27, and viii. 23, 43, 47, and x. 1-6; also xiii. 33, and
viii. 21; also vii. 21, and v. 1-16.

† The temple cleansing, ii. 13-17; the feeding the five thousand, vi. 5-13;
the walking on the sea, vi. 17-20; the anointing by the woman at Bethany,
xii. 3-8.

no links of consecution, and leave the new story completely outside the old. The ministry of Jesus is spread upon a different ground plan of *time;* including, instead of one great national festival, no fewer than five, and claiming apparently, in the writer's conception, not one year but three. And it is transposed, in the main, to a different *local theatre*, its Galilean passages being a mere accidental by-play, and the whole stress and glory of the mission being concentrated and retained in and near Jerusalem. Even if these contrasted representations were two fragments of one integral history, no writer designing to remedy the imperfection of the first could contribute the second without giving the key to their union. Far from attempting this, the last evangelist has constructed his Gospel into an organic whole, more complete than we obtain from the previous compilers; nor is there the least appearance of his having left large acts of the drama for others to supply. As mere varieties of the same original testimony, these differences are utterly inexplicable. And, if we have to choose between their historical values, the decision can hardly be doubtful. That Jesus of Nazareth should be elevated into Jesus of Jerusalem; that the divine appeal of which he was the organ should shift its scene from provincial villages to the holy city, and test the nation at its responsible centre; that the incarnate Logos should be supposed to present himself, not so much to private peasants, as to the hierarchy, and at the sanctuary which claimed a sort of property in the true God,—this is an intelligible turn which the history might receive, as the theory of the founder's person became strained to higher intensity. But, if he had really devoted his chief efforts to the capital ; if he had seized on festival after festival for the most public proclamation of his divine nature and his authoritative claims ; if he had habitually encountered there those strangely coupled foes of his, the " high priests and Pharisees," and year after year been the object there of wonder, admiration, and conspiracy, —it is impossible that history should forget or suppress all this, and tell us instead that all his brilliant day was spent in Galilee, and only in the evening did he come to Jerusalem to die.

These several features do not encourage us to look for the

fourth evangelist anywhere within the circle of the twelve ; and
against his identification with John in particular special objections force themselves upon us from his recorded character.
The few traits of him which are historically attested would
never help us towards the Christian ideal of the "beloved
disciple." The younger son of Zebedee, he is counted indeed,
with his brother James, as an apostle from the first ; * and
these two, with Peter, appear as selected associates of Jesus in
some of the private moments of his life, e.g., when called to
raise the daughter of the synagogue ruler,† and on the Mount
of Transfiguration : ‡ and their mother, presuming on this
more intimate relation, tried to bespeak on their behalf the
chief seats in Messiah's kingdom.§ This daring request, to
which the answer of Jesus shows that they were parties, was
not out of keeping with the stormy, self-asserting nature
which made Jesus call them "sons of thunder ; "‖ which
impelled them to invoke fire from heaven on an inhospitable
village of Samaria ;¶ and led John to put an interdict on a
seeming disciple, because he did not join their company.**
After the departure of Jesus, John, still the companion of
Peter,†† selected Jerusalem for his field of labour, quitting it
only on a short excursion to Samaria ;‡‡ and, as late as the
year A.D. 50, he is found by Paul to be one of the "seeming
pillars" of the disciples' church there,§§ though by outside
observers he is regarded as an " unlearned and obscure " man.
Slight as these hints are, they present to us the picture of a
man fiery in temperament, not ashamed of intolerant anger and
even exclusive ambition, entirely preoccupied with Messianic
expectations, and a trusted representative of the Judaic section
of the Christian Church.

C. *Relation to the Apocalypse.*

If these traits of character and this cast of imagination are
reversed in the Evangelist they are exaggerated in the Seer
of the Apocalypse. And if, in conformity with tradition, wo

---

* Matt. iv. 21 ; x. 2. Mark i. 19 ; iii. 17. Luke vi. 14.   † Mark v. 37.
‡ Matt. xvii. 1 ; Mark ix. 2 ; Luke ix. 28.   § Matt. xx. 20.
‖ Mark iii. 17.   ¶ Luke ix. 54.   ** Mark ix. 38.
†† Acts iii. 1 ; iv. 13, 19.   ‡‡ Acts viii. 14.   §§ Gal. ii. 9.

might resort to that work in order to complete our picture of the Apostle, the lineaments, as they sketched themselves in, might more strongly define the John of the synoptics, but would utterly efface the image of the fourth evangelist. Never will the same mind and hand produce two such books, till " all things are possible " to men as well as " to God."

If this were all, we should only be driven to make a choice, and, probably at the cost of the gospel, save the Revelations for the Apostle. Yet this we cannot do, consistently with the story of his exile in the Domitian persecution, A.D. 95, and his return to Ephesus under Nerva's mild reign, commencing the next year. The Apocalyptic visions thus fall in the tenth decade of the first century. Yet from some of them we learn, in express terms, that they were written fourteen or fifteen years earlier, prior to Domitian's accession to the purple. In ch. xiii., the composite beast, made up of leopard, lion, bear, with seven heads and ten diademed horns, represents imperial Rome; the seven heads doubly symbolizing, as explained in xvii. 9, her seven hills and first seven emperors; in the latter sense, being regarded as successive, so that each in turn is identified with the whole organism and called " the beast." Of these seven heads it is said,* " The five are fallen ; the one is ; the other is not yet come ; and when he cometh, he must continue a little while. And the beast (i.e., the head) that was, and is not, is himself also an eighth, and is of the seven ; and he goeth into perdition." It is of the *fifth* that these enigmatical things are spoken ; somewhat less darkly hinted in the corresponding words, " I saw one of the heads as though it had been smitten unto death : and his death-stroke was healed."† The fifth Roman Emperor was Nero, abhorred by Jews and Christians. Deposed in June, A.D. 68, and flying from his pursuers, he died by his own hand, and that of his freed man Epaphroditus: but though his funeral was public, a strange belief got hold of the popular imagination that he had not really died,: but had found refuge among the Parthians beyond the Euphrates, and would reappear to take vengeance on his

* xvii. 10, 11.   † xiii. 3.
: Tac. Hist. II. 8. Dio. Cass. 63, 64. Sueton. Nero, 57.

Western enemies and the city of the seven hills. There were not wanting pretenders to take advantage of this belief; one of whom found followers enough to raise a formidable Parthian war, after the rumour had run through ten futile years. The Apocalypse is not the only book on which it has left its trace. In the Ascension of Isaiah (a Christian production of probably the second century) occurs a prediction that Belial will appear in the form of a godless *matricide* of a king, who will rule for three years, seven months, and twenty-seven days (Daniel's 1335 days, and the forty-two months of Revelation xiii. 5), and then be thrown into Gehenna by God and his angels.* And in the Sibylline Oracles† Nero is described thus : " Then will a mighty king fly unexpectedly out of Italy, unheard of, like a meteor, beyond the Euphrates, after perpetrating the atrocious guilt of matricide, and with wicked hands committing many other crimes." And then a few lines further on,‡ he thus reappears : " But the conflict of raging war will then come to the West ; and the fugitive from Rome will also come thither with lifted spear across the Euphrates with many myriads of allies."

To complete the identification of the wounded head with Nero, the author goes as near as he can to spelling his name ; taking its component letters, only not in their *phonetic* but in their *numerical* function, and, while hiding their series, reporting their sum, " the number of the man " as 666. For a reason which will presently appear, he works out the total from the *Hebrew* spelling; the successive letters of which (answering to *Cæsar-Nero*) stand for the numbers 100 + 60 + 200 + 50 + 200 + 6 + 50 = 666.

This fifth head, then, of heathendom, was to have his "second coming," like the crucified and risen king of saints ; and, at that coming, was to consummate his blasphemies and play the part and suffer the doom of Antichrist. He would belong to the crisis of " Last Kings," and when his term was over, would leave no successor. There were but seven heads, and when the seventh had fallen, Rome would be no more.

---

* xii. 2. † B. IV. 119, written probably A.D. 79-80.
‡ Sib. Or. IV. 137.

A Western writer possessed by this prophetic vision might find his reckoning at a loss during the confused eighteen months which followed Nero's fall. For seven of them only, Galba exercised a precarious authority; and for the rest Otho and Vitellius received but partial allegiance, so that the whole term is described by Suetonius as a *rebellio trium principum*, and they were never counted as emperors in the East. To a writer, therefore, in Asia Minor Vespasian would be the sixth, and when he says "five have fallen, one *is*," it is within *his* reign that he declares himself to stand, i.e., between A.D. 69 and 79. He is on the look-out for "the other," that "is not yet come, and when he cometh, must continue a little while." But that "other" will be the seventh and last; and is not that place reserved for the returning Nero? and has not the "little while" of his continuance been defined as forty-two months, or three and a half years?* So apparently has the prophecy hitherto run: invented and delivered under the Prince who succeeded the fallen fifth, it had to take account of a sixth: but on no seventh would it venture other than the returning blasphemer, who was to close the series and hasten the world's catastrophe. A Seer, possessed by the current belief and writing under the sixth "head," would have nothing in view beyond but the conflicts which ushered in "the end of all things." Yet, to our surprise, the next words to the passage just quoted introduce us to "*an eighth*" : "The beast (i.e., the head) that was and is not is himself also an eighth, and is of the seven. And he goeth into perdition."† A writer under Vespasian who could say this must have reckoned on Titus ("the other not yet come") succeeding his father, and "continuing but a little while" (A.D. 79–81). If we think this more than we learn from Daniel, and take it rather as a *vaticinium post eventum*, may we not say that it looks like a correction of a disappointed prophecy, intended to make room for its proving right after all? There was always an ambiguity in the reckoning of the seven heads, caused by the double apparition of Nero among them. Were we to count *persons*? or, to count *reigns*? seven persons, with one taken twice over, would give eight reigns. Of this ambiguity

* xiii. 5.   † xvii. 11.

advantage is taken by the interpolating writer of xvii. 11, to explain away the non-appearance of Nero at the date when he was due, viz., at the fall of the sixth head, Vespasian. The seventh place was filled, not by the convulsions of the advancing Antichrist, but by the tranquil two years of Titus, the *deliciæ humani generis;* had not then the prophecy failed?   Not so, was the reply: this is but the seventh *reign* that is now consummated, " continuing for a little while," exactly as was said ; and it is of seven *chiefs* that the prophecy speaks, and *their* story is not yet told to the end : for one of them who has vanished midway has yet " to be revealed in the last time," and he will supply an eighth chapter to the history, though himself the fifth of their number.   The author of this verse, by his recognition of Titus' reign, betrays his date, as not that of Vespasian's writer.   If assigned to A.D. 81, prior to the accession of Domitian, he would probably be looking for the literal fulfilment of the Neronic prediction.   If to a later time, when the detested brother of Titus had revealed his character, he may conceivably have been content with a figurative interpretation, and, regarding Domitian as an *alter Nero*, have identified their personalities, for the purposes of the prophecy, as indistinguishable incarnations of Belial.   But this interpretation, though favoured by Weizsäcker,* seems hardly to satisfy the condition that " the eighth is to be one of the seven."   Resemblance to another is not self-identity.

The dates which the text itself thus supplies for its own composition lie between A.D. 69 and 79, with a supplementary comment extending to a couple of years further.   If, instead of stepping on to Vespasian, we accept Galba as the *sixth* " head," the only difference will be that the former date must be thrown back and compressed within the concluding half of A.D. 68.   Yet, according to the Patmos and Johannine tradition, the visions themselves were not experienced till about A.D. 95.

Nor are there wanting other traces of a no less early chronology.   At the opening of the eleventh chapter the Seer

* Das apostolische Zeitalter d. christ. Kirche. v. Karl Weizsäcker.   S. 518, 519.

in his vision is sent with a surveyor's rod to the beleaguered
Holy City, with commission to measure the Temple and the
Altar and the Worshippers assembling there, but not the
outer court; for that is given up, along with the city, to be
trodden down by the Gentiles for forty-two months. The
purpose of this ideal survey evidently is to mark off the
sacred area which, under Divine protection, is to remain
inviolate, from the environment already abandoned to desolation. The passage transports us to the penultimate stage of
Jerusalem's defence against Titus, before the zealots had
driven matters to the last despair, or the thought had become
possible that the Temple was to fall. In the autumn of A.D.
70, however, it had fallen; and the prophet who could give
it assurance against such fate, and even promise the cleansing
of its outer court in three and a half years, must have written
his word several months before.*

If here the record of the Seer's visions proves its existence
twenty years before the alleged date of their occurrence,
elsewhere it betrays its origin just as long after he had left
the world. The signs of such later date are not indeed as
simple and exact as the marks of time furnished by the
succession of the Cæsars. Being read off, not from the
biography of persons or the chronology of events, but from
gradual changes in the usages of language, the development
of doctrine, and the constitution of societies, they speak with
their full force only to those who are familiar all through with
the special lines of growth on which they stand. In appropriating their meaning, others must needs take something on
trust. When a reader conversant with the early Christian
literature comes upon the words, " I was in the Spirit on the
Lord's Day," his attention will be arrested at once by the
phrase *ἐν τῇ κυριακῇ ἡμέρᾳ*, an ecclesiastical name for Sunday
which, like the term *καθολικὴ ἐκκλησία*, occurs for the first
time in the Ignatian Epistles;† and carries us into the
middle of the second century. Elsewhere in the N. T. the
day is known as "the *first* day of the week";‡ in the Epistle of

* See this interpretation extended to other parts of the same-chapter in
Die Entstehung der Apokalypse, v. Dr. Daniel Voelter, 2te Aufl. pp. 58, 59.
  † Magnes. ix.   ‡ Acts xx. 7.   1 Cor. xvi. 2.

Barnabas,* and the writings of Justin Martyr, as "the *eighth day*," or, as "the so-called day of the Sun."† That, when once introduced, it passed into rapid currency is evident from the disappearance in it of the word ἡμέρα, and the retention of κυριακὴ alone as a noun, as in the "Teaching of the Twelve Apostles," and later writings of the second century.

Nor can the attentive reader fail to notice an extension of the familiar predicates of Messiah introduced with an air of mystery betokening something both unexpected and significant. The secret is but hinted at in the message to the church at Pergamum.‡ "To him that overcometh will I give of *the hidden manna*, and I will give him a white stone, and upon the stone *a new name written* which no one knoweth but he that receiveth it." For the symbol of this esoteric wisdom we have to wait till "the Faithful and True," who sends the message, appears on "a white horse," followed by "the armies which are in heaven, upon white horses, and clothed in fine linen, white and pure." "He hath a name written which no one knoweth but he himself." Yet the Seer is an exception; for he adds, "His name is called the Word of God."§ The writer of these passages obviously stands at the initial stage of an expanding Christology, nutritive perhaps as "bread from heaven," but not yet palatable except to a few who had felt its power to stay their spiritual hunger. That Christ is here called "the Word of God," in the full sense of the Logos doctrine, I do not affirm. The phases of that doctrine, in the Book of Wisdom, in Philo, and in the Hellenized Christianity of the Alexandrine school, are various and progressive. But the appropriation of its characteristic predicate to the Christ of the Apocalypse certainly assigns the writer to the post-apostolic period in which the conceptions of the school first gained a hold in Asia Minor.

Nor can we find the heresies which are denounced, any more than the Christology which is implied, at an earlier date than the fourth decade of the second century. The letters to the seven churches contain warnings against several varieties of pernicious error. However difficult it may be to fit

* xv. ad fin.† Apol. 67, Tryph. 24, 41.
‡ ii. 17.§ xix. 11-13.

each descriptive term—"Nicolaitans," "the teaching of Balaam", "the woman Jezebel who calleth herself a prophetess", "the synagogue of Satan", to precisely its intended personage or type, the characteristics condemned, the lapse from self-denying faith, the ungodly carelessness, the concessions to heathen dissoluteness (even to "the exploring of the depths of Satan"), the inward alienation from the spirit of Him that is Holy and True,—all point to the gnosticism of Carpocrates and Basilides, with its orgiastic variations in the usages of Phrygia. The Pauline antithesis of Law and Gospel pressed to its extreme and unintended consequences, assumed with them the form of absolute antinomianism, treating all moral distinctions as illusory, and resolving the ideal life into unrestricted freedom. Christianity, instead of being the development and fulfilment of the Jewish religion, involved a total breach with its fundamental principle of *Righteousness*. The Old Testament system was the Revelation of a lower or demiurgic nature; while the Christian worship is directed to the Highest God, who is above the distinction of good and evil, and is best served by those to whom "all things are pure." Marcion, like Paul, saved his protest against legalism from giving any excuse for licence. But in the schools most prevalent in Asia Minor, about A.D. 130–140, the antinomian theory of indifference undoubtedly led to the practical libertinism which is so vividly painted in the letters to the churches.

Combining these several marks of time, we find in the Apocalypse passages which cannot have been later than the seventh decade of the first century, and others that cannot have been earlier than the fourth decade of the second century. The irresistible inference, viz., that the book is a composite product, made up of contributions from several hands, moulded by a final editor, was announced in 1882, and supported with remarkable critical skill, by Dr. Daniel Voelter, a Privat-docent in Tübingen, in a Treatise* which, though destined to be superseded, will always mark an epoch in the true interpretation of the Apocalypse. On one point only Voelter adheres to the older criticism : all the components of the book

---

* Die Entstehung der Apokalypse: 2te Aufl. 1885.

are " *Jewish-Christian* " ; and it is just here that his position is already shaken, and *that* by the independent labours of a still younger theologian.   This ulterior movement cannot be better described than by the distinguished Professor, Adolf Harnack, its first witness and generous reporter.   In commending to the reader the Essay by his pupil, Eberhard Vischer, of which the title is given below,* he says :—

" In June last year, the author of the foregoing treatise, then a student in Theology at our University, came and told me that in working at the theme prescribed for his department, ' On the theological point of view of the Apocalypse of John,' he had found no way through the problem but by explaining the book as a Jewish Apocalypse with Christian interpolations, set in a Christian frame.   At first he met with no very gracious reception from me.   I had at hand a carefully prepared Lecture Heft, the result of repeated study of the enigmatic book, registering the opinions of a host of interpreters from Irenæus downwards : but no such hypothesis was to be found among them : and now it came upon me from a very young student, who as yet had made himself master of no commentary, but had only carefully read the book itself.   Hence my scepticism was intelligible : but the very first arguments, advanced with all modesty, were enough to startle me; and I begged my young friend to come back in a few days and go more thoroughly with me into his hypothesis.   I began to read the Apocalypse with care from the newly-gained point of view ; and it was—I can say no less—as if scales fell from my eyes. After the too familiar labours of interpreters on the riddle of the book, the proffered solution came upon me as the egg of Columbus.   One difficulty after another vanished, the further I read ; the darkest passages caught a sudden light; all the hypotheses of perplexed interpreters—of ' proleptic visions,' ' historical perspectives,' ' recapitulating method,' ' resting stations,' ' recreative points,' ' unconscious relapse into purely Jewish ideas,' melted away at once; the complex Christology of the book, hitherto a veritable *crux* for every historical critic, resolved itself into simple elements, and the

* Die Offenbarung Johannis eine Jüdische Apokalypse in Christicher Bearbeitung; mit einem Nachwort von A. Harnack. 1886.

sections, XI. XII., by far the most difficult of all, at once became plain and intelligible. But, above all, the severance of a Jewish original text from a Christian redaction resolved the main problem of the Apocalypse of John, viz., the peculiarity of the author's Christianity. What pains have been spent upon this question for the last ten years! What arguments of high repute lent support to those who held the book to be strictly Jewish-Christian, and therefore anti-Pauline, and yet how easily were they refuted by other proofs drawn from the book itself! How plainly might the author's Christian universalism be proved; and what insuperable considerations presented themselves against it! Vischer's hypothesis removed these difficulties at a stroke. There can be no further question of a Jewish Christianity. We have before us, as the basis of the work, a purely Jewish document, clearly traceable in its outlines and the mass of its details, supplemented and revised by a Christian, who has nothing whatever to do with the Ἰσραήλ κατὰ σάρκα, but thinks only of the Gentile world, out of which the Lamb has purchased with his blood a countless multitude."*

In this generous tribute to his pupil, Harnack does not, in my judgment, overestimate the convincing effect of his analysis.

After indicating the lines of cleavage between the original text and the recension throughout the book, and accounting for each interpolation, Vischer exhibits the results in a reprint of the entire Jewish part, extending from iv. 1 to xxii. 5, with the Christian insertions rendered conspicuous by different type: followed by an Appendix, containing the first three chapters and the Epilogue xxii. 6-21, which form the Christian framework of the whole. The effect of this recast of the composition is most striking. For a reader who is at all conversant with the Jewish apocalyptic literature the impression can scarcely fail to be irresistible, that the prophetic oracle which has darkened so much has at last revealed its own origin.

It does not follow, from the mixture of the two elements, that the work is due to only two contributors, and referable only to two times. From the second century B.C. the Jewish

---

* Vischer's Offenb. Joh. Nachwort, S. 126, 127.

eschatology was ever producing fresh varieties of vision ; and the play of Christian fancy upon them fitted them with new meanings for new times.   Reasons which it would need a complete commentary to set forth warrant the conclusion that the Judaic groundwork owes part of its text to the zealot period of the first Jewish war, A.D., 66–70, and part to a time about eight years later ; and that the Christianized recension shows the hand of two editors, one, in Domitian's time, responsible for all the twenty-nine passages speaking of " *The Lamb*," the other, belonging to Hadrian's reign, answerable for the letters to the churches, as well as for the introduction and conclusion of the whole work.   It cannot therefore have been issued before A.D. 136, and is altogether post-apostolic. How strange that we should ever have thought it possible for a personal attendant on the ministry of Jesus to write or edit a book mixing up fierce Messianic conflicts, in which, with the sword, the gory garment, the blasting flame, the rod of iron, as his emblems, he leads the war-march, and treads the wine-press of the wrath of God till the deluge of blood rises to the horses' bits, with the speculative Christology of the second century, without a memory of his life, a feature of his look, a word from his voice, or a glance back at the hillsides of Galilee, the courts of Jerusalem, the road to Bethany, on which his image must be for ever seen !

What then is the effect of the new discovery (if such it be) respecting the Apocalypse on the question of authorship for the fourth Gospel ?   Simply this : the Apocalypse is put out of court altogether as a witness in the case.   Stripped of its own apostolic pretension, it has nothing to say either for or against that of the Gospel : and the old argument against either from its violent contrast with the other can no longer be pressed.   Deprived of this source of comparison, we return to the purely internal features of the Gospel, so far as they bear on the probable authorship.

D. *Relation to the Paschal Controversy.*

Among the peculiarities of the fourth Gospel there is one which seems to displace the author both from the list of Apostles, and from his traditional residence and authority at Ephesus. His reports of events in the Passion week is inconsistent with the Synoptic narrative, whose source must be regarded as apostolic. And his interpretation of their meaning is at variance with their memorial celebration in the churches of Asia Minor. It will be simpler to take the latter discrepancy first. To render it clear, some account must be given of the controversy about Easter, which preceded the establishment of the present church calendar.

There is no reason to believe that in the earlier half of the second century the Western Christians observed *any annual festival at all.* Justin Martyr, writing in Rome, and professing to give to the Emperor a complete account of the Christian usages,* mentions only baptism, the eucharist, the Sunday assembly; and is silent about any Christmas, Easter, or Whitsuntide. Their commemorations went by the week, not by the year; and within the week, Wednesday and Friday (the latter especially) were kept as fast-days (*stationes*),† in memory of the sufferings of Christ; but, above all, Sunday, as the festival of the resurrection. The attitude of the early Christians was altogether prospective, on the watch for the return of Christ and the last act in the drama of human things; and the tension of this amazing expectation was inconsistent with the commemorative mood, which sees its brightest glories in retrospect, and repeats them as beacon-lights to intersect the routine of future years. But when the world had sufficiently vindicated its permanence, and it seemed settled that Christ was to remain in heaven, and his church to organize itself below, disappointed prophecy withdrew, and historical veneration came to the front, eager to save the Christ of the past, in proportion as the form dissolved away of Christ in the near future; and the same portion of the second century which discredited Chiliasm, and threw it into the shade, concentrated interest upon the earthly life of Christ, and created the anniversaries which celebrated its main epochs. Especially was the desire felt to emphasize *that one* of the weekly resurrection days which fell nearest

* Apol. I. c. 65 *seqq.*
† Hermæ Pastor, Simil. v.; and Tertull. de Jejun. 11.

in season to the original event; and how to hit upon this with the requisite precision became a question. In the history, that week was picked out from all the weeks of the year, by the occurrence of the passover; and the passover was a spring festival, determined in date by the equinoctial full moon, which marked the mid point (or fourteenth day) of the first Jewish (lunar) month, Nisan. Here, then, without consulting any rabbi or submitting to his law, was a conspicuous astronomical event which detected the *right week;* and the rule emerged, that the Sunday next after that particular full moon should be *Easter Sunday.* This was the regulative day: from this, the reckoning was taken backward to the previous Friday, in order to alight upon the memorial day of the crucifixion; which was chiefly kept by intensifying the usual weekly fast, prolonging it through the time when Christ was in the sepulchre, and terminating it only with Easter morning communion. Thus the Western usage established an anniversary *week*, rather than an anniversary *day*, and, when the full moon came, paid no attention to it, but waited for the following Sunday; refusing to disturb the incidence of the passion and the resurrection on the original week-days which witnessed them, although if they had been brought on at the passover of some earlier or later year, they would have fallen on other days than the sixth and the first.

In Lesser Asia, the consuetudinary rule had formed itself in a different way. The Christians there had never, from the first, been without an *annual* festival; nor had they to find for themselves the right date on which to hold it; for what they meant to keep was just the passover which, according to the synoptists, their Master had kept with his apostles; and that must be found, as he had found it, by the Jewish rule, and always fall upon the 14th of the spring lunar month. As the moon in her fulness pays no regard to the days of the week, but in a series of years looks down on every one, the paschal observance shifted through them all, and had no preference for one above the rest. Hence it might happen that in Asia Minor the commemorative season was over before it had begun in Italy; and, while the West was bending in the most solemn worship of the year, the churches across the

Ægean had resumed their routine again.   Thus there was no *Good Friday* among these Eastern Christians, no *Easter Sunday;* nor was the primary object of their commemoration either the *crucifixion* or the *resurrection,*—to which these were respectively dedicated,—but the *Last Supper,* which was their prelude, and stood for the disciples as the dividing mark between the earthly ministry and the heavenly retirement of their Master.   And upon this feature depends another difference between the West and the East.   That paschal supper, which was the uppermost thought with the latter, was a *feast* of thankfulness and joy; and, as soon as its celebration came, the *fast* which preceded it was ended, and the regimen of austerity was dismissed, just at the time when the former, contemplating only the dark hours of the cross and the sepulchre, imposed a rigorous self-denial, and filled the churches with plaintive prayer, refusing to dissolve the fast till the resurrection morning broke.   Thus the Asiatics simply continued the Jewish usage, importing into it Christian memories and ideas; not of course unmindful of the Master's death and resurrection, but concentrating the remembrance of them into *one* commemoration copied from the night of forecast and of parting, when the catastrophe waited only for the morrow, and its reversal for the next sabbath's close.   With what observances these Christians celebrated their paschal days; whether they actually imitated the Jewish rite and partook together of the lamb, or merely administered the eucharist with some special solemnities, there is no distinct evidence to show.   Certain it is that in some Eastern Churches the former practice prevailed for many centuries; but a usage so strongly at variance with the customs of the West could hardly have escaped mention and protest in the controversies of the time, had the Romans been able to charge it upon their opponents. Probably, therefore, there was only a communion service of exceptional sanctity.

Divested of its accessories, the question in dispute fell into this form, Are we to celebrate the *passover* which Jesus kept with his disciples the day before he suffered, or his *sufferings* which followed?   And, if the latter, what *paschal* character has our celebration?

Of this dispute vestiges remain to us from three of its stages; in which the opposite sides were represented, first by Polycarp of Smyrna, and Anicetus, Bishop of Rome (about A.D. 160); next by Melito of Sardes, and Apollinaris of Hierapolis (about A.D. 170); and lastly, by Polycrates of Ephesus, and Victor, Bishop of Rome (about A.D. 190). Of these, Apollinaris alone gives us any clear insight into the pleas, other than of example and authority, urged on either side. Notwithstanding his geographical position, he supported the Western usage, adducing on its behalf a consideration which, repeated as it is by Clement of Alexandria and Hippolytus, was evidently the *stock-argument* of the Roman party. It takes us at once to the point where the kernel of the problem lies. The contention of his opponents, he tells us, is that "on the 14th of Nisan the Lord ate the lamb with his disciples, and on the next day, the great day of unleavened bread, himself suffered," and they appealed to Matthew in proof. Against this he advances his own position, that "the genuine passover, the great sacrifice, is the Son of God instead of the lamb, the bound captive who binds the strong one, the judge who judges quick and dead,—from whose pierced side flow the two purifiers, water and blood, and who was entombed on the paschal day."* Hippolytus places the two opinions in still stronger antithesis. The Christian of Asia Minor, he tells us, puts his case thus: "Christ kept the passover, and then next day he suffered: therefore it is my duty to do as the Lord did." To which Hippolytus replies, "He is mistaken, being unaware that, at the season of his passion, Christ did not eat the legal passover, being himself the passover of promise that fulfilled itself on the prescribed day." Again, "He partook indeed of *a supper* before the passover; but the passover he did not eat: instead of this he suffered. Not even was it the time for eating it."†

Nothing can be clearer than that the two parties here represented were at issue upon a question of historical fact,— the Quartodecimans affirming, the Westerns denying, that

---

* Chron. Pasch. p. 14. Ed. Bonn : more fully cited ap. Hilgenfeld's Pascha-Streit der alten Kirche, p. 256.

† Chron. Pasch. p. 12.

Jesus kept the last passover with his disciples: both appealing to the "Gospel;" the former, by name, to Matthew; the latter, by citation and allusion (observe the pierced side, the blood and water, the entombment on the paschal day, the supper *before* the passover, the time for eating it not having come, the passion on the paschal day and as the fulfilment of the typical rite), to the fourth evangelist; thus establishing, as Apollinaris himself remarks, *a variance* between the Gospels.*

That variance is no perverse invention of either party. It plainly exists, and survives all the good offices of indefatigable harmonists. The case stands thus. The Gospels all agree in their *hebdomadal* chronology of the passion; that Jesus was crucified on the Friday; that he held a last supper with his disciples on the Thursday; that he rose from the dead on the following Sunday: nor have any critics with whom we are here concerned ever doubted their unanimity in this program.† But to these dates the synoptists fit the numerical days *of the month* differently from the fourth evangelist; letting the 14th (with its passover in the evening), which he identifies with the Friday, fall already upon the Thursday. The evidence of this discrepancy is of the simplest and most conspicuous kind: the paschal meal is declared by the synoptists to be the Thursday's supper, and to be over, therefore, before the crucifixion; by the fourth evangelist to be due on the Friday evening, and therefore to be still to come at the hour of Christ's passion. When the day came (says Luke) for the passover to be killed, Jesus sent Peter and *John*, saying, " Go and make ready for us the passover, that we may eat it": these disciples having carried out their instructions, and " made ready the passover," he placed himself at table, when the hour came, with the twelve apostles, and said, " I have earnestly desired to eat this passover with you before I

---

* σταστάζειν δοκεῖ κατ᾿ αὐτοὺς τὰ εὐαγγέλια. Chron. Pasch. p. 14.

† Dr. Sears attributes to the "Tübingen critics" the opinion that the fourth evangelist "places the crucifixion on Thursday," and the supper on Wednesday. This misapprehension runs through his whole Appendix on the Easter Controversy, and renders its reasoning a labour in vain. " The fourth Gospel," &c., p. 537.

suffer." * This, at all events, is unambiguous. The fourth
evangelist, on the other hand, in citing the symbolic proof of
love,—the washing the disciples' feet,—which Jesus gives at
the last supper, places it still *before* the feast of the passover.†
When Jesus, still at table, addressed a few words to Judas
Iscariot, after giving him the sop, he was supposed, by some of
the twelve, to be ordering the purchase " *of things needful for
the feast.*"‡ In the early morning following, Jesus being
brought up for examination before Pilate, his Jewish accusers
will not enter the prætorium, lest they should *disqualify themselves for eating the impending passover.*§ At noon, when Jesus
is delivered up to be crucified, the day is again defined as the
" *preparation day for the passover.*" ‖ Again, in the afternoon,
provision is made for removing the bodies before sunset,
that they might be out of the way before the Sabbath began :
for " that *sabbath was a great day;* " why? because it was not
only an ordinary sabbath, but the first day of the feast, the
paschal day, which had a special sanctity. And why does the
evangelist lay solemn emphasis on the fact that the *crurifra-
gium* was not applied to Jesus? Because in him is thus
literally fulfilled the law of the passover that "not a bone
shall be broken"; and he became in this, as in the hours of
his doom to death and of his execution, the Lamb of God, the
fulfilment of all passovers.¶ And here comes out, unmistakably, the doctrinal conception which underlies the writer's
historical variation from his predecessors. He is possessed all
through with the idea that Jesus was the true paschal lamb ;
and that the story of his life and death must be so presented
as, by its mystical conformity with the paschal ritual, to
declare him the corresponding antitype. In this interest it is
that he fixes the anointing of Jesus by the woman of Bethany

* Luke xxii. 7-14. Compare Matt. xxvi. 17-20 ; Mark xiv. 12-17.

† In spite of the tangled construction, which would allow πρὸ τῆς ἑορτῆς
to be attached as a date to any one of several nearer words, the meaning of
the whole passage evidently requires this initial phrase to be held on till the
action of taking the towel and basin is reached (xiii. 4, 5 ; 1-5).

‡ John xiii. 29.

§ John xviii. 28.

‖ John xix. 14. The attempt to make out that παρασκευή means Friday,
and πάσχα Easter week, is a mere subterfuge.

¶ John xix. 36.

—her dedication of him " against the day of his entombment " —" six days before the passover," * i.e., on the 10th of the month, when the Jew was to provide himself with " a lamb without blemish," to be reserved for the paschal day: and perhaps also, that he introduces the mention of " the tenth hour " in connection with the Baptist's words of testimony, " Behold the Lamb of God !" and the visit of the two disciples to see where he dwelt; † for that was the time when the lamb was slain, and became the passover, and the door-posts of the house were sprinkled with its sacred blood.

A minor feature in this discrepancy between the narratives deserves a passing remark. The fourth evangelist will not allow the last supper to have been the passover, which, he tells us, was not due till next day. And who was this fourth evangelist? That very John, we are told, who, with Peter, was charged by his Master with the preparation of that supper as the passover, and who did prepare it accordingly. ‡ Those assiduities of the *apostle* in the guest-chamber it is the main business of the *evangelist* to undo and remove out of the way: how, then, can these two be the same person ?

We find, then, exactly the same variance between the synoptists and the writer of the fourth Gospel which divided the churches of Lesser Asia from the Western Christians in the paschal controversy. And how did they share the evangelical authority between them ? The Asiatics had Matthew and his companions on their side: the Europeans were in accord with both the facts and the doctrine of the last evangelist; and his Gospel, though not at first put forward by them as their authority, is an unanswerable manifesto in their favour.

Yet, if we believe the Irenæan tradition, the author of that Gospel was the very John who had lived and died among the Ionian Christians: whose tomb was at Ephesus; whose name was a sacred word to old and young; and whose mode of life,

---

* John xii. 1-8. As, in the account of the resurrection, Sunday is called the " third day," or " three days " after Friday (Matt. xxvii. 63; Mark viii. 31); so, inversely, would Friday be described as three days before Sunday. Similarly, three days before the 15th would be the 13th; four days, the 12th; five days the 11th; six days the 10th, when the lamb was set apart for its sacred purpose.

† John i. 37-39; Ex. xii. 3-7.   ‡ Luke xxii. 8.

outward look, and casual sayings were the subject of reverential remembrance. Nowhere was he so well known; and the churches of that region declared that they had nothing which they did not owe to him. And, strange to say, they persistently affirmed, at every stage of this controversy, that their paschal usage was what he had taught them, and what he himself had always practised. In a friendly conference at Rome, about A.D. 160, " Anicetus could not induce Polycarp to forego his observance, to which he had always adhered *along with John, the Lord's disciple*, and the other apostles with whom he had associated; nor could Polycarp persuade Anicetus to the observance, bound as he declared himself to be by the usages of his predecessors." * In reply to the same Victor's attempt to enforce a uniform observance of the Western practice, Polycrates vigorously defends his Ephesian Church and its neighbours, by appeal to the authority of their martyrs and spiritual guides. This roll of honour included seven bishops (relations of his own), Melito of Sardes, Polycarp of Smyrna, the apostle Philip in Hierapolis, and his daughters, and " *John, who lay on the Lord's breast*, who became priest, and wore the Petalon": " all these kept the paschal fourteenth day, according to the Gospel." †

Here, then, is the whole authority of the Apostle John, his personal habit, and the usage which formed itself under his influence, brought to bear against the historical statement and doctrinal conception of the fourth Gospel. How could this be, if at Smyrna, at Ephesus, and throughout the region where his name was a power, that Gospel had been current as his legacy, and its representation of the last earthly days of Christ had been received as accredited by him? The features of his life and thought which these traditions preserve are precisely what this Gospel resists and banishes. They give us the seer, and not the evangelist: he is the Chiliast, the Quartodeciman, nay, the priest who wears the sacerdotal headgear,—all of them characters of lingering Judaism, detaining him still among the sacred λαός, and totally at variance with that spiritual humanism, that dislike of " the

---

* Letter of Irenæus to Victor, ap. Eus. Hist. Eccl. V. xxiv. 16.
† Letter of Polycrates to Victor, ap. Eus. Hist. Eccl. V. xxiv. 2-7.

Jews " and leaning to " the Greeks," which pervade the last Gospel.

E. *Marks of Time.*

Not only is the evangelist other than the apostle, and other than the Ephesian John of the Apocalypse: he plainly belongs to another age. He uses a dialect, and speaks in tones, to which the first century was strange, and which were never heard till a generation born in the second was in mid-life. True it is, that period of Christian development is shrouded in impenetrable darkness, and can be interpreted only by a kind of historical divination, comparing its resulting faith with its initial, and supplying the silent and invisible links that must lie between. Were an unexpected sunshine to be shed upon that time of struggling religions and dissolving philosophies, one of the most curious passages of human experience would doubtless be laid open to us. A craving in the Jewish mind to escape the limited service of a national and historic God, and find room for some sacred relations within the wide realm of men and nature ; a craving in the heathen mind to bring the too spacious divineness of the universe nearer home, and see and feel it in contact with human life,—led to their approximation from opposite directions, till, in fields of thought not far apart, they alighted on some mediating conceptions helpful to the desire of both, expanding the religion of the one, concentrating that of the other. Among a host of these abstractions,—σοφία, φῶς, ἀλήθεια, χάρις, πίστις ζωή, δύναμις, ἑστώς, παράκλητος, πλήρωμα,—many were tried, and after playing a brief part, fell into silence, and disappeared ; but there were two which so served the common want as to hold their ground, and give final form to the universality of the Christian faith. The first of these—πνεῦμα—came from the Jewish side, and was especially the vehicle of Paul's ascent from the level of his holy land till his horizon embraced the " circle of the earth ; " and whoever has accompanied the movement of his thought knows how he steers and commands this " chariot of fire," to show him all the abodes of men in the light of comprehensive mercy beneath him. The second,—λόγος—came from the heathen side, and supplied a common term and link of union between the divine and the human nature; first applied by Philo to all the media, whether in the *cosmos*, in history, or in the individual soul, through which God passes from being into manifestation; then incarnated by the Christians in the person of Jesus during the *annus mirabilis* of his ministry on earth. In this form it did not come upon the stage till the middle of the second century; when Christianity, released from its first enemy by the destruction of the Jewish State, turned round to face and to persuade its Pagan despisers, and searched the philosophic armoury for weapons of effective defence; and most of all when converts from heathenism, as Justin Martyr and Athenagoras, addressed themselves on behalf of their adopted faith to those whom they had left behind. From the apostolic age this conception was entirely absent: not a trace of it is to be found in the Pauline letters, which work their way to similar issues by other tracks of thought; and not till we listen to the Apologists in the time of the Antonines does this new language fall upon the ear. It was borrowed from the Greek γνῶσις, so fruitful of speculative systems in that age of peace and letters, and was compelled to take up into its meaning the Christian facts and beliefs. The fourth Gospel breathes the very air of that time: it weds together the ideal abstractions of the Gnostic philosophy, and the personal history of Jesus Christ; and could never have been written till both of them had appeared upon the scene. It is, indeed, itself a Gnosticism, only baptized and regenerate; no longer lingering aloft with the divine emanation in a fanciful sphere of æons and syzygies, but descending with it into a human life transcendent with holy light, and going home into immortality. This internal character assigns the Gospel to the same time which is indicated by the external evidence,—about the fifth decade of the second century.

The distance of this Gospel from the events of which it speaks admits of illustration, and of some approximate measurement, from another point of view. The doctrine respecting the person of Christ passed through three centuries before it reached its acme, and found its definition; the tendency throughout being to invest him with new predicates of the Godhead, till the deification was complete. Of the several stages into which this history divides itself, three at least fall within the limits of our Gospels, and of the literary fragments which stand on the same line with them. They may all of them be regarded as interpretations successively put upon the phrase "*Son of God*," applied to Jesus by his disciples from the moment when they recognized him as the Messiah of prophecy. What was the meaning of this metaphor? of what reality was it the symbol? It plainly attributed a divine element to the nature of Jesus. When did it enter?—and how adjust itself into partnership with his humanity? These were questions irresistibly thrown up by the phrase; never contemplated, indeed, by those who first used it in its stereotyped Jewish sense, but sure to be started as soon as it came with the surprise of freshness upon hearers who had to construe it for themselves. The oldest type of answer to these questions is embodied in the account of the baptism of Jesus; but, in order to see it in its purest form, we must pass behind the synoptists, and consult the "Gospel according to the Hebrews," a fragment of which preserves probably an earlier tradition. There, as in Justin Martyr and in the Acts of Peter and Paul, the heavenly voice addresses Jesus in the Psalmist's words, "Thou art my Son; this day have I begotten thee." For this declaration it is that the heavens are opened, the Spirit descends, and the supernatural light shines upon Jordan.* According to this primitive representation, the investiture with the attribute of *sonship* was reserved for the day of baptism; *then* it was that, with the descent of the Spirit, the divine element entered its human tabernacle, and the heavenly adoption was proclaimed. And this belief long lingered among the Ebionites, who, through the changes of the second and third centuries, still

* See Hilgenfeld, Novum Testamentum extra Canonem receptum: Librorum deperditorum Fragmenta, pp. 15, 33. Compare Adnott. Among the several versions of the heavenly voice, the presumption is strongly in favour of the direct citation of prophecy, as the original form of the tradition. And though Epiphanius had got hold of a later edition of the Ebionite Gospel (for, to omit nothing traditional, it makes the voice say *two* things), this does not impair the probability that it *contains* a representation older than that of Matthew.

represented the faith of the first, and held the simple humanity of Jesus to have been in no way distinguished from that of other men till the act of divine selection and consecration on the banks of Jordan. And whoever opens the Gospel of Mark, and finds that the baptism is with him " the *beginning of the Gospel of Jesus Christ, the Son of God,*" can to this day receive no other impression. Nor can anything be plainer than that the genealogies which give the pedigree of Joseph, and are intended through him to link Jesus with the house of David, must have been drawn up under the influence of this belief as to the conditions that were to meet in Messiah,—an earthly lineage and a heavenly investiture. They supply the human element, to which the events at the baptism add the divine. Not till the second condition followed did the " Son of David " become the " Son of God." To this change the Apostle Paul, who knows nothing of the baptism, and whose faith in Jesus starts from the other end of his career, assigns a different date : with him, it is the *resurrection* which constitutes the heavenly filiation, and in which the Holy Spirit bears its testimony : " Jesus Christ was born of the seed of David according to the flesh ; and declared to be the *Son of God* with power, according to the Spirit of holiness, by his *resurrection from the dead.*"*

So long as the new faith remained only an inner variety of domestic Judaism, and addressed chiefly those whose thought flowed freely into Hebrew moulds, this title " Son of God " would suggest no attribute or function except such as might be conferred at any selected moment of initiation. The national poetry rendered the term familiar in figurative applications, and left no temptation to scrutinize it closely for the detection of lurking mysteries. But, when it fell freshly upon minds less touched by Hebrew custom, it naturally spoke with a different power, and seemed to hint at some divine relation more than official, and beyond the range of conferred credentials. How could " *sonship* " be taken up and laid down ?—how be *given* to one who had it not before ? Did it not belong to the personal identity itself, and determine the very nature from the first ? If a Son of God has lived

* Rom. i. 3, 4.

and moved upon this earth, it could only be from dull eyes that the sacred lineaments have been entirely hid: to a deeper and discerning gaze some exceptional divineness would distinguish him from the common crowd of contemporaries— some visible converse with the invisible, some grace of child-hood, some marvel in his nativity. The working of thoughts like these cannot appear unnatural to any who have studied the history of religion among men; and will readily explain how the original date of Christ's divine filiation was pushed back from his baptism to his birth, and the story arose of his infancy and nativity. In this second type of Christology, the divine and the human are already woven together in the very personality, the divine instead of the manly, and the human of feminine origin; and fore-shadowings of the future mission appear in the premonitions and dropped words of boyhood. Among the "Gospels of the Infancy" which were thus brought into existence, the prefatory chapters of Matthew and Luke are perhaps the most ancient. They could not be pre-fixed, however, to the original baptismal scene without an obvi-ous discordance: if the sonship dated from the nativity, it could not at the baptism be announced as beginning "this day:" and so the phrase from the Messianic Psalm was removed; and in its place the prophetic Spirit supplied the fitter words, "This is my beloved Son, in whom I am well pleased."[*]

But the exigencies of reverential feeling, when once they are allowed to shape history, find no natural point of rest. It was not enough that the divine element in Christ was drawn back from the opening of his ministry to the opening of his life. The story of the miraculous birth is, after all, but a drama, though a sacred one, of *human history:* its scene is laid entirely in this world, and may be found upon the map; and he who thus commences his providential career is, with all the wonders of his infancy, not less a *new* being, fresh to existence, and having to learn all its ways, than

---

[*] Evidently an adapted citation from Isa. xlii. 1, "Behold my servant, whom I uphold; my chosen, in whom my soul delighteth; I lay my spirit upon him,"—a passage which the same Gospel applies to Jesus (Matt. xii. 17). In the baptismal scene *παῖς* becomes *υἱός*, to give expression to the sonship as a permanent fact.

any of his village kindred.   For the human side of him this conception would serve; but can the *divine* be *born?* and shall he whose nature it takes up have no advantage, in his range of being, over the usual measure,—

Οἵη περ φύλλων γενεή, τοιήδε καὶ ἀνδρῶν ;

This could never satisfy a mind trained, directly or indirectly, in the Greek schools, where the distinction between the divine and the undivine is tantamount to that between what *ever is*, and what *comes and goes;* and every higher essence that becomes incarnate is in itself eternal, and though entering and quitting the phenomenal field, neither begins nor ceases *to be.* It was inevitable, that, under the influence of this mode of thought, the sonship to God should yet retreat back another step beyond all temporal limits, and become pre-existent to the whole humanity of Jesus; so that nothing in him should be new to this world, except the corporeal frame and mortal conditions which were needful to his relations with men.   Thus there arises, for the transcendent element in Christ, a history prior to its personal manifestation in Palestine; a " glory before the world was;" an eternity " in the bosom of the Father ; " a subsistence blended in intimate union with God.   And when this transcendent perfection " became flesh," and " dwelt among us, full of grace and truth," it was not to give a mere refinement to a human organism and elevation to a human character, but to manifest, under the disguise and amid the shadows of a life like ours, the light of a divine nature belonging to the eternal world ; so that, as he moved along the ways of men, whenever the winds of change and circumstance stirred the folds and parted the garb of his humanity, there was a flash of mystic splendours which kindled the face of disciples, and drove the guilty from his sight.   Such is the being presented to us in the fourth evangelist's figure of Christ, not only in the memorable proem which gives his attributes " before all worlds " and in the origination of all worlds, but in the whole construction of the Gospel where it tells of his sojourn among men.   In what it narrates, in what it utters, in what it suppresses, in the order of its incidents and the tone of its

R

discourses, in its selection of miracles, in its interpretation of the cross and of the resurrection,—the one pervading purpose of the author is to illustrate this loftier theory of the "Son of God." There is no baptismal adoption, only a sign sent for the information of the Baptist. There is no miraculous nativity, as if the heavenly and earthly in him were connate. For the origin of the divine element, we are carried past the banks of Jordan, past the cradle in Nazareth, or the manger at Bethlehem, to "the beginning," which in itself is eternal, and has no beginning.

It is surely not a small interval that separates this third stadium from its antecedents. But, waiving all attempt at nicer measurement, I am content to say, it is at all events greater than could be traversed by a single mind. Who that appreciates the tenacity of religious conceptions can believe that one and the same person could not only live through the genesis of these three successive types of opinion, but himself adopt them all? Yet, if the son of Zebedee were the writer of the Logos Gospel, no less than this would be demanded of our credulity. If this is inadmissible, we must fall back on the real probability, that these three doctrines span no fewer than four generations; and that even the second of them is altogether post-apostolic.

From all quarters, then, does evidence flow in, that the only Gospel which is composed and not merely compiled and edited, and for which, therefore, a single writer is responsible, has its birthday in the middle of the second century, and is not the work of a witness at all. Nor, in the moulding of it, does the author proceed under the control of an historical purpose,—to tell objective facts in the order and the form of the best accredited tradition. His animating motive is *doctrinal*, as he himself declares,*—to convince his readers that Jesus is "the *Son of God*," in the transcendent sense which this phrase bore to his own thought; and he had so long looked at the evangelical biographies through the glorifying haze of that idea, that whatever would not take its richer light dropped into the shade and disappeared, and those elements alone stood out on which the heavenly tints would

* John xx. 31.

lie. As the story had transfigured itself to him, so did he present it transfigured to his readers; in a form true, as he held, with a deeper truth than that of outward circumstance; rendering, if not the very words as they were heard, the inner meaning that they carried; and comprising nothing but that which *might have been*, and the equivalent of which could hardly fail to be, when such a nature was moving on such a scene. This kind of historical drama is full of interest as an exponent of its own time, but is not a new witness for the time of which it speaks.

For our knowledge, then, of the life of Jesus, except so far as certain features of it are assumed in some of the Epistles and the Apocalypse, we are thrown upon the remains of popular tradition collected by our synoptists,—remains which are doubtless rich in fragments original and true, but which are assuredly of mixed character and worth, and cannot pretend to carry the guarantee of known and nameable eye-witnesses. Priceless as sources of probable history, they are unserviceable for a theory of documentary authority.

§ 3. *The Acts of the Apostles.*

The life of Jesus does not exhaust the Protestant sources of authority. Beyond the tragic catastrophe on Calvary, beyond the day of ascension, the divine drama still runs on, and enters upon new acts, with ever widening stage, and scenery more quick to vary. The holy visitant was personally withdrawn; but from his changed abode he still held communion with the " little flock " he had left behind, and sent a guiding inspiration to replace the presence they had lost, to interpret the past they had so little understood, to reveal the future which they were entitled to promise, and "lead them into all truth" related to their immediate needs. This second stadium of supernatural history had for its object the formation of the Christian Church: it crystallized in a sacred society and permanent institution the consecrating influence which for a season had dwelt among mankind, and, by warding off for a while the intrusion of error and infirmity, secured an interior space within which the pure model might compact itself and grow, and leave its image and its record as an ideal for all times.

If the claim of authority is thus to be extended over the apostolic age, so must its credentials; and, for the miraculous phenomena on which it rests, we must repeat the demand for appreciable and unexceptionable testimony, which has already been preferred in the case of the Gospels. Our only historical sketch of Christian affairs in the years succeeding the personal ministry of Jesus is found in the Acts of the Apostles; and on the value of the recitals in that book it depends whether we recognize in the teachings and methods of the primitive church the expression of authoritative inspiration. Who is it, then, that here tells the story of a nascent Christendom ? Does he report his name ? and, if so, does it guarantee the adequacy of his knowledge, and the trustworthiness of his narrative ? Or, if we know not who he is, have we the means of checking and testing any of his statements, so as to gain an approximate measure of the credibility of the rest?

Fortunately, the Book of Acts, from various causes, admits of historical appreciation more readily than the narratives to which it gives the sequel. It is not entirely insulated. It stands in literary relation with the third Gospel, professing to proceed from the same hand, and to continue the same story. It stands in substantive relation to the Pauline letters, telling over again biographical incidents of which the apostle has given his own account, and drawing of him a portraiture which we may compare with his self-presentation. It furnishes a picture of the early Christian community, with the interior life of which every page of the apostle's writings ferments : so that, apart from its occasional points of contact with external secular history, we have resources within the New Testament itself for critically estimating the contents of the book.

A. *Relation to Luke's Gospel.*

The preamble of the work, which addresses it, like the third Gospel, to a certain Theophilus, and refers to his previous reception of just such an account of the ministry of Christ, has naturally linked together tho two writings as successive chapters, from the same hand, of one continuous history. The reality of this relation between them has recently, it is true, been called in question by Scholten, who, finding in tho Gospel a tone of hostility to Jewish Christianity, which has died away in the Book of Acts, refers them to different sources; and will allow to the author of the latter no hand in the former, except as editor and interpolator.* This conclusion, however, seems to overstrain the difference of tendency in the two writings. It is founded on the idea, that, in the early struggle between the Pauline and the Petrine Christianity, the evangelist takes sides with the former, while the author of the Book of Acts balances and reconciles the two. But in fact all that the writer cares about, in either case, is the *universality of the Gospel:* he will not have it limited to Israel, but accessible to the Samaritan and the heathen. Only so far as they infringe this principle, does he disparage the Jewish disciples : only so far as they represent it, does he favour the Pauline school. The Catholicity of the third Gospel seeks no support from the special theology of the apostle of the Gentiles; and that of the Book of Acts is worked out by his predecessors and opponents. The characteristics of both parties are washed out, and a comprehensive unity is sought by condemning or ignoring them as exceptional extremes. No doubt this common preconception works to a different end in the two writings,— in the Gospel, to vindicate the universality of the religion against those who would narrow it; in the Book of Acts, to claim the credit of this universality for both the parties alike, that entered as constituents into the early Church. There is nothing in this difference to require the hypothesis of separate authorship; while the literary evidence, from the complexion of the language, and organism of the style, clearly indicates the action of the same mind and hand.

Admitting, then, on behalf of the Book of Acts, a complete community of interest with the third Gospel, i.e., that it is a

---

* Is der derde Evangelist de Schryver van het boek der Handelingen? Critisch Onderzoek. J. H. Scholten : Leiden, 1873. I have only a second-hand knowledge of this treatise, through German reviews. An abstract of it is given by Hilgenfeld in his Zeitschrift für wissenschaftliche Theologie: 17 Jahrgang. Heft 3, p. 441 *seqq.*

sequel furnished by the same writer, in further prosecution of
the same object, and with no very important interval of
time, we may apply to its case some of the conclusions already
reached in tracing the history of its companion.   The external
testimony which shows us the text of the evangelist in Marcion's hand gives, also, the lower limit to our search for the
later treatise; and the date, which, on internal grounds, we
have assigned to the Gospel, will approximately serve for its
sequel; unless, indeed, its own contents should carry in them
fresh marks of time which oblige us to correct our former cal-
culation in favour of an earlier time.   Such mark of time,
though only of a negative character, some critics have detected
in the entire silence of the book respecting the destruction of
Jerusalem under Titus.   No reader could suspect that the
city, with its temple and its local hierarchy, which supplied
the scene of so many incidents, no longer existed; and, had
they already perished, this calm presentation of them, as
though nothing had happened to them, would have been
impossible, it is said, to the Christian historian.   On this
ground we are asked to fix the publication of his work as early
as the year A.D. 69.*   This argument would apply with some
force to a writer in the reign of Titus, while the fall of Judæa
was still fresh, and, perhaps, to a Jewish Christian writer till
the end of the century.   But the impression of even national
disasters, still more of foreign ones, does not long remain
intense; and in the second generation a Gentile writer
might draw scenes from the life of the sacred city, without
thinking of the siege which it had suffered in the days of his
grandfathers.   Historical silence about particular events is in
itself but poor evidence of literary chronology; for it may
exist either because they have not yet happened, or because
they have happened long enough to be occasionally forgotten.
In the present instance, the latter is plainly the operative
cause.   In the author's earlier production, clear traces appear
that he is already looking back on the destruction of Jerusalem;
for no one who compares the definite words (Luke xxi. 20–24)
about Jerusalem being compassed with armies, and trodden
down by the Gentiles, and her people falling by the edge of

* Schneckenburger, Ueber den Zweck der Apostelgeschichte, p. 231.

the sword, and being dispersed among all nations, with the indefinite description of the future Parusia in which they are imbedded, can fail to see in them a *raticinium post eventum.* It is, indeed, one of the characteristic features of the third Gospel, that, throughout its alleged prophecies of the latter days, " the coming of the Son of man " is disengaged from its immediate connection with the Roman war, and thrown vaguely forward, as the thing signified is separated from the sign; and, though it is still promised within the lifetime of some who had been present at its preaching in Galilee, it is mentioned with an anxious sense of disappointed waiting and delay. It is illustrated by the story of the lord of the vine-yard, who will indeed return, but not till after he has dwelt in a far country "*for a long time.*" * God will assuredly avenge his own elect; but ah! not till he has "*borne long with them,*"—so long as to weary out what faith there is upon the earth.† The disciples must gird themselves up for a patient vigil, and not look for the Deliverer at the opening of the night. The second watch may pass, for aught they know; nay, even the third, ere the sound of his approach is heard; and their blessing lies in their being awake to meet him, however near the morning.‡ It is not to make immediate way for him that Jerusalem is to be trodden down; it is to be handed to Gentiles first: and not till their history is worked out, and their " times fulfilled," will it become the city of the great King.§ This language unmistakably speaks the feeling of almost exhausted patience which marked the years near the border of the two centuries, and refers even the first of our author's productions to the period rather of Trajan than of Titus.

* Luke xx. 9 ; comp. Matt. xxi. 33, where this expression of delay is absent.
† Luke xviii. 7, 8.
‡ Luke xii. 38. How late must be the date which would oppress the writer with the sense of delay we cannot, perhaps, safely infer from his language. But if the term which he thus divides is taken to be the possible lifetime of one of the children whom Jesus blessed (using the measure given in Luke ix. 27), and estimated at eighty remaining years, each of the " watches " (which are quarters) will be twenty ; and three of them, reckoned from the death of Christ, would bring us to about A.D. 95 ; and the fourth would not expire till about A.D. 115. The expression about the watches is not found in Matt. xxiv. 43.   § Luke xxi. 24.

Nor is the Book of Acts itself entirely without indications of age which accord with this estimate. The witnesses against Stephen are made to charge him with ominous prophecies against "the holy place,"—that this Jesus of Nazareth should destroy it, and change the Mosaic customs.[*] The author, who wished to exhibit Stephen as a true prophet, even when misunderstood, would not have ventured on this representation till history had verified the word.[†] There are also traces of an ecclesiastical constitution, and hierarchical ideas, quite out of character with the apostolic age, and belonging to a more advanced religious organization. The imparting of the Holy Spirit is reserved as the exclusive prerogative of the apostles, and cannot take place in Samaria

---

[*] Acts vi. 13, 14.

[†] It is a difficult question what the author could mean in calling these witnesses "*false*"; but certainly he did not intend to disclaim for Stephen words of slight and disparagement with regard to the temple; for the very speech which follows, in reply to the charge, condemns the building of the temple, and contrasts it as the gratuitous attempt of Solomon (vii. 47) to localize the abode of God (οἶκος τοῦ θεοῦ) with the construction, after a divine pattern (vii. 44), of the shifting tabernacle which symbolized the presence of God on every spot (σκηνὴ τοῦ μαρτυρίου). Instead of denying his alleged threats against the temple, the speaker inveighs against its existence as an example of the perversity and violation of covenant which ran through the whole national history. This is virtually to own the charge, and not to refute it. How, then, are the witnesses "*false*"? In two ways:—

1. They represented Stephen as denouncing not only *the temple*, but *the law* (vi. 13): whereas he treats it as divinely given (vii. 53) "by the ministration of angels"; and rests his whole case against the Jewish people on this, that they have never kept the law; but while God has always done, and more than done, his part, they have never been true to theirs.

2. The witnesses, in reporting Stephen's words about the temple, made its threatened destruction the direct act of Jesus of Nazareth, as if it were to proceed from some vengeance of his, and he were personally answerable for it. So far, however, is this from being true, in the writer's estimate, that it is the Jews themselves who are responsible for the inevitable disaster. By their attempt to *appropriate* God, whose essence escapes all exclusive relations, they have rendered it necessary to destroy the stronghold of their unrighteous monopoly, and to carry the divine meaning of the law and the prophets direct to the Gentiles, instead of trusting any longer to the mediation of Israel. The disposition to distinguish between the Old Testament dispensation and the temple, to condemn the latter as a human limitation, but develop from the former the principles of universal religion, is in harmony with the whole theology of the Acts of the Apostles. The phrase "false witnesses," in Matt. xxvi. 60, 61, raises a similar difficulty, which must there be met in a different way.

till Peter or John has gone down to put hands on the
baptized.* The Ephesian disciples are "a flock" under the
pastoral charge of "elders," duly appointed by the Holy
Spirit; and these "overseers" are regarded, not simply as
local administrators, but as office-bearers in a general "*church
of the Lord*, which he has purchased with his own blood."†
This conception of a catholic body, under governance of a
sacred order, and the application to it of the doctrine of
redemption, betrays modes of thought prevailing not before
the end of the first century. The language, also, in which
Paul is made to speak of the theological dissensions which
will break out among the Christians of Asia,—"of grievous
wolves" that will enter the fold, and even rise up from
among themselves, drawing after them a train of followers by
their perverse teachings,‡—suits nothing so well as the outbreak of the Gnostic sects, which so agitated the Church of
the second century. If these are instances of anachronism,
they invalidate, no doubt, the authenticity of the speeches
and narratives in which they are contained. But for this we
are prepared by so conspicuous an example of invention, that
the unwelcome character of the inference cannot excuse any
apologetic colouring of the facts. In the deliberations of the
Sanhedrim on the defiant attitude of Peter and the other
preaching apostles,§ Gamaliel counsels non-interference, and
a surrender of the cause to the judgment of results. He
supports his advice by appeal to two analogous cases which
may serve for precedents; viz., that of the pretender
Theudas, who set up for a prophet, and drew a multitude
after him, with no result but death to himself, and dispersion
to his people; and, "*after this*," of Judas of Galilee, who
raised an insurrection against the Roman assessment under
Quirinus, only to perish, and bring his followers to a ruinous
break-up. Now, these instances, which are expressly cited as
consecutive, occurred in just the opposite order; and that of
Theudas took place under the procurator Cuspius Fadus, in
the reign of Caligula, ten or twelve years after the date of

---

* Acts viii. 14-17.   † Acts xx. 17-28.
‡ Acts xx. 29, 30.   § Acts v. 33-40.

Gamaliel's reported speech.* This positive proof that the address is fictitious cannot but make us less reluctant to accept elsewhere at their proper value slighter indications of the same freedom of invention.

So far, then, there is nothing to prevent the date assigned to the third Gospel serving also approximately for the Book of Acts. But, as the one is a sequel to the other, some interest attaches to the probable interval between them. To guide our judgment here, we have only one uncertain clew. The earlier book closes with a notice of the ascension of Jesus: the later one opens with a more explicit account of the same event. So far as they are in accordance, they might have been written on successive days; but, if they materially differ, time must be allowed for the first type of tradition to be replaced by another; and it is reasonable to say, that, the larger the difference, the longer the time.

The concluding chapter of the Gospel comprises within the compass of a single day everything subsequent to the entombment of Jesus; the resurrection opening the morning, the ascension closing the evening.† The Book of Acts expands this one day into forty, and, for two meetings of the disciples with their risen Master, substitutes an indefinite number of such "infallible proofs" by living intercourse.‡ In the Gospel the ascension is despatched in a phrase ("was taken up into heaven"), supposed by Scholten to be an editorial addition to the original text:§ in the Acts, it is presented with descriptive detail,—the uplifted form, the receiving cloud, the gazing disciples, the white-apparelled angels and their message.‖ The place also, which, in the earlier account, is at Bethany, fifteen furlongs from the city, is shifted to the Mount of Olives, one-third of that distance from Jerusalem.¶

* For Theudas, see Josephus, Ant. XX. v. 1; for Judas, Ant. XVIII. i. 1, 6, XX. v. 2; B. Jud. II. viii. 1. In one of these passages, Josephus happens to mention Judas just after Theudas: is this the source of our author's mistake? It is not the only indication of an apparent acquaintance with Josephus.

† xxiv. 1, 13, 33, 36, 50, 51.　　‡ i. 3.　　§ xxiv. 51.　　‖ i. 9-11.

¶ Luke xxiv. 50; Acts i. 12. It has been said that, Bethany being on the Mount of Olives, the two terms may be used of the same spot. But the additional definition in Acts i. 12 ("distant from Jerusalem a sabbath day's

In both narratives, but more fully in the latter, Jesus enjoins his apostles to await in Jerusalem the descent of the Holy Spirit upon them : and the only new feature in the second recital is this,—that when pressed to say whether, with the descent of the Spirit, will come also his Messianic restoration of the kingdom to Israel, he gives a twofold answer : as for the *season* of the kingdom, he desires them to leave it to God ; as for its *range*, he bids them preach it not to " Israel " alone, but to the ends of the earth.   Need we say that the historian who thus writes is sure of the *universality* of the "kingdom," but has had to put its *date* into the indefinite ?   No usages of regular literature enable us to conceive how a writer could ever give two such reports of the same incident with apparent indifference to their discrepancy.   Had his mind been simply occupied with the historian's proper end, wholly intent on seeing things as they really lie in the past, the phenomenon would have been impossible.   But where an author writes with an object, or under the pre-engagement of a dominant feeling or idea, it is surprising how historical materials, now reduced to a secondary and instrumental place,—still more how tradition that has never firmly set,—may become soft under the pressure of his hand, and mould itself to the shape of his own thought ; and if twice, with different purpose, he should have to work up the same elements to the needful symmetry, they will insensibly take incompatible forms, which he will not care to bring to coalescence.   He cannot, however, be supposed to produce the two representations at once, or close together : there must be time for the impression of the one to grow faint before he can set himself to create the other,—time for a second interest, or drift of feeling, to succeed to the first, and throw itself on some new problem.   In the present case, there is both this inward necessity for time between our author's two works, and also an outward necessity, founded on the modification of the materials with which he had to deal.

Early Christian tradition held together, as two phases of the same event attached to the same day, the resurrection

journey," equal to two thousand paces, or between five and six furlongs), takes us only to the top of the hill, twice as far from Bethany as from Jerusalem.

and the ascension of Christ; and in this form it still appears, as we have seen in the Epistle of Barnabas. So long as this was the case, the reports of appearances on the part of the risen Christ must have been extremely few: accordingly, in Mark there is actually not one;[*] in Matthew, who, with John, knows nothing of the ascension, only two, of which one is subordinate to the other; and, in Luke, only two, on the same day. But as reports accumulated of interviews with Jesus, or visions of him, as far apart as Galilee from Jerusalem, room had to be found for the growing series; and his departure from the world was separated from his resurrection and variously postponed,—eight days for the conversion of Thomas,[†] indefinitely for the scene at the Sea of Tiberias (declared to be the third appearance),[‡] forty days for the "many infallible proofs," and the instructions "respecting the kingdom," which completed the apostles' preparation to become organs of the Holy Spirit. Other causes concurred to throw the ascension forward into a time of its own, and give it prominence as an independent event. In the oldest accounts of the manifestations of Jesus after death, beginning with those of Paul, he is presented in an impalpable or phantasmic form, now as an inward revelation,[§] now as a vision,[‖] or a voice;[¶] and, again, as something that might be mistaken for "a spirit," or open to a doubt;[**] as able to vanish in an instant;[††] as coming through shut doors.[‡‡] This representation seemed to lie too near the borders of possible subjective illusion; it left the means of personal identification obscure or inadequate; and, even apart from the question of evidence, it favoured a *Docetic* view of the person of Christ,—that the divine nature, which lived on earth, and passed into heaven, was other than the man Jesus who died upon the cross, and separated from him on Calvary. In reaction from these dangers, stress would naturally be laid on all reported appearances which carried in them local and personal features, and

---

[*] i.e., excluding the later appendix, which does not belong to the original Gospel, xvi. 9, to the end.

[†] John xx. 26.   [‡] John xxi. 14.   [§] Gal. i. 16.

[‖] 1 Cor. xv. 8.   [¶] 2 Cor. xii. 9.

[**] Luke xxiv. 37; Matt. xxviii. 17.

[††] Luke xxiv. 31.   [‡‡] John xx. 19. 26.

assimilated the risen life to an ordinary human life. The traces of individuality, and even organic continuity, would be collected, and pushed to their furthest consequences ; for, if the sameness were disturbed between the past Jesus and the future Christ, the whole Messianic theory which had been wrought out would break down.   Hence the insistency of the later evangelical records on acts of the risen Christ corrective of the former impression,—on his *eating* with the apostles,* on his offering them his hands and feet to feel,† on his bidding Thomas put his finger into the nail-prints on his hands and the wound in his side.‡   This escape from one difficulty induced, however, another : the human body with which tradition had thus encumbered itself remained as a serious burden on its hands, which had again to be removed by recourse to a physical and visible ascension.   For the growth of belief, often as we may trace the stages of its modification, we have no exact chronometer ; and how long it would require for the faith in the risen Christ to emerge into this stupendous form, it is impossible to define ; but certainly it could not be till the supposed witnesses were beyond the reach of questioning, and the conception of his heavenly life and expected return had so fastened itself in the scenery of the Christian's real world as to render easy the insertion of this one link of marvel more. Our author, therefore, is dealing, in his second work, with far later elements of tradition than in his first.

The relative age of his materials, however, is not necessarily that of his own later work upon them ; indeed, he incorporates with the Acts of the Apostles large portions of a traveller's journal, evidently proceeding from some companion of Paul, and so mingles in the same production the newest and the oldest records of Christian things.   But some further light on the relation of the two books may, perhaps, be gained by comparison of their characteristic aim and ruling idea.

Christianity, in its primary spring, is the power of a unique personality.   That power, exercised upon minds pre-occupied with Jewish conceptions, inevitably burst into a belief, not realized, it is probable, till after the departure of Jesus, that

<hr>

* Luke xxiv. 43.   † Luke xxiv. 39.   ‡ John xx. 25-27.

he would prove to be the promised Messiah, the inaugurator of the kingdom of heaven upon earth. Looking back upon the marvellous year which had wrapped them in a trance of reverence, and suffusing with new love and sorrow that gracious and majestic presence, his disciples could not but think, that, though he was not yet Messiah, he was marked out to be so : that his past life was but a preluding disguise ; and that the real history enfolded within him was yet in reserve. That death could not detain, but only glorify him ; that he was on its brighter side, and on the eve of returning thence to bring in the consummation of human history, speedily became their fixed conviction. This persuasion, however, did not fit in with the established program of the "last days" and encountered the strongest resistance from minds unsoftened by the personal impression of the great Teacher's life. No apocalyptic dream, no writing accepted as a divination, had ever presented Messiah, except as invested from the first with attributes of splendour, and functions of power. To other men of God, to prophets who foretold him, and warned the people to repent betimes, suffering and ignominy might attach, and even martyrdom be assigned ; but that the last elect of God, the representative and assertor of the divine sovereignty over men, should utterly fail, and die in shame, was nowhere written, and was incredible. Here was the first difficulty which the disciples had to encounter, no doubt in their own minds, as well as among their compatriots: it was necessary to recast the Messianic theory, and find room within it for the stage of humiliation prior to the period of triumph ; and, for that purpose, to read again, with more discerning eyes, through the lines, and between the lines, of the old prophets and seers. To an uncritical people, with whom historical poems have come to stand for oracles, all literary interpretation is in fluid condition, and will take any direction ; and passages were soon found which held the preconceived thought, and spoke in the desired tone. Who was that "servant of Jehovah" that was "despised and rejected of men, a man of sorrows, and acquainted with grief," who was "led as a sheep to the slaughter, and as a sheep before her shearers is dumb, so he opened not his mouth " ?* Is there not proof here " that the Christ ought to have suffered these things, and only thus to enter his glory " ?† And, if thus it was appointed and foretold, that lowly lot, that gentle humanity, that inward conflict in the garden, that outer agony upon the cross, are no contradiction, but rather the very sign of his Messiahship. Far from constituting failure and defeat, they were all entered on the providential plan, and all, under the guise of necessity, voluntarily contemplated and assumed; and though his disciples did not see it at the time, do they not remember now the forebodings that fell from him in his dark pathetic moods, and penetrate their mysterious meaning ? This state of mind, it is probable, long controlled the formation of the earliest Christian traditions, and modified what was purely historical in their groundwork; and in the same interest were the materials thus constituted subsequently combined into the several selections presented in the synoptical Gospels. They recite such portions of his teaching and labours as have reference to the " coming of the kingdom : " they mark the crises and the hints which seem to let out the secret of his own appointment, and to show, that, in what he suffered, he purposely assumed the will of God : they regard his whole ministry as a preamble or presage, relating to the impending real Messiahship, as the Baptist's mission to his own career in Palestine, and are less anxious to make it shine with the light of history than with that of prophecy. The third Gospel has other subsidiary characteristics ; but the thesis so intently dwelt upon in its last chapter—that the future Christ was meant to be a sufferer first, and that the tragic scene on Calvary is but an act of the divine drama—is the expression of its deepest thought. It would harmonize the cross with the theory of Christ's function.

To work out this doctrine, of a Messiah emerging through the baptism of suffering and death, was the first achievement of early Christian thought. In order to give it its hoped-for success, Jesus should have early fulfilled the promise made on his behalf, and returned from heaven with his full investiture of power. This, certainly, was the disciples' expectation ;

* Isa. liii. 3-7. † Luke xxiv. 26.

this, the purport of their preaching; this, the needful justification of the theory they had formed. A notice sent that the last days were at hand, the appearance of a herald to make ready for them, the nomination of the person who is to introduce them, are measures full of meaning, if addressed to those upon whom also the sequel quickly comes, but lose all fitness and significance, if the warning is given to one generation, and the fulfilment falls upon another, and the eager haste which has been urged is proved by death to have been superfluous, and has to be handed on to the next age. Hence a new difficulty gathered with lapsing years around the early Christians. They were not prepared for an indefinite postponement of the advent ; and their first doctrine had no place for it. It was necessary to revise their construction of the providential scheme, and find some worthy design to fill the intermediate time which they had so much under-estimated ; and to this second problem it is that the post-evangelical literature, represented by the Acts of the Apostles, specifically addresses itself. The solution is gained by setting up a second stage of divine preparation for the great end, a dispensation of the Holy Spirit which shall take the place, for a generation, of the immediate presence of Jesus, now withdrawn. To his *personal* preliminary visit is to be added a *social* proclamation of the coming kingdom through the constitution of a witnessing church, organized, not, indeed, for permanent history, but for provisional protest till the hour strike. As the body of Christian believers gradually increased and ramified, and absorbed into itself both Jewish and Gentile elements, and, settling down into regular usages of its own, found itself isolated from society around, this was the interpretation which it naturally put upon its own life and meaning : it stood there as representative of the absent and waiting Christ, to prolong his night of warning, and "show forth his death till he come." As the Church became a fact of larger dimensions and more various elements, this theory of it hastened to overtake it, and shaped itself into a connected system, which found a place for all the parts. The apostolic age was thus set up as furnishing a second volume in the divine history, parallel to the first, and by new agency doubling its warning to the world. It opens, like the first, with visits of angels, announcing, not now the earthly, but the heavenly nativity of Christ.* It starts its new mission, like that of Jesus on Jordan, with a spiritual baptism, no longer, however, of water, but of fire,† and then, simply substituting the apostles and evangelists for the Master, conducts them through a similar career, of preaching, of miracles, of exorcism, of bestowment of spiritual gifts, of persecution, transfiguration, and martyrdom. In the Book of Acts we stand in presence throughout of a theory of the apostolic age, under the influence of which the recorded facts and words are selected, moulded, and balanced; and this feature alone, apart from all questions affecting its truth in detail, throws light upon its date. For no generation as it lives on, least of all a generation plunged in hot conflict and intense anticipations, has time, and sufficient distance from itself, to speculate upon its own position in the system of the world; and ere it can all lie in symmetrical order before the eye, and be exhibited as part of an intended plan, foreshadowed in the past, and needful for a future long decreed, it must already be well over, and seen in retiring perspective by the observer. The work, therefore, is certainly post-apostolic. It deals with a later stadium of the Messianic theory than that on which the Gospel pauses, and addresses itself to an ulterior state of mind. It is obliged to throw the Parusia more into the indefinite, and let it rest in comparative silence. And its representation of Christian affairs approaches visibly nearer the settled existence of a society no longer provisional, but rapidly passing into the Catholic Church of history. These features would not naturally make their appearance in the first century. And the favourable feeling everywhere shown towards the Roman Government would be most in place, notwithstanding some partial persecutions, in the reign of Trajan. In the latter part of that reign (which extended from A.D. 98 to A.D. 118), at an interval of, perhaps, ten years, the author may probably have compiled his two works. Accuracy, however, is here certainly unattainable; and definite dates are admissible only as approximations, which,

* Acts i. 10, 11.   † ii. 1-13.

s

till corrected by further evidence, may serve in aid of clear conceptions.

B. *Relation to Paul's Epistles.*

Laying down the third Gospel, let us now take up the Pauline letters as our second term of comparison for the Book of Acts. In order to appreciate their relation and points of contact, we must take a rapid glance at the historian's scheme, and the disposition of its contents.

The story which he tells arranges itself around two great figures, presented in succession,—that of Peter, so long as Jerusalem is the centre of his scene ;* that of Paul, from the moment when it widens into foreign parts :† and so nearly complete is the separation of their action, that only once does each apostle appear in the section devoted to the other.‡ The founding of the parent Church at Jerusalem, after the college of apostles has been filled up,§ opening at Pentecost with the descent of the Spirit and the gift of tongues,‖ so effectually turned to account by Peter's exposition as to bring in three thousand converts,¶ is confirmed by a miraculous cure of a cripple in the temple,** by a vain attempt to restrain the apostles through imprisonment,†† and by further addresses of Peter to the people, converting five thousand more,‡‡ and to the council,§§ and culminates in a life of enthusiastic brotherhood, carried even to community of goods,‖‖ visiting reservations of private interest with instant supernatural death,¶¶ and glorified by such signs and wonders, that crowds from neighbouring cities competed for the passing shadow of Peter upon their sick.*** But this human society, thus far distinguished from orthodox Judaism only by its belief that Messiah has been nominated, soon outgrows its first compactness, and carries within it elements at once of division and of expansion. Greek-speaking colonists and foreign proselytes are there,

---

* Acts i.-xii. inclusive.   † xiii. 1, to end.

‡ Saul in viii. 1-3, ix. 1-30, passages which practically form one subject; Peter in xv. 7-11.   § i. 15-26.

‖ ii. 1-13.   ¶ ii. 14-41.   ** iii. 1-11.

†† iv. 1-3, 17-22.   ‡‡ iv. 4.   §§ iv. 8-12.

‖‖ iv. 31-37.   ¶¶ v. 1-11.   *** v. 12-16.

who have been held or drawn to Judaism, not by its temple
cultus and its Levitical law, but by its pure theism and its
ideal hopes; and they bear with impatience the legal rigour
of the twelve, and the preference shown towards the disciples
who are natives of Palestine. The outburst of their feelings
represented by Stephen, with its consequences on the interior
spirit and outward relations of the Church, forms the subject
of our author's next section. To allay the complaint of the
Hellenists, the poor's fund is handed over to seven of their
number, appointed, however, only as secondaries, by the laying-on of the apostles' hands.* But this vantage-ground of
recognition gives scope enough for the fervour of Stephen to
break forth in that daring speech of his which spiritualizes
the history and law of Israel, disapproves the temple, rebukes
the national blindness, and brings down martyrdom upon
himself.† While this first explosion of revolt against Jewish
hardness and exclusiveness sprang from within the parent
Church itself, Saul, its future representative, steps upon the
scene as the agent of sacerdotal resistance to it.‡ By that
fierce resistance, the disciples, especially the Hellenists (for
the apostles seem to have been safe enough at Jerusalem),
were scattered over Palestine,§ and, far from limiting themselves to the synagogue, made Christians of Samaritans,‖
baptized Simon Magus himself,¶ and the treasurer of the
Ethiopian queen.** Not that these cases were without some
affinities with Judaism. Its separation from Samaria was
somewhat of a domestic quarrel; the treasurer was at least a
proselyte, for he had been to the temple to worship : but they
were at one remove from the close circle of Jerusalem, and
formed an intermediate link between the first narrowness and
the last universality. Accordingly, the way being thus prepared, our author's next section unfolds the provision for
advancing on the Gentile world. First, Saul is converted by
the mid-day miracle on the Damascus road ;†† the secret of
his mission being confided, not to himself, but to the disciple
who was to receive him, and cure his three-days' blindness at

---

* Acts vi. 1-8.   † vi. 9-vii. 60.   ‡ viii. 1-3.
§ viii. 1-4.   ‖ viii. 5-8.   ¶ viii. 9-24.
** viii. 27-40.   †† ix. 1-9.

Damascus,* and taking at first no practical effect; for both there† and at Jerusalem, where Barnabas immediately introduces him to the mistrustful apostles, he preaches his new convictions only in synagogues,‡ and comes into conflict, like any other Jewish Christian, only with Hellenists and Jews.§ The historian, therefore, is here simply providing this conversion for further use: for the present, he sets it aside, ere a single Gentile had been addressed, and, reverting to Peter, invests him with a direct divine commission to bring the first heathen into the faith and brotherhood of the baptized,‖ and attributes to him the very motto of Christian universality, that "God is no respecter of persons; but in every nation he that feareth him, and worketh righteousness, is accepted with him."¶ As if eager to mark with an exceptional sanction the conversion of Cornelius's household, the Holy Spirit does not wait, as usual, for their due baptism, but ere Peter was silent, fell upon them with the gift of tongues;** asking for their baptism, instead of crowning it. Does the author, then, mean to dispossess Paul of any concern with the first life of Gentile Christianity? Not quite so. He tells us that some Cypriots and Cyrenians among the disciples dispersed by Stephen's death had, of their own accord, though primarily addressing Jews, turned their preaching to the heathen, and gathered a great harvest of converts, chiefly at Antioch.†† To report upon this first experiment of a mixed church, Barnabas went down as commissioner of the Jerusalem apostles; and, accepting the good results as a sufficient seal of divine approval, he fetched Saul from Tarsus to work with him for a year in organizing a community so encouraging, yet so precariously balanced.‡‡ Paul has thus a hand in the earliest Gentile work, but by human invitation, not divine commission; by authority from Jerusalem, not in his own right; and in garnering the harvest raised by others, not in sowing the seed himself. During this year, at Antioch, a deputation of prophets from the parent Church came thither to announce a famine impending at some future date, and to

* Acts ix. 10–18. † ix. 20. ‡ ix. 26–29.
§ ix. 22–25. ‖ x. 1–33. ¶ x. 34, 35.
** x. 44–48. †† xi. 19–21. ‡‡ xi. 22–26.

seek help for the evil times ; and, a collection having been made, Saul, in company with his patron Barnabas, visits Jerusalem to deliver it into the elders' hands.* He thus appears in a position thoroughly recognized at headquarters, but wholly subordinate; and, for the second time since his conversion, is thrown into intimate and friendly relations with the original apostles. Before conducting the bearers of the collection back to Antioch, the historian, casting a last glance upon the revered Church at Jerusalem, relates the particulars of Herod Agrippa's persecution and subsequent death, the beheading of James the son of Zebedee,† the rigorous imprisonment of Peter, his deliverance by an angel through spontaneously opening doors, and his reappearance among the astonished friends to whom he was given back.‡ Whether among them we are to look for Barnabas and Paul, we are not told ; but from the house where the gathering was held, they took John Mark (who lived there with his mother) to help in their labours in and beyond Antioch.§

With this episode the narrative bids adieu to the parent Church and its representative apostles, and, taking up its second thread, follows the movements of Paul till he is brought to Rome. On looking back over this section of the history, we notice a gradually changing attitude of public feeling in the city towards the Christians. At first their cause is described as popular ; and its active opponents are found only among the aristocratic Sadducees and chiefs of the state.‖ When Stephen and the Hellenists step to the front, the favour of the citizens falls away ;¶ and at last the local king finds no more persuasive means of courting the people than by lifting his sword against James, and closing his prison-doors upon Peter ;** so that the perverseness is universal which turns away from the divine light in the midst of them. Hence the way is now fully prepared for the quest of new fields and the introduction of the new Agent, who, if his countrymen reject his message, will obtain a hearing for it among the Gentiles.

* Acts xi. 27-30.　† xii. 1, 2.　‡ xii. 3-17.
§ xii. 12-25.　‖ iii., iv., v.　¶ vi., vii.
** xii. 2, 3.

As Paul's conversion had, according to our author, conveyed to him no commission, he has yet to receive the authority which shall start him on his special career. With this, accordingly, the section devoted to him begins. From whom, then, does he obtain it? A body of prophets and teachers in the Antioch congregation, engaged in fasting and prayer, are divinely impelled, as they believe, to set apart Barnabas and Paul for a missionary enterprise; and, in obedience to this nomination, the two friends are consecrated by the laying-on of hands, and sent forth to their work.* Drawn first to Cyprus, as the native place of Barnabas, they passed through the island, from east to west, with Mark as their associate, but without recorded result, till, at Paphos, Paul, encountering Elymas the sorcerer, strikes him miraculously blind, and converts the proconsul, Sergius Paulus.† From this critical moment, Barnabas, hitherto the patron, is withdrawn into the secondary place; and the growing importance of the heathen mission induces a change of the Hebrew name Saul, to the more current Roman form of Paul.‡ On their crossing over to the opposite mainland, Mark, to the displeasure of Paul, returned to Jerusalem.§ The other two advanced into the interior, through the Pisidian and Lycaonian towns; always, it is affirmed, proceeding by the same rule,—of preaching first in the synagogue, and usually with the same result,—of incurring the hostility of the Jews, and being driven to seek a heathen audience, and form an independent community.‖ Wherever they went, their steps were marked by supernatural signs;¶ and the healing of a cripple at Lystra induced, it is said, that monstrous scene in which the missionaries were first worshipped as gods, and then, on Jewish instigation, stoned and expelled.** Returning on their steps, they rendered account at Antioch of the execution of their commission, and, resuming their residence there, are lost sight of for several years. When we consider that their first journey occupied about two years, we cannot but be struck with the scantiness of the historian's record. It gives us one

---

* Acts xiii. 1–3.   † xiii. 4–12.   ‡ xiii. 9.
§ xiii. 13; xv. 36–39.   ‖ xiii. 14, 15, 44–52.   ¶ xiv. 3.
** xiv. 8–19.

speech of Paul in the synagogue, one personal conversion by a miracle of terror, one dramatic outburst of superstition, brought on by a miracle of mercy, but else, only the most general statements of method and result; that the first chance was always given to the synagogue; that the Jews were perverse and rancorous; that the Gentiles asked to hear the word. The heathen mission is everywhere exhibited not as within the primary intention of the preachers, but as an incidental consequence forced upon them, and justified by the infatuation of the men of Israel.

Their proceedings, however, though ratified by their constituents at Antioch, were called in question by a party in the parent Church; and messengers came down from Jerusalem to insist that no Gentile should be baptized, unless he submitted himself to the entire Jewish law.* If this were to be the rule, the whole work of the late mission was invalid; and Barnabas and Paul, thus challenged, determined to seek at headquarters the legitimation which the complainants threatened to withhold from them.† Taking a deputation to Jerusalem, they submitted the question, with the narrative of their labours, to a meeting of the apostles and elders,‡ curiously characterized by great breadth of speech, dwindling into narrowness of result. Peter, appealing to his own initiative in the case of Cornelius, unreservedly declares that the intolerable yoke of the law is broken, and there is no difference before God between the Gentile and the Jew.§ And even James supports the same thesis, out of the prophets, yet induces the assembly to lay four restrictions on heathen converts,—abstinence from meats that were the remains of Pagan sacrifices, and from such as had the blood in them, and from the flesh of animals snared or strangled, and from marriage within the prohibited degrees, and from other irregularities of the same class.‖ This decision is said to have been accepted by Paul and Barnabas, conveyed by letter, and authenticated by deputation, to the Church at Antioch, and established as the basis of common action among all sections of Christian believers.¶

---

* Acts xv. 1.   † xv. 2, 3.   ‡ xv. 4-6.
§ xv. 7-11.   ‖ xv. 13-20.   ¶ xv. 22-31.

Armed, now, with a full recognition, not, indeed, as apostle, but as missionary, Paul is sent by the historian on his second and greatest journey, which is to establish his character as chief founder of the Gentile churches. Here, too, Barnabas drops away, offended with his colleague's displeasure with Mark,* and disappears from the story; and Paul, emerging into complete independence, and taking Silas, and soon, Timothy, as assistants, begins upon his old track, leaving with every church the rules adopted by the apostolic assembly at Jerusalem.† In his own conduct he is said to have even gone beyond their restrictive requirements, compelling Timothy, who had a Jewish mother and a Greek father, to submit to the Jewish rite before entering the Christian service.‡ The historian hurries the travellers through Phrygia and Galatia,§ without mention of any of the important churches,—Colossæ, Laodicea, Hierapolis,—which so soon became renowned, and barring them by divine prohibition from proconsular Asia on the south-west, and Bithynia on the north, brings them rapidly to Troas, the verge of that European enterprise which he is eager to describe. First pausing at Philippi, he tells of the pious and hospitable Lydia, with whom the missionaries were guests;¶ of the soothsaying girl, whose master, provoked by Paul's successful exorcism, had him and Silas beaten and imprisoned;** of the miraculous deliverance from jail, and conversion of the jailer;†† but does not explain how it was that the plea of Roman citizenship, which would have protected them from stripes, was not urged till after the punishment had been inflicted.‡‡ Three weeks at Thessalonica serve only to show how at once the Jews are rendered inveterate, and the " devout Greeks " are profoundly attracted, by the Christian message.§§ Driven forward by the hatred of their countrymen, the travellers are at last at Athens,∥∥ the culminating point of the historian's interest, for which he has reserved the speech¶¶ characteristic of this section. The city

---

* Acts xv. 36-40.
† xv. 41-xvi. 5.
‡ xvi. 3.
§ xvi. 6.
∥ xvi. 7, 8.
¶ xvi. 12-15.
** xvi. 16-24.
†† xvi. 25-34.
‡‡ xvi. 37-39.
§§ xvii. 1-9.
∥∥ xvii. 10-15.
¶¶ xvii. 22-31.

of the schools was not a place congenial to the Christian
gospel ;* and, forming no church there, Paul passed on to
Corinth, and spending a year and a half there, under the
friendly roof of Aquila and Priscilla,† he met with the
usual experience,—enmity and persecution from orthodox
Judaism,‡ indifference or protection from the Roman
authorities,§ and a large following among the religious
Gentiles and Jewish proselytes.‖ Here was the limit of his
second mission. Wishing to show himself once more at
Jerusalem as a faithful observer of the law, he put himself
under a vow, which begins its effect in Greece, and completes
it in the temple ; and, calling at Ephesus and Cæsarea,
reports himself to the parent Church, and thence returns to
Antioch.¶

The third missionary journey assumes the character of a
passing survey of the previous work ; and it follows so much
the lines already traced, through Galatia and Phrygia,** to
the coast of Asia Proper, and by Troas to Macedonia and
Achaia, followed by a return but little varied, that scarcely
would new ground be broken at all, were it not for a stay of
more than two years†† at Ephesus. Here the author gives a
sample of Paul's encounter with three influences menacing to
his work,‡‡—the imperfect gospel of Apollos and his friends,
who are preaching the promissory message of John the Baptist
(that Messiah is at hand), but have yet to be brought up to
the baptism of Jesus as the Christ, and to receive the gift of
the Spirit ;§§ the impenetrable Jewish conservatism ;‖‖ the
interests and passions of Pagan superstition. The representatives of the first, recognized already as " disciples," need only
further instruction ; and the laying-on of Paul's hands after
baptism, followed by the gift of tongues, at once declares their
enrolment complete.¶¶ The second shows itself not only in
the hardened opposition in the synagogue, which, after three
months, drove Paul to remove to the school of Tyrannus,***
but in the attempt of the Jewish exorcists to trade in the name

* Acts xvii. 34. † xviii. 1-3. ‡ xviii. 5, 6, 12, 13.
§ xviii. 14-17. ‖ xviii. 7-11. ¶ xviii. 18-22.
** xviii. 23. †† xix. 10. ‡‡ xviii. 24-xix. 3.
§§ xix. 4-7. ‖‖ xix. 8, 9. ¶¶ xix. 4-7.
*** xix. 8, 9.

of Jesus as a spell of power in their art. The possessing demon, however, being up to this device, declines to stir, and goads on his victim to beat the impostors, and turn them out of doors.* The third find voice in the outcry of the craftsmen, and the worshippers at Diana's shrine ;† and being not properly encountered by the Christian missionaries at all, but turned aside by an adroit and tolerant city officer, are adduced, apparently, only in proof of the public alarm at the spread of the new religion.   It is, doubtless, with a view to leave the same impression of growing popular success, that the historian cites the "special miracles" wrought not only by "the hands of Paul," but by "handkerchiefs and aprons brought from his body to the sick or the possessed," and the voluntary burning, by converted and repentant sorcerers, of their books of divination, to the value of above two thousand pounds:

It was between Troas and Philippi, in the second journey, that our author first availed himself of the Pauline itinerary, which he often quotes ;‡ and it is on the return from Philippi to Troas, in the third journey, that he resorts to it again.§ With the dry memoranda of this journal are interspersed passages more fully descriptive, which betray themselves by the historian's pervading feeling that Paul is on his last circuit in the East, and is taking leave of the disciples, whom he gathers round him.   This it is which explains the lingering of his address at Troas, till Eutychus has fallen asleep, and given occasion to the miracle answering to Peter's recall of Tabitha from death.‖ This it is which gives its pathetic character to the speech before the Ephesian elders at Miletus.¶   And this it is which introduces the prophecy at Tyre and Cæsarea, of Paul's seizure at Jerusalem,** although the author has here concealed his hand by interweaving his additions with his materials, and adopting the borrowed form for the whole.   It is natural for the writer, who knows his own drama to the end, to give impressiveness to this last visit to Jerusalem, by auguries of calamity, growing louder as the

* Acts xix. 13–17.   † xix. 23–41.   ‡ xvi. 10–17.
§ xx. 4–15.   ‖ xx. 7–12.   ¶ xx. 18–38.
** xxi. 4, 8–14.   M. Renan perceives that xxi. 8, is no part of the journal, and treats it as an interpolation.—ANTICHRIST, p. 564.

city is approached. But it is not natural that Paul, whom a heavenly intimation so easily turned aside from Bithynia and the province of Asia, should now, in defiance of emphatic warnings of the Holy Spirit, persist in taking the road to bondage or death.

The last section of our book presents the apostle in a new character, not of aggressive action, but of endurance and defence. It conducts him from Jerusalem to Rome,—the persecuted, the accused, the prisoner on appeal. His missionary life is over; and when he speaks, whether to his countrymen from the steps of Fort Antonia, or before the council, or to the court at Cæsarea, his addresses, though telling the story of his religious change, are rather forensic than prophetic. Finding himself still an object of suspicion among the Judaic Christians of the Holy City, he is described as taking on himself, with four zealots for the law, the obligations and charges of a conspicuous vow, that he may seem no less loyal to Moses than they.* Whatever soothing effect this might have upon the Church, it did not avail with the unconverted Jews. On the rumour that he had brought a Gentile within the interior temple courts, a riot is raised among the worshippers, from which he is rescued only by the Roman guard.† Every attempt of the officer in command to obtain a distinct charge against the prisoner, which shall justify his arrest, is frustrated by orthodox vehemence. Paul's speech to the people, immediately after his apprehension, is silenced by tumultuary cries the moment he mentions his preaching to the Gentiles.‡ His own examination by scourging is stopped by his claim to Roman citizenship.§ The reference of his case to the Sanhedrim is rendered fruitless by the outburst of clamorous dissensions.‖ And, after all, he is sent off to the Roman governor at Cæsarea, without any definite indictment against him, merely to place him beyond the reach of a Jewish conspiracy against his life.¶ Summoned before Felix, his accusers can bring no legal charge, but only try to make him responsible for their own disturbance in the temple.** And

----

* Acts xxi. 20-27. † xxi. 28-40. ‡ xxii. 21, 22.
§ xxii. 24-29. ‖ xxiii. 1-10. ¶ xxiii. 12-35.
** xxiv. 1-9.

when, after two years' unintelligible imprisonment, his case is brought up for hearing before Festus, the succeeding governor, the court, though aided by the presence of Agrippa, the Jewish prince, and Berenice, is still unable to draw up any regular bill against him ;* and he is sent to Rome, not to answer for any alleged offence, but merely in compliance with his own appeal.† In all his speeches, the ground of his defence is remarkable. He pleads his full Jewish orthodoxy, and denies that he teaches anything which is not covered by the faith of a consistent Pharisee.‡ And in two of them he repeats the story of his conversion, with circumstantial variations from the historian's account, and from each other, which indicate how little was exactitude regarded in even the most important Christian traditions.§

The voyage to Rome is evidently drawn, for the most part, from the journal of an eye-witness, very unevenly kept ; for while the earlier portion is related with consecutive explicitness,‖ from the shipwreck at Malta the narrative hastens to its end, three months being compressed into a few verses,¶ and marked only by the mention of four days, to two of which miracles are referred. Paul, on reaching the city where for two years he was to live as a prisoner under little restriction, soon sent for the leading Jews, to explain what brings him there, and to remove any prejudicial rumour that might have preceded him, and is assured that no report of him had reached them, and he had no evil impression to fear.** The way being thus open, he devotes a day with them to the exposition of his gospel; and as, with few exceptions, they withstand his persuasion, he denounces their blindness in the words of Isaiah, and tells them that the Gentiles should have what they had refused.†† The author, having conducted

---

* Acts xxv. 1-27.   † xxvi. 30-32.
‡ xxiii. 1-6; xxiv. 15-21; xxv. 8; xxvi. 4-7, 22.
§ xxii. 6-21; xxvi. 12-20. In ix. 7, it is said that Paul's companions "heard the voice"; in xxii. 9, that they "saw the light, but did not hear the voice." In the first account, the commission to the Gentiles is not confided to Paul, though mentioned to Ananias: in the second, it is given to Paul, not in the Damascus vision, but in a later trance, at the temple: in the third, it forms the main part of what Jesus says to him at his conversion.
‖ xxvii.   ¶ xxviii. 1-10.
** xxviii. 17-21.   †† xxviii. 22-28.

Paul as the organ of conveyance for the Gentile gospel from its birthplace to the centre of the heathen world, has reached the goal of his design, and leaves him at the climax of his mission, though possibly descending into the shadow of personal danger, or even the martyr's death.

The picture thus drawn of Christian affairs in the apostolic age is in itself distinct, symmetrical, and fairly consistent ; and it represents, no doubt, the conception which the Church, when its first contrarieties had been levelled, formed of its own nativity.   Its chief features, however, we can fortunately compare with paragraphs from the life, handed down in the epistles of Paul ; and they will reward a scrutiny.

I. The spiritual gifts showered down upon the disciples on the day of Pentecost, and especially that "speaking with tongues," which is described as usually following baptism and the laying-on of the apostles' hands, are the subject of a special discussion between Paul and his Corinthian converts ; and as he writes about them to the very people whom he had introduced to them, at the very moment of their habitual exercise, and with a view to a right estimate of their relative value, we are thrown by his allusions into the midst of the facts, and can see for ourselves what was really going on.

To the author of the Book of Acts, the miracle of Pentecost undoubtedly consisted in the power conferred on a set of Galileans to speak intelligibly to a mixed audience of foreigners, without requiring from any one a knowledge of more than his own language.   Fifteen different countries had their representatives present ; while the disciples, new fired by the Spirit, set forth " the wonderful works of God ; " and not one of them missed the inspired story.   Each "heard in his own tongue in which he was born."[*]   Whether the historian planted the supernatural phenomenon in the speaker, who delivered himself in a language he had never learned, or in the hearer, who received in one tongue what was uttered in another ; whether, in his view, this happened now to one, and then to another, of the listeners, or to all at once,—are secondary questions, which may be left to curious interpreters : the essential point is, that to these Christian recipients of the

[*] Acts ii. 7–12.

Holy Spirit is attributed the faculty, without human means of communication, of preaching to foreigners not less intelligibly than to their own countrymen.   True it is that in subsequent instances which the author adduces of this "sign," viz., the conversion of the Cornelius household,* and the baptism of the Apollos school,† there seems no room for the exercise of such a gift, all the persons present being speakers of Greek; but that the phenomenon is here *meant* to be still the same is evident from Peter's own account of his mission to the centurion: "As I began to speak, the Holy Spirit fell on them, *as on us at the beginning.*"‡

The gift thus described by the historian of its origin evidently played only too conspicuous a part in the early assemblies of the Christians; for we find the apostle of the Gentiles disapproving its display at Corinth, and treating it with marked disparagement; and, in the reasons which he assigns for his judgment, we obtain a lively picture of its nature and results.   He attributes to it the following characters :—

1. It is a mode of speaking, *not to men, but to God.*§   One who resorts to it edifies *himself*, and not the assembly.‖   "If," says the apostle, "I come to you speaking with tongues, what shall I profit you?"¶   "Except ye utter with the tongue intelligible words, how shall it be known what is spoken? for ye will be speaking into the air."**   The gift, therefore, isolates the individual, and constitutes a private act of devotion, in which the assembly cannot participate.

2. It is an *unconscious act of impulse, not attended by the understanding*, an expression of "the Spirit" without "the intellect:" "My spirit prayeth; but my understanding is unfruitful."††   "If thou shalt bless with the spirit, how shall the unlearned say Amen at thy giving of thanks, seeing he understandeth not what thou sayest?"‡‡   "I had rather

---

* Acts x. 44, 46: "While Peter yet spake these words, the Holy Spirit fell on all them that heard the word . . . and they heard them speak with tongues, and magnify God."

† xix. 6.	‡ xi. 15.	§ 1 Cor. xiv. 2.
‖ Ibid. 4.	¶ Ibid. 6.	** Ibid. 9.
†† Ibid. 14.	‡‡ Ibid. 16.	

speak five words with my understanding, that I may instruct
others also, than ten thousand words in a tongue."*

3. Hence it needs *an interpreter* to bring out the thought,
even for the speaker himself, and still more for others : "Let
him that speaketh in a tongue pray that he may interpret."†
"If any man speak in a tongue, let one interpret; but if there
be no interpreter, let him keep silence in the church, and let
him speak to himself and to God."‡ Else no other impression can be produced on occasional attendants coming
in, than that the Christians are mad.§

In consistency with these statements, the effect of this gift
is compared with the tinkling of metal,‖ with the note of
a wind or stringed instrument,¶ with the sound of an
unintelligible language ;** and, by its unmeaning and
unedifying character, it is contrasted with the prophetic
function.††

What is here described and deprecated has evidently nothing in common with miraculous power of communicating with
foreigners ; for the favoured possessor of such a gift would
certainly use it for the expression of conscious and coherent
thought : he would address that thought to men, and not to
God : and he would need no interpreter, the gift itself having
no function, except to save interpretation. Listening to the
apostle's graphic hints, we find ourselves in an assembly, where
member after member rises and pours forth, with the air of one
possessed, a torrent of vehement, inarticulate sounds ; breathing
forth, it may be, distinguishable tones of varying emotion,—
now plaintive and pathetic, now hopeful and jubilant, or again
stormy and indignant,—but like music without words, or like
a laugh or a wail overheard, betraying no definite thought,
except to the Reader of all hearts. There seems to be a certain
point of tension at which every kind of emotion, escaping the
restraints of reason, takes possession of the powers of utterance, and bursts into involuntary voice ; and those who have
witnessed the reproduction, at Edward Irving's church, of the
Corinthian phenomena, will not claim for the religious affec-

---

* 1 Cor. xiv. 19.
§ Ibid. 23.
** Ibid. 10.

† Ibid. 13.
‖ 1 Cor. xiii. 1.
†† Ibid. 2–4.

‡ Ibid. 27, 28.
¶ 1 Cor. xiv. 7.

tions any exemption from this general law. That such hysterical or ecstatic excitement should bo regarded, like other enthusiastic spontaneities, as a divine inspiration, can occasion no surprise. Nor is it difficult to see how *interpretation* would bo possible: it would consist in at once finding, doubtless from the rich poetry of prophet and psalmist, words that chimed in with tho mood and tone of tho speaker, and filled in with clear images his vast and formless feeling.

If this is at all a true representation of the objective facts, how long would it take for tradition to give them tho form thoy assume in the Book of Acts? Without pretending to measure tho interval, wo may safely say, that they must have long passed out of experience, and even of memory. The apostolic ago must have been not only gone, but completely idealized, beforo tho power of speaking foreign languages which had never been learned could bo reckoned among the gifts of tho Spirit, and identified with a phenomenon so completely opposite in its character. Tho story, probably, arose from a misinterpretation of tho language employed, when tho facts described by it had been forgotten. In tho oldest form of phrase, " to speak with a tonguo " (γλώσσῃ λαλεῖν),[*] tho word "tonguo" does not mean "*language*" (for which a different word, διάλεκτος,[†] would bo used), but tho bodily member most active in speech; and it is resorted to on account of tho inarticulate nature of tho utterance; because, to tho hearer who understands nothing of what is said, tho act of talking appears a purely physical performance, a mero *gabble*, in which his attention rests upon tho organic machinery. Next tho phraso passed into tho plural: acts of " speaking *with tongues*" (γλώσσαις λαλεῖν),[‡] and "*kinds of tongues*,"[§] wero mentioned; because, in different cases, distinct types of feeling perceptibly prompted tho utterance, so that a plurality was cognizable in tho phenomenon. And, finally, tho fuller phrases, "other tongues" (ἑτέραις γλώσσαις λαλεῖν),[‖] and "now tongues" (καιναῖς γλώσσαις),[¶] camo into uso, in order to contrast tho act with common speech, and givo it an origin *other than*

---

[*] 1 Cor. xiv. 2, 13, 27. [†] Acts ii. 8. [‡] 1 Cor. xiv. 5, 6, 23.

[§] γένη γλωσσῶν, 1 Cor. xii. 28; compare γένη φωνῶν, 1 Cor. xiv. 10.

[‖] Acts ii. 4. [¶] Mark xvi. 17.

human, and *new to experience.* It was the *tongue of the Spirit,* an *instrument unfamiliar* for the expression of feeling, which was here concerned. At a distance from its origin, this real meaning of the words was lost: " tongues " was construed into " *languages* "; * and " *other* tongues " were supposed to be dialects different from the speaker's own; and out of a misunderstood phrase was born a stupendous miracle.

II. The Epistles of Paul supply several autobiographical particulars, which enable us to check the story of his life as presented in the Book of Acts.

It has been already shown that the three accounts given by the historian of the apostle's conversion (two of them in speeches of his own) are not circumstantially consistent; and to disregard as trivial the particulars in which they are at variance involves an obvious confusion of ideas. In itself, it is pretty much a matter of indifference whether his companions on the journey were standing or prostrate; whether they only saw, or only heard, the elements of the miracle; whether Jesus said a little more or a little less: any one of the assigned forms for the event would be nearly as compatible with its efficacy as another. But these varieties, though neutral to the character of the incident, are not neutral to the value of its evidence. The question, whether the vision of Jesus was purely subjective, limited to the consciousness of Saul, or was an objective perception of external facts, can be determined only by appealing to other witnesses than the person himself entranced; and our trust in their testimony cannot but be shaken, if they tell us, — now that they were on their feet, then that they were on the ground; now that they heard the voice, then that they did not hear it, but only saw the light; now that the voice spoke twenty-six words,† then that it spoke eighty-six words,‡ including a commission unmentioned in the shorter form. To all who lay great stress upon the outward phenomenon which arrested the journey, these differences are of undeniable importance; but they are slight in presence of the broader contrast between each and all of these recitals, and the

---

* As in Acts ii. 11: ταῖς ἡμετέραις γλώσσαις.
† Acts xxii. 7-10.   ‡ xxvi. 14-18.

picture of his change, which we incidentally gather from Paul himself.   Though occasions repeatedly occur in his Epistles when, as in his defensive orations in the Acts, an appeal to a splendid miracle at noonday, publicly installing him into a divine office, would be conclusive for his purpose, and save many a superfluous circuit of argument, he never once describes such an occurrence, but speaks of his change in terms more suitable to an inward than to an outward revelation.   He says, indeed, in relation to the risen Christ, that he " has seen " him,* and that, too, at a time later than his appearances to the original apostles; † but the nature of this personal vision, its place, its occasion, its contents, are left in silence.   No scene or circumstances are named by which it can be identified, no companions mentioned whose partnership in it would settle its objective reality; nor is it made either the moment of his conversion, or the medium of his summons to preach a gospel of his own in a new and special field.   The phrase, indeed, "I have seen Christ," does not fit well the noonday scene on Damascus road; for in no one of the accounts of it is it said that Jesus was seen.   A voice declared him; but, in the dazzling light which alone was visible, it is not pretended that any form was discerned.   And, while all allusion to an instantaneous conversion by external miracle fails us in the apostle's letters, the internal origin of his new conviction seems to speak in the words, " When it pleased God to reveal his Son *in* me," ‡—a phrase which no one could transfer to the narrative in the Book of Acts, without feeling its incongruity.   Strangely, indeed, would so splendid a miracle be thrown away upon a convert who had everywhere to confront the impugners of his apostolate and enemies of his mission, to defend the rights of his disciples, and make good the authority of his gospel, yet instead of simply reciting the facts on which all the legitimacy of his action depended, and appealing to the witnesses who had part in it, rested his case partly on the fruits of his labours, but chiefly on an elaborate scheme of theology reasoned out from the nature of man, the government of God, and the analogies and intimations of the Old Testament.

* 1 Cor. ix. 1.   † 1 Cor. xv. 8.   ‡ Gal. i. 16.

If Paul is reticent about his conversion, he is not so about its sequel. Does he, then, confirm the main statements of our historian; viz., that, in the very synagogues at Damascus to which he had been sent as a persecutor, he immediately preached as a Christian; that, "after many days," he escaped a design against his life, and fled to Jerusalem; that there, through the intervention of Barnabas, he overcame the first distrust of the Christians, and consorted with the apostles, and preached boldly, till the enmity of the Hellenists compelled his retreat to Tarsus? On the contrary, he tells us, that, "immediately" on his change of mind, he avoided all contact with men, and did not go up to Jerusalem to those who were apostles before him, but went away into Arabia; and, on returning, sought Damascus again; and only after three years presented himself at Jerusalem, and spent fifteen days with Peter, seeing no other apostle except James, the brother of Jesus.* It is surely impossible to conceive a more precise and thorough-going contradiction, point by point, than between these two stories. If they both refer to the same period, this must be admitted; but it may be said, considering the absence of chronology from the Book of Acts, may we not suppose its visit of Paul to Jerusalem, and preaching there, "and in the country of Judæa,"† to come in *after* the events which he himself enumerates, i.e., at the end of his three years' absence from the holy city? Happily, of this time, also, his own words supply an exact report; "next," he says (i.e., after his fifteen days with Peter), "I came into the regions of Syria and Cilicia; and *my face was unknown to the churches of Christ in Judæa;* and they had only heard that their former persecutor was preaching the faith which once he destroyed."‡ Thus it appears that he had never shown himself to the Christians of the metropolis and its neighbourhood, but remained to them an object of rumour from a distance, throughout the period spent, according to the Book of Acts, in consorting with them, and everywhere boldly preaching to them. And how long did he continue thus a stranger to them? This, also, he distinctly tells us: "Then, after fourteen years, I went up again to Jerusalem with

---

* Gal. i. 16–19.   † Acts xxvi. 20.   ‡ Gal. i. 21–23.

Barnabas."   The visit was, "by revelation, privately, to lay
before the reputed leaders " " the gospel which he preached to
the Gentiles ; " and so to obviate the risk of any frustrating
opposition.*   Up to the time, therefore, of his writing to the
Galatians, i.e., to the middle of the third missionary journey,
by the reckoning of the Acts,† Paul had been only twice at
Jerusalem, on both occasions without any public appearance ;
and we must set down as fictions two out of the four visits
which the historian distributes over the same period.‡   And
further, as the second visit was designed to settle terms, by
private agreement, with the elder apostles, for the recognition
of Paul's Gentile gospel, it is plain that no public understanding, much less any formulated treaty, had thus far
defined the conditions of this gospel ; and that, for seventeen
years, he had made himself its independent organ in thought
and action, without approaching the Jewish-Christian field,
and now brought in, not its principles for judgment, but its
fruits for acknowledgment.

It must be already obvious that these inconsistencies
between the two writers are too uniform in character to be
treated as mere historical inaccuracies : they are the signs of
divergent literary purposes.   The object of the apostle is to
establish the originality of his Gentile movement and doctrine,
to show that they arose as a sacred commission given personally to him, and lay entirely between God and himself,
indebted for no help, and needing no authority, from men.
With this view, he does not shrink from disclaiming, even in
a tone of contempt, all obligation to " those apostles who
passed for something considerable," and stood for " pillars "
at Jerusalem, and plainly declaring that he had nothing to

* Gal. ii. 1, 2.

† The chronology is obtained thus : when Paul escaped from Damascus,
Aretas was in possession of the city ; for the gates were watched by order of
his commandant (2 Cor. xi. 32).   The city did not belong to him, but was
temporarily under his control, through political complications, in the spring
of A.D. 37.   This gives the date of Paul's conversion.   Seventeen years from
that time brings us to A.D. 54.   The Epistle to the Galatians was written
either from Ephesus, about A.D. 55, or from Corinth, about A.D. 58.

‡ Viz., from Damascus, after his conversion (ix. 26) ; from Antioch, to relieve the Jerusalem Christians (xi. 27–30) ; from Antioch with Barnabas, to the
" first council," after the first journey (xv.) ; from Cenchreæ, after the second
journey, under a vow (xviii. 18, *seqq.*).

thank them for ; while they, on the other hand, were too much struck with the practical evidence of divine blessing on his ministry to exclude it from fellowship, or hesitate to leave its field to him ; reserving to themselves the Jewish mission, and stipulating only for a considerate remembrance of the poorer brethren.* The author of the Book of Acts works throughout to precisely the opposite end ; insisting at every step on Paul's dependence on those who were Christians before him, on his direct apprenticeship to them as their agent, on his accord with them in principle and method, and difference from them only in his geographical area of life. Consigned, at first, to the care and instruction of the Jew Ananias, taken up into the patronage of Barnabas, called in as a subordinate helper in the first community open to Gentiles, at the end of every journey appearing at Jerusalem to render an account, to bring a tribute, or to exhibit himself under the most rigorous Jewish vows, he is exhibited as called, indeed, by Christ, but as trained and employed by the Church, and loyal to its leaders and decrees. While this difference of purpose between Paul and his historian occasions discrepancies in many biographical particulars, it also goes much deeper, and leads to our next contrast.

III. The whole personality of Paul, his characteristic thought, his method of work, as presented in the Book of Acts, are inconsistent with his own self-revelations.

Whatever obscurities may be found in the Pauline theology, and whatever estimate may be made of what is clear in it, it cannot be doubted that he was a *theologian*, if he was any-thing ; that he had wrought out for himself a comprehensive theory of human nature, of the divine government, and of the stadia of history in the past, and to the close of its drama ; that with this theory his Christianity was identified, so that he required its leading conceptions and characteristic terms for every exposition of his gospel. The whole problem of the world was for him resolved in the person of Jesus Christ. The central point in which the solution lay was the cross of Christ : the redeeming efficacy of the cross presupposed both a particular conception of humanity and a double nature in

* Gal. ii. 6–10.

Christ, to appreciate which we must be familiar with the relation of "flesh" and "spirit," of "sin" and "transgression," of "knowledge" and "power," of "faith" and "law," of "life" and "death;" and, while the "righteousness of God" was freely open to all who had faith thus to receive it in place of their own, that faith was conditional on a whole system of prior thought and feeling. Hence the apostle's simplest modes of formulating the essence of Christianity carry in them psychological, ethical, and theosophic postulates, which are tantamount to a scheme of the universe; nor can he, in a short letter, defend his Galatian teaching from its Judaical impugners without furnishing a text-book of dogmatic theology for the construction of future confessions of faith, and the use of thousands of evangelical professors through the successive ages of the Church. In proportion as his influence has been in the ascendant have all subsequent forms of Christianity assumed the same character, —of vast doctrinal constructions, more or less closely compacted, and covering almost the whole ground of philosophy as well as of religion. And in his day, as in ours, there stood, in direct antithesis to this, that simpler type of belief, which, in dealing with sin, is content with bringing it to repentance, and offering it mercy on self-surrender; and which, thinking no more of the death than of the life of Jesus, makes a whole of both, as the realization of the true filial union of soul with God. The primitive Christian samples of these opposite ways of thinking were, indeed, far from identical with ours; but the central motto of each has remained,—for the one, "salvation by the cross;" for the other, "return unto God through repentance and faith."

Now, in the second section of the Book of Acts, we have a speech of Paul's for each of his three missionary journeys,— the first addressed to Jews,[*] the second to heathens,[†] the third to Christians,[‡]—and, after his apprehension, reported defences of himself before the people,[§] the council,[‖] and the court at Cæsarea;[¶] all of them professing to give the substance of his faith: yet in no one of them do we find a trace

<hr>

[*] Acts xiii. 15-41.   [†] xvii. 22-31.   [‡] xx. 18-35.
[§] xxii. 1-21.   [‖] xxiii. 1-6; xxiv. 10-21.   [¶] xxvi. 2-29.

of his characteristic doctrine, or a single thought which serves to identify him with the writer of his Epistles. In short, "*his gospel*" *is not there;* and to shift from the Church of Chalmers to that of Channing could scarcely change the atmosphere more than to pass from the Epistle to the Romans to the address on Mars Hill. Instead of his own, the opposite gospel is thrown to the front; and a prominence is given to the lesson of repentance and moral reformation,* which is by no means Pauline. Scarcely is anything attributed to him which, in its essence, might not have fallen from any liberal Jew; and what Christian element there is consists of historical rather than doctrinal statement. To apply another test, there is not a speech of Paul's which might not—*mutatis mutandis*—have been set down to Peter: the vehement contrast between the two, which created in the Clementines a special literature, is all chafed away, and a smooth level left, from which all personality has vanished in favour of a superficial catholicity. If ever, for a moment, there is a phrase with the Pauline *ring* in it, it turns out, when put to the proof, to be but an echo without the thought; as in the sentence, "By him all that believe are justified from all things from which ye could not be justified by the law of Moses,"† where the "justification" is used only in the negative sense of *acquittal*, and quite misses the positive appropriation of a foreign divine righteousness, which lies in the meaning of the apostle's word.

The Pauline doctrine of the cross not only involved as a consequence, but carried in its very essence, the absolute extinction, already accomplished, of the Mosaic law, and the emergence of the human soul, in its relation with God, into a faith and love possible alike to all. The apostle unconditionally cuts out the whole *legal* period from Sinai to Calvary as a parenthetical interpolation, interrupting the proper religious history of mankind, and designed only to prove, by its fatal spiritual barrenness, the incapacity of humanity for its own salvation, and reverts in the free faith of Christ to that free faith of Abraham which made him "the friend of God," linking these two together as contiguous

* Acts xvii. 30, 31; xxiv. 25. . † xiii. 39.

phenomena in the divine life of men. Nothing can be more repugnant to him than any half-view upon this matter: he is Antinomian to the heart of him ; and at the least pretence of continuing, as if sacred, any residue of positive Jewish enactment, he fires up with indignation, and treats it as a disloyalty to Christ, and a rejection of the grace of God. When Jewish Christians, "spying out the liberty which he has in Christ Jesus," and frightened at it, come to him with recommendations to compromise, he calls them "false brethren ;" and when they want him to naturalize Titus, who was a Gentile, by passing him through the Jewish rite, he would not for a moment submit to such miserable counsels, so as to build up again what he had destroyed.* Yet the Book of Acts attributes to him throughout a course of conduct directly at variance with this uncompromising conviction and habit. It would persuade us, that, though he would not have the heathen personality of Titus touched, he thought it prudent to turn the half-caste Timothy into a Jew, as a qualification for preaching the gospel.† It represents him as twice taking upon himself, without apparent motive beyond the display of a Judaic zeal and piety, vows of special asceticism, which, under the Nazirite law, could be discharged only at the temple.‡ It exhibits him in his speeches, especially after his indictment, as a good orthodox Jew, entirely loyal to the national law and traditions, and absolutely limiting his teachings to the contents of "Moses and the prophets,"§ holding, therefore, a Christianity which was not the opposite, but the development, of Judaism. It sends him forth as a missionary primarily to the synagogue, and makes any extension of his preaching beyond, conditional on the prior rejection of his message there ; so that the universality of his gospel is not in its principle, but in its accident ; and, if the Jews were not stupid, the heathen would not be saved. It sets him forth as a consenting party to the treaty at Jerusalem, defining the conditions of Gentile discipleship ; though they make essentials of some things to him indifferent, and forbid the sacrificial meats, which, except where tenderness to weak

* Gal. II. 3–5, 18.   † Acts xvi. 1–3.
‡ xviii. 18 ; xxi. 20–26.   § xxvi. 22.

consciences came in, he unhesitatingly allows.* How different was the real feeling towards him, and the estimate of his attitude with regard to the εἰδωλόθυτα in the parent Church of the apostolic age, may be gathered from the bitter invectives in the Apocalypse of John against "the doctrine of Balaam," which allows of "eating things offered to idols." † In short, all the burning characteristics of the apostle of the Gentiles are paled down in the artificial picture of the Book of Acts; and no one who has caught the focus of his thought, and become possessed of the intense image which it leaves, can recognize his personality in the liberal, courtly, and compromising Jewish Christian of the historian's narrative.

IV. If, from the Pauline section of the Book of Acts, we turn to the other, the faith and work attributed to Peter present variances no less marked from the picture sketched, though faintly sketched, elsewhere. The one personal appearance which he puts in within the range of Paul's Epistles is singularly significant both of his character and of his position. He is on a visit at Antioch; and, moving in the society of its mixed church, he is daily thrown among Christians of heathen origin. Falling in with the liberal manners of the place, he meets them on equal terms, sits down at table with them, and enables them to forget that he is a Jew. This, however, continues only so long as he is unwatched. Some disciples who are his neighbours at Jerusalem, arriving, apparently with commission from James to keep their eye upon what is going on, Peter's catholicity disappears; he can no longer take a meal with a Gentile; he sets up an exclusive Jewish table; and drawing to it all the Israelitish Christians, not excepting Barnabas himself, he leaves the Gentiles to discover that, although called brethren at Church, they are aliens at dinner.‡ The rebuke which Paul publicly gave to him was probably too subtle for his understanding; § but his conscience would sufficiently convict him, only we would fain know whether its conflict was permanently settled on the Antioch side, or, as is rather to be feared, by relapse into the ways of Jerusalem. Be that as it may, one thing is clear

* 1 Cor. viii. 4–13; x. 25–31.   † Rev. ii. 14–20.
‡ Gal. ii. 11–13.   § Ibid. ii. 14–21.

from this transaction,—that at the headquarters of the Twelve there was no communion between Jew and Gentile, and that, under the eyes of disciples thence, Peter dared not break bread in ethnical company ; that, in the central church, the law still drew the line between sacred and profane ; and that no door was open to the heathen, except through the passage of prior naturalization. The usages of the community were evidently established upon this basis, and Peter lived in habitual conformity with them ; else he could have felt no fear or shame in the public adoption of a freer life. The very fact that James had sent down a commission of inspection to Antioch, which completely cowed all the leaders, except Paul, shows a jealous assertion of a Jewish-Christian primacy, re-solved to sanction no breaking of the ancient bounds.

If this was the character of the original Church, assembled under the very shadow of the temple, and if Peter was fully committed to its principles, what are we to think of the part assigned to him in the Book of Acts? There he appears em-phatically as the first Gentile advocate and apostle. Senti-ments of unqualified universalism flow from his lips ; and, while Paul is still in the synagogue, he has already been bap-tizing Romans : and he alone admits them on the avowed principle that they are as near and dear to God as he ; while the " man of Tarsus " turns to them only of necessity, when the priority of Israel has come to nought. It is Peter to whom the call of the Gentiles is revealed, and who learned from it that he was "to call no man common or unclean ; " who finds that the Holy Spirit falls as graciously on the household of Cornelius as on the company at Pentecost ; who pleads, in the church convention, against laying on any believer the legal " yoke which neither they nor their fathers were able to bear," on the ground that God, who knoweth the hearts, hath put no difference between Israelite and alien, but gives the witness of his grace to both. How could thoughts like these be pub-licly and repeatedly uttered by a man whose daily life was in utter and notorious contradiction to them? And how could they be approved and echoed by the very people, including James' himself, the threat of whose opinion frightened Peter from acting them out? The representation, for those who trust the Epistle, must stand as unhistorical, due to a treatment of ecclesiastical materials which credits Peter with Pauline universality, and Paul with Peter's legal loyalty.

V. That the author of the Book of Acts wrote with a purpose, or at least preconception, not purely historical, is apparent from his anxiety to hold the balance of eminence even, between the two great apostles whose work about equally occupies his treatise. No advocate of either can quote from him a brilliant act or generous speech which eclipses the glory of the other. If at the "beautiful gate," a "cripple from birth" springs to his feet at Peter's word, and, leaping with joy, fills all beholders with wonder at the power of God; so, by the precincts of a Pagan temple, does Paul at Lystra meet with another "cripple from birth," and sends him bounding among the people, till they cry, "It is the hand of a God."* It is sufficiently marvellous that the very shadow of Peter should be found to shed healing on the line of sufferers over which it swept; but no less "special miracles did God work by means of Paul:" for "from his body were brought unto the sick handkerchiefs or aprons, and the diseases departed from them, and the evil spirits went out of them." † Do the prayers of the Church avail to bring down an angel of rescue into the prison at Jerusalem, and strike off the chains of Peter, and open the gates of cell and city, and restore him to the disciples while still at worship? Just as effectual are the prayers and hymns of Paul and Silas in the jail at Philippi, to rouse an earthquake of deliverance, and shake the walls till every door stood open, and the keeper owned the hand of God, and was baptized.‡ The Holy Spirit plainly bears witness to the authority of Peter and John, by taking no notice of Philip's converts till they have been touched by their apostolic hands, but equally withheld itself from the disciples of Apollos till the hands of Paul have been laid upon them.§ Peter, brought face to face with the prince of magicians, Simon Magus himself, puts him to shame; but only go with Paul to Paphos, and you shall see him baffle Elymas the sorcerer, and strike

* Comp. Acts iii. 1-10; xiv. 8-12.   † Comp. v. 15; xix. 11, 12.
‡ Comp. v. 18-25; xii. 4-17 (probably a duplicate tradition), and xvi. 25-39.
§ Comp. viii. 5-8, 14-17; xix. 1-7.

him blind.* Not even death is found too strong for the chief of the Twelve; and the departed spirit of the exemplary Dorcas comes back to her at his prayer; but so, too, does the embrace of Paul suffice to restore life to Eutychus, when he had been taken up dead.† And we have seen how the message to the Gentiles, which was the special pride and boast of the missionary of Tarsus, is not allowed to be appropriated by him, but is allotted, with a kind of equilibrium, to both; the priority and the divine initiative being set down to Peter, the large field, the copious results, and the crowning recognition of the Holy Spirit when the work was done, being accorded to Paul. This parallelism is too marked to be unintentional, and too artificial to be historical; and even though all the materials thus balanced should be drawn from previous sources (such as the " preaching," or the " Acts of Peter," and some itineraries of Paul), without any mixture of conscious fiction, yet the organizing principle which has disposed them thus is evidently not the simple service of fact, but some interest in persons, or schools of doctrine, which cannot but weaken our confidence in the carefulness of the writer. Whoever imports into a professed history anything of the structure and the effects of a romance is inevitably regarded with serious distrust.

Of the apostolic age, then, judged by its genuine memorials, the Book of Acts gives a distorted and highly ideal representation, changing the characteristics of its principal personages, suppressing its most serious dissensions, and assimilating its incompatible theologies. The author stands at a distance from its inner conflicts, and sees only the results which in their subsidence they have wrought out. He has been called a Pauline disciple; but he betrays not the slightest insight into the system of thought which distinguished the apostle of the Gentiles, or sympathy with his special genius: he simply glorifies his agency as one of the two great factors of the Christian Church, discerning only the extension he has given to it, not the element he has infused into it. He has been regarded as representing the Catholic, as opposed to the Judaic version of the gospel; but he does so only by abolishing the difference between them, attributing the broadest

* Comp. viii. 18-24; xiii. 8-12.   † Comp. ix. 36-42; xx. 7-12.

liberality to the apostles at Jerusalem, and treating Christian universality as Judaism rightly developed. This is the view natural to an observer stationed in the post-apostolic age, who saw the two elements, once mutually exclusive, adjusted together in the Church ; who knew that, in fact, that Church had spread from Jerusalem, used the sacred books of Israel, and claimed to be the true heir of their ancient promises, but whom the controversies and heart-burnings leading to this settled result had reached only in the faintest echoes. His work is a retrospective reconstruction of a drama which has long passed from the stage, and which can be recovered only by shreds of scenery preserved, by rumoured memories, by portraits and costumes of the chief actors, and by reasoning backwards from the known catastrophe. Passages of successful restoration there may be ; but the life and genius of the whole are not there. The imitation could hardly change so seriously the colouring and proportions of the original, without the refracting power of a generation between.

BOOK III.

DIVINE AUTHORITY INTERMIXED WITH HUMAN THINGS.

CHAPTER I.

THE HUMAN AND THE DIVINE IN HISTORY.

IF neither the hierarchy nor the canon can make good a claim to dictatorial authority, it by no means follows that the sacred function ascribed to them is gone, and that nothing divine is committed to their keeping. It may well be true that, for the religious guidance of men, there is a real order of dependence of the multitude upon the few, and of ordinary ages upon special crises and transmitted products of fresh spiritual insight, though the relation has degenerated into servility. But the oscillations of unreasoning impulse always shoot past the true centre without a pause. The easy credulity of mankind first insists on investing the priest with magical powers, and then, on discovery of their failure, turns upon him fiercely as an impostor. The blind idolater of " Holy Writ " will have it all infallible, that it may spare him the cares of thought and conscience, and serve him as *sortes faticinæ* for the solution of every question, and the relief of every scruple ; and then, when his moral sense has outgrown the Israelitish standard, and with his critical discernment he finds himself in the midst of myth and legend, of *vaticinia post eventum*, of conflicting histories and incompatible doctrines, he vents his displeasure, not upon his own arbitrary expectations, but on the written text which was in no way bound to fulfil them, and the persons whom he had himself arrayed in hieratic robes, and now disclaims as mortals in working dress.

Thus to stipulate for everything or nothing, and fling away whatever is short of all your fancied need, is the mere waywardness of the spoilt child: it is a demand absolutely at variance with the mixed conditions of any possible communion between perfect and imperfect natures. Not heaven itself can pour more or purer spiritual gifts into you than your immediate capacity can hold; and if the Holy Spirit is to "lead you into *all truth*," it will not be by saving you the trouble of parting right from wrong, but by the ever keener severance of the evil from the good through the strenuous working of a quickened mind.

Those whose dependence has been upon the Church are not without excuse in their demand for unconditional truth; they do but too passively acquiesce in a positive claim of infallibility already put forth by their own guide. But the Christians who have wrested that pretension from the Church only to transfer it to the Scriptures, charge upon the writers a wholly fictitious arrogance, utterly at variance with their prevailing humility and their quiet assumption of the simply human level. Who can better state the condition of all Revelation than the Apostle Paul at the very moment of imparting it,—" We have this treasure *in earthen vessels*, that the excellency of the power may be of God, and not of us"? Far from affirming that the gift incurs no liability in its transmission, he plainly says, "It cannot come to you without the alloy of humanity: whatever you find in it that is less than perfect, charge upon us: for all the rest give glory to God." But such modest terms are simply distasteful to the lazy will, that would like to have the vision, while the eye that apprehends it sleeps.

Yes: the heavenly essence in the earthen jar, the ethereal perfume in the tainting medium, the everlasting truth in the fragile receptacle,—this is just the combination which does not content the weakness and self-distrust of men. They want not the treasure only, but the casket too, to come from above, and be of the crystal of the sky; they are afraid of having the water of life spilled, like the rain, upon the meadows, and trickle through the common mould to feed the roots of beauty and of good; and they would store it apart,

and set it aloft, and secure for it a sacred inclosure to which
common men may come for their supply. This craving for
some accessible resort where the divine may be found pure
and simple, some blessed island fast anchored in the fluctuating sea of things, has created all the " holy places " of the
world ; and so, the ancient oracle, the mediæval church, the
Protestant Bible, have been severally detached from the scene
and conditions of natural humanity, and regarded as mere
media of unerring truth and grace. That this turns out to
be a dream of vain desire, that in this world no spot, no body
of men, no set of books, can be insulated as the peculium of
the Holy Spirit, will surprise no one who remembers that, in
the weaving of history, two agents are inseparable partners ;
and that, even where the pattern is most divine, the web that
bears it must still be human. Whatever higher inspiration
visits our world must use our nature as its organ, must take
the mould of our receptive capacity, and mingle with the
existing life of thought and affection. How then can it both
assume their form and escape their limitations ? how flow
into the currents of our minds without being diluted there ?
how dissolve itself in them without any taint from their
impurity? You cannot receive the light on a refracting surface, yet expect it to pursue its way still straight and colour-
less. And the soul of a man, especially of one fit to be among
the prophets of the world, is not like a crystal, a dead medium
of transmission, which once for all deflects what it receives,
and has done with it; but a living agent, whose faculties
seize on every influence that falls upon them, with action intenser as the appeal is more awakening. If, in your silent
musings, some deep word of God were to come to you, some
tone of solemn and tender conviction, lifting and placing you
where you had never stood before, would you not think of it ?
Would you not adjust its place with the faiths that were
dearest to you before ? Would it not run up into every love
and hope you have, and flow from your lips in their speech,
and pass into your life in their guise ? Instead of suspending
the natural faculties, and coming out of them as it went in,
it would but quicken reason, imagination, affection, and
multiply their combinations without yet perfecting their

U

resources. The flash of vision which bursts into the mind may itself be a light of heaven; but it can illuminate only the scene on which it falls; and while it pierces every recess, it does but touch with glory what already lies around, the thoughts and admirations which furnish the chamber of the soul, and the far-stretching ideals which spread as the night-field beyond the windows of her home. Come whence it may, from Nature or from Grace, new truth, once committed to the mind, falls into fallible custody; and the more it possesses the soul, the more will it be worked into the tissue of prior conceptions, retinting their imagery, reasoned into their theory, flung into the forms of their language; so that it cannot even issue at first hand from the inspired prophet himself, except on the intellectual air of his time, and in the dialect of his people or his school. The questions with which the age is already charged, and towards which eager spirits are bent with painful tension, are precisely those on which every hand will instantly turn the focus of any fresh heavenly light. "Is it this mountain, or Jerusalem? Is it Messiah, or that prophet? What about the tribute to Cæsar? How shall we know the end of the world?" Such are the problems, chiefly creations of pure fancy, and all perishable with their time, for solution of which the first witnesses of Christ rushed to his authority, and in which his religion was compelled at the outset to become a partner. By this instant crowding round of human interests and transitory elements wherever a sacred centre rises into life, the divine agency is inevitably lost from distinct and separate view, and indistinguishably mingled with the ferment and development of our humanity. But must we on that account deny that it is there? On the contrary, these are its recipient conditions: the higher agency could live on, only by entangling itself with the lower in every fibre, and making the joint harvest richer from the infusion of a purer sap. As the divine element does not suspend the human, the appearance of the human does not disprove the divine; everywhere in history, even in Christendom—their supreme product—their work is blended; like a single drama by two authors, or like the melody and harmony of the same piece.

This mingling of God's Spirit with man's in the education of our race is illustrated in the singularly mixed impression which every student must receive, when he steps across the line from the ancient Pagan civilization into the early centuries of Christian history. If he has heard of the " Fathers " only as they are quoted by Catholic divines ; if he has dreamed only of an age of saints and martyrs ; if he has been prepossessed by the Protestant ideal of the primitive church, as the spotless witness of heaven upon earth, which it is the highest aim of faithful men to reproduce ; great must be the shock of his disappointment on finding himself in communion with writers not only barbarous in speech and rude in art, but too often puerile in conception, passionate in temper, and credulous in belief. The legends of Papias, the visions of Hermas, the imbecility of Irenæus, the fury of Tertullian, the rancour and indelicacy of Jerome, the stormy intolerance of Augustine, cannot fail to startle and repel him ; and if he turns to the milder Hippolytus, he is introduced to a brood of thirty heresies which sadly dissipate his dream of the unity of the Church. The very questions on which polemic passion was habitually expended, whether Easter should be computed by the day of the month or of the week,—whether returning heretics should be baptized,—whether it was not impious to believe in antipodes,—whether Christian women might cut their hair,—with the perpetual fire of excommunications and intrigues which was maintained till they were settled by some stroke of power, must offend the feeling of all but trained ecclesiastics. Forged literature, spurious miracles, fanatical courting of the martyr's crown, episcopal contests in Antioch, Alexandria, and Rome, councils where the religion of truth and love was put to the vote of rival antipathies, leave upon the mind the most painful sense of shame and mortification, of a sinking intellectual civilization and a lost spiritual ideal. Yet we have only to look a little deeper, to pass through the noise of the front ranks and move quietly through the Christian commonalty behind, to recover from the depression of that first half-view. Nay, if we return with a larger purpose into this very crowd of disappointing men and repulsive phenomena,—if, piercing through the angry clouds and pelt-

ing storms that shut in the lower region of their life, we seek
for the ultimate heaven in which their true self hides—for the
supreme ideas, the dominating worship, the expanse of inner
thought and trust in which their characteristic essence is to
be found,—we shall feel ourselves in the midst, not of the
fretful and impotent decrepitude of a decaying world, but of
the passionate exuberance of a young enthusiasm, too much
carried away by new and sublime relations to be capable of
calmness and self-control. It soon becomes evident that the
very centre of gravity in human interests has changed; that
the old Nature-world is passing away, and the sense of a
supernatural life is seizing the vacant place; that while for
heathen thought the divine principle lay distributed and
buried in the matter of the world, now, from some marvellous
cause, God and Man had both of them burst from the cere-
ments of a dead philosophy, and stood face to face, spirit to
spirit, person to person, heedless of the physical realm, which
bends and sinks before their mutual approach, yielding itself
to miracle, and ready even to pass away, that they too may
be alone together. This is the grand revolution which we
find accomplished when we cross from Pagan on to Christian
ground,—the transfer of life into the immediate hand of the
living and personal God; and the assumption by each individual soul of man of its own answering personality. The
Church was everywhere the witness and the shelter of the
communion of these two; where the humiliations of servitude
could be forgot, the stains of sin be lightened by true tears,
and the shadows of death vanish before the light of eternal
life. So great was the effect of this fresh power, that you
had only to step from the forum to the Church to find quite a
new edition of human nature, with altered ethical proportions,
and a reversal of established sentiments and manners; in the
young a reverence and simplicity, in the slave a dignity and
quietude, in the woman a modest self-forgetfulness, in the
man a frank humility, not ashamed to stoop to the smallest
service or lift the voice in highest prayer;—all proclaiming
that here an ideal of character and an order of affections prevailed, quite different from the fevered and festering world on
which the sunshine glittered without. I do not apologize for

the coarseness of Tertullian, or the immodesties of Augustine. Doubtless, in the desperate struggle for a higher purity, a wild vehemence of defiance, and absurd reactionary asceticism, carried many a powerful genius beyond all bounds of reason. But we are not to charge the residuary corruption of a dissolving society, brought by converts into the Church, upon the community which sought to heal it. After all, and in the main, the purity was won. Domestic life fell under a rule simple, severe, and sacred; and in the social relations of class with class; there arose a mutual fidelity, a pity for suffering, a relaxation of dependence into sympathy, which reflected the compassion of God in the new affections among men. I know not how any one can appreciate these great changes without owning the presence of an intense Divine agency; or, if he owns it, can pretend that it is not everywhere,—in priests and people, from the central altar to the outskirts of lay life, —mixed up with the natural workings of humanity, and melted down into the indivisible forms of our weakness and our strength.

Such was the blending, and such the strife, of the δύναμις τοῦ πνεύματος and the ἀσθένεια τῆς σαρκος, in the Church of the first four centuries; of which the former was unmistakably the new and cleansing element, while the latter was but the old and degenerate organism which it had come to heal and renew.

Perhaps, however, we are turning our attention to too late a time, when causes of corruption had already been long at work to destroy the first simplicity and unity of the Christian life; and by simply retreating to the fountain-head, we may leave these imperfections of thought and temper behind, and see the new dispensation clear as yet of every taint. Thither let us ascend, therefore, and approach as near as we can to the very sources of our religion. It can hardly be denied that there also we still receive the same mixed impression. Is there any one among us to whom the New Testament itself speaks with a tone invariably true and sacred, dispensing with selection, and never compelling avoidance? Do the pictures which it gives to us of that first age always win our hearts, and make us sigh that we were not there, to hear the preaching of Peter,—to see Ananias and Sapphira carried out,—to support Paul against the factions at Corinth,—to ask the Seer John of the phials and the dragon of his visions at Patmos? Those whose minds are not shut up by an undiscriminating reverence,—those to whom it has become a necessity to think and feel as they read, must surely own their disappointment that the divine gleams which kindle them are so sparse and transient, and so soon quenched by the mists of an obsolete world and the dust of its crumbled controversies. There are few more pathetic experiences than that of the young enthusiast, whose devotion has consecrated every page of Scripture, but whose intellect wakes to read it critically at last; and who has to reduce his prophecies into history,—to find the drama of the parables played out long ago in Galilee and Jerusalem,—to discover that the Last Judgment, which art and poetry have solemnized in vain, is the lost dream of a world that has outlived its end ; and whose sacred thirst, increasing with the fever of disappointment, has to retreat to fountains ever narrowing, till he has drunk so often of the beatitudes, the parting discourses, and the remaining dews of scattered sweetness here and there, that he goes for a draught of fuller refreshment to à Kempis or Tauler. To whichever of the primitive versions of Christianity, contained in the New Testament, we turn, the human admixtures are instantly felt. Paul, our earliest witness, weaves the living fibre of a true spiritual philosophy into a texture of rabbinical dialectic, from whose windings he himself cannot always emerge into the clear. Firm as his grasp is of truths, unspoken before, yet ever present in the deepest moral consciousness of man, that to live in yourself, however rightly, is to live in prison, and to go captive to a diviner is alone to be free,—and glorious as are his outbursts of thanksgiving for an emancipated nature, that has escaped the conflict of sin, though not the thorn of suffering, we sometimes wish that he would let them speak for themselves, instead of trying to extort them from cross-questionings of Hagar and Ishmael, or striking again the desert rock to make them flow; and sometimes fear lest, in his exulting scorn of conquered sin, he should negligently guard the ways

of return possible to that subtle power. And though no
writings bear more strongly than his the impress of profound
and disinterested conviction, how is it possible not to be
disturbed by his liability to paroxysms of ecstasy, to look
regretfully at his flight to the third heaven, and to wish he
had not heard those unspeakable words ?   If from his Gentile
gospel we turn to the teaching of the Judaic twelve, we are
indeed relieved from the theosophic strain of the Pauline
reasoning, and left upon the plainer ground of the elder
monotheism, with a Christ who is but " a man approved of
God " on earth and reserved by him in heaven.   But then,
in holding to the simplest, they cling to the narrowest too,
and by setting themselves against the daring Pauline revelation in thought and act, they miss the universality and
spiritual depth of the religion, and leave Christianity a mere
interior variety of the Israelitish history.   An horizon bounded
in the Past by fancied promises to David, or even forecasts of
Moses, and in the future by the apocalyptic scenery of the
returning Nero's fall before the returning Christ, and the
substitution of the New Jerusalem for the perished Rome,—
an horizon which therefore shut up human history at once,
and turned men then living into the millennium, or out of
it,—can have no serious interest for us who belong to a still
persistent and expanding humanity: and it is no wonder that
we, whom it never contemplated, look on its wild and rugged
pictures as on a mythology foreign to ourselves, and listen to
the hymns that mingle with its drama, as to a sublime poetry,
the dream-voices of many waters, murmuring from afar.
The Book of Revelation embodies a form of apostolic
Christianity which, if it had been finally ascendant, could
have had no attraction, except as a curious past phenomenon,
for any future age.   It owes its very preservation only to the
forbearance of the Gentile universalism which it denounces ;
and remains to engage the fancy, to baffle the predictions,
and alarm the fears, of those who are blind alike to the early
history and the everlasting spirit of their religion.   If, again,
we open the page of the Gospels and approach the person of
Christ himself, no reverent prepossessions can secure us from
painfully mixed impressions.   How broken, and at times

distorted, is the image which the record presents! Glimpses of divine beauty, lost as soon as seen; openings of insight immeasurably deep, caught by a flash that leaves the denser darkness; tones of majestic trust and tenderness, that float upon a momentary wind, yet linger on the heart for ever; a form of grace and power, free and firm because at disposal of a highest Unseen Love, gentle and flowing because surrendered to lowliest service; yet with many an adjunct which it is impossible to bring into the outline, and many a look that will not sit upon that face: such are the fragmentary features which alternate, as it seems to me, our joy and our discontent; and which show that we have no sun-portrait of the reality, but only a pieced picture, half memory that is dim, and half tradition that is blind. Everywhere the individual personality is confused by identification with a Messianic ideal; nothing is left to speak in its own concrete simplicity; all is turned to some official or evidential account. If Jesus quotes the prophets, the historians twist them into some incredible application to himself. If his path is strewed with deeds of mercy, and his calm look quiets many a troubled mind, it is that the demons are disturbed at his approach and cry aloud in witness that he is Christ. If he teaches the uttermost self-forgetfulness and pure imitation of God, he must be made, within a few lines, to balance this by the directest appeal to the hopes and fears of retribution. If he wishes the temple and the priests away, that he may deal with the naked human spirit, and in a trice raise up an imperishable temple not made with hands, he is thought to be talking of his own body, instead of the soul of humanity. From beginning to end there is every trace of a divine life once realized in history, but partially lost through the persistent self-assertion of human theory and doctrine. The two elements thus given to us we can therefore know from one another by no mechanical severance, by no chemical precipitation. We cannot say, 'This doctrine is divine, because it is found in a canonical book, and that is human, because confined to the apocrypha:' or, 'This moral rule is binding, because enforced by Peter or by Paul, and that is open to question, as given only by Apollos or by Clement:'

or ' This argument, is demonstrative, because attributed to Jesus himself, and that is subject to doubt, as reported only of Stephen or of Timothy.' Neither Church nor Scripture can serve on these easy terms as our " Rule of faith and practice ; " and yet both may provide adequate guidance to the highest truth and goodness. To reach it, however, without use of the discriminative faculties, and be carried blindfold into the eternal light, is impossible. Other than mixed materials, possibilities of true or false, of good or ill, transient or everlasting, are nowhere offered to our acceptance ; and we have not simply to *take*, but always to *choose*. And the tests by which we distinguish the fictitious from the real, the wrong from the right, the unlovely from the beautiful, the profane from the sacred, are to be found within, and not without, in the methods of just thought, the instincts of pure conscience, and the aspirations of unclouded reason. These are the living powers which constitute our affinity with God, and render what to Him is eternally true and good, true and good to us as well ; and their selecting touch alone can part asunder the entangled crowd of acts and things, and from their conflicting meanings single out for us the idea which is His, and the spirit which He loves.

In applying these tests to the materials of early Christian history, we shall see considerable portions of them fall away to the account of the human agent's store of local prepossession and temporary error, while the divine essence is concentrated in a spiritual focus, simple but intense. But when this severance has been effected, it would be hasty to dismiss the discarded elements as mere refuse, out of all relation to the Divine Will. For, though they may be false as attached to the new religion, and fail of the end contemplated by its teachers, they are not inoperative, and will produce other ends, like all active beliefs, false as well as true. These effects, undesigned by men, must be referred to the causality of God. They will turn up in the courses of the world, and would have done so, though there had been no new infusion of his Spirit to be confused by their alloy. The illusions of men, which disappoint their expectations and frustrate their purposes, such as the notion of demoniacal possession, the outlook for a near end of the world, and the trust in the supernatural virtues of rites and sacraments, are influences of great power in human affairs, and work out results which cannot be foreign to the scheme of Providence in history. Our errors are controlled, our blindness disarmed, by God's omniscience, and their erratic lines deflected into place within his diagram of universal good. Just as the animal instincts continually provide for the exigencies of descendants they will never see, and conform in the dark to the conditions of a season beyond their date, so do our impulses and passions, working in an imperfect light of thought, move on paths which they know not, and realize ends which they never contemplated. Through some misdirection or infirmity, most of the larger agencies in history have failed to reach their own ideal, yet have accomplished revolutions greater and more beneficent; the conquests of Alexander, the empire of Rome, the Crusades, the ecclesiastical persecutions, the monastic asceticisms, the missionary zeal, of Christendom, have all played a momentous part in the drama of the world, yet a part which is a surprise to each. Nay, what is the very principle of that law of Evolution which we have learned to take as our clew through the history of the universe and man? that each living being, in simply following its own impulse in the "struggle for life," helps to build up a constitution of organic nature, not only replete with adaptations and interdependencies infinitely varied and refined, but secure of progressive development through higher stages of physical growth, of skilled instinct, of reflective intelligence, and of moral elevation. If we acknowledge that birds and insects, without knowing what they do, could never alight on infallible provision for an unsuspected future, were not their activities directed by a foresight other than their own, how much more must we feel that when men, not simply blind to the right goal, but straying towards the wrong, are nevertheless secretly deflected into the curve of truth and beauty, and made involuntary instruments of an issue sublimer than their boldest dreams, it can only be through the controlling presence of a Reason and a Will transcendent and divine. Here, then, in the sphere of ends which, absent from human intention, yet obviously lie within the embrace of an intellectual system of the world, we have a further test, no longer intuitive, but susceptible of outward application, for discriminating the divine and human agencies in history. Instances of its use will not be wanting, as the story of Christendom unfolds.   But the inner tests must be our chief dependence in tracing our way along the fragments of a path to the fountain head of that marvellous and fertilizing power.

CHAPTER II.

WHAT ARE "NATURAL" AND "REVEALED RELIGION?"

IF either Church or Scripture could for a moment be constituted a *sacrarium* for secluding all that is simply divine, the first movement of historical change, through the play of finite powers, would break the holy bounds, and interfuse the thoughts of God and man. Nothing can arise on the field of history that is not the product of them both ; nor can they be shut up, apart from each other, in any portion whether of space or time. Are the beginnings human? The divine will not be wanting in their ends. Are the beginnings divine? There will be plenty of human outgrowth ere the end, it may be of strength and beauty, or of sickly and degenerate development. For the fallen angels are not the only heavenly natures that "do not keep their first estate." Whatever is "born of God," simply because it *lives*, is ever on the move: be it a light for thought or a rule for will, it may be given to a rudimentary intelligence, on purpose to be outgrown ; or, it may fall into unfaithful custody, to be turned to corrupt account ; or, it may be genially received, and quickened, as a seed of grace, into ulterior truth and good, which transcend and supersede it. There can be no surer characteristic of a divine dispensation, than that it lifts its disciples to a position higher than the level from which it originally spoke, and so widens their horizon as to dwarf the little circle which then fenced them round.

The free handling of the ancient Law and its teachers " of old times " in the sermon on the mount, and the whole preaching of Jesus, might have opened the eyes of his personal followers to these things. But it was reserved for the apostle who never heard his voice to treat the ancient " oracles of God " as by no means final, to assume that the Revelation of one age might be the superstition of another, to declare the

Law " the schoolmaster to bring us to Christ," to claim escape from an inherited Divine institution into spiritual religion, with free permission to throw away canonical theology and go straight to the living reality of God, as if Moses had never been. Has not " God revealed his Son in him ? " And now that he " knows God, or rather is known of Him," he has no more to do with " the weak and beggarly elements " which have hitherto held him " in bondage." What are these " elements " which he visits with such contempt ? They are the very " Law given to the fathers," the words that burst from the thunders of Sinai, which made the nation " a holy people," and Jerusalem the hope of the whole world. And why does he fling these things aside ? Is it because he thinks them false? No : but because he has learnt a directer way to the truth they hold and to truth beyond it : because the time has come when the life of God is its own witness and is accessible anew : when the human spirit, now clearer and larger, feels after Him not in vain : and his Spirit, finding the latch lifted in many a mind, steals in, and speaks the secret of his presence. The apostle was accused of apostasy from revealed religion, because he put the whole Mosaic economy into a parenthesis and resumed the world's history as if it were not there. He was denounced as a latitudinarian, because he let the Pagan come to the living God without asking leave of the Jew and taking Zion by the way. He was set down as a " mere Theist," because he said that Abraham and the pious men of old times had direct relations with the Most High, and so might we have. And he was charged with bare negative teaching, because this was the chief burthen of his gospel—that the divine light was impartial, the divine worship spiritual, and regenerate humanity the inmost resort of the divine glory.

In every age, and not least in our own, the same treatment awaits those who bid men look straight into the clear heaven, instead of peering at it only through the cloister window, so dark with age, and rich with the colours of the past, that it uses the sunshine but to paint the figures of the saints. Every veil which has once transmitted a sacred ray, every medium of expression, by word or symbol, frequented by the soul in her devout ascents, becomes so consecrate that a frightened piety will not dispense with it, even to stand face to face with the living God.

But though we cannot *sever* the Divine thought and action from the human, so as to isolate it in a literature or an institution, may it not be possible to *distinguish* the two conceptions, notwithstanding their admixture in fact? especially if, to simplify the question, we limit our attention to the one field of experience which we are trying to explore, viz., the grounds of our religious knowledge and beliefs?ˑ In the *method* of acquiring these and the *tenure* by which we hold them, there is a familiar distinction drawn, for the express purpose of solving this problem, viz., between *Natural* and *Revealed* religion : and if we can give exactitude to the meaning of these terms and exhibit their true relation, it may clear our way, and save us from some prevalent illusions.

Shall we say, " Natural religion is that in which man finds God : Revealed religion is that in which God finds man ? " This surely is the distinction which the phrases are intended to mark : on the one hand, the ascending effort of the human faculties towards their Supreme Object: on the other, His spontaneous descent into the field of human apprehension. The knowledge of him is the reward of thought, the crown of long endeavour, in the first case : but in the last, the surprise of an unsought light, that illumines what is in us but is not ours. The Agents therefore are different in the two cases, and proceed from opposite termini, with movements in inverse directions.

If this be so, we may next ask why the first is called " natural " religion, a term which does not happily balance the epithet " revealed." " *Nature*," in its ˑoriginal and largest sense, means the whole realm of things *that are born*, that enter and quit the field of existence ; and, as naming the sphere of phenomena, stands opposed to *God*, the eternal ground and cause of all that sweeps across the stage. In this view, the religion of nature is that which we gather from the world of appearances, from the changes with which time and space are populous. If they speak to us not simply of themselves, or of antecedents like themselves, but as expressions of a higher cause; if their laws seem not to have scrambled into equilibrium, but to take the dispositions of intending Thought; if their order, which when recorded makes our science, and when copied makes our arts, must be, we think, an intellectual organism in its primal seat; if their beauty everywhere, and their play of light and shadow upon human life, which press from the soul the tones of poetry, report to us a creative artist who has set the strain; if, in short, as we look around us, we find a passage from the world to a Divine Mind as author of the world, we are disciples of " Natural religion." The phrase marks simply the source whence the impression comes,—the objects in contemplating which it is forced upon us ; and whether we are able to give a rational account of it, or it streams in upon us we know not how, from the very aspect of the earth and sky, it falls under the same designation.

We speak, however, under the same word "*Nature*," of something else than the external universe in face of which we stand. We appropriate the term to *ourselves;* and talk of "*human nature*," when we wish to mark the distinguishing endowments and tendencies of man. He too is a creature *born*, and bringing up into this scene of things a *constitution* or *system* of faculties, which at once open and limit his range. He belongs therefore to the same field which other transitory beings occupy, and takes his place as an object with the groups of animals and the catalogues of stars. His phenomena must be added on to theirs in order to make up the book of the world; and must be taken into account by one who, through the world, would seek to know its author and its end. But when we speak of " the natural religion of man," we use the phrase in a different sense; to denote the religion, not in which man is the object thought of, but in which he is the thinking subject,—which is the characteristic expression of his mind, and without which he would be an exception to the rule of our humanity. In describing God as apprehended thus, we refer to the faculties we know him with, not to the vestiges we know him by. Phrases there are which lie between and look both ways. If we say that the ancient philosophers were left to the "*light of nature*," we may mean either the light of *their own* nature, or the luminous characters written *on the heavens and the earth.* In the one case, we regard their religion chiefly as depending on their personal and moral characteristics, as giving direction to their reverential faith: in the other, we look on it as intellectually gathered by survey of the realm of Law.

Take it in what sense you will, whether as collected by inference from external nature, or as worked out by meditation within our own, Natural Religion is a human elaboration which sets more or fewer steps between ourselves and God. It is a method of *mediate* knowledge, carrying us, by successive stages of advance, out of the finite into the infinite: there are media without, as we pass the facts of the world in review before us, and move from the narrower through the wider order to the cause which embraces all: there are media within, as our own reason weaves up feeling and perception into its premisses, and so marshals its premisses as to conquer its conclusion. So far forth as God *naturalizes* himself in order to be discerned, constructs a cosmos to be the mirror of his thought, covers it with greater and lesser circles of intersecting laws, executed by a delegated physiology from within, he is not *presented*, but *represented :* the knowledge of him belongs to the *religion of nature;* it requires that we know another object, or series of objects, on the way to an apprehension of Him. Every interposed term requires a corresponding step of reasoning in us; the final inference attenuating its security by every link in the catena. True it is that God's agency in outward nature is just as immediate as in the soul of man; its forces, though imagined to be his deputies, being simply his modes of energy, so that in spreading out the universe he is showing himself. But it is on *it*, and not on *us*, that his physical action is immediate, and it would still have its object and its field, though we were away. The material world is interposed to bridge the interval between his living thought and ours; and one and the other must cross before they meet.

This is the feature which has made men sigh for something more assured than natural religion, and has left its chaste and modest temple to gather only a sparse company of worshippers: where, it is true, you may number many a pale and lofty brow, many a pure and noble will, and see hung upon the walls some crowns of highest martyrdom, and lyres of sweetest song; but whence spirits more fervid or less choice turn aside to crowd around some bolder prophet and kneel in worship of deeper tone. *Thus* to reach God by effort and discovery of ours is esteemed too great an act for our humanity; and, since it must be by mediate reasonings on mediate phenomena, is too precarious for yearning hearts to bear. "If he be really there" (they cry), "behind the folds of the visible order, will he throw all the hazards of the search on us, and coldly wait until we have found the eternal secret? Will he not rather take the initiative himself, make us his object, and so enter our mind as to be *immediately* known?" Such is the feeling which has made men impatient of the bare probabilities of natural religion, and prepared them to look for assurance more direct. To answer that feeling, the one condition which the desired Revelation must fulfil is plainly this: it must be *immediate*, living God with living man, Spirit present with spirit; knowing Him, indeed, but rather "being known of Him." The whole road of human ascent must be cut away, and the painful climbing spared; or if, besides, any ladder now should be left, it must not matter whether it stands upon the plain, or its visionary steps are the air-stations of a dream; since they are but for the feet of men and angels, and are dispensed with by Him whose presence makes earth as well as sky the very house of God and gate of heaven. Where the Agent is Divine, and the recipient human, there can be nothing for the mind to do but to let the light flow in, and by the lustre of its presence turn each common thought to sanctity: the disclosure must be *self-disclosure;* the evidence, *self-evidence;* the apprehension, as we say, *intuitive;* something given, and not found. Here then we have the essential distinction,—the only one which we can not merely state but verify, between natural and revealed religion,—that the one is what is worked out by man through processes which he can count and justify: the other is there by gift of God, so close to the soul, so folded in with the very centre of the personal life, that though it ever speaks it cannot be spoken of; though it shines everywhere it can be looked at nowhere; and because presupposed as reality it evades criticism as a phenomenon.

But does not this reduction of Revelation to Intuition carry us too far, and involve us in the idea of a revealed Science as well as a revealed Religion? For we certainly have intuitive apprehensions of a reality in other fields than that of spiritual truth. Our beliefs in Space and Time, the bases of geometry and number, in Substance and Causality, assumed in Physics and embodied in the structure of all language, are no less immediate than the directest consciousness of God. Are they then entitled to the same place, as a communion between the Divine mind and the human? To a certain extent they are so; but not without an important qualification. They have precisely the same claim to absolute trust, and, in exercising that trust, we ground ourselves simply on the veracity of God: his report to our perceptive and intellectual capacities we accept just as it is, and use as a *datum* for all that we have to learn. Only, what we get to know by means of them is *not God per se*, but the *external world:* they are the conditions under which we interpret our place and life as creatures of Nature, and not our spiritual relations as personal beings; and these alone it is which constitute the object matter of religious knowledge; and beyond this sphere it is not usual to carry the word *Revelation*. Else, these primary cognitions, simply as *data* at first hand, might well be called intellectual revelations; and as not found among phenomena of nature, but standing as prior conditions of them all, might even aspire to the epithet *supernatural*. But as this also has been appropriated to religious use, the equivalent Greek word, *metaphysical* is accepted instead. The reason of this jealous guarding of its special terms on the part of religion lies in the difference of its object of knowledge from that on which science rests. The field which is entered through the scientific intuitions is the field of *Necessity*, either eternal and unchangeable as the nexus of mathematical properties, or simply durable as empirically unchanged, like the persistent sequences of physical law; and if this field were all, its lesson might be delivered and learned, from end to end, without a conception beyond this necessity, or a suspicion of the higher infinitude which lies around our prison walls. The field, on the other hand, which is entered through the intuitions of conscience, is the field *of freedom, of possibility, of alternatives,* i.e., of *spiritual action,* amenable, not to natural antecedents, but to preferential obligation, carrying in it the relation of mind obeying and mind commanding, both on the ground of a common righteousness. Here we are ushered by our own supernatural life (i.e., life beyond the range of Nature-necessity) into cognizance of our supernatural affinities : we walk in the presence, not simply of animals in the same cage, but of spirits other than our own ; with whom we pass from creatures of nature into children of God. This is the specialty which properly reserves for the *moral* intuitions alone among the cases of immediate knowledge, an identification with re-vealed *Religion.* It may be true that God is not less immediately present with us in the energies of nature than in the authority of conscience. But it is an external and dynamic presence, simply executant of what is predetermined to be, and, as such, might as well be purely automatic ; and is short of the volitional and personal character which alone entitles to the name of *God.* The world is no doubt " immediate " both to him and to us : to him, however, as effect, to us as cause ; it therefore lies between, *revealing* itself as here, and only *implying* Him as there.

From this analysis flow several inferences corrective of prevalent illusions.

1. If Revealed Religion is an immediate divine knowledge, it is strictly personal and individual, and must be born anew in every mind. It admits of no condition separating the Self-revealer from the recipient Soul : it is a light for which they two alone are needful, alone are possible. " The secret of God " is with the " pure in heart," taken one by one. As many minds as there are that know him at first hand, so many revealing acts have there been ; and as many as know him only at second hand are strangers to revelation : they may hold, or think they hold, what has been revealed to another ; but, in passing through media to them, it has become Natural religion. Take away the fresh Divine initia-

tive, and the immediate apprehension which it gives cannot pass *laterally* from man to man : no one, in the absence of God's living touch, can put us into communion with him, and make him known to us as his own spirit would. Nothing spiritual, nothing Divine, can be done by deputy; and the prophets are no vicars of God, to stand in His stead among alien souls, and kindle in them a flame unfed by the Light of lights. And yet, so close and deep is our interdependency that their mediation is indispensable. For

2. The Divine life in our humanity exists in various intensities, and in more or less unveiled form; with some, never passing beyond dim yearnings and impersonal ideal images of something right and noble that draws them on; with others, clearing itself into the personal presence and real communion of the supremely Holy. When a mind kindled with this inspiring consciousness comes into contact with natures still groping in the half-lit cloud, and simply tells its tale, nothing has so much power to turn the implicit feeling and suspicion of the Divine reality into explicit apprehension of it : the truth of the mystery being struck, it becomes imperative and demands recognition by surprise. In this way there is certainly a lateral transmission of faith from mind to mind. But it gives no new reality : it only interprets what is already there; flinging a warm breath on the inward oracles hid in invisible ink, it renders them articulate and dazzling as the hand-writing on the wall. There is no change in the object within sight; only the film is wiped away that concealed or confused what was close at hand. The divine Seer does not convey over to you *his* revelation, but qualifies you to receive your own. This mutual relation is possible only through the common presence of God in the conscience of mankind : that the sacred fire can pass from soul to soul is the continuous witness that He lives in all. Were not our humanity itself an Emmanuel, there could be no Christ to bear the name. Take this Divine ground away, shut up each individual mind under its own non-conducting glass, and no inspiration given to one can avail to animate another. He may indeed tell others what has been revealed to him, and they may take it on his word, and pass the

report on; but this is not repeating his experience: it is believing testimony, not seeing God.

3. Physical phenomena, whether observed or reported, cannot in any form convey a revelation. They do not fulfil the condition of direct contact between the revealer and the recipient, but on the contrary are interposed between, proceeding as effects from the one, and entering as a spectacle through the senses of the other. All that they can give is something seen, something heard, something felt; and whatever else they bring to light must be elicited and elaborated by thought, and stand among the inferences of natural reason or piety. This will be readily admitted with regard to all the familiar changes of the world. Whatever lineaments of disposing intellect we trace behind the order of the seasons or the course of life upon the globe, whatever vestiges of Providence we find in the history and culture of mankind, are confessedly reached as deductions of our own, with authority contingent on their logical validity. But it is supposed to be otherwise, if the events should be of that exceptional and irreducible kind which men call *miracles*. Yet they too, appearing in the same field, addressing the same senses, are at precisely the same remove from God on the one 'hand and from us on the other; so that from them too, if they are to win any higher significance, it remains that we have to reason up to Him. Do you say, ' But miracles are his immediate act? ' Be it so: still, they are his immediate action on the world, and not on us; or, if on us, only on our senses or our limbs: while, as we gaze, our immediate knowledge is of them, and not of Him. They stand, no less than the commonest events, between ourselves and Him, and leave us to make of them what we can; and as we ponder them, and work out their theory to its result, we are still upon the lines of natural religion, only dealing with exceptional phenomena, whose law is as yet unknown. And how far their teaching is from any simple and invariable voice, into how many divergent paths of inference it may break, is attested by every age of belief and unbelief. To refer them to the secret fund of power in the superhuman world is not to give them a source sacred and supreme. That invisible scene represents itself to

human thought by no means as a divine solitude, but as teeming, like this earth, with beings of various will; any one of whom may supply the imagination with an adequate source of each startling event; and Beelzebub and Mephistopheles, the demons and the ghosts, the sorcerer's fiends and the medium's prompters, have all in turn found recognition as depositaries of supernatural power among men. Granting that their claim must be disallowed, yet, even for this it must be heard and answered; and so we are unrelieved from our conditions of subsidiary reasoning and mediate relief, and pass by a circuit no shorter than before to the assured presence of the living God.

If such phenomena, instead of being observed, are *reported*, they themselves, with all that they contain, are known only through an estimate of evidence; and being reached by more or fewer steps of probability, are foreign to the category of Revelation. Should they be of the miraculous kind, the inferences from them will even compare unfavourably, in respect of the risk of error, with those of the familiar "Natural religion;" for *there* the consecutive links are supplied by considerations rational and moral, the conclusion is congruous in character with the premisses, and the whole intellectual structure is homogeneous throughout; whereas, in the supposed teaching of attested "signs and wonders" no arch of appreciable relation spans the interval between the attestation and the thing attested; and the believer has to take at a leap the chasm that separates them, in blind trust that the witness has power to land him safe. Moreover, be the value of such inference what it may at one remove from the fountain head, its assurance suffers reduction at every step of transmission, and rapidly passes into the precariousness of a tradition. In the case of ordinary history there are critical resources for minimizing this precariousness, by rules of analogy and measures of probability; but where the facts attested lie out of all analogy, and are amenable to no standard of probability, where they are unconditionally staked on an authority silent in the sleep of ages, these safeguards fail us: so that the mere inheritance of a reported revelation, dealing with matters which we cannot verify, would but leave us with an organism of natural religion of far more attenuated strength than that which usually goes by the name. As a logical problem, it will always be more difficult to establish the adequacy of a personal authority for a religious truth, than to establish the truth itself. And as for the moral problem,—if you deny or disparage the spiritual apprehensions of humanity, your authority has nothing to speak to ; if you admit them, it ceases to be mere authority ; for the revelation verifies and renews itself.

4. In virtue of its immediate or intuitive character, Revelation must always open our eyes to what really *is* or *ought to be*, not to what *has happened, is happening, or will happen.* The organs and processes of Sense are our provisions for noting phenomena as they pass ; the registers of memory and computations of the understanding, for reading their series back into the past and forward into the future : to these faculties it is,—which move by steps of thought,—that all the contents of Time are amenable and come up for judgment ; but the Time itself in which these contents are found we bring with us as intuitively given. In like manner, the properties of all figured spaces are determinable by deduction from their definitions ; but not without the Space itself, already known as a condition of them all. The immediate self-disclosure of God to the human spirit, similarly carries in it the consciousness of a present Infinite and Eternal, behind and above as well as within all the changes of the finite world. It brings us into contact with a Will beyond the visible order of the universe, of a Law other than the experienced consecution of phenomena, of a Spirit transcending all spirits, yet communing with them in pleadings silently understood. But it recites no history ; it utters no Sibylline oracles ; it paints no ultramundane scenes ; it heralds neither woes nor triumphs of "the latter days." So foreign are such apocalyptic things from the essence of "revelation," that they exemplify the lowest aberrations of "natural religion." Whether or not God could impart to us knowledge of this type I will not presume to say ; but, certainly, neither the capacities he has given us nor the scene in which he has placed us are provided with the means of receiving and authenticating such phenomenal foreknowledge.

5. The analysis which has been given requires us to invert the accepted order of dependence between natural and revealed religion. In treatises which assign validity to both, the former invariably occupies the prior place, and is taken as the necessary presupposition of the latter; on the obvious ground that, till the existence of a Revealer is assured, the pretensions of a revelation cannot be tested, and its indispensable marks determined. The conclusion therefore which terminates the reasonings of natural religion must be reached in order to furnish the first condition of revealed : and on the solidity of that borrowed premiss all that follows inevitably depends. The Theism which is thus the $\dot{a}\rho\chi\dot{\eta}$ of revealed religion must therefore, as the $\tau\dot{\epsilon}\lambda o\varsigma$ of natural religion, be won by non-religious premisses, such as a mere logician, dealing only with intellectual concepts, will be competent to wield. A theologian who follows this order of procedure, from purely scientific data at one end, to the contents of the creeds at the other, can hardly escape two fallacies. On passing to the treatment of revealed religion, he pleads for its necessity on the ground of the inadequacy and uncertainty of natural religion ; not observing that the whole of this weakness he himself imports at the outset into his evidence of Revelation, so as to double the precariousness from which he proposes to save his conclusions. And in the first half of his task he deceives himself by secreting in his premisses more than he supposes them to contain, the additional element being no other than the conclusion itself: for whether he works from the principle of causality, or from the signs of a perfection higher than the realized world, he hides within them the assumption of living Will, of supreme excellence, of eternal Authority, which come out at the last in concentrated form under the name *God.* The implied *datum* on which his mind proceeds in his interpretation of the universe is the impersonation of causality and the ideal of righteous life : when it is charged upon him as a *petitio principii,* he resents the imputation of unconscious blindness : rather let him own it as a Divine revealing. It truly is the ground intuitively assumed in all his reasonings on nature without and life within : they lead to explicit Theism, because they start from implicit

Theism : which therefore stands as an initial revelation, out of which is evolved the whole organism of natural religion needed for the ulterior proof of what, under the name of historic revelation, is in fact, as a reasoned product, a second part, or supplementary development, of natural religion.

Thus the intuitive and personal character of revealed religion necessarily places it first in the order of thought, and hands it over into the conditions and the denomination of natural religion on the delivery and subsequent history of its influence. Whatever records it secures, whatever usages it creates, whatever doctrines it brings into form, whatever types of character it moulds, are mixed products of the original grace and the recipient natures, and may develop, under right direction, into higher truth and purer good : or under wrong direction or none at all, sink to lower levels of abject superstition and ignoble aims. The actual history of Christendom presents examples of both. For how much of what has arisen in its train the religion of Christ himself must be deemed responsible can be determined only by surveying, in their chief groups, the concurrent historical conditions which have either perverted or fostered its spirit, as it passed through the ages, and then turning back, after withdrawing these foreign elements, to contemplate, in its rescued personality, the solitary form of the Son of Man.

BOOK IV.

CHAPTER I.

REVEALED RELIGION AND APOCALYPTIC RELIGION.

THE distinction insisted on in the foregoing chapter, between immediate intuition as Divine, and reasoned conviction as human, has been expressed in modern language, but is by no means an innovation of modern thought. In other forms it presented itself to both Greek and Jew. Plato, indeed, is said to have fallen short of the conception of *Revelation*, because he identified the knowledge of truth with the highest Good, and this again with the " Idea of God," and regarded that knowledge as accessible to human reason, and apparently, therefore, left nothing beyond the compass of the mind's own faculty. But the inference vanishes as soon as we remember that Plato's " idea of God " does not, like ours, denote a mere thought of the human subject, but also the reality of the Divine object, turning up into intellectual consciousness ; and this unification of the infinite with the finite intelligence, giving the former to apprehension by the latter, is the Hellenic equivalent both of intuition and of revelation. Whether we say that the theory of God in the human mind is the real presence of Himself, or that he reveals Himself immediately to man, we do but record the same spiritual experience in the terms of somewhat different schools.

Place the same experience at the disposal of the *Jewish* Platonist, Philo, and the expression of it is modified. The human mind is indeed cognizant of God, the primal reality ; not, however, through the reach of its own faculties, which are quite transcended by the Divine essence ; but by special revelation, which thus sets a crown of preternatural glory on the head of the highest intellect. This communicated idea, being super-rational, plants the Supreme Good beyond the range of all philosophy, and reserves it to be conditional on inspiration. In this feature of Philo's theory, Harnack* finds the Greek principle of the supremacy of knowledge to be not so much rejected, as outbid ; and room henceforth provided for an over-topping heaven of revelation, to which no wing of thought can lift the Reason. And when we observe, that for the *dialectic* on which Plato relies for ascending to the Idea of God, Philo substitutes the prophet's *ecstasy*, the interpretation seems accordant with the colouring of the text. But the contrast drawn is illusory. Plato does not deny that the enlightening power is divine : Philo does not deny that the illuminated field is the seer's intellect. The ecstasy of the latter, as a Divine act attended by a flash of human insight, i.e., as a *revealing* moment, is simply *intuition*, *as immediate consciousness of God ;* and that this consciousness means, for the Platonist, the co-presence of the Object with the Subject *is* no new thing, but is already involved, as we have seen, in the twofold aspect of his " Idea of God." All else that the word *ecstasy* suggests, beyond its *cognitive* significance, the absorbing emotion, the transcended self-consciousness, the prophetic fervour,—is foreign to its comparison with other theories of knowledge, and forms the corona of atmospheric flames investing the central substance of spiritually apprehended fact. I cannot perceive, therefore, the alleged fundamental and structural difference between the two philosophies of religious knowledge ; or anything more than is due to the intenser affection and deeper enthusiasm inseparable from the strong hold of the personality of God upon the Jewish mind.

At all events, in order to effect this supposed advance upon Plato, Philo had but to fall back upon the history of his own nation, and listen to the voices of its ancient seers, especially in the utterances wrung from them in times of trouble, which sifted the true men from the false. Every reader of the

* Lehrbuch der Dogmengeschichte, Band I. S. 96–98 (2ᵗᵉ Auflage).

Hebrew Scriptures must have noticed, not without questionings of wonder, the frequent contrast of two competing classes of prophets, false and true, and the rules provided for distinguishing them from each other. For the prophet's hearers, no other test is available than the experience whether his words come true. But the prophet himself intuitively knows the touch of God by the authoritative consciousness of his immediate communion, which never really attends the subjective phantasmagoria of his own imagination. With what precision, and what dramatic irony, does Jeremiah thus distinguish between what is given to the human mind, and what is elaborated by it, when he introduces God himself as speaking thus: "I have heard what the prophets said, that prophesy lies in my name, saying, 'I have dreamed, I have dreamed.' The prophet that hath a dream, let him tell a dream ; and he that hath my word, let him speak my word faithfully. What is the chaff to the wheat? saith the Lord."*

As "the chaff to the wheat," it seems, so is the prophet's "dream" to the real "word of the Lord." Such is the relative value of "apocalyptic" as compared with "revealed" religion,—of the special pictures and visual representations of divine things in a single mind, as against that universal appeal of God to our humanity which the prophet's voice first makes articulate. If he comes to me, saying, "I have dreamed, I have dreamed," and tells me of seas of glass and cities of jasper, and fills me with a drama of trumpets and vials, and armies of angels, and a dragon enchained, how am I to know whether it is indeed his dream, or whether he "prophesies lies"? None but God can tell. And who shall say, be it ever so veraciously told, whence it comes, and what it is worth? or shall pretend to learn anything from it of the constitution or course of this universe? There can be no more hopeless task than to verify another man's visions of scenes beyond our reach ; and to seek nourishment for the soul from such things is, indeed, to feed on "chaff." But if the prophet comes to me with "the word of the Lord," with the inspiration of a higher insight, and the authority of a

* Jeremiah xxiii. 25. 28.

purer will; if he tears away the veil of my inward dreams, instead of spreading the images of his own, and reveals me to myself as I am and as I ought to be; if he wakes me from my bed of selfish ease, and sends me out on thorny ways to do the tasks and bear the sorrows of compassion ; if he shames me out of the doubts which hang around the lower mind by lifting me into the light of a more trustful love; I am sure, of myself, that he has spoken to me a Divine word; that I live in a light I never had before; that whether I know or not who he is, and whence he cometh, this one thing I know, that whereas I was blind, now I see.

As even prophets may be self-deceivers, perhaps this distinction between the vision which cannot be verified and the spiritual truth which verifies itself,—let us say between apocalypse and revelation,—may not always, in the first instance, exist for the prophet himself, and may not be fully realized, till he tries to carry his " burthen " into other minds. So long as he is alone with God, all that surrounds an immediate action of the Divine Spirit upon his own may indiscriminately affect him as a revelation, the light from some flash of moral conviction, spreading itself over the scenic images of invisible things already painted on the corridors of thought. The universal truth that enters from beyond the boundaries of his personality, while clearing away an illusion here, and imparting a fresh faith there, may meet, in the special contents of his nature, much that is *neutral;* that may thus, by its tacit presence, get mistakenly covered by the new reverence. But let him quit his solitude, and try his message on the hearts of men, and the two elements will instantly fall asunder ; the personal vision, the creation of fancy, will be believed, if at all, on his word; the Spiritual truth, on God's; the one loses its revealed character at the first step; the other doubles it : the one sinks into a marvel of individual biography ; the other rises into a new human consciousness of relation to God. The reason is obvious. The prophet's apocalypse is a specialty which lies outside the apprehensions and sympathies of others ; while his revelation is flung into recesses of their nature which peal with multiplying echoes, and speaks what, yet unspoken, was already there. So far only as his inspiration touches the chord of a universal inspiration, and repeats in others his own immediate divine knowledge, does he do the work of heaven upon earth, and wield any blessed power among men.

It is objected, however, that, if the range of revealed religion is simply co-extensive with that of human intuition, it is superfluous: for, if God himself brings his living Spirit to every soul, there can hardly be room for the mediation of prophets to plead in his stead. If a private revelation be given to each of us what occasion is left for any historical revelation to all? Is not the whole function of the inspired messenger to give us, what else we could not find? If he never ascends beyond the resources given to our humanity at large, and can never authenticate for us any tidings from the further darkness, is not his occupation gone?

Not so, if we only consider how all human culture, spiritual as well as natural, hangs upon the inequality of souls ; and as the child depends upon the parent, and the sick lean upon the healthy, so too the weak conscience is lifted by the strong, and the dim-sighted grow towards the sphere of more luminous natures, and the faint whisper of a pure inspiration in the inmost vault of the soul wakes up with answering resonance, and swells and comes out into the air in presence of a fuller tone. The grace of spiritual insight, though never withheld from any responsible being, exists in every variety of clearness and intensity ; remaining, at one extreme, a bare possibility not yet brought to the birth ; and reaching, at the other, the realized maturity of the large and saintly mind. In matters of the inward life, among the deep springs of goodness, beauty, and faith, a thousand things which it is given us to know may lie unsuspected in the dark : a whole world of truth is there, but, for want of light, not a flower, perhaps, has ever opened on its Elysian field, and, for want of warmth, not a stream has ever flowed. It is the realm of *implicit* knowledge, knowledge still shut up and fast asleep, with blossom waiting to be born, but meanwhile shapeless and tintless in its prison. The prophet, like the poet, is he for whom the creative hour has come upon this inner world, and the word been passed, " Let there be Light ! " and beneath the vernal sky and the soft breath of a season of the soul that never wanes, every possibility of beauty is nourished at the root, and the divinest secrets burst into bloom. The very same field has here become a realm of *explicit* knowledge; what is unconscious and latent in the one case having, in the other, passed into the daylight of clear apprehension. To carry the minds of men from the earlier to the maturer stage, nothing is so effectual as contact with one by whom the transition has been made, and who can tell the story of the way. He remembers the darkness while he feels the dawn; he pities the blind as they grope along the wall, while he freely moves upon the open grass, and directs his course by the everlasting hills: and as he describes what he sees, his breath falls upon an invisible picture in the listeners' souls, and brings out its lineaments to verify his word. Being simply in advance of their moral intuition, he does but break the seals of an oracle which they have kept and never read. He articulately speaks the silent inscriptions, on which they had never turned their eye, on the inner chamber of their nature. And as thus they know it to be true, the moment it is uttered, it draws towards him a reverence, and invests him with an authority, due only to one who can interpret the God within us all. The prophet then still has his specialty; consisting, however, simply in the higher intensity of a grace common to our humanity. He is himself the subject of a real revelation, i.e., of an immediate action of the Divine Spirit upon his own. And he is the occasion of a real revelation to others, by putting them into susceptibility for like immediate unveiling of God.

When we thus limit revelation to the sphere of intuitive apprehension, i.e., of moral and spiritual truth, the question will perhaps be asked, whether then we are to pronounce it impossible for God to give us a proper apocalypse,—i.e., an immediate disclosure of eternal facts and realities, which lie beyond the compass of our faculties or our opportunities, such as the existence of living beings on other worlds, or the provision of successive lives for man, or a plurality of personal natures within His own unity. Two brief remarks suffice for a reply.

1. It is not a question of what it is possible for God to give, but of what it is possible for us to receive: and it is no limitation of His power to say, that into capacity such as ours, and through media such as our dwelling-place affords, the ultra-mundane knowledge supposed could not pass and be authenticated. We are not made for its reception; and the earth is not made for its display.

2. Whether or not means might be found for revealing other than moral and spiritual truth, the media actually present are available simply for this end. They all resolve themselves into testimony; and who can attest such facts of ultimate being as the constitution of the Godhead, or the eternal life of the Son of God? or such invisible scenes as the superhuman abodes of the spirits bad and good? or the mysterious drama of the future which lies beyond the realm of death? In order to bring upon the earth an adequate witness of such things, the incarnation of a Divine person has to be presumed; and that in its turn is a kind of fact which transcends all evidence, and which human testimony never can approach. An apocalypse of such things is incommunicable by veracity ever so faithful: to me who only hear it, it is simply a *reported vision*, not a discovery of *what is*: it takes me into the mind that has seen it, but it takes me not beyond. And even this it does, only by a *rote of confidence* in the seer, which rests on other grounds, and is resolvable at last into the authority of his moral and spiritual insight. It is on the faith, or rather the experience, of his true account of the divine facts *within*, that he is accepted as interpreter also of the divine facts in the infinitude without.

In this distinction between apocalyptic and revealed religion we have, I believe, a mark by which the truest prophets may be discerned. Pretenders and self-deceivers are fond of knowing what no one else can know; they have been let into some special turn of the heavenly economy which shall startle the wonder of mankind. They have always their apocalypse, which amends the program of the scenes beyond the world. They think it nothing great and solemn to frequent the shrine within, and commune with Him that seeth in secret: but the darker they are on that side, the more do they strain on the other for light they can never find; and the more dim-eyed they are, the further do they take their look. The Mormon prophet, who cannot tell God from devil close at hand, is well up with the history of both worlds, and commissioned to get ready the second promised land. The Anabaptist of West-phalia, after flinging all the sanctities away in the name of the Holy Ghost, announces a kingdom of the saints, that is to hold the earth for ever as its own. To trumpet forth, like such noisy interpreters, the external scheme of God, is a missive of empty breath, which almost any storm-wind of human fancy may send forth. From the very echo in his thought of such audacious gospel the true prophet shrinks.˙ He will neither strive or cry; nor is it thus that his voice is heard in the street. He is not at home in the politics and revolutions of the universe,—has not seen the measures in reserve,—cannot discuss the questions of the spiritual clubs; he knows not the day nor the hour. But he is at one with the Spirit that governs all; and keeping close to the centre, cares not to lay down the map of the circumference. He loves the com-mon elements of human religion, in which he mingles with the affections of his kind, yet feels the consecrating presence of his God; the susceptibilities and simple trusts which may be less fresh in the priest than in the child, nay, in the decorous than in the outcast, which the cares of the world so often wither, and intellect alone will not avail to keep. From these it is, and not from his own " dream," from what is exceptionally his, that he speaks; and to these he carries his appeal; sure that he does but anticipate what others can verify, and make them partners of an inspiration meant for all. This holds pre-eminently of Jesus; who again and again thrust aside apocalyptic questions, or gave them an ideal turn, and floated them away on the current of spiritual religion. The sublimest things which he told the people he assumed that they in their secret hearts must know; he gave them a higher truth than they would hear from the scribes in Moses' seat; but nothing that they might not realize in their closet, when alone with the heart-Searcher. In this feature, I believe, was the root and essence of his power. Thus it was that he established a link of communion between the human soul and God; who never before had the same confidences together, as in the highest religious life of Christendom.

In the first effect of such pure power there is something singularly deep and winning; and it is easy to believe that among the waiting and aspiring minds that he had lifted out of their shadows into the light of God, his image, especially when touched with the infinite pathos of the Cross, would be enshrined in an unspeakable reverence. The change which he had wrought in them, the transition from implicit to explicit consciousness of divine things, is unique and entrancing;—a waking-up to find that the dull weight and the troubled dream of sleepy habit were illusions of the night, and that the real world is sweet and fair with the touch of morning. The first deep contrition for sin, the first real daily walk or midnight watch with the living God, the first opening perspective of a life in death,—these things are to many like the emergence from a dark chill cave to the flood of warm and beautifying light; and the hour that brings them is full of an excitement that is long ere it subsides. But every burst of dawn must settle into daylight; and every opening of revealed religion must become habitual, and leave behind its first surprise. The truth which it has given takes its quiet place within, fuses itself into the very texture of our thought, and becomes an integral part of us, and no longer carries on it the mark of its nativity. The level of life is permanently raised, but over an area so large that, looking quite natural all round, it suggests nothing of the fact or the source of its elevation; and it seems to us as if it could never have been otherwise. The more the insight given is complete and has passed into self-evidence, the less are we able to wonder at the gift; and the fervid veneration of the first conversion declines into a cold historic recognition, or dies away into absolute forgetfulness. The influence of countless forgotten benefactors, organs in their day of God's spirit, and centres of a healing love and trust, mingles insensibly with our present life, and makes it, unawares, from first to last, an All-Saints' Day; and often, perhaps, we celebrate them better when we know them not, and merely think the truth and love the good and feel the beauty which they dissolved into the air we breathe, than when we count out the conscious reasons for our reverence, and crystallize them into forms of commemoration. For, somehow, with every secret inspiration, as it passes outward to be looked at, a certain falsehood and artifice of thought is sure to mingle, and it takes quite another shape and colour beneath the eyes of men, and more and more hides what it really is under the growth of what it is to seem ; and so it comes to pass that the falsest reasons are given for the truest things.

Christendom, from end to end, is one gigantic example of this. It was impossible that such a trustful affection as its author had drawn upon him should die away into an invisible trace upon the life of men ; yet equally impossible that the simplicity and depth of its real power should be consciously apprehended as well as inwardly felt by the generation nearest to him. And had its ground been truly stated a little after, when the new colours he had shed on life had grown familiar and undistinguishable from the common light of day, it would have seemed to give too poor an account of so divine an agency ; and the vulgar pomp of theological imagination (which appears unsusceptible of the baptism of humility) would have cried again, 'Can any good come out of Nazareth?' Scarcely was he gone, therefore, when his disciples, not excepting those who had been nearest to himself, began to quit the pure ground of trust to which his presence held or recalled them, and to work out reasons of their own for clinging to him and proclaiming him as the organ of a new divine life for the world. They must have a theory of his person and his work, and be able, when asked, to tell all about him,—whence he came, and where he is, and what he will be ; thus turning their attention and that of others from the interior of his life to its surrounding and invisible relations. Schemes of thought rapidly consolidated themselves about what he was and what he meant to do and what he left behind that was unique and superhuman, and set him at a height unapproachable by men. And so it came to pass that his own revealed religion retired from the front and took shelter within ; and in its place there advanced an apocalypse respecting him. But where, in such a life, could invention find its point of departure? What excuse could it extort, from a story of such meek service and teachings of such spiritual tone, for constructing an elaborate pile of creeds about him, and inscribing it all over with the titles of his grandeur? Alas! they found perhaps in what fell from him when hard pressed with the questions of his time,—a few dropped words to which others gave a personal meaning they had not from him,—rudiments to start from in the building-up of such a scheme. He too was human; he too stood in an historic place, and was woven in with the living texture that twines before and after into one, and renders mental isolation impossible; and with the divine intuitions of his mind were inevitably mingled undivine traditions of his country and his time. On these, little congenial as they were, silence could not be maintained. And on his share of these, though they were not his specialty, but his inheritance, his disciples seized, and laid them as the corner-stone on which to raise the ecclesiastic pile of Christendom. Of the outward and inward, of the earthly and the heavenly part of his thought and teaching, the one has been taken and the other left. On this small and mistaken base there has been heaped up an immense and widening mass of Christian mythology, from the first unstable, and now at last apparently swerving to its fall. And let it fall: for it has corrupted the religion of Christ into an apocalyptic fiction ; and *that*, so monstrous in its account of man, in its theory of God, in its picture of the universe, in its distorted reflections of life and death, that if the belief in it were as real as the profession of it is loud, society would relapse into a moral and intellectual darkness it has long left, and the lowest element of modern civilization would be its *faith.* The chief earlier stages of this mythologic growth, already clearly marked within the Christian Scriptures themselves, must next be passed under review.

CHAPTER II.

THEORIES OF THE PERSON OF JESUS.

§ 1. *As Messiah.*

THE " Gospel of Jesus Christ," revealed to him and constituting his personal religion, was delivered to a very various world, over which its message spread in successive stages, through families of men preoccupied with modes of thought dissimilar to it and to each other. Taken up by these, and mingling with their speech, its voice was inevitably changed, and, like a border dialect, passed into a patois pure to neither heaven nor earth. Three, at least, of such modifying media it had been called to traverse before our New Testament writings were complete : viz., the popular Judaism of Israel at home ; the Hellenistic theology of mixed Israelites and proselytes abroad ; and the Gentile sects of gnostic speculation ; influences of which the Temple, the Synagogue, and the School may be regarded as respective symbols. Each of these in turn presented the field on which the new divine light, and the personality possessed by it, had to work ; and only by adjusting relations with what was already there, and therefore binding up together much that was perishable with the treasure that was eternal,—leaving the pearl within its shell,— was it possible to provide a vehicle for the gift, and prevent its being lost as soon as found. So long as the scene was laid in Palestine, and the action was conducted in the language, and appealed to the preconceptions prevailing there, it was limited by impassable assumptions, of the perpetuity of " the Law," the exclusive prerogative of Israel, and the validity of the predicted Messianic theocracy. These ideas were crystallized into the very substance of the religion of the land ; and whatever rays of fresh light might come from heaven must pass through their seat and report their colours. How pervading is their presence throughout the evangelic narrative, from the Star in the East to the Apostles' parting question, " Lord, dost thou at this time restore the Kingdom to Israel?" how they seem to form a common ground of reasoning and ultimate appeal in every difference between Jesus and his opponents, so that he tests them by their own standards, and declares that "not one jot or tittle of the law shall fail :" how it is said that he too expects, on his speedy return, to reign over an elect people and a subject world, and promises to place his apostles on " twelve thrones to judge the twelve tribes of Israel ;" is well known, not perhaps without sorrowful regrets, by every reader of the synoptic gospels.

Not that any one can now-a-days suppose these things to form any part of the Divine message of Jesus to the world ; for with him, at all events, they are not original : if he is responsible with regard to them at all, it is only for letting them alone.   The whole mind of the Palestinian Jews had become saturated with the high colouring of a rude apocalyptic literature which, in imitating the Book of Daniel (b.c. 167–164), had put new meanings into its symbols, widened the horizon of its historic survey, filled in its blank futurities with fresh visions, and found scenery and incident for the whole sacred drama to its consummation.   In the Jewish production which forms the fundamental text of the Book of Revelation* we see how definite had become the stages in the mythology, the actors of its parts, even the date of its catastrophe, and the splendour of its issue.   Of that writing we cannot positively say that it was prior to our era.   But it can no longer be reasonably doubted that the nucleus of the Sibylline oracles† and the main part of the Book of Enoch‡ are productions from the second half of the second century b.c., and faithfully reflect

---

* See above, pp. 225–227.

† For an account of this production, see a paper in the National Review, No. XXXII., for April, 1863, p. 466, on "The Early History of Messianic Ideas."

‡ Of this book an account is given in a second paper under the same title, National Review, No. XXXVI., April, 1864, p. 551.   For a thorough and masterly treatment of the whole literature bearing on this subject, see The Jewish Messiah : a critical history of the Messianic idea among the Jews, from the rise of the Maccabees to the closing of the Talmud, by Rev. James Drummond, LL.D., 1877.

the pictures acceptable to the prophetic imagination of the people who heard the word of Jesus and wondered who he was. From these sources we know for certain that it was not *he* who filled with its meaning their question, "Art thou he that should come, or look we for another?"—who drew in their fancy their picture of the "Son of David": who introduced them to the expectation of his Advent with an angelic host, to make an end of all that opposes, to open the last assize, and reign for centuries in the new Jerusalem; and who named for them the harbingers of these last things, the wars and rumours of wars, the convulsions of nature and distress of nations, and mustering of Gentile armies against the elect. The whole drama had already been written, and photographed in thought, and might haunt the believer's conscience by day, and startle him in dreams and visions of the night. And if Jesus spake of it, it was as of something given, and not of what he brought.

But though the pre-existence of the Messianic idea relieves Jesus of responsibility for its contents, it leaves the question open how far he shared it with his contemporaries, and carried its influence into his ministry. At a time when all the "just and devout" in the land were, like Simeon, "waiting for the consolation of Israel," the home at Nazareth could not fail to be imbued with the common hope, to read it into the prophets, to hear of it in the synagogue, to breathe it into many a prayer, and throw its prospective look into the whole attitude of life. Nor is it possible to put any other interpretation upon the self-dedication of Jesus to his missionary labours than that he had a message to deliver, "The Kingdom of Heaven is at hand." This sense of a divine crisis and new spiritual birth is more than the subject of a parable here, and a denunciation or a blessing there; it is, throughout, the very spring of conviction that disposes of his will, and shines through all his public compassions and lonely devotions.

It is one thing, however, to admit his belief in a reign of truth and righteousness as a promise made "to the Fathers," and now approaching its fulfilment; it is quite another to affirm that in his own person he claimed to realize it as its Prince and Head. That this also is universally assumed is not surprising, seeing that the synoptists assure us that it was so, and tell it as if it were an attested fact and not a later inference. Yet they add (what surely is not without significance), "He strictly charged his disciples and commanded them to tell no man that he was the Christ."[*] If the disciples had only kept that injunction instead of spending their lives in reversing it, Christendom, I am tempted to think, might have possessed a purer record of genuine revelation, instead of a mixed text of divine truth and false apocalypse. For, the first deforming mask, the first robe of hopeless disguise, under which the real personality of Jesus of Nazareth disappeared from sight, were placed upon him by this very doctrine which was *not* to go forth,—that he was the Messiah. It has corrupted the interpretation of the Old Testament, and degraded the sublimest religious literature of the ancient world into a book of magic and a tissue of riddles. It has spoiled the very composition of the New Testament, and, both in its letters and its narratives, has made the highest influence ever shed upon humanity subservient to the proof of untenable positions and the establishment of unreal relations. Knowing as we do, that Messiah was but the figure of an Israelitish dream, what matters it to us English Gentiles to-day whether its shadowy features were more or less recalled to mind by acts and words of the Galilean prophet? Tell us only, we are apt to cry, the things he really said and did: and how far they fitted in with your lost ideal may be left untold, as belonging to *your* life and not to *his*. Yet, however natural this thought may be to us, when we grow impatient of the strange evidence which the demons and the prophets are said to give to his Messiahship, it is hasty and inconsiderate. For, had it not been for this Jewish conception of him, we should probably have had no life of him at all. It is chiefly in this primitive school of disciples, gathered in the upper chamber at Jerusalem, that the interest felt in him was essentially personal, and hung around his image in the past, and watched his steps, and listened for the echoes of his words, to detect under his disguise the traces of what he was and was to be. In the larger gospel of Paul,

* Luke ix. 21. Matt. xvi. 20.

which swept over the Gentile world and ultimately reduced the original community to the position of a sect, the biography of Jesus, the traits of his mind, the story of his ministry, play no part at all: it is from heaven, after he has done with the hills of Galilee and the courts of the temple, that he begins with his last apostle; and it is in heaven alone that that apostle knows anything of him,—in his glorified state and immortal function, and not in the simple humanity and prefatory affections of his career below. The Pauline gospel therefore opens where the others cease. And had their narrative not pre-existed, the fourth gospel could scarcely have been; for it does but spiritualize and reconstruct, with change of scene and interweaving of new incidents, a portion of their historical material; working it up into the service of a later and more transcendental doctrine. That we have memoirs of Jesus at all we owe therefore to the very theory about him which has so much coloured and distorted them; and we must accept the inevitable human condition, and patiently strip off the disfiguring folds of contemporary thought, and gain what glimpses we can of the pure reality within.

Those to whom the personal figure of Jesus still appears beautiful and sacred are often said to substitute for the reality an ideal of their own; because they rely on a small selection of the deepest sayings and the most pathetic incidents, as if these were all, and refuse to balance against them the countervailing mass of questionable pretension and false prediction and habitual exorcism which the narrative presents. The charge would be unanswerable, if the story were all upon one level, and the credibility were equal of the part that is taken and the part that is left. But this could only be the case if the gospels were the products of pure history, with the risks of error impartially distributed over their whole surface. What however is the fact respecting (let us say) the first of them? (in the order, that is, not of time, but of place in the canon.) It is compiled throughout in a dogmatic interest, and is historical in the same way as the recital of an advocate shaped for the support of the case he undertakes to plead. The position which it aims to establish, viz., that the life it relates is that of the future Messiah, is present everywhere: it supplies the principle of selection with which the writer passes through the traditions and records ready to his hand: he drops as irrelevant whatever does not help his thesis: he weaves together exclusively the incidents and sayings which admit of being turned to its support.   And when we remember that ere the Aramaic copy of the Gospel was put together, forty years separated the writer from the latest event which he records, and that our Greek edition is in parts a generation later still; and that during all that time the same Messianic belief had been busy among the memorials floating in the air, sifting the very leaves that drifted to the compiler's feet, the only wonder is that, with so strong a set of the wind, any shred of history should have slipped beyond the margin and be found upon the field outside.   If here and there, in the intervals of the compiler's logical vigilance, words that transcend his theory or incidents that contradict it lie embedded in his story, the truth is betrayed by the only signs of which the case admits ; and such rare instances, like the solitary organic form de-tected in rocks that never showed such traces before, may tell a story of the past significant out of all proportion to their size.   It is only by reasoning from such internal marks, that we can ever hope to recover the simple outline of the truth : for our gospels, instead of securing to us, as commonly sup-posed, the personal testimony of reliable eye-witnesses, are really (as in part already shown) of unknown source, of mixed material, and to no small extent of gradual growth. They are essentially anonymous compilations, without re-sponsible authorship ; and do but collect into a focus the best elements of popular tradition respecting the author of Chris-tianity current in the second and third generation of his disciples.   If we want an earlier word than this, we have it in the letters of Paul ; but there, Christ is already in heaven, and we learn nothing of his ministry on earth.

That the Messianic theory of the person of Jesus was made for him, and palmed upon him by his followers, and was not his own, appears to me a reasonable inference from several slight but speaking indications.   The difficulty, however, of penetrating to the truth on this matter is so considerable that the prevailing critical verdict on the other side is by no means surprising.*   Our only sources of evidence are the synoptical gospels, proceeding, even in their oldest constituents, from disciples who had long convinced themselves, not only that Jesus *was* the appointed Messiah, but that he knew himself to be so, and gave sufficient signs of his authority as such.   Looking back on his earthly ministry through this posterior conviction, they viewed all things in its light; it served as the interpreting medium to all the historical elements of the current tradition, assimilating its pictures of the past to the later version of their meaning.   When once they had learned to explain away the disheartening features of his life and thought, his fatal failure and unresisted death, and found in them just what *ought* to have happened in order to prove what they seemed to disprove, the whole story would assume a new aspect; and whatever they missed in it, or found to disappoint and shock them, would appear but as part of an intended scheme, consciously carried out in obedience to the divine will.   No doubt would longer be entertained that Jesus saw everything and chose everything that met him on the way; and no hesitation be felt about making him speak out what he really was, and reading into his occasional words of pathetic foreboding definite predictions of the tragedy on Calvary.   Were the gospels *uniformly* suffused with the colouring of a later time, as they would be were they the production of that time alone, it would be impossible to withdraw the veil that dimmed the historic truth.   Since, however, they are composite works, not only with their several characteristics, but each put together from successive layers of tradition, the more recent overlying the oldest, they admit of being dealt with like a palimpsest MS., on which the underwritten characters are indelible by the process which washes out the superficial text.   There is a corresponding critical chemistry which is not without resources for recovering at least some fragments of the first faithful record.

* Harnack, for instance, says, "Dass Jesus sich selbst als den Messias bezeichnet hat, ist von einigen Kritikern—jüngst noch von *Havet* Le Christianisme et ses Origines, T. iv.1884, 15 ff—in Abrede gestellt worden. Allein dieses Stück der evangelischen Ueberlieferung scheint mir auch die schärfste Prüfung auszuhalten."   Lehrbuch d. Dogmengeschichte, I. 57, 58, note.

It is usual to assume that the several titles *Son of Man, Son of David, Son of God*, are interchangeable as names of the Messiah, and that each, when appropriated, carries in it precisely the same official claim as the others. And this is true, when we are speaking of the *apostolic age*, and the usage of its missionaries and churches; true therefore of the meaning attached to these phrases by the writers or editors of the synoptical gospels. But that it is *not* unconditionally true of the prior age of which they tell the story they unconsciously betray by an unequal use of the terms that is plainly not accidental. Thus, the phrase ' Son of God ' received its Messianic significance from the Christians themselves; neither in the true text of the anterior apocalyptic literature, nor in the Hebrew Scriptures, does it ever appear in that sense; and in the oldest gospel (Mark), it is a title which only beings of superhuman insight—the demons he cast out,* and the Satan who tempted him,† are described as applying to Jesus. One exception indeed is reported in the High Priest's question to Jesus, " Art thou the Christ, the Son of the Blessed ? " and the affirmative reply.‡ It is hard to reconcile this public avowal with the repeated shrinking from this claim, and absolute prohibition to make it on his behalf. And when we realize the conditions under which the High Priest's examination took place, that no friendly witness was present but Peter, who was not within hearing ; when further we remember that, ere it could be set down as matter of history, it had become the equal wish of Jewish accusers and of Christian disciples to fasten upon the crucified the highest Messianic pretensions, the one as proof of imposture, the other as a warrant for their faith ; it may be reasonably doubted whether dependence can be placed upon the accuracy of an exceptional detail. The total absence from the fourth Gospel's report, of any question about the Messiahship (on which, in the synoptists, the whole judicial sentence hangs) shows how great may be the influence of an evangelist's preconception on the colouring of his narrative.

It is hardly necessary to remark that in the only other instance of the phrase, viz., the centurion's exclamation be-

* Mark iii. 11.   † Matt. iv. 3, 6.   ‡ Mark xiv. 61, 62.

neath tho cross, "Surely this was a Son of God,"* tho Roman speaker can havo had no Messianic meaning, but only ono compatiblo with his heathen conception of divino things.

In truth, tho namo " Son of God " becamo appropriate to Jesus in virtue, not of tho Messianic offico, but of the heavenly nature, discovered in his person: and was, therefore, first freely given to him by his disciples after his passago to immortal life. This is strongly marked by the Apostle Paul's distinction,—that ho was " born of the seed of David according to tho flesh, but declarod to bo tho *Son of God* with power according to tho spirit of holiness, by *the resurrection of the dead*." † It was tho spiritual constitution of beings moro than human which was conceived to bring their nature into antithesis with the animal lifo and affinity with tho essenco of God,—an affinity that might bo abused by fallen spirits to their perdition, or with tho faithful turn to undying blessedness. When tho author of tho Book of Daniel describes tho fourth angelic figuro seen in tho fiery furnaco with tho three intended martyrs, ho says that "his aspect is liko a Son of God." ‡ If tho plan of tho Messiahship had been different, and had fulfilled itself on earth alone, in tho person and tho career of another David, only with wider dominion and moro glorious reign, ho would hardly havo received tho titlo " Son of God." It is specifically duo to tho Christ in heaven; invested now with somo glorious form of light, and capablo of being revealed in inward vision to tho spiritualized minds of men. This titlo, therefore, by its very nature, posthumously gained its placo among tho predicates of Jesus.

When onco " tho heavens had received him," and revealed his higher naturo, tho question could not fail to present itself, *when* did this divino affinity, this enrolment in tho ranks of spiritual life, take its origin ? for it is not said, and it was not thought, that by his resurrection *he became*, but only that ho was '*declared*' tho 'Son of God'; and if tho fact were already there, it was impossible to repress tho inquiry, 'how did it ariso'? at what dato did tho Divine element take possession of that transient human personality? and where

* Mark xv. 39.   † Rom. i. 4.   ‡ Daniel iii. 25.

was it before?   The earliest reply undoubtedly was, the Spirit of God descended and united itself with him *at his baptism;* the tradition assumed the form preserved in the Ebionite gospel,* and twice quoted by Justin Martyr,† that as the Spirit alighted on him, a voice from heaven said, ' Thou art my son, this day have I begotten thee.'   The filiation consists in the communication of the Divine spirit, and is synchronous with it.   This Messianic application of Psalm ii. is, I believe, a purely Christian invention; and had probably the effect, when the accounts of the baptism came to be written, of carrying back the title ' Son of God ' from the heavenly to the earthly life of Jesus.

The secret of this godlike essence in him was supposed to be instinctively read by the superhuman intelligence of the evil spirits exorcised by him; so that they could cry out in their dismay, ' Art thou come to destroy us?   I know thee, who thou art, the holy one of God.'‡   ' What have I to do with thee, thou Son of the most High God ?' §   ' Thou art the Son of God.'‖   But from his sane countrymen we do not hear this mode of address : it is as the ' *Son of David* ' that they own his Messiahship, and appeal to his compassion. The blind who follow him on the way, till he stops and touches their eyes ;¶ the Canaanitish woman, who, for her suffering child, prays for the crumbs of mercy that may fall from Israel's table ;** the multitudes, astounded when the blind mute both spake and saw ;†† or descending the hill to Jerusalem with cries of Hosanna :‡‡ all, in short, who represent the vernacular speech of the time and place, address their prayers and their enthusiasm to him as the ' Son of David.' This phrase is undoubtedly the nucleus of the popular pre-Christian Messianic faith.

In speaking of himself Jesus habitually employs the remaining expression ' Son of Man ': and on its meaning, when thus appropriated, depends the question as to the range

---

* See Hilgenfeld's Nov. Test. extra Canonem Receptum. Evang. sec. Hebræos, &c. II. Ebion. Evang. pp. 34, 36.

† Dial. cum Tryph. C. 88, 316 D. and 103, 331 B.   ‡ Mark. i. 24.

§ Mark v. 7.   ‖ Luke iv. 41.   ¶ Matt. ix. 27.

** Matt. xv. 22.   †† Matt. xii. 22.   ‡‡ Matt. xxi. 9.

and character of his self-conscious mission. That for the evangelists themselves it had settled into its Messianic sense, and that they attributed the same to him is not disputed. The point to be determined is whether this is historically true, or is a Christian afterthought thrown back upon the personal ministry of Jesus. The previous history of this phrase certainly gave it sufficient elasticity to leave room for reasonable doubt. The use of it as the name of a personal Messiah was supposed to be sanctioned by the pseudo-prophecies of Daniel, but was drawn thence only by a misinterpretation of the author's symbols. As the Seer has described successive heathen empires—Babylonian, Median, Persian, Macedonian, —under the image of brute forms, the lion, the bear, the ram, the goat,—so does he contrast with them the hoped-for kingdom of righteousness reserved for " the saints of the Most High," under the superior image of *Humanity* embodied in the " likeness of a Son of Man : "* of a *personal Agent* he no more speaks in this symbol than in the previous cases of representative animals. And where, as in the vision by the river Ulai ;† and in that by the Tigris,‡ an individual figure is introduced instead of a generic type, it is not any Messiah, but, in the one case, God himself, who speaks—in the other, the archangel Gabriel, Michael's πρωταγωνιστὴς in the wars of the upper world.§ Whether the misinterpretation of these visions which appropriated the phrase 'Son of Man' to a supposed personal Head of the future theocracy was prechristian, and furnished the disciples in Palestine with a familiar Messianic title, cannot be conclusively determined. In the Book of Enoch it is similarly applied : " Beside the Ancient of Days there sits another, whose countenance is as the face of a man, full of grace, like one of the heavenly angels : this is the Son of Man : "‖ " the Son of Man was named by the Ancient of Days before the world was."¶ But there is much reason to suspect that the section in which this language occurs is a Christian addition to the original work ; and the text, when

* Dan. vii. 13, 18, 22, 27.   † Dan. viii.   ‡ Dan. x., xi.
§ For fuller exposition see Early History of Messianic Ideas. National Review, April, 1863, pp. 471–476 : and more at large Drummond's Jewish Messiah. B. II. ch. vii.
‖ xlv. Das Buch Henoch. Dillmann.   ¶ xlviii. 1, *seqq.*

critically sifted, becomes divested of the characteristic evangelic phraseology. The known Jewish literature prior to our era, whether within or without the canonical Hebrew scriptures, throws no satisfactory light on the Messianic use of the term " Son of Man."

Two other applications of the phrase, however, are perfectly clear. It is used as a common noun, to denote any member of the human race; and it is given to a selected individual, employed as the herald of a Divine message. In the former sense the Psalmist says, " What is *man* that thou art mindful of him, and the *son of man* that thou visitest him ? "* and the answer of Job, " the stars are not pure in his sight; how much less man that is a worm, and the *son of man* that is a worm ? "† Constant familiarity with this *generic sense* so completely obliterated, in the minds of those who used it, all separate reference to the component elements of the phrase that in the Syriac version of St. Paul's 1 Cor. xv. 45, the curious rendering occurs, " Adam, *the first son of man*, became a living soul ! " In this application the phrase passes into the gospels also; else, from the answer " the sabbath was made for *man*, not man for the sabbath," the inference could not be drawn, " therefore the *son of man* is lord even of the sabbath."‡

The individualized use of the phrase in prechristian literature occurs exclusively in Ezekiel; where the prophet, in receiving a commission, is invariably accosted by Jehovah, " thou son of Man." It is no doubt possible to construe this address also into the mere equivalent of " O man ! " but invariably connected as it is with the initiative of a special prophetic function, it can hardly fail to carry in it some additional connotation relative to the Seer's office: especially as it is so uniformly adhered to that it occurs eighty-nine times in this single book, while there are but eleven instances of the phrase in its general sense throughout the previous Hebrew scriptures. The supplementary idea is probably no more than an intensification, in the awful presence and communion of the Most High, of the conscious weakness, unworthiness, nothingness, of the human agent, when called to

* viii. 4.   † xxv. 6.
‡ Mark ii. 27, 28.   Cf. Matt. xii. 8, Luke vi. 5.

bo the organ of a Divine intent: that so feeble a voice should
bo charged with tho mighty word of God could but cast the
prophet down in utter dependence, save that it also snatched
him upwards into an unfailing trust.   As tho human figure,
brought by tho pseudo-Daniel into comparison with the lower
animal forms, serves for the symbol of rational and moral
majesty, so, when placed in the person of Ezekiel, face to
face with tho infinite perfection, is it emptied of all its semblance of dignity, and "talking no more so exceeding proudly,"
can only yield itself to bo disposed of by the hand of God, and
move with lowly and equal sympathy among the brotherhood
of mankind.   This is probably tho thought which commended
the term " Son of Man " to the preference of Jesus ; and as
it thus comes from his lips, it exactly expresses tho trustful
self-surrender, the blended fearlessness and tenderness before
men, tho shrinking from words of praise, " Why callest thou
mo good ? ", tho pathetic calmness of the uplooking and uplifting life, which speak in all the features of his portraiture.
In adopting this name ho takes the level, not of tho Messianic
grandeur, with its political triumphs and earthly glories, not
of tho heir of David destined to crown and render millennial
the splendour of his reign, but of simple Humanity in its
essence and without its trappings, endowed and called to be
the child of God, but through the discipline of many a need
and sorrow and temptation.   It is in harmony with this
attitude of character and conception of his mission, that ho
discouraged from following him all those who were not prepared to move with him on the same level of the common lot,
and find tho beauty and sanctity of life in its inner affections
and possibilities, and not in its outward possessions ; neither
tho rich who could not forego his treasures, nor the poor who
could not face further privation, would ho have in his train,
" The foxes have holes, tho birds of tho air have nests, but the
Son of Man hath not where to lay his head." *   ' The prophet,
who has only to bear tho message of heaven to his followers,
must live as a man among men, taking no more account than
God himself of any one's lot or of his own : and if you would

* Matt. viii. 20. See an interesting essay by Ferd. Chr. Baur, in Hilgenfeld's Zeitschrift für wissenschaftliche Theologie. 1860: pp. 274, seqq.

share his work, you must, with him, bo ready to dispense with even the shelter and security of tho creatures of the field and air.' This sympathetic self-identification with the lowliest conditions of human life, in tho service of its divine ends, appears to mo truer both to the connection of the passage and the characteristics of Jesus, than the evangelist's own apparent construction, viz., that Jesus, in words of touching lament, was here contrasting the protected lot of the lower creation with the homeless exposure and prospective sufferings of the King of glory in his disguise.

If, then, Jesus occasionally spoke of himself as the "Son of Man," it by no means implied any Messianic claim. It might, on the contrary, be intended to emphasize the very features of his life and love which are least congenial with the national ideal. That in tho days of his Galilean ministry it had not passed into a Messianic title is proved by the startling effect of Peter's first recognition of him as "the Christ;" or, as Luke has it, "the Christ of God;" or, as Matthew has it, "the Christ, the son of tho living God."* The apostle's outspoken declaration is in answer to tho questions, "Who do men say that I am?" and "Whom say ye that I am?" or, as Matthew puts the former, "Who do men say that I, the Son of Man, am?" Now, if the term "Son of Man," was only a synonym for "the Christ," and Jesus had been habitually applying it to himself through the previous year or years, there is no room for his question addressed to them, and their answer was a mere tautology; and if he actually framed the question in Matthew's words: "I, the Son of Man," he dictated the very answer which, when uttered, produced so intense a sensation, and was ordered to be suppressed and told to no man. His appropriation of the phrase, in public address and in private converse, had left the way open to various interpretations of the character in which he appeared: and needed the supplementary influence of his personality on his constant attendants to lift them into the hope to which Peter had given voice.

To this memorable turning-point in tho life of Jesus I shall have to return for another purpose: at present I draw

* Mark viii. 29; Luke ix. 20; Matt. xvi. 16.

only the inference that at that date the phrase "Son of Man" was not tantamount to "the Messiah." Yet, on the other hand, in numerous discourses attributed to Jesus by the evangelists the term is undoubtedly restricted to this meaning: the "Son of Man shall send forth his angels:"* then shall they see the Son of Man coming in clouds with great power and glory:" † "him shall the Son of Man confess before the angels of God." ‡ To such passages as these it is impossible to apply Holtzmann's remark that the phrase "Son of Man" is a *verhüllender Name*,§ covering one knows not what tender and mystical significance: it is distinctly Messianic, referring, moreover, to the least spiritual eschatological features of the Jewish expectation. What then are we to say? could this meaning be absent from the phrase during the first part of the ministry of Jesus, yet get exclusive possession of it before the close? Not so: for it is found in discourses on both sides of Peter's confession, and, if you follow Matthew rather than Mark, equally all through. To allow of such a change in the use of a current term, a greater interval is needed than between the stages of a fifteen months' ministry. And the interval will be found between the date of Jesus' living voice, and the period from forty to seventy years later, during which our synoptic gospels were compiled. In that interval the first disciples and their Palestinian converts had wrought out their doctrine, that Jesus, now reserved in heaven, was to be Messiah, and that the kingdom of God which his earthly life had been spent in fore-announcing, was to be realized in his person. And at the same time, and through the century, the deepening darkness and confusion and ultimate ruin that fell upon the Jewish state, mustered all the wild forces of fanaticism in Israel, and threw insurrections into the hands of zealots, and left religion at the mercy of visionary seers. How prolific the time was in apocalyptic dreams, dazzling with glory or lurid with horrors, the Book of Revelation, as now understood, may suffice to convince us. The strong resemblance between the national sufferings in the

* Matt. xiii. 41.   † Mark xiii. 26.   ‡ Luke xii. 8.
§ Lehrbuch der Einleitung in das Neue Testament, 2er Aufl., 1886, S. 369.

Jewish wars with Rome, and the tragic experiences under Antiochus Epiphanes, would naturally place the Book of Daniel in an intenser light, and lead men to seek oracles there, and find relief from an afflicting present in its promise of deliverance for the faithful people, when "the wise shall shine as the brightness of the firmament, and they that turn many to righteousness as the stars for ever and ever." Nor is it any wonder if, " under the likeness of a Son of Man," they saw, not simply the predicted sway of a true Humanity, but a personal Head to the saints on earth, as Michael was leader of the loyal angels in the conflicts of heaven. It was during this period then,—I conceive,—between the ministry of Jesus and the fall of the Jewish State,—that the term " Son of Man " came to be used as a Messianic title ; and this new sense, having once usurped the phrase, affected the composition of the Gospels in two ways. The evangelists, themselves possessed by it, and unconscious of any perversion, threw it back upon the name as it passed from the lips of Jesus. And, being unaware that it was a characteristic expression of his, by which he loved to designate himself, they too readily fitted to him whatever any prophetic writing said that the Messianic Son of Man would be and do ; and hence were tempted to patch his discourses with shreds of Jewish apocalypse, and even to attribute to him, as what he must have meant and might have said, whole masses of eschatology, borrowed from Israel, in which the signs of the " Son of Man," on his coming to conquer, to judge and to reign, are unveiled in their succession, and identified in their commencement with the events passing before the writer's and the reader's eye. That the expositions of " last things " in the synoptical gospels are just as much Christianized Jewish apocalypse, as the Book of Revelation, it is hardly possible to doubt ; though the written leaves which have furnished the excerpts have fallen upon the stream of time, and been swept away without a name.

Yet not entirely without a trace. Every reader who, in his study of the life of Jesus, has freed himself from the unhistorical chronology of the fourth Gospel, and followed the steps of his ministry under the guidance of the synoptists, must have been as much struck by the inopportuneness as touched by the pathos of the lament over Jerusalem, whether uttered, as Luke reports,* while Jesus was still in Herod's territory on the eve of departure for Judæa, or, as Matthew states,† in the Temple courts, on the first day of his arrival at Jerusalem. In the former case, it is spoken in the Northern province, while as yet his voice has never been heard in the city: in the latter, it winds up his first day's teaching there. And yet in both its burden is "*How often* would I have gathered thy children together, as a hen doth gather her brood under her wings; and ye would not!" Such a reproach, whether flung from a distance by a stranger, or coming from a visitor within his first twenty-four hours, would be simply inane, and can be rendered credible by no evangelist's authority. By a comparison, however, of the two evangelists, the passage is saved, and its enigma resolved. In Matthew, the apostrophe to Jerusalem is introduced by the words, "I send unto you prophets and wise men and scribes : some of them ye will kill and crucify : and some of them ye will scourge in your synagogues, and persecute them from city to city; that upon you may come all the righteous blood shed upon the earth, from the blood of Abel the righteous unto the blood of Zachariah, son of Barachiah, whom ye slew between the sanctuary and the altar. Verily, I say unto you, all these things shall come upon this generation." In Luke, this passage, with change of only a word or two, has been already worked up into an earlier discourse at a Pharisee's dinner table in Galilee;‡ and there it is introduced, not as spoken by Jesus *in propriâ personâ*, but as a quotation of *Another's* words,—evidently *God's* : "Therefore said *the Wisdom of God*, I will send unto them prophets," &c. The speaker, therefore, who has *so often* appealed to the Holy city and its perverse people is the God of their fathers, their providential guide through all their history. The only question is what is denoted by that " Wisdom of God " from which the words are

* xiii. 31-35. Cf. xi. 37-52 and xix. 41-44.
† xxiii. 20-39.   ‡ xi. 49-51.

cited.   Not surely the canonical Hebrew scriptures, which are never quoted under such a title, and which do not contain the passage here adduced.   The phrase, moreover, must cover a much more recent production : for in the reproach which it utters it includes as its last term, the murder " between the temple and the altar " (i.e., in the court of priests) of Zachariah, the son of Baruch,—an act perpetrated, as Josephus tells us, " in the midst of the temple " by two of the zealots shortly before the destruction of Jerusalem by Titus.* The disastrous events of that time, interpreted as judgments on the past and omens of a redeeming future, were fruitful in homilies of denunciation and oracles of prophecy,—fugitive fires discharged in the collision of despair and faith, and kindling both wherever they touched.   That one of these, or a collection of them, should receive the title " The Wisdom of God," is accordant with the taste and style of apocalyptic authorship.   That the impulse to produce them or turn them to account would operate alike on all who are imbued with the Messianic faith, whether simply Jews or Jewish Christians, is obvious : the difference would only be that the one would ignore, the other would accept, the historic episode of Jesus' life, as the key to the downfall of Jerusalem.   That the first evangelist already looked back upon that downfall is plain from the words, " Behold, your house is left unto you desolate."†

We have here, therefore, an example of quotation by evangelists from an apocalyptic writing, called the " Wisdom of God," Jewish in essence, Christian in application, so incorporated with their biographical narrative as to be thrown back some thirty-nine years before its origin, and appear as a vaticinium *ante* eventum.   The upbraiding of Jerusalem being thus transferred from Jesus who is supposed to cite it, to God with whom it sums up the long history of Israel, is no longer out of character in its manifold indictment of unfaithfulness.

* Jewish Wars.   B. IV. v. 4.

† Luke, feeling the impossibility of attributing this sentence to Jesus, more than a generation before, has dropped the word ἔρημος ; escaping the incongruity, but leaving the sentence empty.   On this whole passage, see an excellent paper by Strauss in Hilgenfeld's Zeitschrift für wissenschaftliche Theologie.   1863 : p. 84, *seqq.*

This particular citation proves no more than that the troubles of the perishing Jewish State in the apostolic and post-apostolic age did actually produce more Messianic literature than has come down to us by name. It does not throw light upon the part which the phrase " Son of Man " plays in such writings. But it provides a fund from which a reasonable explanation may be drawn of the remarkable fact, that this phrase, as applied by Jesus to himself, had still its non-Messianic sense, while in the eschatological discourses which worked themselves into the traditions of his life during a half century of Jewish Christianity, the Messianic meaning is in full possession. I believe it to be entirely posthumous. But as we have no contemporary record, and are dependent on writers with whom everything was fused down into a Messianic faith, who could neither speak nor let speak in any other sense, the evidence can only be indirect and reached by critical combinations. Our earliest Christian witness, the apostle Paul, though himself imbued with the Messianic belief, even to its doctrine of " last things," never once uses the phrase " Son of Man." By the synoptic evangelists it is put into the mouth of Jesus on about thirty-two occasions. Out of these it is used fifteen times not of himself, but as of a third person. In all the remaining instances it is given as applied to himself, seven times in a Messianic sense, ten times in a non-Messianic. And, on comparing the parallel passages in the three gospels, it will be found that the Messianic profession is at its minimum, or has its most modest expression in the oldest, Mark's. Thus, Peter's confession he gives in the words " thou art the Christ ; " Matthew adds " the Christ the Son of the living God ; " Luke, " the Christ of God." And in the account of the entry into Jerusalem, the popular cry, as given by Mark, is " Hosanna, blessed *is he* who cometh in the name of the Lord," and " Blessed is the *kingdom* that cometh,—of our father David ; " words which imply no more than the *announcement by a prophet* of the coming kingdom ; while Matthew has it " Hosanna *to the Son of David* ; " and Luke, " blessed is the *King* that cometh in the name of the Lord : " plainly marking the growth in the tradition.

The gradual loss by the term " Son of Man," of the *human* meaning in the Messianic, is indicated by this further peculiarity of the oldest gospel : that in it Peter's confession forms a dividing line between the two meanings, starting the Messianic conception and quitting that of Jesus himself. Whereas in Matthew and Luke the official sense is given to the phrase before as well as after that date, and distributed equally all through the ministry.*

* Mark ii. 10, may seem not to fall under this rule. When Jesus, intending to cure the palsied man, tells him " Thy sins are forgiven thee," the scribes ask " Who is this that speaketh blasphemy? who can forgive sins but God alone?" Jesus replies, 'Why this reasoning? what difference does it make whether I say 'Thy sins are forgiven,' or 'Arise, take up thy bed and walk'? but that ye may know that the 'Son of Man' hath power on earth to forgive sins, I say unto thee 'Arise, take up thy bed, and go unto thine house.'' It is usually supposed that Jesus here justifies his act of forgiveness by asserting his Messianic rank, to which it would admittedly be appropriate, and, as proof of his competency, offers the man's discharge from his physical penalty. In this view, his objectors then were not aware,—as indeed their question Who is this? implies,—that he spoke as Messiah ; else they would never have questioned the fitness of his words to his assumed character. His answer, therefore, consists simply in telling them who he is: he virtually says, 'Do you not know that I am the Christ?' giving them the information under the name " the Son of Man." This, however, is not the way in which Jesus treats their doubt. If it were, he would have to offer proof that he was "the Son of Man." Instead of this, he proposes to prove that it is within the competency of " the Son of Man " " to forgive sins on earth," a point undisputed and in no way relevant, if " Son of Man " means Messiah, to whose office the judicial function primarily belonged. The scribes' objection was founded upon precisely the opposite assumption, viz., that the unpretending character of " Son of Man " under which, like Ezekiel, he moved among his people, carried in it no authority to forgive sins. How does he answer the objection? *Sins in heaven* (i.e., in their spiritual aspect) whose moral heinousness, relative to the secret conscience, is measurable only to the Searcher of hearts, are certainly reserved for the mercy of God alone. But sins *on earth*, in their temporal expression by visitations of incapacity and suffering, he has from of old permitted his human prophets to remit, and when such a son of man takes pity on a stricken brother, what matters it whether he goes up to the sentence and pronounces it thus far reduced, saying, 'Herein, the sin is forgiven,' or whether he goes down to the prison doors, and opening them, bids the captive 'Arise and go to his house' ? Thus understood, Jesus simply tells his hearers, 'I speak in conformity with your preconception, viz., that at the back of all physical evil there lies some moral cause of which it is the outward mark and record.' How far he was himself from sharing this misconception, how ready, on fitting occasions, to protest against it, is attested by his comments on the fall of the tower of Siloam (Luke xiii. 1, *seqq.*). He repudiates the idea that the victims crushed by it were suffering execution for their sins: he warns his hearers against judging either others or themselves by what happens to them : they have the

Thus much respecting the history and contents of the current Messianic terms it was necessary to premise, ere we attempt to determine for how much of the claim which they seem to imply Jesus himself can be deemed responsible. The materials for a true judgment must be sought in the synoptical gospels; and yet are so largely moulded by conceptions first blended with these terms in and after the apostolic age, that they can be used only under great restrictions, if they are to lead us up to the historical figure of Jesus.

The foregoing account of the phrase " Son of Man," has against it the serious weight of Harnack's authority, who categorically affirms that the term means " nothing else than Messiah."* If this be so, it is certain that Jesus, who indisputably assumed it from the first, gave himself out for " the Christ " with uniform emphasis from the baptism to the crucifixion ; and yet Harnack himself says, in a note immediately preceding, " From the Gospels we know for certain that Jesus did not come forward with the announcement, Believe on me, for I am Messiah."† He attached himself to the mission of John the Baptist, and only slowly and with reserve prepared his adherents for anything more than the repentance in expectation of the kingdom. To escape from the contradiction between these two positions, by differencing his conception of the Messiahship from the popular one, is to put into the name " Son of Man " *something else than Messiah*, and so to retract the first proposition. The theory, however, of a gradual disclosure and advance of Messianic pretension has a plausibility which secures it an increasing amount of critical approval ; and in particular has its evidence very

inward power to " know even of themselves what is right ": to this let them look, and see what *they are*, and not mind *how they fare*, and then they will never mistake calamities for judgments.

Baur gives a different turn to the dialogue about the palsied man, founded on the closing words of Matthew's parallel passage (ix. 8), " the multitude glorified God, who had given such authority *unto men*." Taking the phrase *son of man* as simply equivalent to *man* without any special reference to Jesus in particular, he understood the lesson inculcated to be that the pure human consciousness places man in such a relation to God as to give him a well-grounded trust in the Divine forgiveness of sins. Hilgenfeld's Zeitsch. 1860. 282, 283.

* Lehrb. d. Dogmengeschichte, p. 68, note 2.   † Ibid. note 1.

skilfully presented by Holtzmann in his comparison of the gospels of Matthew and Mark.* Its plausibility is not surprising; for it is in truth the very theory of the evangelists themselves,—at least, of the common tradition at the base of their work; and it is easy to draw out of their text the speculative thread on which they have constructed it. But the question still lies behind, whether the assigned series of phenomena, from the impersonal message "the Kingdom of heaven is at hand," to the climax of personal faith in the messenger as himself the coming King, represents a progressive claim asserted by him, or a growth of belief naturally matured in them and retrospectively read back between the lines of his reported life. To determine which of these explanations is the more satisfactory we must recur to the chief landing-place in the ministry of Jesus, the scene of Peter's confession near Cesaræa Philippi.

The scene of his ministry opened in Galilee, and closed in Jerusalem; all but a few weeks of it being spent in his native province, in the fields and villages around Capernaum, or on the hills that overlook the sea of Gennesaret. Between these two unequal periods a memorable week of transition is interposed,—the farewell to Galilee,—the venture upon the city of the priests. It could in no case be an ordinary week that had so critical a place; but a time of pause, to gaze back upon a past which could never be repeated; and a time of misgiving, to look into the mists of a future which he could not pierce. In brief, three things are said to mark this week: (a.) he asks his disciples the popular opinion of his person, and receives from Peter the confession that he is the Christ; (b.) in the same breath he declares to them his impending death at Jerusalem; and (c.) six days after, the immortal prophets of the old time meet him on the mount of transfiguration and put a glory into that death by speaking to him of it. Whatever mythical materials may be embodied in this report of a memorable week, there are certain historical elements which must be admitted as the necessary base of its very existence. It is clear that (1.) up to that date, i.e., through the whole of his career except seventeen days, no word had been ever

<hr>

* Lehrbuch d. Einleitung in das N. T. 368, 369.

breathed about his Messiahship; for not only does popular rumour limit itself to explanations short of this, but even within the inner circle of his personal attendants it is only now that Peter's boldness itself ventures on the startling claim. That we may rely on this I conclude, because it is the story told by the oldest evangelist alone, while it has vanished from the others, who write under the conception that Jesus acted and was confessed as the Christ all through. The later version must yield, as unhistorical, if only through its unconscious inconsistency; and Jesus must be relieved, for the whole period, of a pretension uncongenial with his spiritual character, and the source of all that is perishable in the religion which bears his name. Nor does this affect our estimate of himself alone ; for the claim having not been made by his disciples for him, any more than by him, we do them wrong if we suppose them to have become followers in his train through hope of some great thing in the "Kingdom of our father David ; " he was but the human herald of a Divine event; and they were but the herald's servants. They were drawn to him and held fast by the power of a penetrating and subduing personality, the effect of which was a mystery to themselves, and their vain attempts to solve the mystery have left us the unfortunate legacy of a Christian mythology.

(2.) From the same date, i.e., on "setting his face to go to Jerusalem," Jesus himself experienced forebodings of danger and public death, sometimes openly expressed to his disciples, oftener perhaps overheard in the wrestlings and quieted in the composure of prayer. These deepening apprehensions needed for their source no changed intention, no heightened claims, no more aggressive calls to repentance, on his part : it was enough that the same message, 'The judge is at hand,' was to be flung upon a new scene, addressed not to listening ears and simple hearts, but to the threatened interests of blind guides and traffickers in spurious righteousness. Even in Galilee he had come across scribes and Pharisees enough to know that it was one thing to speak in the village synagogue or on the hill-side to a people "looking for the consolation of Israel," and quite another to lift the prophet's voice in the temple of the priests, who dreaded all reform, who wanted no purification but such as they could administer with hyssop or with blood, and thought less of mercy than of sacrifice. For him therefore it was a declining path that led from the sunny uplands of his home to the strange and stately city, in whose shadows the outlines of possibility were hid. All that he knew was that already the very message with which he was charged had been fatal to John the Baptist, though " all the people held him for a prophet," and only " the Pharisees and lawyers rejected for themselves the counsel of God."

(3.) At the very time then when the disciples, fresh from the crowds and the enthusiasm that for above fourteen months had followed his steps in Galilee, were at last approaching, as they thought, the crowning joy of conveying his glad tidings to the centre of the nation's life, their exaltation of spirit, instead of meeting response from him, seemed to sink him into a more pathetic silence, or even to force from him a look of compassion or a word of remonstrance. It was precisely this contrast of moods that was sure to elicit from him, in check of their exuberant confidence, prophetic hints of impending ignominy and sudden sorrow. And this close combination is the most striking feature in the scene of Peter's confession, and the most helpful for its right interpretation.

If we look beneath the surface of that scene, removing the films with which the touches of after-thought have painted it over, nothing can be more simple and true to character, as tested by the foregoing historical assumptions. The impetuous apostle breaks out, 'Thou art the Messiah.' Does Jesus accept the part? His answer is peremptory. ' Silence! to not a creature are you to say such a thing again !' and he instantly adds that at Jerusalem he expects the cross and not the crown. That Peter takes this for a disclaimer and contradiction of the pretension just proclaimed on his behalf is evident from his drawing his Master aside and privately rebuking him for his melancholy prophecy, and pressing him to a bolder use of his opportunities. Does Jesus set him right by telling him that there is no contradiction, the glory and the shame being blended in the same part? On the contrary, he goes with Peter in accepting them as alternative, and treats him as a *tempting Satan*, counselling the easier and the worse of two open possibilities: "Thou mindest not the things of God, but the things of men." The state of mind implied in both the speakers of this dialogue is exactly what would exist if the one had heard and the other inwardly seen nothing beyond the tragic issue at Jerusalem. If Peter had just been told not only of the cross but of the resurrection, could he have deprecated the death and taken no notice of the immortal glory to which it was but the prelude and condition? His remonstrance is plainly occupied with a humiliation pure and simple, and relieved by no reversal. And if Jesus knew and had just said that he should "lay down his life that he might take it again," if, having explained that this was the Divine gateway to the Messiahship, he was going to Jerusalem on purpose to pass through it, how is it possible that he should meet the apostle's suggestion as an alternative, and thrust it away as a temptation? It is only in the deep darkness of the soul, where nothing is clear but the nearest duty and its instant anguish, and the issue is shut out by the midnight between, that any Satan can slink in with pleas of ease and evasion. I infer therefore from the relation described, with all the internal marks of truth, between the disciple and the Master, that Peter felt his assertion of the Messiahship to be *repudiated*, not accepted, in the reply of Jesus; that his reply included no mention of a resurrection, but received this addition after the Messianic theory had been fitted to the facts and had modified the traditions of his life; and that even of his death it did not amount to the present definite and detailed prediction, but only to such prognostication as the fate of John the Baptist and the temper of the city sects and hierarchy too clearly warranted. If he had really set himself " to teach them that the Son of Man must suffer many things, and be rejected by the elders and the chief priests and the scribes, and be killed, and after three days rise again:"* if, a few days after, he had charged them to say nothing of the transfiguration vision " till the Son of Man should arise from the dead: "† if, by two special acts of later teaching, once while still in Galilee,‡ and

* Mark viii. 31.   † Ib. ix. 9.   ‡ Ib. ix. 31.

once on the road to Jerusalem, "he took the twelve, and began to tell them the things that were to happen unto him, saying, behold we go up to Jerusalem, and the Son of Man shall be delivered unto the chief priests and the scribes; and they shall condemn him to death and shall deliver him unto the Gentiles; and they shall mock him and shall spit upon him, and shall scourge him and shall kill him; and after three days he shall rise again;"[*] what can we possibly make of the strange statement that " they questioned among themselves what the rising again from the dead should mean;"[†] and that "they understood not the saying, and were afraid to ask him?"[‡] Was then the idea of "rising from the dead" foreign to the Israelite of that day? Was it not the very matter in dispute between the Pharisee and Sadducee, and, as such, discussed before these very disciples by Jesus himself? Had they not reported, as one of the popular notions about Jesus, that he was "one of the old prophets risen from the dead?"[§] Is there any obscurity in these "teachings" of Jesus, that a child could mistake them? Something far more dim it must have been, some ominous surmise quite other than these lists of clear details, that left the little band so utterly unprepared for the events from the Passover eve to the Easter morn, and scattered them in dismay. Every feature of the tragedy, as it occurred, took them by surprise; and not till they afterwards discovered that just these things "the Christ *ought to suffer* and to enter into his glory," did they feel sure that he must have known and voluntarily met it all, and have said enough to let them know it too, had they not been "slow of heart to believe what the prophets had spoken."[‖]

If we suppose Jesus to accept Peter's confession, and, at

---

[*] Mark x. 32–34. [†] Ib. ix. 10.
[‡] Ib. ix. 32. [§] Luke ix. 19.
[‖] The *post eventum* discovery by the apostles of the need and fore-announcement of the resurrection must have been notorious, for as late a writer as the fourth evangelist to say of Simon Peter and "the other disciple," even after they had gone into the tomb and found it empty, that "as yet they knew not the Scripture, that he must rise again from the dead." (xx. 9.) If they must "know the scripture," before they could interpret the empty grave, they could hardly have had the key to it which Christ's alleged and distinct prestatement placed in their hands.

least from that moment, to regard himself as Messiah, what are we to make of the instant injunction, renewed again and again, of absolute *secrecy*, sometimes unconditional,—" to tell no man," at others provisional,—" till the Son of Man should have risen again from the dead " ? Was then the Messiahship a *private* prerogative, which could be clandestinely held? Was it not rather the ultimate national test which he was bound to offer for the judgment of Israel? Might not his unbelieving " brethren " have reason for urging him to declare himself on the public theatre of his country—" No man doeth anything in secret and himself seeketh to be known openly. If thou doest these things, manifest thyself to the world " ? [*] If he knew himself to be offered to the faith of his people, as their predicted Prince of Righteousness; if he saw in their rejection of him the ruin which drew forth his tears; if his own death was to be incurred by the rejected witness he had to bear to his own Messiahship, how was it possible to tell no one he was the Christ? Why, it was the very message of God with which they were all charged; the touchstone of Jerusalem ; the hinge of perdition or salvation; and to keep it out of sight, not to press it passionately and always upon the nation at an hour so critical, were simple betrayal of the divinest trust. The injunction to conceal the claim is inconsistent with his having made or sanctioned it; and the evangelist, we may be sure, would never thus have provided for its secrecy had it not notoriously been publicly unheard of at the time, and waited to be posthumously discovered. It is not impossible, indeed, that we have here some remaining trace of a fatal difference between the disciples and the Master : that, as soon as their faces were turned towards Jerusalem, their excitement could restrain itself no more, and when the beauty of Zion rose before their eye the sunshine on it seemed a prophecy of joy, and they more than suspected him to be the hope of Israel, and the long-sleeping hosannas burst from their hearts. It was in vain now that he had forbidden that they should commit him to it. Had he been able, in doing so, to tell them, in some stereotyped formula who he was, and to say outright that he was Elijah or Jere-

* John vii. 4.

miah, they might perhaps have obeyed him. But as they must have some story to tell, they slipped through the too modest prohibition, and told their own tale; and, when out of hearing, whispered that he could be no other than the King that was to come. When by thus setting up a dangerous popular rumour at the passover, they had actually brought their Master to the cross, they would long to discover that the thought on which they had acted he had secretly cherished himself; they would search among the deep mysterious words that lingered in their memory for the needful signs of the Messianic consciousness; and to reconcile them with the foreboding and the fact of death, they worked out from the old prophets the theory of the suffering Messiah, and put it back into his history as if it were his own. And so have come together, as three ingredients of one incident, the prohibition to say that he was Christ; the acknowledgment that he is so; and the announcement of his death as if inseparable from the character. The combination is historically impossible; but it is explained by the retrospective anxiety of tradition to force upon him a theory of his person of which first himself and then his religion has been the victim.

But nothing perhaps has left so strong an impression of the Messianic self-announcement of Jesus as the eschatological discourse in which he answers the apostles' question about the " sign of his coming and of the end of the world." * The question arose at the end of his first day's teaching in the temple, when on leaving he met the disciples' admiration of the great buildings by the startling prediction, " There shall not be left here one stone upon another which shall not be thrown down." Seizing on this as the date of his coming, they draw from him, it is said, an account of its precursory symptoms, with the addition, in Matthew, of its issues in the judgment of nations and the eternal severance of righteous and accursed.†

Since the writers of the Gospels certainly intended to present all these things as announced by Jesus respecting himself, the reader, in so taking them, understands the evangelists aright: but that in doing so he understands Jesus wrong, two slight

* Matt. xxiv. 3. Mark xiii. 4. Luke xxi. 7.   † xxv. 31–46.

but significant indications enable us, without detailed analysis, to render more than probable.

1. Throughout the prophecy, said to have been privately given to his disciples, of the fall of Jerusalem, of the world's last throes, leading up to the arrival of the Son of Man on the clouds of heaven to part the sheep from the goats, and gather his elect into their divine inheritance, and similarly in all the parables about the kingdom of heaven and the harvest of which the reapers are the angels, never once does an evangelist venture to make him speak of that drama as belonging to *himself.* The inquiry addressed to him in the second person, " What will be the sign of *thy* coming? " is answered not in the first person, " After the tribulation of those days, ye shall see the sign of *my* coming with power and great glory," but in the *third*, the sign of the Son of Man, "and of *his* coming on the clouds of heaven." Nor, in the account of the judgment, does he place himself on the throne and declare, " *Before me* shall be gathered all nations "; it is again "*the Son of Man*" who has his escort of angels, and takes the seat of his glory, with the nations summoned to his bar. In explaining the parable of the sower he does not say, "*It is I* that sow the good seed," and "*I* will gather out of my kingdom all things that offend, and them that do iniquity, and will cast them into the furnace of fire "; these things are still given as predicates of the indeterminate " *Son of Man.*" Not even is it otherwise when he says, " Whosoever shall be ashamed of me and of my words in this adulterous and sinful generation, *the Son of Man* shall be ashamed of him when he cometh in the glory of his Father with the holy angels." This also might have been uttered by John the Baptist, or any prophet of any unknown Messiah, for whom he was commissioned to sound the note of warning and prepare a purified people; ' he that found it too low a thing for him to be seen in the track of the ascetic of the desert and his pool of baptism, would meet with the penalty due to a divine message despised.' This constant avoidance by the biographers of any self-identification on the part of Jesus with the eschatological functions of Messiah, explains itself at once if we assume that, in an age which had become convinced of his investiture with these functions, memorialists of his

earthly ministry would not hesitate to interweave with the floating traditions of his acts and words apposite fragments of Jewish apocalypse filling in the picture and completing the drama of his work. The matter of these supplementary elements would be in the third person; the historical colloquies in the first and second; and where the literary art of the compiler has not effaced the difference, the phenomenon which I have pointed out would result.

2. If Jesus, speaking in his Messianic capacity, fore-announced to his disciples all the particulars of his Parusia, he certainly would describe it, not as a "*coming* of the Son of Man," but as his *return*. Was he not there, present with them now? Had he not said that the Son of Man was going to be betrayed and put to death, and to rise again, and go forth into a "far country" ("even a heavenly") and "*to return?*" Why then does the revisiting phenomenon so habitually introduce itself as an unprecedented arrival of a personage known only to prophecy? Why caution the companions who know him so well, not to run after false Christs, whose "great signs and wonders" will be such as, if possible, to deceive even the elect?—as if it would be nothing, to them and to him, to meet again while all is fulfilled. This peculiarity of language and conception (which is not, however, found in the parables, but only in the literal apocalyptic statements) appears to me a clear indication of the unhistorical character and secondary source of the eschatological passages affected by it.

The identification then of Jesus with the Messianic figure is the first act of Christian mythology, withdrawing man from his own religion to a religion about him. What has been its effect? I do not deny that it may have been the needful vehicle for carrying into the mind and heart of the early converts influences too spiritual to live at first without it. Nor do I forget that it has saved the Hebrew Scriptures for religious use in the Christian Church instead of leaving them no home but the Jewish synagogue. But the moment the conception is seen to be false and unreal, this secondary plea disappears, and the whole system of images and terms that hang around the primary fiction and have no life besides,

A A 2

require revision.   It does not escape me how wide is the sweep
of this rule, and how the very scenery of the traditional drama
of faith, the pictures with which Art and Poetry have rendered
the invisible world beautiful and terrible, nay, much of the
symbolism consecrated by the hymns and prayers of centuries,
must shrivel at its touch, roll up and pass away; only, however, to leave us alone with God in a universe imperishable.
If its magic should dissolve the theatre in which we sit, and
the stage lights go out, we should but find ourselves beneath
the stars.   Must we not own that, purely in his character of
Messiah coming shortly with his saints to reign, was he called
Lord; or only as presiding at the great assize which was to
open his reign, was he called *Judge;* and because in that hour
his verdict would reserve from the sentence which swept the
rest away all those who knew him and bore his name, he was
called their *Saviour?*   And can we pretend that, when that
advent-scene has been turned into a dream, its language can
remain a sincere reality?   For those who, instead of letting
the Messianic vision break up as an Israelitish illusion, perpetuate it as a Christian apocalypse; for those who believe
that Jesus of Nazareth will send forth his angels and gather
his elect, and set up his throne and divide the affrighted world
with a " Come, ye blessed," and a " Depart, ye cursed," these
titles of sovereignty, of judicial award, of rescue from perdition, have still an exact and natural meaning, as the symbols
of a definite though monstrous mythology.   But, when once
our relation to him has become simply spiritual,—a relation
of personal reverence and historical recognition,—a looking-
up to him as the supreme type of moral communion between
man and God,—must we not own that these terms not only
cease to represent any reality, but become either empty or
misleading as imagery?   Between soul and soul, even the
greatest and the least, there can be, in the things of righteousness and love, no lordship and servitude, but the sublime
sympathy of a joint worship on the several steps of a never-
ending ascent.   The language which marks external differences
of rank and function can no more enter into the fellowship of
the spirit, than robes of office and patents of nobility can go
to heaven : the august presence of the Divine reality shames

these things away. With the throne and the glory, and the chariot of clouds, and the retinue of saints in the air and the trumpet of the herald and the voice of the archangel, must disappear the lordship too; and God alone, as Ruler of Nature, as well as Light of Souls, and so, disposing of us where we have no disposal of ourselves, must be owned as the Sovereign whom we unconditionally serve. To no other being (the political organism apart) do we stand under this two-fold relation,—of outward dependence in the sphere of physical power, and of inward communion in the sphere of spiritual good : and nowhere else can the double attitude and the mixed language befit us, of natural surrender and of moral aspiration. There alone the theocratic terms remain at home, and keep a meaning pure and firm. If you strain them thence, and carry them over to the realm of conscience and affections, you confuse the region whence you take them, and vulgarize that to which you apply them. For mere figurative speech indeed, which flings a transitory light and passes on, which settles into no formula but moves with flitting gleams, the old Hebrew and apostolic types of conception remain as open and as rich as any other store : and of the " promised land," the " heavenly Jerusalem," the " Kingdom of heaven," the " City of our God," the " holy place behind the veil," we shall never cease to speak, so long as there is a divine love and hope in the human heart, and a faith in everlasting Righteousness. But it is precisely where there is no flash of poetry and no glow of fervour, in the most literal and well-weighed speech, in professions of belief, in definitions of doctrine, in forms of prayer, that the Messianic language has settled with the most tenacious hold ; and, unless it be loosened thence, our religion will perish in its grasp. Are we quitting an ancient sanctity in doing so ? it is to enter on a truer and a higher. It is time to ascend to a more enduring order of spiritual relations, binding us to a larger world of sympathy, while infinitely deepening the long familiar ties. Let us take courage to be true, and make no reserves in our acceptance of the inward promptings of our ever-living Guide.

§ 2. *As Risen from the Dead.*

The Christian Religion, at its fountain-head, and in its imperishable essence, is the religion of Jesus. Not that it includes *the whole* even of *his* thought about divine and human things : for he too, born in time and place, had his heritage from the past as well as his power over the future ; and the new life in him wrought amid old materials of habit and idea, and struck out its light in dealing with many a problem traditional then and obsolete now. From the mere scenery thus given for his agency we must still retire within, till we reach its hidden springs in his own individuality ; and there at last, in the characteristics of his spirit, in its attitude towards the Heavenly Father and the earthly brother, in the secret faiths which shaped these tender and expressive lines, we look upon the pure source itself, the crystal waters as they lie among the hills in their basin of living rock. The more the type of mind thus coming into view approaches the unique, the more difficult it is to define its lineaments in analytic words. An impersonated religion can have no equivalent in propositions. They may enumerate some indispensable conditions ; but the inner unity, the tempering power, the delicate harmonies, which blend and proportion them, evade the resources of language. Every enumeration must be false which gives in succession elements which can only live together. But, if we must try to state in words the religion embodied in the person of the Christian Founder, we may perhaps resolve it into an intimate sense of filial, spiritual, responsible relation to a God of righteousness and love ; an unreserved recognition of moral fraternity among men ; and a reverent estimate of humanity, compelling the faith that " the dead live." This is the combination of which his person is the living expression ; and he in whom they reappear is at one with Christianity ; consciously, if recognizing their representation in him ; unconsciously, if repeating them apart from him.

From this primary Religion of Christ, which simply speaks out the native trusts and unspoiled reverence of the human soul, which lies hid in all its justice, breathes in its pity and its prayer, and inwardly hears a pathetic poetry as the under-tone of life, transfer yourself suddenly to the Christendom of today : watch the worship; listen to the creeds ; mark the picture of the universe and the theory of existence that pervade it,—the assumption of ruin, sin and hell as the universal ground of all, the eager seizure of an exceptional escape into a select and scanty heaven : see how he who throw open the living communion between the Divine and human spirit is set to stop the way and insist that no suppliant cry shall pass except through him ; and what can be more astounding than the contrast between that pure spring in the uplands of history and this dismal stream of horrors ? Who could imagine that the one has flowed from the other ? that the candle-and-posture question comes from that scene at table in the upper chamber at Jerusalem ? that he whom litanies and hymns without number implore today, is the same whom we see on the mountain all night in prayer, and prostrate and broken in Gethsemane ? It would be inexplicable, were it not that all ideal truth must apparently build a mythology around it, in order to realize its power ; and then, hiding itself among the current ideas and inherited affections of men, disappears from the foreground, and is replaced by secondary opinions about it,—whence it comes, and whither it would go. And so it has happened that for the religion of Christ has been substituted, all through the ages, a theory about him,—what he was in nature, what he did by coming into the world, what he left behind when he quitted it. These are the matters of which chiefly confessions and churches speak ; and, by doing so, they make him into the *object*, instead of the vehicle and source of their religion ; they change him from the " author," because supreme example, into the *end*, of faith ; and thus turn him, whose very function it was to leave us alone with God, into the idol and the incense which interpose to hide him. If his work is not to be utterly frustrated in the world, the whole of this mythology must be taken down as it was built up : if once it was needed to conciliate the weakness of mankind, it now alienates their strength : if to Jew or Greek it made some elements of his religion credible, with us it runs the risk of rendering it all incredible : if ever it helped to give to Christianity the lead of human intelligence, to secure for it mastership in the schools, authority in the court, and the front rank in the advance of civilization, it now reverses these effects, irritating and harassing the pioneers of knowledge, compelling reformers to disregard or defy it, and leaving theological thought upon so low a plane that minds of a high level must sink to touch it, and great statesmen and grave judges and refined scholars are no sooner in contact with it and holding forth upon it, than all robustness seems to desert their intellect, and they drift into pitiable weakness.

It would be much easier to untwine the mythological attributes from the person of Jesus, were it not that the process of investing him with them had begun long before our New Testament books assumed their form. No one takes it amiss if we ascribe a fancy to Barnabas or Apollos, a superstition to Papias, a theory to Justin Martyr, a blunder to Irenæus. But the moment we stand among the canonical writings, it is thought shocking to say, "This was Paul's speculation;" "That was Matthew's mistake;" "Here the fourth gospel is at variance with the rest;" and "There the Galatians and Acts cannot both be true:" as if the writers were lifted above opinions and were not allowed to think. Yet, except that it contains (not however without exception) an earlier Christian literature, and in the case of the Pauline letters productions of the first age itself, the New Testament does not differ, in the conditions of its origin, from the mass of writings whence it was selected; and its living interest, as best reporter of facts and traditions of the first century from the baptism of Jesus, is lost in a haze of illusory uniformity, unless we may trace through it the evident growth of doctrine from the baldest Jewish Chiliasm to the confines of a Trinitarian theology; a growth conspicuous even in the single mind of Paul himself, and vastly broader when he is compared with the preceding stage in the second gospel, and the succeeding in the last.

The growth of the Christian mythology which has taken the place of the Christian religion was continuous through six centuries, and received, at intervals, some important additions afterwards. Within the limits of the New Testament, we can follow it for nearly a century and a half; and we find there the vestiges of three successive theories respecting the person of Jesus. He was construed into (1.) the *Jewish* ideal, or Messiah; (2.) the *Human* ideal, or second and spiritual Adam; (3.) a divine *Incarnation*, whose celestial glory gleamed through the disguise of his earthly ministry. The personal attendants on Jesus worked out the first; the apostle of the Gentiles, the second; the school whence the fourth gospel proceeded, the third. They were not mere interpretations of his historical mission and past life in Palestine. They all demanded room for him beyond the term between the birth and the sepulchre; one of them at least required his pre-existence; and *all*, his post-existence. If he were Messiah, he had yet his work on earth to do; if he were the second Adam, the ideal of humanity, he was the head of an immortal race, and must be the first-fruits himself; if he were the divine Logos in the form of Man, he must return whence he came, and reassume his place with God.

Of these three theories, the first alone was already formed during the later days of his ministry. It possessed the minds of his companions from Galilee to Judæa, without (as I have endeavoured to show) any sanction or adoption by him. It kindled them with excitement as the towers of Jerusalem came in sight: it broke out in Hosannas as the procession descended to the gates: it was ever present in their minds as he taught in the temple, and gathered the people, and shamed the officers away: it suggested the conversations of the evening walk across the hill to Bethany: it came to a crisis on the last night, when Judas at all events would wait no more, but would drive him from his ideal pieties to assert his real character and assume his place. They all probably shared the feeling of impatience at delay which in the betrayer had taken its extreme and fatal expression: they had all more or less committed themselves to the Messianic claim for their Master, and contributed by it to bring him to the cross. Struck down with dismay at the issue of their own dream, tossed between compunctions which they dare not meet and a love for him which they would not let go for ever, " scattered abroad like sheep when the shepherd is smitten,"* and flung back into Galilee, to hide from danger, brood in solitude, or whisper their grief and wonder in twos and threes, could they discern no light through all that gloom? Must they say that the divinest vision of their life was an illusion? that the priests were right, and Calvary was just? No, it was impossible; if he was not what they had thought, he was something higher, and not lower: if he had refused their way, it was because it was not pure enough for him, and through sorrow and death he could find a better. Had they not read the Prophets with eyes only half awake and been dazzled by brilliant colours of Messiah's glory? 'For see here,—is he not "led as a lamb to the slaughter?" seemingly "smitten of God and afflicted?" "despised and rejected of men?" And yet, "because he had poured out his spirit unto death," is it not said that he shall still "prolong his days" and "divide the spoil with the strong," and that "the design of the Lord shall prosper in his hand?" † Is it not this that we have unwittingly fulfilled,—the humiliation of Messiah which must go before his glory?—of which glory his father David spake for him in the Spirit, when he said, "Thou wilt not leave my soul in Hades; and, Thou wilt not suffer thy holy one to see corruption; Thou wilt show me the path of life."‡ Nor would such deductions from Scripture have been without some support from the disciples' own memory of the recent weeks. Could they forget the pathetic shadow that seemed to fall upon their Master's face, as soon as it was set towards Jerusalem? —or the hints of suffering and wrong with which he had met Peter's exulting zeal? Was not his whole mood, from that moment, a preparation for self-sacrifice rather than for triumph? Was he then perhaps first learning the will of the Father concerning him, that not on this side of death was he, any more than the Baptist, to see the Kingdom which he had to announce? It was called the "kingdom of heaven:" what wonder then that from heaven it should come, and that to heaven he should go to bring it? For *there* surely, and not in Hades, must he be,—this Son of God more beloved

* Mark xiv. 27.   † Isaiah liii. 3–12.
‡ Psalm xvi. 10, 11.   Acts ii. 27, xiii. 35–37.

than Moses, more august than Elijah ; and as they, his two
witnesses and fore-runners, chiefs of Israel's Law and Israel's
prophets, were already there among the angels, where else
should he be on whom they are both to attend at his coming ?
' Nay, what is it that I half remember,' might Peter say to
James and John, ' of that night upon the mount, made up
of dream and waking, of cloud and light, when we overheard
the prayer go forth from the darkness of his soul and beheld
it return in a divine glory on the "fashion of his countenance," and words escaped him as if communing with the
earlier messengers of God?   Was it perhaps in that very
hour that he learned that the will of God was by the way
of the cross?   Who could be so fitly sent to tell him, as
just those two who were to "go before" and "prepare the
way for him" to tread?   Our eyes "were heavy with sleep ;"
I was beside myself with joy and fear, and "knew not what I
said ; " but now there comes from that memory the one clear
voice, " This is my beloved Son, my chosen ; hear ye him." '

If the Messianic doctrine of the time did not directly invent,
it would at least admit, such trains of thought as these ; for,
like all ideal pictures, it had but wavering outlines and colours
that changed with the glow or chill from the breath of circumstances.   The enthusiasm of trust and love, beaten back by
the tragedy of Calvary, was sure to reassert its elasticity ;
nor could anything sooner bring the reaction than the return
to Galilee, where every familiar scene recalled his image and
his voice, and the villagers and children who gathered round
to hear the story to its end, bore witness to him by their
dismay and tears.   It was impossible to tell the tale without
the intensest assurance that never had he been truer and
dearer to God than in those last days, which were but as an
offering himself up to a diviner will, and a passing through
into more heavenly life ; so that there was something in them
which neutralized the shock of the Cross itself.   To this state
of mind it would cease to be a thing incredible that Messiah
should be "cut off from the land of the living:" it was only
that " the heaven should receive him until the time for the
restoration of all things."

Thus far then, that is, to the belief that Jesus, the crucified, *still lives*, and only waits the Father's time to fulfil the promises, an intelligible process might well bring the disciples; and *this is the faith in his resurrection.* The conviction depended, in its two parts, on different sources : that the cross, instead of forfeiting, realized the Messianic character, rests, for its evidence, on the prophetic writings ; that Jesus, on yielding up his earthly life, passed, not, like other men, into the storehouse of souls in the underworld, but, like the two or three great spirits that had "walked with God," into the abodes of the immortals, where even they that have been human are "as the angels of heaven,"—this faith was only what was already held by contemporary Israel respecting their own Lawgiver, and was not conditional on any supposed resuscitation of the earthly corpse ; as may be seen from a curious fragment of a Jewish Apocalypse, called the Ἀνάληψις Μωυσέως, the *Assumption of Moses*, and quoted in the letter of Jude.* When Moses ascended Pisgah to look down on the promised land, and die, it is said, the Lord buried him.† But his successor, Joshua, the "Assumption" tells us, being carried in vision to the spot at the moment of decease, beheld a double Moses, one dropped into the grave, as belonging to the earth, the other mingling with the angels.‡ This exceptional assignment to the ranks of the blessed is the instinctive award of reverence and gratitude to the diviner lights of the world ; and in the case of the disciples attests the transcendent power of the personality of him to whom their very souls had clung, and from whom neither wrongs from men nor the fate of death could part them. Whatever momentary cry the parting anguish might wring from his lips or theirs, they now know him to be taken away, not as the forsaken, but as the beloved of God, elected to be the Prince of Life to all who grew like him by seeing him as he is. This dependence of their faith in immortality on the irresistible suasion of a single supreme and winning personality explains the order of *their* inference, from the one to the many, " because he lives, we shall live also ; " whereas *we* should

<hr>

* Verse 9.   † Deut. xxxiv. 6.

‡ xiv. ap. Hilgenfeld, *Messias Judæorum*, p. 459. Drummond's *Jewish Messiah*, p. 77.

more naturally say, " because man is immortal, he is in heaven, a chief among souls," seeming to reason from the many to the one.   Yet I know not whether, so far as there is difference, theirs be not deeper truth.   For surely with all of us it holds good, that only through the presence of spirits akin to his, does any diviner world of human possibility, any inward demand on life eternal, open upon us and plead in our prayers.   All our higher faith enters as we stand before those saintly and commanding natures to which perishable attributes refuse to cleave, and fall off, like the moss and mould from the finest marble, leaving the form clear against the stainless sky. As their silent appeal finds the spiritual deeps within us, it is from them that we draw the faith in immortality, and learn to deem nothing too august for a soul of such high vocation. Thus far we move on the same line with the first disciples. If at this point we diverge, it is that they could not yet assume, as we now do, that all human souls have the same high vocation, but treated it as a particular calling, conditional on something else than the common humanity.   They had not yet fully emerged from the religion of an " elect people " into the universalism of Christianity, though the key to it had been given by Jesus himself in his great saying that " All live unto God."   Nobly and beneficently has the conviction worked, that God would have " all men to be saved," and has endowed all alike with the conditions of probation and the potentiality of holiness.   It has softened the antipathies of race, and shamed the excesses of power ; has precipitated the higher consciousness of the world in labours of missionary mercy upon the lower ; has lengthened the arm and multiplied the appliances of compassion ; and has been the palladium, guarding every threatened sanctuary of hope.   Unavoidably, however, what is gained in diffusion is more or less lost in intensity ; and the ideal which is practically believable for all men, and is therefore measured by the standard of the lowest, cannot inspire the devotion and love with which Mary sat at Jesus' feet, and Peter exclaimed, " Lord, to whom shall we go ? Thou hast the words of eternal life."   We may well admit then that there was a concentrated power in the disciples' direct personal limitation of the immortal life to the case before them. They had simply gained the assurance that on Calvary Jesus had finished nothing but his sorrows, and had passed to a divine retreat till the hour should strike for him to open the kingdom of God upon the earth; his heavenly life, in its human relations, remaining solitary and exceptional; in the presence, no doubt, of angels and of God; but with no human society, except the two or three favoured prophets who had mysteriously vanished from their "walk with God," or in the clouds of Nebo, or on the chariot of fire.

Supported at least, but not induced by influences like these, the belief that their Master lived in a higher world was certainly intensely held by his personal disciples, and in the course of a few years (viz., four) it started up afresh, from some marvellous cause, in a mind of very different order,—the very enemy in whom it might least be expected to appear. It is impossible to doubt that all alike,—the new convert and the prior apostles,—flung themselves with unreserved confidence on the faith that Jesus was in heaven, to die no more, and accepted it as their mission to spread this faith among their nation, and beyond.

In carrying out this mission, they affirmed something more than their faith in the resurrection of Christ: they declared that they had *seen* the risen Christ; and had they not been able to do so, they could hardly have conveyed to others the profound assurance of his heavenly life which, in their own minds, so largely depended on the impressions of their personal experience. It is no wonder then, that, in the traditional accounts of their life-work, and in the autobio-graphical passages of the Pauline letters, Christophanies play an important part, and come to the front as the credentials of their gospel. In fixing attention on these, the chief point to be determined must be, whether they were the cause or the effect of the faith in the immortal Christ. In order to approach this question to the best advantage, we must take up the documentary testimonies in the order of their production, and not in the historical order of appearances which they relate.

Under the hand of one writer alone, the Apostle of the Gentiles, have we any contemporary report of the Christophanies; of those which he enumerates, one only, and that the last, occurred in his own experience; and his earliest mention of it dates nineteen years after its occurrence. This single personal testimony naturally becomes, in our endeavours to penetrate to the ultimate historical truth, the clew to the rest; and the terms in which it is given have an important significance in what they express, and what they exclude. The apostle, referring to his conversion, says, at a pre-determined time, it "was the good pleasure of God *to reveal his Son in me*"; and, as to the gospel thus given, "It is not after man; for neither did I receive it from man, nor was I taught it, but it came to me through revelation of Jesus Christ."* The two facts here asserted, that for the contents of his gospel he wanted and received *no human testimony*, and that the revealing of Christ to him was *internal*, are in harmony only with a process of ideal change occurring in his spiritual history, and are announced in terms wholly inapplicable to the flash of physical miracle upon the senses, or the visit of an unknown person walking and talking in the space around. The language would have its natural meaning completely satisfied by a sudden discovery of thought, throwing a new light upon some painful problem, or setting free from pressure a struggling will; and could be appropriated by many of the impassioned souls that have had a story to tell of religious conversion. True it is, that Paul comes nearer to the language of perception, when he says, "Am I not free? Am I not an apostle? Have I not *seen* Jesus our Lord?"† In all language, however, it is usual to extend the terms of visual perception to acts of mental apprehension; and here there is a particular reason for using the same word to cover both; for the writer's argument is, that the apostleship of the twelve, which rests upon the former, is no better than his own, which rests upon the latter: the qualifying knowledge in either case is adequate, as is shown in the resulting fruits.

But Paul's testimony does not stop short with the "revelation of Jesus Christ" at his own conversion. He also ranges this in line with the whole series of Christophanies known to the first Christians: he tells the Corinthians, "I

* Gal. i. 12-16.   † 1 Cor. ix. 1.

delivered unto you first of all that which I also received, how that Christ died for our sins according to the Scriptures, and was buried ; and that he has been raised on the third day according to the scriptures ; and that he appeared to Cephas ; then to the twelve ; then he appeared to above five hundred brethren at once, of whom the greater part remain until now, but some are fallen asleep : then he appeared to James ; then to all the apostles ; and last of all, as unto one born out of due time, he appeared to me also."* The whole of these facts he *"received ;"* but from two different sources which he is careful to distinguish ; the first half, including the resurrection on the third day, were "accredited by the scriptures ;" the second half, consisting of the Christophanies, were personal experiences related to him by others, or felt in himself. These are presented in the list as if they were perfectly homogeneous, his own case being distinguished by nothing except its occurrence after an interval and at the end. Beyond this relative position, no date is given for any of them ; nor is any locality assigned ; provided *the order* were not disturbed, there is no one of them that might not be on the third day or on the three-hundredth,—in Jerusalem,—at Bethany, or on the hills of Galilee. This inclusion of all under the same category could hardly be, if the writer were conscious that his own experience, as inward and spiritual, was strongly contrasted with that of the others, as a return of the earthly body from the grave, to walk upon the roads, and partake of meals, and be handled by testing fingers, and recognized by characteristic marks. If the same word (ὤφθη) is to mean the same thing, the "appearance" to Peter and James and the twelve was no other than the "appearance" to Paul, and may be construed by what he predicates of himself, and by the conceptions which we know him to have had of Christ's "spiritual body." By his resurrection, Jesus, we are told, became the "first-fruits,"†—the preluding sample of them that sleep : their change, on emerging from death, is simply into the likeness of their forerunner ; and is described by the apostle in terms which, on the one hand, negative all the properties of mere σάρξ and ψυχή, and, on the other,

* 1 Cor. xv. 3-8.   † Ibid. 23.

affirm those of πνεῦμα,—incorruptibility, immortality, and, as manifested, a brilliancy as of a glorious light.[*] This ideal of the heavenly nature as conformed to Christ's " body of glory," is repeated in the letter to the Philippians ;[†] and by its aid we must interpret not only the apostle's own appealing and subduing vision of the Christ he had been persecuting, but the earlier Christophanies of which he had only heard from others.

After what has been said in the section upon the Acts of the Apostles, it is needless to explain why we cannot accept from this book, with its three inconsistent accounts of the apostle Paul's conversion, any correction of the inferences warranted by his own letters.

It appears then, that, up to a quarter of a century after the event, the apostle of the Gentiles had no other idea of the resurrection of Jesus than of his exchanging the earthly organism for the investiture with the spiritual essence of heavenly life ; and no conception of a Christophany but as a manifestation of this life to the spirit or inward vision of the believer. As the eye of spiritual apprehension is different in different men, and the outward senses alone are common to all, it was natural for the Jew or the Pagan to demand from the disciples something other than their own subjective vision in proof that " Christ lives " ; and to beg that the appeal might be carried from the inner experience to the outer perceptions : and it is not surprising that the traditions were so moulded as to answer this demand. For, where a number of persons are thrown into the same attitude of mind, pre-occupied by one intense image, eager with a fixed expectation, fired by a sympathetic enthusiasm, the common affection answers the same end as the identical constitution of the eye and ear in all of them. A movement of thought, a glow of feeling, a turn of will, beginning in one, will run through all, and induce a common impulse of belief and act, precisely similar to the effect of the same objective experience. The two sources of common conviction are easily confounded ; and the Christian missionary who, in his contact with unbelieving auditors, felt the want of support from the former, was under

<hr>

[*] 1 Cor. xv. 42-50.   [†] iii. 21.

constant temptation to imagine and substitute the latter.
There were also current, as we know, grosser ideas than the
Pauline of what was meant by the resurrection from the dead,
ideas involving no more than a reinstatement in the old
conditions of the earthly life ; as when it was imagined that
Jesus was " John the Baptist," or " one of the ancient
prophets risen again."*   Among persons under the influence
of such preconceptions, there would be a persistent desire for
more palpable evidence, and a stream of questions about the
empty grave, and, if they were unbelievers, about the disposal
of the body, or, if believers, about the witnesses' interviews
with their risen Master, the signs of identity by which they
knew him, and the time, place, and mode of his final parting
from them. Ten years later, these questions, which are
without meaning for the Pauline Christian, but in Judaic
circles had probably long been stirred, had come to the front
and almost displaced the earlier type of faith ; so that in
Mark's gospel, which had no Christophany at all,† but only
gives notice, at the sepulchre, of the distant theatre of their
occurrence, it is the surprise of the stone rolled away and the
tomb without the corpse, that is superfluously offered as the
plea for this notice. To Paul and his believers it would have
made no difference, if the Jewish authorities had rifled the
tomb and publicly replaced the body upon the uplifted cross ;
this would no more prevent the spirit he had committed into
the Father's hand from putting on its garment of heavenly
light, than the contest between Michael and Satan for the
body of Moses could detain the Lawgiver from his welcome by
the angels. This hovering of interest about the tomb,
natural as a tribute of retrospective memory, is out of place
when turned into the supposed condition and sign of the
visible realization of the immortal hope, and implies an
incipient materializing of the first faith. In Mark, it enters
into its mere slight beginning, not yet touching the chief
figure, but presenting only a white-robed messenger to tell
where he will show himself to those who seek him. The

* Luke ix. 7, 8.

· † The proper close of the Gospel, I need hardly say, is with chap. xvi. 8 ;
the Appendix which follows being a summary, by a later hand, of current
traditions respecting the appearances of the risen Christ.

women who receive the message are to send "the disciples *and Peter*" forthwith "into Galilee; there they will see him, as he had said to them." This allusion is to the last of his alleged prophecies, given on the way to Gethsemane, of his passion and resurrection, "Howbeit, after I am raised up, I will go before you into Galilee."[*]

From this narrative it is clear (1) that the evangelist knew of no Christophany on the third day, either near the sepulchre or at Jerusalem; (2) that he regarded Galilee as the theatre of the first appearances of the risen Christ; (3) that apparently he knew of no other; (4) that in these Galilean appearances Peter's experience took the lead, in agreement with the order of Paul's enumeration. According to this conception, the events conformed themselves to the anticipation attributed to Jesus; "the shepherd being smitten, the sheep were scattered abroad:"[†] by the disciples' flight the scene was at once transferred to Galilee, and was there re-opened, when, amid the quiet hills or by the lapping waters of the beach, the ineffaceable impression of his life stole over their dismay at his death, and in spite of themselves breathed into their sorrow the reviving faith which had so often subdued his own. There, where the tones of his voice had scarcely died away, but were still heard in the memory of his beatitudes, his parables, his prayers, and they could now see how, in its divine calm, his form stood out against the city throng of carping scribes, and angry priests, and noisy traders, he would more than ever appear as the "holy one of God," to whom by the very way of death, "He will show the path of life,"—whom "after two days," as the Scripture saith, "He will revive," and "raise up on the third day to live before Him."[‡]

Of the Galilean Christophanies which responded to this natural reaction of thought tradition has preserved two doubtful traces, both of them introduced at the latest evangelistic date, and both misplaced at the end instead of the beginning of the resurrection story. One of them closes Matthew's gospel with an appearance thus described: "The eleven disciples went into Galilee, to the mountain where Jesus had appointed them; and when they saw him, they worshipped

* Mark xiv. 28.   † xiv. 27.   ‡ Hosea vi. 2.

him ; but some doubted."* This expression of objective uncertainty favours the idea of something visionary in the manifestation, or some affection of consciousness which was not common or equal to all. The other instance constitutes the appendix to the fourth gospel ;† in which is described an appearance of the risen Jesus to seven disciples at the sea of Tiberias, terminating with the well-known prophecy of Peter's martyrdom, compared with John's indeterminate continuance in life. Notwithstanding the obviously mythical character of this narrative, it is still of historical interest, as retaining the connection of the resurrection tradition with the Galilean localities.

If the faith and evidence that " Christ has risen " and lives in heaven arose and regathered his scattered " little flock " in the seats of his chief ministry, the time usually allowed for the consolidation of this belief must be considerably extended. The return to the homes in Galilee,—a walk of 100 miles,— would need the interval between one Sabbath day's journey and another ; nor can we treat the occurrence of the first spiritual communion between the forsaken disciples and their rediscovered Lord, depending as it did on the inward chronometry of their souls, as an appointment that could be punctually and uniformly kept. Nothing forbids us to allow whatever time may be required. The fancied necessity of forcing the whole process through within a few days, is imposed only by the later conception of a bodily resuscitation while the organism could still resume its suspended functions; and belongs to the materialistic forms of tradition so curiously blended, in the Evangelists, with the primitive and Pauline mode of thought. When, with an obvious awe, they transport the risen Jesus mysteriously from place to place, making him vanish from table,‡ and enter through closed doors,§ and appear now in one form and now in another,‖ so as not always to be recognizable even through long conversations,¶ by disciples familiar with his person, they seem intent on showing that he is invested with the attributes of immortal spirits. Yet, on one of these very occasions, he is made to say, " See

* Matt. xxviii. 16.   † John xxi.   ‡ Luke xxiv. 31.
§ John xx. 19-20.   ‖ Mark xvi. 12.   ¶ Luke xxiv. 14-31.

my hands and my feet; handle me and see: for a spirit hath
not flesh and bones, as ye behold me have." *   And, in disproof of this same incorporeality, stress is repeatedly laid on
the palpable signs of identity,—the eating of broiled fish,† the
print of the nails, the scar in the side.‡   It is the second of
these two layers of tradition that has both shifted the scene
of the Christophanies to Jerusalem as the place of interment,
and thrown back the time of the occurrence upon the third
day (the date, probably, at which the human soul was conceived to be released for its descent into Hades) and the few
more that could be spared from the waiting life in heaven.
The extreme case of this scant allowance of time is in Luke's
gospel, where the last chapter brings all the appearances of
the risen Jesus within the resurrection-day, on the evening of
which "he was parted from them" over against Bethany,
and "carried up into heaven."   Yet so regardless is the author
of consistency, that, at the opening of the second part of his
history (the Acts of the Apostles) he expands his one day into
forty, during which Jesus had many interviews with the disciples, and at the end of which he gave them their commission
as witnesses of him, and visibly ascended through the clouds
into heaven.§   Nor is Luke's contradiction of the Galilean tradition less direct in regard to place than in regard to time; for
he definitely detains the whole of the apostles at Jerusalem, by
an express order from Jesus not to leave it till the day of Pentecost shall have armed them with their divine credentials.   We

* Luke xxiv. 39.   † Ibid. xxiv. 42.   ‡ John xx. 27, 28.

§ Harnack remarks on the wavering character of the traditions about the
Ascension: "Paul has as yet no knowledge of it; nor is it mentioned by
Clement, Ignatius, Hermas or Polycarp.   It had no place in the oldest pro-
mulgation of the gospel.   The formulas often combine the Resurrection and
Sitting at the right-hand of God (Eph. i. 20 and Acts ii. 32, *seqq.*).   According to Luke xxiv. 51 and Barnabas xv. 9, perhaps also John xx. 27, the
Ascension took place on the day of the Resurrection, and is hardly to be
understood as an event happening only once (for the origin of the idea the
passages John iii. 13, and vi. 62, are very instructive; see also Rom. x. 6,
seq., Eph. iv. 9, *seq.*, 1 Pet. iii. 19, *seq.*).   According to the Valentinians
and Ophites (Iren. I. iii. 2, xxx. 14) Christ was taken to heaven eighteen
months, according to the Ascensio Isaiæ (ed. Dillmann, p. 43, 57, &c., s.c. ix.
16) 545 days, according to the Pistis Sophia eleven years after the Resurrection.   The statement that the Ascension took place forty days after the
Resurrection appears first in the Acts of the Apostles."   Lehrb. d. Dogmengeschichte, B. I. p. 172, note 1.

must conclude that, since the composition of his gospel, something had brought home to the evangelist the need of a larger allowance of time to find room for the known historical order of development of the young community.   That an interval of suspense still more considerable followed on the crucifixion may be fairly inferred, as Weizsäcker remarks,* from the account which Tacitus gives of the origin of the Christian denomination: "It had its origin from Christus, who in the reign of Tiberius had been executed by the procurator Pontius Pilate.   The deadly superstition, though suppressed for a time, broke out again and spread not only through Judea, which was first to suffer from it, but through Rome also, the resort which draws to it all that is hideous and shameful." †
The interruption and period of suppression which are here implied, and which are consistent with all that we learn from the apostle Paul, disappeared from view, under the influence of the later tradition of bodily Christophanies, and left in its place the continuous story, around the tomb as its centre, which the harmonists gather from our evangelists. Yet, even here, there are unobliterated vestiges of the historic truth in the mention of the " scattered sheep," of the " going before " of the risen Christ "into Galilee," of the appointed and the actual meeting with the disciples there, under conditions so far mystical that, in the absence of adequate spiritual preparation, "some doubted."   If the life of the Crucified with God were revealed by "heavenly vision," the reason is plain why he appeared only to his disciples.   But were it announced by a return of the human personality in its bodily frame, it is impossible to account for his having never appeared to the enemies and blind multitude who most needed to be convinced. In such case, well might Peter say to them that had "killed the Prince of Life," "I know, brethren, that in ignorance ye did it." ‡   If Jesus would neither, before his passion, suffer his Messiahship to be told to any man, nor, after it, present himself in living evidence of it to those who knew it not, how is it possible, on the strength of a single refusal at his trial to disown the character, to treat the downfall of the Jewish state and what is called the " casting-off of Israel," as the righteous

* Das apostolische Zeitalter, S. 1.   † Tacitus, Ann. XV. 44.   ‡ Acts iii. 17.

judgment of God on a people who laid hands upon his Son, misled by his reserve and his disguise?

The dependent and supplementary character of the traditional Christophanies at or near the sepulchre is indicated by their aimlessness. They simply serve the purpose, already served by the message of the angel, of referring the disciples to the real rendezvous in Galilee; or else, of merely verifying the fact of "the rising on the third day" already known as a necessity "according to the scriptures." The real object of the interview appointed by the heavenly Christ with his disciples was that they might receive from him their mission to take up his gospel of the Kingdom and proclaim it to the world until his return. This was the end of his appearing; and the idea of reducing it to a mere evidential instrument, as if prophetic certainty needed eking out by palpable perception, plainly belongs to the temper of a later time.

And in the whole series of traditions, whether referring to Galilee or Jerusalem, we cannot fail to observe, as a mark of their visionary character, their conformity, not to the relations of the universe as it objectively exists, with its infinite space sown with scattered worlds, but to the little cabinet picture of the Jewish imagination,—the angels in white, the celestial home just above the clouds, from which the heavenly messengers promise Messiah's return, and to which the person of Jesus visibly ascends, the throne of God and the seat of Jesus beside him. So long as we find ourselves in scenery like this, we evidently stand within the mind of the seer who paints it, and must seek the whole drama for which he prepares it in his own experience.

From this review of the early Christian traditions we issue with one indisputable historical fact,—the intense belief of the personal disciples of Jesus and of their quondam persecutor Paul, that, in spite of the cross and the sepulchre, he had passed into a heavenly life whence he would visit or whither he would lift those who were his by the pure power of faith and love. That belief was the essence of their message, the inspiration of their labours, the creative energy out of which Christendom was born. If we find that it did not come to them by physical experience, by handling a resuscitated body, by talking on the road with a mysterious stranger, lost as soon as identified in the breaking of bread, by ascension of a standing figure from their midst into the clouds, is it stripped of its validity and dropped out of the religion?   If we find that of no one else, under like external conditions, would they have had this belief, that it was contingent on their state of mind towards him alone, that it was due to a personality of unique power to enshrine itself in reverence and love and render Death itself conceivable only as a new birth, do we on this account turn it into an illusion? On the contrary, no physical fact, simply as perceived, touches the essence of religion, but lies within the knowledge of the seen; while all faith in the unseen, inseparable from trust in the Divine Perfection, is born out of the inner experiences of the soul in looking up to one who at once lifts and humbles it, out of the infinite moral ideality of the human affections. When I am told that, to be his disciple, I must believe in the resurrection of Jesus, I invert the order, and reply, to believe that Jesus is risen and lives the heavenly life, I must be his disciple.   Unless, with the little flock who could not leave him because he had the words of eternal life, I recognize in him the attributes that are worth immortalizing,—indeed, cannot dispense with it,—I shall not invest him with immortality; and if they bring me to his feet, I shall not go in quest of his body out of the tomb, as if it were the Holy Grail.   Not only do I conceive that the disciples' visions of him as risen depend on their entrancement by his transcendent personality, and could never have visited them had he been of lower spiritual stature, but I also admit that for us these visions cannot in themselves serve as objective proofs of his immortal life.   As psychological facts in the consciousness of others, their validity is simply for the persons to whom they were present; and to us the only thing they attest is, the intense power of his spirit over the springs of veneration and trust in them.   We may be sure that if there were a cynic or a Sadducee, or even an indifferent stranger, mixed up with the five hundred brethren at once on the Galilean mountain, the vision could not come to him.   And if the indifferent stranger, though seeing nothing himself, were to let himself be borne down by the multitude of affirming witnesses and accept their report on trust, it will have no hold upon him as a personal faith like theirs, but sit outside, ready at any call to drop away.   Take away the interplay of soul on soul, in the direct moral experience of higher character, and you dry up the very sources of conception for any divine humanity.   They are not felt in their fulness of power except in such living relations as those between the disciples and their Master, where the personal impressions are conveyed through voice and eye and kindling features which bring the inner thought on to the transparent plane of imagination; so that in the front of the saints in heaven are ever the greatest and loveliest we have known on earth.   But where the materials adequately exist of historical portraiture, of a life too simple for invention, too human to be less than real, and so deep in thought and pure in spirit as clearly to be fed from springs divine, the record carries in its representation no little of the power belonging to the personal presentation.   It furnishes a new measure of the contents of the nature it exemplifies: it expands the possibilities of humanity to godlike dimensions, and, with the possibilities, its aims, its duties, and the scope of its being and its hopes.   The faith that thus becomes irresistible towards one who rises to the spiritual headship of our race can certainly become universal in its application only on the assumption that the essence and destination of a nature are not overpassed, but simply developed and brought to light, in its supreme example; below which there is ever an assimilating power and even an upward pressure, which make the ultimate standard one for all.   This is no other than the apostle's thought " As he lives, we shall live also."   Now that Christendom has well learned this generalization, and that as the disciples reported it by their personal experience, now dim and secondary for us, so we rather let it rest on saintly souls we have known and loved, it is not unnatural to turn the inference round, and including the historical instance in the human, say, " As we shall all live, he has risen also." In either case, the last secret of the faith is the same; the " loved and like of God are loved and more like for ever."

§ 3. *As the Spiritual Adam.*

The interval between Romanism and Rationalism in our time is not wider than that which, in and before the apostolic age, separated the different schools of Jewish Messianic theology. As the whole theory was a product of fancy, working upon obscure and shifting prophetic limits, it broke into as many forms as the poets' pictures of the golden age. Men asked one another, " What think ye of Christ? Whose son is he? Whence will he come? Who will go before him? Who will be with him? What will he do?" and quarrelled about the answers; and never thought of raising the question whether they were not disputing about a personage entirely imaginary; just as they now debate whether the efficacy of the sacraments depends upon the form of words, whether it lies in the objective act or in the recipient's condition, whether it is rightly expressed by this or that elevation of the arms or bending of the knees: and forget to determine the previous question whether, in their sense, there is any efficacy at all. Happily, in these ideal worlds, extensive unity is rarely possible, or the blindness would be truly terrible : the diversities of error, pressing against each other, yield at last, as their resultant, the simple line of truth. So was it in the earliest years of Christendom as in the latest. There was latitude enough in the conception of Messiah for adaptation to differing wants, and wholesome conflict between minds of various scope. Whether he was to be some old king or prophet sent back in person to inaugurate the final glory of Palestine, or some heir of the royal line; whether he was to be of human kind, or a delegate from the powers of the upper world ; nay, whether even the promise might not be fulfilled, without personal representative at all, in a Divine outpouring of the Spirit of Truth and Righteousness : these were questions which the prophets had left open, and which were differently answered by the scribes in Jerusalem, the Hellenists of Asia, and the schools of Alexandria.

There was ample room, therefore, for a new theory about the person of Jesus and the meaning of his death, as soon as a fresh and original mind was awakened to see the promise realized in him; and no sooner had Saul of Tarsus obeyed his vision of the risen Christ, than he framed from it a scheme which has scarcely anything in common with the Petrine gospel except the central name. It was impossible that he should rest satisfied with the doctrine which sufficed for the Galilean twelve, of a suffering Messiah, whose advent was simply *put off* a while by death. About a mere postponement of date and gain of time, if that were all that could be got out of the cross, he little cared. He wanted something larger, freer, more humane, than any national glory under a resuscitated David or perpetuated Moses. His school-days in a Grecian city, his daily contact with its manners and its arts, his trade with the shepherds on the hills above and the captains of the port below, had opened to him a world which it were more divine to save than to destroy; whose idolatries had not sealed up the springs of pity, justice, and fidelity, and whose children were as bright and as susceptible as any Israelitish nursery could show. At the same time, his own vehement and capacious nature moved uneasily, though on that very account with the more intensity, within the narrow discipline of his inherited religion; and was ready to burst its ligaments and, if only the lash would be quiet on the will, to achieve a double fleetness on the wing of love. With this larger view of the world, this leaning to Gentile sympathies, this secret sense of the dead-weight of the Mosaic law, this inability to contemplate the universal government of God shrinking in its consummation to the dimensions of Palestine, he would seize on *any plea* for substituting a *human* in place of a *Jewish* hope. This plea he found in the present abode of Christ.

Saul, to whom the person of Jesus was unknown, in whose memory were no lingering echoes of his voice, who could rehearse in thought no tender and solemn passages from the Galilean ministry, had a mind blank as to that human drama. In his letters, the whole contents of that sacred life, from the nativity to the last passover, are left without any allusion; nor from them alone would the reader ever know that there was a baptism in Jordan, or a temptation in the wilderness, or a sermon

on the mount, or a mighty work of pity, or a parable of tender
wisdom, or a scathing of hypocrites, or an uplifting of penitents, or an agony in Gethsemane, of one who bore the name
of the " Son of Man."   His apostleship had been exercised
for three years, before he had contact with the predecessors
who could tell him of these things; nor could the historical
knowledge thus rendered accessible fill in the theoretic outline
of his teaching with any forms and colours of the past, or any
living traits of his inspirer's personality.   The whole space is
reserved for a single thought, flashed upon him in his conversion and conveying to him his mission—" *Messiah the crucified
lives with God in heaven.*"   That one conception suffices as the
seed of a new faith.   Was he indeed in heaven ?   Not in the
caverns of Hades among the shades of the dead, where
Abraham and David and Isaiah waited for the latter days,
with the frequent sigh, " Oh Lord, how long ?" but exceptionally lifted into the upper light where angels dwell and no
human being is found, save the three glorified prophets,
Enoch, Moses, and Elijah ?   Then he surely is of like nature
with the beings there,—the spirits who form that divine environment of God ; and has been *invested with that nature,*—
nay, rather has returned to it as already his,—after having
lived the traditionary life of men below.   Was it then to be
supposed that once exalted to transcendent rank in the spiritual
world, he would come back a little later to the earthly conditions which he had just laid down, and set up the national
kingdom in Jerusalem ?   Had he burst the chains of humanity
only to resume them, after the blessed vacation of a divine
freedom ?   No: if Messiah had to die and to go to heaven, it
was for something better than that.   He had escaped the
restraints of nationality ; he looked down upon the earth from
a station at whose height the frontier posts of jealous lands,
and the complexions of peoples, and the confusion of tongues,
disappear, and the rivers and the mountain-chains run through
the silent picture and dispose of the human race as one.   He
was living in a divine society where no pedigrees are kept, and
lineage is of no account, for they are immortals, and have one
Father, God.   He was the associate of natures intrinsically
holy, who served the perfect Will with saintly joy ; and had

his own obedience released from the strain of conflict and the exaction of tears. Who could believe that, from such a scene, he was to come, only to pick up the broken thread of his career, and finish what he had begun? To set his apostles on twelve thrones for judging the twelve tribes of Israel? to unlock the doors of the outer darkness and sweep into it the unbelieving nations "to weep and wail and gnash their teeth"? and to rule over the select minority of men still subject to the appetites of flesh and blood? No, if indeed he is to return to us, it will be not to reassume our nature, but to transform us into the likeness of his own: *we* shall be caught into the contagion of his glory, not *he* descend again into our limitations. No longer Israelite, he listens to no muster-roll of tribes. Among the immortal scenes of God, the earthly order dies, and the first-born can talk no more so exceeding proudly. Born under the law, he has emerged from it in death, and loves all minds in the proportions and by the affinities of holiness. Clothed with an imperishable spiritual life, he will gather around him when he comes, and perhaps before he comes, a society similar to himself, abolishing the weakness of humanity and changing its "vile body" into the likeness of his "glorious body."

This was the light that broke upon Paul, when the scales fell from his eyes: this, the meaning of the *heavenly man* (ὁ ἄνθρωπος ἐξ οὐρανοῦ) whom God sent to commune with him and bid him stand on his feet in newness of life: it meant the inauguration of a *heavenly humanity*, freedom from the burdens of an earthly nature, and quickened by the "spirit of holiness," from a divine and immortal Head. To the other apostles Jesus might be Messiah, because he was the "Son of David;" and to them the tragedy of Calvary was a shock of postponement which it cost them some faith and patience to endure. To Paul there was no Christ till he appeared, in his spiritual essence and power, as "Son of God" and "Lord" in heaven. This it was that defined his title and opened his living energy as realizer of the Divine purpose for humanity. "He was born of the seed of David according to the flesh, but defined to be the Son of God with power, according to the spirit of holiness by the resurrection of the dead."[*] His death was not his casting down but his "lifting up," that he "might draw all men unto him :" it was the step to his enthronement : it was not his temporary absence in "a far country," but the beginning of his intimate presence with his disciples, his inseparable union with those who found their spiritual life in him. His personal followers, scattered from his tomb in dismay, "as sheep when the shepherd is smitten," had relieved their recoil from his fate by fitting to it passages from the prophets which might have prepared them for it, and they reconciled themselves to it, as a supreme example of the sufferings of the righteous, which were still left, after every plea, among the pathetic mysteries of God. To them, it could never quite cease to be an ungrounded and arbitrary event, prophesied in the Old Testament because it was to happen, and then happening because it had been prophesied, but serving no obvious end except to gain a little time and swell the number of disciples to meet him on his return. This was a lame and inadequate account of a suffering Messiah, if, when he came at last, he was to be the same and to do the same, which had been expected from him at first, viz., "to restore the kingdom to Israel." To Paul, it flung both the adopted Israel and the outcast Heathendom into the cancelled Past, and delivered the race which embraced them both to its ideal representative in heaven ; that, by assimilation to himself, he might give forth a new edition of humanity, released from the tyranny of sense and self, and consecrated to the service of the pure and perfect will of God. He who was thus to abolish Sin and Death must emerge from the scene which they overshadowed : to deliver from the mortal weight, he must escape it : to found a regenerate society, quick with the powers of spiritual life, he must be "the first-born of many brethren." Thus Calvary becomes the very pivot of the whole design, the critical hour when it begins to work, the negative deep, in which, as it is crossed, are dropped the fetters for ever loosed : as the exaltation to heaven is the crown and completion of his investiture, his active assumption of the spiritual headship of mankind. It is no

* Rom. i. 3, 4.

wonder then if, on this account alone, apart from other grounds on which something will be hereafter said, the cross is, with Paul, never excused and left at the door of the prophets, for the scribes to deal with as they may; but is his boast, his joy, his strength; the central fact from which he reasons, and without which, whatever Jesus might historically be, there would have been no gospel for the man of Tarsus. It is the symbol and the opening of the universal change, not only in the character and feeling, but in the very constitution, and with the constitution the destiny, of human nature.

To understand the apostle's language on the new life in Christ that radiated from him in heaven, we must possess ourselves of his conceptions of the actual constitution of the two worlds, human and divine, of the measure of their contrast, and the conditions of their reconciliation. Their opposition was not, in his view, a gradual divergence that slowly spread from a primary similarity: nor even any sudden fall that disappointed an intended order in which all was good: but was based on the very material out of which the Creative hand had moulded the parents of our race. His words, that the first man was "of the earth, earthy" (ἐκ γῆς χοϊκός)* and that he "became a living creature" (ψυχὴ ζῶσα),† show that he started from the statement in Genesis, that the Lord God formed man of the dust of the ground, and breathed into his nostrils the breath of life" (πνοὴ ζωῆς).‡ The substance thus arising from the infusion of breath into dust (χοῦς) was *flesh* (σάρξ); and this it is of which the human being, as an animal, with conscious senses and moving limbs, is made: it is, as we should say, inorganic matter become organic and sensitive. The vital element put into it by the divine πνοὴ, though coming from God as πνεῦμα and, when separately named, called ψυχή (breath), is by no means regarded as carrying in it any share of the divine Essence; for it does not avail to save 'Flesh' from the most absolute antithesis to 'Spirit,' as no less the distinctive substance of the Divine nature than σάρξ is of the human. As a transient whiff of a breath that has left his source, all it can do is to convey a new property into the matter which it

* 1 Cor. xv. 47.   † Ibid. xv. 45.   ‡ Gen. ii. 7.

penetrates, waking it into consciousness of what it feels and where it is. But all the added power thus set up is given to the stuff of which the man is made; and the change to him, when lifted into a feeling Self, is in simply knowing it and becoming his own spectator. There is henceforth an "inner man" that stands off from "the outer," to notice and apprehend its contents: and this aspect of the human ψυχή as subjective intelligence undoubtedly receives, in distinction from the σάρξ-factor of the composite man, the name of νοῦς,— and even πνεῦμα, seeing that this is the seat assigned for the corresponding intellectual function in God. Thus the apostle asks "Who among men knoweth the things of a man, save *the spirit* of the man that is in him; even as the things of God none knoweth, save *the spirit* of God:"* implying that, in respect of conscious self-knowledge, the human and the Divine natures were similar, having an attribute which was beyond the resources of "flesh," and was so far "spiritual." But this " spirit " of the finite person detached from its infinite source, is empty of all initiative power, and goes no further than theoretic insight: it sees, but only like the dreamer through some inward tragedy in which he never stirs; and so is utterly opposite to the real essence of spirit, i.e., to the Spirit of God, which is eternally active, and in its thinking creates, and in conceiving the holy and the true, institutes the ordered steps that shall bring them to pass.

'Spirit' in heaven then is quite another thing from that which bears the same name on earth. In its proper home, it is as truly the essence of all living natures as "flesh" is here below; of God himself, rendering him intrinsically invisible; of his angels, charged with his gifts and messages of power and righteousness; of Christ, the well-beloved first-born of the regenerate and sanctified family of man; and of all the saints that may be gathered to him there. As the viewless air and wind serve for symbols of the invisible power of the infinite God, so does light supply the means of giving form and celestial beauty to the finite ministers of his will and children of his love: their body (σῶμα), unlike our organisms "of flesh and blood which cannot enter into the

* 1 Cor. ii. 11.

kingdom of heaven," is conceived by the Apostle as woven of sunbeams or luminous air, and described as "glorious," "heavenly," "spiritual;" unburdened by material hindrances, and a fit vehicle of the immortal life and love which transcend all earthly experience and mould it into the service of the eternal Will. "There is a natural body, and there is a spiritual body;" the former, our heritage from Adam; exchanged for the latter by union with the heavenly Christ.

From the defect of this divine element in man, and his surrender to the properties of a carnal organism, the apostle deduces all his infirmity and misery. It is the very essence of "flesh," in his view, to be the seat of Sin and Death; of Sin, because the susceptibilities of Sense awaken desire and stimulate action, which carry away the natural man untouched by spiritual power, and deliver him as a bond-slave, "sold under sin;" of Death, because, as intrinsically perishable, it spontaneously executes the sentence, "the soul that sinneth, it shall die." Of $\sigma \acute{\alpha} \rho \xi$, as substance, $\epsilon \pi \iota \vartheta \upsilon \mu \acute{\iota} \alpha$, its essential activity is, in the Pauline sense, $\dot{\alpha} \mu \alpha \rho \tau \acute{\iota} \alpha$,—the very principle of evil which leads men astray; and is still regarded as such, although, in the instinctive life not yet submitted to law, it is without the consciousness of the guilt of sin. To us this seems a strange conception, that men may be sinners without knowing it, accustomed as we are to apply it only to cases of voluntary choice; but the apostle, in order to seize it in its objective reality, thinks of it as it would look to the Divine mind, that sees what ought to be instead. He treats it as in itself the same fact, whether hiding its character in the animal darkness, or turned by the true light of a Divine $\dot{\epsilon} \nu \tau o \lambda \acute{\eta}$ into positive transgression ($\pi \alpha \rho \acute{\alpha} \beta \alpha \sigma \iota \varsigma$).

In either case, whether aware of his wretched fate or not, man is subjected to sin by the very constitution of his nature. If simply disposed of by his uppermost impulses, he cheerfully goes into all that is unrighteous. If he "assent to the rule of right that it is good," and even "delight in the will of God after the inner man," still, alas! it makes no difference; for this is only vision, not power; 'he finds another law in his members, warring against the law of his mind, and bringing him into captivity'* so that he cannot cease from sin, and is tied to "a body of death." Nor is it merely the appetites of Sense that drag him down to what he secretly despises; they not only tyrannize over what he does, but mingle a venom with what he thinks, and give rise to the whole brood of selfish hates and greeds,—strife, envy, jealousy, suspiciousness, revenge; † so that, from the hot-bed of σάρξ the taint universally spreads, and covers the whole surface of life with a rank growth of poison-plants. Before a being thus constructed the Divine Will itself is exhibited in vain; it may excite wonder at the spectacle of its beauty, and awaken thirst by its refreshing flow: but it leaves him on the ground, hopeless to follow the beckoning light, or to cool his lips at the regenerative stream.

As this fatal defect lies in the material itself of the human body, it was inherent no less in the first man than in his descendants, and was as truly "original sin" in him as in them; being in fact the cause, and not the effect, of his transgression. Else, if set up as a spiritual being, how could he fall before the first temptation? Neither in the Hebrew story, nor in Paul's application of it, is there the slightest hint of any change in the composition of Adam's person, by a metamorphosis of it into flesh, on his expulsion from Paradise. He is expressly treated as "made of the earth, earthy," to be the founder of an "earthy" race; so that his παράβασις was but the outcome in him of the ἁμαρτία inherent in his kind, and transmitted to his offspring nothing (beyond a first example) which he had not himself received. The universal sinfulness of mankind is never referred to the fall of Adam, as if his act could be also theirs, either really, because they were in germ within his person, or by "imputation," because he was the representative sample that stood for them all. These ideas, the one Jewish, the other Augustinian, are quite foreign to the Pauline anthropology, and are only futile apologies for the paradoxical but actual conception of unconscious sin as an attribute of organized matter. The apostle is not content with assuming this conception as an admissible premiss of his reasoning; to vindicate the stress which he

* Rom. vii. 17, 22, 23.† See Gal. v. 19.

lays upon it, he supplies it with a special proof, which runs thus: in the human sphere, Death is linked to Sin as an inseparable appendage, and so, wherever it appears, it is a sure mark of Sin.   Death visited all the generations between Adam and Moses: therefore, Sin was universal throughout. But *transgression* there was none; for outside the gates of Paradise no Divine commands were given till the Law was delivered from Sinai; nor could there be any *imputation* of Adam's transgression: "for where there is no law, sin is not imputed."   The sin, therefore, was personal to each, yet was disobedience in none; and was simply the same sway of natural impulse that had play in Adam, while yet untempted, and floating on the eddies of an epithumetic nature.*

According to this unquestionable purport of the apostolic reasoning, Adam's certainty of ἀμαρτία and subjection to Death were provided for *ab initio* in his sarkical constitution, and were only *evinced*, not *caused* by his trespass.   Yet the immediate context curiously verges towards the opposite account, which fastens the responsibility for the facts of Sin and Death not on the essential nature, but on the historical act of Adam's fall.   "Through one man," it is said, "Sin entered into the world, and death through sin, and so death passed unto all men, for that all sinned."†   These first words seem already to make more of Adam's agency than would be due to it if regarded as merely an early exemplification of a universal constitution: yet, if no more were said we might perhaps read in them only this meaning,—' See here what is to be expected of a race thus carnally constituted.'   But, as we pass on, we find the stress distinctly limited to the particular act of disobedience, and the consequent death treated as its sentence of judicial condemnation: "by the *trespass* of one" (not by the constitution of all) "the many died:" "the judgment came of one unto condemnation:" "by the trespass of the one, death reigned through the one:" "through one trespass the judgment came unto all men to condemnation:" "through one man's disobedience the many were made sinners."   And this involvement of all in the lapse of one is rendered the more striking by the parallel provision for

* Rom. v. 13, 14.   † Ib. v. 12.

c c 2

its reversal in the unique obedience of Christ which brings acquittal " to the many," and " abundance of grace " and a " righteousness of God."[*] It is impossible to harmonize the penal institution of death with the natural necessity of sin as its cause : and impossible to doubt that both conceptions co-existed in the mind of Paul. They are fragments of two different systems of thought, both indispensable yet never perhaps entirely unified ; for when the moral convictions which are the authoritative interpreters of human life are carried into the transcendent sphere of the divine Infinitude, their relative characteristics are liable to be swallowed up in the stupendous demands of absolute Being. The apostle's intense and lofty ethical feeling appropriated the national faith in the holiness of God and His righteous government, and applied to it the judicial ideas of the Pharisaic school. When, on his conversion, the universality of that government burst upon his view, and spread before him as its scene and story, instead of the family of Israel, the groups also of Gentile nations in their march through all the ages, the Divine economy became so vast and all-pervading as to dwarf the agency of man, and take up all his phenomena into the meshes of one design, now hastening to its consummation : so that all that had seemed to baffle the Providential intent, the Sin of man, with its entail of Death, the multiplication of offences by the very law which prohibited them, the train of hideous or beautiful idolatries, the stoning of the prophets, the captivity of the saints, the cross of Calvary, the persecution stopped by the vision on the Damascus road, were all of the counsel and ordination of God, leading up to the revelation of Christ in heaven, and the assimilation to that second Adam of all the redeemed who would throw themselves upon the offered power of His spirit. It is no wonder if the enthusiasm of this great Theodicy carried its author too lightly over the logical joints in its structure.

However obscure may be the inseparable linking together of Sin and Death in the apostle's thought, one thing, most needful to his interpreter, is clear, yet apt to escape attention ; viz. that to him the word Death denoted not the mere

<hr>

[*] Rom. v. 15-21.

dissolution of the bodily organism into its elements, but the consignment of the ψυχή to the caverns of an underworld, either never to return into the sunshine, or to await Messiah's recall of his elect to share his reign on earth, while all the rest were exiled to the nadir furthest from him. This dim psychical continuance was as much a part of the conception of death as the decomposition of the flesh : it lingered behind as a faint penumbra of a consciousness that had passed, and the reserved possibility of one that might be yet to come; but was just as much the privation of spiritual life as the mere ψυχή of man is alien to the πνεῦμα of God. Heaven alone is the realm of Spirit in its divine essence and life-giving power : the earth and the vaults which it hides are peopled by sarkical natures and their ghosts ; and nothing can cross these confines of death into the living light, unless caught up by the immediate Spirit of God, or lifted by the attracting love of a Christ,—the image and the medium of His perfection.

Since Sin and Death are the inherent accompaniments of the human organism, they are the impartial doom of Adam and all his race, from which no device can save them which leaves them "in the flesh" at all. Will the apostle,—himself " a Hebrew of the Hebrews,"—dare to proclaim this to his fellow-citizens of " the chosen people," " the holy nation," so self-assured of being the favourites of heaven ? Have they not been divinely organized under a revealed Law, to be disciplined in righteousness and made well-pleasing in the sight of God ? ' Yes,' is his reply : ' and so have the Gentiles in their secret thought, "clearly seen " "what may be known of God," and received his " law written in their hearts : " but neither the tablet of stone, nor the invisible hand-writing on the conscience, has been obeyed : both have been shamelessly violated, and left Jew and Pagan alike exposed to righteous condemnation from Him who " judgeth the secrets of men." [*]
Thus, the Pauline universality begins with the universality of Sin, and flies directly in the face of Israel's pride of spiritual primogeniture. Nor is this all : a shock more startling follows : He who bowed the heavens to throw His voice from Sinai gave indeed a Law intensely holy, just, and good : but

* Rom. 1. 18-29.

instead of being meant to make a people holy, just, and good, it was intended to demonstrate its own futility for this end :— nay, its own inevitable tendency to multiply transgressions by suggesting temptations that else would sleep. "The Law entered, that the offence might abound."* "I had not known sin, except through the law; for I had not known coveting except the law had said 'Thou shalt not covet:' but sin, finding occasion, wrought in me all manner of coveting: for, apart from the law, sin is dead."† In short, we are for ever haunted by the dream of a righteousness which we are radically incapable of realizing. The commandments do but clear and brighten the dream, and leave the nightmare on the rigid and writhing will more dreadful than before: for precept deepens the consciousness, without conferring the power of good: nay, by letting in the moral light among instincts once free and unquestioned, it casts the shadows of guilt on many a track undarkened by them before. Something more is wanted with the paralytic will, than to tell it whither to go and bid it "rise up and walk!" It can only answer with a groan, and turn to the wall to hide its tears. The appeal to the personal consciousness thus confirms the witness of history by which the apostle proves the inefficacy of Law, either natural or specially revealed, for forming a righteous humanity, at one with the holiness of God : in the mind of a carnal race it can only implant a baffled idea, overpowered by the tyranny of impulse. And the whole object of the world's Providence thus far has been to convince mankind of their sin, and humble them to the verge of despair, by the anguish of conscience and the wreck of law, and the failure of every polity, whether human or divinely lent on experiment, in order that at last they may fling their self-reliance away, and lie open in faith to the promised gift of a new righteousness from heaven.

But is not that an incommunicable gift? who can be found to convey across the worlds a living grace that must be born *within*, that cannot be laid as a crown on the nature already there, but only grow as a flower from a root which, alas! it has not? For want of this it is that the light and air of

<hr>

* Rom. v. 20.   † Rom. vii. 7, 8.

heaven play around it in vain, and the natural mind misses its beauty and its joy, without approaching the angels except with the sense of exile. Nothing short of a reconstitution of humanity, infusing into it the divine principle absent from it in its first edition, and dissolving or neutralizing its carnal elements, can give it power adequate to its intelligence, and lift or throw off the dead weight that holds it down. And as no creature can reconstitute itself, this is a deliverance which can only come by supernatural gift, or descend from some spiritual Adam on a new race, as the slavery has passed on all the family of the natural Adam. And lo! this is just what has happened to Paul himself from the day when God " revealed his Son in him," and showed him how the crucified, though fashioned as a mortal man, was in essence a glorious spirit, and could not be holden of death, and had passed not into the underworld of departed souls, but into the home of God as the first-fruits of a pure and divine humanity. Ever since that kindling vision, and the commission to proclaim it as the promissory opening of holy and immortal life for all, the bonds have fallen from the anxious and labouring Pharisee, and he " can do all things through Christ who strengtheneth him :" he has received " the spirit of adoption," that brings him to God as a Father, and makes him one with the beloved Son, with whom he has died to the burden and power of sin, and risen to the new life of faith and love. Carried out of himself by the enthusiasm of a heavenly affection, and finding his saddest problem solved, not by his will, but by the " Spirit of God that dwelleth in him," he has in his own experience the true key to the enigma of the world's Providence. First were the resources of the flesh, with their desires, activities and intelligence, to be instituted and tested by full development : and when their creaturely pride had been brought low by their story of failure, sorrow, and death, the secret should be revealed that man is meant to belong to the Divine and not to the animal realm, that his essence is akin to that of God : and at this crisis an economy of Spirit is to enter and be administered by an ideal or heavenly man, who shall effect the transition by bearing the flesh that with him it may die and its contents perish, and yet living in the spirit and returning to its source that he may send it into the heart of his brethren still "travailing in pain" and "waiting for the redemption of their body." The new era is now opening : the sonship to Adam is succeeded by the sonship to God, through the agency of one who united both and took the sorrow of the one to inaugurate the glories of the other. By what method, in the Apostle's view, this Mediator accomplished the transition, how he so cleared away the accumulated failures of the past, as for the future to free the track of spiritual righteousness between heaven and earth, must be reserved for consideration till we treat of the doctrine of Redemption. The one indispensable condition with which at present we have to do is the Humano-Divine personality that spans the interval between the two periods, that knows to the uttermost the experiences of both, and shows the way through the most pathetic shadows into the eternal light.

Though in the world's history the periods of the carnal and the spiritual Adam were successive, not so was the existence of their heads. The *revelation* indeed of the second, and his entrance upon his term of *Lordship* ἐν δυνάμει, were reserved till the term of the first was appointed to end. But, for all that, he must have been "ready to be revealed in the last time :" for spirit, "the spirit of holiness," being an efflux of the essence of God, is not put together and moulded into this or that creature, like "flesh :" and as soon as the apostle came into communion with the heavenly Christ, clothed with immortality, he knew more than the future function of this Son of God : his exaltation reflected back a light upon his past, and made it impossible to think of him as now, or within his human span, first beginning to be. His pre-existence therefore is undoubtedly implied throughout even the Pauline letters which find no occasion to give it direct expression : could the birthday of a new human being be announced, for instance, in these terms, " When the fulness of time was come, God sent forth his Son, born of a woman, born under the law, that he might redeem them that were under the law."[*] Or, again, thus, " God, sending his own Son in the likeness of sinful flesh, and for sin, condemned sin in the flesh."[†] One

* Gal. iv. 4, 5.† Rom. viii. 3.

who is "sent" is presumed to be there in readiness for the mission; and the predicates enumerated, his being made of flesh, and having a mother, and being under the law, might be taken for granted of a Palestinian Jew, and would not be specified except of one to whose nature they did not properly or necessarily belong. Such language is applicable only to a spiritual being, passing into the conditions of an incarnate life. If more unmistakable statements are required, they are supplied by passages in which the appearance of Jesus on earth, instead of being referred to the grace of God, is described as his own voluntary act: " Ye know the grace of our Lord Jesus Christ, that, though he was rich, yet for your sakes he became poor, that ye through his poverty might become rich :"* and, still more explicitly when the acceptance of the human life is set forth as the ideal of humility: "Have this mind in you, which was also in Christ Jesus; who, being in the form of God, counted it not a prize to be on an equality with God, but emptied himself, taking the form of a servant, being made in the likeness of men; and being found in fashion as a man, he humbled himself, becoming obedient even unto death, yea, the death of the cross."†

Except as presupposed in his incarnation, sacrifice, and resurrection to immortal life, Christ's pre-existence is left almost a blank in the Pauline theology. One brief allusion shows that he was regarded as the divine Agent in shaping the history of Israel; for he is identified with the rock-fountain which assuaged the people's thirst, and was traditionally reputed to have accompanied them through their desert wanderings; "which rock is Christ."‡ Other words are found which seem to assign him even an instrumentality in the creation of the world; "to us there is one God the Father, of whom are all things, and we unto him; and one Lord Jesus Christ, through whom are all things, and we through him."§ The "all things" here mentioned refer, however, not to the objects constituting the universe, but to the current Providential courses of human affairs: as the antithesis, in the context, to the "Gods many and Lords many" of the heathen clearly shows; for their supposed

* 2 Cor. viii. 9.   † Phil. ii. 5–8.   ‡ 1 Cor. x. 4.   § Ib. viii. 6.

function was not creative, but only interventive. It would not have been in character for the apostle, as " a Hebrew of the Hebrews," to trench upon the undivided prerogative of Him "who *alone* stretched out the heavens, and treadeth upon the waves of the sea, who maketh the Bear, Orion and the Pleiades, and the chambers of the South."[*] But the subordinate agency attributed to the pre-existent Christ in the national history and in the voluntary descent into the humiliations of mortal life, can belong only to a being conceived as *personal*, and therefore forbids us to interpret the personality as due to the incarnation and limited to the contents of the human nature. The subtle questions afterwards raised respecting the relation between the heavenly and the earthly factors of the suffering Redeemer, whether he had a compound personality, made of a Divine will and a human soul, and how in that case the two consciousnesses were adjusted into the needful unity, never emerge in the apostle's letters, and doubtless were foreign to his thought. The general tendency of his treatment is to identify the active affections and determining energies of the character with the spiritual personality brought from heaven and returning thither, while charging on the incarnation the passive sufferings, the moral conflicts, and the sympathetic sorrows, inseparable from the human lot. This was probably roughly conceived as the planting of a personal divine essence in a sarkical organism ; the susceptibilities and ἐπιθυμίας of the latter being subjected to the authoritative hegemony of the former.

It has indeed been inferred, from the expression " God sent his own Son in the *likeness* (ὁμοίωμα) of sinful flesh," that the corporeal material of the incarnate Christ was something *other than* the ' sinful flesh ' of mankind, the imitation being not *homogeneous*, but only *homœogeneous* with the original.[†]   But though this interpretation, essentially Docetic, is the first which the language of " likeness " would suggest, it involves the apostle's doctrine in a contradiction to which

* Job ix. 8, 9.

† F. Chr. Baur, Theol. Jahrbücher, 1857. S. 106, *sqq.*, and Vorlesungen üb. N. T. Theologie. S. 190 *sqq.*, and Das Christenthum und die Ch. Kirche. I. S. 295, 1te Ed., 310, 2te Ed.

he could hardly have remained insensible; for if it was not the σάρξ ἁμαρτίας that suffered on the cross, the sin and death of man was not, as he affirms, carried off and annulled in that sacrifice; and there is the less need, on exegetical grounds, to run into this contradiction because, although homogeneity is not *implied* by likeness, neither is it *excluded*: an exact copy, or reduction, identical in attributes, being also a facsimile.*

In " the heavenly vision " then of the glorified Son of God, there burst upon the view of Paul not the Galilean prophet taken into retreat till he could fulfil the prophecies, but God's own idea as originally projected in spirit, of what man was to be; a nature already divinely constituted in the invisible world when the earthly Adam was set up to institute his poor terrestrial copy. But if the second Adam thus co-existed with the first, it was not in active plenitude so much as in latent possibility, ready to declare its contents in the fulness of time. He was there, among God's eternal stores, like " the true tabernacle " in heaven, " the pattern shown to Moses on the mount,"† of what was yet to be for the worshippers' courts below, till they also passed " behind the veil " above. For the apostle, himself not called till the prelude was over and the πλήρωμα had come, all the interest was concentrated in the realization: the cross was the prologue, the surrender of " the kingdom " to God, as all in all, was the consummation, the communion and assimilation between the Son of God above and the adopted sons below, made up the intermediate acts of his divine drama of redeemed humanity. Hence in his love of Christ there was nothing retrospective, no personal image, no memory of moving incidents and startling words, no regret even that he had missed all contact with that sacred life. Its whole story is compressed for him into a single conception, of a god-like human person, passing himself through the darkest conditions of earthly experience, that, on emerging, he may bear off to heaven in his train all of his race that will trust and follow him. This one act, at once lowliest and most transcendent, is so all-sufficing

---

* See this well argued in Holsten, zum Evangelium d. Paulus und d. Petrus, p. 439.   † Heb. viii. 2, 5.

for the apostle that, with his immediate knowledge of it, he feels no want of the particular experiences of the earlier apostles in their attendance upon the ministry of Jesus: to have known him as "the Son of David," as born at Bethlehem, as duly registered under the law, as in conflict with scribes and Pharisees, and with tempters worse than they, is but familiarity with the detail of his incarnation,—a γιγνώσκειν κατὰ σάρκα χριστόν,—such matters of biographical concern for a person defined by the national, family, individual incidents of his earthly lot, vanish from the foreground, where behind them the glory of a heavenly essence is kindled, and draws the eye to their only meaning: one to whom it is revealed that Christ has died and lives in heaven for all, knows him κατὰ πνεῦμα, and knows him no more κατὰ σαρκὺ.*

Thus it was that, from the hour of his conversion, the Apostle of the Gentiles consciously stood in an immediate relation with the glorified Son of God,† his commissioned servant in the winding up of the long design of history; and, impelled forwards by the inspiration of that trust, set little store by the past, whether national or personal, which had done its work and shown that it was there chiefly in order to be humbled and transcended. Thus it was that when called to serve, not the Messiah of Israel, but God's living ideal of humanity, he cared not to "confer with flesh and blood," and learn his lesson from those who were apostles before him, but retired into Arabia,‡ to conform his startled thought and affections to the scale of the universal gospel, and the deeper insight of the Spirit. The companions of Jesus, "the Son of David," in his journeyings, could "add nothing unto him:"§ they had seen the mortal form; had he not seen the immortal Christ?|| The incarnate life belongs also to the past, like Israel's prophecy, and was all summed up in the cross and the resurrection, which established the present open com-

* 2 Cor. vi. 15, 16, i.e., "In *his* Sarkical character," e.g., as Son of David: had it been κατὰ τὴν σαρκὰ, the meaning would have been "in *my* fleshly character," e.g., with my bodily eyes: for, with a similar arrangement of the words, the article usually appropriates the flesh to the *Subject*, not to the *Object*.

† Gal. i. 11, 12.   ‡ Ib. i. 16, 17.   § Ib. ii. 6. || 1 Cor. ix. 1.

munion between the saints on earth and the home in heaven.

The full significance of this variation on the doctrine of the earlier disciples will become more evident after treating the Pauline interpretation of the cross. Meanwhile, one feature which goes deep into it is already evident. The identification of Jesus with Messiah by his original followers, lifted him into an indefinite distance from them, as their king, hid for awhile among the host of heaven, but coming back on the clouds with power and great glory to gather his elect, indeed, under his beneficent sway, but to rule the nations with a rod of iron. A few " who had been with him in his temptations " might be in office under him, with functions of delegated judgment ; but the multitude were to be subjects under sovereignty, he on the throne, they at the footstool ; the majesty to be his, the obedience theirs. Though human in his first experience, he had been invested with the supernatural prerogatives of a god. Here, an original community of nature is practically lost by a miraculous leap of exaltation, amounting to virtual apotheosis. Paul, on the other hand, instead of identifying an individual man with Messiah, identifies Messiah with the spiritual essence of ideal humanity ; so that all through, he is what man is meant to be ; and, to bring it to pass in spite of baffling failures, takes all the hindrances upon himself, and having made them null, returns to heaven as the spiritual Adam, made perfect through suffering, and henceforth drawing all men into his likeness by the quickening affinity of his spirit. In the Palestinian gospel he begins from a level indistinguishable from that of his disciples, limited to the same nature and the same nation, but is promoted, without change of either, to an unapproachable elevation of rank. In the Pauline, he lives at first among heavenly natures, to which the children of the earthly Adam could only distantly look up.; but only to show, by change of form to theirs, that they may change to his, and to plant them consciously on the same plane of being, as one family in God. The one induces the dependence of willing obedience : the other inspires the blending enthusiasm of divine affections.

In this latter aspect of his being, Christ, whether in his

heavenly or in his earthly life, is no mere individual. He is a representative personality at the junction of two ages;—the suffering medium in whom the miseries of the one expire; the divine energy from whom flows the free and glorious life into the other. He stood for mankind, as children of Adam, below ; stood in the flesh which was foreign to his original self, and died in it, that God might condemn it and have done with it, and let the spiritual essence emerge from it to its native home. He stands for mankind, as sons of God, above; to dispense among them, by the awakening affinities of faith and love, the power of the Spirit which henceforth is to make all akin and form one family in earth and heaven. Of this new family, not gathered by lineage or lying as a clan between the river and the sea, but linked to each other by the invisible sympathies of pure affection, and to God by the trust and aspiration of them all, he is the founder and head : the " Spirit of holiness " is the common element of life for them and him, as it has been eternally the perfection of the heavenly Father himself.

In this Pauline doctrine we have the second form of the Christian theory respecting the person of Messiah ; separated by a vast interval from the first ; and remaining, to this hour, the depository and monument of some of the deepest truths and most awakening influences of religion. Whatever the historic and logical critic may have to say of its technical form, of the adequacy of its premisses, the security of its reasoning, and its selection and application of historical analogies, it is impossible to deny the grandeur of its main conception, or the depth of insight and pure passion of aspiration with which, when once free from the tangle of its dialectics, it rushes upon its sublime conclusions. It resolutely makes over to humanity at large whatever was glorious and divine in the personality of Christ, and claims for all a participation in the spirit of his heavenly life. It vindicates the marvellous power of a free faith and trustful love to transcend the achievements of the labouring will, and to give at once atmosphere and wings to the spirit in its upward ascent. And it carries in it the principle which lies beneath all the communion of souls, that minds, wherever placed, and however ranked, are blended into one kind by the divine element of all, living upon the same truth, owning the same righteousness, thrilled with the same affections, and folded within the same eternal love.

§ 4. *As " the Word."*

A. *The Alexandrine Logos.*

It is hardly possible to appreciate the change of intellectual climate which every reader feels on entering upon the fourth Gospel, without adverting to the contrasted position of the Israelites at home and their settlers abroad. In the religion of the two, nominally the same, the fixed and fluid elements were curiously different. The monotheism which both of them inherited was in its origin a privilege of race, an ignoring of " strange gods," and undivided loyalty to Jehovah, as the divine Guardian of their fathers and their tribes ; and by slow degrees alone did the national God become, not only the greatest but the only one. Thus revealed to them as author and director of their family drama, he was traced chiefly in its vicissitudes, as for ever weaving the pattern of history, and mingling with human affairs as the field of his living will. His agency moved through Time as its scene, and worked out the idea of Man as its central object, intending to realize its aim in a society brought at last to complete righteousness. In this faith the dominant ideas are given in the One Righteous Will, evolving through the ages the type of perfected Humanity, reflecting the Divine. They are the measure of every value in the universe ; the heavens and the earth, with all their contents, are but the theatre on which their denouement is wrought out ; and whoever and whatever is too intractable to subserve the end will have to perish. On this mode of thought, founded in the conception of a Moral Government, the Palestinian Jew retained an unrelenting hold. He could let the cosmos burn and go out like a firework in the night,* and see " the armies of heaven " wade in blood even unto the bridles of the horses,† and " the false

* 2 Pet. iii. 10.   † Rev. xiv. 20.

prophet and them that worshipped the image" "cast alive into the lake of fire,"[*] and all would be right, if only God were just and true to his promise. That promise was of a final kingdom of righteousness, a heavenly Jerusalem, where nothing that defileth should ever enter, and for the glory of which the doom of myriads would not pay too dear. This national vision the apostle Paul also shared and cherished, but, carrying it with him into an Hellenic city, found its limits intolerable and its sacrifices too great. He could not part off the fellow-citizens greeting him in the streets of Tarsus into the eternal light and the outer darkness: he was tempted to feel that, of the two, he would rather consort for ever with this young heathen poet than with that priggish Hebrew scribe, and would save the wrong one, if it were left to him. The working of such thoughts incessantly chafed away for him the hard lines of national election, and supplied an interpretation of the Law and Prophets of his people which universalized the hope of Israel, by transferring its conditions from the flesh to the spirit. This expansion made him the Apostle of the Gentiles; but, except in the widening of his panorama of salvation, it left him still, in his whole cast of thought, a Hebrew of the Hebrews; with a Messiah who was indeed no stranger in heaven, yet only such an image of God as Adam ought to have been; with a Law which, though no longer binding, had never been repealed, but came to an end by using its received provisions for its own release; with an eschatology which would bring back Christ to this world for judgment at the last assize, and for union with his disciples of the living and the dead, to be for ever with them till he surrendered all to God. To the last as to the first of the apostles, the whole scenery was that of a supernatural drama, the winding up of human history, in which all the agents, whether on earth or in heaven, are distant by an infinite dependence from the One eternal and invisible Spirit whose will they subserve: although the Messianic personality, from the great part it plays in evolving the design, is lifted "above every name," and called the "Son of God."

For the Jews of the dispersion, natives of non-Semitic lands,

<hr>

* Rev. xix. 20.

this cluster of ideas lost its centre of cohesion, and from time to time threw off large portions, especially from its outer shell of local and political conception, retaining at last little more than its monotheistic and ethical nucleus. For the first two generations indeed of our era, while some semblance of national life was left in Palestine, and the festivals were kept, and the smoke of the sacrifice ascended, and the hierarchy stood, and the sects disputed, and the synagogue usages remained, Jerusalem might still be as sacred to the far-off Hebrew as Mecca to the Moslem pilgrim now, and his dreams of heaven itself might be but dissolving views of the fatherland from Lebanon to Hebron. But when alien armies had scattered the chosen people, had confiscated their patrimony, and made their law of no effect; when the priesthood had no altar and the Sanhedrim passed into an empty name, when over the temple site first the ploughshare was driven and then a sanctuary raised to Jupiter Capitolinus, when Israel became a race without a home, their sacred books, which could be carried anywhere, came to be their sole inheritance; and of these a large proportion fell away from all present application, and could be snatched from the grip of a "dead Past" only by miracles of allegorical resurrection. A religion thus released from geographical concentration and ritual polity, and embodied only in the literature of an ideal faith, is free to seek its rest and growth wherever favouring conditions may be found; and it may well be that the lost pre-eminence of Zion should migrate to one or other of the great colonies which attracted Jewish enterprise and culture. On the delta of the Nile the Macedonian conquests had provided the most tempting of these foreign seats, by appropriating one-third of their memorial city of Alexandria to Jewish settlers from Palestine; and curious it is that while by escape from Egypt Israel consolidated itself into a nation, by return thither it melted its nationality away, and gave its essence forth as the spirit of a universal faith.

Nothing more was needed for so great a change than a prolonged contact with Greek civilization and the gradual interfusion of Semitic and Hellenic thought; and in Alexandria this was rendered inevitable by the mere necessity of speaking, writing, and reading Greek; and of resorting to it, not only as the currency of daily intercourse, but as the vehicle, through the translated scriptures, of their religious ideas to a mixed society unacquainted with the Hebrew tongue. The difference between the genius of two races is never so sensibly felt as in the attempt to lodge the conceptions of one in the words of the other; nor does any discipline so quickly correct the rude crystallizations of concrete thought and disenchant the illusory creations of abstract thought. The Septuagint version affords abundant evidence of the shrinking of the Hellenized Jew from the strong anthropomorphism of his sacred books, and the desire to soften in it what would be repulsive to a more refined people. It was not the Greek *polytheism* that he thus sought to conciliate; rather would he earn a better right to denounce it by sacrificing a semi-mythology of his own. It was the Greek *philosophy*, afloat in the intellectual air of Alexandria, that, in certain of its ideal terms came into comparison with his religion, and opened to him a region of thought undreamt of in his traditional heaven. While the "Gods many and lords many" of the Gentiles, being for the most part ancestral and national divinities, patrons of only those who had the same fathers, the same heroes, the same history, were discredited and dethroned by the merging of states and tribes in universal empire, and retired to the Roman Pantheon as a museum of Statuary Art, there arose from the schools of Athens a philosophical mono-theism that touched the very minds most averse to the popular superstitions; and though in the strife of rival theories at home it was no serious power, it found a more genial reception in Alexandria, and was carried with enthu-siasm over the boundary which separates metaphysics from religion. The field in which both Platonists and Aristo-telians found themselves in presence of the Divine was not, as with the Israelites, the field of Time and the processes of historical development, but that of Space and cosmical order spread through its infinitude, within and through and behind which must be hid the Thought of its thought, the Ideal of its beauty, the Goodness of its good. The eternal Reason which made it an intellectual system, the infinite synthesis which made it one, the insight of moral proportion and harmony that made it a hierarchy of interdependent affection and noble life,—these are what we mean, or should mean, when we speak of God; who is therefore the indwelling cause and archetype of all that can be known and loved, as well as of the knowledge and love themselves. This idea of the immanent Deity, the primal, continuous and co-extensive source of whatever exists or acts in the universe for fair and excellent ends, is even more strictly monotheistic than the Israelitish conception : for it begins from the notion and belief of unity, instead of ending with it: it is there for the sake of unifying the indivisible cosmos, and constitutes the very formula of its inmost essence. The Jewish Jehovah, on the other hand, emerges into Oneness only by the defeat and suppression of rival claims, and reigns at last in Imperial sovereignty over tributary heathens, whose idols have been driven ·to enlist among the demons under " the Prince of the power of the air." The unity of a *national* god can hardly be called *a truth* at all, held as it is side by side with the admission of similar foreign gods. It can only *become* a truth if persisted in with tenacious loyalty till not only the collateral belief has been flung away, but the constitution of Man and Nature has been read into an inseparable whole, permeated by One mind, and directed to harmonious ends.

That the Unity had reached that stage in the Greek philosophic thought is evidenced by one very simple mark in the language of the schools, whether of the Academy, the Lyceum, or the Stoa. They never speak of "*minds*," though habitually attributing the functions of reason to both men and God. The word $\nu o\tilde{v}\varsigma$ has no plural : Intellect, in whatever Subject manifested, being *all one*, just as a *truth* is one and the same in however many persons' consciousness it may present itself. All the particular cognitions are unified in the single cognitum ; and thought can be rightly regarded only as a cosmical element that alights upon distributed points of life with identical undulation, as Space reveals its own dimensions by carrying them into every room. The animal organism of man was was not more intimately dependent for its vitality on the material products of the outer world which form its nutriment, than his mind for its energy on the universal Mind which is the source of its supplies and the essence of its being. And perfectly parallel with this Greek conception is the simultaneous Jewish and Christian notion of *Spirit*, as the common element of all that is Divine, whether it be God in his eternal essence, or the heavenly natures nearest to him, or the human souls that die to sin and live to him, through the new birth that makes them his true sons.

The old Hebrew monotheism was sure to be modified into this Hellenic form, as soon as it was brought into the focus of philosophical reflection. The fiat of Jehovah could not, as an act of Will, be permanently accepted as an absolute beginning: for it presupposes the presence of alternative possibilities waiting for its determination; take these away, and it becomes a blind force, no more imperative than the weight of a millstone. Volition, the starting-point of action, is itself the issue of prior thought and impulse: and for this there must be provision in the background of the nature which puts it forth. In the constitution of that nature, therefore, we must conceive a plurality of spiritual powers, all functions of one essence and initiative of one type of will. It was not difficult, from the analogy of the human mind, to borrow names for the Divine δυνάμεις expressed in volition: and in the play of relation which Philo invents for the reason, the authority, the goodness, the wisdom, the spirit, and the words of the Most High, there would be almost a mythology constructed, were it not that the changes of his fancy prevent it from settling into fixed form. But the Supreme Essence of which all these are but the manifold expression is an infinite and inscrutable Unity compassable by neither thought nor name. The human soul cannot even know its own essence, any more than the eye can see itself; how vain therefore to imagine that it can apprehend Him who is the soul or mind of the universe!* He alone is self-knowing in the highest sense, uniting at once the subjective and the objective conditions of such cognition: "before there was any universe, He saw, using Himself as light."† Unlike man, or the heaven, or

---

* Legg. Alleg. I. 29; III. 9. De Gigant. 10.
† Quod Deus sit Immut. 12. φωτὶ χρώμενος ἑαυτῷ καὶ πρὸ γενέσεως.

tho world, Ho is beyond finite conditions, therefore without
discriminative predicates, therefore no object of intellectual
apprehension, except as to his *existence:* that is a fact which
we understand; but beyond that we discern nothing.* This
incomprehensibility of God in his absolute essence is tho
basis of the whole doctrine of Philo, often giving it the
momentary aspect of a complete agnosticism; from which
however it escapes by more than one ingenious turn. It is
only the primal and inmost unity of the Divine existence,
the fountain of all ere yet it flows, that is incognizable by
human intelligence; when it breaks the eternal silence and
comes forth in modes of thought and power, these emana-
tions from tho infinite Source speak to the understanding
and make its sciences; and when followed out into the
phenomena under which they terminate, define the laws to
which life and its expectations must conform. From the
many characteristic expressions which this distinction receives, it suffices to take the following: Moses, inquiring
after the Divine nature, prays to learn it from God himself,
yet finds it inaccessible, and is told 'Thou shalt see what is
behind me, but my face thou shalt not behold;' and indeed
it is enough for tho wise man to know *what is sequent upon
God:* but he who would behold his essence would be struck
blind ere he could see it. It is glorious to contemplate, but
impossible to comprehend, the unoriginated and divine Being,
the First good and beautiful and happy and blessed, that in
truth is better than good, more beautiful than beauty, more
blessed than the blest, more happy than happiness itself, and,
if possible, transcending whatever is more perfect than these
perfections. Were tho universal heaven itself turned into an
articulate voice, it would fail of fitting terms in which to
speak his essence. No created nature is susceptible of knowledge so high; or able to appreciate, except in their effects,
even the attributes at one remove from God's inner essence.†
From our conceptions of Him all that is changeable and
created must be kept at a distance: He is the uncreated,

---

* Quod Deus sit immut. 13.
† De Profugis, 29. De virtut. et legat. ad Caium, 1. De monarchai. I. 6.

immutable, immortal, and holy, and only blessed God.* It is safest not to open our lips to speak of Him, but to contemplate Him in the silence of the soul alone, as He exists in indivisible unity.†

As it would be impossible, by any effort of silent abstraction, to "contemplate" an infinite blank, we must allow for some over-statement of the author's meaning in these remarkable sentences, and take them as severely limiting, rather than as totally excluding, access for the human mind to God himself. He does not really mean to leave us in the dark even with regard to the Divine Essence. He warns us that effort of ours can never reach so far, or go behind the properties and powers that radiate from that unsearchable unity; but expressly allows that when God takes the initiative, His knowledge can find us, though we cannot attain to it. He is the archetypal light and needs no other to see with,‡ whether he takes cognizance of the world or of his own infinitude; and of himself he has imparted a share to us; considering that created souls could not, of their own intrinsic power, apprehend divine things, yet that such knowledge was indispensable to blessedness, he breathed into men from above something of his own divine nature,§ and became the archetypal pattern of what is highest in ourselves. Thus, our knowledge of God is regarded as his dwelling in us, and is contingent, not on any exercise of our faculties as created beings, but on the presence with us of the uncreated Spirit, constituting a communion, like with like. Within the thoughts of the truly perfected, the God and ruler of all noiselessly walks, invisible and alone : there is his house, his holy temple.‖ In this view, all religious apprehension has the character of proper inspiration, and by its immediate nature discriminates itself from scientific knowledge, the method of which is logical and mediate. God imparts himself to us in various degrees, proportioned partly to our capacities,¶ partly to his designs for us, partly to our aspirations towards him.** But once commencing our communion,

---

* De sacrif. Abell and Caini, 90.   † De Gigant. 11.
‡ De Cherubim, II. 28   § Quod deterior potiori insid. soleat.
‖ De somniis, I. 28.   ¶ De posteritate Caini, 43.   ** Ibid. 41.

we may attain to ever higher degrees; for as the fountain is perennial, it can never fail our thirst; * as its amplitude is illimitable, our spiritual growth may be without end.* Some men are born of the earth, and never seem to escape slavery to the pleasures and interests of sense; others are born of heaven, and live in the pursuit of scientific culture; others, again, are *born of God*, and are the true priests and prophets of mankind, denizens not of this or that visible portion of the world, but of the spiritual whole of this universe.†

It is an easy thing to God thus to make the human mind his own; for if the strong winds of nature, sweeping over earth and sea, can lift the waves, and snatch up objects that of themselves gravitate downwards, much more can the Divine Spirit carry off the soul and take it aloft into a region of thought truly kindred with itself.‡ In all such living inspiration there is a glorious contagiousness. No mind that gives it loses what it gives; rather does it more intensely kindle as it spreads; and just as one torch suffices to light a thousand and multiply the flames, so does the touch of the Divine Spirit pass from soul to soul, and the holy fire become brighter as it flies.§ Nay, so far does Philo press this conception of the converse of essence between the source and the recipient of divine light, as to say that he who is truly inspired "may with good reason be called God."‖ The higher mind, indeed, is no individual or personal possession; rather is it a common spiritual element pervading both natures, God's and our own, the medium of spiritual understanding and harmony.¶ The true prayer therefore for every pious man will be, that he may have the Supreme Ruler as a guest within, to raise the little tenement of the mind in which he dwells to a great height above the earth, and ally it with the heaven.**

It is only, however, to the truly initiated,—the souls "born of God" and visited by him, that this immediate contact with his essence is possible; they alone go beyond the shadow

---

* De posteritate Caini, 44.
‡ De plant. Noe. 6.
‖ De nom. mutat. 22.
** De sobrietate, 13.

† De Gigantibus, 131.
§ De Gigant. 6.
¶ Ibid.

to the abiding substance, and bring its inmost meaning as
the key to the knowledge of created things. Ordinary men,
by an inverse process, receive a humbler gift, the constructive
interpretation of God by the issues of his living power,
whether in self-conscious natures that reflect the direction of
his thought, or in physical laws and tribes of creatures that
render that thought explicit in a visible world. It is in dealing with these mediating steps of divine knowledge, whether
as the track of diluting light that softens our darkness, or
that of progressive illumination that draws us to the intenser
borders of heaven, that Philo's language assumes its most
marked characteristics. He introduces us to a hierarchy of
mediating agencies, at one time appearing as abstract qualities, at others decked out with the features and dress of
prosopopœia so strong that but for the rapid change of
imagery, it would be taken for a mythology.

The term "Father" is appropriated to God in his absolute
Unity, with the connotation, of course, of a derivative
plurality; the Oneness means, says Philo, "not that he
exists in unity, but that unity subsists in him;"* i.e., the
universe is a coherent single reality as his idea. This phraseology is curiously strained in more than one connection which
might have tempted Philo to relinquish it. Thus, the world
being treated as the father of Time because supplying
measures to its lapse, God as Father of the world is pronounced to be the Grandfather of Time; the Divine life itself
presenting no time, but only the beautiful archetype of time,
viz., Eternity; in which nothing is past and nothing is
future, but everything present only.† This play upon the
family relations is allowed to run a step further; the Father's
creative efficiency has its partner in his σοφία (wisdom), which,
as feminine, may be called the Mother of the world; who,
when her time of travail was due, brought forth the only
and beloved Son perceptible by sense, viz., this universe.‡
So little does Philo shrink from this idea that he more than
once recurs to it and calls σοφία the wife, the virgin wife, of
God, Source especially of the virtues of pure souls.§ In this

* Leg. Alleg. III. 1.   Quis rerum divin. hær. 38.   † Quod Deus sit immut. 6.
‡ De ebrietate, 8.   § De Cherubim, 14.

connection, however, he suggests that the word "Father" would be more appropriate from its higher dignity; and he says that doubtless σοφία is feminine towards God, as secondary to him, and masculine towards men as having precedence over them.[*] The Wisdom which is ancillary to God has rightful lordship over mankind.

The relation of Fatherhood involves in it the two ideas of new existence, and of continued essence. In the former aspect alone, as a derivative product, the universe would never have been called by Philo "the only and beloved Son of God;" the phrase befits it in virtue of the second mark, as embodying in its constitution the essential order of the Divine perfections, so far as things visible can express their significance. Not as a perceptible creature offered to Sense, but as an ideal system, the living projection of the Infinite Spirit, can this supreme filiation be claimed for it. Hence it is that, for the sake of more exact expression, the Sonship is sometimes limited to the intellectual ground-plan or inner meaning of the cosmos in the Divine consciousness, as distinguished from its material presence to human perception: the λόγος (ὁ ἔσω λόγος) of the universe,—its *idea*,—is separated, as a prior step, from its ἔργα, or concrete objects; and is called the firstborn Son (πρωτόγονος υἱός)[†] of God. The *theory* or Divine *program* of the world, as the condition of its genesis, lies nearer, by one remove, to the essence of the Creator, than the visible heaven and earth; and so intercepts and appropriates their title to be called his Son by primogeniture.

Having once interposed this intellectual term between the absolute source and the cosmical phenomena, Philo might be expected to repeat at the second step the language selected for the first, and to claim the universe as Son of the Logos, now that the Logos occupied the place of Son of God. By parity of expression he had called Time the grandson of God, because determined into being by His "world." And this might the more be expected because, of the two elements in the meaning of the word λόγος,—*thought* and *speech*,—he emphasizes the first as the living source of the second; it is

<hr>

[*] De profugis, 9.   [†] De Agricultura, 12.

the fountain whence by nature the channels of uttered speech receive and are filled; and the fountain is mind.* Logos, both in the universe and in man's nature is twofold; in the universe there is that which has to do with the incorporeal idea whence the world was constituted a thought-system, and that which has to do with the visible objects which are representations and copies of these ideas, and of which this perceptible world was composed. In man, again, logos is on the one hand conceptual (ἐνδιάθετος), and on the other express (προφορικός): the former a fount, as it were; the latter, flowing from it aloud; the former having its seat at headquarters, (τὸ ἡγημονικόν); the latter and express, in tongue and mouth and other organs.† This analogy,—that as speech is to thought in man, so is the visible creation to its intellectual ground-plan,—is the key to much of Philo's doctrine; and the only difference which he points out as crossing the analogy is this, that while the human voice is made to be *heard*, that of God is literally to be *seen*; for whatever God says consists not in words (ῥήματα), but in works (ἔργα), appreciated by eye rather than by ear.‡ It would be only consistent in Philo to treat the visible cosmos as no less an offspring of the Divine Logos than is the speech and literature of mankind the offspring of the human logos. Why does he never claim for the world the title "*Son* of the Logos?" Because, I imagine, he reserves this relation exclusively for that which comes straight out of the *essence* of a spiritual nature, and will not extend it to what issues from an attribute, like Logos, itself subsisting in the essence.

Another anomaly in this language of Philo has some significance for his interpreters. In spite of his comparison of the universe with *speech* in man (*explicit* logos), he never, I believe, directly applies the word Logos to the visible world, but only to the thought that lies behind. The universe, he tells us, is "the only Son of God;" and so is the Logos; "the *Son*" therefore is one object with two Synonyms; and yet the Synonyms are not interchangeable! The reason is the same as in the previous anomaly. So far forth as each

---

* Quod deter. potiori insid. soleat. 25.
† Vita Mos. III. 18.   ‡ De decem orac. 11.

(the world and the Logos) is " *Son of God*," both must be immediately from the Divine essence, and have their filiation only in that which such proximate position makes common to both, i.e., in the ideal ground and meaning immanent in the cosmos, and connoted in Logos as a name for thought, to the exclusion of the word's other sense, of spoken words. The universe, when treated as "only Son of God," is regarded as itself the thinking out of the Divine idea, and not as a second step of physical utterance, the outcome of a prior plan, and falls into coincidence with only the intellectual meaning of Logos, severed from the vocal. Nor does it cover the whole, even of this ; for Philo's cosmos did not exhaust the resources of God's infinite reason, so as to leave his Logos no more that it is possible to do ; transcendent as well as immanent, the scope of thought-construction thus far realized is no measure of its unknown reserves ; so that even in giving the universe, the Logos does not give the whole of itself. The relations are difficult to adjust : if the two are made successive, the universe loses its sonship ; if they are identified, the Logos is shorn of its infinitude.

Though, however, Philo's Logos winds a changeful way through his fantastic imagery, and now Immanent, is scarcely distinguishable from the world as a realized divine order, and now Transcendent, lapses into God's own essence ; yet, on the whole, the attentive reader will find its middle place obviously intended and fairly preserved : and at the upper end, especially, its distinction is unmistakably marked from God as its prior no less than its superior term. The Logos is his creative and administrative instrument ; he needs no material media for action : in dispensing his gifts, Logos is his minister, by which also he fabricated the universe.* The precise relation of this deputed to the original agent is distinctly indicated when it is said respecting the universe, " The *cause* of it you will find to be God, by whom (ὑφ' οὗ) it comes into being : the *matter* of it, the four elements of which it is composed : the *instrument* of it, the Logos of God, by whose means (δι οὗ) it was constituted : and the motive source (αἰτίαν) of its constitution, the goodness of the maker."† This Logos

<hr>

* Quod Deus immut. 12.   † De Cherubim, 35.

of God, which he used as his instrument in forming the
cosmos is the shadow of himself; and this shadow or model is
the archetype of all else; for as God is the pattern of his
image or shadow, so does this again become the pattern of
other things.*

This favourite image, of the model and the copy, suits well
enough the analogy between the Divine preconception and the
cosmical presentation of the scheme of things; but is an
inadequate rendering of the author's entire doctrine. Pattern
and copy are both of them *objects* contemplated by a comparing artist distinct from both; and would naturally occur
as illustrations to Philo the Jew, already familiar with the
translation of the visionary " tabernacle on the mount " into
its miniature below. But Philo the Platonist had more to say
than that two separate things were made like to a third
which was different from both. He meant to affirm that the
εἶδος of the first was present in the second as its objective
essence, and in the third as its subjective perception of
resemblance and clew to imitation. One and the same Logos,
the base of a common understanding, did it all, constituting
a unity rather than an analogy; subsisting in the order of
the universe and living in the consciousness of man, it carries
into his nature as *intelligent* the attributes and epithets it has
already attached to the world as *intelligible*, unifying the
categories of thought, thinking, thinkable. The human soul
is made after the image of God; is stamped with his seal;
is the abode of his Word, his interpreter, his son. To the
soul God gives a seal,—a glorious gift,—to teach it that on
the indeterminateness of all things he impressed a determinate
essence, and shaped the shapeless, and defined the character-
less, and, in perfecting the whole, stamped the universe with
an image and idea, viz. his own Logos.† The soul of man
was a copy taken from the archetypal Logos of the Supreme
cause.‡ Hence the attraction to him of those who are drawn
upwards;§ their love of retirement, and longing to attend
alone on God;‖ for the soul is, in man, what heaven is in

* Leg. All. III. 31.   † De somniis, II. 6. Cf. De prof. 2.
‡ De plant. Noe, 5. Cf. De mundo, 3.
§ De plant. Noe, 6.   ‖ Quis rerum divin. hæres, 48.

the universe. The two natures, that of reason in us and of the divine Logos above us,—the mind in us and the mind above us,—are indivisible and correspondent; each engaged similarly and in sympathy with divine things by essence and kind, one in the world of being, the other in the world of thought.* Reasoning indeed is but a fragment from the soul of the universe, or, in Mosaic language, an answering impress of a divine image.† These various attempts to establish the homogeneity of the Logos in God, in Nature, and in Man, would seem to rank Philo amongst those Jewish writers to whom Spinoza attributed a hazy apprehension of the truth that God, God's understanding, and the things understood thereby, are one and the same.‡ Yet the " indivisibility " of " the mind within us " is so constantly crossed by the insertion of a *mediation* between these terms that an explanation is needed of the apparent contradiction. A conflicting tendency is evidently at work, and presses the author's thought into a deviation. It is found in his estimate of *matter* as undivine and antithetic to the intellectual and spiritual life of the natures burdened with it. From a confusion of the two senses of the word " *corruption*," to denote *organic dissolution* and *moral depravation*, it was deemed necessary to keep the immaculate Holiness of God clear of all responsibility for the constitution of perishable things, and to hand over the story of their vicissitudes to secondary agencies. Pure and original good he himself may give; but even the *remedies* for ill must come through commissioned instruments, and especially his Logos, the physician of human maladies.§ Well may he be compared with the Sun, if Sun there be that casts no shadow; " He is light, and in him is no darkness at all."‖ Yet even this is but a symbol: he is not only light, but the archetype of all light besides; or rather, older than the archetype and prior, containing the intellectual essence (λύγον) of the model: for his own Logos in its plenitude was the model; light, it may be called; but he himself cannot be compared with things that come to be.¶

* Quis rerum divin. hæres, 48. † De mut. nom. 39.
‡ Ethica. II. vii. Schol. § Leg. All. III. 62.
‖ 1 John i. 5. ¶ De somniis, I. 19.

The cosmos, as an assemblage of mixed natures, subjected for the most part to change and death, did not, in consistency with this principle, owe its genesis to the immediate fiat of the Most High: hence it is that, to alight on the creative Agent and procedure, Philo descends one step, and finds the work committed to the most ancient Logos, neither created nor uncreate, and thenceforth administered by him : for it is not God himself who is the indwelling principle, invisible and inappreciable except to the soul; but no other than the Logos which is older than originated things, by hold of which, as by a helm, the Pilot of all steers the system, and by use of which, as an instrument, when he was forming the world, he accomplished the faultless constitution of his work.* In this withholding of the world from immediate relation to God in himself, man also is involved, as may be gathered from the turn of expression in the account of his creation ; for observe, he is made, not "*an image*," but "*after the image*," of God, i.e. in the likeness of his primary reflection, viz. the Logos.† Nay, a deeper look into this language discloses an authority for even deifying the Logos. "Why," asks Philo, "is it not simply said, ' God created man in *his own* image ? ' Why does the scripture say rather ' God created him *in the image of God*,' as if, besides the Creator who made, there were another God who served as a pattern in the making? Most beautifully (he replies) is this oracle expressed : for no mortal nature could be formed in the immediate image of the Supreme Father of all, but only in that of the *second God*, which is his Logos. For the type of thought in the soul of man must needs take its impress from the divine Logos, since the God prior to the Logos is superior to every thinking nature; and it was not permissible for any creature to be made like the God who is above the Logos in a type of being uniquely best and subsisting alone."‡

The distinction, in Philo's theology, between the inaccessible perfection and the express thought and life of God repeats itself in his anthropology : the man whose creation is described

---

* De migratione Abrahami, 1.　　　　　　　　　　† Quis rer. div. hær. 48.
‡ Fragm. ex Euseb. Præpar. Evang. Lib. VII. xiii.　Cf. Quæst. et Solut. in Gen. ii. 62.

in the first chapter of Genesis being the generic type of ideal humanity modelled after the divine Logos; while the Adam of the second chapter is the concrete individual, in whom the bodily features reflect, and are made to express, that generic type, under the conditions of the particular instance. "The latter is the visible man, in his likeness to the conceptual model: the former is the incorporeal and spiritual man, in the likeness of the archetype, and so representing a higher character, the divine Logos, the first principle, the prototype, the original measure, of all nature."[*]

In virtue of the analogy, in their divine origin, of the outward and the human world, God may be said "to have two temples," in which he is concurrently, yet differently served: viz. (1.) the Universe, where his own primary Logos is itself permanent High Priest as well as constructive architect, and is the source and security of unswerving law, the bond of all things, clothed with the world like the soul with the body; (2.) self-conscious creaturely Reason ($\lambda o\gamma\iota\kappa\dot{\eta}$ $\psi\nu\chi\dot{\eta}$) whose Priest is *Man in his true essence* ($\dot{o}$ $\pi\rho\dot{o}\varsigma$ $\dot{a}\lambda\dot{\eta}\vartheta\epsilon\iota a\nu$ $\ddot{a}\nu\vartheta\rho\omega\pi o\varsigma$), the ideal mind and will, clad with the virtues.[†] Here, the administration of the sacred Logos deals, not with necessary nature which cannot go astray, but with free spirits which may cut themselves off from its guidance and get lost in the wilds. Its function, therefore, becomes not simply intellectual as the "interpreter of God,"[‡] "the true and genuine philosophy,"[§] "the heavenly manna," "the bread of God," "the dew of the soul," the "pupil of the inner eye;"[||] but *moral*, as the "frost" that lays a congealing hand on the current of earthly desires,[¶] "the honey-bearing rock,"[**] "the convicting conscience,[††] which gives the knowledge and with it the reality of sin,[‡‡] and at once humbles and heals us with a correcting shame.[§§]

How completely, in this moral relation, it answers to the conception of "the Holy Spirit" may be seen from a single

---

[*] Quæst. et solut. in Gen. i. 4.
[‡] Quod Deus immut. 29.
[||] Leg. Alleg. III. 59.
[**] Quod det. pot. insid. 31.
[‡‡] Ibid. 28.

[†] De somniis, p. 37.
[§] De poster. Caini, 30.
[¶] Ibid. 60.
[††] Quod Deus immut. 37.
[§§] Quod det. pot. insid. 40.

passage : so long as this most holy Logos lives and abides in the soul, it excludes by its own natural unsusceptibility of all sin, the possibility of involuntary perversion entering there; but if it die, not of course by any perishing in itself, but by parting from the soul, an entrance is immediately given to voluntary offences: banished while it remained in its vigour, on its departure they will be reinstated. For this choice privilege has been assigned to Conscience, our undefiled high priest; that it allows no slippery place in it for the will to fall.* Under this aspect the Logos is at one time termed "the divine angel "† that guides us; at another the true man, the convicter of the soul;‡ the Logos of God being thus the living source of moral law and righteousness, the actions of the wise and good are but articulate expressions of its mean-ing; they are truly "divine words":§ here words and deeds are all the same, and both may be admitted to the name of 'angels.'‖ The righteous are thus all enrolled as sons of one and the same Father, not a mortal but an immortal, the Man of God who, as the Logos of the eternal, must needs be him-self imperishable.¶ If as yet a man is not worthy to be called a Son of God, let him give diligence to order himself by God's first-born Logos, the eldest angel, or, in truth, arch-angel of many names; for he is called the beginning ($\mathring{\alpha}\rho\chi\acute{\eta}$), and the name of God, and Logos, and Man in the image, and beholder of Israel. This it was (he says) that led me just now to praise the excellent who say "We are all the sons of one man." For if we are not yet fit to be deemed sons of God, yet we may, at least, be called sons of his eternal image, the most sacred Logos; for the most sacred Logos is his image.**

As the spotless holiness of the Most High is saved by com-mitting the creative process to a "second God" to convey his ideal purpose into the materials it has to mould, so does the corporeal investiture thus commenced mingle more and more alloy with that pure primal light at each successive step of

----

* De prof. 21.   † Quod Deus immut. 57.
‡ De prof. 23.   § De migr. Abr. 23.
‖ De confus. ling. 8.   ¶ Ibid. 8.
** Ibid. 28.

derivative genesis. Hence, the entrance of imperfection, and the ulterior ills that arise upon the track of life, are to be charged not on the infinite Source, but on the intermediate agencies, which partly execute, but partly spoil, his thought. In the Logos itself indeed there is as yet no incipient shade; second in order only, not in purity, it is but infinite Reason turned into definite truth, possible righteousness kindled into conscious aspiration: so that it seems often indifferent to Philo whether he attributes what is excellent and beautiful to God himself or to the "sacred Logos," or even to the human soul possessed by it. But again and again he insists that God is the cause only of the good; that in the creation he was himself the author of whatever is best, but had assistants who were charged with all admixture of evil; and that he still operates all the good in the human mind. Nor is this rule content with protecting the Divine agency from contact with the moral failure of mankind. Even natural disturbances, such as "earthquakes, and plagues, and lightning strokes," are improperly though commonly said to be heaven-sent; for God is the cause of no ill at all; and they are due to changes in the physical elements belonging, not "to the leading phenomena of nature, but to those which follow in the train of such by necessary laws." The rule explains the plural form, so startling to the strict monotheist, of the final creative project, "Let *us* make man?" Why does the Creator invite the *co-operation of others* in this particular work? That he himself, the guide of all, might be responsible for the faultless purposes and acts of man in his uprightness, while the opposite class lay at the door of his subordinates; for it was right that no evil should be chargeable on the Father by the children.* To God, he elsewhere says, it belongs to plant and raise the virtues in the soul; and it is self-love and atheism in the mind to put itself here on an equality with God, and fancy itself Agent, when on closer view it is but Patient: for when it is God that sows and plants the good in the soul, it is impiety in the mind to say, "I am the planter." †

It is not, however, only of the entrance of evil that the

* De mundi opif. 24. Cf. 46; also de confus. ling. 34, 35; de prof. 13; de mutat. nom. 4.   † Leg. All. I. 15.

relation between the First Cause and his subordinates gives account; it also opens a way for its redemption. The intermediaries demanded by the infinite elevation of God above the world, while serving as messengers and menials and penal agents of his realm, are themselves akin both to Him and to the created natures receiving from them the orders of his will; and being touched at once by devotion to him and sympathy with them, are qualified, when alienation arises, to warn, to intercede, and pray for reconciliation. The main host (στρατός) of them is supposed by Philo to consist of incorporeal and happy souls," * "identical with the beings called demons (δαίμονες) by the philosophers,—souls flitting in the air : " † by Moses happily designated as angels, sent on missions of good from the Ruler to his subjects, and serviceable to the King in the concerns of their obedience.‡ They are subordinate ministers and priests of God in the temple of the universe.

But as these ministering natures owe all their beneficent influence to their indwelling share of the sacred Logos, so is it in that Divine Logos itself that the redeeming function is centred. The unique feature of his intermediate position fits him for a mediatorial office. The Father who gave origin to the universe intrusted to the most ancient and archetypal Logos a special function, to stand on the confines and mark the limits between the created and the Maker ; at once constant suppliant (ἱκέτης) to the Immortal on behalf of the perishing mortal, and ambassador of the Ruler to the subject. And the Logos delights in the function and announces it with exultation, 'I was appointed to stand between the Lord and you ; being neither uncreate as God nor created as you, but as midway between the extremes, serving as hostage for both : with the Parent, a pledge that the race shall never utterly perish and rebelliously prefer disorder to order ; with the offspring, that the merciful God would never, it might be confidently hoped, disregard his own work.' 'For I am to be the herald of peaceful tidings to the creation from Him who has decreed the abolition of strife,—God, the Guardian of peace

<hr>

* Sacrif. Abell et Caini, 2.   † De Gigant. 2.
‡ De plant. Noe. 4.   Cf. De monarch, II. 1 ; de mundo, 3.

for ever.' * It is partly in virtue of this function that Philo repeatedly compares the Logos, as we have seen, with the priest in the temple who makes the worshippers' peace with God. And it is interesting to find the word *Paraclete* applied to him in precisely the sense which it bears in 1 John ii. 1. " If any man sin we have an advocate with the Father, Jesus Christ the Righteous." The passage affirms that for consecration to the Father of the universe it is needful "to have as advocate the Son perfect in virtue (the Logos), for the oblivion of sins and the unsparing supply of blessings." † This conception of the mediating function of the Logos can hardly have been without influence on the author of the Epistle to the Hebrews, when he wrote, " We have not a high priest that cannot be touched with the feeling of our infirmities, but one that hath been in all points tried as we are, and yet without sin:" to stand on the confines of the heavenly and the earthly life, and be at one with the affections of both, is the qualifying condition of the perfect mediator. *That* is the common thought of the Jewish and the Christian writer.

From the vast and various assemblage of predicates accumulated upon the Logos the modern student will not feel that he issues with a clear result, unless he can say whether they constitute a *Personal* being, or are mere personifications of something *Impersonal.* And this question is one which can never be answered, for the simple reason that the conception of " Personality," as now held, is a later acquisition of the West-European mind, and has no equivalent in the philosophy which threw itself into the old Greek moulds of thought. The space therefore is blank where we should seek an answer to the question most interesting to us. But this disappointment is no more chargeable on Philo than on the early writers of the Catholic Church, and on the very creeds which authoritatively defined its faith : for, there also, the word selected for the supposed distinctions in the Godhead meant nothing like what we understand by " person." In the absence of this

---

* Quis rer. div. hæres. I. 42, paraphrasing Num. xvi. 48.

† Vita Mos. III. 14. Heinze's doubt about the interpretation of this passage seems (in the last result even to himself) superfluous: Die Lehre vom Logos in der Griech. Philos., von Dr. Max Heinze, p. 283 *seqq.*

idea, recourse was had to one or both of two antitheses, Substance—Attribute and Source—Derivative, or, with a view to combine both in one, Essence—Phenomenon; and it is vain to test the position of the Logos by other standard than these.

If all that there is must be either substance (hypostasis) or attribute, i.e., an existence in itself, or a character of something else, the Logos must certainly have place in the former category. For, as the instrumental agent in creation, as the interpreter of the Divine idea into physical law and concrete fact, as the vehicle of spiritual light into the consciousness of mortal man, he spared the Most High the need of dealing with material conditions inconformable with his absolute holiness. There is therefore a substitution of one acting subject for another; which could not be if he were only a property or function of that other. His relation to God therefore is not that of attribute to substance.

Is it then that of Derivative to Source? It is so often illustrated by the imagery of effluence or emanation, of the stream from its fountain, of the rays from the stars, of the moonlight from the sun, and by instances of successive genesis, as of spoken or written words from inward thought, or of the Son from the Father, that we are naturally tempted to look for our answer here. And the hope receives support from the metaphors of archetype and ectype, of reflected images and shadows. It seems even to be realized when we alight upon the assertion that he who has reached the divine Logos is still far from the more distant God (ὁ πρὸ τοῦ λόγου θεός), whom no man can apprehend.* Here, as in every instance in which the Logos is described as next to God on the way from the eternal to the perishable, the conception of an originated being is irresistibly suggested. And yet, if it be accepted, what becomes of the *substantive* character of the Logos as an hypostasis? That word, applied to anything *born*, forfeits its distinctive meaning, of "that which is self-subsisting," and is at the disposal of any effect out of which further subordinate effects may arise. Besides, we have been explicitly instructed to think of the Logos as "*neither created, nor uncreate*," and are

* De somniis, I. 11.

thus forbidden to go behind it for any origin, and yet warned against regarding it as the primal and eternal Being.

From this contradiction Philo does not offer, or even seek, any way of escape. His own mind,—a curious repository of the mixed and incoherent culture of Alexandria,—appropriated, without reconciling, the religious elements of the Hebrew transcendental and the Greek immanental monotheism, and wrought them into a texture of thought in which the philosophical relations are of the loosest kind, and form not so much the tenacious web as the ornamental pattern of the whole fabric. He probably conceived, under the supreme Divine Name, of an infinite potentiality of thought and perfect will, eternally existing and implicitly containing all the combinations that might be; and, under the name of the Logos, the definite system of intellectual relations which explicitly emerged from that infinitude into the actual laws of the rational and moral cosmos. Such a conception, of the development of the Divine spiritual essence into an instituted order of living expression, would easily take on, in its applications, all the characteristic imagery which clusters around "the second God" of Philo. The logical straits into which, when hard pressed, it may easily be driven, were unfelt if not unnoticed, in the relief which it afforded to deep religious wants. It annihilated the severance between God and the world by an approximation in opposite directions; planting Him within its great circles as the intellectual essence of all that they contain or bring to pass; and lifting man into conscious assimilation with Him by communion of moral life and love. That the movement towards this union was conceived by Philo as an object of Divine intent, supreme among the ends of creation, cannot be doubted: whether the Logos intrusted with it was regarded by him as a personal Agent separately knowing his appointed task, or as a distributed spiritual influence at work both in heaven and on earth, it is impossible to decide. It was at all events something over and above either the absolute self-existence of God or the moulding of man "out of the dust of the ground:" it was a separate mediatorial provision, forming a distinct department in the inner thought and outer activity of the Divine nature; and so, prepared the way, if it should ever, through the reverence of man, become identified with some transcendent personality, for that peculiar notion of humanized Deity, which has infringed in Christendom on the simplicity of the ancient monotheism. In a world penetrated with the tastes and brilliant with the art of heathendom, the path was but too easily entered ; and it did not take long for the Logos to "become flesh."

B. *The Word "made Flesh."*

Nothing could be more natural than that, as the figure of Jesus receded into the historic distance, and was seen through a brightening haze of reverence, a more and more ideal theory of his person should form itself in the mind of his disciples, and spoil them for the simplicity of its first impression. So long as the interpretation of his nature and office remained in the hands of his Galilean companions, it was exercised under the restraint of positive memory, and the living colours were too fresh not to betray themselves below the films of later fancy ; and so, when we have cleared the surface from the Messianic doctrine which, like some monkish homily written over the text of an ancient monument of genius, hides the sacred poem underneath, the lineaments come out, fragmentary but clear, of the real human life unique in its beauty and its power. All the reverential interest awakened in the reader of the synoptic gospels, all that fastens on his memory by shaming his littleness and winning his affections, all that sacred art most aspires to paint,—the child in the temple, the synagogue at Nazareth, the blessing on the infants, the counsel of perfection to the rich youth, the preference of the woman's penitence to the Pharisee's righteousness, the swift transition from the calm of the last supper, through the anguish of Gethsemane to the *ria dolorosa*,—all are scenes from the interior of an experience intelligible through our own ; and owe their subduing influence to the characteristics of a surpassing personality. However modified by admixture of supernatural elements in the narrative, the essential groundwork of its marvellous appeal is biographical and human ; and fitly claims to be the story of the " *Son of Man*."

That the apostle Paul never once uses this touching phrase is significant of a very different state of mind. " Born out of due time," called into his new life by a voice out of the invisible, he knew not the Jesus of history, but the immortal Conqueror of death, and construed him in thought, not by individual affection and remembered traits, but by inward revelation and ideal faith, both of them concentrated on what that beloved " *Son of God* " already was in his present heaven, and hereafter was to be and do. What he had been in his earthly part was lost in eclipse behind those transcendent relations in which henceforth the whole interest of the world-drama lay. So that the Pauline Gospel thinks itself out free from the restraints of personal memory, and identifies the crucified and risen prophet with the new type of regenerate humanity that shall realize the Divine idea.

In both these forms of doctrine, the respective disciples look up to Christ as the bearer of divine endowments at an elevation far above them. But these endowments are *conferred* upon him : in the Petrine gospel, by miraculous investiture : in the Pauline, by preordination of the creative will " when the fulness of time should come " for the " spiritual Adam " to be revealed from heaven as " the Son of God," and show the meaning of the first " natural Adam," who himself was no son of man. Thus, both these Christologies are strictly *anthropological:* not to the Galileans only was Christ simply *Man :* to the Gentile apostle also his essential nature was measured in its pre-existence, as in its post-existence, by the human standard,—or rather, was invoked to supply it,—the truly " first-born among many brethren." Though living among the angels, he was not one of them ; but remained linked to our kind, " touched with the feeling of our infirmities," consoling the humiliation he has escaped, and by the first-fruits of his spirit drawing us to the glory he has reached. In the order of this faith, he is followed from earth to heaven, from the shadow of the last sacrifice to the light of eternal Love : but only as the forerunner of the race he represents. In him, humanity rises from its low beginnings towards its perfect end, and reaches some fitness for society diviner than its own. The direction of thought in these theories is from below upwards; and its range lies entirely between the inferior and superior limits of human capability.

It is impossible to open the Gospel which bears the name of John, without feeling ourselves in a totally distinct world from this. The point of departure is no longer (as in Matthew and Luke) the home of the Nativity, or (as in Mark) the baptism in the Jordan, or (as with Paul) the death on the cross, or anything else that lies in history. The story opens in quite another field of time, indefinitely prior, not only to the life of Jesus, but to the creation of the visible universe itself: it plants us amid the silent eternity ere yet there was anything but God. There, as its "beginning," it introduces us to an interior view of the Divine life, and shows it to be not an Absolute Solitude, but a relation between two varieties of spiritual being: one, the infinite and unapproachable Essence, for ever hid from all inferior apprehension: the other, the explicit Thought and manifesting Word, which is like him as Son to Father, and may be the organ for breaking the ancient silence, and putting forth a universe to take his invisibility away. This is the scene,—if such we can call that transcendent retreat,—on which the curtain of the drama rises; and this associate of God "before all worlds" is the personage whose history it proposes to exhibit, with at least the moral unity which never changes place or time except to link together the beginning, the middle, and the consummation of an eternal purpose. Two stages of activity are spread for him as the steps by which he passes to the central incident of his existence: he called up the natural cosmos, to hint by a finite sign how much behind could not be signified: and he came in transient visits of revelation and prophecy, to the people who, as the channels of promise, were more especially "his own." But to be this divine Agent for nature, and divine Agent for history, could not accomplish his supreme end; and, to realize this at last, he assumed our humanity, became incarnate in the person of Jesus of Nazareth, and, after tarrying among men for awhile as the visible impersonation of the infinite " grace and truth," returned to " the bosom of the Father " whence he came ; not, however, without sending the Holy Spirit to take his place below, to continue his work, and blend into one organism the children of God in both worlds.   From this mere outline it is evident that here we have the story, not of ascending humanity, but of descending Divinity ; of a god entering into the disguise of an earthly life, and, when the mantle has fallen, resuming his home on high.   The movement of the writer's thought is from above downwards, its range from the beginning to the end of time ; and his interest in the biography he follows out is not so much in the human incidents and experiences, which only mask the reality, as in the vestiges of irrepressible glory which escaped in gleams with every gust that stirred the robe of his humility.   The Christ of this gospel has no infancy, no youth of growing wisdom and stature, no dawning suspicions of a sacred call mocked by taunting voices from the desert of temptation, no deepening of self-devotion by conflict and widening of spiritual affections through a life of tender mercy, till all that is pure on earth or in heaven is drawn into his love.   Nor does he here begin, from "a day of small things," with a set of first disciples who scarce know why they follow him, who rebuke as often as they trust him, and who but slowly emerge into the feeling, though not the understanding, of his greatness.   These gradations of human experience are here unknown.   Not even his enemies, with all their disputings, are allowed to *doubt:* in spite of their pretence he tells them " Ye both know me, and know whence I am."   On them, as on his followers, it is with a sudden burst that his Divine nature breaks, and is self-revealed.   This third form of Christology is in no respect a development of the others, simply advancing a little further in the same direction.   It is no longer *anthropological,* lifting a human being into exaltation ; it is *theological,* bringing a Divine being into incarnation.   It is a theory starting from the opposite end of thought, worked out from different assumptions, by the methods of a different school ; nor do the highest expressions of Paul (even if we refer to him the epistles of later and doubtful authorship) respecting the heavenly humanity of

Christ afford any steps of gradation between the Son of David that went up on high and this "Person" of the godhead who came down below. Take away the *manhood* of Christ, not as his temporary accident, but as his supreme essence and the whole idea of his celestial existence, and there is not an argument or exposition of the Apostle Paul's which will not be simply stripped of all its sense and point, and reduced to an assemblage of incoherent thoughts. And on the other hand, take away the *godhead* of Christ, as the entire real meaning of even his ministry in Palestine, and there is not an incident or a speech in the fourth gospel which does not lose its significance, and leave on the mind the hazy impression of a half-understood discourse in a foreign tongue. To carry the same key to both is only to make sure of opening neither.

This contrast of doctrine implies a separating chasm of time and circumstance; and the very language of the new theology tells us where to seek it; for it is the nomenclature and thought of the Platonic Judaism; nor could the Proem have been written where Philo was unknown.

When Paul wrote, Palestine was still the fatherland and home of Israel, where the national sanctuary yet stood; and here and there in the village synagogues where prayer was wont to be made, some venerable man might still remember hearing the gracious voice of the prophet of Nazareth. The conditions under which the "common tradition" was formed, conditions of locality, society, sect, ritual and faith, were undisturbed, and left his brief career an unforgotten episode in contemporary history. To the apostle who never saw him he had been known, in his earthly life, only as a provincial enthusiast, a disturber of the people, an assailant of the priests, a disparager of the law, and his figure would appear conspicuous as an example of the fanatical excitability of the time. Throughout the apostolic age, the whole scene, as it lay before the Christian imagination, was redolent of the soil and air of the holy land; and the incidents that filled it found their occasion in the local habits and relations, and their meaning in the current beliefs and dominant passions of the population. The anthropological Christology belongs to the time when the Jewish State, however dependent, was still guardian of its theocratic institutions and monotheistic faith, with all the accessory fictions and usages that clustered round them: "Beelzebub" is available in argument: "demons" are quite "familiar spirits:" Pharisees make broad their phylacteries: Sadducees draw sceptic quibbles from the levirate marriage: lepers bring their entreaties as near as they dare from their sad exile: dilemmas are started about the tribute money: and the strangest Messianic cloud of dreams broods over the near future of the world.

When the fourth evangelist wrote (who knows nothing of these things), the whole of this scene, with all its characteristic ideas, had vanished from life and broken into fragments of memory. Jerusalem captive, the temple razed, the priesthood banished, the ritual and law superseded, the nation, in its local organization, practically dissolved, the Semitic Judaism, whether with or without Messiah, had lost its central seat: its people were dispersed, its problems silenced, its promises discredited. The vitality which it vacated had passed to a new dynasty, of Hellenic Judaism, in Alexandria,—an influence purely speculative and theosophic, but powerful as a solvent for taking up and diffusing through all thought the most quickening elements of Hebrew monotheism. How a Jew had prepared this solvent in his doctrine of the Logos, and how he had applied that conception to both God in heaven and man on earth, without either dividing it or confounding them, has been shown in the preceding chapter. It remained only for some Christian thinker to let the Divine Logos play the part of soul to a human body, and use the living mask through the scenes of an earthly drama: and, thus interpreted, the story of Jesus of Nazareth at once became a Theophany. And this is the purpose the Johannine author begins by avowing, and ends with accomplishing.

The link which connects the two Christologies is found in the phrase "Son of God." To the Pauline Christian the risen Jesus was declared in heaven the unique "Son of God." To Philo, the Logos was the "only Son of God." The fourth evangelist had but to combine the two, in order to unify the person of Jesus with the Logos, and make over to him the same divine attributes and relations. Philo's doctrine was cosmical: Paul's was Messianic: the evangelist's was both. In either case the term itself (Son of God) may here and there be used with more or less of the full meaning of the filial relation which it denotes; and, in the Pauline letters, as in all popular speech and writing, is far from carrying the whole.

Father and Son cannot be, without two conditions,—an order of *derivation*, and an *identity or likeness of kind*. Did we take account of the first of these alone, God might be called the Father indifferently of all that has proceeded from his will, of men and angels, of seas and stars. And in this way Philo, though not consistently, styles the *visible universe* "the only Son" and "the first-born Son" of God. Usually, however, simple *derivation* without sameness of personal type, is not regarded as entitling to so high a name; and a distinction is drawn between the mere living *creature* which is *fabricated* as an object of Divine invention, and the *child* of God who comes into existence as the expression of his nature, and whose lineaments betray a kindred with himself. Still, even in this restricted sense the term would still embrace the "whole family of minds," none being destitute of spiritual capacities which hold them in divine relations; and it is exultingly claimed for Christian men by Paul, and by Jesus himself for all whose affections repeat the universal Love. With the same idea, only further reduced in latitude, so as to leave all finite analogies behind, is the phrase "Son of God" applied to the pre-existing "Word" in the fourth Gospel. The oneness with God which it means to mark is not such resembling reflex of the Divine thought and character as men or angels may attain, but identity of essence, constituting him not *godlike* alone, but substantially *God*. Others may be children of God in a moral sense: but, by this right of elemental nature, none but he: he is, herein, the *only* Son, so little separate, so close to the inner Divine life which he expresses, that he is "in the bosom of the Father."[*] This language undoubtedly describes a great deal more than such harmony of will, and sympathy of affection, as may subsist between finite obedience and its infinite Inspirer: it denotes two natures homogeneous, entirely one,

* John I. 18.

and both so essential to the Godhead that neither can be omitted from any truth you speak of it. So completely reciprocal is their relation over the whole sphere of its extent that there is nothing left to divide between them: "all things that the Father hath are mine;* "all mine are thine, and thine are mine."† So identically applicable to both are the eternal laws of God's own life, that the acts and exemptions of the one repeat themselves in the other. In this connection it is instructive to compare the answer of Jesus, as reported by the Synoptists, to the charge of Sabbath-breaking,‡ with that which the fourth Gospel ascribes to him.§ His plea in the former,—that "the Sabbath was made for man, not man for the Sabbath,"— urges that the institution, being provided for the true wants of man, must bend to his obvious needs, and seek the ultimate rule for its observance from the constitution of his nature and the emergencies of his life. If Jesus, in clenching the argument with the words "therefore the Son of Man is lord of the Sabbath," meant to use this title *of himself*, it was clearly as the *prophet of humanity*, and on behalf of its "weary and heavy-laden," that he claims his free action in the Sabbath fields. In the fourth Gospel, do we find him thus taking his stand upon the human level? On the contrary, he carries the Sabbath at once to the transcendent sphere which knows no rest and can give it no place; and justifies himself by the tests of that world. There, beyond the conditions of measured Time, the Infinite God knows no Sabbath and never pauses on his everlasting way; and the rule which flows from his nature no less embraces the Son, to whom also, even upon earth, all days are sacred alike: "my Father worketh thus far, and I also work." Nay, there is more than reciprocation, such as may take place between two harmonious but separated beings; it is merged in inward unity: "the Father is in me, and I in him:"‖ "I and my Father are one." ¶ They belong for ever to one another, without the thought or possibility of independent life; the Father as indivisible from the Son as from himself: the Son

* John xvi. 15.   † xvii. 10.
‡ Matt. xii. 1–8. Mark ii 23–28. Luke vi. 1–5.
§ John v. 16, 17.   ‖ x. 33.   ¶ x. 30.

so surrendered to the Father as to have no resort to his consciousness of distinct personality: each discovers but himself in that which the other is.

If the evangelist had set forth these thoughts as *his own* interpretation of what the term ' Son of God ' implies, if he had simply taken for granted that it could mean nothing less than the Deity of Christ, we should have recognized at once the production of a writer in the second Century, and settled his more exact chronological place by comparison with the Christology of Justin Martyr and his contemporaries. But when the doctrinal conceptions propounded in his Proem and in his interspersed reflections take possession of his narrative also, and issue in the most startling form from the lips of Jesus himself, and are upheld by him in sharp dialectic with the scandalized Jews, we are asked to put back their historical place by three or four generations, and, instead of treating them as theological commentary on a traditional past, to accept them as personal features of a most authoritative biography. Is it possible to do this? Not unless we utterly discredit the Synoptists' picture of the whole stage and time of the ministry of Jesus. Both in their narrative and in the fourth Gospel the phrase ' Son of God ' expresses the highest claim set up for Jesus and the greatest occasion for offence. But how different in the two cases are the reports of its effect! If in the former it brought him to the cross, it was not as a gainsayer of the *Religion* of Israel, but politically, as a ' *King* of the Jews,' troublesome to Rome: nor did the belief strip him of the modest synonym ' Son *of Man;*' it indicated him only as Messiah. On the other hand, no sooner does the Johannine Jesus express the claim of Divine Sonship, and appeal to what he ' does in his Father's name,'[*] than the Jews ' take up stones to stone him '[†] and make Solomon's porch resound with their cries, that he sets himself up as God's equal, and so blasphemes the national monotheism. The evangelist supplies him with an answer which, founded on their scriptures, is valid *for them,* viz., that the word ' God,' and, a fortiori, the phrase ' Son of God,' need mean no more than one "to whom the word of God came;"[‡]

---

[*] John x. 25.   [†] x. 31.   [‡] x. 33–36.

but at the same time plainly intimated that it is not in this
lower sense that Jesus really speaks, but, as implied in his
words, "I and the Father are one,"* and " the Father is in
me and I in the Father,"† in the far higher sense which
they impugn and cannot understand.

The very existence of this controversy was evidently impossible till the Divine Logos had taken possession of the
term ' Son of God,' and given it a theological in place of a
simply Messianic significance. Prior to the time when the
' Father' and the ' Son' were both within the Godhead,
there could be no complaint of tampering with the Divine
Unity: an *anthropological* predicate, however armed with
' signs and wonders,' cannot encroach on the sovereignty of
the Most High. The pure calm Theism of the Synoptists,
common to the disciples and the opponents of Jesus, and
disturbed by no imputation of religious disloyalty, is undoubtedly historical. The differences on which the narratives
and their discourses turn are differences between two varieties
of Israelite, both alike true to the same ancient worship. The
recurring topic in the fourth Gospel, that the Sonship of
Christ militates against the Unity of God, with the polemic of
attack and defence, came to the front only as the tendency to
glorify the person of Christ reached its highest stages ; and
in the form assigned to it by the evangelist, could not present
itself till the Alexandrine philosophy had turned the gospel
history into a theosophy, and the elevation of Christ into an
object of worship had completely severed Christians from Jews
as votaries of irreconcilable religions.‡

Intense as the language of identity is between the Logos
and God, amounting to an apotheosis of the ' Son,' it must
not be taken as equivalent to the assertion of ' co-equality ' in
the Church creed. The evangelist, in saying that the relation
subsisted " in the beginning," only means to place us at a
point prior to creation, and does not commit himself to the
eternal existence of the Word ; and probably, like Philo, he
conceived of him as intermediate, in posteriority as well as in

* John x. 30. † x. 38.
‡ See this argument admirably enforced by J. H. Holtzmann, in his Lehrbuch d. hist. krit. Einleitung in das N. T. pp. 464, 465.

agency, between the Infinite God and his finite universe. Be this as it may, the Son, whether originated in time or not, is intrinsically subordinate to the Father, and the very unity between them carries in it this relation of dependence. The initiative is ever with the Father as absolute cause, the effect only with the Son as agent relatively to the world. "The Son can do nothing of himself but what he sees the Father doing : for what things soever He doeth, these the Son also doeth in like manner."* The divine " Word " cannot speak save what the divine Thought may give him to say : "I have not spoken of myself, but the Father which sent me hath given me a commission what I should say and what I should speak : " " the things therefore which I speak, even as he said unto me, so I speak : "† "I speak the things which I have seen with my Father : " "I have told you the truth which I have heard from God."‡ He does not come of himself, but is no less sent into the world than the disciples whom he commissions as his ambassadors in turn : " As thou didst send me into the world, even so send I them into the world."§   Nay, more ; the distinctive glories embodied in his person, the " truth," the " life," the " light," conspicuous in him, are not his own. If he is 'the truth,' his disciples " know that all things whatsoever thou hast given me are from thee, for the word which thou gavest me I have given unto them ; and they know of a truth that I came forth from thee, and have believed that thou didst send me." If he is the life-giver, it is because the " Father who hath life in himself gave to the Son also to have life in himself : "‖ " as the living Father sent me and I live to the Father, so he that eateth me shall live because of me."** If he is the light of the world, and if, when he leaves it, he passes into purer brightness still, it is an *investiture* of glory which, before the world was, the Father imparted and the Father would renew. The most intimate terms of equal union stop short of absolute Unity of being, and break into expression of relation and distinction : we read " All things that the Father *hath* are mine ; "†† but

---

* John v. 19.   † xii. 49, 50.   ‡ viii. 38, 40.
§ xvii. 18.   ‖ xvii. 7, 8.   ¶ v. 26.
** vi. 57.   †† xvi. 15.

never " All things that the Father *is* am I :" the promise of the Spirit, and its dispensing, comes from both ; but of God alone it is said, He "*is* Spirit." The very blending of their natures, which seems so intimate, is with a difference : the " Father is *in* the Son,"* as the greater in the less ; (" the Father is greater than I.")† leaving nothing which escapes sanctification in the nature occupied, but not exhausting the whole infinitude of the indwelling Deity. The Son is in the Father, as the less in the greater, where he finds the ground of his being, in coalescence with which is his only power and his perfect rest, and apart from which his integral existence would be gone. Thus, even in this high and mystic doctrine, the co-equality variously gives way. The relation cannot be turned round ; and though the Son is of the Supreme essence and an intrinsic function of the Divine life and love, the Father preoccupies and for ever keeps the name of " the true God," and *is* the invisible perfection which the Word is commissioned to manifest.

From the relation of the Logos upwards towards God, we may turn to contemplate the relation downwards towards the world which he becomes incarnate to visit. What kind of scene does it present to him ? It is the very world which he created in the execution of the Divine idea: does it reflect that idea ? and is the work of his hand such as he is well-pleased to behold ? Had the Logos been commissioned to look after the world which he had set up, to uphold as well as institute it, and animate it as its indwelling principle of thought, some conformity must surely be found between the perfect source and the finite product. The evangelist, in spite of his leanings to the conception of Immanence, strangely gives to his *Divine* " Son " less to do with the world he has made, than the apostle Paul assigns to his pre-existent *Human* Son, the spiritual Adam, who at least accompanied the providential history of Israel and left his traces there. After invoking an infinitely greater agent (Philo's " second God ") for spreading the scene of the world drama, the fourth Gospel silently withdraws it from all sacred guardianship and direction ; so that its Creator, on returning from the bosom

* John xvii. 21. † xiv. 28.

F F

of the Father, finds his work under the dominion of an anti-god. In descending from the heavenly to the earthly sphere of life, he invades the territory of an enemy, and has to break up the administration of "the Prince of darkness," who in this Gospel alone is acknowledged as in possession under the title of "Prince of this world."[*] How a cosmos set up by "the best of causes" came to be overrun with the worst of effects; how, especially, a Creator absolutely good could include in his work a spiritual being of will absolutely evil, and free to quicken all possible seeds of evil in others, is left unexplained. Certain it is that the author neither regarded Satan as an uncreated rival of the true God, nor supposed him *fallen* from "a first estate" of pure obedience; but in his view of the world of experience stationed him, at the opening, as the true *fons et origo* of moral alienation from the government of God. I say "*moral*" alienation, because the author does not lay to his charge the *physical* maladies and mental disorders which in the other evangelists are referred to the "evil spirits" and treated by methods of exorcism; but he is at one with them in saying that "Satan put it into the heart of Judas Iscariot" to play the traitor.[†] To the author's religious consciousness, refined by more than a century of Christian thought and life, the actual world of human experience presented itself as a scene of intensest contrasts of pure evil and pure good, no more capable of blending than two rival wills; and personally concentrated respectively in the διάβολος, the father of lies and murderer at the outset, and in the Logos, the Son of God, who having been with him from the beginning, brought the truth, the light, the life, the love of heaven to "his own," if such there were whom it could reach through the darkness of the earth.

This intense moral dualism in the Johannine writings, which allows no gradations, drives all antitheses into contradictions, and invokes God and devil to settle every disputed cause, doubtless indicates that the interval had become practically hopeless between the spiritual ideal of life and character reached by the Christian conscience, and the low types of motive and conduct into which the unconverted

<hr>

* John xii. 31, xiv. 30, xvi. 11.   † xiii. 2, 27.

Judaism and heathenism had set. The Christian mission had carried its appeal into both their fields for now three generations, and had drawn thence the great mass of the baptized; but had long spent all its available persuasion on the former and seen itself scorned as an apostate; and from the latter had, it would seem, attracted the front rank of its susceptible and waiting minds into its own communion, till the supply had flagged, and the residuary paganism spake to ever meaner passions and sillier dreams, and to every pure eye seemed simply an ungodliness. From the point of view of an Alexandrian Christian in the fourth decade of the second century, all the Divine presence and expression in life might well seem to be sheltered within the Church, beyond which was a heterogeneous anarchy of selfish, fleshly, devilish elements; the sanctuary of the former being in the world, though not of the world, which was surrendered to the latter. This extreme opposition, due to his historical position, the author carries back into his reading of the religion in its birth and revelation through the personal visit of the Son of God. Hence, both the lights and the shadows of his picture are painted in with the colours of another age, and give a false kind of glory to the leading figure, while flinging the forms of opponents into too black a shade of wrong.

This would be a serious fault in a production announcing itself as simply and strictly historical; but wears another aspect in a selection of excerpts from a larger store, avowedly made for a purpose of religious persuasion: "many other signs did Jesus in the presence of his disciples, which are not written in this book; but these are written that ye may believe that Jesus is the Christ, the Son of God; and that believing ye may have life in his name."* The author who knows Christianity in its spiritual development and could measure it by its fruits, might legitimately wish to reflect back its highest characteristics on its inconspicuous beginnings, and find its essence and its future, while as yet they lay hid: and having possession of the secret in his conception of "the Word made flesh," he brings its intense light to bear upon the evangelistic story, and detects its vestiges in many a passage

* John xx. 30, 31.

ill understood before. His gospel is thus set forth, not as either a new or a supplementary biography, but as a theological construction of actions and events on record as facts, yet unappreciated in significance. To reveal their transcendent character, to lift them out of the plane of earthly things and refer them to their source Divine or devilish, and make them tell their inner meaning, was the very purpose of the author. His Proem gives notice at starting of the very thoughts which he intends to read into the facts and colloquies as he relates them. And his selection or reconstruction of historical material from previous evangels is so made as to vindicate for the seeming " Jesus of Nazareth " the very predicates attached in the Proem to the Divine Logos : to exhibit him as Life-giver, Light-bringer, Spirit-quickener, Truth-essence and Truth-reader. Similarly, the selection of all that opposes itself to him is so made as to exemplify only utter perversity or hardened wickedness, to the serious injury of historical verisimilitude, and a deterioration still more serious of the moral portraiture of Christ in controversy with perplexed gainsayers.

With this severance of " the world " as the playground of " the Prince of darkness," from the sphere of God and his " Word," is connected a theory of human nature and a division of human beings peculiar to this evangelist. He sees them in two classes opposed, not morally alone of their own free choice, not arbitrarily, of God's electing or reprobating will,—but by *heredity* that goes behind the world of time and nature,—as " children of God " and " children of the devil," known from each other by the infallible mark of aversion to sin or proneness to it.* It is a distinction that may arise in the same family, having, indeed, its prototypal instance in Abel and Cain ;† that forces itself on the attention of every observer of mankind who follows the heroisms and tragedies of their history. Seldom in the darkest times are there wanting a few choice spirits in whom the heavenly fire has not died out, the feeling for truth, the openness to love, the

---

* 1 John iii. 8-10.

† Ibid. 12. I doubt, however, whether we can appeal to the Epistles as from the same author.

enthusiasm of right: the sanctity of a divine lineage remains in them and rallies to them "such as may be saved" from the vaster host that is hurrying to infernal darkness escorted by the lusts of the flesh. Nothing so soon *finds* and draws these unspoiled natures as the appeal to them of a congenial yet higher Son of God; and nothing, on the other hand, can lie further from the intelligence of a godless world than the deep truth he is sure to speak, and nothing be more humbling to its self-esteem than that summons to a new birth from which he will never recede. In presence, therefore, of the. incarnate Logos in his sojourn upon earth, the mixed multitude of men spontaneously divides; the "little flock" who constitute the true kernel of humanity gather round him, and go in and out with him, and understand and trust his voice; for they are the children of light, and he is from "the Father of lights, in whom is no darkness at all." But the rest are wrapped in a darkness which no revelation of God can pierce,—children of "the Prince of darkness," shut out from the life of God, and given up to falsehood, hate, and death; and in their blindness can only be affected either with supercilious scorn towards the Divine appeal, or murderous passion towards its "faithful witness." To sift out these classes from each other was at once the effect and the purpose of Christ's visit, "For judgment am I come into this world; that they which see not may see, and that they which see may become blind."* "I know mine own, and mine own know me, even as the Father knoweth me and I know the Father:" "my sheep hear my voice, and I know them and they know me:" "but ye believe not, because ye are not of my sheep."† This kind of "crisis," it is evident, is no new act of judicial power, altering the relations or rights of men: it only tests and reveals the exact posture of things as they are, tearing away the veils of semblance from the souls of men, and showing them in their true affinities. Hence it is not a contradiction, but only a more precise affirmation, of this conception of judgment, when the evangelist says, "God so loved the world, that he gave his only-begotten Son, that whosoever · believeth in him should not perish, but have

* John ix. 39. viii. 42–47. † x. 14, 15, 27, 26.

eternal life. For God *sent not the Son into the world to judge the world*, but that the world should be saved through him. He that believeth on him *is not judged:* he that believeth not *hath been judged already*, because he hath not believed on the name of the only-begotten Son of God. And this is the judgment, that the light has come into the world, and men loved the darkness rather than the light; for their works were evil."* The same idea, that the personal life of Jesus on earth as the Divine revealer is the test which of itself discriminates the children of God from the unsifted mass, recurs in even condensed expression: "I am come a light into the world, that whosoever believeth in me may not abide in the darkness. And if any man hear my sayings, and keep them not, I judge him not; for I came not to judge the world but to save the world. He that rejecteth me and receiveth not my sayings, hath one that judgeth him; the word that I spake, the same shall judge him in the last day; for I spake not from myself; but the Father which sent me, he hath given me a commandment what I should say and what I should speak."† In spite of the not very consistent, perhaps conventional, allusion to a future "last day," this present, self-acting "judgment" through the operation of Christ's personality and religion on the hearts of men, is the only one in the evangelist's theology; and is the spiritual substitute there for the mythological scenery of the Parusia and eschatology of the Jewish apostles.

And if the great assize of the synoptist and Pauline Christology is thus shifted back from the "last days" to the ministry of Christ, so too must the resurrection be which is to muster the subjects for judgment. And accordingly we hear, "Verily, verily, I say unto you, The hour cometh, and *now is*, when the dead shall hear the voice of the Son of God, and they that hear shall live: for as the Father hath life in himself, even so gave he to the Son also to have life in himself."‡ So quickening is the presence of that Living "Word," that it pierces the ears of spiritual death and wakes slumbering souls to open their eyes on a new heaven, and become the conductors of its spirit to the earth. Whether

* John iii. 16-19.   † xii. 44-49.   ‡ v. 25, 26.

or not the evangelist meant to leave room for another and
more literal understanding of the summons of the dead from
their tombs by the voice of the son of man,* it is obvious
that the material conception had no significance for him
except as symbolical of the regenerative power of Christ
which raises a new creation and drops the old in death.

All the peculiar features which have been noticed converge
upon one result, viz., to make the whole Christian revelation
consist in lending to the world the Divine personality of the
Son, as an object of faith, and a power of sanctification.
He is not (as with the synoptists) the prophet of an era, the
medium of a message, the herald of a future; warning men
that, in view of what is coming, they must repent and seek
forgiveness, and get their "wedding garments" ready; the
very words "repentance" and "forgiveness" never once
occur in the Gospel. There is no initial hindrance in the
way of discipleship, needing to be removed either by voluntary

* The Johannine theology translates the incidents of the Messianic drama,
as far as possible, into a system of spiritual truths already visible in experience. The knowledge of God was itself a heaven : faith in Christ was eternal
life in possession : rejection of him was the darkness of death : the drawing
of believers and unbelievers into their separation was self-executed judgment.
But, however far this process of translation was carried, the immediate relations of the Father, the Son, and mankind did not supply equivalents for all
the essential parts of the apocalyptic picture. Resurrection of the *spiritually
dead* at the "voice of the Son of God" there might already be, and the doom be
determined of those who would not hear. But what of the generations and
tribes who have died, or yet will die, without being put to the test? Were
there only the departed Christians to be considered, they might pass, one by
one, to be where Christ is, while their and his enemies might be left dead in
their sins. But other provision was needed for the fathers of Israel to whom
the promises were given, and the heathen nations from whom they were withheld : and for these apparently it is that the evangelist reserves, from his
early Jewish belief, "the last day," when the tombs shall render up their
dead ; and sets up, as the principle of judgment, the universal rule of conscience, the "doing of good" or the "doing of ill." I find it impossible to
doubt that the words of v. 25 quoted above speak of the spiritually dead
among the hearers ; while the following passage (28, 29), which does not
contain the words "*now is*," refers to the literally dead : "Marvel not at
this ; for the hour cometh in which all that are within the tombs shall hear
his voice, and shall come forth ; they that have done good, unto the resurrection of life ; and they that have done ill, to the resurrection of judgment."
Oscar Holtzmann thinks that, in thus treating the judgment by the Son of
Man as a public future event, the evangelist speaks in "accommodation " to
the traditional Christian conception. His reasons are ingenious, but do not
convince me. Das Johannes-evangelium, pp. 54, 55.

discipline or by foreign atonement: the children of light "need no repentance:" the sins of darkness are past redemption. "No man can come to me except the Father which sent me draw him:" "every one that hath heard from the Father, and hath learned, cometh unto me."[*] The entire meaning and effects of the dispensation were centred in the mere presence among men of the Incarnate Logos; whose subsistence in the Father enabled him to lay open the confidences of heaven, and do and be whatever was according to the pattern of His will; whose life-work upon earth, so "full of grace and truth," so pathetic and sublime in its finite self-limitations, was the pure expression of the Divine essence; and who accomplished the end for which he was sent by simply passing over the human scene, mingling with the human relations, and carrying into the heaven which had spared him for awhile the august and subduing image of his spiritual perfection. So intense is the evangelist's preoccupation with this conception of Christ as the Divine self-manifestation, that he even makes Jesus himself proclaim it, "He that hath seen me hath seen the Father."[†] Over and above all that he may have to testify as an organ of Divine truth, he is himself its very reality, borrowed from the invisible, and recognized by "his own" as their mysterious life-bringer, making them conscious of new powers: the fountain of living waters assuaging an eternal thirst: the bread of life, that never fails the hunger of souls, however various: the source of an abiding peace, which the world cannot give.

So significant is this peculiar Christology, that, to bring it more strongly into view, I will allow myself a momentary over-statement which, after serving the purpose of exposition, shall be corrected to its proper dimensions. For the synoptists, the whole contents of the story they relate are important as evidences of the Messiahship of Jesus, proving, that is, that he was the person marked out for a future function, not to be assumed till the heralds had been sent forth and the world got ready for his Parusia "on the clouds of heaven." Nor was it otherwise with the apostle Paul; except that, of the manifold evidences spread over the Galileans' narrative,

<hr>

[*] John vi. 44, 45.　　　　　　　　　[†] xiv. 9.

he limits himself to the single one,—the resurrection,—which came into contact with his own experience. For them, therefore, the whole matter revealed lay beyond the ministry of Christ on earth, and did not even propose to begin till that was ended: the revelation was purely promissory, and referred, not to truth eternal, but to dramatic events to be thrown upon the stage of Time. The objects of Christian faith were certain futurities secured on adequate data of expectation which it was the mission of Jesus to supply. In the Johannine view, the Revealer is himself one with the object revealed, the manifested God, the apprehension of whom fulfils the meaning of the dispensation, and *is* eternal life without waiting for anything more : the preliminaries become the substance, the evidences are no other than the things evidenced, the futurities are brought into the present, the heavenly and transcendent life walks the earth, leaving its vestiges in blind eyes opened and souls newborn. The whole secret of the disciple's initiation is in his recognition of Christ as Divine: nothing more is needed, nothing else will serve ; but within this secret is contained a participation in Christ's own divine experience, a dependence, only less immediate, on the same aliment of immortal spirits, which seals his consecration as among the sons of God. Here then the essence of the divine truth disclosed is contained in the life of the Incarnate Logos ; and, lying between its opening and its close, might be said to withdraw at the point where the Pauline revelation begins. And this would be true, were it not that the fourth evangelist, intent on writing up the inner experience of the Christian life to his own time, crosses the boundary of the incarnate term, and continues to characterize the ulterior development of the Church when its Living Word has returned to heaven. By taking account of this sequel, which the author, in the form of a prophetic discourse, has inwrought into the narrative of the last days in Jerusalem, we shall supply the qualification which the previous over-statement required.

If the Logos became incarnate to manifest the Living God, and bring his light and life to tabernacle awhile among men, the bowed head on Calvary and the last words " It is finished," must apparently bo the terminus of tho revelation. Yet the death upon tho cross is singled out not for sad regret, as tho fading trail of a vanishing glory, and soon to livo in memory alone, but for a joy in it doubly justified : viz., in its relation to tho past, as a culminating act of self-identification with God, and voluntary preference for tho Father's will : and in relation to the future, as releasing tbo Logos from the human vehiclo in which fow could " behold its grace and truth," and setting it free as the pure Divine Spirit, to spread overywhere, and, from tho historical baso already firmly fixed in tho souls ho had renewed, to " draw all men unto him."* In tho former aspect, the death of Christ is signalized only as tho superlative crown of his divinely perfect lifo, his entiro self-renunciation, in lovo to tho Father and to his " friends."† It is not a humiliation forced upon him by any other will, and passively borno as by a shoop led to tho slaughter ; but is a froo act which the Father himself contemplates with love : " therefore doth tho Father lovo me, becauso I lay down my lifo, that I may tako it again. No ono taketh it away from mo, but I lay it down of myself. I havo power to lay it down, and I havo power to tako it again."‡ Ho resigns human life, as ho had taken it, to reveal, from end to end, tho truo way from man to God, through a blending of will and centring of lovo in a common righteousness ; and, that nothing may bo wanting to the sacrifice, ho quits it by no sudden flight into a safo heaven, but by tho well-trodden path of mortal pain : it is the supreme fulfilment of his mission to " show us tho Father " by perfect realization of what is contained in tho spirit of sonship. 'For tho sako of them whom thou hast given mo I sanctify myself, that thoy themselves also may bo sanctified in truth.'§ In presenco of this climax of moral sublimity, tho evangelist cannot look upon tho cross as a descent into servilo ignominy and shame, and treat it, liko tho Epistlo to tho Philippians, as tho tragic midnight that must precedo tho overlasting day : ho calls it a *lifting up* (ὑψοῦσθαι),¶ drawing tho eyo of tho disciplo to tho loftiest point of tho incarnato episode. There is in tho word, no doubt, a play upon tho physical

* John xii. 32.   † xiv. 31, xv. 13.   ‡ x. 17, 18.

§ xvii. 11, 19.   ‖ Phil. ii. 7–10.   ¶ John iii. 14, viii. 28, xii. 32, 34.

height of the cross itself: but it plainly commends itself to choice only as symbolizing the spiritual elevation whence that suffering form looks down. He does not *wait* to be exalted till the death is past.

Not only is the closing passage of Christ's visit no mere limit, but an integral and even consummating part of its Divine manifestation as viewed from the past: it also provides and institutes for it a prolongation and indefinite expansion of the future; so that, though natural sorrow filled the hearts of the disciples on the point of severance from their Lord, it was yet "expedient for them that he should go away." Why this should be so is not difficult to understand, from the Johannine point of view. It was one and the same Divine Logos that in the beginning was with God, who in due time appeared in human form and showed forth the Father's pure perfections in relation to mankind, who then returned to his eternal life, with the spiritual ties unbroken which he brought from his finished work. The evangelist who opens with the first of these stadia of being was not likely to close without reference to the last, though the main thread of his gospel is engaged with the intermediate term. His own Christology supplies a principle of continuity which carries him past the period of the incarnation still in the presence of the same beloved Son. Intensely as the light, the life, the truth of God had been concentrated in that Divine personality, they were even then essentially diffusive, not passively looked at and owned, but creative of souls un-born or half-born before, and lifting them out of themselves into the love and incipient likeness of God. So long as the living Word was in the midst of those whom the Father had thus given to him, they hung upon him in reverent depend-ence, and he 'kept them in God's truth and guarded them that none should be lost, save the son of perdition.'* He was at hand to keep alive their trust, to shield them from the evils of the world, and be their protector, the advocate (Paraclete) to watch over their Spiritual well-being. Is all this to come to nothing when he is seen no more? Does the quickening influence emanate only from his bodily form, and

* John xvii. 12.

will the new birth fall back into death when that is gone? No: it is only "the world," and not the disciples, that 'cannot receive his spirit of truth, because it does not *see* it or know it' when it is there: but they in whom the consciousness of it has been awakened by Christ himself can never lose it and take back their old selves in exchange for it again; it has gone forth as a spirit from heaven into them, to abide with them for ever, whether he be in the visible or the invisible world. Nay, more: till they are left to live by it alone as an inward power of light and love, they will never know the hidden treasures of insight and peace which it contains. Not without reason therefore is it said that the Spirit which should replace the personal presence of Christ would "guide them *into all the truth;*"* for it is only under the developing action of human experience and reflection that the "good seed" flung from the Sower's hand could manifest the range of its fertility. Though this "Spirit of truth" which was to make the posthumous influence of Christ greater than the personal, is called "*another* Paraclete,"† it is plain that this only contrasts the external and internal form of the guidance, and involves no breach of identity in the Divine Guide himself throughout. 'The holy spirit, whom the Father would send in Christ's name, would teach them all things,'—how?—Not by drawing on any new sources, but by 'bringing to their remembrance all that he had said to them;'‡ by 'bearing witness of him:'§ by 'taking of his and declaring it unto them:'‖ it was still the Logos in his heavenly personality interpreting and unfolding the words and acts of his earthly incarnation. An immanent divineness runs through the consciousness of the whole hierarchy of spiritual beings and links them in graduated relation with Him who is κατ' ἐξοχήν "Spirit."¶ The Son reveals the Father: the Spirit interprets the Son: the new birth and sanctification of disciples bear witness to the Spirit: "that they may all be one; even as thou, Father, art in me, and I in thee, that they also may be in us:" and "that they may be one, even as we are one."**

* John xvi. 13.   † xiv. 16.   ‡ xiv. 26.
§ xv. 26.   ‖ xvi. 14.   ¶ Πνεῦμα ὁ Θεός, iv. 24.
** xvii. 21, 22.

As the application of the Logos idea to the person of Jesus places the fourth Gospel far on in the post-apostolic age, and makes it coeval with the gnosticism prevalent in the fourth and fifth decades of the second century, so the conception of the Paraclete as a supplementary source of revelation is an evident provision for the large development of doctrine which by that time had eclipsed the primitive tradition, and transformed the historical Christ from Prophet to God.   Time had wrought in the Judaic Christianity the same kind of change as that which had befallen Judaism itself through severance of place from its ancient home.   The Messianic belief, like the Semitic Monotheism, was essentially *national*, bound up indissolubly with patriarchal inheritance and tribal law, and consecrated places, and dreams of theocratic empire: and just as the rise of a colonial Hebrew culture in Alexandria modified the jealous Jehovah into the immanent Divine essence of the Hellenic cosmical Theism, so did the utter break-up of the Jewish national organization during seventy years from Vespasian to Hadrian's final blow, leave the Messianic apocalypse with nothing to cling to, and compel the interpreter to get rid of it by reading in between the lines some spiritual substitute already realized in the soul.   Hence it is that the Parusia, the raising of the dead, the judgment, are all taken out of the future and found in the present.   And hence too it is that the evangelist makes little or no disguise of his own post-apostolic date, or of the novelty of doctrine or usage that characterizes it.   He makes Jesus speak of the Gentile influx into the Church, " Other sheep I have, not of this fold : "[*] and even treat it as the peculiar glory for which he is brought to the hour of his exaltation in death.[†]   He attributes to Jesus on the eve of his departure a special instruction new to the disciples, and attaches a promise to its observance : ' If ye will ask anything of the Father, he will give it in my name : hitherto have ye asked nothing in my name : ask, and ye shall receive, that your joy may be fulfilled.'[‡]   " Whatsoever ye shall ask in my name, that will I do, that the Father may be glorified in the Son : if ye shall ask anything in my name, that will I do."[§]   Here it is plain, as Weizsäcker remarks, we

[*] John x. 16.   [†] xii. 20–32.   [‡] xvi. 23, 24.   [§] xiv. 13, 14.

alight upon *a new practice*, viz., of prayer to Christ, and prayer in his name, the natural consequence of the recently developed doctrine of the Godhead of the Son.*   Not till the incarnation was over could occasion arise for such a change: it was the work of the Paraclete to dispense with the human person in which for awhile the glory of the Father was seen by a few within reach, and to set free the light from that nucleus to radiate upon the whole sphere of souls, and wake their springs of life and bring truth out of truth to sight, and love upon love to blossom. The theology of the fourth Gospel thus attests and vindicates the Hellenized Christianity of its era, when its Jewish conflicts were obsolete, and Gentile needs and influences alone resorted to it.

It was a dark world, according to the evangelist, into which the light of the revealing Word shone: *so* dark, that but for this lonely altar lamp, the eternal midnight would never have been broken.   Had the Divine Logos remained in his heavenly seclusion, the earth would have been left without its vivifying source of spiritual life. He instituted and realized the redemption by *taking our nature* and traversing our experience. How does the writer understand this act of " taking our nature," and what truth does he draw from it? Was the incarnation, in his view, the first Divine assumption of *personal existence*, and offered to mankind in rebuke of their pantheistic dreams of a transcendental power without thought or will or love? Does he sanction the modern assertion that the divinity of Jesus Christ is our sole warrant for believing in the personality of God? If so, to be " *made flesh* " is tantamount here to becoming personal; and till the bodily organism was appropriated, the prior knowledge and love of the Father, the seeing whatsoever thing he did, the acting for him in the creation of all that has been made, and the voluntary descent into the incarnate life, were insufficient to constitute him a person ! Nothing can well be more at variance with the genius and purpose of the gospel than this notion, that flesh and blood were charged with the high dignity of conferring personality on that which had it not before, and inducing on a spiritual nature its last glory of intending intellect and love

* Das apostolische Zeltalter. 1856, pp. 537, 538.

and will. The very name of the Divine Logos which dwelt in Jesus carries in it already the whole contents of perfect reason and volition; and the end of his episode on the historic field was not to insist on an attribute never questioned, but to divert it from outward acknowledgment to inward hold upon the conscience and affections: not to humanize Deity, but to consecrate humanity. The idea of incarnation presupposes, instead of authenticating, a personal Divine nature: were it *impersonal*, what interest could it have, as a blind force possessing itself of a machine, for the foreign observer before whom it figures in unmeaning acts? The whole drama, as conceived by the evangelist, is constructed on the largest prior assumption of spiritual personalities: the Father being a person, the Son being a person, the human disciple being a person, relations of likeness, of love, of trust, may 'and do subsist among them, and link them into one communion of life, before the world, in the world, beyond the world. The instrumentality of " the Son of God" in establishing these relations has its three stadia, with the earthly visit in the centre. If the post-existence is meant to be personal (which admits no doubt), the pre-existence must be so too; for they balance each other, and are always covered by the same terms. "No one hath ascended into heaven but he that descended out of heaven :"[*] " What if ye should behold the son of man ascending where he was before?"[†] "My testimony is true; for I know whence I came and whither I go:"[‡] "And now, O Father, glorify me with thine own self with the glory which I had with thee before the world was."[§] There is no meaning in words like these unless the prior and posterior glory are homogeneous, and the eternal love which receives him home is the same affection of person to person which, in the bosom of the Father, he had " before the world was."[‖] Far from lifting the incarnate life into ontological distinction, the evangelist rather treats it as a brief disguise inserted between two periods of personal existence. He does but " tabernacle among us," pitches, as it were, his tent for the night, and in the morning is away: but in the prior world he has done all things for

* John iii. 13. † vi. 62. ‡ viii. 14.
§ xvii. 5. ‖ xvii. 24.

the Father from the beginning, and he returns thither to share the perpetuity of God. So strongly is this feature marked, of higher and fuller reality in the life before and after, that scarcely does the incarnation escape the aspect of a mere semblance, pretending to be human. All the acts of will, the words that are spoken, the deeds that are done, the traditions which are accepted, are expressions of the same personal subject,—and that subject the Divine Logos that was and is and is to be. How else could his historic life manifest the Father ? Instead of representing, he would misrepresent the Godhead, if he offered a set of personal volitions as the guiding clew to the secret of an impersonal essence.

This third theory respecting the person of Christ could never have existed face to face with the passing facts and colloquies of his village ministry. No audience in Palestine would listen for a moment to a "carpenter's son" who gave himself out as "the only-begotten son of God" just come down from heaven and charged with words that gave eternal life. And they would be right. For a being divine enough really to be "a second God" would be the last to think or say it, and would leave the sacred place at the disposal of others' veneration, and of himself would rather say, "Why callest thou me good ? none is good save one, that is God." Historical, in the literal sense, that is, faithful as a representation of objective incidents and real discourses, this Christology certainly is not. It is an idealization of the evangelistic tradition, in which the essential materials, severed from Jewish dross, are cast into the crucible of an intenser fervour, tempered by the breath of a less fitful philosophy. The meaning which the author is intent on extracting from his recital controls the selection and modelling of his narrative, so that they tell rather what might have been than what actually was. And that meaning doubtless corresponds with the contemporary theology and piety dear to the church of his allegiance. And in that theology there is contained one vital element which, however questionably reached, transcends in truth and power the level of the synoptists' gospel. It so construes the personality of Christ, so avails itself of his characteristics, as to abolish the difference of essence between the Divine and the human nature, and substitute for the obedience of dependence the sympathy of likeness and the fellowship of trust.   In appearance, it unites the qualities of God and man in *one* case only, and centres the blended glory in a single incarnation.   But there it does not end.   The unexampled spectacle of such "grace and truth," of heavenly sanctity penetrating all human experiences, startles and wins hearts that never were so drawn before, and wakes in them a capacity for that which they reverence in another.   This attraction of affinity there could not be, were there not divine possibilities secreted and a divine persuasion pleading in each soul.   There cannot be a chasm of forbidding antipathy and alienation, rendering for ever inaccessible to man the very "beauty of holiness" which he already adores: nor is there any hindering curse to be bought·off, before he can enter on the new life of self-consecration.   There is no longer need of despair at the seemingly hopeless task of climbing the heavens and finding the unapproachable God.   For He himself comes unsought, and lifts the latch of our nature when we thought the door was shut, and makes his abode with us,* seeking us with his love, finding us with his truth, and claiming us with his righteousness.   Thus does the Paraclete perpetuate and universalize the impersonation of the Son of God in the Son of Man, and carry it through the spiritual history of the world, and convert the life of Humanity itself into a Theophany.

* John xiv. 23.

CHAPTER III.

THEORIES OF THE WORK OF JESUS.

§ 1. *The Sense of Sin in Christendom.*

In the foregoing chapter it has been shown how the historical life of Jesus of Nazareth fell upon a time and related him to a people charged with preconceptions which threw a variety of false colours upon his figure, and have handed down the image of it in several editions, no one of which can claim photographic truth. To a large extent, the disciples' representation of what he was conformed itself to their previous idea of what he had to do; and that this was all contained in their recognition of him as Messiah, afforded no security against wide divergence; the Messiah being a wholly imaginary personage, whose attributes admitted of variation almost indefinite. Each disciple, looking for what he had been led to expect, and finding what he most needed, interpreted the history in the way congenial with his thought, and helped into existence this or that of the several portraitures which tradition has preserved.

When, however, we come to reckon with the chief preconceptions of the appointed work of Christ in his mission to the world, their number, though considerable if every *nuance* of theological distinction be counted, rapidly thins away for any one who will look beneath the logical forms of statement, and penetrate to the spiritual fact of human experience that is hid within. Or, if he prefers it, as more congenial to him than this deep search, he may carry an objective criticism through the successive ages of Christendom, and elicit from the life and literature of even contrasted churches the true springs of their piety; and, through all the different languages, he cannot fail to be struck by the breathing of the same thoughts, and so modulated that the severed voices from all directions, flow together into one chorus of harmony. This implies no more than some common affection characteristic of religion. What that common affection is it may be well to determine, by distinguishing the forms of doctrine under which it has justified itself to the understanding. It is an affection so inwoven with the deepest root of Christianity, yet so exclusively developed by it, that it is hard to describe it except from within, and express it in terms familiar to other religions. It has, indeed, to borrow from their vocabulary its first faltering words; but only to charge them with a meaning which was never there before, and which their exoteric use can but ineffectually simulate. It is in truth a passion essentially new to the human soul, notwithstanding its rudimentary tentatives before, which constitutes the inner genius of Christianity, and gives a peculiar complexion to its whole history.

It is a favourite maxim with the satirical observer of the world, that the way to make men religious is to *frighten* them. The churches, he says, are never so full as in time of public alarm; and the prayers that are slow to come from the lips of health and the heart of joy, find voluble voice when life is wasting away in sickness and sorrow. The priest who tries in vain to reduce the pulse of hopeful vigour is soon invoked by the humble penitent, and leads him hither and thither as a little child. Place a Whitefield and a Wesley before the rude multitude on the hill-side, and, in spite of their differences, they instinctively fling all their impassioned fervour upon one primary aim,—to *convict of sin*, to exhibit an immeasurable danger, and cast down the strong will with sobs for rescue. The fact, no doubt, is truly stated, and marks a striking difference between the terror of the brute and the terror of the man. Whether it means what the satirist's contempt assumes, and bespeaks a weakness from which the happier animals are free,—whether it is a fall from the true light of life into a delusive shadow of death, is a question of which perhaps he never seriously thought. Plainly, however, it is in virtue of some endowment *purely human*, something added to the groundwork of the animal nature, that we are liable to this experience; and this alone might lead us to suspect it to be not an infirmity, but an insight and a power.

G G 2

The truth is, Fear can never be the occasion of religion, except in a nature which ought to be above fear. It is the shrinking of the creature before the decrees of the Creator,—the cry of the finite being under the laws of the Infinite; and wherever there is consciousness of this its relative character, wherever the Creator and his infinite order are present to the thought, it ceases to be a mere sensitive recoil, and by attesting a variance between the human will and the Divine, carries a secret compunction with it, and turns the shriek into a prayer. Had we no vision of heavenly things, pain would be only pain, and fear would be but its shadow on the path before us; and the passing moan and the sudden start would tell all the tale. But the depth and significance of human unrest comes of this: that we live for ever seeing what is Invisible; that we suffer before the face of the All-blessed; that we resist the dispositions of the All-loving; that we sin in the sight of the All-holy; and so are not at one with Him to whom we belong, and in whose perfection our imperfection should be lost, if not in fact, at least in faith. Haunted in thought and affection by the Absolute Goodness, and scarcely rising by our poor strength above constant failure, we can never lose the sense of humbling separation; nor can the Divine light stream through the bars of our narrow nature, without parting with its outer brilliancy, and melting into a thousand pathetic hues. It is this entrance of the Infinite within finite conditions, this transcendency of our knowledge beyond our strength, this inward homage to the Supreme Sanctity while rendering it a mixed and tainted service, which saddens us with that inextinguishable sense of estrangement from God, which it is the aim of all religion to acknowledge and to escape. This secret consciousness it is, of variance from the only True, of distance from the only Real, of alienation from the only Holy, which wakes up at the touch of human suffering and fear, and turns them from a bare quivering of the flesh into a fruitful anguish of the spirit. It is by appealing to this that the true prophet breaks the contented sleep of instinct,—rings the alarm in the chambers of the soul,—flings the animal nature convulsed with shame upon the ground, and by a purifying sorrow lifts it up into responsible manhood. In vain would the preacher light his torch from fires of hell, did he address only physical susceptibility and abject consternation ; it is the moral history written within, the felt interval between what is and what might have been, which these things passionately express and which makes them credible at all. The terror is born of religion, not the religion of terror.

As it is the function of the *prophetic* spirit to keep alive this ideality of conscience, and interpret it as God's own light within the soul, so is it the business of the *priestly* office to lay its disquietudes to rest, and by outward methods specially its own to reinstate the broken harmony. The priest could never be, but for the noble discontent, the divine sorrow, with which the prophets electrify the murky air of life, and divide it into heavenly gleams and stormy glooms. The priest lives upon the shame and misery of stricken souls that are in haste to find peace with themselves and with their God : he offers to take them to their rest, not by pure and inward reconciliation that would speak for itself in its own harmonies, but by magic ways which ask no aid of the human will, and make no report to the human heart. The whole institution of sacrifice, which forms the very substance of all ancient worship, and the proper business of a sacerdotal order, arises, it cannot be doubted, from the consciousness of imperilled peace between earth and heaven, and the desire to do something which might conciliate the smile, or break up the frown, of the Supreme Powers. It was an attempt to restore right relations between the visible and the invisible world ; and however low the expiatory conceptions that mingle with it, it still attests the conscious variance between the human and the Divine, and proclaims its perpetuity by never-ceasing effort to get rid of it. But every priestly device for this end is but a pretence at wiping out the shadow while the substance that casts it still is there ; and when the process is over and the magician is gone, the darkness lies as before within its silent outline.

If ever a religion could subsist without this feeling, it would be the Nature-worship of the old heathen world, whose Olympus and Tartarus were almost parts of its geography, and whose gods were scarce diviner than its men. Yet tradition consecrated many a fearful and pathetic sacrifice, which, reproduced upon the tragic stage, hushed and solemnized the gayest populace of history. Not even the Attic sunshine could dissipate the shadows from the Furies' grove.

Infinitely more profound was this feeling in the Hebrew race; their whole polity being in fact an organized method of assuaging it, and for ever renewing the for ever broken covenant with God. Their history, their culture, their literature, are little else than its prolonged expression; their prophets dissipating the false repose of the national conscience, and flinging the fresh light of heaven direct upon their sins; their priests ever ready with an atonement, and soothing them again with remission of the past; till the alternation ended in the triumph of the temple and the altar, and Jerusalem, having killed the prophets, and stoned them that were sent unto her, could sit at ease upon her hills, look out for her Messiah, and clap her hands at the sinking world.

. Now when we ask, throughout Christendom, what it is that its Author has characteristically done for men, the first element in the answer is this: he has awakened in them a sense of Sin entirely unlike the servile fear and mere deprecation of retributory anger which had set up the priest and the altar of earlier religions. *They* brought their expiatory sacrifices at crises of terror or special crime, when the heavens scowled upon them and could hardly hold their thunders in: *He* breathed into the soul a permanent sorrow of humility, kindling on its upper side with a glory of aspiration. Their impulse was to fly from the track of the pursuing gods, and hide "in caves and dens of the earth" from the capturing enemies: He put it into the offender's heart to say, "I will arise and go to my Father," and to expect the embrace of restoring love. Their whole device was to buy off and escape the pains and penalties of their wrong-doing, and be no worse for it: He brought his penitents to just the opposite mind: so that nothing is further from their desire than to throw their burden off; it is the fitting sequel to their sin, and it would leave a stain upon them not to bear it to the last: nor is the suffering unsanctified, for the spirit now reconciled to God. It is this genuine moral assent to the requirements of the Divine Holiness,—this inward acceptance of all that it appoints, and loves, and is, which lifts the Christian sense of Sin into quite another region of character from that in which self-interested hope and terror assail the will.

Hence it is only natural that, in carrying on their work among men, the true missionaries of Christ make it their first aim to reach the springs of compunction and extort the cry for relenting love. And it is impossible to deny that this sentiment of Divine need has played a part in the Christian history of mankind which it never played before. The very eagerness with which the new religion, in spite of its un-promising origin, was seized on as " the desire of nations," the rapidity with which it stole into the heart of great cities, and into the cabin of the slave, the resorts of commerce, and even the palace of the Cæsars, the welcome it found with "devout women," and dissatisfied scholars, and passionate natures pining for nobler life, show that it interpreted aright the weariness of a world trying to live upon the present and the visible, and looked with eyes not too sad on a humanity lost to God. In that universal death of nations which coin-cided with the consolidation of the Roman empire, the most generous and delicate springs of energy collapsed ; on the spent level of that subjugated area, where genius breathed heavily and self-interest had the chief play, natures with higher wants found nothing quickening to think, and nothing worthy to do ; and humanity, at the moment when it reached its unity, was made conscious of its degradation too. It is impossible to read, I do not say the satirists, whose business it is to lash the vices of mankind, but even the historians of that period, without per-ceiving that it was an age of portentous moral corruption, fostering every shameless license, permitting every cruelty, rewarding every daring crime which law and right are consti-tuted to prevent ; so that whoever looked, from the depth of a purified conscience, at the ethical physiognomy of society, be-held an objective image of all that he most loathed in his own worst possibilities, and that warned him how far he might fall into the darkness away from God. And just when the disease was at its height, the physicians were beneath contempt. As the world lay festering in wickedness, the priests of Paganism could not even carry about the cleansing incense of a believing presence, or charm misgivings or despair with even an imaginary peace; for the gods had become a fable, the temples a trade, and their expiations a pretence; so that the earth seemed cut off from all higher life, and doomed, like a plague-stricken city, to nurse its own fever and infuriate its own delirium, deserted by all that could heal or pity or even drop the cold water on the tongue.

In such a world then, if it can be caught in listening mood, let the Beatitudes fall upon the ear and tell the secret of the meek, the self-sacrificing, and the pure in heart; let the infinite heaven open, and the Living God become all in all; let the image be shown, on the distant hills of Palestine, of One who was transfigured with the blended glory of Divine and human love, now flushed with compassion, now pale with prayer, with the child in his arms, or the penitent at his feet; let the tone be heard in which he thrusts his very essence away, and says, "There is none good save One, that is God:" and what light must such revelations bring with them? Will they not come upon the rarer and better minds like a waking into the stainless morning from a night of fevered dreams? and yet, while justifying their purest enthusiasm, filling them also with an awful despair? Who can wonder that, when the Divine light is brightest, the human deformities on which it shines, and to which it leaves no shade, look most appalling? that the more deeply the conscience is touched, the more heinous should appear not only its own unfaithfulness, but the collective guilt of mankind. Let it not be said that this shadow so broadly flung upon human life falsifies the parting prophecy of Christ, "Peace I leave with you:" for does he not qualify it by adding, "*My* peace I give unto you," and warning his disciples, "*Not as the world giveth*, give I unto you?" The religion bequeathed under such conditions could not fail from the very first to take the false brilliancy away from a scene that had lost the innocence and truth of simpler days, and should speak home to the exceptional minds that turned from that scene in weariness and were waiting for better things.

The same character, so striking in its marked contrast with the gay and reckless heathen life, has maintained itself through the whole length of Christian history. The question nearest to the heart of it has been, not 'how stands the life of man with physical nature?' but, 'how stands the life of man with the spiritual God?' and as the finite has thus been confronted with the Infinite, and the actual been tried by the Supreme ideal, the sense of short-coming and the sigh of failure could never die. An eternal longing, an unwearied pressure, a beating of the labouring wings, however far the height and lone the track, mark the spiritual tendencies of Christendom. There alone even shame does not wear the downcast face, but turns an uplifted look, with the full eye on heaven, and only its tears given to the ground. Throughout its ages, penitence has been recognized as a condition inseparable from the human soul, and the provisions for it have been wrought into an institution. Sacred Art has caught the same inspiration. It instinctively aims to suggest more than it displays; giving to its human forms depth of expression rather than the balance of repose ; and to its great churches, not the compact outline and satisfying symmetry of the Greek temple, which had no shadow except what the sunshine brought with it through the peristyle, but the deep perspective, and the high-clasped space, and the intersecting arches showing marvels of distance and hiding more, and the shrined chapels and retreating oratories solemn with coloured lights and hinted glooms,—everything that can be born into shapes of stone out of the sense of mystery and immensity embracing in pity the child of sorrow and vain endeavour. The very forms of speech were remoulded by the tender pressure of the same constant feeling working itself into thought ; and the old Roman tongue, so firm and round, so clear and true to the business of civil life, scarcely knew itself when it was transported from the fórum to the church, and heard with what plaintive voice and delicate turns and musical simplicity it could tell the drama and sing the lyrics of an inner life unknown before. The hymns and litanies of Christendom are the perpetual sigh of the human spirit for the Divine, now sinking into a *Miserere* for their separation, and then swelling into a *Jubilate* at their reunion. Nay, even upon its philosophy and polity the same unresting and prospective temper has left its mark. The dream and tendency of modern society has been, not to conform to the world as it is, but to make it what it ought to be; not to stereotype some best condition which should adequately repress the incurable evil and set free the given store of good, but to repent of every wrong in the past and press on to every right in the future; to open boundless possibilities, and own with shame how few of them have yet been realized ; to treat humanity as no perpetual self-repetition, but as a spiritual organism of unlimited growth, with ills deciduous as each season falls, but roots that can feed on the very decay they make, and branches that answer with a fuller foliage to every vernal wind. So much for living in presence of the Infinite God, instead of finite Nature: the mingled sense of possible righteousness and actual guiltiness has at once humbled and inspired the human soul, and impressed a *movement* upon Christendom out of the dead past into the living future, which had never been owned by men before.

Do I refer this sense of sin and mood of penitence and pressure of aspiration to an inadequate source, when tracing it to the awakened ideality of conscience, touched by the majesty of grace and truth in Jesus himself? Shall I be reminded that by the first preachers of his word there was a terror spread abroad, the thunder-clap of which startled many a soul insensible to the sweet persuasion of the divinest life ? Yes, they doubtless did go forth with a clarion of alarm, announcing " the end of all things " as "at hand," and bidding men make haste to repent and leap into the life-boat, for the world had struck upon a rock and would ride the seas of time no more. And it cannot be denied that this stupendous expectation, wherever it got hold, would intensify the plaint of penitence and the prayer for rescue in every soul weighed down by guilty memories. But which of the two horrors, physical and moral, that mingle in that cry is answerable for the other? Could the vital struggle of impending wreck set up a compunction in a nature either above or below the capacity for guilt? To the mere instinctive creature the disorders of life bring pain alone, with neither self-reproach nor care. And from a Christ, on the other hand, the cross itself can wring only the prayer of a Divino love, "Father, forgive them, for they know not what they do." But where there is already a haunting consciousness of many a sinful stain unwashed by cleansing tears, of selfish aims ascendant over sacred calls refused, of the manifold confusions of a heart not right with God, the last hour of probation cannot threaten to strike without hurrying into it a crowd of moral arrears and a train of shadowy forebodings, such as fitly visit spirits that "believo and tremble."

Nay, more. The very possibility of belief itself in such a prophecy as that there is to be no morrow for a world, is dependent on a secret anarchy of the private conscience and a terrible prevalence of corruption in social life. A prediction so monstrous would not be listened to in a community under righteous sway, where there were no odious vices and no flagrant wrong, and personal purity and mutual service maintained the equilibrium of peace. Innocent, faithful, well-ordered and disinterested people cannot be made to believe in the near ruin of the heavens and the earth: it must be a world not worth preserving which they can reckon on seeing immediately burnt up. Tragedies of judgment and visions of the last despair are the outward projection of inward remorse, or of the torture of baffled righteousness. Fevered passions and a paralytic will, waves of infinite desire rolling over a soul in moral decrepitude, spread an answering universe around, and will render any portentous vaticination credible. And similiar predisposition may be wrought in the lonely servant of God, or some small band of his rejected witnesses, at the spectacle of hopeless greed and cruel wrong and shameless indulgence, in a "faithless and perverse generation." It is everywhere the same; the insight of conscience and the sense of Sin are the source and not the fruit of religious fear; and whatever is fabulous in the scene on which it looks is but a distorted shadow cast from the truest light. And that this truest light shines as it does into our hearts we owe, as I believe, to its reflection in the face of Jesus Christ, the mediator between God and man, by realizing a type of holiness and ground of spiritual fellowship relative to both.

It is true that the first missionaries of Christ, through whom this characteristic was conveyed into the heart of Christendom, were themselves unconscious that they drew it from his personality; and, in imparting it, they did not commend it as a trait of his own spirit, but rather rested it on dogmatic grounds, adopted as axiomatic from anterior or contemporary theologies for which he was in no way responsible. The Judaic gospel, assuming a national instead of a moral and spiritual division between the lost and the saved, confounded the sense of sin with a despair of election, or under proselyte conditions, with a frightened resort to ritual compliances. Overleaping these invidious limits, the Pauline gospel universalized Sin, and made it dreadful by linking it with Death; but, attaching it as an irresistible attribute to all flesh so as to be inborn in all the children of Adam, reduced it to a constitutional necessity, to be deplored with the sigh of the slave rather than the tears of the penitent; and regarding it as equally present with its entail of moral penalty, whether the act is of blind instinct or of conscious wrong, expelled it from the moral province altogether, and planted it among the sequences of objective phenomena. To rescue the race of the terrestrial Adam from this fatalized condition, the apostle, we have seen, invokes the Celestial Adam, the failure of the Natural being reversible only by intervention of the supernatural. The process of redemption which the apostle constructs and applies will be noticed in the next section. It is based, like the Galilean evangel which preceded it, on Jewish preconceptions which have neither validity for us, nor foundation in the personal religion of Jesus. It is a theory in which the accepted facts of his death and resurrection are wrought into their place in a vast Theodicy embracing the providential drama of humanity from its opening to its consummation. Being the theory of one whose knowledge of Jesus began with his revelation from heaven, it naturally made no use of the features of his earthly life and personality. Considered as the afterthought of a posthumous disciple, it is a wonderful construction, full of original combination and deep experience and large sweep of thought and sympathy. But it presents us rather with the

outer contour of the Christian faith as organized for a world's
history, than with the inner secret of God which lives as its
kernel in each Christlike soul.

§ 2. *The Apostolic Doctrine of Redemption.*

It has often been remarked by the critics of religion that
its tone of intense penitence and its assurance of Divine
acceptance do not adjust themselves well together, and
can hardly be alike sincere. How, it is asked, can the
worshipper who confesses himself so steeped in sin receive
any light of hope on the eye he lifts to heaven? How pass
from his passionate cry of self-abhorrence to his hymn of
repose on the love of God? how, within an hour, look down
from the brink into an abyss of despair, and then be lost
in visions of everlasting peace? If penitence were only a
slavish terror of a wrathful hell, it certainly could not pass
so soon into the joy of assured salvation. But, strange as it
may seem to one unfamiliar with the laws of spiritual belief, these
opposite states, far from being incompatible, are inseparable,
—the two sides of one and the same faith, which only completes its expression in transition from the one to the other.
Let God but lift the veil from the human spirit and appear
before it and within it, the infinite to the finite, the perfect to
the imperfect; and by their co-presence and their contrast,
the self-consciousness, whether of sinner or of saint, loses its
contentment and sinks away towards nothingness, while the
consciousness of Him becomes all in all, and takes up into its
plenitude more than all that has been lost. The humiliation
is no absolute darkness, hopelessly there upon its own
account, but, like an eclipse, the witness of a flood of light
around; the shadow of the earthly nature, whose very depth
measures the heavenly brightness by which it is cast. Hence
the feeling of failure and the sadness of evil are attended by
an absorbing faith in the Divine perfection which rebukes and
cancels their despair, and flings them out of the sorrows of
self into the embrace of God. If it be the revelation of the
Divine holiness which fills me with the sense of sin, and of
eternal love which makes me know my selfishness, the glory

which I see lifts me from the contrition which I feel; and there is healing in the very light that shows my woe. It is no accident then, and no inward contradiction, that the penitential mood of Christendom should be but the prelude to the joy of Redemption; that the discovery of alienation should be the first sign of reunion; and that the prophets of terror should melt into the organs of Pity and Grace. It is of the very essence of religion to detect the actual disharmony, and proclaim the possible harmony, between the human spirit and the Divine.

In every doctrine of redemption, the provision for recovery will correspond to the preconception of the ill; and the Saviour's work will be measured by the ruin he has to reverse, the wrongs to redress, the spoiled ideals to reinstate. This dark side of the world presented by no means the same aspect to all sections of the early Church; and its variations were concomitant with those which we have noticed in the theory of Christ's person. To the twelve apostles the range of evil was ethnological, and divided Gentile from true Israelite; to Paul it was human, and divided the natural from the spiritual man; to the fourth evangelist it was cosmical, and divided the devilish agency in the universe from the Divine. And the offices of redemption received corresponding measures of extension; having an interest, in the first case, for a people; in the second, for mankind; in the third, for the whole creation. Under each mythological form was couched the confession how deeply, in minds of various scope, the religion of Jesus had penetrated the conscience, and with what force it had touched the trembling strings.

In his attempt to discriminate these three types of doctrine, and still more to exhibit their order of development, the historical critic meets with serious difficulties from the defective sources of information on which he must rely. It seems a plain enough rule to take the Synoptists and the Book of Acts as his authority for the teaching of the original body of Jerusalem disciples; the undisputed letters of Paul as embodying the first Gentile gospel; and the Johannine writings as giving the later modifications of the Alexandrian school. But in the second case only is direct contact gained with the sole authentic guide; and after following him through his four primary letters to the Galatians, Corinthians, and Romans, the reader is, on some points, still held in suspense till he decides how far he may invoke the witness of the less certain Pauline texts. In the case of the Johannine writings (excluding the Apocalypse) the conclusions yielded by the Gospel are by no means identical with those required by the Epistles. And though the synoptical gospels and the Book of Acts no doubt contain the doctrinal conceptions of the earliest disciples, it is certain that they contain much else that is due to afterthoughts of the apostolic and post-apostolic age: the writings assigned to Luke, in particular, bearing marks, on the one hand, of the Pauline spirit, and on the other, of a time when Pauline controversies were already laid to rest. So that the only gospel of redemption which we know at first hand from its own preacher is that of the apostle of the Gentiles; and into that of his predecessors we gain insight, more by subtracting the distinctive features which he himself accentuated, than by any extant report authentically theirs. This subtraction the auther of the Book of Acts has so far done for us with the advantage of his near point of view, that we may reasonably rely on his representation of the first preaching of Peter and his companions in Jerusalem. Nor is it impossible for the comparative critic of the synoptists to remove into the margin the vestiges of later thought, and gain a detached view of the state of mind which the disciples carried from the scene of the Cross to that of the Resurrection. An unprejudiced use of these aids sets before us, in clear lines, the growth and the differences of the prevalent conception respecting the nature and range of the redeeming work of Christ.

In the eye of the Jewish Christian the alienation of men from God was an affair of race, with its concomitant in ancient times, the inherited religion, and, but for one national exception, it would have been universal and hopeless. As he looked over the world, it divided itself before him, much as it does now in the view of the orthodox missionary; the heathen nations lost in their idolatries and reserved for the wrath to come; and only the Israel of God, and its naturalized citizens, the chosen remnant of the faithful, separated as heirs of his purposes on earth.* To the eye of the immediate observer this tremendous distinction in the statistics of the Divine favour was not apparent on the surface: the mark of the beast,† and the saving name,‡ were hid by the folds of the outward dress; it was yet a mixed world; and in the forum at Rome, and the schools of Athens, and the Museum of Alexandria and the colonnades of Antioch, elect and cast-away jostled each other on equal terms, and looked and spoke and felt so much alike that, without the assurance of faith, you would not know the difference. But it would not long be so:§ the term was expiring for the affluence of the world to be flung into the lap of corruption and its diadems to glisten on unbelieving brows. The classification now latent would soon be visible enough; a divine crisis was at hand when the elements of human society would be sifted out, the sheep from the goats,‖ the wheat from the chaff; the one to be the first-fruits of a new and purified earth; the other to be cleared out into the unquenchable fire.¶ This external form of expectation, this belief that a Theocracy was about to be set up, introduced by a great assize for the cleansing of the field, and gathering the enrolled disciples into a sacred and happy commonwealth under the presidentship of Messiah, is evidently what the Jewish Christians meant when they declared that the "Kingdom of heaven was at hand."** It differed in no respect from the Messianic belief which all their compatriots held, except in venturing to *name the person* in whom it would be shortly fulfilled. That Jesus was to be the Christ did not alter in the least their picture of what the Christ was appointed to do. Of this we have the clearest proof in the resort of Christian evangelists and prophets to Jewish apocalyptic writings for the expression of their own Messianic visions, and even for their version of what Jesus himself must have said or meant to say. The eschatological discourses of the Passion-week in Matthew and Luke, and the mass of the Book of Revelation are mainly made up of material

* Acts ii. 30.   † Rev. xiv. 9.   ‡ Rev. xiv. 1.
§ Luke xii. 46.   ‖ Matt. xxv. 32, 33.   ¶ Matt. iii. 12.
** Mark i. 15; Luke xix. 11, xxi. 31.

common to both religions ere they finally parted ; and present
the same succession of scenes as that which passes before the
reader of the Book of Enoch and the fourth of Ezra ; the
confederation of all the Pagan powers against Messiah, and
their total overthrow ; the opening of the valley of Hinnom to
swallow them in its fires, while the disciples live happily in
sight of them on the hills and around the temples of Jerusalem ; the return to life of pious Israelites to share the
glorious reign, be it of a thousand or (as Ezra has it) of four
hundred years ; and then, the winding up of even this last
stage of terrestrial history and, after final judgment by God
in person over the whole universe, human and superhuman,
and the casting of Death and Hades themselves into the lake
of fire, the emergence of a new heaven and new earth where
immortals alone shall dwell, and God shall be all in all.   Even
that eternal scene, when the Kingdom of Messiah was over,
delivered up into the hands of the Father, was conceived of as
exclusive to the believers, and none were to enter whose names
were not of the true Israel of God and on the roll of the
Lamb.

What then could be the *redeeming function* of Christ, working
within the conditions of this picture?   *From what* could he
redeem? From forfeiture of all share in the glories of Messiah's
reign.   His missionaries were sent forth with the summons to
" repentance " as the condition of " remission of sins " ; and
charged, if their message was rejected, to shake off the dust of
their feet, with the warning, " Nevertheless be sure of this,
that the kingdom is come nigh " ; * and " unless your righteousness exceed the righteousness of the scribes and Pharisees, ye
shall in no wise enter into the kingdom of heaven." † *Into
what* could he redeem?   Into the citizenship of that kingdom.
Hence the exhortation, " Repent, and be baptized every one of
you in the name of Jesus unto the remission of your sins,"
and " save yourselves from this crooked generation." ‡   *Whom*
could he redeem? Not any in the vast Gentile world, embraced as it was by a hard and fast line cutting it off from
the promise ; nor could any name thence pass on to the register
of life, unless by prior naturalization in the family of Jacob.

* Luke x. 11.   † Matt. v. 20.   ‡ Acts ii. 33, 40.

It was " the God of Abraham, of Isaac, and of Jacob, the God of our fathers " who " had glorified his servant Jesus," and " thus fulfilled the things which he foreshowed by the mouth of all his prophets."   " Let therefore the house of Israel know assuredly, that God hath made this Jesus, whom ye crucified, both Lord and Christ."   " To you is the promise, and to your children, with as many of those that are afar off as the Lord our God shall call unto him." *   The redemption of this *Israel* the appointed Prince and Saviour was now commissioned to effect ; chiefly, when he came to take his power, by gathering them from the mixed world into his commonwealth ; but, meanwhile, by sending them notice of his approach, giving them time to prepare their hearts and stand ready till the hour struck.   Thus, the main act in the drama of redemption lies in the *future ;* and the preluding notice which his *past* has left consists of two parts: (1) his living ministry and personal warning that a diviner age was about to dawn : a warning so certain to be fruitless that, as it drew to its close, he wept over the unheeding city, saying, " If thou hadst known in this thy day, even thou, the things which belong unto peace ! but now they are hid from thine eyes." †   (2) His dying sacrifice of himself, which withdrew him from the world till the warning had had time to work.   There was yet an interval of Divine longsuffering ere the account was closed : " Repent, therefore, " might Peter well say, " and turn again, that your sins may be blotted out, that so there may come seasons of refreshment from the presence of the Lord ; and that he may send the Christ who hath been appointed for you, even Jesus, whom the heaven must receive until the times of the restoration of all things, whereof God hath spoken by the mouth of his holy prophets which have been since the world began." ‡   Those who had turned a deaf ear to his voice upon the hills or in the streets, who had rejected and despised him, and whom, if he had set up his kingdom at once, he would have been unable to admit, could not fail, if they had since seen their error and taken refuge in the Christian brotherhood, to feel that their hour of repentance had been an hour of salvation, that *they* must have perished if *he* had not, and

that, but for his cross and its delay, there had for them been
no redemption.

For the exercise of this function, the attributes of the
ancient prophets and the will of pure self-sacrifice were alone
required. It made no demand on him which human nature,
kindled by the spirit of God, and dedicated to the love of man,
was inadequate to render. To teach the truth, to win over to
the good, to snatch from blind illusions, to be patient with the
froward and stricken lest they die,—all this is not beyond the
province of the man of God, and had been exemplified long
ago in the history or the visions of the elder times. There is
here no magic office needing an Agent superhuman or divine.
Accordingly, this Jewish-Christian conception of the redeeming
work of Christ stands in connection with the humanitarian
doctrine of his person, and looks on him simply as the last
and supreme of the prophets. And so too the result which he
wrought out upon the minds of his disciples lay within the
compass of humanity; they were persuaded, they repented,
they renounced the world, they lived in faith, they formed a
holy brotherhood; not indeed without the helping spirit of
God, but only in such union with Him as faithful souls have
always found,—a union which neither suspends their nature
nor absorbs it. Human therefore is the Mediator of this redemption, and human remain its recipients. In this feature,
and in the limitation to Israel and its proselytes, and in the
ascendency of the national over the personal idea, the primitive gospel is distinguished from the later forms of the same
doctrine.

Totally changed does the whole theory become, the moment
we enter the school of Paul. All the actors in the drama,—
Jew, Gentile, Christ and God, stand in altered relations and
fill different parts. The evil which demands a Redeemer is
not shut up within the boundary of the idolatrous nations;
nor anywhere on the surface of the world is a line to be seen
which parts the shadow of alienation from the light of hope.
Israelite as he is, a Hebrew of the Hebrews, the apostle cannot keep all that is divine at home, and fling all the unre-
conciled elements abroad. He finds the Jewish .nature, he
finds his own nature so crippled for good, so compelled to

wrestle with evil, so drawn to own yet failing to fulfil the perfect law of God, that he dare not, while so little true to his heart's inmost worship, taunt the Gentile with his offences. No ; the estrangement is nothing outward, that can be cured by a sifting of mankind, and thrusting the corrupted populations of unbelievers, idolaters, and liars into the pit of Sodom. It is *human*, and discernible alike in Jerusalem and in Rome ; it is in the very *make* of the race, and, coming from Adam, runs through the line alike of Jacob and of Esau. Whilst men are moulded of flesh and blood, the very material of their composition carries the taint of sin and makes them due to death, not by any arbitrary law, but by a natural necessity attaching to every fabricated creature that is "of the earth, earthy."

The great scale of the apostle Paul's gospel depended on his profound impression of the universality of Sin, and his assured faith in a promise of final righteousness. The magnitude of the ruin measured that of the restoration ; and if the one attested the broken forces of the human will, the other could be looked for only from the recreating energy of God himself. Through what personal agent, in the Pauline theory, he effected this reconstitution of humanity, has been explained in a former chapter ; and after the sketch of anthropological doctrine there given, the subjection of our whole race to sin may be assumed as the primary axiom of the apostle's scheme. There are questions within this on which doubts may be raised ; for example, whether the sin everywhere present is a fatality of nature, or a freely incurred guilt : the apostle argues from both positions, content to resolve their contradictions into the irresponsibility of God. But for his starting-point it is not needful to look with speculative eye behind the actual fact of the moral condition of mankind : the Gentiles have a law written on the heart ; the Jews, a law divinely given to their fathers : both are flagrantly and universally violated, " so that there is none righteous, no, not one "; " they have all turned aside, and altogether become unprofitable "; " every mouth must be stopped, and all the world brought under the judgment of God." * This state of the world, revolting to

* Rom. ii. 14-29, iii. 10, 12, 19.

every observer's better mind, is rendered too intelligible by the conflicts and humiliations of his own inner life, which for ever sees what it fails to reach, and incurs an alternation of hope and shame more constant than day and night.[*]

Neither as a Jew nor as a Pharisee was the apostle bound to throw so dark and unrelieved a shade upon his estimate of the world. It was an extension, through the ideal pieties of his own nature, to Israel's sacred enclosure, of the Hebrew abhorrence of Pagan life and manners. It was otherwise with the next link in his chain of thought, "The wages of Sin is Death."[†] This he derived and accepted simply as a dogmatic axiom from "the Law and the Prophets," only applying it in uncontemplated ways. From the fact that the first mention of Death in the Hebrew Scriptures is as the fore-announced penalty of transgression, "Of the tree of the knowledge of good and evil thou shalt not eat, for in the day that thou eatest thereof thou shalt surely die,"[‡] it became a fixed idea that there could be no sin without death, and no death without sin; and the maxim, "the soul that sinneth, it shall die,"[§] was accepted as the statement of an irrefragable law. The Divine alternative had no room for halting wills; "I call earth and heaven to witness against you this day, that I have set before you life and death, the blessing and the curse;"[‖] and "Cursed be he that observeth not the words of this law to do them."[¶] Certain it is that the apostle unconditionally assumed this principle; affirming both the entrance of Death as the curse upon sin,[**] and the incidence of the curse upon every transgressor,[††] and taking the rule directly home to the personal experience in the startling words "I was alive apart from the law once; but when the commandment came, Sin revived, and I died: and the commandment, which was unto life, this I found to be unto death; for sin, taking occasion through the commandment, beguiled me, and through it *slew* me."[‡‡] As this fatal concomitant of sin completes the apostle's conception of the human ruin, and gives therefore the measure of the redemption needed, it is

* Rom. vii. 14–25.   † Rom. vi. 23.   ‡ Genesis ii. 17.
§ Ezekiel xviii. 4.   ‖ Deut. xxx. 19.   ¶ Ibid. xxvii. 26.
** Rom. v. 12.   †† Gal. iii. 10.   ‡‡ Rom. vii. 9–11.

important to determine correctly what range of ill he includes in its name.

At the lowest it has of course the privative meaning, of a cessation of this life. Even when it takes in no more, it may mark, instead of the actual fact of cessation, the liability to it which we call *mortality;* as the passage " In the day that thou eatest thereof thou shalt surely die," announces, not that Adam would not survive that day, but that by removal out of the reach of the tree of life, he would become subject to the law of all flesh ($\vartheta\nu\eta\tau\dot{\eta}\ \sigma\dot{\alpha}\rho\xi$). It was impossible for this negative idea long to keep the word to itself; the cessation of life is followed by a dissolution of the body which, once known, would cling to the thought; and when the question arose whether these visible phenomena were all that was happening, or whether others that were invisible might not also be occurring to what had been invisible in the living man, the answers supplied by guess or thought would add themselves on to the previous conception and enlarge its significance. Thus, even in its literal application, the word Death obtains no slight latitude of variation in its meaning, and compels the interpreter to ask his author what he supposes to take place when a human life is closed.

Shall we find the Pauline conception by keeping close to the naked negative meaning, and say that by Death, as the penalty of sin, he understands the " complete extinction of the individual " ? This opinion, very ably supported by M. Eugène Menegoz,* rests on the assumption that the apostle's anthropology is strictly *monistic,†* regarding " the flesh " not as a companion factor with the $\nu o \bar{\nu} c$, but as "*the whole man*,"‡ whose will, intelligence, and desires are functions of it and constitute it "a personality." A Sarkical doctrine of this type would be equivalent to the modern physiological materialism ; and would certainly be in similar alliance with an interpretation of death as "complete annihilation of the individual."§

If the choice lay between this reading of the apostle's

---

* In his interesting and valuable treatise, *Le Péché et la Redemption d'après St. Paul.*   1882.
† p. 41.   ‡ p. 48.   § p. 76.

thought and the assumption that his death-penalty of Sin contained in it eternal retributory suffering, exegetic reasons, entirely apart from moral, would decide in favour of the former. The Pauline Epistles, it is true, are not without terrible denunciations of Divine displeasure and personal punishment against evil doers; "wrath against the day of wrath and revelation of the righteous judgment of God;" " unto them that obey not the truth but obey unrighteousness, wrath and indignation, tribulation and anguish upon every soul of man that worketh evil, of the Jew first, and also of the Greek; for there is no respect of persons with God."* " The unrighteous shall not inherit the kingdom of God;"† but shall meet with "eternal destruction from the face of the Lord and from the glory of his might."‡ But in these warnings there is not a word which assigns these awards to scenes beyond this world. They obviously refer for the most part to the " day of the Lord,"—the reappearance of Christ, expected without delay,—" the night is far spent, the day is at hand."§ And there is the less reason to interpret them of the state of the wicked after death, because in not one of his Epistles does the apostle ever mention or imply a resurrection of the unrighteous : he contemplates no other witnesses of that " great day " than the living people whom it should overtake, and the departed Christians called back into life to meet it. Whosoever of these should receive a sentence of " eternal destruction from the face of the Lord " would surely fulfil it by a " complete annihilation of the individual." It must be owned that temporal death gives an adequate account of the apostle's language of retribution : which, in truth, is not more intense or appalling than we find in the denunciations by the ancient prophets, and in the fearful volley of curses on the unfaithful in the 27th and 28th chapters of the Book of Deuteronomy. And the reader must be on his guard against importing into the apostle's writings images and conceptions, associated, it may be, with similar phrases, occurring in other portions of the New Testament. His eschatology is not free from obscurity and self-variation; but it has one clear character-

---

* Rom. ii. 5, 8, 9.   † 1 Cor. vi. 9.
‡ 2 Thess. i. 9 (doubtful whether Pauline).   § Rom. xiii. 12.

istic; it knows nothing of any hell, of any worm that dieth not, and fire that is not quenched, or other vision of infernal torment: it has nothing eternal but a "weight of glory," unbalanced by any everlasting shame; and if it is not without "vessels of wrath," the worst that it says of them is that they are "fitted for *destruction*."[*]

But if the Pauline "*Death*" does not carry in it so much as the pains of hell, neither, I believe, is it reducible to a mere blotting out of the individual. The alleged "monism" of the apostle, constituting the human personality of flesh alone, with the dissolution of which all is gone, rests on no sufficient grounds. It is admitted on all hands that ψυχή, νοῦς, and πνεῦμα, are attributed to man; the only question is, whether in *subordination* to σάρξ, as its properties, or in any *co-ordination* with it as a separate condition of the compound being. That the apostle ever set himself to solve such a metaphysical problem and deliberately took sides upon it, is inconceivable, unless we suppose him to be beforehand with the antitheses of scholastic and modern philosophy. But that his habitual language, instead of identifying the proper Self of the natural man with "the flesh" (as understood by him) invests it with the indefeasible though baffled rights of a superior, and plants it at the level of a self-conscious Agent looking down on a meaner territory of impulse, is beyond dispute, and clearly shows the answer which must be given for him. "If what I would not, that I do, it is no more I that do it, but Sin that dwelleth in me. O wretched man that I am! who shall deliver me from the body of this death? I thank God through Jesus Christ our Lord. So that *I myself* with the mind serve the law of God; but with the flesh the law of Sin."[†] No form of words can more clearly identify the "I myself" with "the Mind," in direct contrast with "the flesh," as "the body of death," from which that Self cries out for "deliverance." No less marked is the duality of our nature, when the apostle turns from the confessions of inner experience to the observation of character in the disciples: marking off their respective fields to the two opposites,—Sin and Christ,—he says, "If Christ be in you, the *body* is dead because of Sin,

<hr>

[*] Rom. ix. 22.   [†] Ibid. vii. 20, 24, 25.

but the *Spirit* is life because of righteousness."*   Here he no doubt speaks, not of the natural man, but of the Christian touched by the fellowship of Christ; and the "spirit" may be taken to mean, not the personal soul of the recipient, but the indwelling presence of his Sanctifier.   Sanctifier, however, there cannot be without a subject susceptible of sanctification; the spirit that comes cannot be the spirit that receives; and this it is that is quickened to life and light by the influx of grace from the communion of Christ.   Such a partition of human nature, surrendering the body to the operations of sin, and the spirit to those of Christ and his righteousness, is surely not what might be expected from a monistic thinker. Nor would he be more consistent if, in dealing with an offender against Christian purity, he proposed, like the apostle with the Corinthian transgressor, to "deliver him to Satan for the destruction of his flesh, that the spirit may be saved in the day of the Lord Jesus."†   Whatever be intended by this apostolic act of discipline, there are two points indisputably clear; that the flesh which is destroyed cannot carry as its property the spirit which is saved; and that the spirit saved cannot be the spirit of the Saviour, but is the personal essence of the lapsed man.   There is therefore no reason to doubt that Paul distinguished, in the constitution of humanity, between a perishable organism which closed its history with the last breath, and an element susceptible of survival and ulterior development, and opposed them to each other as the flesh and the spirit of a man.   Else he would have been a Sadducee, and we should never have heard of his Pharisaic challenge to King Agrippa, "Why should it be thought a thing incredible with you, that God should raise the dead?"‡ for it is as a hope given to the fathers, and including them and their historic tribes, that it commends itself to him in the resurrection which he attests and proclaims.   To render individual resurrection possible, the soul's essential type, moulded in the past, must abide as the germ of the new life in the future. And hence, unless among embalming nations, the disposal of the corpse was not conceived to give complete account of the lodging of the dead; subterranean chambers were provided in

---

* Rom. viii. 10.   † 1 Cor. v. 5.   ‡ Acts xxvi. 8.

Sheol or *Hades*, as tarrying-places of faint survival in nocturnal existence, till possibly a burst of sunrise should invade the gloom, and wake the sleeping souls to a new morning, and weave around them vestments of etherial light and glorious form.   Can we fail to see the traces of this view of Death in the apostle's yearning, amid his many trials, for the immortal life ?   " We know that, if the earthly house of our tabernacle be dissolved, we have a building from God, a house not made with hands, eternal in the heavens.   For verily in this we groan, longing to be clothed upon with our habitation which is from heaven ; if so be that being clothed we shall not be found naked.   For indeed we that are in this tabernacle do groan, being burdened ; not for that we would be unclothed, but that we would be clothed upon, that what is mortal may be swallowed up of life."*   He could wish for release from an overburdened existence ; not indeed to be left among those whom Death will only *strip to the* $\psi v \chi \dot{\eta}$ and leave "naked ; " but to emerge into the new birth of the children of the resurrection, and put on the likeness of Christ's "glorious body."   The apostle evidently thinks that, when the cast-off clothes of the dissolving organism are gone, there is a psychical remainder, admitting of being either let alone as a bare unrealized possibility of ulterior life, or quickened by the breath of heavenly powers, and borne off into conditions of endless spiritual growth.

In this view, Death, as the penalty of Sin, would be confinement of the $\psi v \chi \dot{\eta}$ in perpetuity to Hades, bereft of organs, whether of activity or of feeling.   And redemption from it would be a repeal of the decree of perpetuity, and a provision for resuscitating the sleeper, if already there, or imparting to him, if still in the sunshine, such grace and spirit of holiness as may neutralize the power of sin, and mark him out as among those whom God will raise.   It is surprising how little the apostle's imagination dwelt upon the line of division, in the great assembly of the dead, between those that would be taken and those that would be left, in the day of the Parusia. He tells the relative order of procedure as between the disciples that had fallen asleep and the survivors upon earth ;

* 2 Cor. v. 1–4.

that " the dead in Christ " shall rise first, and that the living undergo their change ;* but he is absolutely silent respecting the countless multitude of generations gone, who are not included in either class, though we throw in, as we probably must, all the prior Israel among " the dead in Christ."   The omission is strange in the missionary of the Gentiles and the preacher of a universal gospel, who, when treating of his contemporaries, had no hesitation in admitting to " eternal life " Jew and Gentile alike " who sought for glory, honour and incorruption, by patient continuance in well-doing ; "† and by making the most of his statement that the Gentiles who " do by nature the things of the law " " show the work of the law written in their hearts," and pass judgment of approval and disapproval, we might infer, if we looked no further, that the righteous heathen of generations past had a place, along with the Israelites, in his " eternal life."   But when he insists that no possible conformity to Law, natural or revealed, can invest either Jew or Gentile with any availing righteousness, and that the indispensable condition of redemption is a Faith possible by anticipation in Abraham and his seed, impossible to the Pagan who had " exchanged the truth of God for a lie,"‡ it is clear that his ethnic hope cannot go behind his own generation, and refers only to the converts of his own and his fellow-labourers' toil.

The Pauline " Death " is summed up thus : To *all*, bodily dissolution ; to *the redeemed*, a waiting in Hades till re-investiture with life; to *the unredeemed*, permanent disappearance in Hades.

In this interpretation of " death " in its literal meaning as the ultimate effect of sin, there is nothing to prevent the inclusion within the connotation of the word, of other effects, simply moral, on the way to the last issue, or even the application of it to these alone.   The blunted affections, the drifting will, the slavery to passion, the proneness to hate, which mark the descent down the ways of sin, are treated as the signs and beginnings of death ; they are in fact that withering-up of the soul in its innermost essence, which will bring it to Hades as a virtual but lost possibility of life.

* 1 Thess. iv. 16, 17.   † Rom. ii. 7.   ‡ Ibid. i. 25.

There is therefore nothing overstrained in the phrases which denote these threatening antecedents of spiritual blight: "She that giveth herself to pleasure is *dead*, while she liveth :"* "The carnal mind is *death*, but the spiritual mind is life and peace :"† "He that loveth not abideth *in death* :"‡ and the prodigal's return is welcomed with the words, "This thy brother was *dead*, and is alive again; and was lost, and is found :"§ and the two meanings, the moral and the literal, are brought together in the saying, "Let the dead bury their dead."‖

Such was the "condemnation," the "curse," the alienation from God, the penalty of violated law, natural or spiritual, under which the sons of Adam lay. Redemption from it required the reversal of it all; riddance of Sin, and mortification of the flesh as its seat; creation of new life, and quickening of the Spirit, as its element; reconciliation with God, by reparation for the past; and reunion with him in relations of peace and righteousness. What are the resources which the apostle deems available for the solution of this problem ?

One thing is certain to him: Man, as he is, can answer no appeal for self-redemption; his present nature has long enough been tried and found wanting, and the experiment must come to an end. The evils of his case arise from his constitution, and will never cease till he is reconstituted in proportions truer to the Divine model which he dishonours and distorts. Now that he has lost his Paradise, it is as vain to call for repentance, as to cry, "Turn ye, turn ye," to the fallen angels flung from heaven. He can no more lift himself than the bird can fly without an atmosphere. Nothing short of a re-creation of him, casting off the dross of accumulated sins, and charging his nature with the tension of new affections, will be of any avail. The rescue, therefore, must come from superhuman power; the initiative must be with heaven; *there* must provision be sought for the fresh departure.

How Paul, after his "heavenly vision," found there this new departure for humanity in the "second Adam," reserved through all ages, and now installed as the Head of the

* 1 Tim. v. 6.   † Rom. viii. 6.   ‡ 1 John iii. 14.
§ Luke xv. 32.   ‖ Matt. viii. 22.

spiritual family of man, and how, by inward union with the Father and the Son, he and his converts " escaped from the bondage of corruption into the glorious liberty of the children of God,"* has been already shown.   It remains to be seen what specific part, in the apostle's view, the Cross, as distinguished from ordinary modes of death, bore in preparing for these effects of the resurrection.

In his persecuting days, Saul the Pharisee had intensely shared the popular aversion to the new Galilean sect, and regarded, not only with social scorn, but with religious horror, the claim, on behalf of one executed as a rebel and blasphemer, to be the Messiah of Israel.   If death in any form was the penalty and evidence of sin, who could deny that *such* a death raised the evidence to the highest pitch, and exhibited a transgressor offensive to the justice of man as well as God? Rightly did the people who knew the Law throw in the face of the Galilean agitators the word of God, " He that is hanged is accursed of God ; "† and was it not revolting to see this besotted rabble pointing to *such* an object as the Holy One of the Most High?   How could he curse his own Messiah? This was the "scandal of the cross " which Saul also wielded against the disciples from city to city, and which " made him exceeding mad against them."   As he dashes at one of the nests of these low fanatics, something suddenly arrests him : what has he seen, or heard, or thought, that prostrates, and calms and silences him?   The Crucified Blasphemer has come to him and looked on him with holy eyes, and appealed to him with a grace and pity so Divine, as to tell him not only that the dead was living and the accursed blessed, but that the " malefactor " was the " Son of God."   His favourite proof is not only confuted but reversed : instead of insisting, ' the malefactor and curse cannot be the Messiah of heaven,' he has now to say, ' the Messiah from heaven is no malefactor and curse ; on the contrary, it was not possible for him to be holden of death, and he was snatched from it by the Lord of life who conjoins immortality and holiness.'

As the curse of the cross thus lost all application to a victim declared individually sinless, another meaning was

* Rom. viii. 21.

† Deut. xxi. 23.

needed for it; and was found in the apostle's conception of Messiah as the Head of a new humanity which should set aside the failure of the Adamic race, and fulfil at last the Divine idea. Under this aspect the ἄνθρωπος ἐξ οὐρανοῦ at the world's end, like the ἄνθρωπος ἐκ γῆς at its beginning, became a representative impersonation of his collective race; so that what he did and what he suffered was no less theirs in being his, than the acts and treatment of a sovereign are responsibilities incurred and received by his nation. An unexpected light is thus thrown upon the Cross: the sufferer there belonged to both the earthly and the heavenly type of Man, and stood between the closing term of the one and the inception of the other; he had the susceptible affections and the mortality of the former, without its sin; he had the spirit of holiness and capacity for immortality of the latter. As intermediary between the ages, he has to clear the past, and to inaugurate the future. To wind up the sad tale of Adam's dynasty, he takes on himself the penal curse due to all but him: to open the new life of spiritual humanity, he passes through the agony of shame, into the hands of Him who raises the dead and had never failed to hear his prayer and answer his trust. And thus were enacted and unified in his person the penal expiation of past sins of his earthly kindred, and the emergence into undying union with the Father of spirits and the home of saints.

Under the influence of this mode of thought, the apostle undoubtedly regarded the death of Christ as incurred, not only *for our advantage*, but *in our stead*; what was legally due to the collectivity being concentrated upon the personal Head. "Him who knew no sin God made to be sin on our behalf; that we might become the righteousness of God in him."* In no other passage is the express reference here found to the sinlessness of Christ repeated, though implied perhaps in the title by which he is named. Elsewhere, it is not expressly the individual holiness of Jesus, but the impersonation of humanity in Messiah, in virtue of which his experience and his essence became ours; the many were included in the one; they died in his death, and lived anew in his resurrection, and

* 2 Cor. v. 21.

were taken up into his relations with the Eternal Father.
" We thus judge, that one died for all; therefore all died :
and he died for all, that they which live should no longer live
unto themselves, but unto him who for their sakes died and
rose again."[*]   The discharge which we could never work out
was effected for us : " While we were yet weak, in due season
Christ died for the ungodly ;" "God commendeth his own
love towards us in that, while we were yet sinners, Christ died
for us ;" and " if, while we were enemies, we were reconciled
to God through the death of his Son, much more, being reconciled, shall we be saved by his life."[†]

That the apostle did not shrink from this conception of
ricarious sin and retribution seems strange to us, schooled as
we are in individualism and its lonely responsibility.   The
transference of guilt *from one individual to another standing on
the same plane* involves a contradiction of the first principle of
morals.   This, however, which alone is próper vicariousness,
is not exactly what was present to the apostle's thought ; nor
is it conceivable that he would have deemed it possible for
Peter to take on himself the guilt of Judas, or for John to
relieve Peter of his three denials.   To him the Crucified, as
revealed in his resurrection, was no mere individual sample of
the sons of men, related to those whom he gathered as James,
and Andrew, and Philip to one another ; but, as the realizer
of God's idea for this type of being, he was the essence of
humanity itself, and could speak and act and suffer for it all ;
as vice versâ all its members could find themselves in him.
This εἶδος of Man it is, impersonated and dramatized, that the
apostle sets up as redeemer of the individual ; and if he treats
the wounds of the whole genus as equivalent to those of each
member, and the glory of the whole as extending to each, he
adopts a mode of thought familiar in ancient times, and not
consciously involving the moral paradox of vicarious character.

Wherever indeed the spirit of *clan* exists in anything like
the intensity with which it still keeps possession of Israel, the
intercommunity of responsibility naturally leads to something
verging on the principle of moral substitution and justice by
average.   It does not shock the conscience of such a com-

<hr>

[*] 2 Cor. v. 14, 15.   [†] Rom. v. 6, 8, 10.

munity, that " the sins of the fathers should be visited upon the children to the third and fourth generation ;" or that the righteousness of a small minority should ward off the retribution impending over its guilty multitude.   And if, by a wrong incidence of suffering, it should come to pass that precisely the most faithful and saintly incurred the stripes and scorn which they, of all men, were furthest from deserving, it seemed incredible to the pious observer that so much merit should be wasted and misspent ; and he persuaded himself that it would avail, as the righteous themselves would wish, for the erring kindred or country to which they belonged, and lighten the too heavy debt of their blinded persecutors.   The " servant of the Lord " (be he Israel as a people, outcast among the misguided nations, or some true prophet of their own who cannot get believed) may well be " a man of sorrows and acquainted with grief, despised and rejected of men," " taken away by oppressor's judgment " and "led to the slaughter ;" and the beholders may " esteem him stricken, smitten of God and afflicted ;" but though he " is numbered with the transgressors," he is " wounded for *our* transgressions, bruised for *our* iniquities ; the chastisement of our peace was upon him, and with his stripes we are healed."* Interpret as we may the intended application of this touching and sublime picture, it shows that, in the author's mind, the Providential distribution of suffering was freed from the limits of hard juridical rules, and thrown open to the bold antinomianism and spiritual mysticism of the Apostle of the Gentiles.

The expiatory clearance of the Adamic past was a transaction wholly mediatorial, effected, so to speak, behind men's backs, or while they slept.   The agents in it were God and Christ, by whose concurrent purpose it was brought about. Though the apostle freely attributes it to either, he must have regarded the initiative as with the Father, as the creator of the preexistent spiritual Adam, and the preordainer of the whole world-scheme through its series of ages ; ages, that first reveal his idea only in its frustration, and then break into the glorious sequel which is to fulfil it : "according to the eternal purpose which he purposed in Christ Jesus our Lord."† The

* Isaiah liii.   † Eph. iii. 11.

originating will is accordingly directly attributed to God, who, " sending his own Son in the likeness of sinful flesh, and for sin, condemned sin in the flesh, that the ordinance of the law might be fulfilled in us who walk not after the flesh, but after the spirit."[*]   " When the fulness of time was come, God sent forth his Son, born of a woman, born under the law, that we might receive the adoption of sons."[†]   On the other hand, the spontaneous movement of love is referred also to Christ; for instance, " Walk in love, even as Christ also loved you, and gave himself up for us, an offering and sacrifice to God."[‡] " Let the same mind be in you, which was also in Christ Jesus; who, being in the form of God, counted it not a prize to be on an equality with God, but emptied himself, taking the form of a servant, being made in the likeness of men; and being found in fashion as a man, he humbled himself, becoming obedient unto death, yea, the death of the cross."[§]   These two classes of passages find their connecting link in the exclamation, " If God be for us, who is against us?   He that spared not his own Son, but delivered him up for us all, how shall he not also with him freely give us all things?"[‖]   It is a joint initiative for the same tender mercy in two concurrent wills.   The Son volunteers to take on himself the death due, by retributory law, to his unhappy race; the Father consents to let so divine an act of self-sacrificing love stand as an expiation and be tantamount to an oblivion of the past, and become the occasion of inaugurating the crowning future.

Be it, however, that in the death on Calvary the guilt of humanity dies; this is but the negative half of the needed redemption.   An amnesty for Sin leaves but a blank result; tears out the blotted page behind, but secures no cleaner record for the next.   The acquitted are not yet the righteous and blessed; and it remains to be seen how the exchange of places between the Saviour and the saved is to be completed. He has borne our penalty; how are we to be identified with his righteousness?   The Pauline answer is simple and direct: the Cross expiated the past; the Resurrection consecrates the future: in the one is the death of Sin; in the other, the birth

---

[*] Rom. viii. 3, 4.   [†] Gal. iv. 4, 5.   [‡] Eph. v. 2.

[§] Phil. ii. 5–8.   [‖] Rom. viii. 31, 32.

of righteousness. If, for us, the former alone had been vouchsafed,—if the Crucified had never reappeared, the wiping-out of penalties incurred would have been but a futile grace, unknown to its receiver: the fleshy tyranny would have resumed its course, and no fresh power have rushed in to break the bondage. Instead of this relapse, there came the glorious revelation of the martyred witness of God as his beloved Son in heaven; which at once gave the key to the mysterious tragedy of Golgotha, and brought down to earth the power of his life above. Did not Paul know himself reborn, the very hour when " it pleased God to reveal his Son in him ? " A Divine hand laid hold on him and set him free. " Like as Christ was raised from the dead through the glory of the Father, so we also are to walk in newness of life."[*] " If the spirit of Him that raised up Jesus from the dead dwell in you, He that raised up Jesus Christ from the dead will quicken even your mortal bodies through His spirit that dwelleth in you."[†] " Henceforth the Spirit itself beareth witness with our spirit, that we are children of God; and if children, then heirs; heirs of God, and joint-heirs with Christ; if so be that we suffer with him, that we may be also glorified together."[‡] Here, therefore, is the moment,—in this relation to the heavenly Christ,—in which the supernatural initiative, after removing the dead works of the past, enters on its creative function, of endowing the disciple's soul with a positive righteousness, and carries forward the redemption from reconciliation ($\kappa\alpha\tau\alpha\lambda\lambda\alpha\gamma\acute{\eta}$) to justification ($\delta\iota\kappa\alpha\acute{\iota}\omega\sigma\iota\varsigma$): and hence the preferential stress which the apostle, in spite of his glorying in the cross, lays on the resurrection of Christ. " It is God that justifieth; who is he that condemneth ? It is Christ that died, *yea rather* that was raised from the dead, who is at the right hand of God, who also maketh intercession for us."[§] Between the divine life of Christ in heaven and the inward experience of the disciples on earth the apostle conceived an invisible communion constantly to exist; and to this, as to an effluence from the very sanctuary of holiness, he referred all the intense affections of devotion, trust, and self-surrender, which entered into the new Christian type of

* Rom. vi. 4.   † Ibid. viii. 11.   ‡ Ibid. 16, 17.   § Ibid. 33, 34.

character. The Holy Spirit, in the Johannine sense, was something *sent* from the Father ; in the Pauline sense, it was the personal spirit of the Father and the Son, mingling with the life, and quickening the spiritual energies of their true servants; so that what is called the "mystic" language of the apostle, of "living in Christ,"* and "Christ living in him," of "Christ being formed in "† his disciples, is hardly even figurative to him, but expresses *a fact* of experience, as understood by himself. Nor do I know whether, in case of a profound and commanding love for a venerated being, it is less true to deem him the source of that awakening enthusiasm, than to take it to one's self. The Positivist takes it for the imagination of a mortal dead: the apostle, for the living communion of an immortal.

Thus far, all the agency in the process of redemption has been Divine and mediatorial, carried out in concert by God and Christ. But now that the crowning contact with the persons to be redeemed is reached, there is something to be asked of them : the ruin from which they are to be saved is no external lot whence they can be snatched, asleep or awake, but the transformation of a nature astir and quick in movements of response; and so the Spirit that visits them with its appeal brings its grace on one condition, viz., an answering *Faith*, a loving acceptance of the new vision of higher life for what it claims to be, and a free self-abandonment to it, whithersoever it may lead. Possessed by this pure trust, the disciple will be spontaneously drawn into likeness to the object of his love ; the lower self, shrouded in shame, will die within him ; and he will be invested with the righteousness of Christ. Thus will he, in Pauline phrase, "put on the Lord Jesus Christ," or "put on the new man, which after God hath been created in righteousness and true holiness ;"‡ "new" because not elaborated by his own will ; "after God," because inspired through the Divine mediation of a heavenly humanity. Advancing to an expression still more characteristic of his thought as transcending the ethical plane of religion, the apostle calls the true Christian's spiritual state " the righteous-

* Gal. ii. 20.   † Ibid. iv. 19.
‡ Rom. xiii. 14 ; Gal. iii. 27 ; Eph. iv. 24.

ness of God" (δικαιοσύνη τοῦ Θεοῦ),* as opposed to the agent's own righteousness (ἰδία); regarding it as nothing *earned* by personal volition, but as a *present* supernaturally made by the Source of all grace. It is a participation in "the spirit of Christ," in the sense, not of a voluntary reflection of the character of Jesus, but of a divinely wrought real change of the human nature into homogeneity with Christ's heavenly essence. Without some beginning of this personal self-identification with Christ, a man can be "none of his";† with it he has in his heart "the earnest of the spirit, that he is sealed of God,"‡ and the consciousness that already, as the first-fruits of its 'indwelling in him,' it refines and 'quickens even his mortal body,'§ "while waiting for the adoption," viz., the complete "redemption of the body."‖

The change, therefore, for the completion of which the faithful sighed and waited, was to be but the culmination of a new life,—of deliverance from the thraldom of Sense, and free movement in the power of the Spirit,—not wholly strange to their present experience. By this sign they knew it to be not too soon for them to watch for "the revelation of the Lord Jesus Christ,"¶ and the full entrance on "the glorious liberty of the children of God."** "The time is short,"†† and the powers of heaven are mustering to descend and claim the earth for the kingdom of God. We are thus brought to the eschatology of the apostle, which is in truth only the last scene in his drama of redemption. But it has passed into such close connection with the development in Christendom of beliefs respecting the state of the dead and the future life, that it will be most conveniently noticed in a chapter devoted to that subject.

Every attentive reader must have observed the almost total absence of any personal Satan from the systematic doctrine of the apostle Paul. So few and slight are the references to him in his authentic epistles, that no stress can be laid on them as implying more than transient personification convenient for popular indication of evils of which he had

---

* Rom. x. 3, l. 17, iii. 22; 2 Cor. v. 21.   † Rom. viii. 9.
‡ 2 Cor. i. 22.   § Rom. viii. 11.   ‖ Ibid. 23.
¶ 1 Cor. i. 7.   ** Rom. viii. 21.   †† 1 Cor. vii. 29.

occasion to speak. Neither in his Christology, nor in his theory of redemption, is the Devil brought upon the scene to play any part. The omission is the more striking, from his realistic treatment of Sin and Death, almost as if they were separate agents instead of human acts and phenomena, while yet he stops short of the impersonation which they seem to need. This contrast with the Judaic Messianic mythology of the synoptists and the Apocalypse was not long permitted to remain clear: the ecclesiastics of the next century dramatized the principles of the Pauline scheme by placing a fourth actor on the scene, viz. the Devil,—with alleged rights and wrongs in regard to the Father, the Son, and Man ; and the doctrine was presented thus. The Devil, as Prince of the realm of evil and Death, had acquired, by the transgression of Adam, and the sinfulness of his children, a legal right to have the souls of men for his own world : this surrender into his power was their inevitable curse, witnessed by the deciduous lives of the generations as they pass. But his right was contingent on the sinfulness of humanity ; and the moment he laid his hand upon the sinless Christ, and seized him for the shades below, he overstepped his prerogative, and forfeited his right by usurpation. Two things therefore ensued : having clutched an immortal victim, he could not hold him from passing into heaven, and touching the earth by resurrection on the way ; and having sacrilegiously robbed the treasure-house of divine life, he was condemned to make reparation, by signing a release for the whole brotherhood of Christ. The mythology of redemption here assumed its most consistent and intelligible shape. The subsequent change which in the medieval period removed the person of Satan, putting in his place the " Justice of God," and resolving the whole transaction into a juggle between conflicting attributes of the infinite Perfection, did but replace a childish forensic fiction by a monstrous moral enormity. Yet this, alas ! it is, which mingles its fierce lights of expiation and its massive shadows of despair with the whole theology of Christendom.

The organism of doctrine which the Pauline scheme of redemption constructs around the personal history of Jesus of Nazareth may not be without its perishable elements : but is

shown, by its wide and durable influence, to be the product
of large speculative thought and deep spiritual insight. So
far as it occasioned a breach with the Jerusalem apostles, and
compelled a division of the field of missionary labour, it was
because it constituted a rebellion against all national narrowness and ethical legalism, and proclaimed the Grace of God
on terms of trust and love alone. The facts on which the
apostle lays the utmost stress,—the natural law as binding
on the conscience, the universality of Sin, the misery of
baffled aspiration ; and the positions which he claims to make
good, that God is not defeated by the inefficacy of his laws
and the corruption of mankind, but will turn them to account
in the issues of transcendent good, and that there is an *ideal
humanity* reserved in heaven and operative in kindred souls
on earth,—are among the most profoundly significant bases
and noblest conclusions of religious life and philosophy. If
in the dialectic which deals with them we cannot always find
consistency or adequacy of reasoning, this is in great measure
due to his starting from doubtful postulates dictated to him
by the authority of scripture or of Pharisaic dogma ; or to
the intellectual self-deceptions inseparable from admitting the
play of allegory into the serious business of reasoning. Two
or three examples of difficulties which I find insurmountable
will illustrate what I mean ; and the first shall be one in
which I may well be wrong; as the Apostle is apparently
deemed clear and coherent by so admirable a critic as M.
Menegoz.

1. In his treatment of Sin, the apostle assumes at the outset the moral liberty of man in both its factors, the knowledge
of the right and wrong, and the power of practical choice
between them. Not only does he address to the Christians
warnings and exhortations and reproaches which would be
unmeaning, were there no alternative; but of the natural
man among the Gentiles he speaks as " inexcusable," and as
the object of Divine " wrath and indignation," if he does not
live up to what he inwardly knows to be his duty; or as
praiseworthy if he does, and approved of God. He recognizes
gradations of guilt, according to the differing opportunities of
the Greek or Jewish conscience. He argues throughout on the

principle of retribution as fundamental in the government of God, and regards Death as the penalty of Sin. And his whole doctrine of redemption is the working out of a thesis on the *Justice* of God.

Yet, side by side with these ethical positions stands the assumption of a physiological Necessity, in the fleshly constitution of Man, incapacitating him for resistance to the solicitations of evil, and so enslaving him to the power which he hates, that he is absolutely "*sold under Sin.*" And the very purpose to which he puts this fearful representation is, to prove the hopeless condition of man, unless rescued, and remade by intervention of supernatural agency. I am unable to reconcile these two positions.

2. The apostle, in his statement that "Him that knew no sin God made to be sin for us, that we might be made the righteousness of God in him," means that, through the Cross and Resurrection, there is a change of places between us and Christ; he taking on him our penalty, and we becoming invested with his righteousness. Apart from all moral difficulties, this conception of substitution, viewed merely on its dogmatic side, appears to be illusory. What is the penalty due to human sinners? Death. And what does that mean for us? *Hades for ever:* whereas the death of Christ meant for him *Hades for a day and a half.* On the other hand, *his righteousness* was immaculate conformity to the Divine Will through his entire existence; whereas what is imparted to his disciple is (after expiation of the guilty past) *a birth into the possibility of a stainless future.* In order to pay our penalty, he ought not to have risen from the dead. In order to have his righteousness, we ought to be brought up to the present through as pure a past. It is but a fictitious transference, where the substitute arrives infinitely in defect or in excess of that which it replaces.

3. The apostle's Theodicy is made up, in regard to the past history of the world, of two propositions, which greatly embarrass one another, viz. (1.) that all is divinely foreordained: (2.) that all is merely failure. This appears at first sight a union of Providence and pessimism, without the possibility of escape by throwing the blame on the abused freedom of the

human will.   The Creator, in making man of flesh, doomed him to sin and death; and in giving the Law from Sinai, occasioned "all manner of coveting," and by enjoining on man an impossible condition of life, "*slew*" him.   Boldly facing the consequences of this view, the apostle, as we have seen, declares that the Law was instituted for the express purpose of multiplying transgressions, attended by a full consciousness that "sin was exceeding sinful;" and then perhaps the offenders, reduced to the last despair, would renounce their self-dependence and fling themselves on the grace of God, offering to accept them for their faith instead of for their works.   Since the apostle himself describes the "faithful Abraham" as already so accepted, one does not see the need of waiting till the world's end for turning the example into the rule.   Meanwhile, the generations of men are "subjected to vanity," entrapped in miserable self-deception, "not of their own will, but by reason of him who hath subjected the same in hope,"—of what?   "Of being delivered from" their "bondage of corruption into the glorious liberty of the children of God."   It is difficult to give a sacred aspect to this mere doing and undoing.   It may be fitting work for a holy day, "if an ox or an ass should have fallen into a pit, to draw it out again;" but not, surely, to pitch it in, in order to draw it out.   And how can we deny that to constitute a race, to institute a law, to order and evolve a world's history, with provisions for disappointing the highest ends of their nature and aspirations, is to create and govern on false pretences, and to expend millenniums of cruel illusion, as a prelude to the brief surprise which shall take away the veil from the face of one generation, and save a remnant at last?

These and other minor examples of questionable speculative construction arise, however, in the attempt, inevitable for the Christian missionary, to adjust the original matter of his divine message to the preconceptions occupying his hearers' minds from their antecedent bases of belief; and it is no wonder that in course of time some rents have appeared from sewing the new piece into the old garment.

But quit the apostle's dialectic with Jew and Greek, and seize the central characteristic of his thought and life: look

at it alone, and find its meaning and contents, and you will
leave it to Jew and Greek to quarrel with him over his logical
flaws.   The one thing which he knew, and on which he took
his stand, was the "justification through faith : " that is,
harmony with God through trust and love towards him and
all that is like him : for nothing less than this does the *Faith*
of Paul imply.   As opposed to "*works*" of the will, it is
rightness of *heart*, the true direction of the affections towards
the objects, and in the relative strength, of which God approves.
Not that it dispenses with the practical activities of duty ;
but, seeing that these may be the products of possibly mistaken rules, or the monotonous beat of habits in their mill,
it shifts the accent of spiritual value from the outward to the
inward side of the moral life, and insists that, to be at one
with the Searcher of hearts, the secret spring of what we will
or aspire to do must be that which He loves to see.   The
apostle's formula unconsciously alights upon the very essence
of the teaching, which he never heard, upon the Mount and in
the villages of Galilee, but which throughout, from the beatitudes to Simon's Supper in Bethany, never ceased to strip
away the external semblances of sanctity, and startled self-
deceivers and hypocrites alike, by laying bare the inwardness
and directness of every soul's relation to God.   And is it not
true that the power of moral achievement, which is missed
by the casuistical intellect, flows into self-forgetful affection
directed upon right objects? that under the enthusiasm of
compassion, of love, of reverence, we no longer feel our own
weight, or reckon with our toil, but pass at a bound over
spaces of difficulty which the uninspired will can never face?
And if the enthusiasm does not stop short of the crown of all
its power,—the filial union with the "Father who seeth in
secret,"—even baffled zeal and failing hopes will be guarded
from despair by the one love that cannot be disappointed and
can never die ; we shall cast our own short-comings upon the
infinite Pity of God, and in the simplest trust find the most
perfect rest.

§ 3. *The Work of the Incarnate Logos.*

The impulse which the religion of Jesus gave to the world may be measured by the widening circles of theory thrown out to embrace and explain it. As each was proved inadequate in turn, it was replaced by a more comprehensive, which left the old limits to fall away, and stretched itself to the compass of a larger phenomenon. No amount of failure in the doctrinal schemes of its missionaries, or of disappointment in their prophecies, arrested its progress or interfered with its spiritual power. It was preached from Jerusalem as the tidings of Messiah's nomination and the approach and near fulfilment of Jewish hopes: Messiah came not back from heaven, and those who had promised his arrival died without the sight: yet his name was still the symbol of a spreading union which baffled expectations could not dissolve. It was proclaimed as the harbinger of a theocratic millennium, with the temple for its citadel, and the overthrow of Rome for its inaugural triumph ; * the temple was levelled to the ground, the imperial eagles sought their prey over wider fields, and still no trumpet sounded, no phials were poured out, no seal was broken : yet the seven churches which had watched in vain, far from breaking up in despair, rather became seventy times seven, and at every persecution were enriched by the tombs of new martyrs. From Tarsus, the religion was announced, regardless of national limits, as a reconstitution of humanity itself, a supernatural infusion of a heavenly element, a transference of power from the flesh to the spirit, assimilating the true disciple to higher natures, and preparing him for the society of the descending Son of God : the men and women in the Christian assemblies did not realize this ideal: they were not visibly of other type than that which prevailed around them ; with infirmities of body and soul against which the pity and the discipline of the Church had to provide ; and no sign appeared of such a reciprocation of life between earth and heaven as betokened a new creation : yet, though Paul was gone, and his word was not fulfilled, the Gentile element continued to

---

* Rev. xviii. 16-20, xi. 1-3. Cf. xx. 6, xxi. 22.

pour in, and felt a growing persuasion in his voice a generation after it had ceased. And now the fourth evangelist,
writing, it is probable, not long before the middle of the second
century, looks round upon a scene so large, and animated by
religious characteristics so deeply marked, that no prior doctrine covers the new life which he beholds: no Jewish influence, though in its most consummate form, no agency simply
human, however pure and strong, is adequate to the spiritual
revolution: the partition has given way between man and
God: the Infinite no longer dwells apart and leaves the world
alone, but stoops to finite spirits, and makes one communion
there and here. For the new and higher agency which was at
work upon the private heart and on society, first the Hebrew
prophet was enough: then, as its significance expanded, it
needed a divine man: and at the end of a century, it had
assumed a magnitude and depth which seemed due to nothing
short of an incarnation of God, and a descent upon the earth
of a Divine life. It is easy to dismiss this progression of
doctrine with the contemptuous remark, that, as time passed
on and the true history passed out of sight, the Christian
teachers advanced their pretensions to a bolder distance, and
bid higher for the veneration of mankind. But they would
have defeated their own zeal, had they made any monstrous
over-provision for the facts which they professed to explain:
their grand causes, if applied to insignificant results, would
simply have provoked the rebuke, " Talk no more so exceeding
proudly." There must have been some sort of proportion
between the scale and character of the religion, and the account
which, from time to time, they rendered of it. And as the
latest theology of the New Testament is also the highest, it is
a fair inference that Christianity, whatever doubtful elements
it had taken up, had become clearer and deeper as it flowed,
and swept over human affections with a purifying and fertilizing power, transcending the limits of prior experience and
the resources of existing theory. We are apt to wonder how
it can be that a higher worship can apparently emerge from
conditions of erroneous thought, and Christianity as a whole
be divine, though every successive phase of it be human. And
the perplexity will never cease till we discover that all religion

is deeper than any theology, and we may reverence aright whilst we think amiss.   The spirit of God frequents the regions of the soul below the strata of intellect and speech; and there nourishes, in darkness and in silence, an inner love and trust, which, being the very visual organ through which the spirit sees, cannot look at itself to tell what it is like.   Not only is it possible for men to be possessed by a religion quite other than their theology, and even, when the deeps of their nature are broken up by sorrow, to find there the very faith which they had disputed ; but the greater and more original the inspiration is, the more certainly inadequate will be the forms of conception and language through which it struggles towards expression.   The more we appreciate Christianity as the sublimest of God's revelations to the human conscience, the less shall we be satisfied with any of the schemes of theology, in or out of Scripture, which undertake to define what it is.

The work of Christ, as represented in the fourth Gospel, differs, both in measure and in kind, from the salvation contemplated by either the Twelve or Paul.   The evangelist's picture of the habitable world and of the ills in it which were accessible to redress, was by no means identical with theirs. To them, the universe was a three-chambered structure, consisting of the Heaven where angels and blessed spirits dwelt with the Eternal God: of the Earth, the abode of Adam's race, with the creatures submitted to their sway: and of the Underworld, where Satan had his home, and held the souls of the dead in prison, or sent them forth as demons on his errands of mischief among mankind.   However variously imaged might be this kingdom of the shades, it was plainly regarded as not cut off from communication with the fields beneath the sun ; for the rich man in the parable would fain send his five brethren a message thence by Lazarus, lest they also suffer his " evil things : " * and the early Christians believed that the crucified, on being "quickened in the Spirit," " went and preached to the spirits in prison " ere he ascended into Heaven.†   The fourth evangelist knows nothing of such a Hades, as the realm of the departed in whose waiting-

* Luke xvi. 27–29.

† 1 Peter iii. 19. See Apostles' creed, " He descended into Hell." (Hades.)

halls the prisoners can be converted, or whence they can be rescued. Death, with this evangelist, is no deeper than *the grave;* where Lazarus "*slept*," where Jesus himself lay, whence all who hear the voice of the Life-giver will simply *come forth*, without any complication with an arrival of their souls from the chambers below. Connected probably with this shutting up of the underworld is the total absence of demoniacal possession from this gospel; for the evil spirits were subjects of the Satanic realm, and would naturally pass away when their proper home was gone, and there was no place whence they could make their incursions on the bodies and the souls of men. Not that Satan himself was thus got rid of; he lost a subterranean only to gain an hypæthral realm. Of the two regions now composing the simplified universe, the Heaven above unchangeably remained the abode of the Father and the Son and all immortals; but the earth below, the dwelling-place of men, fell, in spite of prophetic calls and transient visits of Divine light, under the dominion of "the Power of darkness," "the Prince of this world." How it could be that a God-created world, constituted by the eternal Word, "without whom there was nothing made that had been made," should have lapsed into a Devil's territory, the evangelist does not explain; any more than Paul explains the universality of sin under the rule of omnipotent Righteousness; or than Marcion explains the operations of a "malignant" Demiurge, author of Nature and giver of the Jewish law, under the supremacy of "the Good God," who revealed himself in Jesus Christ. All these are but instances of the inevitable but imperfect dualism forced upon human thought by the contrasts of experience. A new religion gives birth to an entrancing affection, and, going apart with its own enthusiasm, sees all else at variance with it, and needing either conversion or rejection. It cannot live without its outcasts: the Israelite has his Gentiles: the apostle Paul his "false brethren," that "make the cross of Christ of none effect," through their "dead works:" and now the mysterious evangelist who finds in union with Christ the whole spiritual distance annihilated between the life of man and God, looks forth upon a world made up of dissolute Paganism and embittered Judaism as in the mass delivered over to the power of evil. Between the low passions that reign there, of greed and lust, of ambition and envy, and the aspirations and trust, the humility and love that breathe through the prayers and sweeten the inner life of a true Christian community, the contrast presents itself to him as little less than infinite; so that only now does the genuine history of humanity open, with the planting of a sacred colony in the midst of the dark continent of earthly sin and shame. Out of such experience he assumes as fact which needs no theory that worldly things are ungodly, that while Heaven is the abode of all perfection, whatever is at variance with the Divine nature, —falsehood, hatred, license, sloth and death,—the vile equipment of "the Prince of this world,"—are in the ascendant here below. It is a scene so hopelessly alien to the whole sphere of Christ's mission, that he disowns it as foreign to him, and is silent at its approach: "I will no more speak much with you; for the Prince of this world cometh, and hath nothing in me:" * "I pray not for the world, but for them whom Thou hast given me, for they are thine." †

If the world be thus given over to the dominion of a supernatural Principle of evil, it would seem that the mere human nature must be overmatched, and an irresistible necessity of sin be laid upon it; and we should be brought, only by another path, to the Pauline doctrine of the utter helplessness of man for all righteousness, and the absolute need, if he is to be snatched from ruin, of investing him with an extraneous righteousness. And language is used in the Gospel which, taken by itself, would undeniably demand such an interpretation. When it is said of his hearers at Jerusalem, "For this cause they *could not believe*," because Isaiah had announced the supernatural blinding of their eyes and hardening of their hearts :‡ when Jesus himself utters the reproach, "Why do you not apprehend what I say? because you cannot hear my word" (i.e., it does not speak to such as you), for it is 'what I have heard of God,' and "you are not of God, but of your father the Devil:" § and when he repeats the expression, "Ye believe not, because ye are not of my sheep:"‖

<hr>

* John xiv. 30.   † Ibid. xvii. 9.   ‡ xii. 39.
§ viii. 43, 47, 44.   ‖ x. 26.

men are described as victims of a fatality which mingles a tone
of cruelty with these upbraidings. So little conscious, however, is the evangelist of abolishing culpability by these representations, that he means to intensify it ; like others who play
fast and loose with diabolic powers, he invokes them to make
guilt portentous, while they play him false by reducing it to
nought. He himself, indeed, lays down elsewhere the principle that the darkness of invincible ignorance respecting true
religion involves no guilt ; and he justifies his condemnation of
his hearers on the ground that they had both competency and
opportunity of appreciating the Divine message with which he
was charged : "If I had not come and spoken to them, they
had not had sin ; but now they have no excuse for their sin :"*
" If ye were blind, ye would have no sin ; but now ye say,
We see ; therefore your sin remaineth."† When he openly
condemns their rejection of him, it is because he sees all its
hollowness and the evil-mindedness of its source : "If I say
truth, why do ye not believe me?" it is "*because* I say the
truth that ye believe me not :"‡ "ye both know me, and
whence I am ; and I am not come of myself, but he that sent
me is true, whom ye know not." § They know not what
spirit they are of : their unbelief is wilful estrangement from
unwelcome truth, a preference for flattering lies, an evasion of
high demands and holy obligations, a setting up of self and flesh
against God, a slavery of habit to sin, till the spiritual night
which hides their shame from themselves is more acceptable
than the day which shows it. This picture is drawn, not of
Heathendom alone, but in even stronger lines of Judaism too :
" Ye are of your father, the Devil, and the lusts of your
father it is your will to do." No truth, no faith, no love,
no purity finds shelter in a world which has given itself up
to the Prince of evil and father of lies. If there is an intensity
of moral passion in the evangelist's appreciation of the state
of mankind, which goes beyond even the apostle Paul's fearful
description in the opening chapter of his Epistle to the
Romans, it is because he sees in the corruption more of
guilt and less of incapacity : and it is, perhaps, but another
aspect of the same characteristic that Satan appears in this

* John xv. 22.   † ix. 41.   ‡ viii. 46, 45.   § vii. 28.

gospel stripped of every attribute of mere physical power, as tormentor of the bodies of men, and keeper of the realms of death ; deprived, moreover, of any retinue of dependent spirits to do his errands, and with the space cleared all around that he may stand alone and centred in himself, without admixture ; all that is odious in itself, ruinous to man, and opposite to God.

Into this alienated world descends the Divine creative Logos to recover it from the usurping ill. He assumes the human personality; presents himself to the nation whose prophets have foreseen his day ; bears witness, by a presence and by works truly unique, to his real character; ascends the cross ; emerges from the sepulchre; returns to heaven ; but never again dissolves the spiritual communion into which he has introduced this sphere. If we ask, wherein consists the redeeming efficacy of this visit, the answer takes us at once to the essential and pervading idea of this gospel. It is simply as the *Light of the World*, the source of truth, the focus whence all purity and beauty radiate, the spring of healing, life and love, that he operates on the darkness around, draws to him the spirits that are pining for a brightness they cannot reach, and repels from him those who are contented with their blindness. Not only does the evangelist emphasize this transforming personal influence, " To as many as received him he gave power to become sons of God ; " " of his fulness we have all received, and grace for grace ; "* but he makes it a theme in the discourses of Christ himself ; " as long as I am in the world, I am the light of the world," " I am the light of the world : he that followeth me shall not walk in darkness, but have the light of life ; "† " I am the living bread which came down out of heaven : if any one eat of this bread, he shall live for ever."‡ And it is especially as the witness of divine *Truth*, fresh from heaven, that he carries this illuminating power : " for this end am I come into the world, that I should bear witness unto the truth : "§ " ye seek to kill me, a man that hath told you the truth, which I heard from God."‖ It is to the mere power of his presence,

* John I. 12, 16.   † ix. 5, viii. 12.   ‡ vi. 51.
§ xviii. 37.   ‖ viii. 40.

—the presence of the infinitely Pure,—that all the efficacy is assigned; and just as the rich and healthful elements of nature come at his call, the wine to the feast, vision to the blind, and life to the dead, so does the secret good of every soul spring forth to meet him, and the conscious ill retire abashed. Nathaniel finds that his guileless piety is known: the woman at the well, that her compunctions speak too true: Nicodemus, that he cannot secretly bargain with the diviner life, but must be born into it, and be and do what it may bring. The Good Shepherd has but to appear and call, and his sheep know his voice and gather together and follow him. A native sympathy of like with like, of aspiring and dependent goodness with the perfect and absolute, sifts the mixed multitude of men, and brings around him the true sons of God. There is an effluence of sanctity from his person, of truth from his words, of cleansing conviction from his look, which reaches every susceptible conscience, and puts every guilty thought to flight. The officers sent for his arrest dare not lay hands on him, and come back with the report, "Never man spake like this man."* The crafty accusers who dragged the adulteress before him to ensnare him in his speech were glad to shrink away from his searching word and silent look.† The chief priest's servants hurried by Judas through the garden to seize him, are met by his advance, and no sooner see his figure in the flash of their lanterns and hear his "I am he," than they "recoil and fall upon the ground."‡ In virtue of this awe-inspiring power of sanctity which the wicked hate and shun, and good hearts love and seek, his very presence begins already the judgment of this world, and marks off by its effect the children of darkness from the children of light; the former turning from him in natural antipathy and going their own way into deeper blindness and more hopeless death; the latter drawn to him by the natural affinity through which "he that doeth the truth cometh" to the absolutely true.§ In this sense it is that Jesus is made to say, "For judgment came I into this world, that they which see not may see, and they which see may be made blind " :‖ and "the Father

---

* John vii. 45, 46.   † viii. 1-11.   ‡ xviii. 6.
§ iii. 21.   ‖ ix. 39.

judgeth no man, but hath committed all judgment to the Son."* The opposite statements, "I judge no man,"† and "if any man hear my sayings and keep them not, I judge him not; for I came not to judge the world, but to save the world,"‡ are no contradiction of the former, for they only disclaim any formal judicial act and verdict on the part of Christ, and affirm that each hearer, in taking his own line, of belief or aversion, shows what he is and pronounces sentence on himself. The presence of the incarnate Word acts as a touchstone on mankind. Everything centres in that one divine figure; whose absence in the "bosom of the Father" had left men under spiritual eclipse; whose presence in our humanity brought the sunshine of an everlasting day. Those in whom he wakes up the "power to become sons of God " have more than the promise, have already the foretaste and beginning of eternal life; the springs of which are consciously renewed every time the broken bread and the communion cup freshen in their hearts the "grace and truth" he brought from heaven. If the statement "I give unto them eternal life" is often and unconditionally repeated in this gospel, it is because, in the evangelist's view, the work of Christ was one not of expiation or redemption, not of repentance and forgiveness, but of *direct sanctification;* and its efficacy was wholly in the manifestation, by the Son of God, of human and Divine perfection, harmonizing earth and heaven. There is no obstacle to the immediate extension of the holiness of Christ, as by the reflection of soul upon soul, to his disciples. "Sanctify them in the truth; thy word is truth. As thou didst send me into the world, even so sent I them into the world; and for their sakes I sanctify myself, that they themselves also may be sanctified in truth."§ Two or three expressions in which the author seems to swerve from this characteristic of his theology will be noticed hereafter. It is sufficient for the present to state the pervading idea of his gospel: in conformity with which, the supreme interest of the drama, the crisis of its saving action, is thrown upon the ministry and human life of Christ; and is thus in strong contrast with the Pauline theology, in which the biography

* John v. 22.   † viii. 15.   ‡ xii. 47.   § xvii. 17-19.

of Jesus is wholly subordinate, and the real Divine economy
opens with Calvary, and concentrates all its light upon the cross.

This does not mean that, in the fourth gospel, the death of
Christ is left without distinct importance for his work. But
the stress laid upon it does not detach it from his historic
life, and charge it with new and magical functions of expiation; but treats it as homogeneous in effect with that life,
and continuing its presence and its power in transcendental
form and on a vaster scale. The incarnation did not begin
that Divine agency, and the crucifixion does not close it, or
anyhow change it except in the deep and intense hold it
must thenceforth have on the human consciousness. The
sacred personality had but passed from earth to heaven, and
would breathe thence the same truth and love as at the well
of Sychar and the home at Bethany. If he gave himself for
us to take our life, he gave himself for us to lay it down : both
alike were pure self-abnegation, a patient treading of the path
of pain, to reveal the Infinite Father to his blind children on
earth. The fruit of that knowledge is nothing less than
eternal life. What wonder then that the evangelist thinks
of Jesus as saying "Greater love hath no man than this,
that a man lay down his life for his friends."* "The son of
man must be lifted up, that whosoever believeth may in him
have eternal life."† That his suffering death, as part of his
whole assumption of humanity, was a disinterested interposition on behalf of "his friends," of "those who believed in
him" and "kept his sayings," and of "those also who should
believe on him through their word,"‡ that it largely developed
their "power to become sons of God,"§ and "took away their
sins" by sanctifying their souls, is perfectly intelligible, and
is consistently affirmed by the evangelist. This only recites
in new words the *selective* power of Christ's presence of
attracting all pure minds to him, and so holding them that of
all 'those whom God gave him out of the world‖ not one
was lost save the son of perdition.'¶ But the correlative of
such "saving" of the elect is the punishing of the rest whom
God had *not* given, i.e., of "*the world*" out of which they

* John xv. 13.
§ i. 12.
† iii. 14, 15.
‖ xvii. 6.
‡ xvii. 20.
¶ xvii. 12.

were drawn. It surprises us therefore to hear the same writer declare that "God sent not his Son into the world to judge the world, but that *the world should be saved* through him;"* and ascribe to Christ the words, "The bread which I will give is my flesh, for the life of the world;"† and speak of him (through the lips of John the Baptist) as the "Lamb of God that taketh away the sin of the world."‡

The evangelist, in defining the end of Christ's mission, cannot have known his own mind so ill as to say, in one chapter, 'it was, to sever and guard such as should be saved from the benighted world doomed to die in its sins;' and in another, 'it was, to take away the world's sins, and dispense with severance by saving the whole.' Nor is it possible to relieve him of the absolute antagonism, pervading his gospel, between the world as wrapped in darkness and ruled by an *antigod*, and the kingdom of light under the Father and the Son. The wonderful discourse and prayer of Jesus on the eve of the betrayal and in full view of the end, are full of the play of this antithesis, and not less plainly treat "the world" as alien and cast-away, than heaven as the home of a spiritual communion no longer local. The solution of the difficulty is to be sought in the different extensions given to the term "World" in different passages. The use of it to denote the Gentiles as distinguished from Israel is familiar to every one; as when the Apostle Paul says "If their (i.e., the Jews') fall is the riches of the world, and their loss the riches of the Gentiles," and "if the casting away of them is the reconciling of the world, what shall the receiving of them be, but life from the dead?"§ Thus used by one of the covenanted people, it was tantamount to what lay outside the religious pale, as marked off from what lay within it. This meaning was naturally carried into Christian usage; of course without reference any longer to lineage or nation, but touching only matters of faith and character; so that it was applied impartially to the whole class of secular-minded people in human society, as opposed to persons of earnest religious life. In the fourth gospel it occurs in both these senses. When Jesus says, "If the world hate you, ye

* John iii. 17.   † vi. 51.   ‡ i. 29.   § Rom. xi. 12, 15.

know that it hath hated me before it hated you : if ye were
of the world, the world would love its own : but because ye
are not of the world, but I chose you out of the world, therefore the world hateth you ; "* and " I pray not for the
world ; " " I pray not that thou shouldst take these out of
the world, but that thou shouldst keep them from the evil
one ; "† it is plain that his language refers, not to the
" World " which he was sent to save, but to the opposite
realm of hopeless unbelief, ruled by " the Prince of this
world." The word is used in its wider extension, to cover all
that is alien to the contents of the Christian pale. When, on
the other hand, it is said that " God so loved the world that
he gave his only-begotten Son, ... that the world through
him should be saved;"‡ that Christ " taketh away the sin
of the world :"§ that he " gives his flesh for the life of the
world ; " the word cannot possibly include those who " did
not take in his words because they were not of God,"¶ but of
the False One ; and who, for not believing on him, were to
" die in their sins ;"** it is used in the Pauline sense, to mark
the cancelling of the Israelite distinction, and the appeal of
the gospel to the " world " beyond : the disqualification of the
Gentiles being removed, there would be found among them
multitudes ready to hear the voice of the good Shepherd, and
follow him because they were " of his sheep." This was the
newly-opened " world " of possible Christians to whom the
bread from heaven would be eternal life. In this sense it was
that Caiaphas was supposed to " prophesy that he (Jesus)
should die for the nation : and *not for the nation only*, but
that he might *gather together in one the children of God that
are scattered abroad*."†† He gave himself therefore " for the
life of the world," by throwing open to great Gentile populations the divine promises in which they had had no part, and
gleaning from their vast field, as well as from the little plot
of Israel, whatever was worthy to be gathered with " the
wheat into his garner :" but this very severance marked out
more clearly the tares reserved for destruction.

* John xv. 18, 19.	† xvii. 9, 15.	‡ iii. 16, 17.
§ i. 29.	‖ vi. 51.	¶ viii. 47.
** viii. 24.	†† xi. 51, 52.	

This universality in the Christian appeal to mankind is the most prominent effect attributed in the fourth gospel to the Cross, and always with expressions of joy. And no wonder: for when the evangelist wrote, the Church had broken with Judaism, after saving and appropriating all its spiritual inheritance from its history and its prophets; and was enriching its own thought and multiplying its members from Gentile adherents of Greek culture, impressed by its monotheism, its pure and disinterested ethics, and its sublime trusts for the human soul: and the outward growth and inward change which are passing before his eyes he describes as if foreseen and taken to heart by Jesus in his last days on earth. When some Greek strangers, happening to be at Jerusalem at the fatal passover, sought an interview with him through Philip and Andrew, something in their tone and purpose, in contrast with the bitter enmity of his own people, realized within him the actual darkness of the present, and the possible glory of a future more at one with his affections, and more ready for a worship in spirit and in truth. Deep as is the trouble of his soul at the tragic parting from the Israel he came to save, the wave of sorrow is turned into light as it breaks and flies through the air of time, with the sprinkling of regeneration for waiting hearts afar. The momentary prayer " Father, save me from this hour," is instantly replaced by " Father, glorify thy name :" and the answer " I have both glorified it and I will glorify it again," receives its interpretation in the words, " Now is the judgment of this world, now will the Prince of this world be cast out ; and I, if I be lifted up from the earth, will *draw all men* unto myself."* The evangelist sees " the Prince of this world " disappointed of his triumph in the cross : the silencing of the divine message was as vain as the entombment of the messenger: both had had their resurrection : and ever since, the armies of Satan were thinned by deserters, and from his favourite heathendom itself multitudes were flocking to the standard of Christ. The grain of wheat was small and lone until it fell into the earth to die ; but, flung away to die, it has borne much fruit.

This idea, of the *fruitfulness* of the cross, is the chief ground

* John xii. 20-32.

of the evangelist's treatment of it, not as a humiliation to be excused, but as the last grace and glory of the Divine visit. It gives indefinite extension to the influence of the manifested "Word"; but it does not change that influence: it is still the new birth into higher life by assimilation to the Father through the Son, the transforming power of a godlike humanity once visible on earth, now self-revealed from heaven. It is a purification that sweeps through the soul on the very light of that vision, and leaves there new truth, new aims, new love, the quickened germs of an eternal life. If it "take away sins," it is not by annulling their guilt, but by withering their power and leaving them dead. The juridical assumption of the apostle Paul that sanctification cannot begin till the score of past transgressions is cleared off by a penalty paid for us on the cross, and that then first the spirit can meet the love of a reconciled God, plays no part in this gospel, and is quite foreign to its pervading genius. The only words which admit, though they do not require, such a Pauline interpretation, are those with which John the Baptist is said to have pointed out the approach of Jesus to him, "Behold the lamb of God, that taketh away the sin of the world."* The passage is so entirely out of harmony with the general tone of the gospel, which does not lay stress on the extinction of sin or ever mention repentance and forgiveness, and assigns no atoning efficacy to the death of Christ, that I cannot but assent to the opinion of Oscar Holtzmann, that "here we evidently come across the reminiscence of an earlier conception of the work of Christ, the language of which the author still uses, without however adopting it as strictly his own."† If however the "taking away sins" be understood not as *carrying off its punishment,*‡ but as *quashing its essence in the soul,* i.e., as purification, another resource presents itself. This gospel identifies the cross, in its date and in its meaning, with the Passover. The Apostle Paul gives it the same meaning: "our passover also has been sacrificed, even Christ." How does he apply this comparison? Is it to show the

---

* John i. 29. † Das Johannes-Evangelium, pp. 50, 51.

‡ The word αἴρειν means in the active "to take away"; and only in the middle voice "to take upon one's self."

Corinthians that their sins are atoned for and cancelled?   On the contrary, it is to reprove their disgraceful continuance in certain members of the Church, and warning them against their spread, and reminding them that the time has come which pledges the disciples to newness of life; and that, as the paschal festival was the signal for clearing the house of all impurity of leaven, and beginning a week for unleavened bread alone, so the Christians had entered upon a term pledged to untainted life.   " Know ye not that a little leaven leaveneth the whole lump?   Purge out the old leaven, that ye may be a new lump, even as ye are unleavened.   For our passover also hath been sacrificed, even Christ: wherefore let us keep the feast, not with the old leaven, neither with the leaven of malice and wickedness, but with the unleavened bread of sincerity and truth."* If among the materials which the evangelist worked up in the composition of his gospel we may suppose the chief epistles of Paul to be present, this passage may have suggested to him the identification of Christ with the passover, described under the phrase "lamb of God;" and in that case the very source from which he drew would determine the words "taketh away sin" to the meaning which I have given them of *purification* from the presence of sin.

The consensus between the apostle and the evangelist in their application of this comparison is not disturbed by the resort of the latter to the phrase ὁ ἀμνὸς τοῦ Θεοῦ, *Lamb of God*, as designating the person of Jesus,—a phrase unknown to the apostle and to the synoptists, and reappearing (without the τοῦ Θεοῦ) only in the so-called first epistle of Peter,† a production belonging to the beginning of the second century. The name, as applied to Christ, is undoubtedly borrowed from Isaiah liii., in which the apostle first found relief from the horror of the cross, and discovered that Messiah " had to suffer these things ere he entered into glory," to " bear our griefs and carry our sorrows;" "to be wounded for our transgressions and bruised for our iniquities"; and to realize the picture, " he humbled himself and opened not his mouth; as a lamb that is led to the slaughter, and as a sheep before her shearers is

* 1 Cor. v. 6–8.   † i. 19.

dumb." This is the text from which the apostle Philip "preached Jesus" to the treasurer of Æthiopia,* and sent him on his way baptized and in the spirit: it is no wonder that a description so apposite to the recent sufferer, "rejected of men" and seemingly "stricken of God" on Calvary, and yet "exalted and lifted up on high," should at last have fixed upon him, from its own tenderest image, the title the "Lamb of God." The phrase denotes no more than the silent and patient endurance of unmerited suffering inflicted by those on whose behalf it is accepted; and is suggested by the experience that it is ever the prayers and tears, the self-devotion and unflinching sacrifices of the righteous, that save the reckless from their ruin and wake the sleeping conscience of an unfaithful world.

No instance occurs of the use of this phrase as a name for Jesus in writings of the apostolic age : and out of thirty examples of it in the New Testament, twenty-eight are found in the Apocalypse, the unusual word ἀρνίον being invariably substituted for ἀμνός to denote the Lamb. As in the Seer's heavenly vision it is " seen as though it had been slain," and is celebrated in a " new song " as having " purchased unto God with his blood men of every tribe and tongue and people and nation, and made them to be unto God a kingdom and priests," it is certainly the *death* of Christ as a redeeming power on which the stress is laid : and as the multitude thus gathered are seen in robes " made white " because washed " in the blood of the lamb,"† the writer may have conceived of the redemption as effected by vicarious incidence of penalty and transfer of righteousness, as in the Pauline theory. His language is consistent with this conception : the robes washed white may be the symbol of past stains of sin expunged by an atoning medium. But they may just as well be the symbol of present purity gained by 'putting off the old man,' and 'putting on the new man' through 'renewal of the spirit of the mind,' re-"created after God in righteousness and holiness of truth."‡ In the former sense, the "washing" would be needed for all men alike; "for there is no difference between Jew and Greek": "all, both Jew and Greek, are

* Acts viii. 27–40.   † Rev. v. 6, 9, 10; vii. 9, 14.   ‡ Eph. iv. 22–24.

under sin."[*] But the Seer's description applies to a Gentile multitude alone: for he has found "the children of Israel," 12,000 from each tribe, already "sealed upon their forehead, with the seal of the living God"; and it is in distinction from these, and in addition to them, that the white-robed multitude "which no man could number" appears "out of every nation and of all peoples and tongues";—an obvious description of the Gentile world, to which the cross and the resurrection threw open the new life of relation to the living God. It is the influx of this host, once estranged, now drawn into the new life of purity and communion with heaven, which the Seer celebrates as the glory of the "Lamb" that was slain.

No light can be thrown upon the doctrine of the fourth gospel from the contents of a production removed from it, like the Apocalypse, so nearly to the opposite extreme of Christian thought. But as there is no other storehouse to which we can resort for instances of the personal use of the term 'Lamb,' it was desirable to ascertain whether the word was limited exclusively to the idea of expiation which has nowhere else any place in the evangelist. The answer that may be given to this question can avail, it must be confessed, only as an evidence of popular usage. All the passages in which the Lamb is mentioned are shown, by critical considerations, which appear to me conclusive, to be the work of a single Christian interpolator, probably in the last decade of the first century, operating upon the text of a *Jewish* Apocalypse which he breaks and confuses, greatly to the discomfiture of all subsequent interpreters.[†] His frequent recurrence to the figure of the Lamb, without being able to assign to him any part essential to the action of the drama, together with the total absence of the image from the interpolations of an editor forty years later,[‡] would seem to point to a usage now and in vogue at the earlier date, but fading away or otherwise shrunk at the later. Hence perhaps the evan-

<hr>

[*] Rom. x. 12, iii. 9.

[†] Eberhard Vischer; Die Offenbarung Joh. eine Jüdische Apokalypse, pp. 35–60.

[‡] Pfleiderer; Das Urchristenthum, p. 351.

gelist, having himself passed beyond it, planted his solitary retrospect of it upon John the Baptist, at a time when the full significance of the ministry of Christ on earth was undeveloped and had not yet escaped its Jewish mould. Even so, it cannot be historically accredited to the Baptist. "That John the Baptist cannot really have uttered these words in reference to Christ," says Oscar Holtzmann, "follows not only from the form of expression, the abstract ἡ ἁμαρτία τοῦ κόσμου being out of character with his practical eye for the individual and concrete (Luke iii. 7–17), but still more from the purport of the phrase; inasmuch as the Baptist, we may be sure, knew at all events just as little about an atoning death of Christ as Paul before his conversion (1 Cor. i. 21–25; Gal. vi. 14). And since the expression accorded no better with the evangelist's own peculiar sphere of thought, to which the idea of forgiveness of sins is foreign, it is plain that he must have written at a time the needs of which were not adequately met within the circle of either the Synoptists' religious view, or of Paul's and his followers' with their various gradations of difference."*

Thus far, the Work of Christ, as presented in the fourth gospel, contemplates the two following ends: To sanctify the children of God, drawn to him through his personal manifestation of what God is, and loves, and eternalizes, and sever them from the cast-off world by selective spiritual affinities.

To throw open the field of selective affinity to the human race at large, by his death and known return to the life with God. Thus "lifted up," and presenting to faith One Living God and a humanity perfected in immortality, he will draw all men, of whatever nation, unto him.

There was yet another end embraced in the work of Christ, as conceived by the evangelist, viz.:

To perpetuate the sanctifying effect of his incarnation, and turn the concentrated glory of his personal appearance on the field of history into a permanent light and spring of growing life for mankind. On the accomplishment of this end by the virtual prolongation of his visible presence in the invisible Paraclete I have had occasion to speak in treating of

* Das Johannes-evangelium, p. 51.

the impersonation of " the Word ; " and need only add a few
words to replace the reader at the point of view to which he
was there led.   So long as Christ was upon earth, he was the
sole focus of vivifying influence ; and to catch the glow of
truth and love that issued thence it was needful to be near.
To his disciples close at hand he was the sacred guide, the
present comforter, the intercessor who prayed the Father on
their behalf, and kept them pure by the power of his spirit.
But this could be no more than a dependent sanctification,
and could not pass the inner circle of his followers.   In death,
the incarnation ceased :   the imprisoned glory escaped its
bounds ; from the human individuality it passed indeed home
to its reunion with the Father ; but no longer to be secluded
in that Divine retreat, but to enfold now the earth which it
had visited as well as the heaven whence it came.   He would
not really leave those who had clung to him and put their
trust in him ; he would come to them, not indeed in the finite
and familiar form, but by the Holy Spirit, the Paraclete, the
omnipresent sustainer of the soul, which he would send them
from the Father.   This,—as soon as the first sorrow of parting had been lifted from their hearts,—would more than take
his place ; and to compel them to this discovery it was
" expedient for them that he should go away."   He could be
with them but for awhile ; the Spirit would abide with them
for ever.   He was their *external* guide ; the Spirit would be
within them, blended with their very personality, an instant
spring of truth and sanctity.   Thus released from limits and
abroad as a luminous atmosphere of the world, the Divine
Spirit would continue as well as diffuse the new and heavenly
life which had made his appearance among mankind so full
of grace and truth.   The bread of heaven, thus broken and
distributed, would feed a multitude which none could count.
Infinite multiplication and development of the higher life of
humanity was thus rendered possible : the implicit sanctity
became explicit ; and the personal passes into the universal.

And so the great end is reached, that the mingling of the
Divine and the human in Christ is not there on its own
account, as a gem of individual biography, unique and
unrepeated ; but as the type and the expression of a fact in

the constitution of our nature.   The intimate relation between God and man which declared itself in the utterance, "I am not alone, but the Father is with me," belongs to the essence of the soul and consecrates every human life.   Nor is it anything but simple and indisputable truth to say, that the consciousness of this has taken its commencement from the experience and religion of Jesus; and has imparted to Christendom its deeper tone of feeling, its higher conception of purity, and its inextinguishable hope for humanity.

NOTE.

In the foregoing chapter, all the inferences respecting the work of Christ, as conceived by the evangelist, are drawn from the contents of his gospel.   If account had been taken also of the first Epistle current under the same name, I am aware that some of these inferences must have given way, or been modified, under the application of the extended test. Such corrections I should have freely made, had I been able to satisfy myself that the gospel and the letter proceeded from the same author.   But though long held in suspense by the apparent equipoise of the evidence for and against their identity of origin, I am at last more impressed by a few fundamental differences of religious conception pervading the two writings, than by several agreements in terminology and secondary categories of thought, which point to some common relation to the same school.   A critical discussion of the question is beyond the scope of my design and of my competency; and I can only indicate the characteristic features in the two productions which, as it seems to me, could not co-exist in the same mind.

(1.) The idea of Repentance and Forgiveness are foreign to the evangelist's conception of the relation between God and man, and the words never occur.   In the Epistle (i. 8, 9) we read, " If we say we have no sin, we deceive ourselves, and the truth is not in us.   If we confess our sins, he is faithful and just to forgive us our sins, and to cleanse us from all unrighteousness."

(2.) The gospel knows nothing of an atoning or propitiatory

efficacy in the blood of Christ. The Epistle says, "The blood of Jesus his Son cleanseth us from all sin" (i. 7). "I write unto you, my little children, because your sins are forgiven you for his name's sake" (ii. 12). "Herein is love, not that we loved God, but that he loved us, and sent his Son to be the propitiation for our sins" (iv. 10).

3. The word *Paraclete* is used in the Gospel exclusively of the Holy Spirit; in the Epistle, of Jesus Christ: "I write these things unto you, that ye may not sin. And if any man sin, we have a Paraclete with the Father, Jesus Christ the righteous: and he is the propitiation for our sins: and not ours only, but also for the whole world" (ii. 1, 2). The word, moreover, is here applied to Jesus Christ in the sense of *Advocate*, and is so rendered in the English version, old and revised. But in the parting discourse of Jesus, as given in the gospel, he declines this intercessory character. "In that day ye shall ask in my name; and I say not unto you that I will pray the Father for you; for the Father himself loveth you, because ye have loved me, and have believed that I came forth from the Father" (xvi. 26, 27).

4. The expectation of the Parusia, or near return of Christ, to wind up human history and establish the theocracy, is absent from the Gospel, with its attendant mythology of premonitory signs. In the Epistle we read, "Little children, it is the last hour: and as ye have heard that antichrist cometh, even now there have arisen many antichrists; whereby we know that it is the last hour" (ii. 18). "We know that, when he shall be manifested, we shall be like him, for we shall see him even as he is" (iii. 2).

5. Notwithstanding the evangelist's silence respecting any "coming of the Son of Man on the clouds of heaven," he retains, as we have seen, a remnant of eschatology in the phrase "the last day." What exactly he included in it is difficult to determine, after he had discharged from it the greater part of its generally accepted contents. To Christ, on the eve of his departure, he attributes the promise: "I go to prepare a place for you. And if I go and prepare a place for you, I come again, and will receive you unto myself; that where I am, there ye may be also," i.e., in one of the "many

mansions of the Father's house" (xiv. 2–4) ; and in his subsequent prayer he adds, on behalf not of his personal disciples,
but of "them also that believe on me through their word,"
"Father, they whom thou hast given me, I will that where I
am they also may be with me, that they may behold my glory
which thou hast given me : for thou lovedst me before the
foundation of the world" (xvii. 20–24). The end therefore
accomplished by this "coming again" would be, not the
abolishing of all rule and authority and power on earth, in
order to "reign till he hath put all enemies under his
feet" (1 Cor. xv. 24, 25) ; but simply to raise up his faithful
disciples to "be with him where he is" and "behold the
glory which God hath given him" in the heavenly mansions.
In the absence of any collective date, the hearer or reader of
such promise would probably look for its intended fulfilment
in each separate disciple successively called away. But the
language is not inconsistent with an intermediate sleep of
the dead till their number was made up and the moment of
awakening should have arrived for all. In this case would be
realized that other word of Christ, "This is the will of him
that sent me, that of all that he hath given me I should lose
nothing, but should *raise it up at the last day*" (vi. 39). The
Gospel then and the Epistle are not at variance as to the
existence of a "last day." But in their account of it they
differ : in the Epistle, it is the "*judgment day*," "Herein is
love made perfect, that we may have boldness in the day of
judgment" (iv. 17) ; in the Gospel, it is the resurrection day ;
and the process of judgment is expressly shifted away from
that future day into the present, and the eternal life or death
determined and self-pronounced already in the devotion or
aversion of each soul to the Holy One of God. "He that believeth on him *is not judged :* and he that believeth not hath
been *judged already*, because he hath not believed on the name
of the only-begotten Son of God" (iii. 18) : "if any man hear
my sayings and keep them not, I judge him not ; for I came
not to judge the world, but to save the world. He that rejecteth me and receiveth not my sayings, hath one that judgeth
him : the word that I speak, the same shall judge him in the
last day" (xii. 47, 48).

In the face of these differences, and of a contrast in the literary moulding of the thought throughout, which is equally striking, the agreements appear to me to plead inadequately for unity of authorship. The antitheses and syzygies,—Light and Darkness, Truth and Falsehood, Love and Hate, Life and Death, God and Devil,—are so akin to the elements thrown into the gnostic speculations, one type of which (the Docetic) the writer of the Epistle encounters in a passionate polemic, that they may well be regarded rather as the common vocabulary of theosophic criticism in a given area and age, than as characteristics of personal thought and taste. Had we larger remains of the religious and philosophical literature of the first half of the second century, we should probably be introduced to stages of development filling the gap which at present we vainly endeavour to bridge by overstraining the possible combinations of our present fragmentary materials.

CHAPTER IV.

THEORIES OF UNION WITH GOD.

§ 1. *Present Media of Grace.*

WHATEVER theories might be formed among the first disciples respecting the person and the work of Jesus, on one point they were all agreed: viz., that they had reference to a crisis yet to come, and that his visit to the world was only suspended for awhile, lest the kingdom of God should be quite too empty. He had set in action, by his life and by his death, the redeeming power adequate for all who stood within its reach; but it needed distribution beyond the "little flock" of his personal adherents; and to allow this expansion of a mere school into a commonwealth ready for his return, a brief interval was appointed, and an administration established for widening the circle of "such as should be saved." The problem of this season of suspense was simply one of spiritual organization: to gather together, and animate by the collective Spirit, the community of the City of God, and hold its members apart from the polluted and perishable elements around; to keep them so minded as if Christ were still in their midst, and to spread round them an influence equivalent to his continued agency upon their hearts. The responsibility rested upon his apostles. This was their field of activity: till he returned, they were to take up and carry on his work, and through the cities of the East and West multiply the stations of the faithful, who should be as sentinels on the watch for him. The question thus inevitably arose, What provision had he left for this period and function of his absence? With what resources, of persuasion or of power that could at all replace his own, had he entrusted them? We know not what passed through their minds from the first dawn of this question upon them to its full answer: for, the result only, and not the process, is laid open to us. But the solution at last assumed this form: He had left them (1.) The *Holy Spirit*, which came to them from heaven to be in his stead, and which, they found, spread by a Divine diffusion through their converts, and united them all in living links with Christ above: and (2.) The redeeming efficacy of *his Death in their stead*, which cancelled the curse of the flesh in humanity, and commenced already the assimilation of the believer to the immortal Son of God. These two,—the Spirit and the Atoning Cross,—were the provisions for carrying on the work of Christ at second hand, and preparing a Divine society for his return. In arming his apostles with these supernatural graces, he had more than compensated his absence from them: he had virtually become everywhere present, and multiplied his points of contact with the world; and the light which had been only local, held to a pure personal centre, passed into a universal element, accessible wherever humanity could be reached.

But who were to share in these supernatural graces? Might any one help himself to them, or pretend to them, or, like Simon Magus, bargain for them, at will? If not, how was the candidate to get into the sacred circle whose proper endowments they were? So long as Jesus himself was there, he could select his own, and keep them "in the Father's name," that "none of them be lost:" but, now that he is gone, and that crowds will be pressing into the kingdom of heaven as if " to take it by force," some conditions of entrance must be defined, some pledges of faithfulness be required; and the Divine graces be withheld till the human acts are performed which publicly commit the disciples' faith and conscience. The ministry of Jesus himself suggested what these acts should be; for it had opened with the baptism, and closed with the last supper: the one followed by the descent of the Spirit: the other by the sacrifice of himself. Let these be the model for every disciple's self-dedication, the beginning and completion of his union with Christ. Does he yearn for the Holy Spirit? Let him be baptized. Does he long " to be delivered from the bondage of corruption," and share in the immortality of Christ? Let him frequent the Lord's supper, and there he will appropriate the benefits of the cross, and be fed on the manna of eternal life. And so was the correspondency established between earth and heaven; and two human usages were instituted which were not the signs only, but the conditions, of the Divine graces respectively linked with them. Here, in this small germ, we have the origin of that ritual and sacerdotal development of Christianity which, at every characteristic point, is a simple reversal of the Religion of Jesus, and, wherever it exists, does but wield his power to destroy his work.

It is one of the significant differences between the fourth gospel and the others, that it represents Jesus himself, during his ministry, as enrolling disciples by baptism, and employing his apostles to perform the rite; and this, with such publicity and success as to surpass even the repute of John the Baptist, and create a panic among the Pharisees.* To the synoptists no such rite is known in the society of disciples, while Jesus is with them. The call of the apostles is complete without it; their investiture with the Spiritual powers of their mission is independent of it; and when he sends them forth to proclaim the glad tidings through the villages and cities of Israel, and minutely instructs them how to acquit themselves in their office, neither in the charge which he gives, nor in the report which they bring back, is there any word of baptism.† This is one of the many traits of historic truth which unconsciously show that, the nearer we approach his person, the more do we leave every outward form and questionable claim behind, and are left alone with the pure elements of spiritual religion. The very account which tells us that at last, after his resurrection, he commissioned his apostles to go and baptize among all nations,‡ betrayed itself by speaking in the Trinitarian language of the next century, and compels us to see in it the ecclesiastical editor, and not the evangelist, much less the founder himself. No historic trace appears of this baptismal formula earlier than the " Teaching of the Twelve Apostles,"§ and the first Apology of Justin‖ about the middle of the second century: and more than a century later, Cyprian

---

* John iii. 22, iv. 1.   † Matt. x.; Luke ix. 1-10.   ‡ Matt. xxviii. 19.
§ Ch. vii. 1, 3. The oldest Church Manual, ed. Phil. Schaff: Edinb., Clark, 1887.   ‖ Apol. i. 61.

found it necessary to insist upon the use of it instead of the older phrase baptized "into Christ Jesus," or into the "name of the Lord Jesus."[*]   Paul alone, of the apostles, was baptized, ere he was "filled with the Holy Ghost;" and he certainly was baptized simply "into Christ Jesus."[†]   Yet the tri-personal form, unhistorical as it is, is actually insisted on as essential by almost every Church in Christendom, and, if you have not had it pronounced over you, the ecclesiastical authorities cast you out as a heathen man, and will accord to you neither Christian recognition in your life, nor Christian burial in your death.   It is a rule which would condemn as invalid every recorded baptism performed by an apostle; for if the book of Acts may be trusted, the invariable usage was baptism "in the name of Christ Jesus,"[‡] and not "in the name of the Father, and of the Son, and of the Holy Spirit." And doubtless the author is as good a witness for the usage of his own time (about A.D. 115) as for that of the period where-of he treats.

How soon the initiatory rite established itself among the Christians, and came to be regarded as the essential prelim-inary of the Holy Spirit,[§] it is impossible to say.   But that it did not at first assume this dignified connection is clear from the disparaging distinction drawn by the Apostle Paul, that he was "*sent not to baptize, but to preach* the gospel," and from the confirmatory fact which he adduces that in all his church at Corinth there were but two or three whom he had baptized.   "I thank God that I baptized none of you, save Crispus and Gaius; lest any man should say that ye were baptized into my name: and I baptized also the household of Stephanas: besides, I know not whether I baptized any other."[‖] How could this be, if the Holy Spirit were an apostolic gift, and baptism its medium and date?   Nay, we are met by a

---

* Gal. III. 27; Acts xix. 5, x. 48.   Cyprian, Ep. 73, 16–18, has to controvert those who still use the shorter form.

† Rom. vi. 3.   ‡ Acts ii. 38.

§ It deserves remark, however, by those who insist on the sacramental doctrine, that in the case of Cornelius and his friends, Peter administers baptism because the Holy Spirit had already fallen upon them, and given him adequate warrant for the act.   Acts x. 44–48.

‖ 1 Cor. i. 14–16.

still more startling fact, viz., that with no knowledge but of the baptism of repentance, and without having even heard of the Holy Spirit, pious and expectant Jews, who had merely listened to the message of John the Baptist, "the kingdom of heaven is at hand," and taken *his* baptism in Jordan, were actually treated already as "*disciples.*" Apollos, who was one of them, "a learned man, mighty in the Scriptures," is described as having been "instructed in the way of the Lord," and as "teaching diligently the things concerning Jesus, and speaking boldly in the synagogue." Then, with only such further instruction as two private Christians (Aquila and Priscilla) could give in conversation with him, and with apparently no additional baptism at all, he is commended as a missionary to the brethren in Achaia; where he "profits much those who had believed through grace;" "publicly showing by the Scriptures that Jesus was the Christ."* Facts like these afford glimpses into a time when the Christian usages had not yet set into separatist forms and been furnished with their ultimate doctrinal interpretation, and when, on the borders of devout and waiting Judaism, there was still a possible communion between those who took, and those who hardly knew, the name of Jesus of Nazareth. There was a Holy Spirit which would embrace them both ; speaking not in any "new tongues," but in the undying language of ancient piety, the tones made sweet and solemn by the voices of prophets and righteous men, the eternal sigh of human prayer and hope ; and they could listen to these breathings hand in hand, and had no occasion to go apart to hear them.

Two ideas, naturally suggested by the baptismal rite, early fastened themselves upon it, and became, through the perversion to which all symbols are open, the copious source of later superstition. As the candidate descended into the stream, and by total immersion disappeared from view, his old self was said to sink away and be buried in the deep water, never to present itself again. In a moment indeed he rose once more above the surface ; but not the same : it was a Pagan that went in : it is a Christian that comes out : and

* Acts xviii. 24–xix. 7.

in this change of identity there is a fresh creation,—a soul new-born,—a rising into life untried and glorious. From this symbolism, hardened into doctrine, and continued in use when the practice of immersion which gave it all its beauty had ceased, sprang the notion of baptismal *regeneration*, the exchange of nature for grace, of alienation for acceptance, of appointment to eternal death for election to eternal life.

"Are ye ignorant," says the apostle Paul, "that all we who were baptized into Christ Jesus were baptized into his death? We were buried therefore with him through baptism into death: that like as Christ was raised from the dead through the glory of the Father, we also might walk in newness of life. For if we have become united with him by the likeness of his death, we shall be also by the likeness of his resurrection."° "Buried with him in baptism, ye are risen with him through faith in the working of God who raised him from the dead."† The other idea is supplied, not by the *look* of the baptized person to the spectator, but by the cleansing action of the water upon himself. He takes into it the stains and dust of a soiling world: he comes out of it pure as from the moulding hand of God. "Arise and be baptized," said Ananias of Damascus to the converted Saul, "and wash away thy sins, calling on his name."; The symbol happily expresses whatever sanctifying change might be involved in assuming the Christian profession: be it the simple self-dedication of a penitent and pious heart, or be it some mystical and transforming grace, of which the human subject is but the passive recipient. The simplicity of the former interpretation satisfied the Christian feeling till near the middle of the second century; the act being regarded rather as that of the human agent voluntarily turning from a tainted past to the purer future, than as a Divine bestowal of a supernatural gift of immunity or positive blessing. The "remission of sins" which was attached to it was conditional on the "repentance" or change of mind expressed in the act, and was in simple conformity with the character and government of God, and did not impart to the baptismal rite any exceptional or mysterious quality as "a means of grace."

* Rom. vi. 3–5.   † Col. ii. 12.   ‡ Acts xxii. 16.

There was still room, however, for recognizing a free gift from God : because the past misdoings now brought into consciousness were due to ignorance of the true relations of man and God and the supreme good for the human soul ; and the new light which reveals them as they are, and induces the change to a better mind, is a Divine mercy quite unearned. With this reservation of a " grace " behind, the remission is often treated as merely covering the sins of ignorance lamented as soon as seen, which in truth are no sins at all. " All such transgressions as you have committed in ignorance, through want of clear knowledge of God, will be remitted to you, if repented of when you came to know him."[*] Remission, sought under these conditions, implies grateful acceptance of a new light of faith, and requires therefore the awakened intelligence of an active human subject, and no mere passive recipient of a foreign gift. It is no wonder, therefore, that the application of baptism to infants made its appearance at a later date : and that when it did, in the latter half of the second century, the pleadings both for it and against it indicated a marked tendency in the movement of the ecclesiastical mind towards magical superstition ; though by no means prepared as yet for the formulas which speak of " the mystical washing away of sin," and in the case of the infant of " washing him " " for the remission of sins," and " sanctifying him with the Holy Ghost," " that he may be delivered from God's wrath."   The cleansing away of the blight on the past, and the entrance on a pure future, were apt to be set forth in terms so unmeasured as to need some more dignified sign than the commonplace act of dipping in water : to qualify it to serve it as " the bath of regeneration " something exceptional must be done to the water : it must be exposed to the prayer of exorcism, and the recitation of the triune name, to clear it of evil spirits; or at any rate be blessed by the priest, to prepare it as the vehicle of the Holy Spirit : or, ere it quits the head of the baptized, feel the hand of the bishop, consecrating its use. Cyprian says expressly " the priest must sanctify the water ;" for, " unless it has the Holy Spirit,

---

[*] Clem. Alex. Strom. VI. vi. 48, quoted from the Preaching of Peter. Harnack, p. 142 n.

it cannot cleanse away sin."* By such accumulation of essentials, all thrown upon the material medium or the official administration of the rite, the personal subject of it is reduced to the condition of a passive recipient, put under an enchantment; and it cannot matter whether he be brought to it by mature thought and will of his own, or exposed to it as a helpless babe may be carried indifferently to be vaccinated or to be christened. So far had this descent into mere magic gone by Irenæus' time as to ruin the spiritual beauty of the words "Suffer little children to come unto me, and forbid them not," by making them mean, "Take your infants to the font."† It was not, however, without resistance that the pædo-baptism which ventured on this plea obtained recognition as a sacrament of the Church. The profession of faith and pledge of purpose which baptism required and the infant could not make had to be assumed by sponsors; whose vicarious responsibility for a personality yet undeveloped was naturally deemed most perilous. Tertullian, who was not apt to strain at gnats of either faith or feeling, protests against the growing practice of baptizing children: "It is well, he thinks, to postpone the rite in adaptation to each person's lot and disposition and age, especially where children are concerned: let them wait for adolescence: let them come with open eyes, when they have been taught what they come to: let them be made Christians when they can know Christ. Why should the age of innocence be in any haste for the remission of sins?" "Those who understand the grave significance of baptism will be more afraid of its arrival than of its delay; conscience as yet inviolate runs no risk of missing its salvation."‡

This curious specimen of third-century theology cannot but affect the modern reader with a strangely mixed feeling. He is pleasurably struck, perhaps, by the boldness with which it snatches "from God's wrath" "the little ones whose angels always behold the face of the Father in heaven." But he will notice with regret that it escapes one superstition only to plunge into another. For, assuming that baptism washes out

---

* Ep. lxx. 1, lxxiv. 5. Harn. 395 n.   † II. xxii. 4.   ‡ De bapt. 18.

the sins of the past, its argument is that, as the rite can come only once, the later you take it, the clearer you will stand : and it is foolish to waste upon the light flakes of childish transgression the power which would equally get rid of the poisonous load of a long worldly life. It is well known in what high appreciation "the first Christian Emperor" held the force of this argument : and that, in taking stock of all that he had done for the Church and perpetrated upon his family and his enemies, and achieved for himself, Constantine deemed it best to be baptized on his deathbed, and secure a favoured place on the roll of both worlds.

From such wretched soteriological calculations modern Christendom has everywhere emerged. Not so, alas! with the other half, withstood by Tertullian, of the baptismal superstition. It is humiliating to think that, in this age, the Anglican Church has reaccented the extreme ritual doctrine, as expressed by one of her own archbishops, "that baptism is necessary for the salvation of infants;" "no baptism, no entrance: nor can infants creep in any other ordinary way."* In the presence of such statements no evidence is needed of the debasing effect of all sacramental doctrine : by attributing moral and spiritual effects, unattested by natural consciousness, to physical acts and material things, it confuses alike the understanding and the conscience, turns the Divine world into a realm of magic, and preserves an inexhaustible fund of credulity for the operations of impostors and the enthralment of mankind.

Not more fortunate than the rite of baptism has been the parallel institution of the "Lord's supper." That it is not now what it originally was, that it has had a history, during which new meanings have been drawn from it or imported into it, and that the change has for the most part been from the natural to the mystical, from the simple to the complex, from the human to the hieratic, few will deny but the officials of the mass. A copious ecclesiastical literature, both historical and polemical, enables us to trace the process of change through sixteen centuries, and take account of super-

---

* Laud's Conference with Fisher, § 15.

stitious accretions which have been added in that time. But
in order to estimate the whole amount of deviation from the
archetypal fact, it is needful to gain insight into the remaining period beyond, and above all into the evening hours passed
by a little band of disciples with their Master in a certain
"large upper room furnished" for the passover in Jerusalem.
In what was then and there thought and said and done is the
standard from which all growths and declensions must be
marked off, and here we are met by difficulties which can no
longer be set at rest by a summary appeal to the authority of
Scripture.

There are four accounts of the memorable incident at the
last supper ; that of the Apostle Paul and those of the three
Synoptists. They are as follows :—

Paul, 1 Cor. xi. 23-26. The Lord Jesus in the night in
which he was betrayed, took bread ; and when he had given
thanks, he brake it, and said, This is my body, which is for
you ; this do in remembrance of me. In like manner also the
cup after the supper, saying, This cup is the new covenant
in my blood : this do, as oft as ye drink it, in remembrance
of me. For as oft as ye eat this bread and drink the cup, ye
proclaim the Lord's death till he come.

Mark xiv. 22-25. And as they were eating, he took bread,
and when he had given thanks, he brake it, and gave to them,
and said, Take ye, this is my body. And he took a cup, and
when he had given thanks, he gave it to them ; and they all
drank of it ; and he said unto them, This is my blood of the
covenant, which is shed for many : Verily, I say unto you, I
will no more drink of the fruit of the vine, until that day when
I drink it new in the kingdom of God.

Luke xxii. 15-18. He said unto them, With desire I have
desired to eat this passover with you before I suffer ; for I say
unto you, I will not eat it until it be fulfilled in the kingdom
of God. And he took the cup, and when he had given
thanks, he said, Take this, and divide it among yourselves :
for I say unto you, I will not drink from henceforth of
the fruit of the vine, until the kingdom of God shall
come.

19, 20. And he took bread ; and when he had given

thanks, he brake it, and gave it to them, saying, This is my body, which is given for you; this do in remembrance of me. And the cup in like manner after supper, saying, This cup is the new covenant in my blood which is poured out for you.

Matthew xxvi. 26–29. And as they were eating, Jesus took bread, and blessed and brake it; and he gave to the disciples, and said, Take, eat, this is my body. And he took a cup, and gave thanks, and gave to them, saying, Drink ye all of it; for this is my blood of the covenant, which is shed for many unto remission of sins. But I say unto you, I will not drink henceforth of this fruit of the vine, until that day when I drink it new in my Father's kingdom.

In estimating the combined and relative value of these statements, it must never be forgotten how dependent we are upon internal evidence: the synoptical gospels being compilations, by unknown hands and of uncertain dates, probably between A.D. 75 and A.D. 120, of the popular traditions respecting the life of Jesus: and the statement of Paul proceeding from one who was no witness of the scene described, and to whom the central figure in it was a purely ideal person modelled in conformity with theory without the check of memory. Narratives produced under such conditions may well contain what is historical; but that they should contain nothing else is simply impossible without a miraculous overruling of natural causation.

It cannot be urged that, when these accounts were written, the incident related was too fresh to suffer from the operation of perverting causes. Those causes are not exacting in their demand for time. And here the earliest report is written by the Apostle Paul to the Corinthians in the spring of A.D. 58, i.e., a quarter of a century after the event, and twenty years after his first opportunity of hearing about it from the apostles present at it: prior to which he had already worked out, and for three years had preached, his independent gospel, with its distinctive doctrine of the cross. That doctrine so possessed him as to absorb or modify all fresh knowledge or conceptions that entered his mind. Nor must it be forgotten that what he heard at Jerusalem would be told him in explanation of a Com-

munion-usage already established in memory of the paschal
night.* Since that evening, not only had the crucifixion of
Jesus happened, and the resurrection caught them up in surprise and turned him into the Son of God, but the theory of a
suffering Messiah had been worked out, and the advent become
a fixed expectation and chief object-matter of the gospel it-

* It will perhaps occur to the reader as an objection to this use of the
apostle's visit to Peter, that he disclaimed all dependence in his work on
those who were apostles before him, and said that they "added nothing to
him" (Gal. ii. 6), and that his account of the last supper is expressly introduced with the words "I received of the Lord that which I also delivered
unto you." The objection opens the difficult question, "What kind of *fact*
is covered by the phrase 'received of the Lord'?" It certainly implies the
apostle's acceptance of what is communicated as verified by Christ. But it does
not on this account exclude information from human witnesses : it is enough
that it includes an authorization to seek it; and this Paul would undoubtedly
suppose himself to have. His second visit to Jerusalem, fourteen years later
(A.D. 52), he himself says was "by revelation" (Gal. ii. 2). By what marks
he would satisfy himself that what he "received" was vouched for by the
heavenly Christ, it is impossible to say; for since that "Christ" was to him
not any human "Jesus" whom he had known, and would know again if they
met and talked together, but an ideal being simply present to thought, and
identified only by distinctive conceptions, it seems certain that anything new
and impressive in close accord with these conceptions would readily find
shelter under sanction of the same invisible personality. The apostle himself, in the counsel which he gives, seems to waver at times between the tone
of the mere adviser and that of the authoritative mouthpiece of Christ
(1 Cor. vii. 10, 12), as if swaying on the verge between inspired and uninspired thought. Those who allow no place to such psychological conditions
have no alternative, consistent with the apostle's veracity, but to represent
it to themselves as an historical fact that Jesus came back from heaven and,
in an interview with Paul, described the scene at the last supper, reciting his
own words in distributing the unleavened cake and handing the wine cup.
If this was what the apostle affirmed, might not the Corinthians have reason
to say, "The experience you relate we do not question as a phenomenon of
your personal life ; but being limited to yourself, and unconformable to the
human ways of knowing, it can have no objective validity for others" ?
The right mode of regarding such language as that of the apostle, where
he speaks of his communion with Christ, was brought vividly home to me
some years ago, while spending some months among a Wesleyan population
in a retired district of the North of England. I was much impressed by the
simple piety of the people, taken one by one, and by the disciplinary power
of their social organization in the diffusion of an affectionate spirit, and the
formation of a standard of character far above the average. They were sufficiently out of the world to have retained the free resort in conversation to
religious conceptions, so that they seemed almost to think in the images and
feel in conformity with the enthusiasms of scripture. One of their elders,
taking a member of my family a drive through the country, pulled up to
speak to a stonebreaker at the roadside ; when a dialogue to the following

self; and all these elements, long taken up into the meaning of the commemorative rite, would inevitably be thrown back into the story of its origin. When, therefore, at the earliest in A.D. 38 (about six years after the event), the passover scene was described by Paul, it had gathered into it the whole gospel of the twelve, and so far as this was less and other than

effect took place:—Good-morning, Nat; glad to see you: I wanted to ask you how did your prayer-meeting come off? Had you a good time of it? —Stonebreaker: Aye, aye, 'twere heart-searching enough to some of us, the Lord knows: but for the chief matter, there were somewhat amiss, as if we had grieved his spirit; for he would not hearken to us, but sent us empty away.—Elder: How so, Nat? what were you putting before him?—Stonebreaker: The troubled soul of sister Margaret. She would have it she is a castaway; she had lost hold of her Saviour: day and night she washed his feet with tears, but he would never say to her, Thy sins are forgiven: she seemed wasting like, and going off into the shadow of death. We besought the Lord to take pity on her, and show her the light of his face; for that she was ever watching for it, as they that watch for the morning. But we prevailed nothing: the poor soul was still sunk very low, and seemed like one forsaken. Howsomever, a way is opening out of her darkness: the Lord has not forgotten her: she will yet praise him for the health of his countenance.—Elder: What makes you so sure of that?—Stonebreaker: Well, you see, when I got home, her woful face was so fast on me I couldna rightly sleep: and as I lay abed, the Lord Jesus came to me, and bid me not be disquieted about the poor sister, and showed me a better way to cast the evil spirit out: saying, You see, you are too many for her, and her heart gets fluttered with all the people and the prayers: go to her, and let her speak out her griefs to you alone: tell her that they are her share in her Saviour's sorrow in Gethsemane: assure her that his peace also he will not fail to give: and in answer to her trust, the promise shall be fulfilled. So in the morning I did as the Lord had said; and as I spoke to her words of comfort, she caught and kindled like at the hope which he had put into my heart; and after prayer together, she seemed, as it were, renewed: her countenance was smoothed and her eye was quiet: and ever since, they say, she takes kindly to her work, and nothing frets her when she is with them: and when she is alone she sings a hymn. No doubt, therefore, the Lord has been as good as his word.

I cannot verbally reproduce the conversation, still less preserve in it the racy vigour of the North country dialect. But its general purport and its dramatic form of impersonation are faithfully presented in the foregoing sketch. There can be no doubt of the perfect simplicity and sincerity with which the tale was told, and of the entire unconsciousness with which inward colloquies of thought and outward dialogues of speech are put upon the same level and reported in the same objective affirmations, the line being crossed like an open boundary overstepped in the night. The student of religions who is not prepared, by divesting himself of his analytical and logical habits, to re-enter the state of mind in which this is possible, must always remain deficient, as it seems to me, both in the sympathy and modes of intelligence which are requisite for a good interpreter.

his own, how could he help, during a score of following years, filling-in and retouching the significance of it as the compend of larger truth ?

His oral informant being out of our reach, we cannot go behind the apostle's own account.   It is the earliest extant, and was in existence for nearly two decades before any of the rest. Nevertheless, it would be a mistake to use his text as an original, to which the others should be required to conform ; for an evangelist may have had access to personal or written testimony fully equivalent in value to that which Paul received at Jerusalem.   The materials which make up even the common tradition embodied in the three synoptists, are not all of the same date ; much less, the sections which are special to each ; and the historical character of the several parts can be determined by no chronological rule, but must be estimated by internal marks, furnished chiefly by a known order in the development of doctrine, enabling the reader to feel an anachronism of thought in the midst of a narrative of fact.   The extent to which theoretical prepossessions may modify, and even mould anew, the materials at an historian's disposal is strikingly exhibited, if we admit the Johannine account of the last supper into comparison with the Synoptists. That both are descriptive of the same occasion is rendered certain by their many marks of identity : in both we have the devil " entering into Judas "; Jesus announcing the betrayal ; the disciples asking which of them it can be ; the answer given by the sign of the dipped sop ; the prediction of Peter's denial ; and the withdrawal of the party after supper to the garden of betrayal.   Yet in the fourth Gospel there is *no communion of bread or wine,* either *personal among themselves or institutive for the future.*   In place of it there is the washing of the disciples' feet ; and, ere they leave the room, there is the long discourse and touching prayer, in which the Paraclete is promised and the orphaned band committed to the Father's benediction and his Spirit's aid.   Whence this entire recast of the story of that night?   Simply from this: that the symbolizing evangelist had made up his mind that Christ on the Cross must be the crowning antitype of the slain lamb of the passover, and must therefore have his death made synchronous with the slaying of the lamb. He could not afford to let him eat of the lamb, and himself celebrate the festival with his disciples the day before, and even institute a commemoration of his doing so. This would be to perpetuate, instead of abolishing, the purely Israelitish significance of his religion. Accordingly the evangelist will not accept the synoptic report of the last days ; he will revise it by shifting the tragedy forwards through twenty-four hours, by removing whatever was thus rendered incongruous, and inserting instead what time had proved to be in true accord with the inner spirit and the intended universality of the new dispensation. If before the middle of the second century the idealization of history had already taken so vast a range, such small beginnings of the process as may resolve the problems of the comparative critic can hardly be denied to kindred productions a century before.

The four accounts of the last supper cannot all be both correct and sufficient, containing as they do several variances.

(1.) In Mark and Matthew the distribution of the bread and the circulation of the cup constitute together an incident of the immediate occasion, appropriate to the crisis and the personal relations of those who were present. But it does not profess to look beyond that room ; no provision is made for its repetition or its extension. There is no hint of an " institution " to be set on foot. Even the prospective terms, " in remembrance of me," which might look no further than that little band of personal companions, are absent. The express appointment of a permanent rite, contained in these words, and in the " This do " (with or without the " As oft as ye drink it "), is limited to the Pauline passage and to Luke, which is taken from it. As Mark exhibits the oldest form of the Jerusalem common tradition, it is probable that he here comes nearest to the oral source of Paul's first knowledge.

(2.) Mark and Matthew also agree in another negative feature. The words of Jesus when giving the bread, " This is my body," stand alone, without the addition of " for you," or " given for you."

(3.) All attribute to Jesus, when handing the cup, the statement it is "my blood of the covenant" (Mark), or "the new covenant in my blood;" Luke adding, "Shed *for you;*" Mark and Matthew, "*for many.*"

(4.) To these Matthew alone adds further, "for the remission of sins."

(5.) Besides these differences in the parallels to the Pauline statement, there is in Luke, as a prelude to his whole account of the institution, a prior handing of the cup by Jesus, as a farewell pledge at parting, with the words, "Take this and divide it among yourselves: for I say unto you, I will not drink from henceforth of the fruit of the vine until the Kingdom of God shall come." And this, again, is preceded by the corresponding statement about the meal, "I have greatly desired to eat this passover with you before I suffer: for I say unto you, I will not eat it, until it be fulfilled in the Kingdom of God." We have thus a duplicate eating and drinking; first, the joint partaking, for the last time, of the usual paschal supper; and afterwards a special passing of the bread and the cup, as the initial act of a usage to be continued till the Advent. By this peculiarity the evangelist does but bring into stronger relief Paul's, "In like manner the cup also, *after* supper," and mark the known custom of the Church in his time; viz., of assembling the members at a common table in expression of their equal brotherhood; and following the actual meal by a Eucharistic offering for the gifts of nature and the grace of Christ. Of these parts, when they come to be distinguished, the first was the "Agape," the second the "Eucharist."

Unless the reader carries to these narratives dogmatic assumptions which bar all historical criticism, viz., that Jesus knew himself to be Messiah, accepted and prearranged his death as a vicarious atonement for Jew and Gentile alike, and his speedy return from heaven to set up "the Kingdom" and preside at its "table with Abraham, and Isaac, and Jacob," as well as his disciples, and that Paul and the Synoptists were exempt from the liabilities of human authorship, he cannot look upon these texts as an untouched photograph of objective facts at the sitting which they represent. The historical

nucleus is doubtless there ; but not without a nimbus of interpretation, and some added colouring by more hands than one.
Reasons already given render it probable that Jesus never assumed the Messianic character, and forbade any claim to it on
his behalf; and more than probable that the doctrine of a
suffering Messiah was worked out to fit the ideal to his case;
and nothing less than certain that the vicarious theory of the
cross, with the admission of the Gentiles to the promises of
Israel, was " the mystery " reserved for the last, and *not* " the
least, of all the apostles."   Yet all these ideas are thrown
back upon Jesus himself, and put into acts and words which
make up the scene at the last supper.   He is made to say, in
his anticipation of death, " The *Son of Man* goeth, even as it
is written of him :"* thus taking that phrase himself in a
Messianic sense which was not appropriated to him till the
resurrection had declared it to be his ; and assuming, as
already familiar, the doctrine of a suffering Messiah, which
first broke on his disciples after he was gone.   The "new
covenant" of which he is said to speak carries an idea foreign
to his teaching (where the words do not occur) and equally
characteristic of the Pauline reasoning.   Not less surely is
the redemption by shedding of blood a *post eventum* interpretation of his death; nor would stress have been laid on
the " *many* " for whom it was shed, before the inpouring of
Gentiles into the Church.   And who that has not indoctri-
nated himself out of all reverent apprehension of the distinctive teaching and mind of Christ can suppose him to make
" remission of sins " conditional on the execution of a substitute, and denied to personal repentance and return of the
wanderer to the Father's arms?   In these phrases I cannot
but see anachronisms.   And though it is impossible to say
exactly how far Jesus might share in the Israelite conceptions
of the future "kingdom," it relieves me to think that the
words " I will no more drink of the fruit of the vine until that
day when I shall drink it new with you in the kingdom of
God," could hardly be addressed to his disciples in that
pathetic hour by one who, in rebuke to the Sadducees, had

* Mark xiv. 21 ; Matt. xxvi. 24.   Cf. Luke xxii. 22, " as it hath been determined."

said, " Ye do err, not knowing the scriptures nor the power of God : for when they shall rise from the dead, they neither marry, nor are given in marriage ; *but are as angels in heaven.*"*

It is one thing however to mark, in the text of a narrative, incongruities inadmissible as history, and quite another to determine how the blank is to be filled when they are removed. Assured knowledge of what was said at the paschal supper is irrecoverably gone : nothing more is in our power than to narrow the range of possibility within which the real facts must lie. While we may be certain that he did not announce his impending death as what he had intended and provided for all along, we may well believe that a shadow of foreboding lay on his spirit that evening, deepening towards its darkest in Gethsemane, and pressing forth the preluding tones of that great agony. While he cannot have told the disciples who for months had been preaching with him and for him the gospel of repentance and the love of God, that to-morrow he was going to purchase their salvation and wash them in his blood, he may rather have called to mind how they had been with him in his temptations and shared the rejoicings of his spirit, and have enjoined them, as they loved him, to remain knit in the bonds of their faith and life together. Though he cannot have promised to put himself, corporeally or incorporeally, into any sacramental bread or wine taken in his name, he may have desired, when the world would not listen to him, that they should not forget him, but when, as now, they brake bread and passed the cup together, should remember with what thankful blessing he sent these symbols round, and should read in them and draw out of them all the meaning of his living presence. These simple outpourings of feeling are all congenial to the occasion. It was a social meal of a band most closely knit around a centre of deepest attach-ment : it was a national festival, stirring to Israelitish piety : it was a joyful celebration, claiming from downcast hearts what they could not give ; for it was a crisis of supreme danger : farewell tones seemed wailing through the air ; and when the moon had set and taken the still night away, they

knew not what the day would bring forth. Times like these
are the divine confessional for tender thought and pathetic
aspiration; but not for instituting rites, explaining emblems,
and defining consubstantiation: their tragic events do not
come on purpose, and preface their catastrophe by telling
what they mean. The "smitten of God and afflicted" are
ever "led, as the blind, a way that they know not:" it is
only afterwards, on the retrospect of mysterious sorrows, that
surviving observers find or fancy what they are for. And
then it comes to be supposed that the sufferer, if he be a
beloved of God, must have been in the secret too; and the
disciples' afterthought steals back into the Master's words.

The historical nucleus of the whole I take to be the joint
observance, by Jesus and his apostles, of their final passover,
as the crown of their common religious life; and his desire
that their union should be unbroken though he were taken
from them, and that in its renewal from time to time the
remembrance of him should be its indissoluble bond, as if his
hand still brake the bread and passed the cup. Here is no
new rite, but merely an assumed continuance of a community
of life begun. And even if there were, it would have to be
taken, not as a perpetual vehicle of grace to mankind for ever,
but as a brief usage to span the watch-hour till Christ returns.
This the apostle Paul expressly says: and if this is what he
"received of the Lord," it shows how wide an interpretation
must be given to such expressions.

Some critic has remarked that the two views of Christ's
death (supposing it to be symbolized by the sacramental
elements), viz., that it was an atonement by blood, and that
it was an antitypal paschal "lamb that was slain," are both
due to the apostle Paul, who in the same epistle whence we
have quoted the first, announces the second, in the words,
"Christ, our passover, is sacrificed for us:" so that, if we
looked to this alone, we should suppose him to have antici-
pated the fourth gospel in referring the crucifixion to the
day of the passover. Were it really so, the apostle must have
lost sight of one of the doctrines, when giving expression to
the other; for if the death of Christ was an atoning sacrifice,
it could not have the paschal lamb for its type; and if it was

the passover's antitype, it could be no sin-offering. That annual celebration was a national and family festival to commemorate the flight from Egypt; the lamb that was roasted whole and eaten in haste by the household standing round, was for the table, and not the altar; and the blood sprinkled on the outer door posts had nothing to do with any cleansing from sin, but told how the destroying angel was signalled to pass on. Whoever had the fancy to treat the death of Christ as the ultimate fulfilment of these ideas, might see in it a deliverance from any bondage not self-incurred, but not from one where sinners were the prisoners, and a borrowed righteousness the freedmen's badge. On the other hand, is any type needed for the cross, regarded as paying the debt of human sin, and investing the transgressor with another's righteousness? Then certainly nothing can be got out of the passover, and the only hope is to go, with the writer of the Epistle to the Hebrews, to the sin-offering of the altar, and the ritual of the great day of atonement. But the apostle is not chargeable with combining these incongruous ideas. In the words "Christ our passover is sacrificed for us," he doubtless finds *something* in the passover which is like *something* in the death of Christ. What is this something? Is it any efficacy in atoning for sin? Not in the least. It is simply that each is the initial term of a festival or season under special vows of blamelessness and purity; the paschal day emptying every house of leaven (the emblem of uncleanness), and opening a week permitting only unleavened bread: and the self-sacrifice of the cross inaugurating a new life for the disciple into which nothing that is impure can be allowed to enter. No more is meant than that for the Christian Church the time was come to fling the heathen laxities away, and live within the bounds of sanctity and truth.

In its origin and central idea,—the remembrance of Jesus,—the Lord's supper was necessarily limited to those whom he had made his personal associates. They alone who had known him could "remember" him: those only who were drawn to him by living contact, as hearers of his word and witnesses of his grace and truth, were deemed and called *disciples:* and often the word was distinctively confined to the constant assistants of his ministry. It marked off their relation to him, as that of learner to teacher, and implied docility in them and access to him for solution of their questions. This was the common bond which held them together around him as their Master; they went where he went, and stayed where he stayed, except when he sent them forth on brief missions to prepare his way or multiply his word. They thus grew together into a social and sacred guild, with the rules and habits of a brotherhood. A common purse provided for their daily wants and daily charities. At the resting-places of their journey, whether on the grass, or by the lake, or within the house, they gathered together round their simple meal, dealt out by Jesus as their presiding head, with giving of thanks for refreshment of body and quickening of the soul. And of such habitual κλάσις τοῦ ἄρτου the assemblage round the passover table was but an example, specialized by the anniversary and the sorrowful tension in the hearts of all. It is evident that this habitual social union, tinged with freer and deeper converse than in the formal Jewish "use and wont," was felt to be an endearing and binding feature in their blended life, and some nameless grace in the personality of Jesus invested it with a sacred charm. It drew the attention of disaffected observers, and raised questions about the manners of the group and their leader: 'Why he came eating and drinking, and with a company of associates, instead of living on locusts and wild honey like the solitary of the desert?'* 'Why his disciples dispensed with the Pharisaic rules of ablution before eating?'† It deepened the claim upon the fidelity of each that he had his place at the common table; and was the most piercing reproach to Judas, "He that eateth my bread lifted up his heel against me.":

When the members of this fraternity, dispersed from Calvary, were reunited at Jerusalem under the eye of their Master in heaven, and in the faith of his early return, nothing could be more natural than that they should resume the order of life so recently suspended; and that, in recurring to that "breaking of bread" together, they should dwell with an

* Matt. xi. 18, 19.   † Mark vii. 2, 5.   ‡ John xiii. 18.

intense stress upon the last evening, when so perplexing a sorrow had filled their hearts. As they were no longer a wandering mission, but stationary in the holy city, the new members who were added to them from the residents there fell into their usages, and, as belonging to their "household of faith," were welcomed to the disciples' gathering at what was now regarded as the table of the Lord. The swelling numbers soon outgrowing the limits of a room, similar centres of brotherhood sprang up in various parts of the city, all on the same principle, and repeating the same type, of religious equality: "day by day continuing steadfastly with one accord in the temple, and *breaking bread at home*, they did take their food with gladness and singleness of heart, praising God and having favour with all the people."[*] The still increasing multitude exceeding ere long the capacity of private houses, and requiring larger organization, places of meeting were found for the ἐκκλησία, to which the members repaired, not for worship only, but for offices of the common table (κοινὸς ἄρτος). When and how this took place in Jerusalem is unknown; but the Apostle Paul describes a painful example at Corinth of "coming together *in the church* not for the better, but for the worse," "to eat the Lord's supper."[†] From this we learn that the provisions spread for the equal use of all, and in express recognition of their brotherhood as children of God, are snatched at by the first comers, and abused to purposes of greed and excess, so that "one has to go away hungry, while another gets drunk;" and thus the festival of mutual affection (the ἀγάπη) is turned into a mess of scrambling appetite and discontent; and the eucharistic distributed bread with the sequel of the communion cup,[‡] whereby the spirit of Christ had consecrated the whole, is dropped out with insult. To a community gathered from the Gentiles, more familiar with the Pagan sacrificial feasts than with the Jewish passover and its significance for the twelve, the remembrance of Jesus on that paschal night did not strongly appeal; and they

---

[*] Acts II. 46.   [†] 1 Cor. xi. 17, 20–22.

[‡] I call it "*sequel*" because the apostle gives this as the order which he had prescribed to the Corinthians ("the cup also *after supper*"); but it is doubtful whether the communion rite was usually severed from the Agape till the second century.

let the religious appendix to the act of fellowship fall through ; and, once bereft of its spirit, abused its elements to the ruin and reversal of even the social influence connected with it.

With the constant influx into the Church of new members who believed only on the word of others, and who waited for a Christ in the future rather than looked on him in the past, the number of those who could "remember" him became ever smaller ; with this inevitable effect : that, of the two relations consecrated at the last supper, viz., that of personal discipleship to him as Head, and that of collateral love of each to all as brethren, the latter gained upon the former, as the living and immediate ever must upon the ideal and remote. The change is marked by the fact that the term "disciples" disappears, as the exclusive right of the personal followers of Jesus, and that the new Christians are habitually called "brethren." The prominence of this relation threw the Agape with its common table to the front of the apostolic institution, especially in Jerusalem, where a large number of indigent converts depended upon it for daily sustenance, and made it not merely an expressive symbol of fraternal fellowship, but a material necessity. The expression in the book of Acts, that they had "all things in common," certainly says too much if understood to denote, in the modern sense, absolute "community of goods." For in this case there could have been no class of "poor" ; yet the one condition on which the Jerusalem Apostles agreed to recognize the Gentile ministry of Paul was, that he should levy contributions from his Church for the Jerusalem poor.* Indeed the historian himself qualifies his own phrase by adding that when possessions were sold by the owner for the common good, the proceeds were available for the relief of each "*according to his need.*" He also tells us of complaints on behalf of the widows of the Greek Jews, respecting favouritism shown towards the Hebrew widows in the daily ministration of alms.† These are symptoms, not of communism, but only of a large and permanent poor's fund, out of which allowances were apportioned by official almoners. The recognition of brotherhood was concentrated in the Sunday Agape ;

* Gal. ii. 10.   † Acts vi. 1.

the more appropriately as that was the usual occasion for the presentation of gifts to the common fund at the disposal of the deacons, or to other requirements of the Church.

We are indebted to Briennius's important discovery of the "Teaching of the Twelve Apostles" for an actual model of the Communion Service as it was administered, probably, in the early part of the second century. It is as follows : "As regards the Eucharist, give thanks after this manner: first, for the cup: 'We give thanks to thee, our Father, for the holy vine of David, thy servant, which thou hast made known to us through Jesus, thy servant: to thee be glory for ever.' And for the broken bread: 'We give thanks to thee, our Father, for the life and knowledge which thou hast made known to us through Jesus, thy servant: to thee be glory for ever. As this broken bread was scattered upon the mountains and gathered together became one, so let thy Church be gathered together from the ends of the earth into thy kingdom : for thine is the glory and the power through Jesus Christ for ever.'*   Now after being filled, give thanks after this manner : 'We thank thee, holy Father, for thy holy name, which thou hast caused to dwell in our hearts, and for the knowledge and faith and immortality which thou hast made known to us through Jesus, thy servant : to thee be glory for ever.   Thou, O almighty Sovereign, didst make all things for thy name's sake : thou gavest food and drink to men for enjoyment, that they might give thanks to thee : but to us thou didst freely give spiritual food and drink and eternal life through thy servant.   Before all things we give thanks to thee that thou art mighty : to thee be glory for ever.   Remember, O Lord, thy Church, to deliver her from evil and to perfect her in thy love : and gather her together from the four winds, sanctified for thy kingdom which thou didst prepare for her : for thine is the power and the glory for ever.' "†   "And on the Lord's day come together, and break bread, and give thanks, having before confessed your transgressions, that your sacrifice may be pure.   Let no one who has a dispute with his fellow come

---

* Ch. ix. 1–4. See Schaff's oldest Church Manual, called the Teaching of the Twelve Apostles.   Edinb. 1887.   P. 190.

† Ibid. ch. x. 1–5, p. 194.

together with you until they are reconciled, that your sacrifice may not be defiled.   For this is that which was spoken by the Lord : In every place and time offer me a pure sacrifice : for I am a great King, saith the Lord, and my name is won-derful among the Gentiles."[*]

This sample of the regular Church ministration of the chief "sacrament," from a date about as early as the book of Acts, is full of interest and instruction ; especially on the following points :—

I. The *Order* of administration has some unexpected features.

1. The *Cup*, with a preluding prayer.

2. The *Bread*, with corresponding introductory prayer.

3. The " being filled," i.e., consuming the provision of the Agape together.

4. The closing thanksgiving prayer.

The confession of sins, which is conjoined with the discharge of alienations from the heart, as a condition of acceptable participation, may be understood, like the reconciliation, as a private act of penitence : or, as a collective acknowledg-ment by the whole congregation through the voice of public prayer.   A similar injunction occurs in an earlier chapter, addressed to the individual catechumen, rather than to the body of communicants: "In the congregation thou shalt confess thy transgressions, and thou shalt not come to thy prayer with an evil conscience."[†]   I think, with Professor Schaff, that this probably refers to open confession to one's fellows of wrong-doing, being equivalent to the exhortation in James v. 16, " confess your sins one to another."   In any case, the confession is to be prior to the service, and not a part of it.

It is clear that in the foregoing order there is no separation of the Communion from the Agape.   They are absolutely identified ; the social meal consisting of the very ποτήριον and ἄρτος τῆς εὐχαριστίας which have been introduced by the first and second prayer, and having for its contents the bless-ing acknowledged in the third.   This feature forbids us, I

---

should say, to seek for the date of the διδαχή much later than the close of the first century.

II. The contents of the three prayers present some points of interest.

1. With regard to what we do *not* find there, it is surely remarkable that there is no allusion to the *last supper* which the service is held to commemorate: no reference to the *death of Christ;* and therefore none to its alleged effects, viz., *atonement, new covenant, remission of sins.*

2. The *positive enumeration of divine gifts* does not modify the impression of these omissions. The first prayer gives thanks for "the holy. Vine of thy servant David," i.e., in evident allusion to Psalm lxxx., the *Church* as the "Israel of God," "the Vine which his right hand had planted"; * the institution of a *holy Society.*

The second prayer gives thanks for "the life and knowledge revealed through Jesus, thy servant,"—a communication of *divine truth.*

The third prayer gives thanks to God for planting in the heart an apprehension of *his name,* i.e., *his nature;* and giving through Jesus the light of *"knowledge, faith, and immortality";* and (in reference to the bread and wine on the table) for the supplies of *food and drink adequate to both natural wants and spiritual life.*

3. The interpretation given to the *symbols* in the Eucharist is not what a sacramentarian would expect.

The Bread, made up of a multitude of corn seeds combined into one substance, stands for the unity of the Church, composed of countless members; and this, without the slightest allusion to the "*body*" *of Christ,* as represented by the visible Christendom.

The Wine is taken to mean no more than *spiritual drink,* the influences which nurture and strengthen faith and love.

4. The title given throughout to Jesus (τοῦ παιδός σου), without even the addition of *Christ,* and identical with that which

* John xv. 1. "I am the true vine" tempts some interpreters to understand the image as referring to Christ himself: but the next words in the text, "which thou hast made *known through Jesus Christ,*" distinguish Christ from the vine. The idea is, that the Church is the *true Israel.*

is given to David, is remarkable in a service supposed to draw its whole meaning from the Incarnation, and to depend on the humanity, only as assumed by the divinity of Christ. No modern celebrant could use such language without incurring the charge of profaning the sacrament.

5. Throughout the prayers there is but one *petition*: viz., that the Church may be perfected in union and sanctity. All else is pure thanksgiving; the pervading presence of which has fixed upon the service the name of *Eucharist*. In this character it is that it is called "a sacrifice" (θυσία); inasmuch as it was essentially, not a supplication for something *from* God, but an *offering* of something *to* God; in which alone consisted, in the eyes of both heathens and Jews, the whole business of a temple service; and without which the Christians presented to them the appearance of a godless race. No incense! no altar! no fire of sacrifice, sending its message aloft to placate an offended Deity! How did such a people hope for the favour of a Heaven of which they took no notice? The answer to such imputations had already been supplied by the prophets and perfected by Christ: the silent devotions of the private heart, the choral fervour of a thankful multitude, were offerings rarer in the giving and more welcome in the receiving than the smoke of censers and the gold of temple gifts. This was the " Christian's sacrifice," not unaccompanied by the free tribute which, on the first day of the week, he had ready to throw into the Church treasury for the aid of the poorer brethren's need. In thus handing over the word θυσία from priestly to prophetic use, the Christian apologists, desiring to free it from clinging ideas of the altar and the knife, often added to it the epithet "spiritual" (πνευματική):—an innocent combination to mark that the offering from man to God was simply an inward act of the soul. But in such attempts to elevate a lower term by the lift of an epithet, it is a question whether the higher will hold up the inferior, or the inferior will drag down the higher. And from following the example of this heterogeneous combination, some mischievous turns have been given to the doctrine of the Communion. As a πνευματική θυσία, the service is an offering to God from the spirit of man, and plainly consists in the *prayer alone*, as the

solo medium of possible communion with him. But when the epithet takes possession of the *bread*, the πνευματικὴ τροφή must bo taken in the inverse order, as the gift *of God to man :* if πνευματικὴ be understood of the *human* spirit, a gift which nurtures the inward life of the natural soul : if of the *Divine* spirit, a gift which imparts a supernatural grace. In the *Didache,* the phrase occurs in the former of these two meanings, and simply includes the Christian faith and knowledge symbolized by the bread among the gifts of God for which thanks are our only possible offering in response. But too easily and too soon the expression, with others like it, slipped into the second of the meanings, and so brought into existence the sacramental idea, the development of which carried Christendom away to the furthest possible point from the religion of its founder. When once it is assumed that, apart from the personal life of the communicant's soul, the material elements themselves are made the media of supernatural grace, they become sacred objects, bringing an incarnation down to things without a soul, and are invested with imaginary powers to heal or harm.

The separation of the Communion from the Agape tended to this result. So long as the assembled brethren ate the bread and drank the wine as parts of a real meal, their perceptible qualities, however touched with an ideal meaning, asserted themselves too strongly to admit of their becoming hiding-places of divine mysteries. But when disconnected from all natural use, and isolated with their symbolized contents, the elements compel the participant to concentrate his mind upon these at a moment when he has nothing else to do, and to make the very most of them by an intense strain of thought and feeling. And where Nature has no place, and Grace claims all, the equilibrium is lost which bars the entrance of superstition. The history of the Church is certainly in accordance with this view. With the enlargement of its boundaries, the semi-communistic feeling of the first age wore away, the differences of social station made themselves felt, and the fraternal supper became rarer, and at last was dropped : the memorial distribution of the bread and wine being alone preserved, and erected into an independent rite. It was a gradual change, stealing on from place to place: but by the end of the second century was apparently pretty complete. From that time the degeneration of the Eucharist from a Thanksgiving to a Sacrament, and even an "unbloody sacrifice," was rapid; taking however, only with accelerated speed, a direction not untraced in the first age, and even marked for a few steps by the apostle Paul himself. The belief which apparently he at first entertained, that discipleship to Christ was a security against death, seems to have connected itself in his thought with the emblems of the sacrifice on Calvary, of which the communicants partook; as if the bread and wine, when taken as the virtual (glorified) body of the Redeemer, were literally what Ignatius calls them, " the antidote of death," " the medicament of immortality,"* and had a mystical antiseptic influence, beginning the assimilation of the disciple's person to that of his risen Lord. Without positively asserting for the elements this efficacy as a charm against natural decay, he negatively implies it, by attributing the sicknesses and death which have cast a shade over the Corinthian Church to their failure of right participation in the communion : " for this cause," he says, " many are weak and sickly among you, and many sleep :" " for he that eateth and drinketh eateth and drinketh judgment unto himself, if he discern not the body."† By missing the real virtue of the rite, and taking nothing but common bread and wine, they fail to appropriate the benefits of Christ's death for them, and remain liable to the lot of his physical nature,—‡ involved in his death, instead of delivered by it. If the apostle had previously encouraged the expectation in others which he avowed for himself, of living into the kingdom of God without passing through the mortal transition, he would naturally be thus driven upon *moral causes*, in order to explain as special exceptions the drooping and failing lives which the disappointed Corinthians had to report.

Not less strongly marked is this eucharistic belief in the fourth Gospel : but with a difference necessitated by the

---

* φάρμακον ἀθανασίας, ἀντίδοτος τοῦ μὴ ἀποθανεῖν. Ad. Ephes. xx. 2.
† 1 Cor. xi. 29, 30.
‡ Not "guilty of the body and blood of the Lord."

evangelist's peculiar Christology. As in his history of the passion-week there is no paschal supper with the disciples, no institution or model of a communion rite, there would not seem to be room for any doctrine respecting a memorial service which is without original. And *as a commemoration* he never directly mentions it, much less interprets it. But when he wrote, he found the usage universal in the Church, as an integral function of its life ; and it was indispensable to provide it with a meaning in harmony with the characteristic thought of his Gospel. This he indirectly does in the strange and startling discourse said to have been pronounced by Jesus in the synagogue at Capernaum :* for when the evangelist makes Jesus insist on the conditions of eternal life under the image of " eating his flesh and drinking his blood," he undoubtedly had in view the elements of the Communion. " He that eateth my flesh and drinketh my blood hath eternal life :" " my flesh is meat indeed, and my blood is drink indeed : he that eateth my flesh and drinketh my blood abideth in me, and I in him. As the living Father sent me, and I live because of the Father, so he that eateth me shall also live because of me. This is the bread which came down from heaven."† This is virtually to say, ' He who realizes the meaning and contents of the Communion rite, and draws the aliment of his spirit from me, shall live as I live.' But when you ask ' What then *is* the meaning of the Communion rite ? ' you find that it has nothing whatever to do with the death on the cross, and would be there just the same if, instead of dying, Christ had been visibly divested of his humanity, and restored to the " bosom of the Father " by some living change. The " bread " does not mean " the body which is *broken* for you," but the body which is *assumed* for you : and the wine does not mean " the blood " which is " *shed* for you," but that which has *throbbed and glowed* for you, and passed to you with answering flush, as the life that kindles your life. It is the whole episode of the Incarnation, and not its catastrophe in the Crucifixion, that is represented in these symbols. " *I am* the living bread that came down from heaven," " the bread of God which giveth life unto the world:" " your fathers did eat

John vi. 22–65.   ·   † Ibid. 54–57.

manna in the wilderness, and they died:" "Moses did not give you bread out of heaven: but my Father giveth you the true bread out of heaven." It is the Divine "Word" that is thus "sent out of heaven," and "made flesh" for the spiritual nurture of mankind: when it is said that they have access to this bread by Christ "giving his flesh for the life of the world," the reference is, not to the flesh of his death, but to the flesh of his living humanity, which brings him into contact with men and enables him to speak to them "the word of God." This, at least, is the interpretation which is added, as from himself, of his own "hard saying:" "does this cause you to stumble? What then if ye should see the Son of Man ascending where he was before? It is *the spirit* that quickeneth: *the flesh* profiteth nothing: the words that I have spoken unto you, they are spirit, they are life."

In accordance then with the dominant thought of the whole gospel, the Communion rite, like the Paraclete, is the virtual prolongation of Christ's presence with his disciples, the former sustaining the renewing and sanctifying power of his Divine humanity: the latter, imparting light and faculty to solve for themselves problems they would once have referred to him. The stress which the evangelist lays on the symbolic acts of eating and drinking the media of this influence, must certainly be taken to imply the conception of a mystic efficacy in them transcending their natural range of operation, and lifting them into indispensable means of grace. The communicant is drawn by a secret process into a nearer assimilation to the *Person* of the incarnate Logos, who has "life in himself," and imparts it to all who are his. He is the centre and sole appointed supply of eternal life to men: as the bread that came down from heaven he renders imperishable all who take it. But, in order to belong to him and be reserved for everlasting life, it is indispensable for the disciples to eat his flesh and drink his blood: for, in the elements of the Communion, they partake of no common food,—no bread that perishes and lets perish,—but a divine manna, a transcendent elixir, of which "he that tastes shall live for ever": he hath Christ abiding in him, and so he shall abide in Christ, and be secure of being raised to eternal life. Whilst the Son of God remains on earth, the principle of immortality is shut up and concentrated in his human personality. He lays down his human life in order to set free its Divine and sanctifying power for unlimited expansion ; that it may become life to the world, and from a finite presence may break into indefinite regeneration. The eucharistic elements are the medium of its distribution and appropriation, drawing together and constituting the family of immortals. Without partaking, no immortality.

Here then, within the scriptures themselves, unless we are to reduce them to the insipid emptiness of a rationalist interpretation, we have the well-defined germ of a truly sacramental doctrine. And after this, the gradual construction of a complete sacerdotal system was only a question of time. Since the mystical efficacy of the elements certainly did not belong to them as they came from the bakehouse and wine-vat, it was supposed to be brought into them by the prayer of consecration : and then the defining fancy of men began to press the question wherein consisted so marvellous a change. As early as Justin Martyr an answer is given, which seems indistinguishable from the doctrine of consubstantiation : he says, " We take these elements not as common bread and common drink : but have been taught that just as our Saviour Jesus Christ, when incarnated by the Word of God, took our flesh and blood for our salvation, so on being blessed by the prayer of his word, the food which is converted into nutriment of our flesh and blood, is also the flesh and blood of that incarnated Jesus."[*] Irenæus gives a somewhat different reply ; suggesting that the divine Logos that assumed humanity in the person of Jesus enters the elements in the Communion and conveys into them their supernatural powers ; repeating in fact the miracle of the incarnation. This, however, seemed to put the wrong constituent of Christ's person into the bread and wine, viz.: the *spiritual and preexistent Logos*, instead of the *flesh and blood*, which are affirmed to be there, and of whose mode of presence an account is needed. In the attempt to amend this answer, a millennium and a half of so-called " developments of doctrine " into better defined but more astounding superstition

[*] Apol. i. 66.

was entered upon, and disturbs us with its ferment still. The very problem discussed invested the bread and wine, as soon as the prayer was said, with properties unknown and awful, to which were attributed all sorts of magical effects. Tertullian, for example, remarks: " We scrupulously guard against any drop of wine or crumb of bread falling to the ground."* In the third century, the administration of the sacrament to infants shows how completely it had passed into a consecrated charm. And a little later the confusion was completed by its habitual use as a *viaticum mortis*, irrespective of any spiritual participation by the dying subject. Whether it was the earthly or the heavenly body of Christ which was in the elements at the Communion remained for ages undetermined. In the ninth century a great ecclesiastic maintained in a treatise, presented to Charles the Bold, that the very body which had been born of Mary was reborn of the bread and wine upon the altar, and sometimes in the visible form of a lamb, or of a boy, with real flesh and blood. When, two centuries later, the word Transubstantiation was introduced, it brought with it new, if not grosser, trivialities : and Pope Innocent III. scrupulously defends the doctrine against the objection that, if the substance is transformed, and what was bread is bread no more, the mice may eat the body of Christ. Consequences like these drove Luther and the Anglicans to their modified conception, that the *Real Presence* in the elements of Christ's person need not involve any *real absence* of the bread and wine in their physical qualities ; and that these may still speak to the senses while the others apply themselves mystically to the soul. The superstition is more decent, but the miracle and its spiritual mischief remain. You cannot have a *supernatural institution* without a *perpetual priest :* nor a perpetual Priest without a hopeless blight upon the freedom and the power of the human soul. Embodied sanctities, enclosed in given material objects, and released from dependence on the living love and moving conscience of mankind, can never be anything but magic spells and charms ; enslaving men with false reverence, while the delusion lasts : and when it breaks, delivering them into a rude irreverence,

* De corona, III.

N N

not truer in itself, but more transient in its duration. The
only centre of repose, remote alike from both, lies in the pure
and direct relation between each naked soul and God.

§ 2. *Future Crown of Life.*

If there is any part of the work of Christ which is owned
alike by the disciple and by the mere observer of his religion,
it is the profound impression he has produced of human
immortality. The fact is undisputed, that Christendom
throughout, and most intensely in its most characteristic
periods, has carried its chief allegiance beyond the immediate
scene to "another country, even a heavenly;" for it is the
ground not less of complaint from the opponents of Christianity,
than of attachment on the part of its votaries. The Church,
it is said, has so preoccupied men's minds with visionary
interests, and so spent itself in providing for them, that
temporal well-being has suffered injurious slight, and in the
flight from invisible evils there is no visible good that has not
been flung away. Dispose as he may of this objection, the
disciple finds something infinitely higher in the Christian
life for an ideal future than in the Pagan surrender to the
actual present ; and thinks it a sublime thing that the heart
of the world should have been held in upward aspiration
for so many ages, and have drawn down, from beyond its
boundary clouds, divine lights upon its passion, grief and sin.
Wherever the genius of Christendom seems to thrill him with
a tenderer tone, and reach him in deeper seats, reducing his
moan of pain to a patient monody, touching sorrow with
sanctity, and turning the strife of conscience into a drama of
personal affection, *there* is secretly present the form of infinite hope which is inseparable from the trust in infinite love.

A certain eclipse of this world by the interposition of
another to intercept the light of God is on all hands attributed to Christianity, with protest by some, with triumph by
others. The concerns of the individual soul have been carried
off into a supramundane region, and raised there to such a
magnitude as to dwarf the simple duties, and flatten the civic
and social claims, which constitute the real material of life.

A religion which takes over all that is choice in beauty, in holiness, in joy, into the space beyond Death, must, it would seem, leave the hither side in shadow, and evince its own power by abating the desires which find their satisfaction here. How then did this transcendent Hope become characteristic of the new Faith? Is it the one great discovery, given by a sudden burst of revelation, and delivered at once in its full force to the human heart? and shall we say that Judaism was the true religion of this life, and Christianity of the other? Was it the work of Jesus, either by his word or by his resurrection, first to open the boundless future, and alter in a moment the whole proportions of our nature and our lot? And did all the pious before him live wholly in the temporal, and all after him chiefly in the eternal? Not so. These paroxysms of transition are impossible to human thought, and uncongenial with the Divine method; and if ever we imagine them, it is because, as we look over the crowded plain, we are liable, with all the aid of our watch-tower and our glass, to catch the figures at intervals of changed place, and miss the movements that have borne them thither. No consciousness appears in the ministry of Jesus of any extension of hope that might not be drawn from the old scriptures and was not familiar to the prayers of every synagogue. It was a Jew who asked him what he should " do to inherit eternal life." It was a doctrine of the Pharisees for which Jesus gave verdict when he proved, from the ancient names of God, that " the dead live."* And his own resurrection was treated by his apostles only as the leading example of a general fact which they believed before, and which, except in its *date*, they believed no otherwise afterwards. It was not by sudden disclosure, but by a gradual growth of faith, which had been in progress for ages, and was still to continue for ages more and is unexhausted yet, that the temporal life of man' became, in Christendom, but a prelude to the eternal, and the real drama of the Divine government was lifted from the level of the present to a higher stage.

The earliest vision of an ideal Future which settled into a

* Matt. xxii. 20–32. Mark xii. 24–27. Luke xx. 34–37.

prophetic hope looked no further than this world, and was simply a political aspiration in a crisis of national distress. The sigh of the captives in Babylon for their native land, their songs of home demanded from them by the stranger, their memory of Zion bathed now in a light that had never clothed it before, were turned by their prophets, as interpreters of the mercy and righteousness of God, into a longing trust in restoration. The God of their Fathers would not desert them, but still, in this new wilderness of exile, would move before them as their guide in cloud or fire, and never leave them till they stood within the borders of their promised land. Had he not given his word to faithful Abraham, and shown in the glory of his servant David how little it had been forgot? And was his Providence in history going to cast them off, and take up with the nations that blasphemed him? Impossible! sooner would the nursing mother forget her child than Jehovah forget the sorrows and disappoint the inheritance of Israel. When he had chastened for a season, he would lift up a reconciled countenance on them again; the story of his ancient mercies would be resumed; a highway would be opened across the desert for their return; the parched land should be fruitful to feed them, water from the rock should cool their thirst, and the river should divide to let them through; the bulwarks and the sanctuary of Jerusalem should be rebuilt; and her people, purified by the bitterness of their afflictions, should be all righteous, and know the Lord from the least even to the greatest. Nor would the disturbed balance of justice fail to be set right; the oppression of the heathen should be known no more; for the godless nations who had ruled, it should now be the turn to serve, and they that would not serve should perish. Arising from the ashes of her long contrition, and clad in garments of beauty, Zion should be the joy and pride of the whole earth, and none that lifted up an arm against her should prosper.

This dream of exile, the imagery of which, painted in the indelible colouring of the prophets, has never faded but become symbolical of higher things, is the original type of every later "*Kingdom of God.*" Its scene was on the map: its hour was within a life-time, and while you spake of it, might strike.   Death did not lie in the midway to distance it, but only a little longer patience of the living.   No super-natural spaces, no night-journey between the worlds, cut it off from the approach of thought ; but only the sunny tracks of the caravan and a few days' evening halt at the margin of the wells ; and then, the bushy banks of Jordan, and the palm-groves of Jericho, and at last the well-remembered ravines that gird the city.   The whole picture was political and patriotic, the image of a State perfected in the faithful-ness of its citizens and the blessing of its God.   In due time, the return of its captives partially ensued ; but as it never realized the brilliant visions of the seers, as new generations witnessed new apostasies and suffered more odious oppressions, as the march of events still increased the dependence and the dispersion of Israel, instead of gathering them home as the sacred caste of humanity, the promise moved on into the future, and the glory of the later days seemed yet to come. New prophets adorned it with fresh features, and spread their canvas on a larger scale ; sometimes softening the harsh self-righteousness of the theocratic spirit ; but for the most part, as the passion of disappointed faith became more intense, deepening the vindictive shadows of the picture, and giving larger space to the extermination of idolatrous nations than to the happy supremacy of the people of God.   But, throughout these changes, and during the ministry of Jesus, and till after the Apostolic age, and not less among the Christians than among the Jews, the essence of the vision was still the same : —of a divine Commonwealth in Palestine, to redress the wrongs and terminate the confusion of history, and realize unmixed the justice and holiness of the providential rule.

In its original form, the conception of the restored and perfected Jerusalem had embraced only the liberated exiles who were to rebuild and establish the sacred city.   It represented the pious work which the enthusiasm of the living generation marked out for itself, or accepted at the prophetic call.   But as the hope became the inheritance of generations undistin-guished from each other ; and as the prophets outvied their forerunners in the splendour of their representations ; as habit fixed and devotion consecrated the scenery of the latter days,

it seemed as if the glory so long deferred would be too great
to be lavished on the degenerate eyes of its last expectants
only; while those to whose fidelity and patience the promise
had been given, in whose glowing words it had been handed
down, who had stood up against terror and death in witness
to it, had no part or lot in that for which they lived and
perished. Were they to lie in the prisons of the Underworld,
and dwell among the shades, while all that they had longed
to see, and tried to hasten, was realized without them, and
their own songs of hope were being chanted in the tones of
triumph? It could not be: it would be a fatal defect in the
action of the drama were a place not provided for them. They
were but in the upper store-house of Hades (" the bosom of
Abraham ") reserved for the souls of the righteous; and doubtless it was placed there, far above the deep dungeon where
the wicked lie, that it might give up its captives to return to
life upon the earth when the trumpet sounds on Zion. For,
what kingdom could be glorious to their children from which
Abraham and Isaac and Jacob were shut out? By such
natural train of thought did the veneration for pious ancestors
enlarge the first register of the Kingdom of God, and open
pages for the names of the historic dead. And this additional
feature, this unlocking of the superior half of the mortuary
world, entering with Daniel (xii. 2), remains constant to the
time of Paul.

There is still another source of enrichment to the original
contents of " the Kingdom." The conception of the *Underworld* was inseparably connected, in the Hebrew imagination,
with their practice of *Cave-burial*, which seemed to introduce
the dead into the interior darkness of the earth, and leave the
soul to explore a way, and wait a guide, to deeper clefts and
lower mysteries. But tradition told of a few exceptional cases
in which there was no burial. Enoch had disappeared, "for God
took him." Moses had passed away, and his sepulchre could
never be found. Elijah had been swept aloft in a chariot of fire.[*]
Of all these, the abode was therefore in the upper and eternal
light of the Divine pavilion; and they mingled, as the only

* Irenæus (Hær. B. V. 3-7) cites the translation of Enoch and Elijah
among his proofs of *the resurrection of the flesh.*

human element, in the society of higher natures. As they too were prophets of the holy nation, nay, the greatest of them all, who could deny to them their share in the later glory? and how could the Kingdom dispense with their presence? They also must come, and, as befits their prophetic character, rather *before* the hour, than at the time, when the hosts are mustering from below.* And so it was the belief of every Jew that " Elias must first come." Out of the elements thus accumulated have arisen all the Christian conceptions of the Kingdom of Heaven in the sense of a life beyond death; chiefly by the interfusion of three additions,—the nomination of Jesus of Nazareth as the Messiah, the doctrine of a suffering Messiah, and the assurance of his resurrection. When this constant supplement had been inwrought into the prior Jewish texture, the expectation gained considerably in definiteness : the person was no longer a secret; he had delivered his notice, and the *time* was near ; he was an *immortal*, and would bring heavenly powers to terminate the imperfection of earthly and mortal things. But these fixed conditions might variously select from the previous less determinate materials ; and by taking more or fewer, and preferring this to that, and filling up ideally the spaces still left open, disciples of different genius might arrive at conceptions of "last things" far from identical, or even accordant. This has actually occurred, not only by development in the course of time, but within the first age and among the writers of the New Testament ; so that scarcely has an eschatological faith been propounded in Christendom, though as different from the rest as that of "the latter day saints " or the Universalists from that of the Divina Commedia, which is without some countenance from the Christian Scriptures.

The prevalent form of the earliest expectation respecting the "kingdom of God " is represented in the Synoptical Gospels, especially in the prophetical chapters of Matthew† and Luke,‡ which so strangely mix up together the downfall of Jerusalem and the " coming of the Son of Man on the clouds of Heaven." It alters nothing in the Jewish preconception, but simply ap-

---

* First expressed by Malachi, iv. 5, 6.　　† xxiv., xxv.
‡ xxi. 7–36.

plies it to the person of Jesus and the conditions of the times. It treats the scenery and contents of the "kingdom" as known from Daniel, and announces it as "at hand." The premonitory signs of the approaching crisis, wars and famines and unheard-of $\vartheta\lambda\tilde{\imath}\psi\iota\varsigma$, lying prophets and desecration of the Temple, are enumerated; and then, at the appearance of "the Son of Man with power and great glory," and the sound of the angels' trumpets to "summon his elect from the four winds," the tribes of the earth that know him not mourn that the hour is come which shall take them all away. Whether mourning or rejoicing, all are gathered together before the throne of the Son of Man, separated from one another as the shepherd's goats from the sheep, to hear the judgment passed upon them: those who had received the Son of Man when he taught in their streets, or had befriended his disciples, being admitted to eternal life: those who had left his invitations unheeded and his people uncared for being doomed to eternal fire, prepared for the devil and his angels.

To measure the interval between this picture and any modern Christian's conception of "the kingdom of Heaven," the reader has only to notice the following points: (1.) The whole scene is *terrestrial*,—the descent of an invading army from heaven upon the earth, on the grass of which the throne is planted and the populations stand before the Judge: (2.) That the multitude includes none but the *living generation*, swept in from their cities and their lands; no resurrection is mentioned and no dead are there; and judgment goes by the reception given to the warning advent and its messengers; it is accordingly said, "this generation shall not pass away till all these things be accomplished:" (3) The judicial test that parts the ways of eternal blessing and eternal curse is purely moral and affectional, conditioned by no redemption, mentioning no cross, and implying no gift of foreign righteousness: (4.) In the absence of any hint of a termination to the reign on earth "prepared from the foundation of the world," it is evidently meant to be taken as eternal, and not as for a term of years, the mere prelude to an ulterior consummation.

In all the writings of this Judaic type, the dominant assumption is, that the work of Christ is mainly yet to come:

the promise is given, the person has been named, and sent as his own forerunner, and the preparations for his return are yet in train, but the "Kingdom" itself is only ready to be revealed. The intensity of the interest is all in the future; the attitude of the present is expressed in a word, "Watch, and again I say unto you, Watch!" "Lift up your heads, for your redemption draweth nigh." Of this prospective out-look several new features, not found in the Synoptic picture, make their appearance in the Book of Revelation. *There* is laid open to the Seer what is passing in heaven during the interval of watching and waiting upon earth ; and among the particulars unheard of before are the following:

(1.) The Crucified appears before the throne of God as a Lamb that had been slain ; and, having with his blood purchased unto God men of every tribe to make a holy kingdom, is celebrated by the heavenly host as worthy to break the seals and open the judgment-rolls of the book of Life, and receive power and glory, and blessing for ever.* The judicial appointment is thus immediately appended to the giving of "his life as a ransom for many."

(2.) Under the altar are seen the souls of the martyrs, slain for their testimony to the word of God, crying out "how long, O Holy and True, dost thou not avenge our blood?" A white robe is given to each ; and they are told to be patient yet a little time, till their number is made up.† The Seer then must henceforth think of these servants of Christ as already taken, one by one, to be with him where he is, and not as in the waiting-halls of Hades, to rise first at his coming.

(3.) The terrible meaning contained in Matthew's phrase, the tribes of the earth shall mourn at "the sign of his coming" is unfolded for the Seer, as he watches the advance of the "Faithful and True Word of God," leading his White Squadrons to the final victory, and sees how "his sharp sword smites the nations" and wreaks on them "the fierceness of the wrath of Almighty God,"‡ and visiting Rome itself, and all that it carries, with such utter destruction, that it vanishes as a millstone flung into the sea. And so the earth is cleansed for the "City of God" that is to rise instead.

* Rev. v. 6–13.　　　　† Rev. vi. 9–11.　　　　‡ Rev. xvii.–xix.

(4.) The forces of Satan being thus broken, he himself is chained and cast into the abyss, which is sealed up for a thousand years. Not that the Gentile tribes are swept away: they still have their place on the habitable world, but un-seduced by their deceiver, are innocuous to the encampment of the saints. Now therefore begins the reign of Christ; and to make up the number of his elect occurs the first resurrection, which calls from the dead all and only those who bear his name: they will surround and serve him for a thousand years, and never know a second death.* Thus is inaugurated the millennium, which plays so great a part in the faith of Christendom during its first two or three centuries, and at many an epoch of its later history.

(5.) Satan when loosed at the end of the thousand years, has been brought to no repentance by his long imprisonment: " deceiving the nations " as before, he gathers an army to invest the commonwealth of the Saints; but it is consumed by a bolt from heaven; and he is cast into the fiery lake, to be tormented day and night for ever. For the final riddance of the strife and vestiges of ill upon the world, one thing only remains; the second Resurrection, viz., of the mixed multitude of dead: they are brought up, from the tombs and from the sea, to stand before the " great white Throne," while the books are opened and searched for every name, both great and small. They are " judged according to their works;" and they " whose names are not written in the Book of Life are cast into the lake of fire; " into which, as " the last enemy " Death with its Hades is also flung.†

(6.) Is not this then the end of the world-history? and for the immortals told off from the book of life will not the scene change to Heaven? On the contrary, the purified earth now at length fulfils its purpose; and, descending on it from heaven, there is seen the New Jerusalem, vast and glorious, watered by the river and shaded by the trees of life " whose leaves are for the healing of the nations :" for, strange to say, there are still Gentiles around the sacred province, who admire its stainless beauty and marvel at its never-waning light of God and the Lamb, and bring their homage and their gifts through

* Rev. xx. 1-6.   † Ibid. 7-15.

tho gates that are always open.*   Thus, even in this ultimate
and eternal scene, the apocalyptic imagination still clings to the
earth, and rather brings down God from heaven to dwell with
men, than bears them away to be "as the angels" with Him.

With the Apostle Paul, as might be expected, the way is
opened to a more Spiritual conception.   To him, Christ's redeeming work was not a merely promised thing, to be apoca-
lyptically contemplated, but a completed fact that looked down
from the cross and penetrated the inmost depths of human
life, and needed only to be met with an answering gaze in
order to reunite the beholder to the family of God, and make
it of small account whether his place were on earth or in
heaven.   To live in Christ, to commune with God, to have
one love, one will with theirs, it was not necessary to cross
the barrier of death ; " the first-fruits" were already here of
all the blessed harvest experiences there.   It is therefore on
the present and known sample of this eternal life, on its
inner springs of power and peace and outward victories of
faith, that the apostle chiefly dwells ; and on the invisible
sequel which they everywhere imply he expatiates only as the
doubts of others, or personal crises of his own, may seem to
require.   But when he does so, it is highly interesting to
notice the still imperfect fusion of the Judaic elements which
he brought and the diviner which he had found, and their
vain efforts to adjust themselves together.

Setting aside the second Epistle to the Thessalonians as
unauthentic, we meet with only two direct expressions of
eschatological doctrine in the apostle's writings, each in
correction of some misapprehension or contradiction on the
part of his own converts.   In his first preaching of the
ascended Christ, his own "heavenly vision" had so absorbed
him, and so eagerly carried his mind on to the Advent which
came next, that he had spoken as if it might happen to-
morrow when he and his hearers would all be there ; for was
it not to be an event for that living generation ?   He had
forgotten to provide for what befell after he had left Thessalonica : Death pursued its way, and did not pass the Christian door-posts by : in this home or that, the place of the

* Rev. xxi. 1–xxii. 5.

father, wife, or child was vacant; and how desolate would be any gathering of saints which *they* had missed by falling asleep too soon! thrown as they are into the miscellaneous company of the unsanctified dead, how shall they ever be recovered and overtake the dear ones who have gone forth to meet their Lord? It may be that the apostle had never before faced this sorrowful problem, and that now, for the first time, he gives definite form to the parts of his own pre-conception. At all events, his answer is distinct: namely, that on the appearance of Christ, the very first thing will be the rising of the Christians who have fallen asleep, and that then the living whom they have rejoined will, along with them, be carried up to meet the Lord in the air, and be thenceforth ever with him.* It is but the case of Jesus over again: he died, and God raised him to heaven: these disciples have died, and them also God will raise, and bring them back with Jesus's return to heaven.† What is here represented plainly is, a simultaneous resurrection of Christians only to eternal life with Christ and God in heaven. And the sole end of Christ's advent appears to be the gathering of his elect from among the dead and living. No hint is given of any other act, or of any prolonged stay in the terrestrial precincts, affording scope for the scenes of a theocratic drama.

Within a year or two of this earliest exposition of "last things," the apostle wrote that grander description of them which is read at every funeral,‡ and has filled-in the Christian conception of immortality with the most impressive images it contains. It agrees with what he had said to the Thessalonians in the Time-order of events: "Christ the first-fruits; afterwards, they that are Christ's at his coming." It agrees further in limiting the resurrection at that date to

* 1 Thess. iv. 15–17. "We that are alive and are left unto the coming of the Lord shall in no wise precede them that are fallen asleep. For the Lord himself shall descend from Heaven with a shout, with the voice of the archangel, with the trump of God: and the dead in Christ shall rise first: then we that are alive, that are left, shall together with them be caught up in the clouds to meet the Lord in the air: and so shall we ever be with the Lord."

† Ibid. 14. "If we believe that Jesus died and rose again, even so them also that are fallen asleep in Jesus will God bring with him."

‡ 1 Cor. xv., especially 20–23, 50–55.

the Christians; for though in the words " As in Adam all die, so in Christ shall all be made alive,"* he seems to make the resurrection to life co-extensive with the reign of death, such an interpretation misses his real meaning; it is not *the same* "*all*" of which he speaks in the two clauses: each is the "all" of its own class; the one, the "all" of Adam's race, the other, the "all" of Christ's: in neither case bringing the entail, whether of death or of life, to those who are "none of his." The relative *order* also assigned to the rising of the dead, and the transfiguring "change" of the living ("we") is the same as in the statement to the Thessalonians: "*the dead* shall be raised incorruptible, and *we* shall be changed; for this corruptible must put on incorruption, and this mortal must put on immortality."†

Here, however, the parallelism ends. If the Corinthians, in reading their letter, asked, " *Where* then shall we share this incorruptible life with Christ?" they would not indeed find any categorical answer, such as, 'It will be in heaven,' or, 'It will be on earth.' But they would learn how the reign on which Christ enters "at his coming" is to be spent, and at what point it is to culminate; its work is to abolish "all rule and all authority and power; for he must reign till he has put all enemies under his feet: the last enemy that shall be abolished is death."‡ But *Earth* is the gathering-place of the "enemies" of God, and thither therefore it is that their appointed conqueror comes; and there too it is that Death prevails over the Divine life-giver, and swallows up every light he kindles; and nowhere else can these foes be met, and their tyranny be ended by their extinction. So long then as this conflict lasts, the throne of Christ must stand upon this world; and the kingdom of God which he administers must be a commonwealth of saints still environed by alien peoples of mortal race. The underlying conception therefore certainly is that of a simultaneous resurrection of Christians only to a Kingdom of God upon earth.

But "*then* cometh the end, when he shall deliver up the kingdom to God, even the Father;"§ "then shall the Son also himself be subject to him that did subject all things,

* 1 Cor. xv. 22.   † Ibid. 52, 53.   ‡ Ibid. 24–26.   § Ibid. 24.

that God may be all in all."* In announcing this sublime consummation, the apostle gives no formal notice of a change of scene. But can we suppose him to see Christ descend the steps of his throne, only to stand and move with his disciples upon the earth which he has just made the cemetery of incorrigible nations, and the hiding-place of vanquished Death? Must he not rather return to heaven to resign his commission into the Father's hands, and take with him those that are his, the immortal host that have been raised to be like him, and through him united in spirit with God himself? The earth was for the earthy: heaven for the heavenly. "The second man is of heaven:" and "as is the heavenly, such are they also that are heavenly." Where but with God above can be the eternal home and such a hierarchy of spiritual life as the apostle plants in the transcendent space beyond "the end"? Unlike the Apocalypse, which builds a new Jerusalem in heaven to let it down upon this world, he creates and gathers a new and Christ-like humanity below, and when it has adequately tried its immortal powers, lifts it to the beatific vision and the Primary abode of Divine Perfection.

Before quitting this memorable chapter, it is worth while to notice a curious illustration which it incidentally affords of the embarrassing questions raised by the prospect of the near Advent. We have seen how the belief in a "first resurrection" at the Parusia started at Thessalonica an anxious problem respecting the relative place and share, in the crisis, of the survivors and of their departed fellow-believers; and how the apostle Paul laid the anxiety to rest. This was not the only trouble which the foreshadowed Advent brought. Its resurrection selected those only who were disciples of Christ, and had been "baptized into his death."† Now in many a Christian family, loved and honoured members had passed away, ere they had been thus sealed with Messiah's name,—perhaps a father too old for new thoughts, or a mother, for new affections, or a heedless youth who could listen to nothing in Syrian Greek; yet all of them with hearts full of ancient piety. Were they really to be left in the outer darkness, while their children, and brothers and sisters,

* 1 Cor. xv. 28.   † Rom. vi. 3.

passed the sacred gates? So intolerable was the thought that the practice established itself of baptizing them by deputy; living friends undergoing the rite and making the requisite profession in their name;—a practice indirectly sanctioned by the Apostle Paul when he asks what would be the use of it, if the dead were not to rise. " Why should they then be baptized for the dead? "* for it is to secure their rising that it is done.

If between these two apocalyptic passages there is a variance in the laying of the *scene*, in one or two others the apostle is betrayed into a deviation from both in regard to the *time* of passing from death to life. And the difference is here the more evident, because it emerges indirectly in the impulsive outpouring of personal feeling, and not in doctrinal exposition as yet imperfectly cleared from clinging shreds of traditional belief. Writing to the Corinthians in a later epistle, he touches on the question whether, to the Christian, life here is worth living, as compared with what would happen if it closed ; and says, " We know that if our earthly house of this tabernacle be dissolved, we have a building from God, a house not made with hands, eternal in the heavens. For in this we groan, longing to be clothed upon by our habitation which is from heaven ; if so be that, being clothed, we shall not be found naked. For indeed we that are in this tabernacle do groan, being burdened ; not for that we would be unclothed, but that we would be clothed upon, that what is mortal may be swallowed up in life. Now he that hath wrought us for this very thing is God, who gave unto us the earnest of the Spirit. Being therefore always of good courage, and knowing that whilst we are at home in the body we are absent from the Lord (for we walk by faith and not by sight), we are of good courage, I say, and willing rather to be absent from the body, and to be at home with the Lord."†

Not long before this problem was settled for him, he adverts to it again. To the flock at Philippi he says, " To me, to live is Christ, and to die is gain. But if to live in the flesh,—if *this* is the fruit of my work, then what I shall choose I wot not : For I am in a strait betwixt two, having the desire to

<hr>

* 1 Cor. xv. 29. † 2 Cor. v. 1–8.

depart and be with Christ, for it is far better: yet to abide in the flesh is more needful for your sake."*

Here, in this longing " to be absent from the body " in order to be " present with the Lord," in this " going to be with Christ," instead of waiting for " his coming," is the unmistakable anticipation of immediate passage of the individual to immortality at death. If this be so, " they that are Christ's " are already gone, and are not here below to " rise at his coming."

These variations occur in the apostle's treatment of questions arising within the Christian fold and involving no glance beyond. But he has to break these bounds ; for the Gentiles were his care; his function was, to bring them within the compass of God's righteous government, instead of applying to them the sentence of Jewish scorn, as the off-scouring of the world. He can place them on the same platform with Israel only by widening the conception of the Divine Law, so as to cover with its sanctity not only the outward legislation of Sinai, but the inward mandates of the human conscience. This code, written "not on tables of stone, but on the fleshly tables of the heart," supplies, he insists, the rule by which the righteous Judge of all the earth will award to the Gentile the same blessing or curse that visits the Jew who keeps or breaks the law of Moses. The same nature has been given to both : the same will has been revealed to both : and if both have failed and have forfeited the promise, the redeeming grace which interposes for the one, and asks for loving faith instead of perfect work, is no less offered to the other. Whichever of the two therefore presumes to judge or despise the other is without excuse : Wherein he judges another, he condemns himself. "Despisest thou the riches of his goodness and forbearance and long-suffering, not knowing that the goodness of God leadeth thee to repentance ? but after thy hardness and impenitent heart treasurest up for thyself wrath in the day of wrath and revelation of the righteous judgment of God? who will render to every man according to his works; to them that by patience in well-doing seek for glory and honour and incorruption, eternal

* Phil. i. 21-24.

life: but to them that are factious and obey not the truth, but obey unrighteousness, shall be wrath and indignation, tribulation and anguish, upon every soul of man that worketh evil, of the Jew first, and also of the Greek: for there is no respect of persons with God."*

This purely ethical doctrine, which attaches eternal life to faithfulness of conscience, and visits unfaithfulness with wrath and tribulation, assumes free power in man to go with the right in spite of temptation to wrong: it is to a righteousness achieved by his personal will that the heavenly promise is given: and if it is not achieved, the dreadful retribution is treated as *deserved*. How can these assumptions be reconciled with the apostle's fundamental principle, that, in virtue of his carnal constitution, man is "sold under sin," and incapable of realizing the moral good which he knows but passes by? Moreover, in the judgment of God before which the Gentiles are here brought, it is plainly assumed that the searching of hearts will deliver over some to eternal life, others to penal anguish: the former being accepted for their holiness of life. Yet, as Gentiles pure and simple, strangers to the dispensation of grace, they cannot have appropriated the redemption and the righteousness of Christ, and taken to the life of faith, without which, according to Paul's gospel, no one can enter the kingdom of God.

It is impossible to combine these various statements into a coherent whole. The apostle would necessarily start from the Messianic doctrine of his nation; and he certainly ended with the consciousness of a life in Christ and of Christ in him, which was already the beginning of an eternal union, and imbued him with a spirit of holiness not his own. And in this mood, the life here and the life there were so much one that the former would naturally seem to flow into the latter without any period of arrest by the icy touch of death. That the immediate transit of each soul at the passing bell from earth to heaven was his last belief may be reasonably supposed. But in reaching this point, it is vain to conjecture what elements of his traditional conception he consciously dismissed as he went along, and what he retained without

* Rom. ii. 4-11, with the context 1-16.

noticing their incongruity with his advancing thought. But
the presence of inconsistent assumptions in one and the same
exposition indicates at least the occasional ascendency of
fluctuating feeling over exactitude of reflection.

If the Messianic eschatology fell away into the background
of the apostle's mind under the growing influence of Gentile
thought and mystic feeling, it vanished altogether from the
theology of the fourth gospel. For the evangelist, as for the
apostle, the work of Christ was already complete on his leaving the world and going to the Father; and if there was yet
in reserve an appendix of futurity, it was not that the Son of
God had half fulfilled the conditions of human salvation, but
only that the operation of the change was large and long, and
needed time to bring to pass all that was bespoken. For both
these writers, therefore, what was yet to come paled before
the glory of the realized past; and to Paul the Cross, to the
evangelist the Incarnation, were the all in all of the revealed
economy. Between them, however, there was a difference as
to the contents of what yet remained to be. To the former,
while still not quite free from Messianic images, the future
included some dramatic incidents, of visible resurrection, of
bodily transformation, of public judgment, on the way to a
final merging in eventless blessedness: to the latter it was
simple continuity, in ulterior development, of that eternal life
in the Father which the Son had instituted in his assumption
and sanctification of humanity. To see God is itself consecration and immortality; as Irenæus says,[*] Ὅρασις Θεοῦ
περιποιητικὴ ἀφθαρσίας; and the mediator of this vision is
the manifested Logos: "No man hath seen God at any time:
the only-begotten Son, which is in the bosom of the Father,
he hath declared him:"[†] and thus commenced in his disciples the emergence into incorruption, as Irenæus also says,
ἡ γνῶσις τοῦ υἱοῦ τοῦ Θεοῦ, ἥτις ἦν ἀφθαρσία.[‡] So that while,
at its opening stage, salvation begins with beholding the Son,
and rises into sanctification and reprieve from death, its
ulterior and heavenly stage begins with the beholding of the
Father, and passes into degrees of assimilation to Him, consummating the resemblance already commenced in a life of

* IV. 38, K. 278.   † John i. 18.   ‡ IV. 36, 7. A.H. 518.

love. Here we take leave of the last remnants of mythology hanging around the Parusia: there is no provision for retributory treatment, but only a continuance of the *self awards* of this life: and for the children of God an eternal growth of light and love through the nearer and purer knowledge of Him. And thus the belief in a crisis of resurrection is transformed into a faith in immortal existence.

From this review of the first records of the evangelic faith, the positions universally accepted are easily selected: Christ is risen: he lives with the Father in heaven: he communes with his people by the Holy Spirit: he will reunite them with himself and God for ever. Whether the scene of that reunion will be in heaven or on earth: whether to each as he dies, or to all collectively at the date of Christ's return: whether after a public judgment, special for the Christians or general for mankind, and, in either case, with what discriminate reward; are questions on which there is no consensus among the different writers, and on which even the same writer is at times at variance with himself. Even the accepted suspense till Messiah's Parusia was not proof against the enthusiasm of the dying martyr who would spring aloft to him, instead of sleeping in the tomb until he came: for was it not Stephen in Jerusalem that cried, as he fell, " Lord Jesus, receive my spirit " ? * In the last strife it was the natural feeling of the Hellenist confessor, as it was of the Gentile apostle, that it were gain to go and be with Christ. And the author of the Apocalypse, who professedly breaks the sleep of the dead only at the first and the second resurrection, could not himself refrain from admitting the martyrs to heaven; though only to lie still beneath the altar, and cry " How long ?" till their Avenger should call "them that are upon the earth" to account for their blood shed upon it.† It is plain that to the Jewish and Christian imagination the heaven of God was no longer reserved for natures exclusively divine, with the addition of the two or three prophets who had been bodily transported thither from the ground on which they walked. It was deemed accessible also to human lives whose lost blood stained the dust, and whose pale forms were still within the

* Acts vii. 59. † Rev. vi. 9-11.

tombs. We know indeed, from the pre-Christian book "The Wisdom of Solomon," that the Hellenic doctrine of the immortality of the soul had found ready acceptance among the colonial Jews, as solving problems embarrassing to a Theism limited to this temporal world: "the souls of the righteous are in the hand of God, and there shall no torment touch them :"* "the righteous live for evermore :"† "their hope is full of immortality :"‡ "to be allied unto wisdom is immortality."§ When this higher scene was once opened to religious hope, and the lifted veil showed "the spirits of the just made perfect" already living in the present, it entranced the finer souls of Israel, and gave them something that touched them more than the imagery of the traditional Messianic mythology. Without conscious disloyalty to the national "Kingdom of God" in reserve for this world's future, their heart was rather in the immediate home above which held not only all that they adored, but all that they had most loved and lost. The two faiths coexisted, and came up by turns, without consciousness of their inconsistency; and the imagination could draw upon either, as private need or social sympathy prescribed. The apocalyptic reasoning and representations which were a power in the synagogues of Palestine, were a hindrance and a repulsion in the schools of Alexandria ; and accordingly they find no place in Philo's theology. And the one feature which commended Christianity to the Gentiles who soon formed the mass of its professors, was its union of a pure monotheism with a faith in immortality and a corresponding standard of ethical life.

It is hardly conceivable that the Messianic and the spiritual versions of the kingdom of God could have been tied up for seventeen centuries together as functions of the same religion, if they had been left to their natural play upon the thought and conscience of mankind. The same influences which brought the apostle Paul to speak of death as a shorter way to Christ than living till he came, and which led the fourth evangelist to treat the eternal life in heaven as already here and now, and never to be broken, would have everywhere alienated the Christian mind from the mythology of its in-

* iii. 1.   † v. 15.   ‡ iii. 4.   § viii. 17.

fancy, and lifted it into a higher stratum of religious experience.   Nay, even the mere lapse of time must have displaced the whole scheme of the Parusia, and broken up its scenery as the images of a dream.   If to the apostle James or Peter, after preaching that " the Lord is at hand," " it is the last hour," the truth had been suddenly laid bare, that neither in " that generation," nor for upwards of sixty more, would any Christ appear, what would have become of the missionary's zeal?   Could he go to the next station, and repeat his tale with mere omission of the date?   Or would he not feel that, with the date, all that was dated had vanished?   Nothing can authenticate a prediction that fixes a time and goes wrong upon it.   He who assures us " it will be fine tomorrow," cannot, when it rains all day, make his case good by saying, " No matter, if you wait long enough, it will still be fine."

Instead of letting these disappointed anticipations fall away by their own self-refutation, the Catholic Church committed itself to them all, as well as to the teachings of opposite tendency, so far as they found expression in the writings declared to be canonical.   By treating all the stages of Christian belief through the apostolic and post-apostolic age—Judaic, Pauline, Alexandrine—as one divine text, of which itself was the one divine interpreter, it arrested the natural disengagement of the permanent from the perishable elements; and by incongruously blending spiritual truth and apocalyptic imaginations in an authoritative *regula fidei*, it no less ensured a history of hopeless contention than if it had laid a tesselated pavement for the floor of its sanctuary, and required every worshipper to declare it all white marble.

Through the first century, the Jewish version of the Gospel, with the Pauline enlargement of its scope, had exclusive possession of the field.   The Christian communities claimed to be the true Israel, released from its law, but heirs of its faith, and the last heralds of its promises.   How completely they could identify their future " kingdom of God " with that of the watchers " for the consolation of Israel " is evident from the mere presence of the Book of Revelation in the New Testament, and from the partnership of Jewish and Christian hands in the elaboration into their final form of such other apocalyptic productions as the Sibylline Oracles, the Book of Enoch, and the fourth Book of Ezra. The retention, indeed, of the Messianic mythology, even in its most repulsive features, by the Church teachers and Fathers of the second century, was largely answerable for the rise and influence of Gnosticism, which, directly under Marcion, and indirectly under Valentinus and Basilcides, was an insurrection against the Jewish God and his world-system as exhibited in the Old Testament law and ritual, and a transference of allegiance to the God of grace and goodness first revealed and represented by Jesus Christ. The prime condition of the new allegiance was to turn away from the Hebrew Demiurge, and leave him to conduct his favourites as he may through the ill-constituted scene on which he has placed them ; and to throw a whole heart of faith into the worship and service of the God of purity and love : that is, Christianity must break with Judaism, and assert itself as religion ideal and absolute ; the salvation it offers is not in the world, but from the world ; and brings such peace of God, even in chains or martyrdom, as to silence the prayer for thrones and Paradise.

No one who reads the records of millennarian belief in the second and third centuries can wonder at this extreme insistence on the special Christian characteristics. The mass of puerile, vindictive, and sensuous imaginations which made up the Chiliasm held in common by Papias, Justin Martyr, Irenæus, Hippolytus, Tertullian, and popular still for a century more, bear a distressing witness to the state of thought and character in the ecclesiastical society of the time, and might well call forth the unsparing protest of reformers to whom Christ was the power of spiritual life and love. Justin makes it an essential element of orthodoxy to expect the return of Christ for his thousand years' reign in Jerusalem,* and therefore to believe in " the resurrection of the flesh,"—an article of faith on which, with strange perversity, an extraordinary stress was laid. So absolute was the assumption of identity between the body of the entombed and the body of the risen person, that Justin says, " the lame, the crippled, and the blind will have to be made whole by Christ, as he healed the

* Dial. c. Tryph. 80. 16.

infirm in Galilee"; and Tertullian asks, "What would be the use of numbering all the hairs of the head, except to make sure that none of them shall perish"? An apologist whose work erroneously passes under the name of Justin, finds in the *σαρκὸς ἀνάστασις* the one addition which Christ has made to what was already known on the subject, Pythagoras and Plato having established the immortality of the soul.* Irenæus, in describing Antichrist, borrows the account of Antiochus Epiphanes from Daniel, and applies it to Rome as the embodiment of Satanic wickedness on earth. As soon as this enemy has planted himself in Jerusalem (which will happen at the approaching six-thousandth birthday of the world), Christ will come and destroy him, and clear the way for the seventh or sabbath millennium, appointed for his terrestrial reign. His saints, whose souls have been somewhere kept in store for this crisis, will recover possession of their bodies by the first resurrection ; and will enter on the blessed life of the kingdom. Its seat will be Palestine, for *there* was the promise of it given to Abraham on behalf of the heirs of his faith. The fields and gardens will yield their produce a myriadfold beyond all experience ; the very chaff of the grain contenting the lion's appetite and changing his habit, to lie down in peace with the lamb. At a table loaded with the abundance of the land the saints will sit down to eat and drink with the Lord ; and so will pass the time which is to compensate the sufferings of the past. When the thousand years have expired, the second resurrection will bring up the rest of the dead, to be disposed of at the general judgment, and the kingdom of Christ be replaced by the sole monarchy of God.† Not only is the reader warned against understanding all this in any but the most literal sense ; but he is particularly protected from the weakness which is offended by the resurrection of the flesh ; those (he is told) who prefer to think of each individual soul passing immediately from death to God, overlook the need of some intermediate steps of preparation for so great a change as that from the purely temporal to the purely spiritual state.

This plea of stages of ascent from earth to heaven was

* Pseudo-Justin. De Resurrectione, c. 10.　　　　† Irenæus, V. 25–35.

turned to better account in the next generation by Origen. He also believed in the continuity of the soul between a first existence and a second ; but provided for it more effectually than by locking it up meanwhile in an asphyxiating closet of Hades. He also believed in a life of passage from this world's experience to a higher yet beyond. But the discipline with which he supplied it consisted, not of eating and drinking with the Lord at a table of miraculous profusion, but of exposure of a nature already free from carnal functions to the purifying fire of a humbled conscience and more fervent aspirations, such as are congenial to a first Paradise, and furnish tension towards an ulterior.* So far did he carry this conception of successive ascents, at each of which some residuary elements of grossness were burned up or dissipated, as to land himself at last in the belief of universal restoration and capacity for life in God.† The theory is remarkable in more ways than one : as illustrating the irrepressible aversion to pay away the soul into Death, on no other security for its immortality than the promise of a general resurrection ; as a mode of combining the faith in individual immortality with that of stages affecting vast multitudes en masse ; and as an early hint of a doctrine of purgatory.

It was inevitable that the apocalyptic faith in the coming of Christ and his reign on earth should lose its hold upon the Church which it had done so much to form. Both outward and inward causes doomed it to decay. Time was ever working against it. It had committed itself to a limit of date which, though somewhat elastic, soon came to be overstrained, and when relinquished, let fall the whole contents of the conception into utter insecurity. As the generations passed on, and the kingdom never came, and the earth still belonged to the mixed multitude of righteous and unrighteous, and no returning Nero ushered in the campaign of Antichrist and compelled the crisis which was to throw off the sinful load, the mythology broke up by force of fact, and altered, first the proportion of its parts, and then the meaning of the whole. Its centre of gravity shifted from the primary to the subsidiary

* περὶ ἀρχῶν, II. x. 1-3.
† περὶ ἀρχῶν, II. x. 4-7 ; I. vi. 1-4 ; III. vi. 1-8 ; contra Cels. VI. 26.

elements. The temporal reign faded away; its table ceased
to be spread; its extermination of "all enemies" vanished
as the trail of a forgotten dream ; the uncounted years of its
millennium suffered its extremities to coalesce in a single
point, the arrival of Christ to end the world and call the dead :
its first resurrection of the saints and its second of the world
lapsed into one; and among the myriads of the departed thus
brought before the judgment-seat, it was vain any longer to
look in the foreground for the living generation that was to
" be changed." But with the last act in the world's drama,
the reign in Jerusalem, thus dropped, and " the end " thus
hastened on, nothing more remained to be done on this scene
of human life ; its functions being closed, the solid earth itself
could hardly retain its characteristics to the thought, its cities,
its mountains, and its seas, and, except as the momentary
platform of transition, must swim away into nothing between
the heaven above and the abyss below. All the interest lay
in the supernatural scene, in the realm beyond death, among
the spirits of the departed and in the eternal home of
God.

With this change of conception, however, new questions are
raised, or, what amounts to the same thing, old ones with
vastly increased urgency. With a crisis close at hand, like
the thunder-roll when the lightning has flashed, time counts
for little, and the interval which may separate us from the
instantaneous does not affect us. For believers standing on
the watch, with loins girt and lamps burning, for the bridegroom
on his way, it was a small thing on which side of death one
or another might be, when his knock was heard at the gate,
and his life-giving call gathered his own around him. But
when his reported approach proved to be an illusion, and
his presence was withdrawn, not only into a " far country "
but into a future quite indefinite, the dreary outlook compelled
men to ask what they were to think about the long interval
between the individual death and the universal summons to
live again. Was it all one unbroken and unbreathing night,
age after age, in the sealed chambers of Hades ? and from so
deep a sleep would anything remain which even an archangel's
trump could wake ? With the corruptible all gone long ago,

and an absolute blank of the consciousness which carries all that is incorruptible, how is the continuity saved which is the condition of personal sameness? Yet this is the answer with which the creeds of the reformed Churches overburden the imagination and the heart of Christians. Many, however, have preferred to turn, if not Hades itself, at least the period of waiting there, into an intermediate state, available, as Origen supposed, for disciplinary purification, and the opening of neglected veins of spiritual development. Neither of these doctrines was willing to part with an ulterior crisis of general judgment, consigning the guilty to a penal underworld, and the righteous to the heaven of the immortals. But the fragments of the broken apocalypse supplied, as we have seen, yet a third answer to the question which every bereavement brings; assigning to each soul, dismissed from its earthly tabernacle, "a house not made with hands, eternal in the heavens," where "mortality is swallowed up in life;" and blending the supreme utterances of Christian enthusiasm into harmony with the majestic voices of pre-Christian philosophy in Pythagoras and Plato. And thousands of the sweetest strains of poetry and piety bear witness that from the larger minds of Christendom the lingering shreds of a worn-out mythology have dropped away, and the simple faith alone remains, that each soul is reborn in death into higher life, and through the silent spaces which we cannot penetrate finds some divine guide into the society of the wise and saintly, and the nearer communion with God.

And in this emergence of an imperishable spiritual trust from the perishable forms of imaginative thought are seen at work the inner causes which render every mythology transient. The transcendental relations which are implicit in the characteristics of the human consciousness and report themselves in the essential postulates of reason, conscience, and ideal affection, cannot be covered by any of the explicit conceptions, borrowed from sensible experience, in which we try to clothe them, and set them before us in the field of time and space. In the earlier stages of individual or social growth, such imperfect symbols shelter the latent feeling of these relations, and convey it from mind to mind, witnessing to it as the common possession of humanity; or, at least, of the family or the tribe. With the advance of thought, and the continuous gain of creative energy upon subjection to the sensory and imaginative life, the inadequacy of the picture-language for the expression of meanings intrinsically infinite, is profoundly felt; attempts at emendation by refining on it give it but a short reprieve, rendering it only a more decorous illusion; the heart of the truth is still within, beating in silence but declining to speak in terms of finite things. When their shell is broken and the fragments flung away, is it that nothing remains? On the contrary, that an infinitude bursts into the field of thought, annulling the limits to the Holiness, the Beauty, the Blessedness, to which the universe is consecrated. And so it is, that out of a national ideal, originally stormy with a righteous yet angry despair of the world and impatience at its idolatries, has arisen a hope before which those clouds have rolled away; a hope at once personal and human, consoling private griefs, warning individual sin, nurturing solitary piety, touching each salient point of life with lights of brighter meaning, and flinging tenderer shadows into every deeper recess; and giving a dignity undreamed of before, to man's nature under all its poor disguises. Disappointed of its earthly millennium, Christendom has nearly doubled its millennium of heavenly expectation; and far though it be from yet growing to the dimensions of its immortality, it furnishes clear evidence, in the deeper tone and purer aspiration and nobler self-devotion of recent ages, how congenial, nay essential, to the human conscience and affections is the sublime faith that "All live unto God."

BOOK V.

THE DIVINE IN THE HUMAN.

———

CHAPTER I.

THE VEIL TAKEN AWAY.

AFTER the separate notice, in the foregoing chapters, of the chief refracting media through which the "Light of the world" has passed into our modern Christendom, it only remains to compute their combined effects, and by clearing away both nimbus and corona, allow the orb to present its true form and features to our thought as once it did to living vision. The problem, however baffling from its complexity, has of late been brought sensibly nearer to a solution by a number of successive approximations; each of which, by registering some unnoticed phenomenon or some obscurity removed, simplifies the task of the successor and deepens his hopeful interest in its prosecution. Nothing indeed is more characteristic of the present tendency of religious thought than the numerous attempts to clear and define the historical image of Jesus of Nazareth. As if the prophecy had come true of him, that his visage "was so marred more than any man's," defaced not less by the human colouring of tradition than by the shadows of unfriendly imputation, one writer after another has resolved, if possible, to suppress all interposing media, and see the reality face to face. A gallery might be filled with the revised portraits which these reproductions have put upon the canvas : and the fewer the lingering adjuncts of artifice and fancy, the more will a comparing eye be fixed by the look of an unspeakable depth and majesty.

For this process, natural as it is to a mind reverent of truth, it is thought needful, in the presence of a sensitive and incurious theology, to apologize: it is timidly suggested that, as there was after all " a human side " in Christ, it can do no harm to look at it for a little while: that the first disciples themselves began at this end, and were only gradually admitted to the mystery of his higher nature; and that his own " method " therefore is followed by those who lead us to " behold the man," provided they lift the disguise at last and bid us " behold the God." Such defence is little better than the attack ; for both proceed upon the same unworthy principle: it is permissible, it seems, to recover the historical Jesus, *on condition* that you do not rest there, but pass on to the eternal Son: the assailant is in terror lest you never take the step : the defendant's plea is that you are sure to go : but they agree that unless the creed is secured, history must be denied its rights. " You may open your eyes, if you will see what we prescribe."

This want of simplicity brings, like all unfaithfulness, its penalty of illusion. What it bargains for as " divine'" is purely human : what it dreads as " human " contains whatever is divine. The " humanity " of Christ, what is it? His inner personality, his individual life, the courses of his thought, the lights and shadows of his affections, the conflicts of his will, as he passed through the drama of his years on earth, and moved before the eyes of man, and was heard by living ear in his teaching by day and overheard in his prayers by night. This assemblage of characteristics belongs to the realm of positive fact, more or less visible and appreciable by observers: and there in the midst, if anywhere, in the foldings of his secret worship and the lines of his spiritual attitude, must whatever was divine in him have worked and told its tale. And on the other hand, what is meant, in distinction from this, by " the higher nature " of Christ? Is it anything that you may know when you see it, or that can be evidenced if unseen? On the contrary, it means something wholly beyond the sphere of our apprehension, in time, in place, in kind: it refers to a supposed existence of his from all eternity, in realms unapproachable, under conditions inconceivable: it denotes in his constitution an exceptional incarnation which it is easy to imagine but impossible to attest: or, at the lowest, it signifies the foresight of him by long previous ages, and his identity with the ideal in the mind of ancient seers. These things, were they even facts, would be intrinsically unsusceptible of verification, lying as completely out of our cognitive faculties as the natural history of the planet Mars or the literature of Saturn. They have no pretension to the character of facts: they are simply doctrines: the reappearance in men's dreams, when the restraints of daylight were gone, of the form which had fixed their venerating eye. In short, they are what *men have thought* about the founder of Christianity and made him out to be, and not what he was in himself; and constitute therefore, instead of the supremely sacred end, for the sake of which the historical portrait may be tolerated as a means, precisely the element which is purely human and precarious, the disappearance of which would only correct the tentatives of fancy, and leave as they were the objective sanctities of God.

And this gives us at once the rule for separating the divine from the human in the origin of our religion. The former will be found, if anywhere, in what Jesus of Nazareth *himself was*, in spiritual character and moral relation to God. The latter will be found in what *was thought about* his person, functions, and office. It was the Providence of history that gave us *him :* it was the men of history that dressed up the *theory* of him : and till we compel the latter to stand aside, and let us through to look upon his living face, we can never seize the permanent essence of the gift. By a standing delusion of theological egotism, this rule has ever been inverted; and in every age, from the apostolic to our own, in every Church, from the most hierarchical to the most reformed, Christianity has been taken to mean, not *the religion of Jesus Christ*, but some doctrine *about* Christ ; and though he might draw you to think his thought, and bear his cross, and pray his prayer, you are no Christian unless you will say what his substance was, and how many natures he had, and what his place, past and future, in the invisible regions which are out of history altogether; or, at least, will own that he was that ideal object of Jewish mythology, the Messiah! We must not mistake all this scholastic dust for the divine radiance that shoots through it and lends it a glory not its own. It is perhaps a blind infatuation that impels us to seek, and a blind incompetence that forbids us to find, the ultimate centre of God's spirit in our life, and leaves it to work in silence and secrecy in the last retreats of affection, where it softens the light and deepens the vision, yet by never coming before the eye cheats us into thrusting forward some conception of our own, as if that which hid him from us were the vehicle of his presence. It is in the subjective tincture of our spirits, not in the objective constructions of our intellect, that his consecration enters and holds us: in the tone of the voice, more than the words we speak; and many are the souls which know themselves one in their religion, though no two of them could say the same sentence of the creed. The appealing personality of Christ has been, through all distortions, the regulative power and the source of unity in Christendom; and the more it stands out clear against the sky, with every cloud from behind and from before it swept away, the more single will be our apprehension of the genius of our religion.

The real figure however cannot, unfortunately, be seen by us except through the medium of human theories and prepossessions. The previous chapters have shown how busy, ere our earliest records were produced, speculation had been with his image, to find a place for it in some prevalent scheme of thought. To Paul, who had never known him, he was a heavenly vision, an impersonated idea; the interest of which lay, not in his past ministry and actual life, but in his position among the ages and his office in the future; so that the Apostle construed his appearance on earth according to the exigencies of a vast and bold theory of history and Providence, which earlier apostles did not share. The fourth gospel was a reconstruction, far in the second century, of the story of Christ's ministry, in the interests of a new metaphysical theology, and gave an aspect to his person quite strange to the older delineations. And the other gospels, together constituting a single source, twice revised and enlarged, have

all the characters, faithful and unfaithful, of popular tradition; embodying a mass of genuine historical materials; but
with many conspicuous patches of later addition; and
throughout, coloured by the Messianic preconception, and
compiled with the resolve that Jesus of Nazareth shall be no
other than the realized vision of the ancient prophets. To
draw forth the objective truth from behind this mist of prepossessions, we are thrown entirely upon internal evidence.
And however great may be the room thus left for fanciful
combinations, there are some critical rules which when applied
with competent historical feeling can hardly mislead us. The
problem before us is amenable to the following three. They
are stated with exclusive reference to the synoptical gospels,
as the source of all that can be known of the earthly life of
Jesus of Nazareth.

1. Whenever, during or before the ministry of Jesus, any
person in the narrative is made to speak in language, or refer
to events, which had their origin at a later date, the report is
incredible as an anachronism.

2. Miraculous events cannot be regarded as adequately
attested, in presence of natural causes accounting for belief in
their occurrence.

3. Acts and words ascribed to Jesus which plainly transcend
the moral level of the narrators authenticate themselves as
his: while such as are out of character with his spirit, but
congruous with theirs, must be referred to inaccurate tradition.

The first of these rules compels us to treat as unauthentic,
in its present form, every reputed or implied claim of Jesus to
be the promised Messiah. In a preceding chapter reasons
have been given for believing that Jesus did but take up the
message of the Baptist, and proclaim and unfold the " Gospel
of the kingdom " about to come: that he made no pretension
to be himself the personal Head of that kingdom : and that
his investiture with that character was the retrospective work
of his disciples, who, once assured of his heavenly life, solved
the mystery of the cross by drawing from the prophets the
doctrine of a suffering Messiah. This affecting theory presented his figure to their memory in new lights, and hid within

it secret meanings which they now first read into moods and hints of his little noticed at the time. And as they must have supposed him conscious in himself of what they now discovered him to be, it is not wonderful that they let that consciousness speak out, here and there, in terms of their interpretation rather than of verbal reproduction. There are clear indications that the subordinate position of forerunner, assigned in the gospels to John the Baptist, was by no means acknowledged by his followers: they treated his alleged self-disparagement "He must increase, but I must decrease," as a Christian invention : nor could it be denied to them that, by accepting his baptism, Jesus, no less than others, became his disciple : or that, by seizing his message the moment John's voice was silenced in prison, he rather co-ordinated himself with the same mission than superseded it. Regarding him therefore, not indeed as John "risen from the dead," but as John's continuator among the living, they neither surrendered nor modified their original fraternity, but under both names preached the same gospel, "the kingdom is at hand." How else are we to understand the curious fact to which I have before referred, that more than twenty years after the crucifixion, a body of "disciples" is found at Ephesus, who have been under the tuition of the fervent and learned Apollos, a man "mighty in the scriptures and instructed in the way of the law," and to whom he had "*taught carefully the things concerning Jesus, knowing only the baptism of John*" ? And this teaching, it is added, was "boldly given in the synagogue." The idea that "Jesus was the Christ," when imparted by some private Christians, came to him as a supplement which "expounded to him the way of God more perfectly." * Here are two co-present schools or sects, the exact relation between which it is not easy to define. Were they agreed that Messiah had already proclaimed himself, the one in the person of John, the other in that of Jesus ? If they were rivals in competition for the same office, each for its own prophet, the claim for the Baptist would set Jesus aside and lose him in the throng of John's disciples : and what then would be "the things concerning Jesus" which Apollos had to teach so "carefully" ? It is

* Acts xviii. 21-28.

evident that in the view of the learned Alexandrine, his relative importance was by no means extinguished by any assumed
Messiahship of John. The whole account becomes clear on
one supposition alone : viz., that for *neither* prophet did the
Baptist's sect assert a higher claim than that of *herald* of
" the kingdom," but regarded both as warning messengers to
prepare the world for meeting its Judge. In this sense, the
doctrine of the school was a simple survival of the very gospel
which riveted the multitudes on the hill-sides of Galilee ; and
attests the living religion of Jesus himself, ere yet his disciples,
left to themselves, had wrought out their proofs of his identity
with the Messiah of whom he spoke. The whole contents of
the earthly life and ministry of Jesus, as of John, were at the
disposal of Apollos in support of the announcement that " the
kingdom of heaven was at hand "; and what he had yet to
learn from Aquila and Priscilla was that reappearance of the
Crucified in heavenly form which first marked him out as
himself Christ the elect.   So readily did he appropriate this
crowning article of faith that he was at once commended as a
fellow-believer to the " brethren in Achaia," apparently without the re-baptism which, in the presence of Paul, was administered to his disciples at Ephesus and ratified by the gift of the
Spirit.*   It could not be expected that all the adherents of the
Baptist's sect would be equally prepared to accept the Christian
sequel to their faith in him, involving as it did his reduction
to a position subordinate to one of his own baptized. Their
society accordingly continued to exist, their rivalry with the
Christians arising, not from their making a Christian of John,
but from their refusing to see more than a prophet in Jesus.

Had John on the banks of Jordan really indicated Jesus to
the multitude as " a mightier than he, who would baptize
them with the Holy Spirit and with fire," or had a vision and
a voice from heaven startled them with the news, as he
emerged from the stream, that this was he, it would have
been the duty of all the baptized to pass on from the forerunner to the fulfiller: the baptism of John would mean
nothing less than the acceptance of Christ in this individual
person. There would have been no possible room for such a

* Acts xix. 1-7.

separate society as that of Apollos at Ephesus. There lies a prior history, now lost, behind the evangelist's account; which has shaped itself, during the apostolic age, into conformity with the relation between Messiah's "great day" and the "Elias," who "would first come."* The actual eclipse of the Baptist's movement by that of Jesus is thrown back upon their personal relations, so as to bring it into the line with prophetic expectation, and give it a divine significance.

In the first and third gospels, the Messiahship of Jesus occupies the very foreground of their picture, and determines the whole story of his birth and infancy. It gives the key both to the external events and the internal experience of his home life. It is no wonder, therefore, that throughout this narrative he plays no other part, and that if ever historic words escape him of more modest tone, he is soon reinstated in his more majestic voice. The second evangelist, not being thus pledged *ab initio*, is freer to leave some ineffaceable traces of the natural truth; and though he too was possessed, when he wrote, with the same interpretation of the life he sketched, it is as if he knew that it had not been always so, but that the Messianic consciousness had but dawned upon the mind of Jesus himself, and hardly perhaps fully risen above the horizon in this life. The scene at the baptism was not, as in Luke, a public communication from heaven to earth, but a breath from an invisible wing, an oracle unheard, perceptible only to the baptized. And whatever surmises might, at such a moment of self-dedication, be stirring in his heart, we have seen that, at "Peter's confession" near the other end of his ministry, he sharply silenced every claim of the Messiahship on his behalf. If indeed, as St. Paul tells us, it was "by his resurrection from the dead" that he was "declared to be the Son of God with power,"† any prior declaration in that sense could be but "idle words," which might well be stopped from repetition. This date, so naturally supplied by the apostle, incidentally lets out the fact that the Messianic character of Jesus was a posthumous disclosure from the other side of death. And it is surely much easier to understand how disciples might read back into his ministry a feature not yet

* Mal. iv. 5. Mark ix. 11.   † Rom. i. 4.

due, than to account, as historical in him, for the alternate
bold assertion and elaborate suppression of the test-pretension
of his mission.

When, therefore, the simplest of the gospels states that
thrice over, near Cæsarea Philippi,* on descending the mount
of transfiguration,† and on the way to Jerusalem,‡ Jesus
definitely predicts, not only his betrayal and his execution,
but his resurrection; and, again, instructs his disciples on
the last evening to seek him in Galilee after he is risen from
the dead,§ I cannot doubt the admixture of historic fact and
retrospective interpretation in these passages: the real basis
of prediction being in the personal forebodings of Jesus, as
the shadows of hopeless conflict closed around him: while the
appendix of interpretation was added by the subsequent belief
in his resurrection to heavenly life, and reappearance in
Galilee. In all these passages (except the last) Jesus speaks
of himself in the third person, as the " Son of Man;" and the
fact is interesting because the phrase is probably here at its
point of transition from the humanitarian to the Messianic
meaning, appropriated by Jesus in the former sense, so dear
to his feeling and so true to the pathetic outlook, but used
in the latter by the evangelist in his belief that, "as it is
written," this is what Messiah "*must* suffer." Here probably
we see laid bare the very process by which so often the bloom
and tenderness of Jesus' words have been swept away in favour
of some hard-cut quibble of the scribes. But in the seven
or eight other instances in which he is said to take the phrase
to himself with its Messianic meaning, we are in contact,
I am persuaded, with the afterthought of the evangelist;
advantage being taken of his Ezekiel-usage to bring him in
as a claimant on the fulfilment of Daniel. If he habitually
assumed the title in its apocalyptic sense, how is it that he
strangely keeps the " Son of Man " at a distance from himself
as a third person? and why does he not say outright " Whosoever shall be ashamed of me and of my words in this adulterous
and sinful generation, of him shall *I* also be ashamed, when
I come in the glory of my Father with the holy angels," instead of "the *Son of Man* also shall be ashamed of him,

* Mark viii. 31, 32.   † Ib. ix. 30-32.   ‡ Ib. x. 32-34.   § Ib. xiv. 29.

when he cometh in the glory of his Father with the holy angels."*

The same rule must apply to other modes of self-assertion, based upon claims similarly transcendent. From my earliest remembered years of attendance on public worship, I could never hear without distress the well-known answer of Jesus to the demand for some sign accrediting his mission; consisting merely of a reproachful contrast of his questioner with the guilty Ninevites and the Pagan Queen, who could listen to a Hebrew prophet and admire a wise king: while "this generation" waited for credentials from "One greater than Jonah" and "wiser than Solomon."† And who that listens to his large plea for sabbatical freedom, that "the sabbath was made for man, not man for the sabbath," can believe that he spoiled it by narrowing its ground to the self-proclamation, "One greater than the temple is here"?‡

Without the same outward pomp, yet affected by the same inner breach of character, are two reports of a burst of exulting thanksgiving from Jesus, shortly after the return of his disciples (the twelve according to Matthew, the seventy according to Luke), from the preaching mission on which he had sent them. The exclamation of joy is the same in both, and is doubtless a remnant of unspoiled tradition, "I thank thee, O Father, Lord of heaven and earth, that thou didst hide these things from the wise and understanding, and didst reveal them unto babes: yea, Father, for so it was well pleasing in thy sight."§ Then with a sudden change from this heavenly flight, he takes the ground of dogmatic assertion, though still apparently in soliloquy: "all things have been delivered to me from my Father: and no one knoweth the Son, save the Father: neither doth any know the Father, save the Son, and he to whomsoever the Son willeth to reveal him." At this point the two evangelists part company: Matthew winds up with the exhortation enshrined through all Christian ages in love and sorrow, "Come unto me, all ye that labour and are heavy laden, and I will give you rest: Take my yoke upon you, and learn of me; for I am meek and lowly in

* Mark viii. 38; Luke ix. 26.   † Matt. xii. 38–45; Luke xi. 29–32.
‡ Matt. xii. 6.   § Matt. xi. 25, 26; Luke x. 21.

heart; and ye shall find rest unto your souls: for my yoke is easy, and my burden is light." Instead of this, Luke says that, turning to his disciples, he said privately, " Blessed are the eyes which see the things which ye see : for I say unto you, that many prophets and kings desired to see the things which ye see, and saw them not ; and to hear the things which ye hear, and heard them not."

That the truth and beauty of both these passages must go home to every disciple, that they invest the person of Jesus with no grace and power that is not there, is beyond all question.   But then the grace, the truth, the power of these lineaments depend on their *not* being proclaimed by himself. What meek and lowly soul was ever known to set itself forth as such, and commend its own humility as the model for others, and *that*, not because it carries a fruitful pain, but because it wins a restful ease ?   A convert who, by sitting at his feet and looking up at the secrets of his face, had learnt to know himself and renounce all but an infinite aspiration, might thus describe the subduing traits which had given him a new birth ; but did a Saviour bear such testimony of himself, his testimony would not be true.   Plainly we have here the reflective experience of grateful disciples.   Nor can wo accept as more historical Luke's alternative ejaculation. Jesus, as the herald of the kingdom to come, regarded himself only as the bearer of a warning and a promise, at the service of which he placed himself, as the Baptist had done. If the fulfilment had for ages been longed for and was now near, this might indeed be regarded as the privilege (or as the terror) of " this generation," as compared with the many that " had died without the sight :" and to this distinction, viz., of living at this final crisis, the " blessing " pronounced by Jesus is often supposed to refer.   The true point of the passage is thus entirely missed.   It is not a chronological contrast of one age with another, but a personal comparison of his little group of apostles as close to himself, with the hearers who from their distance of either time or place, knew of him only at second hand.   The eyes and ears that are blessed are affirmed to be distinctly and exclusively those of his " private " disciples.   This could never have been said during the ministry of Jesus; the gospel of the kingdom was then all in all, and was the same through whatever medium its message came: "he that heareth you heareth me: and he that rejecteth you, rejecteth me; and he that rejecteth me, rejecteth him that sent me."* To "have known Christ after the flesh" carries no privilege and gives no one any "occasion to glory:"† nor, when Paul asserted that he was under no disadvantage from not having seen Jesus in this life, was there any sentiment in the Church of his time to contradict him. So long as the Messianic vision stood right in front and covered the dazzling boundary of "that generation," it concentrated the religion upon itself: the future eclipsed the past; and no wondering importance was attached to the historical personality of the messenger that brought the news. But when "the Lord delayed his coming," till the Parusia was quite overdue, the transcendent glory faded and allowed the pale natural horizon to return; and reverence for Christ, tired out with vain expectancy, fell back upon the vestiges of his transient visit, and made the most of every trait which memory had consecrated, and every incident which tradition had not spoiled. It was not till the post-apostolic age that the biographical figure and personal characteristics and ethical principles of life and love assumed anything like the place due to them in a permanent Church, and presented him as the source of a new Law and new Religion. And then it is that to the true disciple, often perplexed by uncertain lights of history, it would seem the most precious of privileges to have been with him face to face, and heard him with the living ear, and been able to go to him with the sad problems of life. And to this time, and not to his own, belongs the feeling expressed in Luke's benediction. We may relieve Jesus therefore of the alleged rapturous reflection, how blessed a thing it was for anybody to be with him.

To the outburst of thanksgiving from Jesus which the two evangelists have in common, each appends a different close, neither of which could really have come from his lips, breathing as they do the feeling towards him of other persons and another time. Is there anything which carries back the trace

<hr>

* Luke x. 16.   † 2 Cor. v. 12–16.

of anachronism to the prior sentences in which their citations
are the same? There is.   In the didactic passage, which
forms the middle of the speech, it is said, " No one knoweth
who the Son is, save the Father: and who the Father is, save
the Son, and he to whomsoever the Son willeth to reveal him."
This is not the language of Jesus or of his time, as must be
apparent to every one who carefully studies the growth of
Christian doctrine. " My " Father, " your " Father, " our "
Father, these are the terms of relation in which alone he con-
ceives and presents the human spirit or his own before God.
Only from heaven, when his ministry was past, was he
declared to be " the Son of God with power," even in the mere
Messianic and *anthropological* sense : and the absolute antithesis of " *The* Son " and " *The* Father " first came into use
with the *theological* doctrine of his person, when the Logos
theory had need to distinguish two constituents or partici-
pants in the Godhead. Accordingly, it is only among their
latest additions that the synoptists have picked up an instance
or two of this employment of the definite article with the
Divine name. Besides the passage now under consideration,
Luke has 'no example, Mark and Matthew each but one, including the baptismal formula admitted to be unhistorical.
In the fourth gospel, on the other hand, the usage is all-
pervading ; no fewer than sixty-three instances of it attesting
our transference to an entirely new stage of belief, in which
speculation has macerated history and taken it up into solution. Here then, in the very heart of the passage, already
historically discredited in its close, a decisive mark presents
itself of a date long posterior to the earthly life of Jesus.*

The most surprising feature in the Christianity of the
apostolic age was its extension among the Gentiles. No such
thing had been embraced within the message of its founder,
who " was not sent but to the lost sheep of the house of
Israel,"† and would not let his missionaries " go into any way

---

* Even in the use of the *several possessive pronouns* with the name " *God*,"
there is a significant gradation among the synoptists: the closer *personal appropriation* of God as his Father, by the word *My*, rather than *Our* or *Your*,
being greatest in the newest redaction; occurring in Mark, *never* ; Luke,
thrice ; Matthew, *seventeen times*. In the fourth Gospel it is found thirty-six
times.   † Matt. xv. 24.

of the Gentiles or enter into any city of the Samaritans;"* not because he was untouched by traits of heathen worth and piety, but simply because the promise he had to announce was purely national. None could be less prepared than the apostles themselves when Jesus was taken from them and they had received his last commands, to conceive of such a change as possible: "Lord, wilt thou at this time restore the kingdom *to Israel?*"† was their last question. Even according to Luke, the most catholic of the Christian historiographers, nothing short of a divine vision could assure Peter "that God is no respecter of persons: but in every nation he that feareth him and worketh righteousness is acceptable to him:"‡ and but for the supernatural conversion and setting apart of Saul of Tarsus, the gospel of the kingdom would never have found voice beyond the synagogue. Nay, so little was any wider field laid out, that when Jesus sent forth the twelve on their first missionary excursion, he told them "Ye shall not have gone through the cities of Israel till the Son of Man be come."§ If it be deemed doubtful whether he actually used these words (which are not part of the "common tradition"), it is certain that they would never be attributed to him at a date when they were already falsified, i.e., *after* all the cities of Israel had heard the word which had gone forth from Jerusalem. It was evidently thought, therefore, that the Parusia would be upon the earth ere the probation of Israel was complete.

It follows from this that within the historical contents of the ministry of Jesus there can as yet have been no anticipation of a kingdom of God embracing others than the "children of promise," or substituting others for them. What then are we to say to the Parable of the Vineyard-owner,‖ whose tenants withheld his rent and maltreated his agents, one after another, crowning their iniquities at last by murdering his son and heir? and of the retribution with which he visited them, by destroying them and giving the vineyard to others? —so that the "stone which the builders rejected was made the head-stone of the corner." Not less evident is the *post eventum vaticinatio* in the great man's supper, from which,

---

* Matt. x. 5.　　† Acts i. 6.　　‡ Acts x. 34, 35.　　§ Matt. x. 23.
‖ Mark xii. 1–12; Matt. xxi. 33–46; Luke xx. 9–19.

when all was ready, the invited guests absented themselves on various idle pleas ; till he was provoked to fill the room with the common people from the highways, and to say that "not one of the men who were bidden should taste of his supper."[*] In these parables, the kingdom is represented as actually *transferred* to a new people, and "sinners of the Gentiles" become the adopted "Israel of God:" it is the Pauline "olive-tree," with "the natural branch broken off and cast away," and the "wild-olive branches grafted in."[†]   But there is another parable which, in correspondence with the actual mixed composition of the Christian community, typifies the reception of the Gentiles without dispossession of the Jews : for no one can fail to see in the prodigal son, with his wilful aberrations and degeneracy, the picture of the unbridled heathen populations, conscious at last of their own degradation and ruin, and in his elder brother, still at home, the law-abiding but self-righteous Jew, secure of his exclusive inheritance, contemptuous towards the reprobate's folly and forfeiture, and offended at the father's relenting soul.   It is clearly a picture of an inward strife between elements in the Church, recently discordant, but brought at last to the true secret of God in the reconciliation of alienated hearts.   It cannot have been elaborated at a time when the very ground of disaffection had not yet appeared, when neither the younger son had yet come to himself and sought again the embrace of the father's arms, nor therefore the elder betrayed his sullen anger and declared that he " would not come in."

The idea of a *postponed Messiahship*,—i.e., of the advent of the appointed person, with yet a long delay of his accession to his dominion, was wholly unknown to the apocalyptic Judaism, and could have no intelligible meaning to the multitude who listened to Jesus in Galilee or Jerusalem.   It was an innovation on the existing doctrine, devised expressly to fit the case of Jesus, and to extort from the crucifixion and its sequel proof instead of disproof of his being the Christ that

[*] Luke xiv. 16–24. In Matthew's parallel passage, xxii. 7, viz., the additional words, "The king was wroth ; and he sent his armies and destroyed those murderers [for in this gospel they have killed his messengers], and burned their city," the date posterior to the destruction of Jerusalem, A.D. 70, is evident.

[†] Rom. xi. 17, *seqq.*

should come in power from heaven. Not till the epic of his life had passed through all its stages and changed the scene from earth to heaven, could its connected rationale take the form of this new conception. Yet, again and again, he is represented as typifying Messiah by some great one, who absents himself from his domain in some " far country," and returns by surprise in after years to take account of those whom he has left in charge. Thus, the attitude of the disciples is to be that of "men looking for their lord when he shall *return* from the marriage feast; that when he cometh and knocketh they may straightway open unto him; "* a conception which is modified and expanded into the parable of the ten virgins, waiting with their lamps, but five without their oil, till the bridegroom arrives for the marriage feast ;† and is again recast into the parable of the Talents delivered to his servants by "a man going into another country," and requiring them meanwhile to turn his capital for him to good account.‡

The mark of unhistorical character in this and similar passages is the invariable resort to the peculiar idea of the Messianic personage *going away and returning after an absence in another country*, for a wedding, a business, or a throne in the land which he had left. But for this, the mere lesson of *watchfulness*, the exhortation to stand with the loins girt and the lamps burning, might well enough proceed from the lips of Jesus; for the kingdom which he proclaimed as at hand was expected to burst as a thunder-clap upon the world; so that none would be ready then unless they were ready always. Many an expression of his, therefore, may be incorporated in the groundwork of these passages: but ere they reach us, they have taken into their very texture the accretions of a later generation, for which he is not responsible.

Some of these accretions carry in them evidence of their unauthenticity. It is plain, for instance, that the first proclamation of the "kingdom" as "at hand" was deemed

---

* Luke xii. 36.   † Matt. xxv. 1–13.

‡ Matt. xxv. 14–30. Cf. Luke xix. 12–27, where each servant receives the same, "*one pound*"; while in Matthew the sum varies with each, "according to his ability." The same idea of "each his own work" appears also in Mark xiii. 34.

urgent, and compatible only with a very short respite. The original reckoning probably finds expression in the saying that there was scarcely time for the missionary disciples to carry the notice round the cities of Israel. When the idea broke upon the apostles that the news had to be conveyed to the Gentiles too, the term was extended to the limits of the living generation : but even this, I conceive, was only retrospectively attributed to Jesus himself. It was no exact boundary at the touch of which some bell-stroke told the hour : but the watchers said to one another, ‘ Is there no sign yet ? surely the time has passed : why tarrieth the bridegroom on the way ? ’ All language which betrays this state of mind, and either confesses or rebukes wonder and distress at the delay of the Parusia, proclaims its own date, as long posterior to the living ministry of Jesus, if not to the apostolic age itself. Among the passages affected by this rule, which every reader can easily apply for himself, it is a relief to find the very objectionable parable of the “ Unjust Judge ” : so that it may be dismissed from the life of Jesus, with all the shameful ingenuity expended upon it by commentators and apologists.

Though there is no reason to doubt that Jesus shared, under whatever personal modifications, the Messianic expectations of his compatriots, it is plain from many indications that he cannot have uttered, in their present form, the apocalyptic discourses attributed to him by the Synoptists. The most remarkable of these is said to have been elicited by the two pairs of brothers, Peter and Andrew, and James and John, asking him privately why he had just answered their admiration of the Temple by predicting its destruction.* His answer, given from the Mount of Olives, with the holy city full in view, covers much more than their question, and has its climax in “the coming of the Son of Man in clouds with power and great glory, and the sending forth of his angels to gather together his elect from the four winds, from the uttermost part of the earth to the uttermost part of heaven.” But, ere this terminus is reached, a series of premonitory signs, physical portents, political convulsions, social dissensions,

* Mark xiii. 1-13 ; Matt. xxiv. 1-36. Cf. x. 17-22. Luke xxi. 5-36. Cf. xvii. 23-31.

religious persecutions,—is announced, sufficiently specific in parts to carry marks of time; and wherever this occurs they set us down upon a scene far out of sight or conjecture when Jesus spoke.   Take, for example, that which had started the whole conversation,—the destruction of the Temple.   It is conceivable enough, nay certain, that, with his spiritual idea of the relation of man to God, and under the recent shock of recoil from the coarse sights and sounds of the place deemed Holy, Jesus would feel it impossible for the Temple system to survive and pass into the "kingdom to come," and might declare it doomed.   But this is a very different thing from the foresight of the concrete particular "there shall not be left here one stone upon another, which shall not be thrown down ": the thing must have happened before that could be said.   It belongs to the same category,—of history imagined back into prophecy,—with the sign given in Luke, " When ye see Jerusalem compassed with armies, know that her desolation is at hand."   In the omens afforded by the varieties of tribulation, wars, earthquakes, famines and pestilence, it is vain to seek for any definite chronology : they can always be looked up by ingenious eyes in an area so vast as the Roman empire.   But the story of persecutions, as affecting the diffusion of Christianity, is pretty exactly known ; and the description of disciples brought before *governors and kings* to answer for their faith, and of wide-spread family disruptions through religious severance, with martyrdoms through treachery between brother and brother, father and son, is undoubtedly drawn from an experience rather of the second century than of the first.

Even the very language in which Jesus is said to disclaim knowledge of the exact date of the Parusia within the existing generation contains an unfailing mark of a time far beyond it : "of that day or that hour knoweth no one, not even the angels in heaven, *neither the Son, but the Father.*" *   As I have already remarked, this antithetic use of " the Son " and " the Father," with the definite article, was unknown till the doctrine of the person of Christ assumed its *theologic* form.

In short, beyond the repeated exhortation to " Watch " and

stand ready, with heart loosened from the cares and patient under the sufferings of "the latter days," there is hardly anything in these discourses that can have proceeded from Jesus himself: and the more you try to save as historical, the less do you leave to him of the character of a true prophet. Had the things announced happened when and as they are described, they would have borne him a witness worth preserving. But since the generation vanished and all these things did *not* come to pass, since Jerusalem was not "trodden down of the Gentiles" merely "till the times of the Gentiles were fulfilled," since the courses of the world asserted their durability and disappointed the promise of the Advent, surely there need be no regret in letting these apocalyptic leaves drop from the blighted tree of Israel's national life and lie upon the devastated soil of Palestine. They are Jewish growths from the last season of the local history, born from the genius and faith of a stormy time, some decades later than the earthly life of Jesus; and by some disciple have been seized on to supplement his message of the kingdom, and so worked into it as to make his authority seem to cover the whole.

Besides these broad and conspicuous instances of anachronism, many minor indications of a time too late for any uttered words of Jesus will strike a thoughtful reader of the Gospels. We are told of excuses made by hearers attracted to him yet unready at once to follow him; and of somewhat harsh answers to their natural pleas, the wish to bid adieu to the home circle,* the duty of first caring for a father's burial.† Is it not even said, "If any man cometh unto me, and hateth not his own father and mother and wife and children and brethren and sisters, yea, and his own life also, he cannot be my disciple?"‡ The evangelist, living amid bitter conflicts between an aggressive Christianity and a reigning heathenism, transfers the requirements and the passions of a persecuting society to the Galilean ministry; forgetting that Jesus had no personal following except the twelve, and asked no sacrifice that broke up the homes of Israel or the worship of the synagogue, and no devotion but of a heart more loving and a will more faithful than before. These passages reflect the exactions

<hr>

* Luke ix. 61, 62. † Matt. viii. 21, 22; Luke ix. 59, 60. ‡ Luke xiv. 26.

and the irritation of struggling missionaries and irreconcilable
enthusiasms, already organized and entrenched in opposite
camps.   Nay, the very language of the most characteristic of
Christian precepts was not in use till created and consecrated
by his own sacrifice, and could not have passed his living lips,
"If any man would come after me, let him deny himself, and
take up his cross and follow me."*

The second rule of historical judgment is so expressed as to
leave room for assent, at least partial and suspended, in regard
to incidents related as miraculous.   This implies that I do not
mean to base the exclusion of apparent miracle on any a priori
dictum about the universality of Law.   The uniformities
which regulate our expectations we have got to know by
induction from experience; and as they have been gathered
from past facts, they are always open to control by future
facts, which they are incompetent to forbid.   Our stock of
known laws, not being a closed circle, does not shut out an
anomalous phenomenon as impossible and entitle us to say
"It did not happen."   What it does authorize us to say is,
"Granting its occurrence, you can never tell that it was a
miracle;" for there is always room for the unexpected in the
gaps of undetermined law; and when assigned to its place
there, it belongs to the sphere of *Nature*, and not to what is
beyond nature, as you want your miracle to be.   This consideration, which deprives what are called "signs and wonders"
of all religious validity and restores them to the bosom of the
world, I am the less disposed to press, because it accepts from
the theologians the false postulate that the cosmic causalities
and the Divine are mutually exclusive, and that you cannot
be sure of the touch of God till you are outside of nature.

Without being prejudged as impossible, a reported miracle
may, nevertheless, be incredible for the same reason that
induces disbelief in many an alleged commonplace incident,
viz., the want of adequate evidence : and it is on this ground
alone that the historical validity of the evangelists' narratives,
whatever be their contents, must be estimated.   That for
different orders of phenomena there are various gradations of
evidence requisite as conditions of belief is denied by no one :

* Matt. xvi. 24 ; x. 38 ; Luke ix. 23.

or that the chief difference in this respect lies in the conformity or inconformity of the seeming fact with expectations warranted by usage. Even of an event presented to our immediate perception we sometimes say, if it be startling, "I could hardly believe my eyes:" and we keep our acceptance, or our interpretation, of it in suspense, till we have taken special precautions against illusion. At one remove from personal experience, as when we only hear the same thing from another, the element of doubt is, in any case, doubled; and if there be less security for our informant's accuracy or veracity than for our own, the ratio of increase is higher. Every link in the transmission contributes its increment of uncertainty, always enlarging so long as the tradition is oral, then arrested when consigned to a written text and stored among the sources of history, yet by this very process exposed to a new possibility, by which chronicles are revised, filled in, and painted up. If in a court of justice it is often barely possible to elicit the truth, where only recent facts are under investigation, and contemporary documents are accessible and living witnesses are examined and cross-examined, and every safeguard against falsity is provided of which human fear and conscience admit, we may form some conception of what we have to ask from historic tradition, before we can reconstruct in thought the true picture of a life such as that of Jesus of Nazareth, and such a growth as that of the Christian Church. We cannot claim to have any known personal testimony to the contents of the ministry of Jesus ; our earliest witness being the convert "born out of due time ;" and our dependence for the previous time being on the synoptical gospels, which did not come into ascertained existence till the second or third generation after the events they relate, and then doubtless embodied simply the mixed popular tradition moulded by memory, reverence, and faith, in their period of pure but uncritical enthusiasm. While it is thus impossible to reach any original attestation which we can appreciate as adequate to substantiate the tales that would be incredible today, nothing is more certain than that, in the state of mind out of which the Church was born, miracles would have been freely believed, whether they had really happened or not. The known growth of the doctrine respecting the person of Christ through its several stages, as traced in the foregoing chapters, is itself an example, on a large scale, of the tendency which wrought the whole story of Jesus into supernatural form. And though the mode of transformation cannot be traced in detail, the preconceptions and influences of the age supplied inducements to it and facilities for it which serve to explain it.

Thus the belief in demoniacal possession already introduced proternatural agents on to the stage of common life, and assigned to them as their province a large class of nervous disorders peculiarly dependent on conditions of mental excitement or repose, and often amenable to sympathetic control by an intense and powerful personality: and wherever a healing influence seemed to flow from such a centre, the remission, like the access, of the disease, would necessarily be referred to the mediation of the spiritual world. So far, there is a real ground for the old rationalistic explanation of miracles as mis-interpreted natural facts. In other cases, a forgotten parable is petrified into an unmeaning miracle. We cannot, for instance, for a moment doubt the purport of this short symbolic lesson: "A certain man had a fig-tree planted in his vineyard: and he came seeking fruit thereon, and found none. And he said to his vine-dresser, Behold, these three years I come seeking fruit on this fig-tree and find none: cut it down: why cumbereth it the ground? And he answering saith unto him, Lord, let it alone this year also, till I shall dig about it and dung it : and if it bear fruit thenceforth, well : but if not, thou shalt cut it down."[*]   Here, the same Israel which had been, with the Psalmist, " the vine brought by God's hand out of Egypt,"[†] and, with Paul, his " good olive tree,"[‡] appears as the fig-tree; and the complaint of its barrenness, heard already from the lips of many a prophet, is declared to have brought disappointment to its climax. 'See, the sunshine visits it for the last time in vain: cut it down, and let it wither. Israel is cast away. Yet, no! let there be one re-lenting more: and though the probation that should have been final has but brought the crowning failure, and the most

<hr>

[*] Luke xiii. 6-9.   [†] lxxx. 8.   · · ·   [‡] Rom. xi. 24.

glorious season of promise has been thrown away, grant but a supplementary year, and multiply the husbandman's faithfulness and care, and perchance there is yet life enough to ripen some fruit among the leaves.' Here is plainly shadowed forth the mission of the Spirit, as the sequel to the personal appeal of Christ, suspending the rejection of " the people of God," and giving them the apostolic age, as one chance of mercy more.

The parable, thus rounded off to its close, would not be intelligible till the descent and mission of the Holy Spirit had published the reprieve, and extended the term of repentance for Israel. It describes the dealings of God as they appeared to Paul and his evangelist Luke after the middle of the first century. Suppose it conceived and spoken on the verge of the last teachings in the Temple in which Jesus pressed home his conclusive test on the conscience of Jerusalem, it must have been silent about any appendix of mercy, and have stopped short with the sentence, " cut it down, why cumbereth it the ground ? " Did Jesus then, on his morning walk from Bethany, charged with his message that the hour of ingathering was nigh, think within himself, as Zion came in sight, ' What fruit will be ready in this favoured orchard of the Lord ? will he find there " trees of righteousness," " the planting of his hand ? " or, is the foliage so showy because the promised harvest is all dropped ? Alas ! should it be so (and this day may test it), Israel will be doomed as a dead branch ere night.' This half of Luke's parable would cover all that was then within view, and is the probable ground of the strange story in the other synoptists, viz., that Jesus, as he approached the city, being hungry, searched for figs on an actual tree by the wayside, and found none because it was not the season for figs ; and notwithstanding this good reason for its barrenness, he was provoked to doom the tree by an imprecation never to bear fruit again ; and it withered away, either instantly (Matt.) or before evening (Mark).* The two synoptists, having lost the parable with its clew, turned its broken bits into an unworthy and senseless miracle ; Luke, having recovered it, carried it out beyond its date of utterance, by a supplement winding up with long-suffering instead of curse.

* Matt. xxi. 18–20; Mark xi. 12–14, 20, 21.

The true sense of many a reported miracle plainly lies in its symbolical meaning. Why is it that the cures wrought at a distance by a word are accorded to the *Heathen* faith of the Syrophœnician mother afflicted about her daughter,* and the Roman centurion about his servant,† but to show what healing is ready at call for " them that are afar off "? The feeding of the multitudes, already allegorized in the fourth gospel, the walking on the sea with the saving of the sinking Peter, the transfiguration completing and crowning the trio of immortal prophets beginning with Law and ending with Love, speak for themselves in tones deeper and sweeter than the even prose of history. Nor can we mistake, in such episodes as that of the Temptation, the translation into objective drama of inward spiritual experiences of discipline and conflict. In the presence of these indications, and the absence of definite contemporary testimony, there seems no excuse for seeking explanations of the gospel narrative beyond the historical and moral conditions of the time.

The application of our third rule, excluding what is incongruous with the personal characteristics of Jesus, is a much more difficult and delicate task for the critic than he encounters with the other two; nor will his handling of it, however cautious, bring conviction to those who require more definite grounds of belief than are afforded by harmony and disharmony in the shades of character. And yet, to those who cannot help being affected by such phenomena, there is nothing more persuasive. Several traits which might have been brought under this head of incongruity I have preferred to treat, for the sake of more exactitude, under that of anachronism : but the self-proclamation of meekness and lowliness of heart, the pompous self-elevation above Jonah and Solomon and the temple, the joy to think how blessed are the eyes that see him, are just as much out of keeping with the personality as with the time to which they are referred. The unhistoric character of such features cannot be fully appreciated till they are seen side by side with the certainly historical ; but, in passing to this, an additional sample or

* Matt. xv. 21-28; Mark vii. 25-30.
† Matt. viii. 5-13; Luke vii. 2-10.

two may be given, for the sake of completing our scheme of conclusions.

Few readers, probably, of the Sermon on the Mount would be seriously disturbed if an authoritative manuscript were found, the text of which did not contain this verse: "Give not that which is holy unto the dogs, neither cast your pearls before swine, lest haply they trample them under their feet, and turn and rend you."* The tone of ὕβρις is not much relieved by the discussion raised regarding the persons described as "dogs" and "swine." I take it for certain that if this injunction came from the lips of Jesus, its opprobrious terms, conformably with contemporary Jewish usage, could be understood only of *the Gentiles*, and would extend his sanction to the most malign manifestations of Israelitish intolerance. That such an ebullition of scorn and insult should proceed from him who extolled in the alien "a faith which he had not found, no, not in Israel," and who selected a Samaritan as the ideal expounder of the second great commandment, is utterly incredible. The language has its parallel, and doubtless the indication of its date, in the warnings to the Churches of Asia (particularly that of Thyatira),† contained in the prologue to the Apocalypse, guarding them against forms of antinomian corruption which had come upon the Church of the second century from the growth of gnostic philosophy and the misuse of Pauline theology. The verse, wholly unconnected with its context, is doubtless one of the latest interpolations of the most mixed of all the gospels; and expresses the feeling of passionate disgust which the encroachment of heathen licence upon the purity of the Church awakened in its true pastors and people.

Not less repugnant to the spirit of Jesus than this reputed fierceness against the foreigner is the opposite irritation attributed to him by Luke against the obduracy of his own people. In such haste is the evangelist to give prominence to this feature that he opens the Galilean ministry with a striking scene, of really later date, in the synagogue of his native Nazareth. When the carpenter's son, whom the villagers had known from a child, comes before them as a

* Matt. vii. 6.   † Rev. ii. 18, *seqq.* Cf. Phil. iii. 2, 3; Jude 17–23.

young prophet and "proclaims the acceptable year of the Lord," it might seem encouragement enough that "they wondered at the glorious words that proceeded out of his mouth," and recognized in him the divine glow which he could not have caught at home. But instead of leaving the seed to sink into their hearts and find its root in silence, he seizes upon the angry text that "no prophet is acceptable in his own country," and launches forth into reproaches against the perverseness of Israel, so that Elijah had to carry the compassion of God to a widow of Sidon, and Elisha to a leper of Syria.* Is this "the servant of God, who shall neither strive nor cry, who will not break the bruised reed or quench the smoking flax"?† Is not such an outburst, addressed to parents, elders, neighbours, lifelong companions, highly provocative,—the utterance more of temper than of love? The parallel accounts in the other synoptists not only are silent about any such address, but by their remark that in presence of the local unbelief "he could do no mighty work," imply his mood to have been one rather of despondency than of aggression. Pfleiderer's suggestion may well be accepted: that Luke, writing at a time when the Gentile preponderance in Christendom had finally alienated and embittered the Jewish feeling by the wrenching away of the national "election," worked up the Nazarene incident into a miniature, on the village scale, of the passionate resentment of the old Israel towards the successful usurper of its promises.‡

In another instance Luke is betrayed into the same incongruity. He tells us of the acceptance by Jesus of an invitation to dinner at a Pharisee's house, and reports what passed at table. Perceiving his host's surprise at his seating himself without caring for the usual washing of the hands, Jesus breaks at once into the following unsparing rebuke: "Now do ye Pharisees cleanse the outside of the cup and of the platter, but your inward part is full of extortion and wickedness. Ye foolish ones! did not he that made the outside make the inside also? Howbeit, give alms of such things as ye have: and, behold, all things are clean unto

---

* Luke iv. 16–30.　　　　† Is. xlii. 1–3; Matt. xii. 18–21.
‡ Das Urchristenthum, 431.

you."* The invective, thus starting from the usages of the table, then opens out into a general assault upon the Pharisaic hypocrisy and ambition, winding up with the denunciation, "Woo unto you! for yo aro as tombs that appear not, and the men that walk over them know it not." Nor is this enough: an expostulation from "a lawyer" whose class feeling was touched by tho bitter words, only brought down a storm of more scathing indignation, such as must inevitably have broken up any assembly of human beings that had not a hundredfold the patience of Job. But just here tho evangelist, in the excitement of his sympathetic anger, over-reaches himself, and betrays his trespass beyond all historical restraints; for he makes Jesus close his philippic with that quotation from the apocalyptic "Wisdom of God," which brings down the crimes against the prophets to the death of Zachariah in the siege of Jerusalem by Titus. It is as evident as it is natural that these antipharisaic discourses aro throughout tinctured with the feeling of the post-apostolic time when the breach between the Church, now regarding itself as tho true Israel of God, and the Jews exasperated by its apostasy, was complete and embittered. Embedded in these discourses there may be many a pithy saying, and many a piercing rebuke, that really came from tho lips of Jesus; but the tone of intense passion pervading them, with total disregard of all times and seasons, is utterly at variance with the ruling affections and inward repose of his spirit. Not that his inexhaustible heart of mercy, open to forgiveness seventy times in a day, required any Quaker-like suppression of righteous anger, whenever either tho guilty conscience was secretly angry with itself, or it was needful to snatch tho mis-guided multitude from the hands of sanctimonious impostors, and clear their vision to see for themselves what is true and right. But such moral enthusiasm peals forth in the august tones of wounded justice, not in tho shrill rage of mero vituperation : and it would either decline the relation between host and guest, or reserve itself till some less offensive occasion permitted its expression.

There aro perhaps few sincere Christians who have not at

* Luke xi. 39–41.

times been distressed by the strange juxtaposition in the same discourse, and even in the same precepts of Jesus, of ideal elevation and of low self-interest, a juxtaposition psychologically impossible and therefore ethically libellous. His disciples are to be absolutely disinterested, shedding their treasures of love and succour in unstinted measure upon others, "hoping for nothing again"; assured that they would *have their reward* from their Father in Heaven : they are to reserve their hospitable and generous offices for the poor, the lame, the blind, guarding themselves against the possibility of any return ; and they "*shall be recompensed* at the resurrection of the just": their alms, and fasts and prayers are to be private and unseen, lest they should be tainted by the prospect of personal good ; and "the Father who seeth in secret will *reward them openly.*"   This does not seem to rise above the level of an old maxim, "He that hath pity on the poor lendeth to the Lord."* If it be thought that the *futurity* of the compensation sanctifies it, even this feature is not always preserved; as when modesty and humility of behaviour are recommended as the surest means of avoiding rebuffs and obtaining advancement.†   The state of mind that would be formed by surrendering life to the play of these incentives would be utterly at variance with all that Jesus loved and was, and could produce only a hollow mimicry of his spiritual attitude towards God and man. Such righteousness is but a long-headed economy ; an investment in a deferred annuity or the purchase of a reversionary interest by one who can dispense with dividends each quarter day.

These incongruities do but illustrate the irreversible law, that the supreme lights of the saintly conscience retain their purity only in the souls on which they dawn, and become dimmed on their transmission into the next and lower stratum of minds ; so that no Divine revelation can be delivered into human keeping without being shorn of its first lustre by the clouded region through which it has to pass. Jesus himself was not untouched by the consciousness of this and of the loneliness in which it left him : "he sighed deeply in his

* Prov. xlx. 17.   † Luke xlv. 8-11.

spirit and said, ' Why doth this generation seek a sign ? ' "[*]
" He turned and said, ' Ye know not what manner of spirit ye
are of.' "[†]   We have to step downwards from himself to the
apostles, and again from the apostles to the Church, till the
image becomes confused, and its living expression almost
fades from view.   Yet there are discernible a few ineffaceable
lineaments, which could belong only to a figure unique in
grace and majesty.

    [*] Mark viii. 12.   [†] Luke ix. 55.

CHAPTER II.

THE CHRISTIAN RELIGION PERSONALLY REALIZED.

THE portions of the synoptic texts which remain on hand, after severing what the foregoing rules exclude, can by no means be accepted *en masse* as all equally trustworthy. They are relieved simply of the impossible, and contain only what *might be true*. But not everything that might be true turns out really to be so; and from the possible, i.e., that which is consistent with the known conditions, we have still to collect the actual, before the historic image issues from the haze. Nor can this be effected by any mechanical process of further partition. It might seem at first sight a safe resolve to take one's stand upon the *common tradition* as unimpeached and trebly firm. Yet who would say that an uncontradicted story, though it be thrice, or a hundred times told, must be judged free from all that is fabulous? Is it even conceivable that, after its oral repetition through thirty years, its *litera scripta* should at last present an exact photograph of the. reality? Especially if that reality should be, not a visible and palpable event, but the " winged words " of a dialogue or a discourse, can we say that popular rumour is a phonograph which will redeliver it to the next generation? And as, on the one hand, truth, by its very diffusion, may be dissolved away in the media of its transmission, so, on the other hand, may here and there a precious shred of it alight unnoticed and float down on some hidden rill and turn up at last under the eye of a far-off observer, who brings it unspoiled to the light. So that there may possibly be error in the common tradition from which the special may be free; and what is peculiar to any one synoptist is not necessarily to be distrusted as an editorial comment merely for want of corroboration. It must be judged by considerations gathered from the whole field of probabilities.

Thus, at the very outset, we must assent to Mark alone in accepting the Baptist's preaching as the real "Beginning of the Gospel of Jesus Christ,"* the first known awakening in him of a conscious call to speak and act as a witness of Divine things to his compatriots. Whatever may have preceded it in the crypts that underlie the pavement of history is as "the secret of God," read by no human eye; but now, it breaks into a light startling to himself, and, it may be, visible to others in a gracious kindling of new life in his features and his form. Urged to seek the stern prophet of the desert by the same wave of enthusiasm which was carrying multitudes to the banks of Jordan, he no doubt meant what they meant, with only the keener tension and the larger wonder of a soul more rare. He too came in faith that "the times of refreshing from the presence of the Lord "† were at hand, and sprang forward with joy to meet them. But how was it checked when he stood before the tall figure and the piercing eye of the rugged Eremite, and was shaken by the peals of his commanding voice! Short and sharp as broken thunder came the bursts of rebuke, of precept, and of terror : ' Ye viperous generation! do you bring your poison to me? am I to wash you back into children of Abraham? repent: reverse your ways this very hour: judgment is at your heels, to sweep you as chaff into unquenchable fire!' Such was the Baptist's message of the kingdom of God : the Æthiopian must change his skin, and the leopard his spots, or be overtaken by the last despair: it was all warning and exaction, addressed to fear : not a word of promise, not an invitation of hope : the only possibility offered being the bare escape from the axe, the winnowing fan, the consuming wrath.

That within the sensitive conscience of Jesus also these peremptory tones would ring like reverberations of Sinai, and pervade him with an answering awe, we may well believe. But did they adequately render his preconception of the reign of righteousness? did they picture a scene which he could rejoice to see? did they speak to the affection which chiefly made up his relation to the infinite Father, or only to that with which he hid his face from the tremendous Judge?

* Mark i. 1.   † Acts iii. 19.

Hither he had been drawn, "looking for the consolation of Israel," and expecting to meet its foregleams in the prophet's vision : and this stormy prelude interposed a band of cloud and lightning which blotted out the eternal sunshine and shut up the heavens. In his tender humility he too trembled at the message, and went down with the publicans and sinners into the waters of repentance. But it is not thus alone that the pure in heart can see their God : the light of his countenance refuses to be hid : and as he emerged from the stream, the heavens opened to him, and the love of God came hovering down upon him to choose him as its vehicle to the hearts of men. It was the moment of self-dedication to the divine life,—not indeed in the mimic form of self-perfectioning, but in the true passion of self-surrender as the organ of a supreme possessing holiness and mercy,—a crisis therefore not so much of personal resolve, as of delivery into the disposing hand of God, to bear witness of the nearness of holy things and the greatness of the Divine promise. Such an inaugurative moment would hold the same place in his life that is marked in subsequent Christian experience by what is called " conversion," and is seldom if ever absent from minds rightly maturing their spiritual history.

As he stood apart, and watched the mixed crowd, Pharisees and Sadducees, soldiers and traders of the city, husbandmen and labourers from the fields, thronging the banks, or hurrying to the stream, with tumult of competing voices, he would see in them, even in their haste to be cleansed of sin, enough for compassionate sympathy and some gentler reception than the Baptist's severe welcome. Yet the question would haunt him, when he looked across the margin of this ' last age,' ' Are these then the colonists reserved for the commonwealth of God ? are they congenial elements of a society where all shall be holy ? cruel it would be to deal with them as chaff to be driven from the floor : but are they really samples of the precious wheat that is to fill the divine garners ? ' They do not as yet fit in with his pure and saintly vision : something more is needed than setting them right with their broken law : there must be an ulterior stage to the transformation which the Baptist institutes, if the dust of this world is not to settle on the kingdom of heaven, and leave it without its green pastures and still waters. It is no wonder if such doubts and longing sense of incompleteness oppressed the spirit of Jesus, and drove him to the desert to resolve them, and settle accounts between his traditional preconceptions and his personal faith.

That lonely conflict had no human witness, and would certainly remain a secret confidence between himself and the Searcher of hearts. It would be betrayed only in " the power of spirit " with which he issued from it. The oldest reporter left it in its obscurity as a time of inward trial : the other synoptists, affecting a fuller knowledge of its contents, filled them in from their own theory of his state of mind. Had he already, as they imagined, looked on himself as Messiah and been invested with the corresponding powers, while yet something told him that they were not to be wielded till he had received an ulterior commission, then the " temptation " would have been to a premature self-assertion of his claims, and a free use of his control over men and nature for the supply of his wants or the display of his prerogatives. This, in the view of the first and third evangelists, was the Satanic proposal : 'Are you the Christ that is to reign ? then dally no more with these poor scruples ; grasp the sceptre at once, and enter on your rightful glory !' The controversy, thus conceived, was between an immediate seizure, by questionable means, of the Messianic throne, and a deferred accession to it through the Divine method of suffering patience and the martyr's sacrifice. But if, as we have reason to believe, Jesus never claimed the Messianic character, but only took up the Baptist's message and prolonged in new tones his herald's cry that the advent was near, a different aspect must be given to the inward wrestlings of those desert hours. He who proclaims a change of sovereignty over the world must be able to tell what that change is to be : he cannot " make ready the way of the Lord " unless he knows whither his paths are to lead : the harbinger of a fresh order of human life must be at one with the future to which he invites men to conform by anticipation. In his baptism Jesus solemnly joined the band of precursors on the watch for the kingdom : the vows of self-dedication which his repentance carried in it, and the mixed scene at the river's edge, must render impossible a mere return to the routine of secular industry, and overcharge his heart with the burden of a divine message, yet undefined, beginning with John's, but not ending there. When he tries to deliver it and forecast the dwelling of God among men. how shall he speak? Shall he reproduce the temporal terrors and glories of the prophets, threaten the fate of Sodom and Gomorrah, promise the splendours of David and Solomon, and paint the earth with fields and vineyards that yield a hundredfold, and represent all nations as tributary to Jerusalem? Or dropping these things as permitted to "them of old time" only for the hardness of their hearts, may he rather learn for himself from the living Father who communes with him in secret, whose love is the quickening essence of all other love, and whose perfection is for ever working against all imperfection? Between the national and political dream, and the spiritual and human reality, of a kingdom of heaven—*that* was the conflict from which Jesus issued, pale with prayer and fasting, but clear of evil spirits, "for a season" at least, if not for ever.

Sooner than he had expected, he was called to fulfil his vow: the voice of John was silenced in prison, and left its message to be taken up by him. "When he heard that John was delivered up, he came into Galilee," and "began to preach and to say, Repent ye, for the kingdom of heaven is at hand."* The wording was the same, still fixing the eye of faith on the reign of righteousness; but the method was different. He dropped the baptism by which the mission had been centred at a single spot and in an outward rite, and the prophet could but stand still and reiterate the same formula, with little variation, to large classes of unknown men; he set himself free to circulate among the village families, and converse on the roads with husbandmen and mariners, whose every question might supply a text, and every trouble give occasion for a blessing or a prayer. This conversion of a stationary into an itinerant mission, shifts its very centre of gravity. The rush to the Jordan was a movement of panic,

* Matt. iv. 12, 17; Mark i. 14, 15.

started by the cry " Flee from the wrath to come." The attraction to Jesus was the persuasion of a personality rendering all " very attentive to hear him." John had been but " a voice crying in the wilderness :" Jesus himself, by his very presence, taught them more than all he said. "John did no miracle," nor did any one think of ascribing them to him ; but Jesus drew upon him so bright a cloud of love and wonder, that marvels multiplied around him, whether he would or not. This immediate personal influence apparently won for him, almost at sight, his first permanent disciples, the two pairs of brothers, Andrew and Peter, James and John, who formed the nucleus of his assistant train. Little as they could as yet understand him, their reverent attachment sufficed to begin with. They could variously help him on his way, could leave him free to preach or to be alone, could mediate between him and the multitude that soon gathered around his steps, and could sometimes even go before him and bear the main purport of his message to the places " whither he himself should come."

In the story of the life which he henceforth led, there are doubtless many blanks ; nor can we place confidence in all the fragments which have been saved. Yet, scanty as our knowledge is of what he did and said during the great majority of his days, no one can affect ignorance of what he was ; enough is saved to plant his personality in a clear space, distinct from all that history, or even fiction, presents. The authority of the Baptist had been that of censorship alone, as of an officer of justice sent, for discipline, to a colony of criminals. But who will raise the question, whether Jesus could bless as well as denounce? With . him benediction came to the front and sat upon his brow. The flash of his eye was no "dry light," but could be dimmed with tears. The depth to which his words sank into the heart measured the depth from which they were drawn. And though, with the will of a delicate wisdom, he could retain his reserves of thought, no art or disguise clouded the transparency of his spirit ; you knew what he loved and what he abhorred as surely as you saw who they were that loved him, and who that hated. All except those who had lost the key of sympathy in themselves, discerned at a glance what features most moved him in human life, what he required from the human conscience, what he expected for the human soul; and felt as if they witnessed behind the scene, how he realized the hidden life of communion with God.

The aspect of his life most arresting to the observer, was the large place which human need and suffering occupied in his thought and affection; not less, the unconscious needs and contented privations that slept in the darkness of low natures, than the grievous pains of bodily infirmity or of wounded love. Their appealing look was met by such an answering glance that, wherever he went they thronged around him with a thirst for his pity, with or without a hope for his help. You can scarcely think of him but as surrounded by a motley group of the maimed with as various sores as the patients in the waiting-room of an infirmary, all with imploring eyes longing to tell their tale. It is easy to say that this was sure to follow from the popular repute of his miraculous powers. Doubtless, but hardly unless you prefix an inverse explanation, and account for the wide rumour of his miracles of mercy by the wonderful working of his compassion upon the minds of men, and through the mind enabling at times the crippled body to "rise up and walk." The profound impression once made of so unique an agency, more was sure to be told of him than he actually did. But even the physical exaggeration is not without its moral truth,— truth of inward character, if not of outward fact. Nothing short of it can adequately report the range of his humanity. Doubt as you may how many of the broken he made whole, it is certain that he had pity on all that was pitiable, and healed all that was curable.

That this tender insight into the suffering passages of human experience should draw multitudes around him, and make "the common people hear him gladly," is not surprising. As little can we wonder that they were sometimes startled, and even scandalized, by observing that his compassionate affection seemed more deeply stirred by moral degradation than by personal affliction. Did he not consort with publicans and sinners? address himself rather to those who were on the borders of guilt than to the righteous who needed no repentance? and even shield the adulteress from the accusers of her shame? Could a prophet of the Holy One who "is angry with the wicked every day" so lightly treat the breaches of His Law? No more natural question can be asked from the Jewish point of view: it is the legalist's objection to a deeper spiritual discernment. The social treatment of wrong-doing, determined by its outward aspects, may do such violence to right proportion, that the true observer's displeasure at the guilt may be balanced and over-balanced by indignation at too cruel a punishment. And the leniency charged against Jesus was shown exclusively towards *outcast sin*, banished from human mercy and hope less for its heinousness than for its indecorum, though often more open to penitent affection and more amenable to a restoring love, than less glaring forms of guilt. But sin in its court-dress or its priest's robe, sin which shirks natural duties under pretence of holy vows, sin which confesses at church and cheats in the market, which flatters its patrons and fleeces its clients, which gives short measure and makes up by long prayers,—was he lenient to *that?* Did he address himself to it as the physician to heal it, or as the judge to condemn it? Or rather did he not, by the sharpness of his con-demnation, identify himself with the voice itself of conscience and of God, and so bring into play the only living power in which healing could be found?* To the merely ethical mind these characteristics, of severest purity and of gentlest forbearance, are in antagonism, each prevailing at the cost of the other. In Jesus they found their union in the one deep spring of all his life, his relation of devout love to the Father in heaven, as the infinitely perfect. Where this pervades the entire con-sciousness, and the touch is never lost between the human spirit and the Divine, all morals resolve themselves into a personal attitude of affection towards the supremely Holy, a private interchange of secret sympathy, of mutual under-

* Notwithstanding the traces of later conformation in the anti-pharisaic discourses, there is no reason to doubt that they are redactions of earlier texts, and represent the real attitude of Jesus towards the ecclesiastical teaching of his time.

standing, of open trust. As instituted by One "who seeth in secret," it need not and will not talk much of itself and sound its own praises : but, though free from all disguise, will rather be a "song without words" carrying a thrill of varying strength and sweetness through all the life. This one relation, realized as in Jesus, becomes the Supreme good : all other good is but its dependent reflection, whose meaning vanishes in the absence, that is, the oblivion, of its source. Harmony with God is, for the human soul, the only peace, the only right, the only fair : to see things as he sees them is truth : to rank them in the order of his love, is goodness : to act conformably with his rules, is victory. To quit this height and look out from any lower level will inevitably substitute the seeming for the real, and deceive you by the secondary maxim that " Man is the measure of all things,"—a maxim which first becomes valid when "God is the measure of man." If you once set up, as independent objects of pursuit, any of the subordinate ends attractive to the human will, personal pleasure, be it of sense or soul, the prizes of ambition, the advancement of knowledge, even the disinterested service of others ; all these things, cut off from their transcendent support and spiritual significance, degenerate into selfish cupidities or generous idolatries. And even the rules for controlling and proportioning them, that is, their ethical regulation, however anxiously studied, can amount to no more, when worked by a calculating will dealing with forces on its own level, than a sterile art of self-perfectioning. Severed from the uplifting inspiration, it is a mutilated self, that can have no perfection ; and only sham virtues are reached by doing their externals for a foreign object or out of a dead heart. Who can wonder that he who has led us to the Father encountered, on descending from the mount of his prayer, this "righteousness of the Law" with an intense aversion ? The mimicry of holiness by fitting the livery of the virtues on to the figure of an ethical automaton is a sacrilegious traffic in Divine relations, of which the temple of life should be cleansed at any cost. Any fresh converse, spirit to spirit, between man and God, even passion's repentant cry *de profundis*, which lays bare whatever sinks or lifts the soul, touches the true prophet's heart with deeper sympathy.

It is the singleness of this *life in God* that gave its uniqueness to the personality of Jesus; referring back all his experiences to the infinitely Perfect, all his sorrows to the eternal blessedness, all his disappointments to the living Fountain of hope. The deluding impressions of a drudging and suffering world were habitually checked and transcended by a recovered contact with the one and only Good. Stealing out before the dawn, or lingering on the hills into the night, he quenched in the silence the wranglings of disciples and the importunities of the crowd, and received, in answer to his prayer, a fresh share of the Love which overarches and must penetrate the world. Lifted, in these meditative moments, to the Divine point of view, he apprehends the essences of things, sees them no longer as they are but as they are meant to be; and is doubly touched, with a true joy in them, so far as they give forth their intended nature entire and unspoiled; and with a deep longing, where it is left in the dark, or marred in the conscious light, to bring it to the birth or redeem it from its death. The whole hierarchy of created beings, in ascending types from the grass of the earth to the angels of heaven, was sacred and lovely to him as the depository and vehicle of the Divine thought, which could always be read in their possibilities, and only in voluntary agents be missed in fact. Amid the forms of unconscious life, too simple to go astray and appointed only to detain the air and dews and mould them into leafage and blossom, what gladness flashed from his eye and broke from his lips as he looked and said, "Behold the lilies of the field." In the instinctive creatures, moved hither and thither to what they need by an infallible thought that is all done for them, with what a heart-leap of delight did he read for them the providing care which they knew not, when their wings were heard overhead and their shadow floated along the grass, and he exclaimed, "Behold the birds of the air; they sow not, neither do they reap, nor gather into barns; yet your heavenly Father feedeth them!" In the more manifold nature of the little child, still in the play-time of his waking impulses, each with its right to have him as it comes, but intended by revelation of its ordered place to rise from instinctive to divine, how genuine is his embrace of their free innocence, and how pathetic his hinted prayer that, through the guardian angels of life, it may pass unstained into voluntary holiness! In whom else, among the regenerators of the world, do you meet with this tender enthusiasm for natures that are *less than moral*, this sympathy with impulse still at large and waiting for the discipline of thought and will? Their characteristic has usually been a stern and suspicious attitude towards the realm of nature below the sphere of grace, nay, even a disposition to deny the beauty of the world and the blessedness of human life, and designate them together as a howling wilderness; and, on the strength of this theory, to disparage literature, art, science, and all the products of the "natural man" as "carnal" and foreign to the children of God.

Instead of shrouding the real earth beneath this dark pall hiding it from heaven, instead of despairing of any good but by escape beyond humanity, Jesus looked for it nowhere else, and lived on the earth as already bathed in heaven. The illusion of asceticism had no hold on him : there was nothing to kill out and abolish in any nature : in all that was God-given he beheld only what was good, so soon and so long as it kept its appointed place. To him the pure and spiritual was not beyond the material, but within it, ever seeking to clothe itself in form and colour, and breathe out its thought in waves of sound. The outer folds of things seemed to fall away before him, and lay their meaning bare; and hence he so often saw in those around him a light of good, a shade of ill, which they knew not themselves; and by a hint, or even a glance, touched the one with hope, and softened the other with shame and tears. No disguise, of decorum or inde-corum, availed to hide from him the doublings or the simplicity of the soul within. The costume of the Samar-itan, the office of the publican, the rags of the beggar, the sores of the leper, intercepted from him no gleam of goodness, no glow of trust. His very look, like the spring sunshine, searched below the rough unsightly soil, and mel-lowed the seeds of good, till an unexpected verdure surprised the ground. In many of those who were shunned and cast out as sinners his spiritual penetration recognized a class, not of volunteers in preferred wickedness, but of neglected and undisciplined children, swept away, prior to the birth of conscience, by this or that uppermost passion, rather than deliberate rebels abjuring a sworn loyalty: their intense affections, though not yet brought under the comparing and controlling eye of the moral consciousness, were a storehouse of hopeful power, as soon as they looked each other in the face and woke up to the discovery of their respective ranks. The new reverence that would thence arise could be kindled by no touch so readily as the appealing sympathy of Jesus; and many a passionate soul was stopped on its whirlwind as he turned his pitying look upon its madness; and bursting into tears of penitence, found in devotion to him a transcending calm which nature's wildest winds and waves obey.

This habit and power of seeing what is invisible in men, and of measuring affection towards them by what they are in themselves rather than by what they have outwardly seemed, gives the key to his startling solution of the problem of mutual forgiveness. "How often," asks Peter, "shall my brother sin against me, and I forgive him? until seven times? Jesus saith unto him, I say not unto thee until seven times, but until seventy times seven;"* or, as Luke has it, with probably more approach to the original, "If he sin against thee seven times in a day, and seven times turn again to thee, saying I repent, thou shalt forgive him."† This does not imply that you are to renounce your disapproval of his recent sin: if you did, you would fall into variance with him; for he has come to disapprove it himself. It does not mean that you are to interpose and cut off, if you can, its entail of natural penalty: to promise, for instance, to trust him as much in the future as if he had always been faithful: if you did, he would be the first to decline your confidence as misplaced; for in his repentance he knows that he cannot trust himself. He has, in fact, come round to your feeling, so far as it is purely moral,

---

* Matt. xviii. 21, 22.   † Luke xvii. 4.

about his act; and you are to accept and welcome it with entire sympathy: to be angry with him only as he is angry with himself: to be sorry with him simply as he is sorry for himself. But if your feeling towards his past conduct is more than a hurt moral sense, if it has the heat of anger and resentment, because the wrong has been against you in particular rather than against the law of right individualized in another, this personal element must be utterly and instantly blotted out: without recanting the morning's disapproval, the evening's alienation must be unconditionally renounced: you must love him for what he is, and with the more joy because it is other than what he was, and your affections have come into coincidence. And this you must do with free heart and no reproachful reserves: the less you remember his weakness, the more you will nourish his strength, by calling into play the pure and sweet affections before which the spirits of evil fly. Most true is it that human forgiveness thus becomes the miniature reflection of the Divine. When the heavenly Father receives back a wandering penitent on his return, does he repeal any law on his behalf, and treat him as if he had never strayed, so as to abolish the difference between the ever-faithful and the rebel suppliant at the gate? By no means: not a link of the chain of self-incurred habits, of low thought and wrong desire, will be struck off by miracle on his behalf: he must drag them still, till his own heightened energy shall break them, one by one, or his patient will shall wear them out. But he is an alien no more: he is at home again with the All-merciful; and to an energy in touch with the everlasting Love, a patience upheld by the Divine whisper 'Faint on, dear soul, and conquer,' all things are possible, and the forgiven also may be numbered with the saints. Thus is the scope of forgiveness literally exhaustless and eternal, both between finite free natures among themselves, and between the finite spirit and the Infinite.

If the coexistence in Jesus of the strictest construction of the moral law, with an exceptional tenderness towards passionate natures, is referable to his *life in God,* the reason is obvious. Such life is a relation of communion between two invisibles, the Infinite Spirit, and the heart of man. It involves therefore *spirituality* in religion and *inwardness* for the whole seat of morals. It concentrates attention on the point to which the Searcher of spirits looks, the hidden spring of every agent's word or deed; and regards even the same passion quite differently, according as it is a blind impulse that knows not itself, of the animal stage, or the seeing impulse, conscious of its relative place, of the spiritual stage. If it be the former, as it may be in adults that have missed the way to become men and women, it is mere unwrought instinct, the rudimentary material of a conscience that has never been formed, and as little subject to estimate as the brute's hunger and thirst. If it be the latter, and have wrongly swayed the will, the sin may be judged to have any variety of shade, according to the measure of insight and temptation; from the tender condemnation that lays on the child's first transgression a load of arresting grief, to the scathing indignation which invokes retribution on the deliberate traitor and forsworn apostate from known right. In many a slave to evil ways Jesus knows the degradation to be greater than the guilt, and sees the autocracy of a passion never challenged, denoting a nature undeveloped, that has remained in the animal stage past the proper time. It were cruel to heap reproaches on it, ere it is conscious of its probation : the true need is the completion of its inner life into the responsible stage, to waken up the competing host of human affections, and accept their relative appeals, till their authority is owned, and they put shame on the life already in occupation. To his searching eye, the possibility of this unfolding is always there; but it is a possibility that sleeps, till some sweet serenade thrills through the darkness, and disperses the turbid dream, by the dawning certainties of a better day. And so, by his call ' Awake! Arise!' he sought to transfer the monotonous intensity of one tyrant passion to the harmonized enthusiasm of all, and to make the new-born soul compensate its late nativity by the fuller glow of its devotion.

If in these cases of undeveloped humanity, he was intent on calling up new affections and flinging them as fresh battalions on the field, it was naturally otherwise when he addressed himself to riper natures that know their own resources and were already moralized by experience of conflict and temptation. If they went wrong, it is not because they were possessed by some demon passion, but because they were not self-possessed : with the means of victory, they suffered themselves to incur defeat. Jesus fixes their eye upon the chief reason of this, when he tells them to keep watch and control over the intensity of each impulse of the soul, since there is not one that may not, if left to itself, become a despot and make a criminal. Tamper with inward purity, and you may find yourself an adulterer : bind fast your anger, or you may become a murderer : you are at the beginning of these crimes, from the first moment of your relaxed restraint : for yourself the taint of the sin is already there. "From within, out of the heart of men, evil thoughts proceed, fornications, thefts, murders, adulteries, covetings, wickedness, deceit, lasciviousness, an evil eye, railing, pride, foolishness : all these evil things proceed from within, and defile the man."* Be sure therefore, that till you live above the range of hate and anger, to *you* the voice will be awful, "Thou shalt not kill :" and till you breathe only the air of pure desires, there is no shame too foul for you to fear. And ' live above it ' you cannot by any mere resisting effort to repress it and keep it down : but only by surrendering yourself to the lifting power of a higher love, in which the solicitations of sense and the frictions of self are left behind : nor then can you find rest short of the transcendent and supreme aspiration to be "Perfect, as your Father in heaven is perfect."

This is the conception, this the anti-Stoic dynamic of Duty that simply shapes into words the life in God which Jesus lived, and from the light of which he looked on the scenes of human experience and character. It carries in it, may we not say, as its crowning grace and truth, this distinctive feature, that it renders Humility an eternal attitude for all finite minds, rather deepening than declining with their spiritual advance; for it is the spirit's upturned look which, directed upon the All-holy, can never overtake the vision that

* Mark vii. 21-23.

entrances it and draws it on; so that the loftiest of souls is surest to say to a clinging dependent, "Why callest thou me good? One is good, that is God."

The obverse side of this reverence for the inward sanctuary of life must inevitably be an utter aversion to all casuistry of mere external action, which differences right from wrong by insignificant variations of time or place, of word or deed, while the prompting spirit remains the same. Whoever lives, like Jesus, straight out of a spring of affection which needs no rules while it is aflow and cannot use them when it is dry, is necessarily impatient of the moral mimicry that puts on the grimaces and does the postures of goodness without the essence behind: and so, careless of the rabbis and their text alike, he quitted their lines of definition, and seized the determining centre, and would have only the security of love and veneration for every duty. How indignantly he exposed the "blind guides" that at once burdened and misled the people, and the sacerdotal dignitaries with their flaunting texts and empty pretences to superior sanctity! How light he made of the Sabbath restraints, when innocent needs or gentle mercies called! It was impossible that the antipathy to formal rigour and hollow semblance should be anything less than intense in one who had found the unspeakable depth and reality of religion at the supreme Centre, which also gave simplicity to morals and dispensed with the tangle of a thousand rules:—a centre which, though it was everywhere, was yet so far away from "the corners of the streets" and the throng of men that it waits for the soul in the hill retreats, or till the lonely chamber is reached and the door is shut.

This antipathy is in fact but the shadow of that sympathy with ideal aspiration of which every reader will call to mind touching examples. Of one only among the many applicants for his counsel is it said that "Jesus, looking on him, loved him;" and that was the rich young man (or "ruler," as Luke calls him), who asked him the conditions of "eternal life." Reading perhaps in his countenance and voice the sincerity and the secret of his question, Jesus answers it at first as any honest Teacher of the Law in Israel might have answered it; referring him to the commandments, and selecting his examples of them exclusively from the *moral* table of duties between man and man, and with one exception (the honour to parents) all from the prohibitive list "Thou *shalt not*." The test answers its end: by playing the "mere moralist" Jesus immediately reveals the idealist. The questioner's countenance fell: all these he has kept from his youth up: they are but a stale routine, and leave a void in his heart which allows him no peace and only breathes forth empty sighs for more. What is it that is wanting? Just what Jesus has left unnamed, and now supplies: behind and within and above the outward duty the inward enthusiasm of love to God and love to men, whatever be the sacrifice demanded or the enterprise imposed. Whether this also goes with his keeping of the commandments he may easily tell: is he prepared at the call of a divine opportunity, to strip himself of all that he has, and dedicate all that he is, for the sake of those who need his help, and are ready to perish? The answer strikes deep; and he goes away silent and humbled, with perhaps a fruitful sorrow.*

The same relation, of mutual supplementing between practical conduct and spiritual affection involving the desolation of either without the other, which is represented in the self-variance and dejection of the rich youth, reappears with the parts divided between two actors, in the narrative of the sisters of Bethany, the one fuming about her household service, the other drinking at the fountains of faith and devotion, and neither of them sympathetic with the other. The practical Martha is fretted by her cares which turn her duties into task-work. And if there be a shade of melancholy on Mary's upturned face, is there perhaps a secret misgiving whether she is quite considerate towards her worried sister? For probably it is not the first time that the friction between the restless worker and the meditative dreamer has brought out hot words. Where one was behindhand in energy and the other attained to no peace, life was sure to chafe harshly and go out of tune. When the problem was brought to Jesus, he took it up at the same end, and solved it in the same sense, as in the case of the rich man. He would not allow the

* Mark x. 17-22; Matt. xix. 16-22; Luke xviii. 18-23.

listening Mary to be called away from his feet : he would not promise Martha relief from her troubles by merely giving her a partner in them, to be in turn no less harassed than herself. Peace could be infused into the conduct of affairs only by descending into it with a new spirit fetched from a diviner height, an inspiration of sacred love which lightens sacrifice and tranquillizes care. *There* is the source and spring of all the activities of duty ; and in seeking access to it from converse with Jesus, Mary has chosen the good part which must not be taken from her.

Still more readily will the incident of the alabaster cruise of ointment lavished upon Jesus occur to many a memory as exemplifying his direct look, past all externals of action, into its well-spring in the heart, and his sympathy with it if only that were pure.* And so far, in any case, the story does attest his joyful welcome of all that issues from a stainless love. But it is so differently told as to leave it doubtful what the affection was which was so passionately shed on him at Simon's guest table. According to the earliest tradition, it was simply the devout personal reverence of a pious woman from among his disciples, lifted probably to enthusiasm by forebodings of the fatal night which was only two days off, as indeed Jesus himself recognizes when he pleads on her behalf that she is only beforehand with his embalming. According to Luke, on the other hand, who takes back the incident from Bethany to a far earlier time in Galilee, the act was the homage of a sinful woman in an agony of penitence at the feet of him who had awakened it in her ; and Jesus accepts it, against the scandalized murmurings of his Pharisaic host, as a better pledge of final peace with God than Simon's self-righteous respectability, because flowing from a heart that spares itself no sorrow, and offers all it has; "her sins are forgiven, for she has loved much." Not only time and place and person are different, but all the subordinate particulars : the Simon of Galilee is called simply a Pharisee: the Simon of Bethany is described as a " leper " that had recovered. The objections to the woman's act proceed, in Luke, from the host, and are founded on the character of the woman, which a

* Mark xiv. 3-9; Matt. xxvi. 6-13; Luke vii. 36-40.

prophet ought to have known. They proceed, in the other synoptists, from some of the disciples, in anger at the waste of the costly contents of the cruise. The defensive pleas urged by Jesus in reply, following this difference, are dissimilar. But in spite of this, and therefore of the uncertainty regarding the form of historical fact which is the base of the tradition, the one element of its significance which remains untouched is, the invariable penetration of Jesus, in his reading of human relations, of man with God, and of men with each other, to the inward affections in which all good and ill of character reside. Even were all historical claim for the narrative deemed questionable, still the resort of fiction so repeatedly to stories with this same impression, and reproducing the one unmistakable personality, would itself afford a strong presumption that the portraiture was from the life.

Mark yet a further feature. Though in his short personal ministry the mission of Jesus was only to the "lost sheep of the house of Israel," his estimate of men by the springs of their inner life inevitably neutralized this restriction of his influence and became the source of absolute *catholicity* in his religion. For however the tribes of mankind may differ from each other, it is only by varied proportions of the same elements : and there is no motive passion or affection, no type of intelligent faculty, of which any people can claim a monopoly. "God hath made of one family every nation of men for to dwell on all the face of the earth."* And if it be the hidden soul by which he reads them and by which they stand more or less near to him, if the goodness which he loves is not the service of the lips or sacrifice by the hand, but the pure intent of the mind, then all the sacredness of life lies behind language, usage, race ; and there is a path to heaven from every clime, and a spiritual unity among men, which should shame their scorns and enmity away. Hence, the sure emergence of religion, in this rebirth, from the exclusiveness of ruder monotheisms. It cannot but break into universality, comprehensive as the love of God, who makes his sun to shine and his rain to fall upon the evil and the good, patient of everything except the selfish pride which would turn

* Acts xvii. 26.

divine things into a property. Hence too, in Jesus himself, the quick eye for every trace of artless love and pious trust, wherever found ; and his special joy in it if it came to him in the stranger or the alien, the centurion, the publican, the Phœnician, the Samaritan. His sympathy, not lingering on the cultivated plots and ornamental grounds of life, rather hangs around its highways and hedges : and there, exploring among the weeds and lifting their soiled leaves, he turned up the modest face of many a lurking flower,—the child's susceptibility, the widow's offering, the penitent's profuse affection. And when he stood upon the mountain side and taught, never surely did such a dew fall upon the grass as his benedictions dropped upon the arid temper of that age : the poor in spirit, the meek, the pure in heart, the soul thirsting after goodness, —these are the really blest, intent on ends which God also loves and will not disappoint. Nor is it only in the incidental indications of his own personal preferences that this tender catholicity appears : so deeply is it seated in him that it presses to the foreground in his teaching with such dramatic vividness and pathetic power as to reverse the antipathies of his time, and put a light of grace into the most hated names. Has not the ' Publican ' become to us the symbol of humility, ever since we saw him in the temple "afar off" behind the ' Pharisee,' and heard him, as with downcast eyes he beat upon his breast, saying, " God be merciful to me, a sinner " ? And if the artist wants a group that shall most movingly present to the beholder's mind the power and beauty of compassion, can anything come sooner into his thought and his design than the dismounted figure on the rocky heights of Jericho, bending over the wounded traveller, ministering to him with oil and wine, setting him on his own beast and taking care of him ; and ever after called the "Good Samaritan " ?

From the working of these catholic sympathies within the limits of an exclusive Israel arose another feature of the utmost moment to the future of the world, viz., the power of development in religion which, without prejudice to human reverence, saved the old elements from hindering the new, and, instead of stiffening the law, as the Pharisees said, into "*a hedge*," made its boundary elastic, so long as it was described around the same centre of principle.   Far from removing one dispensation to make room for another, or impugning the authority of the sacred books, Jesus taught in the synagogues from the text of the prophets, and justified his most spiritual lessons by the language of the Law.   Wherever it is possible, he charges the narrowness and triviality of the Jewish rules, not on the written code, but on the annotating "tradition of the elders": "ye make void the commandment of God by your tradition."   But it is impossible to deny that he lays himself open to the reply, 'If at our hands the text has its meaning maimed by restriction, in yours it is lost by extension': it is not by legal interpretation but by retreat back to legislative grounds in the nature of man and the purpose of God, that he dispenses with the letter of the Sabbath institution and sets it free for "doing good," though it breaks the appointed "rest."   His concentration of all good in the inward affection whence action flows supersedes at once whole chapters of the Mosaic code, "making," as the evangelist himself remarks, "all meats clean."[*]   And his judgment of the questions of divorce by bill, as the law prescribed, and of re-marriage after divorce, by reference to the story of Adam and Eve, as the ruling instance of the Divine intent, is a direct overriding of admitted statutory ordinances of God by his intimated prior idea in the constitution of nature and the moral life of man.[†]   And surely the personal characteristics that commended the argument to him are full of interest and beauty: see the divine meaning of marriage in its origin: one man, one woman, given to each other by God himself, given for life, when as yet there was no death and no other human life: who can doubt what this contemplates? or fancy Adam sending Eve away, or *vice versâ?*   Could any hardness of heart be greater, or more odious?   Yet it was not that they were sinless, as we know: as they had lived in Paradise together so they quitted it together; and were one, "for better, for worse."   And so he decides that, in allowing the dissolution of marriage, and the remarriage of man or woman, Moses yielded the best to secure the practicable, in concession

* Mark vii. 19.   † Mark x. 2-12.

to the " hardness of their hearts."   This mode of treatment
evidently takes away all final authority from defined systems
of law and usage, and makes them liable to be tested by the
standards of clearer reason and higher sense of right : it makes
living conscience the perpetual amender of historic enactments
and social practice.   The husk is discarded, the true germ is
found within : and it is " as if a man cast seed into the
ground," which could " spring up and grow, he knoweth
not how." *

It was in virtue of this method, of going behind the letter
to seize the spirit of the past, that the early Christianity,
almost captured by the Gentile predominance in the second
century, was saved from total repudiation of its Hebrew
parentage ; and that the precious literature of the Old Testament remained, in the church as in the synagogue, the sacred
depository of divine truth and spiritual experience.

This inward and ideal life in God, wrought out by personal
insight assimilating the finest elements of Israelitish devotion,
could not but remould in Jesus his inherited conceptions of
the " kingdom of God " which he had to announce, and bring
them into some conformity with itself.   The message of John
the Baptist, though remaining in terms the same when taken
up and continued by him, became insensibly enlarged in scope
and elevated in meaning, involving a variance ever wider
from the national aspirations.   So long as he was delivering
it to the mixed population of his native province,—" Galilee
of the Gentiles " as it was called,—there would be hearers
among the crowds around him, and even in the synagogues,
who would yield reverence to his spiritual appeal, and not be
too orthodox for his free handling of the Prophets and the
received traditions.   And it was only natural that as his
characteristic inspirations more and more deeply possessed
him his tone should become firmer, and the movement of his
thought in their defence more fresh and unconventional.

But the time came when the scene must be changed.   The
message to Israel is not delivered, while lingering on the outskirts and hovering among the northern hills : it must seek
the headquarters of the nation around Zion, and demand an

* Mark iv. 26, 27.

audience from the chiefs and in the courts of its sole sanctuary. Recognizing the call, and intending to answer it at the great national anniversary of the passover, Jesus, on turning southwards from "the parts of Cæsarea Philippi," "steadfastly set his face to go to Jerusalem." The very terms of the statement plainly imply that he knows it to be a momentous resolve. With what feeling did he embrace and execute it? Did he go up with the joy of heart which becomes the herald of glad tidings, clearing in advance the highway for the onward march of the Lord of Victory? Do we hear again the exulting words extorted by the Galilean mission, "I beheld Satan as lightning fall from heaven"? When warned to escape from the province, or "Herod will kill" him, does he hasten to secure his refuge in "the city of the great King"? On the contrary, while he can take his time in the dominions of "that fox," he knows what is next before him; "for it cannot be that a prophet perish out of Jerusalem." * Nothing in his life is more certain than that, from this moment of decision, the shadow of a cloud fell upon his spirit, and though softened again and again by pathetic lights of self-forgetting love, was never lifted till after its deepest darkness in Gethsemane.

In this changed mood, the evangelist, in common with his attendant disciples, saw the sorrow of *Messiah* on discovering that a dark zone of suffering and death lay in front of the steps of his throne. It was natural for them to trace in him the prototype of their own vicissitudes of thought: but it has been already shown how little consistent is this explanation with the historical conditions of the crisis. His depression of spirit was indeed due to his anticipation of rejection and martyrdom; not however as *Messiah*, but as *Messiah's herald:* from the city to which he was bearing the Baptist's message he expected the Baptist's fate; all the more because, through the workings of an ever-deepening spiritual experience, the kingdom of God which he now had to announce was far less congenial with the ritualism of the Temple and the fancies of the scribes, than had been the stern words of the "Voice crying in the desert." But that the message, now to be de-

* Luke xiii. 31–33.

livered in divine tones, was identical in purpose with the
Baptist's is doubly evinced by Jesus himself, who, when
challenged for the "authority" of his teaching, at once puts
it on a footing with the authority of John's, and accepts for
himself the answer which may be given to the question,
whether *his* mission "was from heaven or from men," * and
by the witness of both ; for it was the popular belief (a belief
which troubled Herod's mind †), that in the person of Jesus
John the Baptist had risen from the dead : an idea which
could never arise unless, instead of being the *object*, he was
simply the *continuator* of the Baptist's message.

One episode indeed there is in the narrative of his journey,
which seems at variance with this view. The triumphal ride
down the Mount of Olives into the City over scattered
garments, and amid the waving of palm branches and the
shouts of " Hosanna," " blessed is the kingdom that cometh,
of our Father David!" certainly means nothing less than
that the Galilean caravan was possessed by the enthusiasm of
Peter's confession, and proclaimed the arrival of Messiah.
And if, as the synoptists tell, Jesus himself took the initiative
and arranged for a procession which should duly fulfil the
prophecy of Zachariah,‡ he must have emerged from his
dejection, and, fired with the popular excitement, have
announced himself as "the King that cometh in the name
of the Lord."

How far this striking incident can be accepted as historical,
admits of no tests but those of internal consistency with the
antecedent and subsequent course of events and expressions
of character; for testimony there is none; it comes itself out
of the obscurity of tradition; and no witness can be cited to
confirm or contradict it. It is the more open, however, to
judgments of probability, because it is evidently related, not
in the interest of pure history, but as a piece of supernatural
evidence, combining in itself the persuasion of miracle performed and prophecy fulfilled ; Jesus manifesting a divine
knowledge and authority with regard to the ass and its owners,
and being escorted into the holy city in the very manner

* Mark xi. 27–33.   † Luke ix. 7-9.   ‡ ix. 9.

already described by the ancient seer. I need the less remark on the strong temptation which this motive presents to fit the event to the exigencies of the argument, rather than draw the argument from the exact photograph of the event, as an extreme example of it occurs in this very passage, where Matthew, misled by the parallelism of Hebrew poetry, supplies not only an ass, but also its foal, and apparently makes Jesus sit on both.*

The distrust awakened by this symptom, as well as by the miraculous perception of the invisible ass and its owners, is confirmed by several considerations.

(1.) If Jesus sanctioned and led the triumphant enthusiasm of his disciples, and entered Jerusalem to inaugurate "the kingdom of their father David," he had undergone a total reversal of mood during the day's journey; for the whole tension of his spirit on their southern way had been that of heroic pathos in contemplation of ignominy and death, and of compassionate repression of his disciples' illusory hopes. He goes, as he came, to "be as one that serveth," and "to give his life a ransom for many." That a few hours on the road should exchange all this for royal pretensions, and that he should enter the gates counting on the crown where he had expected the cross, is at variance, not only with all probability, but with the narrative of all that follows. Throughout his teaching in the temple, not a trace appears of his playing the part of *king*, or assuming any higher tone than that of *herald* of the kingdom to come. To the demand for his authority, his answer, as we have seen, is pitched low, and he shelters himself from challenge under the popularity of the Baptist. With those who bring him ensnaring questions he submits to stand on the defensive, and answers the problems presented to him on equal terms. And when the public hours are gone, and he is left with his disciples alone, the same undertone of tender sadness is found still there, breathing throughout the converse of the passover, and rising into the passionate tears and prayers of Gethsemane. That in the mood of Jesus the exulting enthusiasm of the triumphal entry should be sharply interpolated in the midst of continuous dejection of spirit

* xxi. 2-7.

under retrospect of failure and foresight of death, seems to me entirely incredible.

(2.) How it was that the evangelist did not feel the violence thus done to truth of character becomes intelligible in the narrative of Luke, in which the opposite states of mind are represented as absolutely synchronous, and the "king of glory" descends into his metropolis in tears, and unites the parts of "Son of God," and "Man of Sorrows." In a Pauline evangelist it is not difficult to see what this means. To him, the Messiahship was first declared by the resurrection from the dead, and was then not to take effect in act until the Parusia; and, therefore, the present appropriation of the office by Jesus was the assertion of only a *deferred* kingship; and as it was the unreadiness of Israel, and the provision for mercy to the Gentiles, which demanded both the delay and intervening sacrifice of the chosen servant of God, the ulterior glory and the nearer griefs might naturally come into view together, and bring the shouts of " Hosanna," and the lament over the city into mysterious accord in the heart of him who knew it all. Under the influence of this conception, Luke makes Jesus *deliver in the temple* the parable of the vineyard-owner, whose tenants first maltreated his rent-collector, and at last murdered his son, and so necessitated their own eviction.[*] Only at the cost of such plain anachronisms is the harmonizing process possible. No such Pauline theory had any preexistence at the historic date : the acclamation of the Galileans, "blessed is the King that cometh in the name of the Lord,"—if that was their cry,—meant something quite other than a *deferred kingship:* and if that alone were in Jesus' mind he cannot have had part or lot in the tumultuary scene. They were escorting him to receive the immediate crown, which to him was thrown into the distance and hid behind the nearer cross.

(3.) For the trial of Jesus a few days later at the house of Caiaphas, witnesses against him were eagerly hunted up from all quarters to make good the charge of treasonable preten-sions which excited and misled the people. Yet no mention whatever is made of this dangerous procession, organized and

* xx. 9–18.

led by the accused aspirant to David's throne. Nothing that was adduced against him was half as apposite to the case of the prosecution as this alleged public act; and as from its very nature it must have passed within the range of hundreds of watchful eyes and ears, testimony in abundance must have been forthcoming, if the fact took place as related in the Gospels. Not even his own alleged acknowledgment to the court of a Messianic claim could avail for so much, in deciding the case, as this incident out of doors; for the indictment against him was not that he personally supposed himself to be Messiah, but that by *giving himself out* to be Messiah he "deceived the people," and occasioned tumult dangerous to the public peace; and of this no completer proof could be desired than the entry into the city of a noisy procession marshalled under the command and in the name of a new King. The silence of the court therefore casts a reasonable doubt on the historical reality of the event.

These difficulties do not oblige us, however, to dismiss the whole scene as a free invention, with no nucleus of fact beneath : and though it is usually a vain attempt to undress an exaggeration till the supporting body is reached, there are here a few data of determinate form, which give shape and limit to the variable additions that may be thrown around them. Jesus did enter Jerusalem, accompanied by many disciples from Galilee. He came from Jericho (some nineteen miles) on foot in the day. He brought (let us assume) simply the message, "the Kingdom draweth nigh." The way was rugged and toil-some to the last degree, over blistered rocks and precipitous steeps, with but one place of pause, the little inn where the Good Samaritan left his wounded traveller. When the last height was surmounted, a few miles of descent, while relieving the strain, would also report the fatigue which it had cost; and it is conceivable enough that Jesus, "having found a young ass" (as the fourth evangelist says*), would accept the rest which, through the attentions of his disciples, it offered him for the two remaining miles of the road : the more so, as the afternoon was already wearing away, and the prospect was before him of the walk back to Bethany for the night. As

* John xii. 14.

they advanced, there lay below and before them the very walls and palaces and temple of the "Kingdom to come:" into it they were escorting the very herald who had to announce its approach: what wonder then that the Galileans devoted to their prophet, and fired by the excitement of Peter and the "sons of thunder," burst into uncontrollable Hosannas? In such a multitude, the cries would doubtless have a various significance, not all within the limits of Jesus' own sanction. But, if we look no further than the oldest tradition, he is celebrated only as "*he* that cometh in the name of the Lord" (a phrase that is habitually applied to *any* prophet):* and the advent proclaimed is that of "*the Kingdom* that cometh," not of the *King*. The later gospels alone develop these expressions into announcements of the personal Messiah.

On such a basis of natural fact may the full-grown tradition have been easily constructed, without involving any pretension, on the part of Jesus, beyond that of the *herald* of the Kingdom.

See, then, this witness of God standing at last on the pavement where his message was to be delivered, and looking round on all things at the time of the evening sacrifice : and remembering the springs of his secret life, and what a "Kingdom of righteousness" must mean to him, think how he would be affected by this sudden contact with a local sanctuary and a blood-stained worship. Knowing neither place nor time where God is not, having found him ever waiting to enter the moment the latch was lifted of the seeking heart, assured that neither words nor silence, neither walls nor spaces, could hinder the communion of his Spirit with ours, what sanctity could Jesus feel in the separating courts of the men and the women, of the Gentiles and the priests? His love and veneration, clinging to the simple social piety of the synagogue in which they had been nurtured, and bringing no offering but that of penitence and trust, could hardly brook the sight of butchering priests and mangled victims, and the smell of burning flesh, once deemed well-pleasing to God, now odious to men. Would the Pontiff's jewelled robe and golden mitre and pompous voice edify or overawe one to whom heaven was never

* See, e.g., Deut. xviii. 22.

so near as when, with bared head and naked soul, he prayed upon the mountain grass beneath the stars in the broken accents of a surrendering love?   Descending from so high and pure an air, he could hardly breathe within those stifling walls, where clouds of incense made pretence of aspiration, and the altar smoke did the work of prayer.   Not less repugnant to him would the whole scene be than George Fox would have found a week of Easter ceremonial observances in Papal Rome: and as the Puritan, in his recoil, flung himself into the absolute and unconditional life of the Spirit, so is it no wonder if Jesus, in the new kingdom of righteousness which he announced, "Saw no temple therein, for the Lord God Almighty and the Lamb are the temple thereof."*   Nor could he doubt, from the series of tricky questions brought to him each day by smooth-faced lawyers amid listening priests, that the whole system of second-hand life, of ritual religion and legalism in morals, hung together, as a conspiracy for evading the divine realities.   The very drift, therefore, of his own inspiration brought it to pass that his few days in the temple opened with the act of cleansing enthusiasm which swept a host of usurping hindrances away,† and closed with emphatic warnings against the scribes and their burdensome impostures.‡   Nay, so overmastering was the vision of the inner life of man with God, and his zeal for realizing it, and so far transcending the apprehension of his disciples, that we owe to his enemies its sublimest and most characteristic expression. It was from the lips of the accusers at his trial, denounced by the evangelist as "false witnesses," that we first heard him say, "I will destroy this temple made with hands, and in three days will build another made without hands:"§ a passionate cry, truly, wrung from the grief and aspiration of an intense experience and an infinite faith,—meaning simply, 'Away with these material walls and works, which only imprison you from the very God they are supposed to contain: and come with me to seek him, spirit to spirit, and ere the next sabbath you shall be united to him in a communion that is imperishable.'   The sacerdotal conscience felt

* Rev. xxi. 22.
‡ Mark xii. 38–40.
† Mark xi. 15–18.
§ Mark xiv. 57, 58.

the shock, though blinded by the light, of this flash from a frowning heaven, and treated it as the unpardonable stroke that must be resented to the death. No further witnesses were called ; and the decisive influence it had on the condemnation is evinced by the taunt of the onlookers at the crucifixion : "They that passed by railed on him, wagging their heads and saying, 'Ha ! thou that destroyest the temple and buildest it in three days, save thyself and come down from the cross.' "[*] How deeply the saying penetrated the souls ready for its touch, whether of love or hate, is evident from its reappearance in the story of Stephen, in whom it repeated both its inspiration and its martyrdom : for against him too the indictment was, that "This man ceaseth not to speak words against this holy place and the Law : for we have heard him say that Jesus of Nazareth shall destroy this place and shall change the customs which Moses delivered unto us."[†] In answer to the question how it could be that the most national and rigidly exclusive of all cults became the historical source of a religion spiritual and universal, great use has been often, and justly, made of Stephen and the Hellenists, in whose colonial life, away from "the scribes who sat in Moses' seat," the hard lines faded and the ideal depths were opened, of their pure theism ; and again, from the fire and the fate of Stephen, dying into the visible embrace of Christ in heaven, have been deduced the compunction and conversion of Saul, with his bolder annulment of the Law and larger gospel of the Gentiles : while to the fusion together in Alexandria of the Jewish and the heathen thought, has been credited that consciousness of God as immanent in the world and in human life, in which the religion reaches its supreme altitude and widest range. These are doubtless stages of development historically verifiable : but they tell only a mutilated story, till you pass behind them all, and ask the 'Whence' of Stephen's divine enthusiasm : and this he himself here reports, when he refers it to the great dictum of Jesus, and his

* Mark xv. 29, 30.

† Acts vi. 13, 14. Luke, however, who here mentions in substance the alleged saying of Jesus as quoted by Stephen, has no notice of it in its gospel place, as playing any part at the trial before Caiaphas. And he transfers the expression "*false witnesses*" to the charge against Stephen.

infinite longing to open the soul of man to the life in God, unhindered by the mediation of priest and ritual. Thus the fountain of all catholicity is in no confluence of philosophies, no combination of external conditions, but in the unique personality of Jesus of Nazareth. That was the fresh and quickening power which broke into new fields of human love and character : all else did but furnish the predisposed conditions of susceptibility which saved that living power from spending itself in vain.

The answers given by Jesus to the polite and learned spies who met him in the temple each morning with their budget of dilemmas are interesting alike in their reserves and their disclosures. To embroil him with either the Roman government or the zealot opposition came the question of the tribute-money; neatly declined and thrown back upon themselves by the production of the coin with the imperial "image and superscription," and the memorable epigram which is still the motto of treatise after treatise on the boundary between the spheres of State and Church ; "give therefore unto Cæsar the things that are Cæsar's, and unto God the things. that are God's." It is said, "This is an evasion of the question. Of course it is : and precisely in this lies the pertinent significance of the reply. The question was one which Jesus could not be called upon to solve ; it was not for the prophet but for the schools ; depending for its determination, not on the right understanding of the inward and spiritual life, but on a true judgment of external and political conditions. The currency of the coinage was evidence of *some* relations from the admission of which duties, whether welcome or not, were inseparable : and all duty is divine in the last resort, though delivered in the form of obligation to man. Religion therefore covers both spheres, and has nothing to do with defining the limits of civil life, beyond securing the conscientious exercise of reason in the work. Jesus therefore declines the functions of the jurists, but lifts their results into the adoption of duty sacred like the rest.

From a still deeper perspective of his thought a gleam comes in the answer of Jesus to the coarse plea of the Sadducees against the doctrine of a Resurrection.[*] The prevail-

* Mark xii. 18-27.

ing belief, which was the topic of dispute, insisted only on a restoration of pious Israelites from former generations, to share with the living upon earth the kingdom which Messiah would be appointed to set up. First addressing himself to the problem of the seven brothers successively married to the same wife, Jesus quietly sets it aside by discharging from that future kingdom, notwithstanding its locality on earth, all relations except such as angels may have, and so leaving us, as his vision of perfect existence, a society linked together by ties of pure affection and growing similitude to God. But the question, it is evident, had struck a finer chord that will not be silent ; and he adds an argument of larger scope to show, not simply that the dead *will rise*, but that the dead *do live*, and that man, once trusted with responsible life, must share the perpetuity of God. This argument he draws from the ancient names under which Jehovah has chosen to hand down the knowledge of himself to distant generations, and which his absolute veracity secures against the least un-meaningness. 'Does he not say, "I am the God of your fathers, the God of Abraham, the God of Isaac and of Jacob"? and at the same time forbid you to construe these into a *past relation*, as if he had said, 'I am he that *was* the God of Abraham, of Isaac and of Jacob,' by expressly insisting on the *present tense* as alone appropriate to Him and so truly constituting the *essence* of his name, that Moses is charged to say, "I Am hath sent me unto you."* This surely means that He *is* as well as *was*, the God of the fathers : for the phrase would be a mockery if he had made away with them, and they were not : the dead can have no God : to the living only can He, the ever-living, stand related.' Say what we may of this plea, characteristic of an expanding thought which had to extort the truth it craved by struggling with a text it could not change, it opens a deep glance into the mind of Jesus. It proclaims, as an element of his religion, the impossibility of human death. It insists that where once the moral union is realized between the all-loving God and the spirits which he loves and trains into his likeness and draws towards himself, it becomes incredible that he should destroy

* Exod. iii. 14, 15.

that union, and put an end to the very object of his culture and affection. By this hint of truest insight Jesus did but say for all, that which his disciples applied from sacred writ to him, "Thou wilt not suffer thy holy one to see corruption!"

Among the listeners to this colloquy with the Sadducees was a scribe determined to follow it up by a question so fundamental as to lay bare the very basis of all his teaching, "What is the first commandment of all?"[*] According to Matthew and Luke, the inquiry, like the previous one, was captious, intended as a trap to catch him in his words: with more probability, Mark treats it as serious, and elicited by admiration for the wisdom of his preceding answer. The reply of Jesus, instead of *selecting* from among the commandments that which is chief, sums them all up in two, the love of God as supreme, and, as its counterpart, the love of one's neighbour as oneself; neither of them, it will be observed, prohibitive rules of action pressing on the will; both of them inward and creative affections carrying us out of ourselves to objects in the one case of infinite devotion, in the other of finite sympathy and equal fellowship; and together covering all the demands of the law and the aspirations of the prophets. The scribe seizes the scope and spirituality of the answer, when he exclaims that to live in conformity with it is "more than all whole burnt-offerings and sacrifices," and so draws upon himself the parting words "Thou art not far from the kingdom of heaven." Can it be denied that to one who thinks thus, the kingdom of heaven which he announces includes the perfection of human life pervaded by the sublimest of human religions?

Notwithstanding the elevated spiritual tone of these "teachings daily in the temple," there was nothing in them directly at variance with the prevailing Messianic idea, of a crisis of

---

[*] Mark xii. 28–34; Matt. xxii. 34–40; Luke x. 25–28: Where Jesus, instead of himself specifying the two chief commandments, elicits them from the "lawyer," and gives approval to the answer, instead of receiving it from him. The original question, too, is not about the relative rank of the commandments, but about the condition of "inheriting eternal life." I need not say that "thou shalt love thy neighbour as thyself" is not among the ten commandments, but appears in Levit. xix. 18.

Divine revolution in human affairs, which should remove "whatever hurts and destroys in all the earth," and set up, under a commissioned Son of God, a rule of perfect righteousness and a worship true to the real relation between God's spirit and man's. They might all come from one who still held by that supposed vision of the prophet's, and had a necessity laid upon him of declaring it near at hand. So far he had a thought and faith in common with his immediate disciples. But the interior contents of that common faith are by no means the same for him and them ; and with the change of scene to Jerusalem, and every day's experience there, have become more and more divergent : the imposing ceremonial of the temple and the dignity of the hierarchy, and the sight of mount Zion, the centre of memories and prophecies so great, intensifying in them every temporal hope, and quickening in him every spiritual aspiration. More and more does he despair of making ready here a holy people and a true city of God : less and less can they forego their suspicion that he himself is Messiah, and, in spite of the darkening outlook, will soon emerge from the herald to the King. On their imagination thus preoccupied his highest teachings in the temple would lay no effective hold, but would rather make them impatient for some practical move towards the issue which he announced : the more so, as the hostility of the priestly party might be entirely neutralized by the favour of "the common people who heard him gladly." Was it perhaps from this variance of his feeling from theirs, that he never trusted them in Judæa, as he had in Galilee, to seek their own audiences as sub-agents of his mission ? He keeps them close to him and assigns them no part. At this maturest end of their association with him, they appear only as silent listeners and learners, unavailable as missionaries. That the questions which in private they are supposed by the synoptists to have put to him have no reference whatever to any spiritual teachings that might transcend them, but only to unhistorical prophecies connected with the Parusia, may be taken as a vestige of the ideas of which their minds were full. That the answer to them is apparently an excerpt from a posterior Jewish apocalypse shows how far, in order to meet them, you must travel from the thoughts and words of Jesus.

As the tragedy deepens, these divergent states of mind become more conspicuous. The passover evening, by its disheartening disclosure of the disciples' inapprehensiveness, indicated that the closing scene was at hand. Iscariot himself, it is probable, did not intend what he brought to pass; but (with whatever taint of lower motives) did but push to its extremity an impatience felt by all at the slowness of Jesus to assert his supposed Messianic prerogative (with the aid, if need be, of " twelve legions of angels "), and resolve to force his hand by driving him to bay. The fatal failure of this design, coming upon Judas as a dread surprise, better accounts for his subsequent horror and death than the faint measure of compunction which can be attributed to a cold-blooded traitor, accomplishing what he intended.

It is hardly possible, by the aid of our synoptists, to transport ourselves back to the position of an observer witnessing the incidents of the Passion-week as they arose, and the persons as they lived and thought; because events define themselves in happening and persons in acting; and the tradition of them, on its way to literary form, takes them up in this finished shape and divests them of all that is inchoate and gradual in their genesis. For its tendency, thus contracted, to strong contrasts and absolute statements reasonable allowance must be made, and sudden surprises be softened by the intervention of an intelligible process. That Judas planned to bring his Master to public execution; that Jesus, knowing this, openly pointed him out as traitor to his comrades at table; that Jesus foresaw and announced as certain, nay, himself willed his own crucifixion, cannot be regarded as probable, but may well have passed into belief from the simpler facts that the betrayer, like Satan in the temptation, proposed to put an end to all shrinking and compel the assumption of Messiahship by planting Jesus in a perilous position; that his design, being more than suspected, was confidentially intimated to one or two of the eleven; and that the presentiment, already avowed by Jesus, of a fatal issue of his Jerusalem mission, became confirmed and gave the ill-understood pathos to the converse and the hymn of the paschal night.

If these were the conditions, Judas would not, as the fourth gospel represents, rise and leave the room by himself, but join in the common departure for the Mount of Olives, and slip away from the rest at the entrance to the footway over Kedron. While he turned aside to carry out his purpose in the city, the little band, pursuing their way up the hill, were again warned that the end was at hand, and that, when the shepherd was smitten, the sheep in their dismay would be scattered abroad : even Peter, who alone would dare to hang about the rear of his Master's danger, being cautioned that by too much trust in his own courage he would be betrayed into denial worse than flight. That they should be simply hurt by these predictions, and meet them, after the example of Peter, with confident professions of fidelity, could hardly be if they accepted in earnest the whole terror of the crisis : they were perhaps sustained by the secret excitement of a lingering incredulity, or, we may rather say, some lurking faith that, at the last moment, some divine turn would open a way for the triumph of Right.

Having prepared them as far as their prepossessions allowed, and arrived at the enclosure which separated Gethsemane from the open hill, Jesus, more intensely solitary from the recent converse, had his own darkest hour to meet. He flew to the only refuge where he could lay his heart to rest ; and withdrawing from his attendants, and taking with him Peter and the Zebedee brothers to keep watch and give notice against surprise, he retired to a remoter spot, where he could be alone with the silent moonlight and the listening God. There he fell on the ground, prostrate with a sorrow even unto death : and his sentinels, ere they dropped off into sleep, overheard his suppliant cry, " Abba, Father, all things are possible to thee : remove this cup from me : howbeit, not what I will, but what thou wilt " :* and twice, in the intervals of their sleep, was the prayer repeated, ere his will was surrendered and he released them from their watch. With a final calmness he looked at them and said, " Sleep on now,

* Mark xiv. 36.

and take your rest ; it is enough : the hour is come : the Son of man is betrayed into the hands of sinners."

It has long been felt that to this "agony in the garden" and its words of prayer a great significance attaches ; and that to read in them aright the state of mind which they presuppose must deepen our insight into the thought and character of Jesus. May we not, for instance, fairly infer from them that for him the possibility was not yet closed, that this "cup might pass from him," and that the will of God might still determine otherwise ? If so, his own expectations were in suspense to this latest hour, and he cannot have delivered to his disciples, three or four times over since Peter's confession, the most positive and detailed predictions of his death in Jerusalem and reappearance in Galilee ; and we are justified in reducing these announcements, if retained at all, to natural presentiments of danger. It is further evident that, in deeming his fate not predetermined, but still at voluntary disposal, Jesus must have looked on it not as the fate of Messiah who had to die in fulfilment of the oracles of God, but only as that of a herald of the kingdom whose message might provoke, as in the Baptist's case, or might escape, the vengeance of murderous hands. Had he really conceived himself to be Messiah, and in that character described and approximately dated his " coming on the clouds of heaven in power and great glory," with all the premonitory signs and the judicial consequences, how, after that, could he possibly pray for leave to stay in this world and dispense with the Parusia ?

And if this prayer is inconsistent with a sincere illusion of Messiahship, still more decisively is it incompatible with the only other suppositions possible : viz. (1.) Renan's, of the rash assumption or acceptance of too high a character, from which, when once committed to it, he would not recede, though persistence was at the cost of life ; and (2.) the Church belief that, as the incarnate Son, he had for ages planned, and through the prophets foreannounced, the very drama which he had now wrought out to its last scene, whose tragic close was to be also its glorious consummation. With each of these doctrines confront the cry, " Father, take away this cup from

me: howbeit, not as I will, but as thou wilt." Must we not
say that if the bitter cup here deprecated were the self-incurred
penalty of inflated pretensions which collapsed at the touch
of reality, the submissive ending could not be there: and
that if, on the other hand, that bitter cup were the crown of
the whole history, contemplated throughout by the sufferer
himself as the essence of God's design in him, the imploring
beginning could not be there? When was it ever known that
detected self-exaggeration, caught in its own trap, poured
forth a "Not as I will, but as thou wilt"? And how could
a Redeemer, brought to the appointed crisis, ask to be
spared the very "cup" he had come to take? All congruity
of character is lost, and the whole scene reduced to a mere
stage-piece, unless the cross were unseen till its approach, and
were incurred, not by overweening profession and half-con-
scious falsehood, but by the purest truth. Here surely we
have the genuine cry of innocence and sanctity, first shrinking
from the crushing heel of men, then sheltering in the eternal
hand of God. The sufferer is so far from courting martyrdom,
that his "will," if that were all, simply recoils from it; and
if it comes, it is from the higher "Will" than his, from the
severe exactions of truth and holiness to which nothing can
be refused. The darkness of that hour is evidently due to
the collision at last brought to a head between the pure
and ideal "kingdom of God" which Jesus announced as near,
and the hollow sacerdotalism of the place, the unready and
refractory temper of the people, that were to form the site
and furnish the population of the "City of God." He could
not deny his vision of the new relation between man and
God: he knew it to be true to the human soul and to the
Divine intent, and he could withdraw no word of witness to
it. And yet to reaffirm it was to tear the mask from the face
of priests, and the pride from the pretensions of sects and
parties: and the clearer the testimony he bore to things
divine the easier it was to prove him an insurgent against the
powers that be, and to make away with him as a blasphemer.

Against the *Roman* civil power, however, he had assumed
no insurgent attitude, but only against the Israelitish
authorities that "sat in Moses' seat," or Aaron's: and unless

the former could be established no capital sentence could be obtained. In order to make the governor the executioner of their own vengeance, the chief priests had therefore to put a false construction on the teachings of Jesus in the Temple, and to suborn witnesses in support of their fictitious case. This was most easily done by a nocturnal arrest and a hurried sitting of the court of first instance before dawn, ere any evidence could be ready to check and contradict the got-up testimony. Hence the dignified protest of Jesus against the clandestine mode of apprehending him, with hypocritical ostentation of military force, as if he and his disciples were prowling bandits of the night: "Are ye come out, as against a robber, with swords and staves to seize me? I was daily with you in the temple, teaching, and ye took me not: but this is your hour, and the power of darkness."[*] Eagerly do the disciples watch him through these words; and seeing that he is content with them and invokes no rescue, but allows himself to be seized, they forsook him and fled, doubtless to Galilee, each, as the fourth gospel says, to his own home,[†] Peter alone lingering and "following afar off."

The object of the ecclesiastical authorities before whom the prisoner was brought in the High Priest's house was not to conduct a trial (which was beyond their competency), but to shape an indictment and prepare a case, to be brought for decision into Pilate's court. To secure a hearing, it needed adoption by a regular meeting of the Sanhedrim, constituted by a quorum of one-third the total number, i.e., twenty-three besides the High Priest presiding. So many could hardly be got together by first daylight; but if the members chiefly interested and already present when the captive was brought in acted at once as a committee of examination, the evidence could be got into order, and a preliminary judgment be formed, which the regular meeting after sunrise would probably confirm. The device succeeded perfectly so far as the unanimous shaping of the indictment was concerned: it charged Jesus with "perverting the nation, with forbidding to give tribute to Cæsar, saying that he himself was Christ a King."[‡] But, for all

* Mark xiv. 48, 49; Matt. xxvi. 55; Luke xxii. 52, 53.
† John xvi. 32. ‡ Luke xxiii. 2.

that appears, absolutely no evidence whatever was forth-coming relative to any of these counts, so that not even was the opportunity afforded of disproving them. Neither the alleged triumphal procession on entering Jerusalem, nor the high-handed act of the cleansing of the temple, either of which might perhaps have been turned to some account by a skilful advocate, is so much as mentioned; and the case, as reported, is left dependent on the saying about destroying the temple and replacing it in three days. As to the demeanour of Jesus in presence of this irrelevant evidence, the only thing secured from doubt by the agreement of the synoptists is that he "held his peace and answered nothing."[*] Not till the judges, having done with the witnesses and their evidence, press him to say for himself whether he be the Christ, is he said to break silence and give (according to Mark and Matthew) a direct assent; or (according to Luke) a dubious answer, which affirms indeed the coming of the "Son of Man," but, as Marcion has pointed out,[†] leaves with his questioners the responsibility of identifying him with that "Son of God": "Art thou then the Son of God? ye say that I am" (ὑμεῖς λέγετε ὅτι ἐγώ εἰμι). If he had wished to say 'I admit and repeat my announcement of the kingdom, but it is you that would make me out self-identified with the king,' he could hardly throw his answer into terser form. I have given reasons, in a former chapter, for distrusting the historical accuracy of this closing incident in the examination, and deeming it incredible that Jesus, after peremptorily forbidding all claim of Messiahship on his behalf, and so refraining from it himself that no evidence of it should be producible by his inquisitors, should choose this untoward moment for the occasion and this malignant audience for the confidant, of his first open profession. But even if it were so, such a belief about himself, extorted from the prisoner's enthusiasm or imprudence in the court, would be of no avail in proof of the indictment, which specified only past acts and needed past eyes and ears to establish their reality and their character. If the alleged acceptance in court of the Messianic claim was

* Mark xiv. 61; Matt. xxvi. 63. Cf. Luke xxii. 67, 68.
† Tert. cont. Marcionem, IV. 41.

an indictable offence, it was a newly committed offence which, in its turn, must be tried on its own merits, and it could in no wise turn the verdict on the prior charge from ' not guilty ' to ' guilty.'. This uselessness for the purposes of the trial, and accordance with the subsequent Messianic theory of the disciples, of the alleged declaration of Jesus to the High Priest, taken in conjunction with its reduction to lower terms in Luke, involve its historical character in the greatest doubt. It comes to us out of the dark, attested by no authenticating witness; for Peter, though in the building, was out of hearing in the court below, where his denial took place, and whence, as he disappears from the scene, he probably fled, like the rest, into Galilee,—the last sheep of the scattered flock.

But even though no Messianic claim were wrung from Jesus, none the less was it charged upon him in the indictment, being the only conceivable way of bringing him, as a royal pretender, under the death-penalty of *læsa majestas.* How ineffectual for this purpose, and even contemptible, Pilate deemed it, when the case was brought into his court, is evident from this, that, though Jesus is again said to have admitted that, as Christ, he cannot disclaim the title of " King of the Jews,"—an admission tantamount to pleading ' *guilty*,'—the Governor declares " to the Chief Priests and the multitudes, *I find no fault in this man*," and proposes to let him go. This is as much as to say, ' a man's belief about himself, however fanatical, is no crime: show me that, acting upon it, he has resisted the law or raised an insurrection, or anyhow infringed the rights of others, and he shall be condemned to the appropriate penalty, though it be death: but your witnesses have proved nothing of the sort: so you put yourselves forward as witnesses, with nothing to say except that he takes to himself the benefit and the peril of one of your own silly superstitions.' That a Roman administrator capable of taking this sensible view of a case so dishonestly got up should nevertheless suffer his sense of justice to be overborne by the outcry of a threatening priesthood and a noisy populace, exclaiming, ' If thou let this man go, thou art not Cæsar's friend,'* is indeed

* John xix. 12.

deplorable, but only too credible in that age of decay of the civil virtues.

The trial over and the sentence passed, the story of Jesus becomes essentially one of passive suffering only, pervaded by the same gracious affections and divine trusts that had given it throughout a radiance of spiritual glory. But in passing from the agent to the victim, he could but carry the personal characteristics which we have marked to their supreme test : they can take on nothing new, but only perfect themselves in their intensest strain. The only features therefore in the narratives of the crucifixion which belong to the right conception of his personality are what are called his seven last words uttered from the cross. They cannot be divested of their interest as expressions of himself : though, like all the sayings of dying men, liable to be charged with an illusory significance, seeing that they are often wrenched without will from a spent and crushed nature, and reveal the mind no more than the wanderings of a dream or of delirium.

The seven words are made up in the usual way of the Harmonists, by combining all that can be found in any evangelist ; though the fair presumption certainly is that each writer would mention all that he knew. Christians instructed only by the gospel of Mark* or Matthew† would connect with the Calvary of their imagination no other utterance than the first verse of the twenty-second Psalm, " My God, my God, why hast thou forsaken me ? " except indeed the inarticulate cry at the moment of death. Nothing can be idler than to bring the commentator's pedantry to such an exclamation and cross-question it about its exact meaning, flashed forth as it is from the focus of concentrated physical agony that burns up for the moment all the ideal dews that would cool or quench it. In the next moment the very Psalmist who supplies the words changes his voice and says, " He hath *not* despised nor abhorred the affliction of the afflicted, *neither hath he hid his face from him :*"‡ and it must ever be that the soul of the sufferer, swept away on the wave of its anguish, should sink into the hollow with a plaintive cry, yet on rising to the crest return to its trust. If however the complaint of being "forsaken" be construed as serious, then it must evidently proceed from one who is taken by surprise and feels himself injured or betrayed by him on whom he calls. With Jesus this is conceivable, if he deemed himself the commissioned *herald* of the kingdom of God, appointed to "prepare the way of the Lord, and make his paths straight:" for how could the bearer of such glad tidings have laid his accounts for so tragic an end? Might he not have reasonably expected protection against it? But if he had been conscious of fulfilling throughout Messiah's part, and knowing all along that the cross was its very essence and crown, had voluntarily accepted it, and frequently told his disciples what he would have to suffer and how the sorrow would be turned to joy, then it is utterly beyond belief that he should treat the exact fulfilment of his own intent as a wrongful "forsaking" of him.

The remainder of the "seven words" have not come down to us in the oldest tradition. For the next three we have to wait till the end of the first century, being furnished to us by the gospel of Luke. They are,—

The prayer for the authors of his crucifixion,—"Father, forgive them, for they know not what they do."[*]

The promise to the penitent thief,—"To-day shalt thou be with me in Paradise."[†]

The final surrender,—"Father, into thy hands I commend my spirit."[‡]

In the absence of any external means of historical verification, the acceptance of these must depend on considerations of internal probability. That we miss them in the common tradition, and first alight upon them further on, is not conclusive against them, though leaving more room for their unauthentic introduction; for fragments of true memory may part company and move down on different lines, to be reunited afterwards. Internal marks however are not wanting, which afford some grounds for discrimination. The colloquy, for instance, of the malefactors with each other and with Jesus is so completely out of time and character as to be

* xxiii. 34.   † xxiii. 43.   ‡ xxiii. 46.

evidently fictitious. That a couple of convicts, under the horrors of their death-struggle, should get into an altercation about the Messianic character of their fellow-sufferer, one of them taunting him as an impostor, the other entreating him as a Saviour,* can be accepted only in defiance of all physical and moral probability. The expectation of the penitent petitioner that, in spite of his death on the cross, Jesus would "come in his kingdom," was one of which as yet his most devoted disciples had no faintest foregleam. Jesus, who had habitually disallowed the claim of Messiahship on his behalf, now accepts it, and makes a promise in virtue of it. And the promise was illusory; for it was an appointment to meet the suppliant within a few hours in an imaginary place, viz., that division of Hades (called Paradise) which, according to the current Jewish belief, was set apart as the waiting-room for the righteous souls reserved for the resurrection. The conception evidently belongs to the age, not of the scene of Calvary, but of the composition of the third gospel,—the age which gave rise to the belief in Christ's *descensus ad inferos*, "to preach to the spirits in prison."† For the scenery of the underworld connected with this conception Luke shows a predilection, not here alone, but also in the parable of Lazarus and Dives. In the absence of any trace of such a conception in the older tradition, there is no excuse for attributing it to Jesus.

No such difficulty attaches to the other two "last words" special to Luke. In the prayer for those who are responsible for the crucifixion, one question only brings with it a faint shadow of doubt: What is involved in the plea on their behalf, "They know not what they do"? If it means no more than might be urged for leniency towards *any* homicide (e.g., that it is done in blind passion, or under vehement temptation, and is no true expression of the perpetrators' permanent character), then it is simply in accordance with the self-abnegation and clemency of Jesus. But if it means, 'forgive them, for theirs is a *sin of ignorance;* they do not know *who their victim really is,* and that they are actually

---

* According to Mark and Matthew, *both* the malefactors reproached him: Mark xv. 32; Matt. xxvii. 44. † 1 Pet. iii. 19.

murdering *their own Messiah ;'* then we must say that this
is the afterthought of the narrator's age, and no suggestion
of the sufferer himself; for in no such character did he meet
his death.   I own my prevailing fear that the latter is what
the evangelist intends.   Yet, if so, it is still possible that by
the mere colouring of a phrase he may have unconsciously given
to a real incident an aspect which in its occurrence it did not
present.   That Luke makes the first martyr die with a like
intercession for his persecutors upon his lips may be adduced
as an author's repetition of what is congenial to his own
feeling, but may also be set down to the natural appropriation by Stephen of the very spirit of his venerated Lord.

The final " word," " Father, into thy hands I commend my
spirit," is certainly what Jesus would most characteristically
say, so long as formed thought and articulate speech were
possible to him at all; and the doubt whether this could be
so to the verge of the expiring moment is chiefly due to the
insertion there by the other synoptists of a mere inarticulate
cry, the desire to interpret which would naturally lead to
such substituted expansion into definite utterances as are
found in Luke and John.   The evolution of a more explicit
account from a meagre one is too familiar to be pronounced
impossible : but whether too little was told at first, or too
much at last, cannot be determined with certainty.

The remaining three of the " seven last words " are found
only in the fourth gospel.   The first alone says anything
material to the interest of the narrative, elicited as it is
by the sight of Mary the mother of Jesus and the beloved
disciple standing together beneath the cross, and consisting
of the words commending them to each other, " behold thy
Son ! " " behold thy Mother ! "*   Unless this touching recital
is to be exempted from question simply on the ground of its
beauty, there will be no slight difficulty in securing its historical place.   The presence beneath the cross of either Mary
or the beloved disciple is inconsistent with the synoptic tradition, the beloved disciple being among those who betook
themselves to their homeward flight from Gethsemane, and
Mary not having come up from Galilee with the disciples at

* xix. 26, 27.

all, or being drawn into his train by any sympathy with his mission. In the original tradition her name never appears with those of the Galilean women, Mary Magdalene, Mary the mother of James, and Salome, who believed in him, or is referred to except in connection with acts of resistance to his course of life. Nor can it be denied that, in his mind also, the greatness of the spiritual call had gone far to dwarf the domestic claim, and replace the ties of the native home which disowned him by those of the second birth which bound him in faith as well as love to many a new brother and sister and mother. That the evangelist should introduce a relation having no foundation in fact will surprise no one who considers the real character and purpose of his work. The fourth. gospel is no history of the actual ministry of Jesus; but an account of what it ought to have been, or would have to be,. in order to exhibit its inner meaning as understood by the author, and fully embody the enlarged theology of his time. He belonged to a school which had no scruple in conforming history to doctrine, instead of controlling doctrine by history. The incident at the crucifixion he conceived in subservience to a design pervading his gospel, namely, to write up "the beloved disciple" into a position of primacy preferable to that of Peter, and under cover of his more intimate relation to Jesus to give authority to a more spiritual theology than found acceptance in the Jewish Christian branch of the Church. The passage ranks therefore with that in which Peter learns the name of the betrayer through the favourite disciple, who was lying on Jesus' bosom ;* with that in which he gets admission into the High Priest's house through the. intervention of the same "other disciple" ;† with that in which, on hearing from Mary Magdalene that the body of Jesus had been removed from its place of interment, "the disciple whom Jesus loved" "outran Peter" in the race to the tomb, and though not the first to 'enter and see the linen clothes lying,' was the first ' to see and believe.'‡ Nor is it without design that the effect of this disciple's presence to the last beneath the cross is heightened by contrast with Peter's denial and desertion, without any mention of the

* xiii. 24, 25.   † xviii. 15, 16.   ‡ xx. 2-8.

bitter tears and repentance which the synoptists do not forget.*
It may be admitted therefore that the evangelist, in his picture
of this anonymous disciple, betrayed the *animus* of an ecclesiastical partisan.   But when it is suggested that the figures
which he introduces and moves upon the scene are *allegorical*,
that the *mother* of Christ means the true Israel, or the Church,
that the "disciple whom Jesus loved" means his *spiritual*
brother in affinity with his *heavenly* Sonship, as distinguished
from his *natural* brother James, the head of the Jewish
Christian community at Jerusalem, and that the sending her
to him for her future home claims for the new gospel of the
Word and the Spirit the final rest of the Church, the search
for hidden meanings seems pushed too far, and diverts
attention from the drift of the original to the ingenuity of the
interpreter.†

The two remaining last words, the exclamation "I thirst,":
and "It is finished"§ stand in a connection which becomes
clear in answer to the question '*What* is finished' (or fulfilled)?
The preamble of the passage gives the answer: "after this,
Jesus, knowing that all the conditions requisite for the
fulfilment of the Scriptures were completed, says I thirst."
He had in his mind all the steps that, according to prophecy,
were to lead up to the last moment, and was conscious that
not one of them was now wanting. Till he was at the
terminus of his suffering he had refused all alleviation : he
had borne his own cross :|| he had refused the stupefying
draught :¶ all that scripture said of him had come to pass :
the last strain was taken from his will : he might cool the
fever of his tongue ere it said ' It is over.'

If this came to us from contemporary sources, and accompanied by evidence that Jesus lived and died under conviction
of his Messiahship, it might easily pass for history.   But
under the failure of these conditions, the certainty that the
fitting of reputed prophecies to the life of Jesus was an apostolic

* xviii. 17, 18, 25-27.
† For an example of this misleading process, see Scholten : das Evangelium nach Johannes, German translation by H. Lang. Berlin : 1867. pp.
164-167, 381-385.
‡ xlx. 28.   § xlx. 30.
|| I.e., according to John xix. 17.   ¶ Mark xv. 23; Matt. xxvii. 31.

and post-apostolic practice, and the obvious tendency of the evangelist to carry this practice to a most artificial extreme, the critic can only treat these unattested expressions, not as the transcript of fact, but as the product of theory.

Though certainty with regard to the details of the crucifixion hours is irrecoverably lost, all the traditions, whether historical or fictitious, represent what in the belief of the nearest heirs of his spirit he would be sure to do and say, till will and voice fainted into silence. And they leave an impression in such complete accordance with his characteristic affections, as to relieve the deepest tragedy in the world with the sacred joy of its highest veneration.

With the expiring breath of the Revealer ends the historic episode of his revelation. That revelation, concentrated as it was in his person, in the drama of his life and the movements of his spirit, had delivered all its immediate light, when the earthly term was closed. The image was complete: the pathetic experiences were all told off: no new traits were in reserve: and whatever power his presence had to "show us the Father," or disclose to us "what spirit we are of," was delivered forth and belonged now to a future store. Not indeed that he himself was at an end: he was truly affirmed to be "alive for evermore": and the absolute conviction of this on the part of his followers is among the most certain of historical facts. But it belongs to *their* history, and not to *his*, which has its continuance in quite another sphere. That "the dead live," when they are such as he, was with them, as it will ever be, an irresistible faith: but the attempt to shift its spiritual warrant to the ground of Sense, and make it good by witnesses of palpable and visible fact, is an illusion like many another false excuse for a true insight. How this attempt wrought itself out into the forms which it assumes in the New Testament writings has been shown in the chapter on the resurrection: I revert to it now only to clear the position that, though to the Crucified himself the crucifixion was but rebirth into higher life, yet to us it is his withdrawal into the invisible, and the necessary close of his historic revelation.

As I look back on the foregoing discussions, a conclusion is forced upon me on which I cannot dwell without pain and dismay: viz., that Christianity, as defined or understood in all the Churches which formulate it, has been mainly evolved from what is transient and perishable in its sources: from what is unhistorical in its traditions, mythological in its preconceptions, and misapprehended in the oracles of its prophets. From the fable of Eden to the imagination of the last trumpet, the whole story of the Divine order of the world is dislocated and deformed. The blight of birth-sin with its involuntary perdition; the scheme of expiatory redemption with its vicarious salvation; the incarnation, with its low postulates of the relation between God and man, and its unworkable doctrine of two natures in one person; the official transmission of grace through material elements in the keeping of a consecrated corporation; the second coming of Christ to summon the dead and part the sheep from the goats at the general judgment;—all are the growth of a mythical literature, or Messianic dreams, or Pharisaic theology, or sacramental superstition, or popular apotheosis. And so nearly do these vain imaginations preoccupy the creeds that not a moral or spiritual element finds entrance there except " the forgiveness of sins." To consecrate and diffuse, under the name of " Christianity," a theory of the world's economy thus made up of illusions from obsolete stages of civilization, immense resources, material and moral, are expended, with effect no less deplorable in the province of religion than would be, in that of science, hierarchies and missions for propagating the Ptolemaic astronomy, and inculcating the rules of necromancy and exorcism. The spreading alienation of the intellectual classes of European society from Christendom, and the detention of the rest in their spiritual culture at a level not much above that of the Salvation army, are social phenomena which ought to bring home a very solemn appeal to the conscience of stationary Churches. For their long arrear of debt to the intelligence of mankind they adroitly seek to make amends by elaborate beauty of ritual art. The apology soothes for a time: but it will not last for ever.

But in turning to the historical residue from these inquiries,

I am brought to a further conclusion in which I rest with peace and hope: viz., that Christianity, understood as the personal religion of Jesus Christ, stands clear of all the perishable elements, and realizes the true relation between man and God. I do not mean by this that he was exempt from an Israelite's interpretation of his national literature and history; that, for example, he could read the Hexateuch and the Prophets with the eyes of a Kuenen, that he knew the date of Daniel, or was secured against misapplying phrases of Malachi. Subjection to the conditions of imperfect knowledge, far from being a disqualification, is an essential, for the true guide of men in things divine. For Omniscience, looking through infinitude along all radii, is beyond the relative perspective which all our spiritual experience involves. Religion is the right attitude of the finite soul to the Infinite, the straining of the vision from within the shadows to the far-off Light, the devotion of goodness still immature and precarious towards the Perfect and Eternal: and no Mediator can help us here but one " who, being touched with the feeling of our infirmities, is tempted in all points as we are, and yet without sin." Even this condition, " without sin," is not to be pressed out of its relative significance for every growing mind into a rigid dogmatic absolutism : it tells simply the impression of his life upon its witnesses, without contradicting the self-judgment which felt hurt by the epithet "*Good.*" Nay, this very susceptibility to possible repentance and consciousness of something short of " Good," rather lifts him for us nearer to the standard of holiness, than detains him in the precincts of sin. It is only in the sphere of mundane phenomena that a Revealer needs to *know more* than we : in the sphere of Divine things the requirement is, that he *be better*, and, in the order of his affections and the secrets of his will, make more approach to the supreme Perfection. This intervening position it is which alone renders the function of a Mediator,—Uplifter,—Inspirer,—possible: and *that,* not *instead of immediate* revelation, but simply as making us more aware of it and helping us to interpret it. For in the very constitution of the human soul there is provision for an immediate apprehension of God. But often in the transient lights and shades of conscience we pass on and "know not *who* it is": and not till we see in another the victory which shames our own defeat, and are caught up by enthusiasm for some realized heroism or sanctity, do the authority of right and the beauty of holiness come home to us as an appeal literally Divine. The train of the conspicuously righteous in their several degrees are for us the real angels that pass to and fro on the ladder that reaches from earth to heaven. And if Jesus of Nazareth, in virtue of the characteristics of his spirit, holds the place of Prince of Saints, and perfects the conditions of the pure religious life, he thereby reveals the highest possibilities of the human soul, and their dependence on habitual communion between man and God.

INDEX.

A CATALOGUE OF WORKS

IN

GENERAL LITERATURE

PUBLISHED BY

MESSRS. LONGMANS, GREEN, & CO.

39 PATERNOSTER ROW, LONDON, E.C.

ABBEY and OVERTON.—**The English Church in the Eighteenth Century.** By CHARLES J. ABBEY and JOHN H. OVERTON. Cr. 8vo. 7s. 6d.

ABBOTT.—**Hellenica.** A Collection of Essays on Greek Poetry, Philosophy, History, and Religion. Edited by EVELYN ABBOTT, M.A., LL.D., Fellow and Tutor of Balliol College, Oxford. 8vo. 16s.

ABBOTT (Evelyn, M.A., LL.D.)— *WORKS BY.*

A Skeleton Outline of Greek History. Chronologically Arranged. Crown 8vo. 2s. 6d.

A History of Greece. In Two Parts.
Part I.—From the Earliest Times to the Ionian Revolt. Crown 8vo. 10s. 6d.
Part II. Vol. I.—500-445 B.C. *[In the Press.*
Vol. II.—*[In Preparation].*

ACLAND and RANSOME.—**A Handbook in Outline of the Political History of England to 1890.** Chronologically Arranged. By A. H. DYKE ACLAND, M.P., and CYRIL RANSOME, M.A. Crown 8vo. 6s.

ACTON.—**Modern Cookery.** By ELIZA ACTON. With 150 Woodcuts. Fcp. 8vo. 4s. 6d.

A. K. H. B.—*THE ESSAYS AND CONTRIBUTIONS OF.* Crown 8vo.

Autumn Holidays of a Country Parson. 3s. 6d.
Changed Aspects of Unchanged Truths. 3s. 6d.
Commonplace Philosopher. 3s. 6d.
Counsel and Comfort from a City Pulpit. 3s. 6d.
Critical Essays of a Country Parson. 3s. 6d.

[Continued on next page.

A. K. H. B.—THE ESSAYS AND CONTRIBUTIONS OF—*continued.*

East Coast Days and Memories. 3*s.* 6*d.*
Graver Thoughts of a Country Parson. Three Series. 3*s.* 6*d.* each.
Landscapes, Churches, and Moralities. 3*s.* 6*d.*
Leisure Hours in Town. 3*s* 6*d.*
Lessons of Middle Age. 3*s.* 6*d.*
Our Little Life. Two Series. 3*s.* 6*d.* each.
Our Homely Comedy and Tragedy. 3*s.* 6*d.*
Present Day Thoughts. 3*s.* 6*d.*
Recreations of a Country Parson. Three Series. 3*s.* 6*d.* each.
Seaside Musings. 3*s.* 6*d.*
Sunday Afternoons in the Parish Church of a Scottish University City. 3*s.* 6*d.*
'To Meet the Day' through the Christian year: being a Text of Scripture, with an Original Meditation and a Short Selection in Verse for Every Day. 4*s.* 6*d.*

American Whist, Illustrated: containing the Laws and Principles of the Game, the Analysis of the New Play and American Leads, and a Series of Hands in Diagram, and combining Whist Universal and American Whist. By G. W. P. Fcp. 8vo. 6*s.* 6*d.*

AMOS.—A Primer of the English Constitution and Government. By SHELDON AMOS. Crown 8vo. 6*s.*

Annual Register (The). A Review of Public Events at Home and Abroad, for the year 1890. 8vo. 18*s.*
⁂ Volumes of the 'Annual Register' for the years 1863-1889 can still be had.

ANSTEY (F.)—WORKS BY.

The Black Poodle, and other Stories. Crown 8vo. 2*s.* bds.; 2*s.* 6*d.* cl.

Voces Populi. Reprinted from *Punch.* With 20 Illustrations by J. BERNARD PARTRIDGE. Fcp. 4to. 5*s.*

ARISTOTLE.—THE WORKS OF.

The Politics: G. Bekker's Greek Text of Books I. III. IV. (VII.), with an English Translation by W. E. BOLLAND, M.A.; and short Introductory Essays by A. LANG, M.A. Crown 8vo. 7*s.* 6*d.*

The Politics: Introductory Essays. By ANDREW LANG. (From Bolland and Lang's 'Politics'.) Crown 8vo. 2*s.* 6*d.*

The Ethics: Greek Text, Illustrated with Essays and Notes. By Sir ALEXANDER GRANT, Bart., M.A., LL.D. 2 vols. 8vo. 32*s.*

The Nicomachean Ethics: Newly Translated into English. By ROBERT WILLIAMS, Barrister-at-Law. Crown 8vo. 7*s.* 6*d.*

ARMSTRONG (G. F. WORKS BY.

Poems: Lyrical and Dr 8vo. 6*s.*

King Saul. (The Trag Part I.) Fcp. 8vo. 5*s.*

King David. (The Israel, Part II.) Fcp. 8vo

King Solomon. (The Israel, Part III.) Fcp. 8v

Ugone: A Tragedy.

A Garland from Gree Fcp. 8vo. 9*s.*

Stories of Wicklov Fcp. 8vo. 9*s.*

Mephistopheles in B a Satire. Fcp. 8vo. 4*s.*

The Life and Letters J. Armstrong. Fcp

ARMSTRONG (E. J.)—
Poetical Works. Fc
Essays and Sketches 5*s.*

ARMSTRONG. — **Elizat** nese: the Termagan By EDWARD ARMSTRONG lege, Oxford.

ARNOLD (Sir Edwin, WORKS BY.

The Light of the V the Great Consummatior Crown 8vo. 7*s.* 6*d.* net.

Seas and Lands. Rep from the 'Daily Telegr numerous Illustrations. 8

ARNOLD (Dr. T.)—WOR

Introductory Lectur dern History. 8vo.
Miscellaneous Works

ASHLEY.—English Eco tory and Theory. ASHLEY, M.A. Part I. Ages. 5*s.*

Atelier (The) du Lys; Student in the Reign of T Author of 'Mademoiselle N 8vo. 2*s.* 6*d.*

BY THE SAME AUTH
Mademoiselle Mori: Modern Rome. Crown 8v
That Child. Illustrated BROWNE. Crown 8vo. 2*s.*
[*Continued o*

Atelier (The) du Lys—*WORKS BY THE AUTHOR OF—continued.*

Under a Cloud. Cr. 8vo. 2s. 6d.

The Fiddler of Lugau. With Illustrations by W. RALSTON. Crown 8vo. 2s. 6d.

A Child of the Revolution. With Illustrations by C. J. STANILAND. Crown 8vo. 2s. 6d.

Hester's Venture: a Novel. Cr. 8vo. 2s. 6d.

In the Olden Time: a Tale of the Peasant War in Germany. Cr. 8vo. 2s. 6d.

BACON.—THE WORKS AND LIFE OF.

Complete Works. Edited by R. L. ELLIS, J. SPEDDING, and D. D. HEATH. 7 vols. 8vo. £3 13s. 6d.

Letters and Life, including all his Occasional Works. Edited by J. SPEDDING. 7 vols. 8vo. £4 4s.

The Essays; with Annotations. By RICHARD WHATELY, D.D., 8vo. 10s. 6d.

The Essays; with Introduction, Notes, and Index. By E. A. ABBOTT, D.D. 2 vols. fcp. 8vo. price 6s. Text and Index only, without Introduction and Notes, in 1 vol. Fcp. 8vo. 2s. 6d.

The BADMINTON LIBRARY, Edited by the DUKE OF BEAUFORT, K.G., assisted by ALFRED E. T. WATSON.

Hunting. By the DUKE OF BEAUFORT, K.G., and MOWBRAY MORRIS. With 53 Illus. by J. Sturgess, J. Charlton, and A. M. Biddulph. Cr. 8vo. 10s. 6d.

Fishing. By H. CHOLMONDELEY-PENNELL.
Vol. I. Salmon, Trout, and Grayling. With 158 Illustrations. Cr. 8vo. 10s. 6d.
Vol. II. Pike and other Coarse Fish. With 132 Illustrations. Cr. 8vo. 10s. 6d.

Racing and Steeplechasing. By the EARL OF SUFFOLK AND BERKSHIRE, W. G. CRAVEN, &c. With 56 Illustrations by J. Sturgess. Cr. 8vo. 10s. 6d.

Shooting. By LORD WALSINGHAM and Sir RALPH PAYNE-GALLWEY, Bart.
Vol. I. Field and Covert. With 105 Illustrations. Cr. 8vo. 10s. 6d.
Vol. II. Moor and Marsh. With 65 Illustrations. Cr. 8vo. 10s. 6d.

Cycling. By VISCOUNT BURY (Earl of Albemarle), K.C.M.G., and G. LACY HILLIER. With 19 Plates and 70 Woodcuts, &c., by Viscount Bury, Joseph Pennell, &c. Crown 8vo. 10s. 6d.

The BADMINTON LIBRARY— *continued*.

Athletics and Football. By MONTAGUE SHEARMAN. With 6 full-page Illustrations and 45 Woodcuts, &c., by Stanley Berkeley, and from Photographs by G. Mitchell. Crown 8vo. 10s. 6d.

Boating. By W. B. WOODGATE. With 10 full-page Illustrations and 39 woodcuts, &c., in the Text. Cr. 8vo. 10s. 6d.

Cricket. By A. G. STEEL and the Hon. R. H. LYTTELTON. With 11 full-page Illustrations and 52 Woodcuts, &c., in the Text, by Lucien Davis. Cr. 8vo. 10s. 6d.

Driving. By the DUKE OF BEAUFORT. With 11 Plates and 54 Woodcuts, &c., by J. Sturgess and G. D. Giles. Crown 8vo. 10s. 6d.

Fencing, Boxing, and Wrestling. By WALTER H. POLLOCK, F. C. GROVE, C. PREVOST, E. B. MICHELL, and WALTER ARMSTRONG. With 18 Plates and 24 Woodcuts, &c. Crown 8vo. 10s. 6d.

Golf. By HORACE HUTCHINSON, the Rt. Hon. A. J. BALFOUR, M.P., ANDREW LANG, Sir W. G. SIMPSON, Bart., &c. With 19 Plates and 69 Woodcuts, &c. Crown 8vo. 10s. 6d.

Tennis, Lawn Tennis, Rackets, and Fives. By J. M. and C. G. HEATHCOTE, E. O. PLEYDELL-BOUVERIE, and A. C. AINGER. With 12 Plates and 67 Woodcuts, &c. Crown 8vo. 10s. 6d.

Riding and Polo. By Captain ROBERT WEIR, Riding Master, R.H.G., and J. MORAY BROWN. With Contributions by the Duke of Beaufort, K.G., the Earl of Suffolk and Berkshire, the Earl of Onslow, E. L. Anderson, and Alfred E. T. Watson. With 18 Plates and 41 Woodcuts, &c. Crown 8vo. 10s. 6d.

BAGEHOT (Walter).—WORKS BY.

Biographical Studies. 8vo. 12s.

Economic Studies. 8vo. 10s. 6d.

Literary Studies. 2 vols. 8vo. 28s.

The Postulates of English Political Economy. Cr. 8vo. 2s. 6d.

A Practical Plan for Assimilating the English and American Money as a Step towards a Universal Money. Cr. 8vo. 2s. 6d.

BAGWELL.—Ireland under the Tudors, with a Succinct Account of the Earlier History. By RICHARD BAGWELL, M.A. (3 vols.) Vols. I. and II. From the first invasion of the Northmen to the year 1578. 8vo. 32*s.* Vol. III. 1578-1603. 8vo. 18*s.*

BAIN (Alexander).—*WORKS BY.*

Mental and Moral Science. Cr. 8vo. 10*s.* 6*d.*

Senses and the Intellect. 8vo. 15*s.*

Emotions and the Will. 8vo. 15*s.*

Logic, Deductive, and Inductive. PART I. *Deduction*, 4*s.* PART II. *Induction*, 6*s.* 6*d.*

Practical Essays. Cr. 8vo. 2*s.*

BAKER.—By the Western Sea: a Summer Idyll. By JAMES BAKER, F.R.G.S. Author of 'John Westacott'. Crown 8vo. 3*s.* 6*d.*

BAKER (Sir S. W.).—*WORKS BY.*

Eight Years in Ceylon. With 6 Illustrations. Crown 8vo. 3*s.* 6*d.*

The Rifle and the Hound in Ceylon. With 6 Illustrations. Crown 8vo. 3*s.* 6*d.*

BALL (The Rt. Hon. J. T.).—*WORKS BY.*

The Reformed Church of Ireland. (1537-1889). 8vo. 7*s.* 6*d.*

Historical Review of the Legislative Systems Operative in Ireland, from the Invasion of Henry the Second to the Union (1172-1800). 8vo. 6*s.*

BEACONSFIELD (The Earl of).—*WORKS BY.*

Novels and Tales. The Hughenden Edition. With 2 Portraits and 11 Vignettes. 11 vols. Crown 8vo. 42*s.*

Endymion.	Henrietta Temple.
Lothiar.	Contarini, Fleming, &c.
Coningsby.	Alroy, Ixion, &c.
Tancred. Sybil.	The Young Duke, &c.
Venetia.	Vivian Grey.

Novels and Tales. Cheap Edition. Complete in 11 vols. Crown 8vo. 1*s.* each, boards; 1*s.* 6*d.* each, cloth.

BECKER (Professor).—*WORKS BY.*

Gallus; or, Roman Scenes in the Time of Augustus. Post 8vo. 7*s.* 6*d.*

Charicles; or, Illustrations of the Private Life of the Ancient Greeks. Post 8vo. 7*s.* 6*d.*

BELL (Mrs. Hu... Will o' the V... trated by E. L. ... Chamber Co... of Plays and M... Room. Crow...

BLAKE.—Tabl... sion of 5 ... from $\frac{1}{10}$ to ... BLAKE, of the ... Limited. 8vo. ...

Book (The) o... Arranged on th... With 96 Illustr... and Title-page ... Quotations for ... Arranged by K... and MABEL B...

BRASSEY (Lad... A Voyage in ... Home on ... Eleven M... Library Edit... Charts, an... Cabinet Edit... Illustratior... 'Silver Libr... Illustratior... Popular Edit... 4to. 6*d.* se... School Editio... Fcp. 2*s.* clo...

Sunshine and... Library Edit... 114 Illustr... Cabinet Edit... 114 Illustr... Popular Edi... tions, 4to.

In the Trade... the 'Roari... Cabinet Edit... Illustratior... Popular Edi... tions, 4to.

The Last Vo... Australia i... With Charts an... in Monotone (2... Illustrations in ... by R. T. Prit...

Three Voya... beam'. Po... 346 Illustration...

BRAY.—The F... cessity; or ... Matter. By C... 8vo. 5*s.*

BRIGHT.—**A History of England.** By the Rev. J. FRANCK BRIGHT, D.D., Master of University College, Oxford. 4 vols. Crown 8vo.

Period I.—Mediæval Monarchy: The Departure of the Romans to Richard III. From A.D. 449 to 1485. 4s. 6d.

Period II.—Personal Monarchy: Henry VII. to James II. From 1485 to 1688. 5s.

Period III. — Constitutional Monarchy: William and Mary to William IV. From 1689 to 1837. 7s. 6d.

Period IV.—The Growth of Democracy: Victoria. From 1837 to 1880. 6s.

BROKE.—**With Sack and Stock in Alaska.** By GEORGE BROKE, A.C., F.R.G.S. With 2 Maps. Crown 8vo. 5s.

BRYDEN.—**Kloof and Karroo:** Sport, Legend, and Natural History in Cape Colony. By H. A. BRYDEN. With 17 Illustrations. 8vo. 10s. 6d.

BUCKLE.—**History of Civilisation in England and France, Spain and Scotland.** By HENRY THOMAS BUCKLE. 3 vols. Cr. 8vo. 24s.

BULL (Thomas).—*WORKS BY.*

Hints to Mothers on the Management of their Health during the Period of Pregnancy. Fcp. 8vo. 1s. 6d.

The Maternal Management of Children in Health and Disease. Fcp. 8vo. 1s. 6d.

BUTLER (Samuel).—*WORKS BY.*

Op. 1. **Erewhon.** Crown 8vo. 5s.

Op. 2. **The Fair Haven.** A Work in defence of the Miraculous Element in our Lord's Ministry. Crown 8vo. 7s. 6d.

Op. 3. **Life and Habit.** An Essay after a Completer View of Evolution. Crown 8vo. 7s. 6d.

Op. 4. **Evolution, Old and New.** Crown 8vo. 10s. 6d.

Op. 5. **Unconscious Memory.** Crown 8vo. 7s. 6d.

Op. 6. **Alps and Sanctuaries of Piedmont and the Canton Ticino.** · Illustrated. Pott 4to. 10s. 6d.

Op. 7. **Selections from Ops. 1-6.** With Remarks on Mr. G. J. ROMANES' 'Mental Evolution in Animals'. Cr. 8vo. 7s. 6d.

BUTLER (Samuel).—*WORKS BY.*—*continued.*

Op. 8. **Luck, or Cunning, as the Main Means of Organic Modification?** Cr. 8vo. 7s. 6d.

Op. 9. **Ex Voto.** An Account of the Sacro Monte or New Jerusalem at Varallo-Sesia. 10s. 6d.

Holbein's 'La Danse'. A Note on a Drawing called 'La Danse'. 3s.

CARLYLE.—**Thomas Carlyle: a History of His Life.** By J. A. FROUDE. 1795-1835, 2 vols. Crown 8vo. 7s. 1834-1881, 2 vols. Crown 8vo. 7s.

CASE.—**Physical Realism:** being an Analytical Philosophy from the Physical Objects of Science to the Physical Data of Sense. By THOMAS CASE, M.A., Fellow and Senior Tutor, C.C.C. 8vo. 15s.

CHETWYND.—**Racing Reminiscences and Experiences of the Turf.** By Sir GEORGE CHETWYND, Bart. 2 vols. 8vo. 21s.

CHILD.—**Church and State under the Tudors.** By GILBERT W. CHILD, M.A. 8vo. 15s.

CHISHOLM.—**Handbook of Commercial Geography.** By G. G. CHISHOLM. With 29 Maps. 8vo. 16s.

CHURCH.—**Sir Richard Church, C.B., G.C.H.** Commander-in-Chief of the Greeks in the War of Independence: a Memoir. By STANLEY LANE-POOLE. With 2 Plans. 8vo. 5s.

CLIVE.—**Poems.** By V. (Mrs. ARCHER CLIVE), Author of 'Paul Ferroll'. Including the IX. Poems. Fcp. 8vo. 6s.

CLODD.—**The Story of Creation:** a Plain Account of Evolution. By EDWARD CLODD. With 77 Illustrations. Crown 8vo. 3s. 6d.

CLUTTERBUCK (W. J.).—*WORKS BY.*

The Skipper in Arctic Seas. With 39 Illustrations. Cr. 8vo. 10s. 6d.

About Ceylon and Borneo: being an Account of Two Visits to Ceylon, one to Borneo, and How we Fell Out on our Homeward Journey. With 47 Illustrations. Crown 8vo.

COLENSO.—**The Pentateuch and Book of Joshua Critically Examined.** By J. W. COLENSO, D.D., late Bishop of Natal. Cr. 8vo. 6s.

COMYN.—Atherstone Priory: a Tale. By L. N. COMYN. Cr. 8vo. 2s. 6d.

CONINGTON (John).— *WORKS BY.*

The Æneid of Virgil. Translated into English Verse. Crown 8vo. 6s.

The Poems of Virgil. Translated into English Prose. Crown 8vo. 6s.

COX. — A General History of Greece, from the Earliest Period to the Death of Alexander the Great; with a sketch of the subsequent History to the Present Time. By the Rev. Sir G. W. Cox, Bart., M.A. With 11 Maps and Plans. Crown 8vo. 7s. 6d.

CRAKE (Rev. A. D.).— *WORKS BY.*

Historical Tales. Crown 8vo. 5 vols. 2s. 6d. each.

Edwy the Fair; or, The First Chronicle of Æscendune.

Alfgar the Dane; or, the Second Chronicle of Æscendune.

The Rival Heirs: being the Third and Last Chronicle of Æscendune.

The House of Walderne. A Tale of the Cloister and the Forest in the Days of the Barons' Wars.

Brian Fitz-Count. A Story of Wallingford Castle and Dorchester Abbey.

History of the Church under the Roman Empire, A.D. 30-476. Crown 8vo. 7s. 6d.

CREIGHTON.— History of the Papacy during the Reformation. By MANDELL CREIGHTON, D.D., LL.D., Bishop of Peterborough. 8vo. Vols. I. and II., 1378-1464, 32s.; Vols. III. and IV., 1464-1518, 24s.

CRUMP (A.).— *WORKS BY.*

A Short Enquiry into the Formation of Political Opinion, from the reign of the Great Families to the Advent of Democracy. 8vo. 7s. 6d.

An Investigation into the Causes of the Great Fall in Prices which took place coincidently with the Demonetisation of Silver by Germany. 8vo. 6s.

CUDWORTH.—An Introduction to Cudworth's Treatise concerning Eternal and Immutable Morality. By W. R. SCOTT. Crown 8vo. 3s.

CURZON.—Russia in Central Asia in 1889, and the Anglo-Russian Question. By the Hon. GEORGE N. CURZON, M.P. 8vo. 21s.

DANTE.—La Commedia di Dante. A New Text, carefully Revised with the aid of the most recent Editions and Collations. Small 8vo. 6s.

DAVIDSON (W. L.).— *WORKS BY.*

The Logic of Definition Explained and Applied. Cr. 8vo. 6s.

Leading and Important English Words Explained and Exemplified. Fcp. 8vo. 3s. 6d.

DELAND (Mrs.).— *WORKS BY.*

John Ward, Preacher: a Story. Crown 8vo. 2s. boards, 2s. 6d. cloth.

Sidney: a Novel. Crown 8vo. 6s.

The Old Garden, and other Verses. Fcp. 8vo. 5s.

DE LA SAUSSAYE.—A Manual of the Science of Religion. By Professor CHANTEPIE DE LA SAUSSAYE. Translated by Mrs. COLVER FERGUSON (née MAX MULLER). Revised by the Author. Crown 8vo. 12s. 6d.

DE REDCLIFFE.—The Life of the Right Hon. Stratford Canning: Viscount Stratford De Redcliffe. By STANLEY LANE-POOLE. Cabinet Edition, abridged, with 3 Portraits, 1 vol. Crown 8vo. 7s. 6d.

DE SALIS (Mrs.).— *WORKS BY.*

Cakes and Confections à la Mode. Fcp. 8vo. 1s. 6d. boards.

Dressed Game and Poultry à la Mode. Fcp. 8vo. 1s. 6d. bds.

Dressed Vegetables à la Mode. Fcp. 8vo. 1s. 6d. boards.

Drinks à la Mode. Fcp. 8vo. 1s. 6d. boards.

Entrées à la Mode. Fcp. 8vo. 1s. 6d. boards.

Floral Decorations. Suggestions and Descriptions. Fcap. 8vo. 1s. 6d.

Oysters à la Mode. Fcp. 8vo. 1s. 6d. boards.

[Continued on next page.

DE SALIS (*Mrs.*).— *WORKS BY.*—*cont.*

Puddings and Pastry à la Mode. Fcp. 8vo. 1s. 6d. boards.

Savouries à la Mode. Fcp. 8vo. 1s. 6d. boards.

Soups and Dressed Fish à la Mode. Fcp. 8vo. 1s. 6d. boards.

Sweets and Supper Dishes à la Mode. Fcp. 8vo. 1s. 6d. boards.

Tempting Dishes for Small Incomes. Fcp. 8vo. 1s. 6d.

Wrinkles and Notions for every Household. Crown 8vo. 2s. 6d.

DE TOCQUEVILLE.—**Democracy in America.** By ALEXIS DE TOCQUEVILLE. 2 vols. Crown 8vo. 16s.

DOUGALL.—**Beggars All:** a Novel. By L. DOUGALL. Crown 8vo. 6s.

DOWELL.—**A History of Taxation and Taxes in England** from the Earliest Times to the Year 1885. By STEPHEN DOWELL. (4 vols. 8vo.) Vols. I. and II. The History of Taxation, 21s. Vols. III. and IV. The History of Taxes, 21s.

DOYLE (*A. Conan*).— *WORKS BY.*

Micah Clarke. A tale of Monmouth's Rebellion. With Frontispiece and Vignette. Crown 8vo. 3s. 6d.

The Captain of the Polestar; and other Tales. Crown 8vo. 6s.

DRANE.—**The History of St. Dominic.** By AUGUSTA THEODORA DRANE. 32 Illustrations. 8vo. 15s.

Dublin University Press Series (The): a Series of Works undertaken by the Provost and Senior Fellows of Trinity College, Dublin.

Abbott's (T. K.) Codex Rescriptus Dublinensis of St. Matthew. 4to. 21s.

——— Evangeliorum Versio Antehieronymiana ex Codice Usseriano (Dublinensi). 2 vols. Crown 8vo. 21s.

Allman's (G. J.) Greek Geometry from Thales to Euclid. 8vo. 10s. 6d.

Burnside (W. S.) and Panton's (A. W.) Theory of Equations. 8vo. 12s. 6d.

Casey's (John) Sequel to Euclid's Elements. Crown 8vo. 3s. 6d.

——— Analytical Geometry of the Conic Sections. Crown 8vo. 7s. 6d.

Dublin University Press Series (The).—*continued.*

Davies' (J. F.) Eumenides of Æschylus. With Metrical English Translation. 8vo. 7s.

Dublin Translations into Greek and Latin Verse. Edited by R. Y. Tyrrell. 8vo. 6s.

Graves' (R. P.) Life of Sir William Hamilton. 3 vols. 15s. each.

Griffin (R. W.) on Parabola, Ellipse, and Hyperbola. Crown 8vo. 6s.

Hobart's (W. K.) Medical Language of St. Luke. 8vo. 16s.

Leslie's (T. E. Cliffe) Essays in Political Economy. 8vo. 10s. 6d.

Macalister's (A.) Zoology and Morphology of Vertebrata. 8vo. 10s. 6d.

MacCullagh's (James) Mathematical and other Tracts. 8vo. 15s.

Maguire's (T.) Parmenides of Plato, Text, with Introduction, Analysis, &c. 8vo. 7s. 6d.

Monck's (W. H. S.) Introduction to Logic. Crown 8vo. 5s.

Roberts' (R. A.) Examples on the Analytic Geometry of Plane Conics. Cr. 8vo. 5s.

Southey's (R.) Correspondence with Caroline Bowles. Edited by E. Dowden. 8vo. 14s.

Stubbs' (J. W.) History of the University of Dublin, from its Foundation to the End of the Eighteenth Century. 8vo. 12s. 6d.

Thornhill's (W. J.) The Æneid of Virgil, freely translated into English Blank Verse. Crown 8vo. 7s. 6d.

Tyrrell's (R. Y.) Cicero's Correspondence. Vols. I. II. III. 8vo. each 12s.

——— The Acharnians of Aristophanes, translated into English Verse. Crown 8vo. 1s.

Webb's (T. E.) Goethe's Faust, Translation and Notes. 8vo. 12s. 6d.

——— The Veil of Isis: a Series of Essays on Idealism. 8vo. 10s. 6d.

Wilkins' (G.) The Growth of the Homeric Poems. 8vo. 6s.

Epochs of Modern History. Edited by C. COLBECK, M.A. 19 vols. Fcp. 8vo. with Maps, 2s. 6d. each.

Airy's (O.) The English Restoration and Louis XIV. (1648-1678).

Church's (Very Rev. R. W.) The Beginning of the Middle Ages. With 3 Maps.

[Continued on next page.

Epochs of Modern History.—*cont.*

Cox's (Rev. Sir G. W.) The Crusades. With a Map.

Creighton's (Rev. M.) The Age of Elizabeth. With 5 Maps.

Gairdner's (J.) The Houses of Lancaster and York; with the Conquest and Loss of France. With 5 Maps.

Gardiner's (S. R.) The First Two Stuarts and the Puritan Revolution (1603-1660). With 4 Maps.

———— The Thirty Years' War (1618-1648). With a Map.

Gardiner's (Mrs. S. R.) The French Revolution (1789-1795). With 7 Maps.

Hale's (Rev. E.) The Fall of the Stuarts; and Western Europe (1678-1697). With 11 Maps and Plans.

Johnson's (Rev. A. H.) The Normans in Europe. With 3 Maps.

Longman's (F. W.) Frederick the Great and the Seven Years' War. With 2 Maps.

Ludlow's (J. M.) The War of American Independence (1775-1783). With 4 Maps.

McCarthy's (Justin) The Epoch of Reform (1830-1850).

Moberly's (Rev. C. E.) The Early Tudors.

Morris's (E. E.) The Age of Anne. With 7 Maps and Plans.

———— The Early Hanoverians. With 9 Maps and Plans.

Seebohm's (F.) The Era of the Protestant Revolution. With 4 Maps.

Stubbs' (Right Rev. W.) The Early Plantagenets. With 2 Maps.

Warburton's (Rev. W.) Edward the Third. With 3 Maps.

Epochs of Church History. Edited by Mandell Creighton, D.D., Bishop of Peterborough. Fcp. 8vo. 2s. 6d. each.

Balzani's (U.) The Popes and the Hohenstaufen.

Brodrick's (Hon. G. C.) A History of the University of Oxford.

Carr's (Rev. A.) The Church and the Roman Empire.

Gwatkin's (H. M.) The Arian Controversy.

Hunt's (Rev. W.) The English Church in the Middle Ages.

Mullinger's (J. B.) A History of the University of Cambridge.

Overton's (Rev. J. H.) The Evangelical Revival in the Eighteenth Century.

Epochs of Church History.—*cont.*

Perry's (Rev. G. G.) The History of the Reformation in England.

Plummer's (A.) The Church of the Early Fathers.

Poole's (R. L.) Wycliffe and Early Movements of Reform.

Stephen's (Rev. W. R. W.) Hildebrand and his Times.

Tozer's (Rev. H. F.) The Church and the Eastern Empire.

Tucker's (Rev. H. W.) The English Church in other Lands.

Wakeman's (H. O.) The Church and the Puritans (1570-1660.)

Ward's (A. W.) The Counter-Reformation.

Epochs of Ancient History. Edited by the Rev. Sir G. W. Cox, Bart., M.A., and by C. Sankey, M.A. 10 volumes, Fcp. 8vo. with Maps, 2s. 6d. each.

Beesly's (A. H.) The Gracchi, Marius, and Sulla. With 2 Maps.

Capes' (Rev. W. W.) The Early Roman Empire. From the Assassination of Julius Cæsar to the Assassination of Domitian. With 2 Maps.

———— The Roman Empire of the Second Century, or the Age of the Antonines. With 2 Maps.

Cox's (Rev. Sir G. W.) The Athenian Empire from the Flight of Xerxes to the Fall of Athens. With 5 Maps.

———— The Greeks and the Persians. With 4 Maps.

Curteis's (A. M.) The Rise of the Macedonian Empire. With 8 Maps.

Ihne's (W.) Rome to its Capture by the Gauls. With a Map.

Merivale's (Very Rev. C.) The Roman Triumvirates. With a Map.

Sankey's (C.) The Spartan and Theban Supremacies. With 5 Maps.

Smith's (R. B.) Rome and Carthage, the Punic Wars. With 9 Maps and Plans.

Epochs of American History. Edited by Dr. Albert Bushnell Hart, Assistant Professor of History in Harvard College.

Hart's (A. B.) Formation of the Union (1763-1829). Fcp. 8vo. [*In preparation*

Thwaites's (R. G.) The Colonies (1492-1763). Fcp. 8vo. 3s. 6d. *Ready*.

Wilson's (W.) Division and Re-union (1829-1889). Fcp. 8vo. [*In preparation*

Epochs of English History. Complete in One Volume, with 27 Tables and Pedigrees, and 23 Maps. Fcp. 8vo. 5s.

*** For details of Parts *see* Longmans & Co.'s Catalogue of School Books.

EWALD (Heinrich).—WORKS BY.

The Antiquities of Israel. Translated from the German by H. S. SOLLY, M.A. 8vo. 12s. 6d.

The History of Israel. Translated from the German. 8 vols. 8vo. Vols. I. and II. 24s. Vols. III. and IV. 21s. Vol. V. 18s. Vol. VI. 16s. Vol. VII. 21s. Vol. VIII., with Index to the Complete Work, 18s.

FARNELL.—Greek Lyric Poetry: a Complete Collection of the Surviving Passages from the Greek Song-Writers. Arranged with Prefatory Articles, Introductory Matter, and Commentary. By GEORGE S. FARNELL, M.A. With 5 Plates. 8vo. 16s.

FARRAR (Ven. Archdeacon).—WORKS BY.

Darkness and Dawn; or, Scenes in the Days of Nero. An Historic Tale. 2 vols. 8vo. 28s.

Language and Languages. A Revised Edition of *Chapters on Language and Families of Speech*. Crown 8vo. 6s.

FITZWYGRAM. — **Horses and Stables.** By Major-General Sir F. FITZWYGRAM, Bart. With 19 pages of Illustrations. 8vo. 5s.

FORD.—The Theory and Practice of Archery. By the late HORACE FORD. New Edition, thoroughly Revised and Re-written by W. BUTT, M.A. With a Preface by C. J. LONGMAN, M.A., F.S.A. 8vo. 14s.

FOUARD.—The Christ the Son of God: a Life of our Lord and Saviour Jesus Christ. By the Abbé CONSTANT FOUARD. With an Introduction by Cardinal MANNING. 2 vols. Crown 8vo. 14s.

FOX. — **The Early History of Charles James Fox.** By the Right Hon. Sir G. O. TREVELYAN, Bart. Library Edition, 8vo. 18s. Cabinet Edition, Crown 8vo. 6s.

FRANCIS.—A Book on Angling; or, Treatise on the Art of Fishing in every branch; including full Illustrated List of Salmon Flies. By FRANCIS FRANCIS. With Portrait and Coloured Plates. Crown 8vo. 15s.

FREEMAN.—The Historical Geography of Europe. By E. A. FREEMAN. With 65 Maps. 2 vols. 8vo. 31s. 6d.

FROUDE (James A.).—WORKS BY.

The History of England, from the Fall of Wolsey to the Defeat of the Spanish Armada. 12 vols. Crown 8vo. 3s. 6d. each.

The Divorce of Catherine of Aragon; the Story as told by the Imperial Ambassadors resident at the Court of Henry VIII. *In usum Laicorum.* 8vo. 16s.

Short Studies on Great Subjects. Cabinet Edition, 4 vols. Crown 8vo. 24s. Cheap Edition, 4 vols. Crown 8vo. 3s. 6d. each.

Cæsar: a Sketch. Crown 8vo. 3s. 6d.

The English in Ireland in the Eighteenth Century. 3 vols. Crown 8vo. 18s.

Oceana; or, England and her Colonies. With 9 Illustrations. Crown 8vo. 2s. boards, 2s. 6d. cloth.

The English in the West Indies; or, the Bow of Ulysses. With 9 Illustrations. Crown 8vo. 2s. boards, 2s. 6d. cloth.

The Two Chiefs of Dunboy; an Irish Romance of the Last Century. Crown 8vo. 3s. 6d.

Thomas Carlyle, a History of his Life. 1795 to 1835. 2 vols. Crown 8vo. 7s. 1834 to 1881. 2 vols. Crown 8vo. 7s.

GALLWEY.—Letters to Young Shooters. (First Series.) On the Choice and Use of a Gun. By Sir RALPH PAYNE-GALLWEY, Bart. With Illustrations. Crown 8vo. 7s. 6d.

GARDINER (Samuel Rawson).—WORKS BY.

History of England, from the Accession of James I. to the Outbreak of the Civil War, 1603-1642. 10 vols. Crown 8vo. price 6s. each.

A History of the Great Civil War, 1642-1649. (3 vols.) Vol. I. 1642-1644. With 24 Maps. 8vo. 21s. (out of print). Vol. II. 1644-1647. With 21 Maps. 8vo. 24s. Vol. III. 1647-1649. 8vo.

GARDINER (*Samuel Rawson*).— WORKS BY.—*continued.*

The Student's History of England. Vol. I. B.C. 55—A.D. 1509, with 173 Illustrations. Crown 8vo. 4s. Vol. II. 1509-1689, with 96 Illustrations. Crown 8vo. 4s. Vol. III. (1689-1865). Crown 8vo. 4s. Complete in 1 vol. Crown 8vo. 12s.

A School Atlas of English History. A Companion Atlas to the 'Student's History of England'. With 66 Maps and 22 Plans of Battles, &c. Fcap. 4to. 5s.

GIBERNE.— WORKS BY.

Nigel Browning. Crown 8vo. 5s.

Miss Devereux, Spinster. A Novel. 2 vols. Crown 8vo. 17s.

GOETHE.—**Faust.** A New Translation chiefly in Blank Verse; with Introduction and Notes. By JAMES ADEY BIRDS. Crown 8vo. 6s.

Faust. The Second Part. A New Translation in Verse. By JAMES ADEY BIRDS. Crown 8vo. 6s.

GREEN.—**The Works of Thomas Hill Green.** Edited by R. L. NETTLESHIP. (3 vols.) Vols. I. and II.—Philosophical Works. 8vo. 16s. each. Vol. III.—Miscellanies. With Index to the three Volumes and Memoir. 8vo. 21s.

The Witness of God and Faith: Two Lay Sermons. By T. H. GREEN. Fcp. 8vo. 2s.

GREVILLE.—**A Journal of the Reigns of King George IV., King William IV., and Queen Victoria.** By C. C. F. GREVILLE. Edited by H. REEVE. 8 vols. Crown 8vo. 6s. each.

GWILT. — **An Encyclopædia of Architecture.** By JOSEPH GWILT, F.S.A. Illustrated with more than 1700 Engravings on Wood. 8vo. 52s. 6d.

HAGGARD.—**Life and its Author:** an Essay in Verse. By ELLA HAGGARD. With a Memoir by H. RIDER HAGGARD, and Portrait. Fcp. 8vo. 3s. 6d.

HAGGARD (*H. Rider*).—WORKS BY.

She. With 32 Illustrations by M. GREIFFENHAGEN and C. H. M. KERR. Crown 8vo. 3s. 6d.

Allan Quatermain. With 31 Illustrations by C. H. M. KERR. Crown 8vo. 3s. 6d.

HAGGARD (*H. Rider.*)—WORKS BY.—*continued.*

Maiwa's Revenge; or, The War of the Little Hand. Crown 8vo. 1s. boards; 1s. 6d. cloth.

Colonel Quaritch, V.C. A Novel. Crown 8vo. 3s. 6d.

Cleopatra: being an Account of the Fall and Vengeance of Harmachis, the Royal Egyptian. With 29 Full-page Illustrations by M. Greiffenhagen and R. Caton Woodville. Crown 8vo. 3s. 6d.

Beatrice. A Novel. Cr. 8vo. 6s.

Eric Brighteyes. With 17 Plates and 34 Illustrations in the Text by LANCELOT SPEED. Crown 8vo. 6s.

HAGGARD *and* **LANG.** — **The World's Desire.** By H. RIDER HAGGARD and ANDREW LANG. Crown 8vo. 6s.

HALLIWELL-PHILLIPPS. — **A Calendar of the Halliwell-Phillipps' collection of Shakespearean Rarities formerly preserved at Hollingbury Copse, Brighton.** Second Edition. Enlarged by ERNEST E BAKER, F.S.A. 8vo. 10s. 6d.

HARRISON.—**Myths of the Odyssey in Art and Literature.** Illustrated with Outline Drawings. By JANE E. HARRISON. 8vo. 18s.

HARRISON.—**The Contemporary History of the French Revolution,** compiled from the 'Annual Register'. By F. BAYFORD HARRISON. Crown 8vo. 3s. 6d.

HARTE (*Bret*).— WORKS BY.

In the Carquinez Woods. Fcp. 8vo. 1s. boards; 1s. 6d. cloth.

On the Frontier. 16mo. 1s.

By Shore and Sedge. 16mo. 1s.

HARTWIG (*Dr.*).— WORKS BY.

The Sea and its Living Wonders. With 12 Plates and 303 Woodcuts. 8vo. 10s. 6d.

The Tropical World. With 8 Plates and 172 Woodcuts. 8vo. 10s. 6d.

The Polar World. With 3 Maps, 8 Plates and 85 Woodcuts. 8vo. 10s. 6d.

The Subterranean World. With 3 Maps and 80 Woodcuts. 8vo. 10s. 6d.

The Aerial World. With Map, 8 Plates and 60 Woodcuts. 8vo. 10s. 6d.

HAVELOCK. — **Memoirs of Sir Henry Havelock, K.C.B.** By JOHN CLARK MARSHMAN. Crown 8vo. 3s. 6d.

HEARN (W. Edward).—WORKS BY.

The Government of England: its Structure and its Development. 8vo. 16s.

The Aryan Household: its Structure and its Development. An Introduction to Comparative Jurisprudence. 8vo. 16s.

HISTORIC TOWNS. Edited by E. A. FREEMAN, D.C.L., and Rev. WILLIAM HUNT, M.A. With Maps and Plans. Crown 8vo. 3s. 6d. each.

Bristol. By Rev. W. HUNT.

Carlisle. By Rev. MANDELL CREIGHTON.

Cinque Ports. By MONTAGU BURROWS.

Colchester. By Rev. E. L. CUTTS.

Exeter. By E. A. FREEMAN.

London. By Rev. W. J. LOFTIE.

Oxford. By Rev. C. W. BOASE.

Winchester. By Rev. G. W. KITCHIN, D.D.

New York. By THEODORE ROOSEVELT.

Boston (U.S.). By HENRY CABOT LODGE.

York. By Rev. JAMES RAINE. •
[*In Preparation.*

HODGSON (Shadworth H.).— WORKS BY.

Time and Space: a Metaphysical Essay. 8vo. 16s.

The Theory of Practice: an Ethical Enquiry. 2 vols. 8vo. 24s.

The Philosophy of Reflection: 2 vols. 8vo. 21s.

Outcast Essays and Verse Translations. Essays: The Genius of De Quincey—De Quincey as Political Economist—The Supernatural in English Poetry; with Note on the True Symbol of Christian Union—English Verse. Verse Translations: Nineteen Passages from Lucretius, Horace, Homer, &c. Crown 8vo. 8s. 6d.

HOWITT.—**Visits to Remarkable Places,** Old Halls, Battle-Fields, Scenes, illustrative of Striking Passages in English History and Poetry. By WILLIAM HOWITT. With 80 Illustrations. Crown 8vo. 3s. 6d.

HULLAH (John).—WORKS BY.

Course of Lectures on the History of Modern Music. 8vo. 8s. 6d.

Course of Lectures on the Transition Period of Musical History. 8vo. 10s. 6d.

HUME.--**The Philosophical Works of David Hume.** Edited by T. H. GREEN and T. H. GROSE. 4 vols. 8vo. 56s. Or Separately, Essays, 2 vols. 28s. Treatise of Human Nature. 2 vols. 28s.

HUTCHINSON (Horace).—WORKS BY.

Creatures of Circumstance: A Novel. 3 vols. Crown 8vo. 25s. 6d.

Famous Golf Links. By HORACE G. HUTCHINSON, ANDREW LANG, H. S. C. EVERARD, T. RUTHERFORD CLARK, &c. With numerous Illustrations by F. P. HOPKINS, T. HODGES, H. S. KING, and from Photographs. Crown 8vo. 6s.

HUTH.—**The Marriage of Near Kin,** considered with respect to the Law of Nations, the Result of Experience, and the Teachings of Biology. By ALFRED H. HUTH. Royal 8vo. 21s.

INGELOW (Jean).— WORKS BY.

Poetical Works. Vols. I. and II. Fcp. 8vo. 12s. Vol. III. Fcp. 8vo. 5s.

Lyrical and other Poems. Selected from the Writings of JEAN INGELOW. Fcp. 8vo. 2s. 6d. cloth plain; 3s. cloth gilt.

Very Young and Quite Another Story: Two Stories. Cr. 8vo. 6s.

JAMESON (Mrs.).— WORKS BY.

Sacred and Legendary Art. With 19 Etchings and 187 Woodcuts. 2 vols. 8vo. 20s. net.

Legends of the Madonna. The Virgin Mary as represented in Sacred and Legendary Art. With 27 Etchings and 165 Woodcuts. 1 vol. 8vo. 10s. net.
[*Continued on next page.*

JAMESON (*Mrs.*).— *WORKS BY.*—continued.

Legends of the Monastic Orders. With 11 Etchings and 88 Woodcuts. 1 vol. 8vo. 10s. net.

History of Our Lord. His Types and Precursors. Completed by Lady EASTLAKE. With 31 Etchings and 281 Woodcuts. 2 vols. 8vo. 20s. net.

JEFFERIES (*Richard*).— *WORKS BY.*

Field and Hedgerow: last Essays. With Portrait. Crown 8vo. 3s. 6d.

The Story of My Heart: my Autobiography. With Portrait and new Preface by C. J. LONGMAN. Crown 8vo. 3s. 6d.

JENNINGS.—**Ecclesia Anglicana.** A History of the Church of Christ in England, from the Earliest to the Present Times. By the Rev. ARTHUR CHARLES JENNINGS, M.A. Crown 8vo. 7s. 6d.

JOHNSON.—**The Patentee's Manual**; a Treatise on the Law and Practice of Letters Patent. By J. JOHNSON and J. H. JOHNSON. 8vo. 10s. 6d.

JORDAN (*William Leighton*).—**The Standard of Value.** By WILLIAM LEIGHTON JORDAN. 8vo. 6s.

JUSTINIAN.—**The Institutes of Justinian**; Latin Text, chiefly that of Huschke, with English Introduction. Translation, Notes, and Summary. By THOMAS C. SANDARS, M.A. 8vo. 18s.

KALISCH (*M. M.*).— *WORKS BY.*

Bible Studies. Part I. The Prophecies of Balaam. 8vo. 10s. 6d. Part II. The Book of Jonah. 8vo. 10s. 6d.

Commentary on the Old Testament; with a New Translation. Vol. I. Genesis, 8vo. 18s. or adapted for the General Reader, 12s. Vol. II. Exodus, 15s. or adapted for the General Reader, 12s. Vol. III. Leviticus, Part I. 15s. or adapted for the General Reader, 8s. Vol. IV. Leviticus, Part II. 15s. or adapted for the General Reader, 8s.

KANT (*Immanuel*).— *WORKS BY.*

Critique of Practical Reason, and other Works on the Theory of Ethics. Translated by T. K. Abbott, B.D. With Memoir. 8vo. 12s. 6d.

Introduction to Logic, and his Essay on the Mistaken Subtilty of the Four Figures. Translated by T. K. Abbott. Notes by S. T. Coleridge. 8vo. 6s.

KENNEDY.—**Pictures in Rhyme.** By ARTHUR CLARK KENNEDY. With 4 Illustrations by MAURICE GREIFFENHAGEN. Crown 8vo. 6s.

KILLICK.—**Handbook to Mill's System of Logic.** By the Rev. A. H. KILLICK, M.A. Crown 8vo. 3s. 6d.

KNIGHT (*E. F.*).— *WORKS BY.*

The Cruise of the 'Alerte'; the Narrative of a Search for Treasure on the Desert Island of Trinidad. With 2 Maps and 23 Illustrations. Crown 8vo. 10s. 6d.

Save Me from my Friends: a Novel. Crown 8vo. 6s.

LADD (*George T.*).— *WORKS BY.*

Elements of Physiological Psychology. 8vo. 21s.

Outlines of Physiological Psychology. A Text-book of Mental Science for Academies and Colleges. 8vo. 12s.

LANG (*Andrew*).— *WORKS BY.*

Custom and Myth: Studies of Early Usage and Belief. With 15 Illustrations. Crown 8vo. 7s. 6d.

Books and Bookmen. With 2 Coloured Plates and 17 Illustrations. Cr. 8vo. 6s. 6d.

Grass of Parnassus. A Volume of Selected Verses. Fcp. 8vo. 6s.

Angling Sketches. With Illustrations by W. G. Brown Murdoch. Crown 8vo. 7s. 6d..

Ballads of Books. Edited by ANDREW LANG. Fcp. 8vo. 6s.

The Blue Fairy Book. Edited by ANDREW LANG. With 8 Plates and 130 Illustrations in the Text by H. J. Ford and G. P. Jacomb Hood. Cr. 8vo. 6s.

The Red Fairy Book. Edited by ANDREW LANG. With 4 Plates and 96 Illustrations in the Text by H. J. Ford and Lancelot Speed. Crown 8vo. 6s.

The Blue Poetry Book. Edited by ANDREW LANG. With 12 Plates and 88 Illustrations in the Text by H. J. Ford and Lancelot Speed. Crown 8vo. 6s.

LAVISSE.—**General View of the Political History of Europe.** By ERNEST LAVISSE, Professor at the Sorbonne. Translated, with the Author's sanction, by CHARLES GROSS, Ph.D.

LAYARD.—**Poems.** By NINA F. LAYARD. Crown 8vo. 6s.

LECKY (W. E. H.).—*WORKS BY.*

History of England in the Eighteenth Century. 8vo. Vols. I. & II. 1700-1760. 36s. Vols. III. & IV. 1760-1784. 36s. Vols. V. & VI. 1784-1793. 36s. Vols. VII. & VIII. 1793-1800. 36s.

The History of European Morals from Augustus to Charlemagne. 2 vols. Crown 8vo. 16s.

History of the Rise and Influence of the Spirit of Rationalism in Europe. 2 vols. Crown 8vo. 16s.

Poems. Fcp. 8vo. 5s.

LEES and CLUTTERBUCK.—**B. C. 1887, A Ramble in British Columbia.** By J. A. LEES and W. J. CLUTTERBUCK. With Map and 75 Illustrations. Crown 8vo. 6s.

LEGER.—**A History of Austro-Hungary.** From the Earliest Time to the year 1889. By LOUIS LEGER. With a Preface by E. A. FREEMAN, D.C.L. Crown 8vo. 10s. 6d.

LEWES.—**The History of Philosophy, from Thales to Comte.** By GEORGE HENRY LEWES. 2 vols. 8vo. 32s.

LIDDELL.—**The Memoirs of the Tenth Royal Hussars (Prince of Wales' Own):** Historical and Social. Collected and Arranged by Colonel R. S. LIDDELL, late Commanding Tenth Royal Hussars. With Portraits and Coloured Illustration. Imperial 8vo. 63s.

LLOYD.—**The Science of Agriculture.** By F. J. LLOYD. 8vo. 12s.

LONGMAN (Frederick W.).—*WORKS BY.*

Chess Openings. Fcp. 8vo. 2s. 6d.

Frederick the Great and the Seven Years' War. Fcp. 8vo. 2s. 6d.

Longman's Magazine. Published Monthly. Price Sixpence. Vols. 1-17. 8vo. price 5s. each.

Longmans' New Atlas. Political and Physical. For the Use of Schools and Private Persons. Consisting of 40 Quarto and 16 Octavo Maps and Diagrams, and 16 Plates of Views. Edited by GEO. G. CHISHOLM, M.A., B.Sc. Imp. 4to. or Imp. 8vo. 12s. 6d.

LOUDON (J. C.).—*WORKS BY.*

Encyclopædia of Gardening. With 1000 Woodcuts. 8vo. 21s.

Encyclopædia of Agriculture; the Laying-out, Improvement, and Management of Landed Property. With 1100 Woodcuts. 8vo. 21s.

Encyclopædia of Plants; the Specific Character, &c., of all Plants found in Great Britain. With 12,000 Woodcuts. 8vo. 42s.

LUBBOCK.—**The Origin of Civilisation** and the Primitive Condition of Man. By Sir J. LUBBOCK, Bart., M.P. With 5 Plates and 20 Illustrations in the Text. 8vo. 18s.

LYALL.—**The Autobiography of a Slander.** By EDNA LYALL, Author of 'Donovan,' &c. Fcp. 8vo. 1s. sewed.

LYDE.—**An Introduction to Ancient History:** being a Sketch of the History of Egypt, Mesopotamia, Greece, and Rome. With a Chapter on the Development of the Roman Empire into the Powers of Modern Europe. By LIONEL W. LYDE, M.A. With 3 Coloured Maps. Crown 8vo. 3s.

MACAULAY (Lord).—*WORKS OF.*

Complete Works of Lord Macaulay:
Library Edition, 8 vols. 8vo. £5 5s.
Cabinet Edition, 16 vols. Post 8vo. £4 16s.

History of England from the Accession of James the Second:
Popular Edition, 2 vols. Crown 8vo. 5s.
Student's Edition, 2 vols. Crown 8vo. 12s.
People's Edition, 4 vols. Crown 8vo. 16s.
Cabinet Edition, 8 vols. Post 8vo. 48s.
Library Edition, 5 vols. 8vo. £4.

Critical and Historical Essays, with Lays of Ancient Rome, in 1 volume:
Popular Edition, Crown 8vo. 2s. 6d.
Authorised Edition, Crown 8vo. 2s. 6d. or 3s. 6d. gilt edges.

MACAULAY (Lord).— WORKS OF.— continued.

Critical and Historical Essays:
Student's Edition, 1 vol. Crown 8vo. 6s.
People's Edition, 2 vols. Crown 8vo. 8s.
Trevelyan Edition, 2 vols. Crown 8vo. 9s.
Cabinet Edition, 4 vols. Post 8vo. 24s.
Library Edition, 3 vols. 8vo. 36s.

Essays which may be had separately
price 6d. each sewed, 1s. each cloth:

Addison and Walpole.
Frederick the Great.
Croker's Boswell's Johnson.
Hallam's Constitutional History.
Warren Hastings. (3d. sewed, 6d cloth.)
The Earl of Chatham (Two Essays).
Ranke and Gladstone.
Milton and Machiavelli.
Lord Bacon.
Lord Clive.
Lord Byron, and The Comic Dramatists of
the Restoration.

The Essay on Warren Hastings annotated
by S. HALES, 1s. 6d.
The Essay on Lord Clive annotated by H.
COURTHOPE BOWEN, M.A., 2s. 6d.

Speeches:
People's Edition, Crown 8vo. 3s. 6d.

Lays of Ancient Rome, &c.:
Illustrated by G. Scharf, Fcp. 4to. 10s. 6d.
————————— Bijou Edition, 18mo.
2s. 6d. gilt top.
————————— Popular Edition,
Fcp. 4to. 6d. sewed, 1s. cloth.
Illustrated by J. R. Weguelin, Crown 8vo.
3s. 6d. cloth extra, gilt edges.
Cabinet Edition, Post 8vo. 3s. 6d.
Annotated Edition, Fcp. 8vo. 1s. sewed,
1s. 6d. cloth.

Miscellaneous Writings:
People's Edition, 1 vol. Crown 8vo. 4s. 6d.
Library Edition, 2 vols. 8vo. 21s.

Miscellaneous Writings and Speeches:
Popular Edition, 1 vol. Crown 8vo. 2s. 6d.
Student's Edition, in 1 vol. Crown 8vo. 6s.
Cabinet Edition, including Indian Penal
Code, Lays of Ancient Rome, and Mis-
cellaneous Poems, 4 vols. Post 8vo. 24s.

Selections from the Writings of Lord Macaulay. Edited,
with Occasional Notes, by the Right Hon.
Sir G. O. TREVELYAN, Bart. Cr. 8vo. 6s.

MACAULAY (Lord).— WORKS OF.— continued.

The Life and Letters of Lord Macaulay. By the Right Hon.
Sir G. O. TREVELYAN, Bart.:

Popular Edition, 1 vol. Crown 8vo. 2s. 6d.
Student's Edition, 1 vol. Crown 8vo. 6s.
Cabinet Edition, 2 vols. Post 8vo. 12s.
Library Edition, 2 vols. 8vo. 36s.

MACDONALD (Geo.).— WORKS BY.

Unspoken Sermons.   Three
Series. Crown 8vo. 3s. 6d. each.

The Miracles of Our Lord.
Crown 8vo. 3s. 6d.

A Book of Strife, in the Form of the Diary of an Old Soul:
Poems. 12mo. 6s.

MACFARREN (Sir G. A.).— WORKS BY.

Lectures on Harmony. 8vo. 12s.

Addresses and Lectures. Crown
8vo. 6s. 6d.

*MACKAIL.—*Select Epigrams from
the Greek Anthology. Edited,
with a Revised Text, Introduction, Translation, and Notes, by J. W. MACKAIL,
M.A. 8vo. 16s.

MACLEOD (Henry D.).— WORKS BY.

The Elements of Banking.
Crown 8vo. 3s. 6d.

The Theory and Practice of Banking.   Vol. I. 8vo. 12s.
Vol. II. 14s.

The Theory of Credit.   8vo.
Vol. I. 7s. 6d.; Vol. II. Part I. 4s. 6d.,
Vol. II. Part II. 10s. 6d.

*MᶜCULLOCH.—*The Dictionary of
Commerce and Commercial Navi
gation of the late J. R. McCULLOCH.
8vo. with 11 Maps and 30 Charts, 63s.

MACVINE. — Sixty-Three Years'
Angling, from the Mountain
Streamlet to the Mighty Tay. By JOHN
MACVINE. Crown 8vo. 10s. 6d.

*MALMESBURY.—*Memoirs of an
Ex-Minister. By the Earl of
MALMESBURY. Crown 8vo. 7s. 6d.

MANNERING. — With Axe and
Rope in the New Zealand
Alps. By GEORGE EDWARD MAN
NERING, Member of the Alpine Club. 8vo.
12s. 6d.

MANUALS OF CATHOLIC PHILOSOPHY (*Stonyhurst Series*):

Logic. By RICHARD F. CLARKE, S.J. Crown 8vo. 5*s*.

First Principles of Knowledge. By JOHN RICKABY, S.J. Crown 8vo. 5*s*.

Moral Philosophy (Ethics and Natural Law). By JOSEPH RICKABY, S.J. Crown 8vo. 5*s*.

General Metaphysics. By JOHN RICKABY, S.J. Crown 8vo. 5*s*.

Psychology. By MICHAEL MAHER, S.J. Crown 8vo. 6*s*. 6*d*.

Natural Theology. By BERNARD BOEDDER, S.J. Crown 8vo. 6*s*. 6*d*.

MARTINEAU (James).— WORKS BY.

Hours of Thought on Sacred Things. Two Volumes of Sermons. 2 vols. Crown 8vo. 7*s*. 6*d*. each.

Endeavours after the Christian Life. Discourses. Cr. 8vo. 7*s*. 6*d*.

The Seat of Authority in Religion. 8vo. 14*s*.

Essays, Reviews, and Addresses. 4 vols. Cr. 8vo. 7*s*. 6*d*. each.
I. Personal: Political.
II. Ecclesiastical: Historical.
III. Theological: Philosophical.
IV. Academical: Religious.

MASON.—**The Steps of the Sun:** Daily Readings of Prose. Selected by AGNES MASON. 16mo. 3*s*. 6*d*.

MATTHEWS (Brander).— WORKS BY.

A Family Tree, and other Stories. Crown 8vo. 6*s*.

Pen and Ink: Papers on Subjects of more or less Importance. Cr. 8vo. 5*s*.

With My Friends: Tales told in Partnership. With an Introductory Essay on the Art and Mystery of Collaboration. Crown 8vo. 6*s*.

MAUNDER'S TREASURIES.

Biographical Treasury. With Supplement brought down to 1889, by Rev. JAS. WOOD. Fcp. 8vo. 6*s*.

Treasury of Natural History; or, Popular Dictionary of Zoology. Fcp. 8vo. with 900 Woodcuts, 6*s*.

Treasury of Geography, Physical, Historical, Descriptive, and Political. With 7 Maps and 16 Plates. Fcp. 8vo. 9*s*.

[*Continued.*

MAUNDER'S TREASURIES.—*continued.*

Scientific and Literary Treasury. Fcp. 8vo. 6*s*.

Historical Treasury: Outlines of Universal History, Separate Histories of all Nations. Fcp. 8vo. 6*s*.

Treasury of Knowledge and Library of Reference. Comprising an English Dictionary and Grammar, Universal Gazetteer, Classical Dictionary, Chronology, Law Dictionary, &c. Fcp. 8vo. 6*s*.

The Treasury of Bible Knowledge. By the Rev. J. AYRE, M.A. With 5 Maps, 15 Plates, and 300 Woodcuts. Fcp. 8vo. 6*s*.

The Treasury of Botany. Edited by J. LINDLEY, F.R.S., and T. MOORE, F.L.S. With 274 Woodcuts and 20 Steel Plates. 2 vols. Fcp. 8vo. 12*s*.

MAX MÜLLER (F.).— WORKS BY.

Selected Essays on Language, Mythology and Religion. 2 vols. Crown 8vo. 16*s*.

The Science of Language, Founded on Lectures delivered at the Royal Institution in 1861 and 1863. 2 vols. Crown 8vo. 21*s*.

Three Lectures on the Science of Language and its Place in General Education, delivered at the Oxford University Extension Meeting, 1889. Crown 8vo. 3*s*.

Hibbert Lectures on the Origin and Growth of Religion, as illustrated by the Religions of India. Crown 8vo. 7*s*. 6*d*.

Introduction to the Science of Religion; Four Lectures delivered at the Royal Institution. Crown 8vo. 7*s*. 6*d*.

Natural Religion. The Gifford Lectures, delivered before the University of Glasgow in 1888. Crown 8vo. 10*s*. 6*d*.

Physical Religion. The Gifford Lectures, delivered before the University of Glasgow in 1890. Crown 8vo. 10*s*. 6*d*.

The Science of Thought. 8vo. 21*s*.

Three Introductory Lectures on the Science of Thought. 8vo. 2*s*. 6*d*.

[*Continued on next page.*

MAX MÜLLER (F.).—WORKS BY.— *continued.*

Biographies of Words, and the Home of the Aryas. Crown 8vo. 7s. 6d.

A Sanskrit Grammar for Beginners. New and Abridged Edition. By A. A. MacDonell. Cr. 8vo. 6s.

MAY.—The Constitutional History of England since the Accession of George III. 1760–1870. By the Right Hon. Sir Thomas Erskine May, K.C.B. 3 vols. Crown 8vo. 18s.

MEADE (L. T.).—WORKS BY.

The O'Donnells of Inchfawn. With Frontispiece by A. Chasemore. Crown 8vo. 6s.

Daddy's Boy. With Illustrations. Crown 8vo. 5s.

Deb and the Duchess. With Illustrations by M. E. Edwards. Crown 8vo. 5s.

House of Surprises. With Illustrations by Edith M. Scannell. Cr. 8vo. 3s. 6d.

The Beresford Prize. With Illustrations by M. E. Edwards. Crown 8vo. 5s.

MEATH (The Earl of).—WORKS BY.

Social Arrows: Reprinted Articles on various Social Subjects. Crown 8vo. 5s.

Prosperity or Pauperism? Physical, Industrial, and Technical Training. (Edited by the Earl of Meath.) 8vo. 5s.

MELVILLE (G. J. Whyte).—NOVELS BY. Crown 8vo. 1s. each, boards; 1s. 6d. each, cloth.

The Gladiators.	Holmby House.
The Interpreter.	Kate Coventry.
Good for Nothing.	Digby Grand.
The Queen's Maries.	General Bounce.

MENDELSSOHN.—The Letters of Felix Mendelssohn. Translated by Lady Wallace. 2 vols. Crown 8vo. 10s.

MERIVALE (The Very Rev. Chas.).—WORKS BY.

History of the Romans under the Empire. Cabinet Edition, 8 vols. Crown 8vo. 48s.
Popular Edition, 8 vols. Cr. 8vo. 3s. 6d. each.

The Fall of the Roman Republic: a Short History of the Last Century of the Commonwealth. 12mo. 7s. 6d.

General History of Rome from B.C. 753 to A.D. 476. Cr. 8vo. 7s. 6d.

The Roman Triumvirates. With Maps. Fcp. 8vo. 2s. 6d.

MILES.—The Correspondence of William Augustus Miles on the French Revolution, 1789–1817. Edited by the Rev. Charles Popham Miles, M.A. 2 vols. 8vo. 32s.

MILL.—Analysis of the Phenomena of the Human Mind. By James Mill. 2 vols. 8vo. 28s.

MILL (John Stuart).—WORKS BY.

Principles of Political Economy. Library Edition, 2 vols. 8vo. 30s. People's Edition, 1 vols. Crown 8vo. 5s.

A System of Logic. Cr. 8vo. 5s.

On Liberty. Crown 8vo. 1s. 4d.

On Representative Government. Crown 8vo. 2s.

Utilitarianism. 8vo. 5s.

Examination of Sir William Hamilton's Philosophy. 8vo. 16s.

Nature, the Utility of Religion, and Theism. Three Essays. 8vo. 5s.

MOLESWORTH (Mrs.).—WORKS BY

Marrying and Giving in Marriage: a Novel. Illustrated. Fcp. 8vo. 2s. 6d.

Silverthorns. Illustrated. Crown 8vo. 5s.

The Palace in the Garden. Illustrated. Crown 8vo. 5s.

The Third Miss St. Quentin. Crown 8vo. 6s.

Neighbours. Illustrated. Crown 8vo. 6s.

The Story of a Spring Morning, &c. Illustrated. Crown 8vo. 5s.

MOORE.—**Dante and his Early Biographers.** By EDWARD MOORE, D.D., Principal of St. Edmund Hall, Oxford. Crown 8vo. 4s. 6d.

MULHALL.—**History of Prices since the Year 1850.** By MICHAEL G. MULHALL. Cr. 8vo. 6s.

MURRAY.—**A Dangerous Cats-paw:** a Story. By DAVID CHRISTIE MURRAY and HENRY MURRAY. Crown 8vo. 2s. 6d.

MURRAY and HERMAN.—**Wild Darrie:** a Story. By CHRISTIE MURRAY and HENRY HERMAN. Crown 8vo. 2s. boards; 2s. 6d. cloth.

NANSEN.—**The First Crossing of Greenland.** By Dr. FRIDTJOF NANSEN. With 5 Maps, 12 Plates, and 150 Illustrations in the Text. 2 vols. 8vo. 36s.

NAPIER.—**The Life of Sir Joseph Napier, Bart., Ex-Lord Chancellor of Ireland.** By ALEX. CHARLES EWALD, F.S.A. With Portrait. 8vo. 15s.

NAPIER.—**The Lectures, Essays, and Letters of the Right Hon. Sir Joseph Napier, Bart.,** late Lord Chancellor of Ireland. 8vo. 12s. 6d.

NESBIT.—**Leaves of Life:** Verses. By E. NESBIT. Crown 8vo. 5s.

NEWMAN.—**The Letters and Correspondence of John Henry Newman** during his Life in the English Church. With a brief Autobiographical Memoir. Arranged and Edited by ANNE MOZLEY. With Portraits. 2 vols. 8vo. 30s. net.

NEWMAN (Cardinal).—*WORKS BY.*

Apologia pro Vitâ Sua. Cabinet Edition, Crown 8vo. 6s. Cheap Edition, Crown 8vo. 3s. 6d.

Sermons to Mixed Congregations. Crown 8vo. 6s.

Sermons on Various Occasions. Crown 8vo. 6s.

The Idea of a University defined and illustrated. Cabinet Edition, Crown 8vo. 7s. Cheap Edition, Crown 8vo. 3s. 6d.

NEWMAN (Cardinal).—*WORKS BY.* —*continued.*

Historical Sketches. 3 vols. Cr. 8vo. 6s. each.

The Arians of the Fourth Century. Cabinet Edition, Crown 8vo. 6s. Cheap Edition, Cr. 8vo. 3s. 6d.

Select Treatises of St. Athanasius in Controversy with the Arians. Freely Translated. 2 vols. Cr. 8vo. 15s.

Discussions and Arguments on Various Subjects. Cabinet Edition, Crown 8vo. 6s. Cheap Edition, Crown 8vo. 3s. 6d.

An Essay on the Development of Christian Doctrine. Cabinet Edition, Crown 8vo. 6s. Cheap Edition, Crown 8vo. 3s. 6d.

Certain Difficulties felt by Anglicans in Catholic Teaching Considered. Cabinet Edition, Vol. I., Crown 8vo. 7s. 6d. ; Vol. II., Cr. 8vo. 5s. 6d. Cheap Edition, 2 vols. Cr. 8vo. 3s. 6d. each.

The Via Media of the Anglican Church, illustrated in Lectures, &c. 2 vols. Crown 8vo. 6s. each.

Essays, Critical and Historical. Cabinet Edition, 2 vols. Crown 8vo. 12s. Cheap Edition, 2 vols. Crown 8vo. 7s.

Essays on Biblical and on Ecclesiastical Miracles. Cabinet Edition, Crown 8vo. 6s. Cheap Edition, Crown 8vo. 3s. 6d.

Tracts. 1. Dissertatiunculæ. 2. On the Text of the Seven Epistles of St. Ignatius. 3. Doctrinal Causes of Arianism. 4. Apollinarianism. 5. St. Cyril's Formula. 6. Ordo de Tempore. 7. Douay Version of Scripture. Crown 8vo. 8s.

An Essay in Aid of a Grammar of Assent. Cabinet Edition, Crown 8vo. 7s. 6d. Cheap Edition, Crown 8vo. 3s. 6d.

Present Position of Catholics in England. Crown 8vo. 7s. 6d.

Callista: a Tale of the Third Century. Cabinet Edition, Crown 8vo. 6s. Cheap Edition, Crown 8vo. 3s. 6d.

[Continued on next page.

NEWMAN (Cardinal).—WORKS OF.—continued.

Loss and Gain: a Tale. Cabinet Edition, Crown 8vo. 6s. Cheap Edition, Crown 8vo. 3s. 6d.

The Dream of Gerontius. 16mo. 6d. sewed, 1s. cloth.

Verses on Various Occasions. Cabinet Edition, Crown 8vo. 6s. Cheap Edition, Crown 8vo. 3s. 6d.

** For Cardinal Newman's other Works see Messrs. Longmans & Co.'s *Catalogue of Theological Works.*

NORRIS.—**Mrs. Fenton:** a Sketch. By W. E. NORRIS. Crown 8vo. 6s.

NORTON (Charles L.).— WORKS BY.

Political Americanisms: a Glossary of Terms and Phrases Current at Different Periods in American Politics. Fcp. 8vo. 2s. 6d.

A Handbook of Florida. With 49 Maps and Plans. Fcp. 8vo. 5s.

O'BRIEN.—**When we were Boys:** a Novel. By WILLIAM O'BRIEN, M.P. Crown 8vo. 2s. 6d.

OLIPHANT (Mrs.).—NOVELS BY.

Madam. Cr. 8vo. 1s. bds.; 1s. 6d. cl.

In Trust. Cr. 8vo. 1s. bds.; 1s. 6d. cl.

Lady Car: the Sequel of a Life. Crown 8vo. 2s. 6d.

OMAN.—**A History of Greece from the Earliest Times to the Macedonian Conquest.** By C. W. C. OMAN, M.A., F.S.A. With Maps and Plans. Crown 8vo. 4s. 6d.

O'REILLY.—**Hurstleigh Dene:** a Tale. By Mrs. O'REILLY. Illustrated by M. ELLEN EDWARDS. Cr. 8vo. 5s.

PAUL.—**Principles of the History of Language.** By HERMANN PAUL. Translated by H. A. STRONG. 8vo. 10s. 6d.

PAYN (James).—NOVELS BY.

The Luck of the Darrells. Cr. 8vo. 1s. boards; 1s. 6d. cloth.

Thicker than Water. Crown 8vo. 1s. boards; 1s. 6d. cloth.

PERRING (Sir Philip).—WORKS BY.

Hard Knots in Shakespeare. 8vo. 7s. 6d.

The 'Works and Days' of Moses. Crown 8vo. 3s. 6d.

PHILLIPPS-WOLLEY.—**Snap:** a Legend of the Lone Mountain. By C. PHILLIPPS-WOLLEY. With 13 Illustrations by H. G. WILLINK. Cr. 8vo. 6s.

POLE.—**The Theory of the Modern Scientific Game of Whist.** By W. POLE, F.R.S. Fcp. 8vo. 2s. 6d.

POLLOCK.—**The Seal of Fate:** a Novel. By Lady POLLOCK and W. H. POLLOCK. Crown 8vo. 6s.

POOLE.—**Cookery for the Diabetic.** By W. H. and Mrs. POOLE. With Preface by Dr. PAVY. Fcp. 8vo. 2s. 6d.

PRENDERGAST.— **Ireland, from the Restoration to the Revolution,** 1660-1690. By JOHN P. PRENDERGAST. 8vo. 5s.

PRINSEP.—**Virginie:** a Tale of One Hundred Years Ago. By VAL PRINSEP, A.R.A. 3 vols. Crown 8vo. 25s. 6d.

PROCTOR (R. A.).— WORKS BY.

Old and New Astronomy. 12 Parts, 2s. 6d. each. Supplementary Section, 1s. Complete in 1 vol. 4to. 36s. [*In course of publication.*]

The Orbs Around Us; a Series of Essays on the Moon and Planets, Meteors and Comets. With Chart and Diagrams. Crown 8vo. 5s.

Other Worlds than Ours; The Plurality of Worlds Studied under the Light of Recent Scientific Researches. With 14 Illustrations. Crown 8vo. 5s.

The Moon; her Motions, Aspects, Scenery, and Physical Condition. With Plates, Charts, Woodcuts, &c. Cr. 8vo. 5s.

Universe of Stars; Presenting Researches into and New Views respecting the Constitution of the Heavens. With 22 Charts and 22 Diagrams. 8vo. 10s. 6d.

Larger Star Atlas for the Library, in 12 Circular Maps, with Introduction and 2 Index Pages. Folio, 15s. or Maps only, 12s. 6d.

PROCTOR (R. A.).—WORKS BY.—continued.

The Student's Atlas. In Twelve Circular Maps on a Uniform Projection and one Scale. 8vo. 5*s.*

New Star Atlas for the Library, the School, and the Observatory, in 12 Circular Maps. Crown 8vo. 5*s.*

Light Science for Leisure Hours. Familiar Essays on Scientific Subjects. 3 vols. Crown 8vo. 5*s.* each.

Chance and Luck ; a Discussion of the Laws of Luck, Coincidences, Wagers, Lotteries, and the Fallacies of Gambling, &c. Crown 8vo. 2*s.* boards ; 2*s.* 6*d.* cloth.

Studies of Venus-Transits. With 7 Diagrams and 10 Plates. 8vo. 5*s.*

How to Play Whist: with the Laws and Etiquette of Whist. Crown 8vo. 3*s.* 6*d.*

Home Whist: an Easy Guide to Correct Play. 16mo. 1*s.*

The Stars in their Seasons. An Easy Guide to a Knowledge of the Star Groups, in 12 Maps. Roy. 8vo. 5*s.*

Star Primer. Showing the Starry Sky Week by Week, in 24 Hourly Maps. Crown 4to. 2*s.* 6*d.*

The Seasons pictured in 48 Sun-Views of the Earth, and 24 Zodiacal Maps, &c. Demy 4to. 5*s.*

Strength and Happiness. With 9 Illustrations. Crown 8vo. 5*s.*

Strength : How to get Strong and keep Strong, with Chapters on Rowing and Swimming, Fat, Age, and the Waist. With 9 Illustrations. Crown 8vo. 2*s.*

Rough Ways Made Smooth. Familiar Essays on Scientific Subjects. Crown 8vo. 5*s.*

Our Place Among Infinities. A Series of Essays contrasting our Little Abode in Space and Time with the Infinities around us. Crown 8vo. 5*s.*

The Expanse of Heaven. Essays on the Wonders of the Firmament. Cr. 8vo. 5*s.*

PROCTOR (R. A.).—WORKS BY.—continued.

The Great Pyramid, Observatory, Tomb, and Temple. With Illustrations. Crown 8vo. 5*s.*

Pleasant Ways in Science. Cr. 8vo. 5*s.*

Myths and Marvels of Astronomy. Crown 8vo. 5*s.*

Nature Studies. By GRANT ALLEN, A. WILSON, T. FOSTER, E. CLODD, and R. A. PROCTOR. Crown 8vo. 5*s.*

Leisure Readings. By E. CLODD, A. WILSON, T. FOSTER, A. C. RANYARD, and R. A. PROCTOR. Crown 8vo. 5*s.*

PRYCE.— **The Ancient British Church:** an Historical Essay. By JOHN PRYCE, M.A. Crown 8vo. 6*s.*

*RANSOME.—***The Rise of Constitutional Government in England:** being a Series of Twenty Lectures on the History of the English Constitution delivered to a Popular Audience. By CYRIL RANSOME, M.A. Crown 8vo. 6*s.*

*RAWLINSON.—***The History of Phœnicia.** By GEORGE RAWLINSON, M.A., Canon of Canterbury, &c. With numerous Illustrations. 8vo. 24*s.*

*READER.—***Echoes of Thought:** a Medley of Verse. By EMILY E. READER. Fcp. 8vo. 5*s.* cloth, gilt top.

*RENDLE and NORMAN.—***The Inns of Old Southwark,** and their Associations. By WILLIAM RENDLE, F.R.C.S., and PHILIP NORMAN, F.S.A. With numerous Illustrations. Roy. 8vo. 28*s.*

*RIBOT.—***The Psychology of Attention.** By TH. RIBOT. Crown 8vo. 3*s.*

*RICH.—***A Dictionary of Roman and Greek Antiquities.** With 2000 Woodcuts. By A. RICH. Crown 8vo. 7*s.* 6*d.*

*RICHARDSON.—***National Health.** Abridged from 'The Health of Nations'. A Review of the Works of Sir Edwin Chadwick, K.C.B. By Dr. B. W. RICHARDSON. Crown, 4*s.* 6*d.*

RILEY.—**Athos**; or, the Mountain of the Monks. By ATHELSTAN RILEY, M.A., F.R.G.S. With Map and 29 Illustrations. 8vo. 21*s.*

RILEY.—**Old-Fashioned Roses**: Poems. By JAMES WHITCOMB RILEY. 12mo. 5*s.*

ROCKHILL.—**The Land of the Lamas**: Notes of a Journey through China, Mangolia and Tibet. With 2 Maps and 6 Illustrations. By WILLIAM WOODVILLE ROCKHILL. 8vo. 15*s.*

ROGET.—**A History of the 'Old Water-Colour' Society** (now the Royal Society of Painters in Water-Colours). With Biographical Notices of its Older and all its Deceased Members and Associates. By JOHN LEWIS ROGET, M.A. 2 vols. Royal 8vo. 42*s.*

ROGET.—**Thesaurus of English Words and Phrases.** Classified and Arranged so as to facilitate the Expression of Ideas. By PETER M. ROGET. Crown 8vo. 10*s.* 6*d.*

RONALDS. — **The Fly-Fisher's Entomology.** By ALFRED RONALDS. With 20 Coloured Plates. 8vo. 14*s.*

ROSSETTI.—**A Shadow of Dante**: being an Essay towards studying Himself, his World, and his Pilgrimage. By MARIA FRANCESCA ROSSETTI. With Illustrations. Crown 8vo. 10*s.* 6*d.*

RUSSELL.—**A Life of Lord John Russell (Earl Russell, K.G.).** By SPENCER WALPOLE. With 2 Portraits. 2 vols. 8vo. 36*s.* Cabinet Edition, 2 vols. Crown 8vo. 12*s.*

SEEBOHM (Frederic).— WORKS BY.

The Oxford Reformers—John Colet, Erasmus, and Thomas More; a History of their Fellow-Work. 8vo. 14*s.*

The English Village Community Examined in its Relations to the Manorial and Tribal Systems, &c. 13 Maps and Plates. 8vo. 16*s.*

The Era of the Protestant Revolution. With Map. Fcp. 8vo. 2*s.* 6*d.*

SEWELL.—**Stories and Tales.** By ELIZABETH M. SEWELL. Crown 8vo. 1*s.* 6*d.* each, cloth plain; 2*s.* 6*d.* each, cloth extra, gilt edges :—

Amy Herbert.	Laneton Parsonage.
The Earl's Daughter.	Ursula.
The Experience of Life.	Gertrude.
A Glimpse of the World.	Ivors.
Cleve Hall.	Home Life.
Katharine Ashton.	After Life.
Margaret Percival.	

SHAKESPEARE. — **Bowdler's Family Shakespeare.** 1 Vol. 8vo. With 36 Woodcuts, 14*s.* or in 6 vols. Fcp. 8vo. 21*s.*

Outline of the Life of Shakespeare. By J. O. HALLIWELL-PHILLIPPS. 2 vols. Royal 8vo. £1 1*s.*

A Calendar of the Halliwell-Phillipps' Collection of Shakespearean Rarities Formerly Preserved at Hollingbury Copse, Brighton. Enlarged by ERNEST E. BAKER, F.S.A. 8vo. 10*s.* 6*d.*

Shakespeare's True Life. By JAMES WALTER. With 500 Illustrations. Imp. 8vo. 21*s.*

The Shakespeare Birthday Book. By MARY F. DUNBAR. 32mo. 1*s.* 6*d.* cloth. With Photographs, 32mo. 5*s.* Drawing-Room Edition, with Photographs, Fcp. 8vo. 10*s.* 6*d.*

SHORT.—**Sketch of the History of the Church of England** to the Revolution of 1688. By T. V. SHORT, D.D. Crown 8vo. 7*s.* 6*d.*

SILVER LIBRARY (The).—Cr. 8vo. 3*s.* 6*d.* each volume.

Baker's (Sir S. W.) Eight Years in Ceylon. With 6 Illustrations. 3*s.* 6*d.*

Baker's (Sir S. W.) Rifle and Hound in Ceylon. With 6 Illustrations. 3*s.* 6*d.*

Brassey's (Lady) A Voyage in the 'Sunbeam'. With 66 Illustrations. 3*s.* 6*d.*

Clodd's (E.) Story of Creation: a Plain Account of Evolution. With 77 Illustrations. 3*s.* 6*d.*

Doyle's (A. Conan) Micah Clarke. A Tale of Monmouth's Rebellion. 3*s.* 6*d.*

Froude's (J. A.) Short Studies on Great Subjects. 4 vols. 3*s.* 6*d.* each.

Froude's (J. A.) Cæsar: a Sketch. 3*s.* 6*d.*

SILVER LIBRARY (The).—
continued.

Froude's (J. A.) **Thomas Carlyle**: a History of his Life. 1795-1835. 2 vols. 1834-1881. 2 vols. 7s. each.

Froude's (J. A.) **The Two Chiefs of Dunboy**: an Irish Romance of the Last Century. 3s. 6d.

Gleig's (Rev. G. R.) **Life of the Duke of Wellington.** With Portrait. 3s. 6d.

Haggard's (H. R.) **She**; A History of Adventure. 32 Illustrations. 3s. 6d.

Haggard's (H. R.) **Allan Quatermain.** With 20 Illustrations. 3s. 6d.

Haggard's (H. R.) **Colonel Quaritch, V.C.**: a Tale of Country Life. 3s. 6d.

Haggard's (H. R.) **Cleopatra.** With 29 Full-page Illustrations. 3s. 6d.

Howitt's (W.) **Visits to Remarkable Places.** 80 Illustrations. 3s. 6d.

Jefferies' (R.) **The Story of My Heart**: My Autobiography. With Portrait. 3s. 6d.

Jefferies' (R.) **Field and Hedgerow.** Last Essays of. With Portrait. 3s. 6d.

Macleod's (H. D.) **The Elements of Banking.** 3s. 6d.

Marshman's (J. C.) **Memoirs of Sir Henry Havelock.** 3s. 6d.

Merivale's (Dean) **History of the Romans under the Empire.** 8 vols. 3s. 6d. each.

Mill's (J. S.) **Principles of Political Economy.** 3s. 6d.

Mill's (J. S.) **System of Logic** 3s. 6d.

Newman's (Cardinal) **Historical Sketches.** 3 vols. 3s. 6d. each.

Newman's (Cardinal) **Apologia Pro Vitâ Suâ.** 3s. 6d.

Newman's (Cardinal) **Callista**: a Tale of the Third Century. 3s. 6d.

Newman's (Cardinal) **Loss and Gain**: a Tale. 3s. 6d.

Newman's (Cardinal) **Essays**, Critical and Historical. 2 vols. 7s.

Newman's (Cardinal) **An Essay on the Development of Christian Doctrine.** 3s. 6d.

Newman's (Cardinal) **The Arians of the Fourth Century.** 3s. 6d.

Newman's (Cardinal) **Verses on Various Occasions.** 3s. 6d.

Newman's (Cardinal) **Parochial and Plain Sermons.** 8 vols. 3s. 6d. each.

SILVER LIBRARY (The).—
continued.

Newman's (Cardinal) **Selection**, adapted to the Seasons of the Ecclesiastical Year, from the 'Parochial and Plain Sermons'. 3s. 6d.

Newman's (Cardinal) **Sermons bearing upon Subjects of the Day.** Edited by the Rev. W. J. Copeland, B.D., late Rector of Farnham, Essex. 3s. 6d.

Newman's (Cardinal) **Difficulties felt by Anglicans in Catholic Teaching Considered.** 2 vols. 3s. 6d. each.

Newman's (Cardinal) **The Idea of a University Defined and Illustrated.** 3s. 6d.

Newman's (Cardinal) **Biblical and Ecclesiastical Miracles.** 3s. 6d.

Newman's (Cardinal) **Discussions and Arguments on Various Subjects.** 3s. 6d.

Newman's (Cardinal) **Grammar of Assent.** 3s. 6d.

Newman's (Cardinal) **The Via Media of the Anglican Church,** illustrated in Lectures, &c. 2 vols. 3s. 6d. each.

Stanley's (Bishop) **Familiar History of Birds.** 160 Illustrations. 3s. 6d.

Wood's (Rev. J. G.) **Petland Revisited.** With 33 Illustrations. 3s. 6d.

Wood's (Rev. J. G.) **Strange Dwellings**: With 60 Illustrations. 3s. 6d.

Wood's (Rev. J. G.) **Out of Doors.** 11 Illustrations. 3s. 6d.

SMITH (Gregory).—**Fra Angelico, and other Short Poems.** By GREGORY SMITH. Crown 8vo. 4s. 6d.

SMITH (R. Bosworth).—**Carthage and the Carthagenians.** By R. BOSWORTH SMITH, M.A. Maps, Plans, &c. Crown 8vo. 6s.

Sophocles. Translated into English Verse. By ROBERT WHITELAW, M.A. Assistant-Master in Rugby School; late Fellow of Trinity College, Cambridge. Crown 8vo. 8s. 6d.

STANLEY.—**A Familiar History of Birds.** By E. STANLEY, D.D. With 160 Woodcuts. Crown 8vo. 3s. 6d.

STEEL (J. H.).—**WORKS BY.**

A Treatise on the Diseases of the Dog; being a Manual of Canine Pathology. Especially adapted for the Use of Veterinary Practitioners and Students. 88 Illustrations. 8vo. 10s. 6d.

STEEL (J. H.).—WORKS BY.—cont.

A Treatise on the Diseases of the Ox; being a Manual of Bovine Pathol gy. Especially adapted for the use of Veterinary Practitioners and Students. 2 Plates and 117 Woodcuts. 8vo. 15s.

A Treatise on the Diseases of the Sheep; being a Manual of Ovine Pathology. Especially adapted for the use of Veterinary Practitioners and Students. With Coloured Plate and 99 Woodcuts. 8vo. 12s.

STEPHEN.—**Essays in Ecclesiastical Biography.** By the Right Hon. Sir J. STEPHEN. Crown 8vo. 7s. 6d.

STEPHENS.—**A History of the French Revolution.** By H. MORSE STEPHENS, Balliol College, Oxford. 3 vols. 8vo. Vol. I. and II. 18s. each. [*Ready.*]

STEVENSON (Robt. Louis).—WORKS BY.

A Child's Garden of Verses. Small Fcp. 8vo. 5s.

The Dynamiter. Fcp. 8vo. 1s. sewed ; 1s. 6d. cloth.

Strange Case of Dr. Jekyll and Mr. Hyde. Fcp. 8vo. 1s. swd. ; 1s. 6d. cloth.

STEVENSON and OSBOURNE.—**The Wrong Box.** By ROBERT LOUIS STEVENSON and LLOYD OSBOURNE. Crown 8vo. 5s.

STOCK.—**Deductive Logic.** By ST. GEORGE STOCK. Fcp. 8vo. 3s. 6d.

'STONEHENGE'.—**The Dog in Health and Disease.** By 'STONEHENGE'. With 84 Wood Engravings. Square Crown 8vo. 7s. 6d.

STRONG, LOGEMAN, and WHEELER.—**Introduction to the Study of the History of Language.** By HERBERT A. STRONG, M.A., LL.D. ; WILLEM S. LOGEMAN ; and BENJAMIN IDE WHEELER. 8vo. 10s. 6d.

STUTFIELD.—**The Brethren of Mount Atlas:** being the First Part of an African Theosophical Story. By HUGH E. M. STUTFIELD, F.R.G.S. Author of 'El Maghreb : 1200 Miles' Ride through Marocco'. Crown 8vo.

Supernatural Religion; an Inquiry into the Reality of Divine Revelation. 3 vols. 8vo. 36s.

Reply (A) to Dr. Lightfoot's Essays. By the Author of ' Supernatural Religion '. 8vo. 6s.

SWINBURNE.—**Picture Logic ;** an Attempt to Popularise the Science of Reasoning. By A. J. SWINBURNE, B.A. Post 8vo. 5s.

SYMES (James).—WORKS BY.

Prelude to Modern History : being a Brief Sketch of the World's History from the Third to the Ninth Century. With 5 Maps. Crown 8vo. 2s. 6d.

A Companion to School Histories of England ; being a Series of Short Essays on the most Important Movements, Social, Literary, and Political, in English History. Crown 8vo. 2s. 6d.

Political Economy : a Short Text-Book of Political Economy. With Problems for Solution, and Hints for Supplementary Reading. Crown 8vo. 2s. 6d.

TAYLOR.—**A Student's Manual of the History of India,** from the Earliest Period to the Present Time. By Colonel MEADOWS TAYLOR, C.S.I., &c. Crown 8vo. 7s. 6d.

THOMPSON (D. Greenleaf).—WORKS BY.

The Problem of Evil : an Introduction to the Practical Sciences. 8vo. 10s. 6d.

A System of Psychology. 2 vols. 8vo. 36s.

The Religious Sentiments of the Human Mind. 8vo. 7s. 6d.

Social Progress : an Essay. 8vo. 7s. 6d.

The Philosophy of Fiction in Literature : an Essay. Cr. 8vo. 6s.

Three in Norway. By Two of THEM. With a Map and 59 Illustrations. Cr. 8vo. 2s. boards ; 2s. 6d. cloth.

TIREBUCK.—**Dorrie :** a Novel. By WILLIAM TIREBUCK. Author of ' Saint Margaret.' &c. Crown 8vo. 6s.

TOYNBEE.—Lectures on the Industrial Revolution of the 18th Century in England. By the late ARNOLD TOYNBEE, Tutor of Balliol College, Oxford. Together with a Short Memoir by B. JOWETT, Master of Balliol College, Oxford. 8vo. 10s. 6d.

TREVELYAN (Sir G. O., Bart.).—WORKS BY.

The Life and Letters of Lord Macaulay.

POPULAR EDITION, Crown 8vo. 2s. 6d.
STUDENT's EDITION, Crown 8vo. 6s.
CABINET EDITION, 2 vols. Cr. 8vo. 12s.
LIBRARY EDITION, 2 vols. 8vo. 36s.

The Early History of Charles James Fox. Library Edition, 8vo. 18s. Cabinet Edition, Cr. 8vo. 6s.

TROLLOPE (Anthony).—NOVELS BY.

The Warden. Crown 8vo. 1s. boards; 1s. 6d. cloth.

Barchester Towers. Crown 8vo. 1s. boards; 1s. 6d. cloth.

VILLE.—The Perplexed Farmer: How is he to meet Alien Competition? By GEORGE VILLE. Translated from the French by WILLIAM CROOKES, F.R.S., V.P.C.S., &c. Crown 8vo. 5s.

VIRGIL.—Publi Vergili Maronis Bucolica, Georgica, Æneis; The Works of VIRGIL, Latin Text, with English Commentary and Index. By B. H. KENNEDY, D.D. Cr. 8vo. 10s. 6d.

The Æneid of Virgil. Translated into English Verse. By JOHN CONINGTON, M.A. Crown 8vo. 6s.

The Poems of Virgil. Translated into English Prose. By JOHN CONINGTON, M.A. Crown 8vo. 6s.

The Eclogues and Georgics of Virgil. Translated from the Latin by J. W. MACKAIL, M.A., Fellow of Balliol College, Oxford. Printed on Dutch Hand-made Paper. Royal 16mo. 5s.

WAKEMAN and HASSALL.—Essays Introductory to the Study of English Constitutional History. By Resident Members of the University of Oxford. Edited by HENRY OFFLEY WAKEMAN, M.A., and ARTHUR HASSALL, M.A. Crown 8vo. 6s.

WALFORD.—The Mischief of Monica: a Novel. By L. B. WALFORD. Author of 'Mr. Smith,' &c., &c. 3 vols. Crown 8vo. 25s. 6d.

WALKER.—The Correct Card; or How to Play at Whist; a Whist Catechism. By Major A. CAMPBELL-WALKER, F.R.G.S. Fcp. 8vo. 2s. 6d.

WALPOLE.—History of England from the Conclusion of the Great War in 1815 to 1858. By SPENCER WALPOLE. Library Edition. 5 vols. 8vo. £4 10s. Cabinet Edition. 6 vols. Crown 8vo. 6s. each.

WELLINGTON.—Life of the Duke of Wellington. By the Rev. G. R. GLEIG, M.A. Crown 8vo. 3s. 6d.

WELLS.—Recent Economic Changes and their Effect on the Production and Distribution of Wealth and the Well-being of Society. By DAVID A. WELLS. Crown 8vo. 10s. 6d.

WENDT.—Papers on Maritime Legislation, with a Translation of the German Mercantile Laws relating to Maritime Commerce. By ERNEST EMIL WENDT. Royal 8vo. £1 11s. 6d.

WEYMAN.—The House of the Wolf: a Romance. By STANLEY J. WEYMAN. Crown 8vo. 6s.

WHATELY (E. Jane).—WORKS BY.
English Synonyms. Edited by R. WHATELY, D.D. Fcp. 8vo. 3s.

Life and Correspondence of Richard Whately, D.D., late Archbishop of Dublin. With Portrait. Crown 8vo. 10s. 6d.

WHATELY (Archbishop). — WORKS BY.
Elements of Logic. Crown 8vo. 4s. 6d.

Elements of Rhetoric. Crown 8vo. 4s. 6d.

Lessons on Reasoning. Fcp. 8vo. 1s. 6d.

Bacon's Essays, with Annotations. 8vo. 10s. 6d.

Whist in Diagrams: a Supplement to American Whist, Illustrated; being a Series of Hands played through, Illustrating the American leads, the new play, the forms of Finesse, and celebrated coups of Masters. With Explanation and Analysis. By G. W. P. Fcp. 8vo. 6s. 6d.

WILCOCKS.—**The Sea Fisherman,** Comprising the Chief Methods of Hook and Line Fishing in the British and other Seas, and Remarks on Nets, Boats, and Boating. By J. C. WILCOCKS. Profusely Illustrated. Crown 8vo. 6s.

WILLICH.—**Popular Tables** for giving Information for ascertaining the value of Lifehold, Leasehold, and Church Property, the Public Funds, &c. By CHARLES M. WILLICH. Edited by H. BENCE JONES. Crown 8vo. 10s. 6d.

WILLOUGHBY.—**East Africa and its Big Game.** By Capt. Sir JOHN C. WILLOUGHBY, Bart. Illustrated by G. D. Giles and Mrs. Gordon Hake. Royal 8vo. 21s.

WITT (Prof.).—*WORKS BY.* Translated by FRANCES YOUNGHUSBAND.

The Trojan War. Crown 8vo. 2s.

Myths of Hellas; or, Greek Tales. Crown 8vo. 3s. 6d.

The Wanderings of Ulysses. Crown 8vo. 3s. 6d.

The Retreat of the Ten Thousand; being the story of Xenophon's 'Anabasis'. With Illustrations. Crown 8vo. 3s. 6d.

WOLFF (Henry W.).—*WORKS BY.*

Rambles in the Black Forest. Crown 8vo. 7s. 6d.

The Watering Places of the Vosges. Crown 8vo. 4s. 6d.

The Country of the Vosges. With a Map. 8vo. 12s.

WOOD (Rev. J. G.).—*WORKS BY.*

Homes Without Hands; a Description of the Habitations of Animals, classed according to the Principle of Construction. With 140 Illustrations. 8vo. 10s. 6d.

Insects at Home; a Popular Account of British Insects, their Structure, Habits, and Transformations. With 700 Illustrations. 8vo. 10s. 6d.

Insects Abroad; a Popular Account of Foreign Insects, their Structure, Habits, and Transformations. With 600 Illustrations. 8vo. 10s. 6d.

WOOD (Rev. J. G.).—*WORKS BY.*—*continued.*

Bible Animals; a Description of every Living Creature mentioned in the Scriptures. With 112 Illustrations. 8vo. 10s. 6d.

Strange Dwellings; a Description of the Habitations of Animals, abridged from 'Homes without Hands'. With 60 Illustrations. Crown 8vo. 3s. 6d.

Out of Doors; a Selection of Original Articles on Practical Natural History. With 11 Illustrations. Crown 8vo. 3s. 6d.

Petland Revisited. With 33 Illustrations. Crown 8vo. 3s. 6d.

WORDSWORTH.—**Annals of My Early Life, 1806-46.** By CHARLES WORDSWORTH, D.C.L., Bishop of St. Andrews. 8vo. 15s.

WYLIE.—**History of England under Henry IV.** By JAMES HAMILTON WYLIE. 2 vols. Vol. I., 1399-1404. Crown 8vo. 10s. 6d. Vol. II. [In the Press.

YOUATT (William).—*WORKS BY.*

The Horse. Revised and enlarged. 8vo. Woodcuts, 7s. 6d.

The Dog. Revised and enlarged. 8vo. Woodcuts, 6s.

ZELLER (Dr. E.).—*WORKS BY.*

History of Eclecticism in Greek Philosophy. Translated by SARAH F. ALLEYNE. Cr. 8vo. 10s. 6d.

The Stoics, Epicureans, and Sceptics. Translated by the Rev. O. J. REICHEL, M.A. Crown 8vo. 15s.

Socrates and the Socratic Schools. Translated by the Rev. O. J. REICHEL, M.A. Cr. 8vo. 10s. 6d.

Plato and the Older Academy. Translated by SARAH F. ALLEYNE and ALFRED GOODWIN, B.A. Crown 8vo. 18s.

The Pre-Socratic Schools: a History of Greek Philosophy from the Earliest Period to the time of Socrates. Translated by SARAH F. ALLEYNE. 2 vols. Crown 8vo. 30s.

Outlines of the History of Greek Philosophy. Translated by SARAH F. ALLEYNE and EVELYN ABBOTT. Crown 8vo. 10s. 6d.